THE OWNED SERIES

BOOKS 1-5

K.L. RAMSEY

The Owned Series

Copyright © 2023 by K.L. Ramsey

Cover design by Sweet 15 Designs

Formatting by Mr. KL

Imprint:Independently published

First Print Edition: April 2023

All rights reserved.

No part of this book may be reproduced, scanned, or distributed in any printed or electronic form without permission. Please do not participate in or encourage piracy of copyrighted materials in violation of the author's rights. Thank you for respecting the hard work of this author.

This is a work of fiction. Names, characters, places, and incidents either are the product of the author's imagination or are used fictitiously, and any resemblance to locales, events, business establishments, or actual persons—living or dead—is entirely coincidental.

HIS SECRET SUBMISSIVE

AIDEN
PROLOGUE

Aiden Bentley stood in the middle of the boardroom feeling as though he had just been blindsided. He must have reread the text from his wife over a dozen times as if he was expecting it to somehow change. It didn't and he was left having to figure out what the fuck he was supposed to do next because he'd never in a million years believe that his Allison would leave him. But according to her very short and not-so-sweet text, she was leaving him to be with her new boyfriend whom she'd apparently been seeing for months now. She told him she had already moved her stuff out of the house that very morning after he left for work, and she left the kids at her mother's. His favorite part was where she tried to justify the fact that she cheated on him by pointing out how he was always busy with his company and his political run for the vacant Senate seat and she was feeling neglected. Her new boyfriend gave her the attention she was craving and fulfilled her like no other man ever had. Allison concluded her text by saying she was too young to be saddled down with a husband who loved his company more than he loved her.

He turned his cell off and cursed and when it didn't help

him to feel better, Aiden threw it across the room watching it hit the wall and smash into three pieces. Of course, his assistant would choose that moment to walk into the conference room.

"You all right, AJ?" she asked. Aiden couldn't help but give her a smile and nod. Rose Eklund was more than his assistant; she was like the mother he never knew. In fact, she was one of the only people to call him by his childhood nickname. Well, she and her son, Corbin. Not too many other people even knew him by that name, but Rose did. She was his best friend's mother and when he and Corbin opened their company together ten years earlier, she agreed to work for them until they got up and running and she just stuck around. They began their little start-up in Corbin's basement and he was sure Rose agreed to help just to keep an eye on them. They were just kids back then, fresh out of college and with enough ambition between the two of them to be cocky enough to believe they could make something from nothing. Now they were a multi-billion dollar corporation with offices all over the world and he and Corbin had Rose to thank for most of their success. She kept them organized, focused, and most of all—grounded.

"I'm fine, Rose," he lied. She shot him a look that told him she wasn't buying what he was selling. Rose could always tell when he and Corbin were being less than truthful with her. As teenagers, they didn't get away with anything. Looking back now, he had to admit he was thankful he had Rose to keep an eye on him. After his mother left when he was just a baby, it was him and his dad. His father did the best he could with Aiden, but he never really got over his wife leaving him. Aiden's dad masked his sadness with alcohol and wallowed in the pit of self-pity that consumed him. Most of his time was spent in bars and when he was able to sober up enough for a job, he worked nights. Rose made sure Aiden had a safe place to hang out over at her house. She made him do his homework and even fed him dinner. Most nights, he'd crash at Corbin's house and Rose would feed him breakfast and make sure he had clean clothes and lunch money. Aiden didn't know where he would have ended up if it hadn't been for her and Corbin basically taking him in.

"Would you like for me to wait here for the truth, or do you want to come and find me after you come up with a better story?" Rose crossed her arms over her chest and cocked an eyebrow at him. Aiden didn't hide his amusement especially when she did her best to try to hide her smile.

"You might be part witch," Aiden teased. "How do you always know?"

Rose shrugged, "Mother's instinct, I guess," she said. "So, would you like to try your answer again?"

Aiden wasn't sure if he should tell Rose about Allison's text. Hell, he wasn't sure he understood everything yet and he needed to pick up the girls before Allison's mother got sick of babysitting them and dumped them off at his office. He knew he didn't want the news of his wife leaving him for another guy to work its way around the company and he damn sure didn't need it leaking out into the press. They'd have a field day with the prospective Senator who couldn't keep a leash on his wife. If they only knew the half of it they'd make minced meat out of him and he could kiss his political career goodbye.

"You can't tell anyone this—not even Corbin yet. Promise me, Rose," he said. She looked him up and down as if he lost his mind. Aiden wasn't sure she was going to make him any guarantees to keep her mouth shut and that would mean he had no one to confide in.

"You can't expect me to keep anything from my only son," she chided. Hearing her call Corbin her only child smarted a little. He had to admit he'd like to think she considered him a son too, but he knew that might be asking too much. Rose was right. Asking her to keep a secret from Corbin wasn't fair to either of them.

"Fine, I'll tell Corbin tomorrow. For now, can this remain

between the two of us?" he asked. Rose gave a curt nod and he let out a breath he didn't know he was holding. "Allison left me. She just let me know, by text," he admitted.

"By text?" Rose shouted. "How could she do that to you? Oh you poor thing," she sympathized. Rose crossed the room to pull Aiden in for one of her famous mama bear hugs he and Corbin like to tease her about. But instead of leaving him feeling like he wanted to poke fun at Rose, he felt more ready to cry on her shoulder. She held him with no signs of letting him go any time soon and Aiden wrapped his arms around her waist, knowing resistance was futile.

"She can't just take the girls away from you, Aiden. Did she tell you where she went?" Rose asked.

Aiden barked out his laugh, "Yeah, I'm pretty sure she went to live with her boyfriend. Apparently my loving wife has been cheating on me for half a year now." He pulled free from Rose's hold and she let him go, seeming to know he needed some space.

"I never liked her," she insisted. Aiden shot her a disbelieving look and she shrugged. "Well, it's true, honey. I thought she was just playing you from the start," she admitted. Aiden knew a good many people felt that way, Corbin included. On the day of his wedding, Corbin pulled him aside and begged him not to go through with it. He tried to convince Aiden that Allison was just out for his money, but he was determined to see marrying her through. Allison was five months pregnant with Lucy at the time and he didn't want his kid to grow up without both parents as he had. He saw no other way around marrying Allison and when she agreed to sign the prenuptial agreement, he thought for sure Corbin and everyone else was wrong about her.

For a while, they were happy; especially after Lucy was born. Two years later, they had Laney and he was sure he'd never been happier in his life. He had a gorgeous wife and two beautiful daughters—what more could he ask for? The answer to that was a hell of a lot more complicated than he'd ever care to admit. For as much as he wanted to blame Allison, she was right. He spent late nights at the office and political functions, trying to fundraise for his run for Senate. Maybe it was all a ruse to cover up the fact he wasn't happy at home, he never really was. He loved Allison and the girls, but he wasn't being completely honest about who he was with his wife or himself. He needed more and that usually left him feeling like a complete ass. Aiden worried there was something wrong with him. Hell, he even went as far as going to see a therapist to help him get over those feelings that plagued him daily.

He was dominant and his need to control and be in charge didn't end when he left the boardroom. He wanted to introduce that side of himself into his marriage, but when he brought up the topic with Allison, she shut him down telling him it wasn't her thing. He tried to tell her they could begin slowly and only incorporate things she would enjoy doing with him in the bedroom but she wasn't willing to even hear him out. His therapist told him he had two choices—either accept his wife's denial and his marriage the way it was or leave. Aiden decided to stay and try to work through his needs and desires, for the sake of his family. His girls deserved more than a father who'd walk away from them so easily. The press shoved the idea of his perfect little family to the masses and voters seemed to eat it up with a spoon. On the outside to everyone looking in, he was a normal business owner with the perfect family life. Aiden was the small-town boy who made good and a loyal family man and that was the persona he decided to stick with. That guy got votes. Aiden wasn't sure if he'd be so public-friendly when everyone found out what kind of kinks he liked in the bedroom. The only people who truly knew who he was were Allison and Corbin.

"I don't want to get into this now," Aiden admitted. Rose shot him a sympathetic look and he hated knowing that once word got out, everyone would be looking at him the same way.

"I have to go pick up Lucy and Laney. Allison left the girls with her mother. She doesn't know if she can be a mom to them right now," he said. He hated how his wife could walk away from their daughters. He knew firsthand what it felt like to know that your own parent didn't want you. He would never let his girls feel unwanted or unloved. At thirty-two he was still living with the demons of being abandoned by his mother after birth and he wouldn't let his daughters be consumed by that same darkness.

"She just left those sweet babies?" Rose choked. Aiden nodded his head, too raw from the emotions roiling through him. He needed to get to his girls and make sure they were both all right. God only knew what Allison had told them and it might be up to him to explain their Mommy wasn't coming home again. He'd just have to find a way to give them the truth without breaking their hearts.

"Okay, you go get the girls and call me later to let me know you are all home safely," Rose ordered. "I'll keep this information to myself but you need to tell Corbin. He loves you like a brother and there isn't anything he wouldn't do for you and the girls." Aiden nodded again and kissed Rose's cheek.

"Thank you," he said. "I'll probably be working from home for the next few days, just until I can get the girls settled and make some sense out of all of this," he said.

Rose shooed him out of the room, "Go, I've got this. You just go and fix your family," she said. Aiden wanted to tell her it was going to take a damn miracle because he was pretty sure his family was broken beyond repair. He just didn't know how to tell her it was just as much his fault as it was Allison's.

Aiden pulled up to his mother-in-law's home to find Connie waiting on the porch for his arrival, almost as if she was expecting him. He wondered just how long she had been standing out there. "It's about damn time," she shouted at him before he was even completely out of his SUV. "I've been waiting for over an hour for you to show up. Allison told me she texted you and you were on your way here to get the girls and then she disappeared. She didn't even say goodbye to them and now they're upset and asking when she's coming home."

"Did Allison tell you where she was going?" Aiden carefully asked. He hated that he might have to break the news to Connie too, but he was starting to see Allison left him quite a mess to have to clean up.

"Nope," she admitted. "Allison just showed up here out of the blue and told me she needed me to watch the girls. When I said I couldn't because I had a doctor's appointment, she promised you would be right over. I've missed my appointment and now I can't get back in to see him for another two weeks," Connie groused. "What am I supposed to do for my blood pressure medicine until then?"

"I'll take care of making you another appointment and getting you your medication," Aiden promised, making a mental note to have Rose do that for him in the morning. He hated that Allison would put her mother's health in jeopardy to run off with some guy. Of course, what he hated even more was that he was going to have to be the one to tell her mother that. "I'm afraid I have some bad news," he said. "You might want to sit down for this next part." Connie found her rocking chair in the corner of the small porch and sat down.

"I'm all ears," she said, smiling up at him. "I have a feeling my daughter has gone and done something stupid and I'm looking forward to the part where you defend her bad behavior." Aiden shot Connie an apologetic look, knowing she was probably right. He was always sticking up for his wife when she would make a decision that seemed to hurt everyone around her. Maybe it was the guilt he lived with for wanting more or maybe he was just blind and stupid.

"I don't know that I'll be able to defend her behavior this

time, Connie," he admitted. "I got a text from her saying she's left me and the girls." Connie's gasp answered his question for him. He wanted to ask her if her daughter had shared the fact she was so easily abandoning her family or if Allison truly just dumped the girls off and left. "So, you really didn't know, did you?"

"No," she stuttered, raising a shaking hand to her mouth. "How could Allison do that to you and her daughters?" she questioned.

"I have no idea, really. I mean, she mentioned something about having a boyfriend for the past six months and well, maybe I don't blame her. She said I wasn't the best husband and she wasn't all wrong. I spent a lot of late nights at the office and campaigning. Maybe if I had paid more attention to her, this wouldn't have happened," he admitted. He decided to leave out the part about craving a kinkier lifestyle and possibly pushing Allison away when she flat-out told him no. Maybe this whole mess was his fault.

"Now there you go," Connie chided. "Allison has admittedly been cheating on you for six months and you blame yourself. God Aiden, you were just providing for your family. My girl was never going to settle down and be happy. Not with you or anyone else, for that matter. Allison was always looking for the next best thing in her life and never stopped to look at what she already had. I'm sorry she did this to you and the girls." Aiden gave a nod not knowing what else to say. She could deny him having anything to do with Allison leaving but he knew the truth. It had been about a year since he came clean and asked Allison to try some of the things he had been wanting. He wasn't asking her to go to a BDSM club from the get-go, but he hoped she'd want to try at least some of the stuff he asked for. It was a lifestyle he knew well, having lived it for most of his twenties. When he met Allison, he was almost twenty-eight and he worried he would never find a woman to settle down with if he didn't leave the BDSM scene and give up his kinky lifestyle. So he did. He started dating Allison and he pushed down that side of himself, never letting on what he needed and everything he craved from her in the bedroom. But Aiden wasn't really happy and he knew if he continued to live a lie, he'd end up hurting them both. He was toying with telling her, but then she announced she was pregnant with Lucy and he got caught up in the excitement of a baby and a wedding. He decided to wait and spring his news on her after Lucy was born and they were officially man and wife. He had some crazy notion that as his wife she'd want the same things he did but he was wrong. In fact, the only thing he had been right about this whole time was the fact his lie would end up tearing them apart. He hated he was correct about that and especially hated how his girls would be the ones to pay the price.

"Listen, I have to get the girls home and tell them about their mother," he all but whispered. He really didn't want to have to do this next part but he had no choice. The three of them were going to have to get used to living without Allison and the sooner he told Lucy and Laney, the sooner they could begin the healing process of moving on. Connie nodded at the front screen door to where both girls stood, watching him. He could tell by Lucy's confused expression she had heard most of their conversation and she had questions.

Aiden opened the door and pulled both girls into his arms. "Hi babies," he murmured. "I'm going to take you home from Nanny's today," he said. Allison was usually the one to pick the girls up from her mother's on the days Connie watched them. Allison called her time away from them her "me time" and insisted it made her a better wife and mother. Now, Aiden could guess her "me time" involved her meeting up with her current boyfriend and he almost wanted to laugh at the irony of it all.

"Where's Mommy?" Lucy questioned. "She usually picks me and Laney up." His four-year-old was usually very inquisitive and he knew now would be no exception. She would ask him for answers and Aiden worried he wouldn't have any to give.

"Mommy had to go away for a while," he said. "I'm so sorry, girls but Mommy won't be coming home."

"Ever?" Lucy questioned. Laney stood next to her sister, watching between her and Aiden as if watching a volley. At two, she wasn't a talker like Lucy had been. Laney was more reserved and observant, but he knew she understood everything they were saying. He wouldn't lie to either of them, ever.

Aiden shook his head, "No baby, not ever. You're Mommy had some things to do but I'm here and I won't ever leave you," he promised. Lucy gave him a look that told him she didn't believe him, but that was par for the course. He knew both girls were closer to Allison; she was the parent who was around most for them. If he was going to earn their trust and help them through this process, he was going to have to make some changes. The first being he needed to be home more often and let Corbin pick up some of the slack around the office. He needed to show the girls he was going to step up and be the parent they deserved, unlike his own dad after his mother left him. He'd never turn into his father. That wasn't even an option —his girls deserved so much better than a drunk who was unreliable at best.

"How about we go home and I'll make us some pancakes for dinner like I used to. Then we can talk this all out and you can ask me all the questions you'd like." Lucy looked him over as if deciding if she wanted to go with him or stay with Connie. He didn't want to admit he was holding his breath waiting for her agreement but he was. Sometimes negotiating with Lucy was like trying to reason with a tiny terrorist who knew the ins and outs of the system. She knew just what to say and how to work over the person she was up against and Aiden worried she was already smarter than he was.

"Can we have chocolate chips in our pancakes?" Lucy asked,

looking at Laney to back her up. When the two-year-old eagerly nodded her head, Aiden couldn't help his chuckle.

"I think I can arrange that," he promised.

"And cream?" Laney chimed in. Aiden was sure his daughters would eat whipped cream on everything if he allowed it.

"Sure, baby girl. We can have whipped cream on top. Any other demands, ladies?" he teased. The girls looked at each other as if silently communicating, trying to decide if they would have any further stipulations to join him for dinner.

Connie giggled from behind him. "I think your Lucy might just become a hostage negotiator," she teased. "They sure do have your number, Aiden."

"They've always been able to twist me around their little fingers, even Allison," he murmured. He knew it was going to take time to get over his wife. He loved her, but that didn't stop the pain or hurt she caused by walking away. Aiden knew from experience that would take time and might never completely happen for him or his girls.

"So, what's it going to be?" he expectantly asked. Both girls nodded their little blonde heads and smiled up at him.

"We'll take your offer," Lucy agreed as if she had just brokered a business deal. "Thanks, Daddy." She kissed him on his cheek and Laney did the same. He watched as they both ran into Connie's house to get their things.

"Thanks, Connie," he said.

"No need to ever thank me," she offered. "Just call me when you're ready to venture back into the world and I'll help keep the girls as much as I can," she said. Aiden appreciated the offer, but knowing his mother-in-law had health issues would put a damper on him asking too much of her. He loved her for making the offer.

"Will do," he said. Lucy and Laney ran from the front door and over to Connie to kiss her cheek, shouting their goodbyes as they raced to his SUV.

"Come on, Daddy," Laney bossed. He watched as his

resilient girls climbed into the back of his vehicle and he wasn't sure how he had gotten so lucky. Aiden wished the promise of chocolate chip pancakes with whipped cream could fix all their problems long term. But for now, he'd take all the help he could get, even if it was only a short-term fix.

Aiden got the girls fed and bathed before Corbin showed up at his house. From the sympathetic expression on his face, Corbin had been completely filled in on all of the sordid details. There was only one person who could have clued him in and Aiden wasn't sure if he wanted to thank Rose or wring her neck for sharing his secret. Honestly, he knew Corbin would always have his back, and having someone to talk to would be a great help. In just two short hours, Aiden had worked through his self-pity over his wife walking out on him and had already moved straight on to anger. He just hoped he could get the girls to bed before he took his newfound feelings out on them. It wasn't their fault their mother had up and left him and he needed to remember that.

He met Corbin at the front door and held it open for him. "So, I'm guessing your mother filled you in?" he questioned, already knowing the answer before Corbin nodded his head.

He shot Aiden a sheepish grin, "Don't be mad at Mom, AJ," he said. "She's worried about you, man. You know she thinks of you as a son and hell, your girls might be the only grandchildren that woman might ever get. I'm not ready to settle down and have any of the little beasties myself." Corbin grimaced and shuttered from just the thought of having kids and Aiden laughed. His best friend never seemed to understand why he wanted to settle down and have a family. When Aiden and Allison announced she was pregnant, Corbin's first question was whether or not she was going to keep the baby. Looking back now, that might have been the first clue he had that his wife and his best friend weren't going to be each other's biggest fans. Aiden had to run quite a bit of interference back then. After the girls were born, they both seemed to settle down and Aiden could let his guard down a little.

"You're not here to say you told me so, are you?" Aiden grouched. "If you are, you can just turn right around and leave."

Corbin held his hands up in defense, "Naw, man. I'm here to tell you I'm sorry you and the girls have to go through this. I love you like a brother, man. I would never want any of this to happen no matter what differences I had with Alli," he offered.

Aiden smiled at the nickname only Corbin call his wife. "You know she fucking hated when you called her that, man," Aiden said.

Corbin's wolfish grin said it all. "I know. It's mostly why I did it," he admitted. "How about a beer?" he asked, holding up the six-pack he had hidden under his suit jacket.

"Sure," Aiden agreed. "Make yourself at home. I'm going to tuck the girls in, and I'll be right back down," he said. Corbin pulled his tie loose and by the time Aiden got back downstairs, twenty minutes later, his friend had stripped out of his dress shirt and was just wearing one of Aiden's t-shirts and a pair of his gym shorts.

"I hope you don't mind me borrowing some clothes," Corbin said.

Aiden laughed. "No problem. Although I'm afraid you're going to stretch out my shirt," he teased. Corbin worked out daily and he was bigger than Aiden, always had been. His arms alone looked like two of Aiden's put together. The women in town seemed to appreciate Corbin's gym efforts and loved the tattoos that banded his arms. Corbin usually kept them hidden under his dress shirt and jacket but when they would all casually go out for drinks, he basically had to turn women away left and right. Women fell for his good guy persona wrapped up in his bad boy image. Aiden had never seen the appeal of tattoos, even if the women seemed to go a little crazy over them. He had one tattoo on his upper arm of a shark wearing swim trunks and sunglasses. Aiden usually kept it secretly tucked away under his suits during the day, but it was his harsh reminder of drunken bad decision made with Corbin while they were pledging the same fraternity in college.

"I ordered pizza too. I haven't had time to eat all day and I'm starving," he said. As if on cue, the pizza delivery guy showed up with Corbin's extra-large meat lovers' pizza that made Aiden's mouth water. He paid the delivery guy and they both settled in the family room with their beer and pizza. Aiden could feel Corbin was holding back with him like he was keeping his hand close to his vest.

"All right, man let's have it. I know you're dying to say your peace, so spill it," Aiden insisted.

"I really don't have anything to say you haven't heard before, man. I hate to say, 'I told you so,'" he lied.

"You'd fucking love to tell me you were right. In fact, I'm betting you love saying those words to me more than you love pussy and that's a whole fucking lot," Aiden teased. Corbin stroked his beard and looked over at Aiden as if he was trying to decide if he was right or not.

"Well, you're not completely wrong but I guess it just depends on the pussy," Corbin joked. Corbin and he might have been the same age but his best friend was always taking lead when it came to their relationship. He seemed to think Aiden needed protecting, being smaller than him growing up, and who knows, maybe he was right. It sure felt good to have Corbin in his corner no matter what he was up against. It was one of the reasons Aiden chose to go to the same college as him, not ready to part ways with the person who stuck by him through thick and thin. Corbin was basically his brother and he wasn't sure what he would do without him.

"So what now?" Aiden asked. "Allison left me with two little girls who are probably going to grow up without a mother. How do I fix that?" Aiden took a swig of his beer and tossed his half-eaten pizza back into the box.

"You don't fix it, man. You be the best dad you can be and show your girls when life gives you shit, you find your shovel," Corbin growled. "How do you know Alli won't be back, AJ?" he asked. Yeah, he hadn't gotten to the best part of his day yet— the part where Lucy handed him her backpack and told him Mommy left something inside for him. Allison apparently told the girls to wait to give him the letter she wrote until they were home from Connie's house. He had to hand it to his wife, she sure knew how to bring the drama. At least he could read her letter in the privacy of his own home and this time, when he finished reading it, he could just tear it up and throw it away. His poor phone bore the extent of his anger at her earlier text and now he was going to have to run out and pick up a new one in the morning.

"Allison left me a letter with the girls. She told them to give it to me when we got home from Connie's," Aiden admitted.

Corbin whistled, "Wow, she had this all planned out, didn't she? What did it say?" he asked.

"Basically, she said she wasn't cut out to be a wife or mother and she wasn't willing to spend her life wondering, 'What if?'. She told me to text her when the divorce papers were ready to be signed and she didn't want anything but the money that was promised to her when she signed the prenup."

"And how much is that?" Corbin angrily barked.

"One and a half million." Aiden shrugged.

"Fuck, man," Corbin swore. Aiden didn't hide his smile. Corbin seemed angrier than he did about the day's events if that was even possible. Honestly, Aiden just felt numb about the whole thing now. He wasn't sure that was going to change any time soon either.

"It's only money, man," he said. He meant it too. He'd pay just about any amount to have Allison be a part of the girls' lives but he knew once his wife made up her mind, there was no changing it. She chose to walk away from him and his daughters and now, the three of them would be the ones paying the price.

"How about you take some time—you know figure out just what you and the girls need. I'll handle the majority of the work stuff and that way you have time to focus on your family and politics," Corbin offered.

"I can't just dump the company on your lap, man," Aiden said. "I'll handle my own shit but I'm going to take the next two weeks off. I need to figure out the girls' schedules and make sure they are both all right with everything that is changing. Maybe we'll take a quick trip somewhere, get out of town for a few days—you know the whole change of scenery thing?" Aiden didn't really have a plan but as far as ideas went, a little family trip sounded like a good one.

"That sounds like a good plan," Corbin confirmed. "Get the girl's minds off of missing Alli and you can take some downtime."

"Right. I'll have Rose book us something in the morning," Aiden agreed. Corbin shot him a concerned look and Aiden chuckled. "Don't worry, man, I'll be fine. Allison made her decision and we will just have to live with it. Life marches on, as your mom likes to say."

"Yeah," Corbin agreed. "I always hated that expression I just never had the balls to tell her," he admitted. Aiden threw back his head and laughed and for the first time since getting Allison's text, he felt normal, as if everything was going to be all right. He just wished he believed it because Aiden wasn't sure anything would be right ever again.

ZARA

6 Months Later

Zara Joy walked into the local club and she wasn't sure how she let her best friend talk her into this. A nightclub was one thing but the town's only BDSM club was quite another. She was sure she wasn't going to be able to follow through with the dare she accepted and would run out of there like the meek little mouse she was. When Avalon tricked her into agreeing to step out of her comfort zone, she had no clue it would be this far out. Her comfort zone was a distant blip on her radar and Zara wasn't sure if she'd ever be able to find her way back again. But once Ava found out she hadn't lost her virginity, as she falsely reported the one and only time the subject came up, she went off and dared her to do the unthinkable.

Truthfully, she wanted a change from her everyday pace and when Ava told her about a new club in town, she was intrigued. The idea of dancing the night away left Zara feeling daring and ready to take on Ava's challenge. But her sneaky friend never mentioned the new club wasn't a nightclub but a sex club that catered to the elite clientele who paid hefty fees to join. Ava's father owned half the town so she had no problem getting Zara into the club as a guest for the night.

Zara's cell rang and she pulled it from her purse. "Hello," she whispered.

"Hey girl," Ava sassed, "did you make it to the club all right?" she asked. Ava knew damn well Zara wouldn't be able to resist a dare. Zara held the phone away from her face and put her on speaker so Ava could hear the moans and groans of pleasure filling the club. A woman was in the corner, sprawled across and bound to what looked like a saddle, having her ass spanked red by a man standing behind her with a leather paddle. She hoped Ava would be able to hear the sound of the paddle every time it made contact with the woman's fleshy ass or the way she cried out and then moaned with pleasure.

"Does it sound like I'm at the club?" Zara asked.

Ava giggled into the other end of the cell. "I knew you wouldn't turn down a good dare."

"Yeah well, I thought you were sending me to an actual club, not a meat market of naked women getting men off," she whispered. "What the actual hell, Ava?"

Her giggle filled the other end of the line again and she knew their conversation was going nowhere. "You should totally take advantage of one of those men, Z," Ava said. "You're a twenty-five-year-old virgin and it's time for you to drop that title." Ava was right but what was she supposed to do? Walking right up to some leather-clad man welding a whip didn't seem like the best idea. Zara was sure that scenario playing out wouldn't end well for her.

"I can't just walk up to a complete stranger and ask him for sex," Zara spat.

"Oh, I don't know. You might find some of us complete strangers are open to a little fun, honey. That is why most of us are here." Zara spun around and found a man standing so close to her, she could feel his breath on her skin. He was sexy as sin, impeccably dressed in a three-piece suit with his light brown hair disheveled as if someone had run their fingers through it already. His blue eyes were what caught her off guard. They were so dark that him looking at her felt as if he could see directly into her soul, even eliciting a shiver from her.

"I'm sorry," she said, taking a step back from him. "I was having a private conversation with my friend." She held up the phone as if proving a point. "Ava," she said into the phone, realizing her so-called friend had hung up on her. "Fuck," she cursed. The sexy man's smirk was nearly her undoing and she found herself smiling back at him for no real reason.

"Seems your friend had other plans than to talk on the phone all night. You have any other plans Miss—" He looked her up and down as if waiting her out. Zara thought not answering him might be her best bet but the way he looked at her as if he wasn't giving her an option but to answer, she had no choice.

"Zara," she answered. He gifted her with his sexy smirk again and she was sure her panties were going to burst into flames from just the scorching way he looked her up and down. It was almost territorial like he was marking her with his gaze.

"Nice to meet you, Zara. I'm Aiden," he said holding his hand out to take hers. She hesitantly took his offered hand and gave a gentle shake, noting the way he didn't take his eyes from hers. "Is this your first time here?" he asked. Zara nodded and pulled her hand back from him.

"I'm here because of a stupid dare," she admitted. God, she sounded like a child and she wished she could take back her words. "Um, I mean my best friend dared me to go out to a club by myself and well, I thought she meant a regular club—you know like dancing and drinks." Aiden smiled at her and she felt like a giddy schoolgirl. "Instead, she sent me here and well, this wasn't what I had imagined," she admitted.

"You don't sound very happy about being here, Zara. Would

you like to leave?" That was a very good question. She looked around the room as if trying to decide her answer. A part of her was curious and she had to admit the chances of her returning were slim to none. What would it hurt to take a look around and maybe get a little bit of experience? No one knew who she was or that she was a virgin, at least she hoped they didn't. The last time she looked, it wasn't stamped on her forehead or anything.

"I think I'd like to stay," she almost whispered. Zara didn't turn to look at him, fixated on the woman in the corner of the room she saw earlier. The man who had been spanking her while she was strapped to a leather saddle released her bonds and was fucking her from behind, in front of the whole room. People had stopped what they were doing to watch the two of them together and Zara felt like an intruder. She wanted to look away but she couldn't. They were seriously hot together and the way he commanded her body made Zara feel things she never had before.

"You like watching them?" Aiden whispered into her ear. She nodded and smiled back over her shoulder to where he stood. He was so close again that she wondered if this guy had any personal space boundaries.

"I—I think I do," she shyly admitted. If she was being completely truthful, she would have told him she wasn't sure what she liked and didn't like because she was never with a man before, not in that way. Sure, she had dated her fair share of guys over the years, but working as a nanny didn't afford her the luxury of meeting too many people on the job. It wasn't like she could have an office romance or go out for drinks with her co-workers after the day was over. She usually lived with the families she nannied for making it hard for her to have any sort of social life. Zara never really had friends over to the family's house, not wanting to presume that was all right. Besides Ava, she really didn't have many other friends but she wasn't lonely.

She loved her work and the families whom she grew to think of as hers especially since she didn't have one of her own.

"Would you like to try the spanking bench?" Aiden asked.

"Um, shouldn't we get to know each other first or something?" she questioned. Zara felt silly asking but this whole thing felt completely foreign to her. When she thought about having sex for the first time, she imagined the guy would at least buy her dinner first. Never in her wildest dreams did she think he'd be asking to spank her ass red while she straddled a leather saddle.

Aiden's chuckle and his warm breath on her shoulder made her shiver. "It was just a question, Zara. Maybe I should have dared you," he teased, causing her to giggle.

"Accepting dares apparently never ends well for me," she murmured.

"Well, maybe tonight will be different," he suggested. "I can help you with that," he offered. Zara wasn't sure how this was all supposed to work but she felt foolish asking.

"I'm not sure I'm ready for all of this—" she said, waving her hands wildly about. "It's just so public," she admitted. Zara felt like a complete fraud standing in the middle of a sexual playroom with no experience of her own.

"Would you like to get a private room?" he asked. She could tell he was trying for nonchalant, but the way he looked at her so intensely, she knew he was hoping she'd say yes. How could she not? He hadn't even really touched her yet and she was sure her panties were wet. She wanted Aiden, that was not the question. Why she wanted a complete stranger might be something she should think about but not now. Right now, she wanted to go with Aiden and take him up on his offer. Zara was done being a coward and it was time she did something about it. She was going to do this for herself. She didn't give a fuck about Ava's dare and when she walked out of that club tonight, she wouldn't have to look back or wonder about what if's because that wasn't what Aiden was offering her. She might be naïve, but she knew enough to know her handsome stranger was going to give her just what she wanted—a night of strings-free hot sex and that was just fine with her.

"Yes," she whispered. "I'd like that, Aiden."

AIDEN

A iden wasn't sure what had drawn him to the pretty little blonde woman with curves for miles and the sexiest smile he had seen in a long time. Maybe it was the way she seemed so nervous and out of place but he couldn't stay away from her and why should he?

Since Allison left, he had been the picture-perfect father. He had taken the girls to the beach for a few days and when they were sick and tired of the sun and sand, he flew them all to Disney and by the time they finally got back home, he felt like he needed a vacation from his vacation. Aiden had worked it out with Connie for her to babysit the girls a few afternoons a week after their preschool let out. He arranged for a car and driver to pick them up from school and deliver them to Connie's to help cut down on her workload. Honestly, it was the very least he could do since she was helping him out so much. Aiden knew it had to be hard on her but she insisted she loved having the girls around. He knew it was good for Lucy and Laney too. Even though they didn't really talk about Allison much, he could tell they both missed her, and being with their grandmother seemed to help lift some of their sadness.

Aiden threw himself back into his work and every night after he'd put the girls to bed, he'd fall into his own bed, dog-tired. He was ready for a change and a little fun. His divorce was finalized two weeks prior and Allison made no attempts to call or see him or the girls. He had his lawyer send her the divorce papers and the check and that was the only contact they had, which was fine by him. Corbin convinced him to stop working so damn hard and blow off some steam. He told Corbin he was fine but they both knew he was lying. Corbin persuaded him to get a sitter and join his local BDSM club. Aiden had to admit he thought his friend was crazy for making the suggestion, but the few times he had been there made him feel alive. And now, the sexy little blonde had agreed to get a private room with him and he was hoping she'd want to play. He could think of nothing he wanted more than to play with sexy little Zara.

Aiden wasted no time showing Zara back to his private room. He kept one reserved knowing anything he did with a woman in the playroom would be in the public eye. When members paid to join the very exclusive club, they were all made to sign a waiver saying what happened in the club would remain private but he knew better. Aiden still had just over six months until the election and there was no way he'd trust everything he'd already built to a simple waiver. People made promises all the time, but enough incentive could persuade anyone to change their minds. He knew he couldn't let anything get in the way of his run for the Senate, not even his driving desires for Dominance. Taking women back to his fully stocked private room seemed to be the only way to ensure privacy. Sure, that meant putting his trust in virtual strangers to keep his secret but what other choice did he have? Meeting women who were into the same kinks he liked wasn't something one could do at a bar or even a dating sight. He couldn't risk the exposure and everything he had worked so hard to build.

He shut the door, closing out the sounds of sultry music, moans, and leather slapping bare skin that seemed to play through the club. He was used to the scene by now after a couple of weeks of attendance but he could tell this world was new to her. Aiden worried Zara might not be ready for everything he wanted to do with her and he had to know she was completely with him; otherwise he wouldn't move forward with her.

"Is this your first time?" he questioned. The look on Zara's beautiful face was almost comical. She shyly nodded her head and he couldn't help his smirk. Aiden wasn't sure if introducing her to kink was a good idea, but the thought of being the first man to give her a taste of the lifestyle he was quickly coming to love, turned him completely on.

"How about you tell me what you'd like to try and I'll do my best to give it to you?" he asked. It wasn't usually how things worked, but he wanted Zara's first experience with kink to be one that brought her pleasure. Him demanding what he wanted from her might turn her off to the whole world and wouldn't that be a shame?

"I think I'd like to try spanking," she said with a shrug. Aiden smiled; his hand literally felt like it tingled at the thought of smacking her sexy, curvy ass.

"I think I'd like to spank you, Zara," he admitted. He wasn't sure what it was about the woman standing in front of him but his whole body seemed to hum to life just being in the same small room with her. Zara looked shyly at the bed and he could see she was still unsure of everything. He closed the short space between them and wrapped her in his arms, pulling her body snugly against his own. Zara gasped and looked up at him, just the reaction he was hoping for.

"If you don't want to do this, honey we don't have to. We can do as much or as little as you'd like. You're in charge here," he admitted. And he meant it too. She was completely in control of everything they would or wouldn't do tonight—he wouldn't push her into anything she wasn't ready for.

Zara giggled, "I thought you were in charge," she teased. Aiden smiled and dipped to gently kiss her lips and those damn sparks felt as if they ran through his entire body. She shyly kissed him back and he wanted to take more from her but he needed to remember his promise. He was going to let her take lead and tell him what she wanted. Then, he'd find a way to hold his inner caveman at bay long enough to give her what she needed and hopefully she'd ask him for more.

"Wow," she whispered, breaking their kiss. He liked the way he seemed to leave her a little breathless.

"Yeah—wow," he agreed. "Tell me you feel it too," he commanded.

Zara nodded her head, not taking her eyes from his. "Sparks," she said. "I feel them," she admitted.

"Thank fuck," he breathed. "Tell me what else you want me to do to you, Zara," he ordered. His body was ready for more and his dick was twitching to be set free but he needed to be patient. Every urge in his body was telling him to forget all the kink and foreplay, throw sexy little Zara onto his bed and thrust balls deep into her. He wanted to mark her, make her hips and never let her out of that fucking room again— but that wasn't what any of this was. He needed to remember she was a stranger in a BDSM club looking for one thing. Sure, it was the same thing he was searching for, but for some reason, he seemed to want to take more from the beautiful stranger.

Aiden couldn't seem to help himself; he ran his hands over her curves, kissing his way down her neck. He wanted more from her. Hell, he wanted everything from her. "Well," she stuttered. He loved the way she shivered against his body, seeming to like the attention he was paying her sensitive neck. He ran his hand up under her tank top to find she wasn't wearing a bra and nearly came in his fucking pants. Aiden tugged at her taut nipple, eliciting a gasp and soft moan from Zara.

"You like that?" he asked, already knowing the answer.

"Yes," she hissed.

"What else do you want, Zara?" he once again demanded.

"I want it all, Aiden, please," she begged. He didn't stop this time, pulling her over to the bed with him. He sat on the edge and ran his hands up under her short skirt, cupping her bare ass. He let his fingers flex into her fleshy globes and pushed his face into her pussy. Even through her clothing, he could smell her arousal and he knew she was ready for him.

"Strip," he commanded. Zara hesitated as if she wasn't sure if she wanted to follow his orders or protest. He took his hands off her body as if letting her know she could refuse him but if she did, he wouldn't touch her again. "You don't have to do anything you don't want to, Zara," he admitted. "I won't touch you again until you tell me it's what you want."

Zara reached for his hands and pulled them back to her body. "I want," she admitted. She tugged her skirt down her body to reveal she wasn't wearing any panties either. He hissed out his breath, greedy to taste her. She was gorgeous; her pussy was completely bare, just the way he liked and he could tell she was soaked and ready for whatever he wanted from her. Zara then shyly pulled her tank up over her body, revealing her perfect breasts to him and this time, he didn't stop himself. He pulled her against his body and sucked one of her nipples into his mouth, loving the way she cried out his name. If he had his way, he'd have her panting and needy within minutes.

"You're beautiful, Zara," he whispered into her ear. She gifted him with her shy smile and rubbed her body against his.

"Will you take off your clothes too?" she asked. Aiden knew if he did, this whole scene would be over way too quickly. It was best if he kept his pants on while she was sprawled across his lap for her spanking. He wanted to at least give her part of her request so he yanked off his dress shirt, loving the way her blue eyes greedily roamed his torso. "You work out way more than I do," she teased. Aiden chuckled against her skin as his lips made their way up to her mouth.

"Working out is a good stress reliever," he admitted. Honestly, sex was an even better stress reliever for him but he didn't get to play like this as often as he'd like. Aiden had only recently joined the club and the first couple of times he went, he found himself watching and learning rather than participating. He was perfectly happy to sit back in the shadows and observe but tonight, when Zara walked in, he couldn't help himself. He knew if he didn't jump on her another Dom would and he didn't want to miss his chance with the sexy blonde. Every man in the club seemed to take notice of her, watching to see if she was with anyone. He knew other men would have given just about anything to take Zara back to their room and he counted himself lucky she agreed to accompany him to his private quarters.

"I'm afraid I don't get much time to work out. I lack the free time to just run to the gym," Zara said. She tried to cover herself with her arms and Aiden growled his displeasure. He wouldn't let her hide from him.

"It's too late for that, Zara," he insisted, tugging her arms down from her body. "I've already seen just about every square inch of your body, baby. You are so fucking sexy and I won't have you hiding from me, understand?" he asked. Zara kept her arms at her side as if accepting his dare and he chuckled. "You really seem to like a good dare, don't you, honey?" he teased.

"Yes," she breathed.

"Good. Let's see how you handle this next one. I dare you to lay across my lap so I can spank that curvy ass of yours," he said. Zara's eyes flared at the mention of him spanking her and he knew he was on the right track with what she wanted from tonight. Aiden sat on the edge of the bed and waited for her to make her decision. He didn't know he was holding his breath until she took a step towards him and he let out his pent-up sigh.

"Like this?" she questioned, laying across his lap with her fleshy ass prominently displayed.

"Yes," he hissed, "just like that, baby." God, this woman might just be his undoing with the way she seemed to obey his every command. She was a perfect submissive and dare he think it—just the type of woman Aiden had been looking for his whole life. He needed to keep his eye on the prize and stop jumping ahead of himself though. Zara was just looking for a hookup, not a marriage proposal and it would do him well to remember that.

Zara squirmed around his lap and his cock protested that he still had his pants on. When she finally settled, he ran the palm of his hand over her ass, loving the breathy little moans and sighs that escaped her lips. "Ready, baby?" he questioned. Aiden needed to be sure Zara was one hundred percent on board.

"I'm ready," she agreed and settled across his lap. He almost wanted to chuckle when she dramatically exhaled but he didn't dare. He knew that this being Zara's first time experiencing any part of the kinky lifestyle might be a little unnerving for her.

"I'll go slowly and you tell me if you don't like something and we can stop," he offered. "You are in complete control here, Zara," he admitted. She turned her head and smiled up at him. "I'd like for you to keep count," he said. She looked back down to the floor and nodded her agreement. Honestly, he was beginning to feel a little nervous from her jitters and it had been some time since any woman made him feel that way.

He landed the first blow on her left globe and then rubbed his palm over where he left his mark. "One," she choked out. Aiden worried this was all going to be too much for her but he also gave her an out. All Zara had to do was tell him to stop and he would. He landed the second blow on her right cheek, liking to mix things up and not concentrate too much on one area.

Although the thought of Zara remembering him every time she sat down tomorrow did strange things to him.

"Two," she said and rubbed her wet folds on his lap. He could feel her heat through his pants and he liked the way she responded to her spankings.

"Hold still, baby," he commanded and brought down his palm again, meeting her fleshy ass.

"Three," she moaned. Aiden couldn't help himself, he needed to know she was enjoying her spanking half as much as he was. He dipped two fingers down into her folds and found her so wet and ready for him that all he could think about was how good she was going to feel when he finally got to the portion of the night where he could take her body. He wanted to be inside of her, claiming her and making Zara cry out his name over and over—but that would come soon enough. First, he needed to finish her spanking and then he'd sink balls deep into her luscious body and take what he wanted from her.

ZARA

Aiden was giving her so much pleasure she wasn't sure if she would be able to take much more. She had just counted out the eighth time his hand landed on her ass and all she could think about was Aiden and what he was going to do to her. Every time his palm made contact with her skin she could feel every promise he was silently making her. Honestly, she knew she should be nervous about what was about to happen between the two of them but she wasn't. Aiden was in control of her body, mind, and soul and that seemed to be just what she needed. Zara was able to finally get out of her own head, not think so much about the next step, and just feel.

The final blow was a little harder than the rest and she yelped in surprise. It really didn't hurt, just caught her off guard. "Ten," he growled and turned her in his lap. He pulled her up his body, so she was straddling his cock, almost cradling it with her slick folds and she forgot all about not knowing what to do next. The way Aiden was kissing her was nearly her undoing. No man had ever kissed or touched her the way Aiden was. She couldn't seem to get enough of the way he almost wanted to consume her.

"On the bed, Zara," he said. He helped her free from his lap and she laid back on the big bed as he ordered. She had to admit she liked his bossy nature; it turned her on. "I'm going to cuff your ankles and wrists to the bed, baby," he said. "Are you okay with that?" Aiden hovered over her body and she wasn't sure how she felt about being bound to his bed. A part of her was afraid that letting a complete stranger shackle her to his bed wasn't such a great idea. For all she knew he could be a crazed lunatic. But when he looked at her, so trusting and hopeful, she wanted to give him everything he was asking for and more.

"Yes," she said, nodding her agreement. "I think I'd like that," she admitted.

"Good girl," he praised. She liked when he called her that. It made her want to please him by continuing to be his good girl. Zara just needed to remember this had nothing to do with emotions or her heart. He wasn't asking her for a commitment. Aiden wanted to use her body for a night of pleasure and that was it. Feelings had nothing to do with what he wanted from her.

Aiden made quick work of securing her ankles and wrists to the bed posts using soft-cuffed handcuffs. She had to admit being completely bound and spread wide for him both excited her and scared the hell out of her. The way Aiden looked at her made her completely hot. He ran a finger along her cheek and down her neck, making his way to her sensitive nipple. He was working his way down her body and just his simple touch, with one single finger, nearly made her crazy with lust. She bucked and writhed against her restraints and he chided her for not holding still for him.

"Do you want me to stop, Zara?" he sternly questioned.

"No," she stuttered. "Please don't stop," she begged.

"Do you think you can hold still for me while I eat your

pussy?" he asked. She wanted to move, to squirm but God she wanted to feel his mouth on her wet core. She wanted to know what it felt like to have a man between her legs in every way and Aiden was promising her that and so much more. All she had to do was hold still. Surely she could do that, right?

"Yes," she hissed.

"Good girl," he praised. Aiden ran two fingers through her drenched folds and moaned. "You are so wet for me, baby," he said. "You are going to feel so fucking amazing when I finally fuck you. I wonder if you taste as good as you feel," he teased. Aiden settled between her thighs and seemed to hesitate. She looked down her body to find him studying her and if she wasn't mistaken, he actually sniffed her pussy.

"You smell so fucking good, honey," he growled. He licked into her folds to find her sensitive clit and sucked it into his mouth. She couldn't help herself, Zara bucked against his mouth, as if trying to take more of what he was already giving her.

"Zara," he warned. She tried to hold still, really she did but just his warm breath on her sensitive core had her writhing and moaning with pleasure. She was so close; she just needed a little more.

"Please," she begged. "Please I need more, Aiden. I'm so close," she cried. She wasn't sure if she was begging him to give her everything or stop. It was almost too much and Zara wasn't sure if she'd ever get enough of the sexy man who was taking complete control of her body.

"I've got you, baby," he promised. "Just lay back and enjoy this and let me take care of you." Zara took a breath and dramatically released it, causing Aiden to chuckle. "Good girl," he praised. Zara wasn't sure why every time Aiden said those words to her, her entire world felt right. Maybe it was the fact he was praising her but really, why should that matter? Aiden was virtually a stranger to her and his opinion shouldn't count —but it did.

Aiden ran his fingers through her wet folds and Zara did everything she could to remain completely still. A soft whimper escaped her lips as she looked down her body to watch Aiden. He smiled up at her and winked and Zara knew he was intentionally driving her crazy. "You're doing this on purpose," she accused.

"Doing what?" he murmured, seemingly distracted by her body.

"Teasing me," she said.

"No, honey," he admitted. "I'm not teasing you. I'm teaching you to hold still for me. You're doing a beautiful job too," he praised. This time she felt less anxious to please him. Truthfully, Zara was feeling a little pissed he might be punishing her in any way.

"That's not fair," she pouted. Aiden laughed against the delicate skin of her inner thighs, working his way back to her aching pussy. He knew exactly what he was doing and it was driving her crazy.

"Fair has nothing to do with it, honey. While you're in this room you belong to me. I do what I please with what is mine and at this very moment in time, you're mine," he said. She wasn't sure how she felt about belonging to anyone but he was right about one thing. At that very moment, she was his and there was nothing she could do about it. Hell, there was nothing she wanted to do about it. She liked the way Aiden controlled her body as if he could read her every need. There was no way she'd want to tell him to stop—not now and probably not ever.

Zara laid back and Aiden seemed to take it as a sign of her compliance. He parted her folds and kissed and sucked at her until she couldn't stand it anymore. "Come for me, Zara," he ordered. She wasn't sure how or why, but her body seemed to do as he asked and she felt as though she was falling and no one would be there to catch her. Zara felt Aiden tug her wrists and ankles free from the restraints and gathered her into his arms, pulling her snugly against his body.

"I've got you, baby," he crooned over and over again and for the first time in a very long time, Zara didn't feel so alone. She wrapped her arms around his neck and looked up at him, wanting to say something—anything but she wasn't sure what would be appropriate in this situation. She had never been in this particular circumstance, so she didn't quite know what to do.

"Thank you," she breathed and nuzzled his neck.

"You never have to thank me for giving you an orgasm, honey," he whispered. "We aren't finished here Zara, not by a long shot. I'd like to see you again, after tonight." Once again, she was struck mute. She hadn't gone out expecting to meet anyone. Honestly, she hadn't gone out expecting to end up in a sex club. Meeting someone as wonderful as Aiden threw her for a loop but she wanted to tell him yes. Zara wanted to see Aiden again and she wasn't about to deny him.

"Yes," she murmured. "I'd like to see you again, Aiden," she admitted. He gifted her with his sexy half-smirk and she knew any resistance she might have been feeling was now completely gone.

"I want you, Zara," he said. No man had ever said those words to her and she could feel her body hum to life again. He rolled her underneath his body and she had to admit, all the feelings of nervousness and worry seemed to dissipate. She didn't know what it was about this man that made her want to trust him but she did. Maybe that made her a fool but she didn't really care.

Aiden kissed down the column of her neck and back up to her lips, giving her soft, slow, passionate kisses that felt like he reignited a fire deep down in her core. "Please," she whimpered and that seemed to be all he needed. He rolled her underneath his body and plunged balls deep into her core. Zara cried out in pain and Aiden stilled.

"What the fuck, Zara?" he growled. She closed her eyes, not really sure if she was trying to hide from his piercing gaze over the fact she kept she was a virgin from him or from the pain of having him sink into her body.

"I'm fine," she lied.

"You want to tell me what the hell is going on here?" he asked. His question felt more like an accusation.

"Well, I thought we were having sex," she sassed. From the look on his face, he wasn't in the mood for her cheeky remarks. Two could play that game because she wasn't in the mood to be treated like a child.

"I mean the fact you are obviously a virgin, Zara," he barked.

"I was a virgin, Aiden. You just took care of that issue for me." Again he shot her a disapproving look that should have made her cringe but there was no way she was going to back down—not now. She was a grown woman and she was capable of making her own choices.

"It's no big deal, really," she added. "I'm twenty-five and up until a few seconds ago, I was a virgin. It was about time I took care of that little problem," she admitted.

"It wasn't a little problem; it was your virginity. You should have told me or at least given me a heads-up. It's almost as if you lied by omission," he accused.

"Are you calling me a liar, Aiden? I might be a lot of things but a liar isn't one of them. I wanted you and you seemed to be pretty into me. I don't understand what the big deal is," she said.

"The big deal is that it was a big fucking deal but you didn't share it with me. As the other person involved here, I had the right to know. Communication is key and you blew that, Zara. You kept a vital piece of information about yourself from me," he said. His tone was harsh and she knew they weren't getting anywhere with their discussion, just moving in circles. She pushed at his body, wanting him out of her. They were still joined and this was definitely not the way she pictured her first time. Hell, none of this was, but Aiden was making fantasies she didn't know existed come true. Maybe this whole night was just a giant mistake but Zara hoped Aiden saying he wanted to see her again was a good sign. Instead, he looked at her like he hated her and all she could think about was getting as far away from him as possible. Aiden took the hint and rolled off her body, allowing Zara to get up. She quickly pulled on her skirt and tank top and found her shoes in the corner of the room. She put them on and grabbed her purse, not wanting to look back at the bed where Aiden was. She couldn't stand the sadness and disappointment that was going to be waiting for her in his eyes. She had already seen enough and all Zara wanted to do was go home and take a long shower, crawl into her own bed, and cry herself to sleep. Tomorrow, she could figure out the rest of her crazy mixed-up life.

AIDEN

Aiden spent the next two weeks trying to forget the sexy curvy blonde who haunted his dreams. Every night, as he was about to drift off, he would see Zara slipping on her shoes and not bothering to give him even a second look back. It hurt seeing her walk away but he knew it was for the best. He just needed to figure out why the hell it hurt so fucking much to watch her go. Zara was the first woman Aiden had felt a connection with since Allison left him. It was silly really. He didn't know Zara and feeling butt hurt over a woman he barely spent an hour with was complete nonsense—but that was where he was at. He had a big fundraiser last night and every blonde woman who came into the room reminded him of her. Aiden found himself wishing Zara would magically appear and when she hadn't, he thought about going back to the club and finding another blonde sub to take her place but he knew that wouldn't work either. He had a feeling no one else would measure up to her and he'd end up disappointed and confused.

"Hey man, you look like complete shit," Corbin assessed.

He walked into Aiden's office, bypassing his mother's shouts telling him Aiden wasn't to be disturbed.

"It's all right, Rose," Aiden offered. "Corbin doesn't listen to either of us so you might as well save your breath." Corbin smiled and agreed with him, watching Rose shake her head at the pair of them and leave his office. "You know, one of these days she's going to lose her shit with you and just up and quit," Aiden accused.

"Yeah," Corbin said with a shrug. "But today's not that day," he teased. "What's up with you, man? You seem grumpier than usual lately if that's even possible." Aiden knew Corbin was referring to his shitty moods since his night with Zara in the club but he wouldn't come right out and say it. Aiden had told him all about his sexy little bombshell and the way she used him to lose her virginity. Corbin thought the whole thing was a lot funnier than Aiden did but that was usually the way things worked between the two of them. Corbin was easier going and carefree while Aiden had adult responsibilities—namely two little girls who counted on him to be the stable parent in both of their lives since their mother left.

"Not now, man," Aiden warned and nodded to the opened door. He knew Rose would see it as an invitation to personally spy on the two of them. She meant well, but sometimes he felt like a little boy again with the way she hovered. What he was doing in a BDSM club or the fact he acted like a complete ass to a perfectly lovely woman, wasn't something he wanted to share with the woman who was like a mother to him.

"Fine, but we aren't finished talking about what happened, Aiden. You need to get over being an ass. I'm sure the pretty woman from the club has already forgotten all about you," Corbin teased, again laughing at his own joke.

"What pretty girl from which club?" Rose asked, pushing her way into the room. Aiden groaned and Corbin seemed to find his discomfort even more amusing.

"Go ahead, man," Corbin taunted. "Tell mom how you fucked up and then I can be her favorite again."

Aiden shot him a look hopefully telling him to shut the fuck up but from the knowing smirk on his best friend's face, he didn't give a shit what Aiden wanted. "We both know you're Rose's favorite. I'm just your annoying best friend who you could never shake off," Aiden grumbled. He hoped he could change the topic, but when Rose put her hands on her hips and stared him down, he knew there would be no getting around her question.

"Focus, Aiden," she prompted. "Girl—nightclub?" she questioned.

He sighed, "Fine," he said. "I met a nice woman at a night club and I fucked things up with her and now I can't stop thinking about her or the way I screwed everything up," he admitted.

"Well, I'm sure it's not the first time you goofed things up with a pretty woman. Maybe you should cut yourself a break. It hasn't been very long since Allison left you and the girls. You should take some time off dating and concentrate on your family. I know that work and your campaign are stressful, maybe you should hire someone to help out," Rose said. He wasn't sure how to explain to her that meeting women had nothing to do with dating right now and everything to do with fucking. Corbin smiled over at him, standing in the corner of his office as if trying to stay out of the way.

"You," he shouted, pointing at Corbin, "need to mind your own fucking business. And, as for the extra help, I have all I can possibly handle. The company is running as smoothly as possible with Corbin taking over some of my caseloads and my fantastic assistant having my schedule nailed down to the very last second for me. My campaign is going well and I have an excellent staff on that end. Hell, they've completely covered up the fact my wife left me. As far as anyone is concerned, Allison is at home lovingly taking care of our family while I'm out winning votes. There hasn't been one single press leak about anything that has happened between the two of us. I signed the divorce papers and thought that would set off a frenzy in the press but nothing, nada—not that I'm complaining." His campaign was headed up by some of the area's best and he couldn't ask for a better campaign manager. Derrika Clayton was highly recommended and cost him a small fortune, but she knew how to put out fires before they were even an ember and he had to admit he was damn thankful for her. His biggest problem was keeping his new social life private and out of the public eye. If anyone found out he had covered up the fact he and his so-called devoted wife were in fact divorced, his whole campaign would be over. He needed to just hang in there a little while longer and then he'd be able to announce his wife had left him and he was trying to pick up the pieces and be the best father he could be to his two little girls. Derrika just wanted to get past the primaries in a few weeks and then he could make the announcement and stop living under the deception that everything was fine. Honestly, he looked forward to the day he could announce to the world he was living a lie. Sneaking around and being under the public's microscope wasn't the kind of life he wanted for himself or his daughters. Plenty of men were in his shoes and he was sure Derrika was making a bigger deal out of him being jilted by his ex-wife than she needed to. Still, he trusted her and she was his campaign manager. He'd do what she wanted, for now.

"I'm not talking about your staff at work or on the campaign, Aiden," Rose said, interrupting his thoughts. "I think it's time you hired a nanny to help with the girls. They hate coming here after daycare while you finish up with work. They're bored and need more stability than hanging out in your office while you try to make phone calls. They need someone who is going to take them to the park or arrange playdates with kids their age." Rose did have a point. Connie tried telling him the same thing a few weeks back. He was sure his ex-mother-in-law was trying to help but at the time, it felt like criticism. Lately, Aiden felt as if he couldn't do a damn thing right, and having Connie tell him he needed a nanny only seemed to drive home his point. If he hired outside help that would mean he wasn't doing a good enough job with his daughters and that was something he couldn't fuck up.

"No," he said. Rose nodded and started for the door, grabbing some files from his desk. He knew he upset her but he was being a stubborn ass.

"You should at least think about it, man," Corbin said. "Mom isn't trying to hurt your feelings or say you're fucking things up. We both see you are struggling and maybe hiring someone to help with the girls isn't such a bad idea." Rose stopped in the doorway to look back at him and he hated the hurt he saw in her eyes. Upsetting Rose was something he hated doing. Having her disappointed in him usually felt like a knife to the gut and he'd do just about anything to avoid hurting her. Aiden knew they were both right; hiring a nanny might be good for his girls. He also knew what he was currently doing wasn't what any of them needed. Lucy and Laney deserved more than he was giving them. They deserved his best and maybe the only way he could give that to them was to hire some help.

"Fine," he whispered. "Can you call some of the local agencies and start the process?" he asked. Rose nodded.

"I'll set up some interviews, weed out the ones who aren't a fit and pick a few for you to look at," she offered.

"Thanks, Rose," he said. She left his office, pulling the door shut behind her, leaving him with Corbin and what he knew was going to become a game of twenty questions. "Please don't start with me," he said, holding up his hands. "I'm spent and just want to get done my work and go home." Corbin's sympathetic look nearly pissed him off again. He could handle snarky and condescending from his best friend but pity or sympathy was another story.

"Don't look at me like that either," he said.

"How am I looking at you exactly, Aiden?" Corbin questioned.

"Like you pity me. I don't need that right now, Corbin," he said.

"I won't hide the fact I'm concerned for you, Aiden. That's what friends do or have you forgotten that?" Corbin asked. "You need to learn to let a few things go and stop beating yourself up every time you fuck things up."

"Yeah, I get that. But I didn't just fuck things up with Zara. I royally fucked things up. I overreacted and blew things way out of proportion. Hell, she seemed fine with the fact I took her virginity and I was the one acting like a catholic schoolgirl over the whole issue," Aiden admitted.

"Well, you can act like quite the drama queen, AJ," Corbin teased. "Have you thought about going back to the club and asking about her? They are members only and would have some record of her I'm sure." Honestly, finding Zara was all he could think about but then what? Once he had her information would he just casually call her up and ask how she was? Starting the phone conversation like, "Hey—it's me the guy who took your virginity and then yelled at you for no reason," didn't seem like a great plan.

"Maybe it's best if you just forget about her, man," Corbin said. Aiden wished it was that simple. He wanted to push the sexy images of Zara from his mind. Remembering the way she looked up at him through her long lashes, watching his every move like she would never be able to get enough of him, wasn't something he would easily forget.

"I don't know," Aiden grumbled. "Right now I just want to finish up this file I'm working on, pick up my girls from Connie's place, and head home. I have a six-pack with my name on it."

"Now, that sounds like a fucking plan," Corbin said. "Just

think about what I said, AJ. If you can't just forget her then find her and do a little groveling."

"As if you've ever begged a woman for anything," Aiden teased. It was true though. Corbin never had to work to get or keep a woman. It had even turned into a problem for him quite a few times when the woman refused to take no for an answer. Corbin wasn't the kind of guy who dated, really. He was a Dom who liked to work his way through subs. When the sub got the wrong idea and started to develop feelings for his friend, Corbin usually found an excuse to end the contract with the poor woman. Most of his subs took the news fine and found another Dom to play with at the club but some didn't like being so easily rejected. Aiden worried sooner or later Corbin was going to piss off the wrong woman and she'd take things too far, but his happy-go-lucky friend didn't seem too worried about the possibility of a disgruntled sub exacting her revenge.

"Yeah well, some of us are just gifted, I guess," Corbin teased. He walked out of Aiden's office, smiling back over his shoulder and Aiden chuckled. His friend was always a rule breaker, but he was pretty sure sooner or later, Corbin would meet a woman who would knock him on his ass. Aiden just hoped like hell he'd have front-row seats to watch that show.

ZARA

Zara had spent two weeks trying to find a new job and she was worried nothing would ever pan out. The family she nannied for found out she ended up at the BDSM club and fired her. It didn't seem to matter to the woman she nannied for how her husband came by this information or that he was also a member of the club. Zara wanted to let the cat out of the bag but ruining a family wasn't her thing. Besides, she believed in karma and knew sooner or later his luck would run out.

She was just about to give up on the whole nanny gig when a new agency called her wanting to interview her for a potentially high-profile client. She was used to working with families who wanted their private lives kept private. Most of her clients consisted of high-profile parents who were usually CEOs or involved in politics at some level. She knew how to keep her lips zipped on the playground while the other nannies droned on about the people they worked for. Zara learned to look the other way and just do her job and until a couple of weeks ago, she never had any issues with the people she nannied for.

"Hey you," Avalon said as she came barreling through their

front door. She and Ava had been roommates for almost five years now. Zara needed a place to live while she was still in college and she was lucky enough to become friends with her biology lab partner—Avalon Michaels. She and Ava instantly hit it off and when she offered to let her move into her townhouse, close to campus, Zara jumped at the offer. It was perfect really, she had her own room and bathroom, and Ava's job, working for a clothing designer, had her working crazy hours and flying to fabulous places like Paris and Milan. Zara had the privacy she needed and when the people she nannied for would need her to spend the night, she could easily just pack a bag with the reassurance that she'd have a place to stay when the job was over. Not every family wanted a live-in nanny. Most families just wanted her to stay over if the parents had a late-night function to attend or just wanted to get away. Still, it was nice not to have an uptight roommate fussing over her not being home all the time. She and Ava were a roommate match made in heaven besides being best friends.

"Hey yourself," Zara said. "You need help with that?" She motioned to the giant suitcase Ava took with her on most of her trips.

"Nope," Ava said, tugging her luggage the rest of the way through the door. "This monstrosity and I have become one. She understands I need to buy everything in Paris and doesn't judge me." Ava patted her suitcase as if she were praising a puppy and set it off to the side.

"Um, I don't think your suitcase cares what you put in her," Zara teased.

"She doesn't mean it, baby," Ava said to her luggage in her sing-song voice. "Honestly Zara, you are no fun anymore."

"Yeah well, while you've been in Paris, I've been here pounding the pavement for a job. Your little dare cost me my job, Ava," Zara grouched.

"And I've apologized for that a gazillion times, Z," Ava said. "I feel horrible that happened, but how were either of us to know your boss would be there the same night as you? Hell, did you know he was into that type of thing?" Zara shrugged, not wanting to tell her best friend not only did she know he was into a whole lot of kink, but he had asked her to join him and his wife a few times; although she doubted his wife had any idea what was going on.

"I didn't even know I was into it until that night," Zara whispered under her breath. Ava apparently heard her, judging from her giggle.

"Well, you at least have that to take away, even if the rest of the night ended in disaster," Ava said.

"Sure," Zara agreed. "And a new agency just called and I have an interview tomorrow."

"That's fantastic," Ava offered. She crossed the room and pulled Zara in for a bear hug.

"Listen, I have a million things to do before tomorrow gets here. How about you unpack then show me all of the latest fashions you brought back from Paris over dinner?" Zara had already started making a mental list of everything she needed to pick up for her interview before Ava even agreed.

"We meet back here at six and I'll order Chinese from our favorite place," Ava said. Zara love the way her best friend's good moods were almost infectious. She couldn't help her smile as she watched Ava tug her luggage up the stairs to her bedroom. She just hoped by this time tomorrow she'd be in a better mood after hopefully getting the job. She could use a win about now.

❋

Zara spent the rest of the day getting ready for her job interview and then the evening eating noodles and listening to Ava go on about what everyone was wearing at fashion week in Paris. Her friend was born with a silver spoon in her mouth. Avalon's family was well-known in the political arena. Her grandfather and father were both congressmen and even though Ava didn't usually act it, Zara knew she came from old money. Ava barely charged her any rent to live in the townhome they shared and she was always treating Zara to dinner and buying her little presents. It was quite different from the way Zara grew up. She lost her parents when she was just nine years old and was moved from foster home to foster home until she turned eighteen. When she finally got out of the system, she ran as far and fast as she could.

It was by chance she ended up at the local university. She was working at a diner in town, waitressing to make ends meet, and trying to afford the shitty little apartment she was living in. One night, the owner sat her down and told her she believed Zara could be more than just a waitress in a rundown diner and she handed her an application and a pamphlet with information about a scholarship she might qualify for. She got a full ride and was pursuing her degree in early childhood education until the scholarship's funds ran dry and she had to quit. She was one semester short of graduation and Ava insisted she let her pay but it just didn't feel right to take her money. It was something Zara wanted to do on her own, so she started fulfilling her credits class by class. She was enrolled in her last class starting in the fall and she honestly couldn't wait to walk across the stage and accept her diploma. She fought so hard for it, there would be no stopping her now.

Maybe not having family left was why she loved the way Ava so easily accepted her. Ava made sure she was never alone on holidays and her birthday. Up until her twentieth birthday, Zara hadn't really celebrated. After meeting Ava, she made sure Zara had a party every year to make up for all the missed birthdays.

"So, any word from BDSM guy?" Ava asked around a mouthful of noodles.

Zara rolled her eyes. Telling Ava about that night might have been a mistake but she didn't have anyone else to talk to. Hell, she made so many mistakes that night she wasn't sure which she regretted most. Not telling Aiden about her being a virgin rated right up at the top of her regrets list but she really wouldn't change much about the night. God, he was perfect in the way he took complete control over her body, mind, and soul. It was as if he could read her every need and gave her what she had been searching for. And just when she thought she was going to get everything she ever wanted, he pushed her away and went radio silent. Aiden asked to see her again but, that was before he found out she was a virgin. Zara couldn't blame him, really. She knew who she was—a twenty-five-year-old virgin and what man would want her? She was a fool to believe a man like Aiden would want someone like her. She was broken and naïve. A man like Aiden was looking for a real woman—one with experience and knowledge of how to pleasure a man. That wasn't her.

"No, and how would he reach me?" she whispered. "It isn't like we exchanged numbers or anything, Ava," she admitted. It was true. After Aiden made her feel like shit for omitting her sexual status, she grabbed her things and high-tailed it out of that club.

"You know I can get his information for you, right? I have a friend who works there, you know in security and I'm sure he'll do a little digging for me. Besides, he owes me," Ava admitted.

"Lord, do I want to know why he owes you a favor?" Zara teased.

"Well, I hooked him up with another friend and so far, so good. They've been going out for a few months now," Ava said. "So, how about it? Want me to track down your mystery man?"

She wanted to tell her friend yes but that would mean admitting to wanting Aiden and if she said those words out loud, Ava would never let her live any of this nightmare down. If it was up to Zara she would just forget the whole night even happened but that was proving nearly impossible. She was pretty sure she'd never be able to forget Aiden or the way he made her completely his even if it was for just one night.

Zara woke early the next morning and went for a run. She had a love/hate relationship with running and for some crazy reason, she just couldn't seem to give it up. Really it was one of the best ways she knew to relieve stress and right now, she had plenty of that. She quickly showered and threw on the outfit Ava helped her to pick out the night before. According to her best friend, it was not only business sheik, but also screamed she wasn't afraid to get down and play with the kids when she needed to. Honestly, it was fancier than most of the outfits she wore on a daily basis. Zara found kids really didn't care what she was wearing as long as she knew the way to the park and where to drop them off at their friend's houses after school, she was golden.

By the time she got to the address for the office building the agency had given to her, she was a full ten minutes early and pretty damn proud of herself for pulling that off. Actually her punctuality was one of her selling points and being early would help to drive that point home when she brought it up in casual conversation during the interview. She had a seat in the waiting area where the security guard told her to hang out and she wondered just whom she was interviewing with. The gold letters on the side of the building said Eklund and Bentley and she knew the woman conducting the interview was named Rose Eklund, so she assumed it was for that partner but that was all she had to go on.

A woman who looked to be probably somewhere in her mid-forties hurried towards her wearing a triumphant smile. It was hard not to return her kind gesture; it was almost infectious. "You must be Zara," the woman said, more stating a fact than asking. "I'm Rose Eklund and I will be interviewing you for Mr. Bentley." She looked Zara up and down and nodded as if happy with what she saw. "Please follow me," the kind woman said.

She led the way to the elevator and when it stopped, Zara couldn't help but admire the view. The top floor had an almost panoramic view of the city and she wondered if she could see her and Ava's place from where she stood. "Impressive, isn't it?" Rose asked, watching her reaction.

"Very," Zara agreed.

"Please have a seat and make yourself comfortable. Mr. Bentley couldn't be here today. He was called out of town on business but has left hiring a nanny for his two girls to me," Rose said.

"That is quite a responsibility," Zara admitted.

Rose smiled at her and nodded. "Well, the girls are like my grandchildren. I've known them their whole lives and practically raised their father. He and my son, Corbin are best friends and they own this business. So, it's really an honor to find a nanny for Lucy and Laney."

"And Mrs. Bentley?" Zara asked. One thing she learned working for high-powered clients was what questions to ask and which to avoid. If she was going to be the family's nanny, she needed to know their dynamics. "Will she be joining us?"

"God, I hope not," Rose protested. "She left Mr. Bentley and the girls a little over half a year ago. She has very little contact with the girls. The last time any of us saw her was at Lucy's fifth birthday a few months back. Other than that, she has nothing to do with them."

Zara felt instantly sad for the little girls she didn't even know yet. She knew exactly what it felt like to be alone and wish for her mother, only to have the disappointment of knowing her mother would never be back. It broke her heart knowing a mother could just walk away from her own flesh and blood so easily.

"I'm sorry," she all but whispered.

"Nothing to be sorry for," Rose offered. "It was hard on everyone at first but we've all adapted. Mr. Bentley has a crazy schedule and is running for the vacant senate seat next fall, so his plate is full. He just needs a little help with the girls' schedules—you know to keep them on track."

"You said Lucy is just five. How old is Laney?" Zara asked.

"She will be three in a few months and she's a spitfire," Rose said, smiling to herself. "Do you mind if I ask you a few questions? The agency sent over your resume and it looks great, but I'm wondering why your last job ended so abruptly." Zara tried not to cringe but she must have given some sign of distress at Rose's question.

"Things didn't really work out. I'm not at liberty to say why, since I signed a non-disclosure agreement with my contract. It's really a matter of privacy, both mine and theirs." Rose watched her as if trying to read between the lines to pick up what she wasn't saying. "Let's just say I was in the wrong place at the wrong time," Zara offered. She hoped that would be enough of an explanation to get Rose to move on to the next question on her list but she wasn't exactly sure it was.

"Well, it's nice to hear you honor your former client's privacy even after you were let go. Your new agency has already vetted you, but are you willing to let us conduct our own background check if we deem it necessary?" Rose asked. Zara nodded, not really having any skeletons in her closet—well, besides going into a BDSM club and having sex for the first time with a complete stranger. She just hoped their background check overlooked her latest indiscretion.

"Sure," she agreed.

"Great," Rose said. "Tell me why you became a nanny, Zara," she asked.

This was her favorite question to answer and also the toughest. She would always be truthful about her past, but sometimes families didn't like the fact she was raised in the foster care system. It was as if they thought she was somehow damaged. "My parents both died when I was very young and I have no other family. I was placed in the foster care system and bounced around a little bit. I've been working my way through college and honestly, being a nanny is right in line with my major," she said.

"Oh, and what is that?" Rose questioned.

"I'm majoring in early childhood education. I want to be a teacher. I have one more class to take in the fall and then I can graduate. But don't worry," she said. "My class is in the evening and work always comes first." Rose nodded again and checked her paper and then sat it back down on the desk.

"It must have been awful for you, growing up without parents. I'm sure they would be proud of the young woman you've become," Rose offered. Zara had always wondered if her mother and father would have approved of her choices and the path she had taken. They would have been so happy she was able to work her way through college, but she wondered if some of her other choices would make them proud. It wasn't something she let her thoughts linger on too long because focusing on them always made her heart ache a little. Sure, she had grown up and learned to live without either of them, but she would always wonder what if and that was a dangerous game to play.

"That is very kind of you to say, Rose," she whispered.

"Well, if you have no further questions for me, I'd like to know when you can start," Rose said. Zara all but stood from her chair, dumping the contents of her purse onto the floor.

"I'm so sorry," she muttered. Rose stood and helped her gather her things from the floor, handing her back her bag.

"No, it's fine. I'm always a bundle of nerves when it comes to these things by myself. You might think it's nerve-racking being on the interviewee side but interviewing someone is just as stressful. Maybe I didn't handle that right. I guess I should have asked if you'd like the job?" Rose waited her out and Zara wasn't sure if jumping up and down, clapping, and cheering was the correct response but she didn't care.

"Thank you so much," she said. "I'd have to meet the family

first but I think I'd love to take the job," she offered. "When would you like for me to start?"

"How about tomorrow morning, eight sound good? You can meet the girls, but their dad will be out of town for a few more days. We'll get you settled in before he even gets back," Rose said. Zara noticed a glint of mischief in the older woman's eyes and she wondered if it was going to turn out to be a good or bad thing for her.

"If you're sure that is all right, then yes. Tomorrow morning works for me," Zara admitted.

"Great. Will you have much to move in?" Rose asked.

"Move in?" Zara questioned. "I was told this wasn't a live-in role." The agencies she worked with usually gave her a heads-up if the position required her to be a full-time live-in nanny. She tried to avoid those jobs but she so desperately needed this one, she really didn't have a choice.

"I'm sorry," Rose offered. "You will need to be there quite a bit during the campaign. I'm afraid the girls haven't had much stability or structure lately. It would help them tremendously if you could be there for them twenty-four hours a day. You can have most weekends off if you'd like." Zara knew she was going to have to make a quick decision, but the idea of leaving Ava high and dry for the unforeseeable future made her feel bad. She also knew if she wanted to finish her last semester of school, she was going to have to have a job to pay her tuition bill.

"Yes," Zara agreed, holding out her hand to shake on it. "I'll take the job and I'll move into their home. It will be on a trial basis, of course."

"Of course," Rose agreed, shaking her hand. "We can re-evaluate when the election is over if that works for you." Zara nodded. "Great." Rose pulled a slip of paper out and handed it to her. "Be at this address by eight tomorrow and bring whatever you will need for the time being. If you need to hire a moving crew, just send me the bill and I'll take care of it for you." Rose walked to the elevator and Zara followed.

"Thank you," Zara said.

"No, thank you," Rose returned. "I hope you like a little chaos because you're about to dive in, headfirst." Zara wanted to laugh at what she thought was a joke but judging from the expression on Rose's face, she wasn't joking.

AIDEN

Spending half a week in boardrooms and one boring meeting after another, Aiden was ready to get home and sink into his own bed. He was just thankful he was able to slip away from his trip two days early because spending one more day away from his girls was going to drive him crazy. Corbin had been handling the business trips since Allison left but he couldn't say no to this one. This trip involved a company that was his baby from the start and he needed to be involved in the negotiations. Sending Corbin in his stead felt wrong and he was glad he made that decision because he had to put out some major fires.

Aiden unloaded his luggage into the corner of the mudroom, deciding he'd deal with it all tomorrow. Tonight, he wanted to peek in on his girls and meet the new nanny Rose hired. She was supposedly staying in his guest room and he wasn't sure how he felt about having a live-in nanny. The press might catch wind of it and have a field day with the news. But, Rose assured him his new nanny wouldn't cause him any trouble and as far as looks went, she described her as frumpy and easily overlooked. Aiden just hoped Rose was right because he didn't have time to squash rumors about his new help.

He checked in on the girls to find them both peacefully sleeping and made his way down to the spare room Rose said she put the new nanny in but he found the room empty. He decided to search for her, hoping she wouldn't just leave the girls alone when he heard the water running in his bathroom. What the hell was the nanny doing in his master bathroom?

"Hello?" he called and no one answered. He rounded the corner and found the door to his bathroom closed. "Hello," he said, banging on the door. No one answered and he had no choice but to try the doorknob hoping his new nanny was decent but not really giving a shit at this point. First, he'd introduce himself and then he was going to lay down a few ground rules; the first being no using his master bath. The second would be to answer the fucking door when he knocked, but he was sure that barging in on her would solve that little problem.

"Hi," he said to the back of the blonde head that greeted him. The woman in the tub full of bubbles didn't answer him and he was beyond frustrated by her complete lack of attention. What if it had been one of his girls who needed her? "Hello," he shouted, going the extra mile to tap her on her shoulder. He tried to ignore the way the bubbles enveloped her sexy curves or the fact she was a whole fucking lot younger than Rose had described her and one hundred percent sexier. He made a mental note to have a little chat with Rose about how she described people and her use of adjectives, the next time he saw her. His new nanny was neither frumpy nor old. In fact, she was damn sexy.

As soon as he tapped her shoulder, she squealed and jumped, pulling her earbuds from her ears. "Sorry," she stuttered, looking him over. "Oh fuck," she swore. "Aiden?" He stood over the tub and realized the woman staring back at him was the same woman he had been dreaming about for the past few weeks, the one he couldn't seem to forget—Zara.

"What the hell are you doing in my house, Zara?" he questioned. She stood from the soapy water, letting the bubbles slide down her curves and he couldn't seem to take his eyes off her. He was immediately reminded of their night together, her breathy sighs, and the way she shouted his name when she came on his tongue. And now, she stood completely bare in his tub and all he could think about was how she ended up there.

"Your home?" she questioned. "Wait—you are Mr. Bentley? Lucy and Laney are your daughters?" Zara questioned. He slowly nodded, trying to catch up.

"Yes," he said. He handed her a towel knowing if she continued to stand in front of him completely naked, he might not be able to regain cognitive thought clear enough to keep up with his end of the conversation. "Can you please wrap this around yourself?" he asked. She shot him a look that told him she wasn't in the same submissive mood she was in the night they shared together.

"What, Aiden," she spat, snatching the towel from his hand, "my naked body offends you now?" He couldn't take his eyes off her as Zara wrapped the towel around her wet body and he felt about ready to swallow his tongue. "My body didn't seem to bother you that night in the club," she spat. God, she was gorgeous and he had to fight every one of his natural instincts to pull her against his body and make her his again. But, she wasn't his—she never was his and he needed to remember that.

"That was before you were my nanny, Zara. So, you didn't know the job was for me?" he questioned. He hated how he sounded like he was accusing her of something but he couldn't help it. If there was any chance she was stalking him or his girls were in danger, he would do whatever it took to make them safe.

"Of course, I didn't," she insisted. "Why would I take this job knowing you will be my boss? As far as I'm concerned, we said everything we needed to say that night. If I remember correctly, you accused me of lying and I ran out of the club half-naked and completely ashamed. Thanks for that, by the way," she said. He hated hearing he made her feel that way. It wasn't what he intended, and he had spent the last few weeks feeling like a complete ass for what he said to her.

"I'm sorry for that, Zara," he admitted. "I handled taking your virginity all wrong and I regret the way things ended that night." She stepped from the tub, pulled the drain, and brushed past him to leave the bathroom. She smelled like flowers and he knew for a fact she tasted like honey. Just the thought of her scent and taste made his mouth water and his cock spring to life. He wanted to push her against the fucking wall and kiss her until they were both breathless and needy, but he could tell that was something she wouldn't allow. So, he let her pass and followed her down the hall to her bedroom.

Aiden stood helplessly in her doorway, watching as the woman who occupied his every waking and sleeping hours, pulled on a pair of yoga pants and a t-shirt, forgoing undergarments. "Listen, I'll be out of your hair by morning," she said. Zara was shoving clothing into a bag and he felt a moment of panic, not knowing if he should feel relief she was going to leave or fear he was going to have to watch her walk away again and possibly this time forever.

"So that's it? You're just going to walk away and leave the girls?" Aiden asked. He hated the idea of his daughters having to lose someone they were getting close to again. The past few nights, when he called home to talk to Lucy and Laney, they seemed so happy about the new nanny. They called her "Z" and Aiden just never put two and two together and why would he? Aiden would have never guessed Zara would not only show up in his life again, but as his daughter's nanny—it was just too much of a crazy coincidence.

"Well, I certainly can't keep working for you—not now, knowing that it's you," she said. She motioned to him as if trying to prove a point and he almost wanted to laugh at her grand, sweeping hand gestures.

"Listen," he started. Aiden knew he had to be patient if he was going to have any chance of talking her into staying with them. Hell, he wasn't sure what he wanted exactly but he knew letting her go would only hurt his girls. "My daughters have been through hell this year. Their mother walked away from them and has very little contact with any of us since the divorce was finalized."

Zara looked down at the clothes she was holding and dropped them onto her bed. "I know," she admitted. "Rose told me some of it and the girls still talk about her. I'm so sorry you three had to go through all of that but I still don't think me being here is a good idea," she said.

"How about if we can work out some kind of agreement? You know, I'll keep my distance and give you some space and you just take care of my girls?" he asked. He sounded more like he was begging but he didn't give a fuck. His daughters were worth any amount of begging he had to do to keep them happy.

"Why would you want me around, Aiden?" Zara questioned.

There really wasn't a clear-cut explanation as to why he wanted to keep her around. Aiden knew part of it was the fact he liked seeing her again. Even in his wildest dreams, he never imagined he'd find Zara naked and wet in his bathtub after he returned from his business trip. He wasn't about to look a gift horse in the mouth though and keeping Zara around just felt like the right thing to do.

"The past few nights, when I've spoken with Lucy and Laney, they both seemed so happy. They went on and on about their new friend, Z and I have to admit it was nice to hear my girls sound excited about something again. It's been months since I've heard either of them sound so happy. I don't know—it was nice to hear. I worried less about being away from either of them, knowing you were here. Well, not you exactly but someone they were both coming to trust. If you leave now, they might never trust anyone to come into our home to take care of them again. Please," he begged.

Zara sat down on her bed next to the pile of clothes she had been working on. "You really know how to work the whole sympathy factor, don't you?" she asked. "I do love your girls. I have to admit in just a few short days, they've really grown on me." She smiled and then broke out into full giggles and Aiden couldn't help himself, he found himself chuckling right along with her.

"Mind sharing what's so funny?" he asked.

"Well, Lucy was telling me her daddy was flying like Superman and he had a red cape and everything. You know she really believes you're a superhero? I guess I was just picturing you in a Superman costume," she admitted. She looked Aiden up and down and then broke out in a fit of giggles, falling back onto the bed.

Aiden flexed his muscles as if trying to show off for her but that only sent her further over the edge. "Is it really so hard to believe I could be a superhero?" he asked. Sure, saying the words aloud made him sound crazy but he had to admit his feelings were a little hurt.

Zara seemed to sober at his lack of hysteria, picking up on the signs he didn't find the whole thing as funny as she had. "I think it's nice your daughters think of you in that way," she admitted. "I'm sure I felt the same way about my dad when he was alive," she almost whispered that last part.

"I'm sorry," Aiden offered. "How old were you when he died?" he questioned. He wasn't sure if her personal life was any of his business, but a part of him hoped she would want to share something like that with him.

"When I was nine," she said. "Both of my parents died in a car crash. They were hit by a drunk driver." Aiden saw the sadness in her eyes and heard every ounce of her heartbreak in her shaky voice. He wished he wasn't dredging up such bad memories for her but a part of him wanted to know more about his new nanny. Hell, he wanted to know everything she'd be willing to share with him but he wouldn't admit that to her.

Telling Zara that might just scare her away and he couldn't let that happen.

"That must have been horrible for you, Zara," he said. Aiden crossed the small bedroom and pushed some of her clothes aside to sit next to her on the bed. He worried about crossing some imaginary line, but when she didn't balk at the idea of him sitting so close to her, he didn't make a move to get up. "What happened to you after they died?" he asked.

Zara sighed, "Well, I was placed in foster care and bounced from place to place," she admitted.

"Shit," he swore. "That sucks."

"No, really it wasn't as bad as you might think. I was lucky enough to be placed with decent families," she said. "You hear horror stories about kids who are abused in some form or another but I got through the system unscathed and I believe I'm a stronger person for the time I was in there. It made me want to become a teacher and taught me to fight for what I want." Aiden took her hand into his, needing the contact. He knew it was silly; he just promised to give her space but none of that mattered at the current moment.

"I'm in college and I have one more class to take and then I graduate. Working as a nanny was supposed to be a part-time gig and give me some extra experience on my resume for after college. But, it became so much more than that. I've grown to love the kids I work with and I honestly find the work fulfilling," she said. Zara paused and Aiden wasn't sure if she was finished talking or if she was going to say what was on her mind.

"Listen, if this is all too much for you, just say the word and I'll have the agency place me with another family," she said. A pang of jealousy ran through him and Aiden shook it off. He had no claim to her professionally or personally, so he had no right to feel that way. The idea of Zara with any family but his own made him inexplicably grumpy.

"No," he said. "I'd like for you to stay. The girls seem to be crazy about you and I promise to keep my distance." Zara looked down to where their hands were joined and smiled.

"Um," she said, holding up their linked fingers as if trying to prove her point.

"Yeah," he said, letting go of her hand. "Sorry about that." Aiden felt anything but sorry but he was going to keep that to himself. "How about we say that rule starts now?" he asked. Zara smiled and nodded. A strand of her long blonde hair fell from her messy bun and he wanted to reach over and tuck it back but he didn't. He was going to have to make an effort to keep his hands to himself but he'd do just that if it meant keeping Zara on. Maybe he was a masochist and having to deal with the realization of having Zara under his roof, but not being able to touch her was just the type of torture he was into.

Zara stretched and yawned and he let his eyes lazily roam her body. Yeah, he was definitely a masochist. There was no other explanation for the self-torture he was putting himself through. "How about I let you get some sleep? I'll get up with the girls in the morning and see them off to school. You take the morning off—maybe sleep in. I'd like to spend some time with Lucy and Laney since this was the first trip I've taken since their mom left."

"Thank you," she said.

"Sure. Will you be free tomorrow for lunch?" he asked. He could see the way she suspiciously watched him, and he worried she was getting the wrong idea. "For a work meeting," he amended. "We need to go over schedules and house rules if this arrangement will work," he said.

Zara seemed to hesitate and then agreed. "Yes, that might be best. Besides, I have to return a few books I borrowed from Rose." Aiden wondered what books Zara had borrowed but he was sure he wasn't going to like her answer. Rose was constantly reading those sappy romance novels and the idea of Zara reading them made him a little hot. The less he thought about his new nanny reading steamy sex scenes from a novel the better.

He stood and crossed the room. "How about noon?" he asked. Zara nodded and he took that as his cue to leave. He was just about to his room when he heard her soft string of curses and he smiled to himself. Zara had just summed up exactly how he felt about finding out she was his daughters' new nanny, but for the first time in weeks, he was looking forward to the next day.

ZARA

Zara slept until just after seven and when she couldn't sleep anymore, she got up, dressed, and ate breakfast. It felt strange being in the house by herself especially now that she knew it belonged to Aiden. She had just enough time to run over to Ava's to pick up the rest of her things and meet Aiden at his office for lunch. He left her a note letting her know they would have to have lunch delivered to his office because his schedule was packed for the day. That was fine with her because it would give her an excuse to leave to finish unpacking before the girls needed to be picked up from preschool.

Lucy would probably try to coax her into going to the park on their way home and honestly, she loved the idea. Being outside always seemed like a good thing and after the restless night she just had, some fresh air might do her some good. Finding out Aiden was her new employer really threw her for a loop. Having him walk in to find her naked and soaking in a bubble bath in his master bathroom wasn't her finest moment. Really, she shouldn't be embarrassed given the fact he had already seen every square inch of her, up close and personally.

But that didn't stop her from feeling awkward about the whole thing. When Aiden insisted she stay on to nanny the girls, she was relieved. Zara wasn't sure her new agency would be so willing to find her a new family to work for. She knew she was under a microscope, being the new girl and she wasn't sure how to explain how she met her new boss. The idea of having to tell anyone about her connection with Aiden made her want to crawl under a rock to hide.

She pulled up to the townhouse she and Ava shared and wondered if her best friend was still angry with her. When she announced she not only got the job but had to move in with the family, Ava was upset. It didn't matter that Zara told her the situation was only temporary, Ava hated the idea of not being roommates anymore. When the small moving company Rose hired showed up to pack and move her meager belongings, Ava left the townhouse in a huff and didn't even bother to say goodbye. Zara called and left a few messages for her but she knew in time, Ava would come around. Zara just hoped it would be sooner rather than later because she could really use her best friend to talk to now.

When she saw Ava's car was still in its spot, Zara felt a sense of relief knowing she was going to get her chance to make things right with her. She knew Ava couldn't resist some good gossip and Zara was about to deliver big time, once she shared the news of her new employer being the same man who took her virginity.

"Ava," she called through the house and received no answer. She smiled knowing she'd probably find her friend still in her bed and once she heard Zara calling for her, she'd cover her head with her quilt and play opossum. Zara made her way to the second floor and found just what she expected—Ava covered like a giant lump, lying in the middle of her bed as still as could be. Zara couldn't help her giggle.

"Hmm- I guess you're sleeping then and don't want the juicy gossip I've come to deliver," she taunted. Zara knew Ava would never be able to pass up gossip. Her friend was the type of woman who lived for that kind of thing and the juicier, the better.

Ava threw down her covers revealing her scantily clad body and Zara knew she had her on the hook. "Gossip?" Ava questioned. "You better not be fucking around with me, Zara. I'm still mad at you for ditching me to live with your new family," Ava warned.

Zara couldn't help but roll her eyes, "You know that's work, Ava. I really have no choice. Besides, this isn't the first time I've had to live with a family."

"Right but those other times were just for a night or two when both parents had to go out of town. This time, you're moving out indefinitely and I hate it," Ava grouched.

Zara sat down on her bed, "I know but I need this job, Ava. If I want to finish my last semester at school, I need a way to pay for it. Besides, I already told you it's not forever. The man I'm working for is running for political office and as soon as the campaign is over, I will have the option to stay as a live-in nanny or move back in here," she said.

"And, you'll choose to move back in here—right?" Ava prodded. Zara smiled at her bossy best friend. Ava was used to getting her way in everything. She was a strong woman who would never understand Zara's desire to be submissive to a man. In fact, the idea of Ava being submissive to anyone was laughable.

"I promise to run everything by you before I make a decision," Zara said, crossing her heart for good measure.

"All right," Ava breathed. "I'll forgive you for now. I reserve the right to be angry again at you later if you chose to stay with that family," she said. "Now, spill your juicy gossip." Zara giggled and pulled Ava in for a quick hug.

"I think you're really forgiving me for the gossip but I'll take the win," Zara teased, releasing her friend. She stood and began to pace, not sure Ava was going to be at all happy about what she was about to admit. "I'm working for Aiden," she blurted out. She wanted to lead up to that point; tell Ava the story of how Lucy spilled her drink all over the both of them and she had to give the girls baths and the way they talked her into bubble baths in their dad's big tub. By the time she got Lucy and Laney to bed, all she could think about was sinking into a tub full of bubbles herself, never suspecting Aiden was her new boss or he'd be home early from his trip. He was supposed to be gone for another two nights, according to Rose.

She gave Ava a second to catch up and judging from the confusion clouding her friend's eyes, she might need some extra time. "Wait—what?" Ava got out of bed and stood in front of Zara, effectively stopping her pacing. "Aiden, the guy from the BDSM club—he's your new boss?"

"Yep," Zara said.

"What the actual fuck, Z?" Ava shouted. Yeah, her friend was definitely not taking this well. "Start explaining," Ava ordered.

"Well, I told you I was called by the agency to work for a high-profile family?" Zara asked.

Ava nodded, "Yes but you never said who it was for."

"I didn't know who it was for until last night when Aiden got home from his business trip and surprised me while I was soaking in his bathtub." Zara grimaced, knowing she should have left the part of Aiden finding her naked in the tub out of her story.

"Fuck," Ava spat. "So, you're working for Aiden Bentley? He's running for my grandfather's vacant Senate seat," Ava said. Zara really didn't follow politics, but she did remember Rose telling her "Mr. Bentley" was running for political office. "You didn't know your Aiden was running for Congress when you hooked up with him?" Ava questioned.

"First, he's not my Aiden. Second, we really didn't do much talking that night. He didn't ask questions and neither did I," Zara admitted. She knew that made her sound like a complete slut, but she wouldn't be ashamed of what happened that night between the two of them. Zara wanted to lose her virginity and try something new and Aiden unknowingly gave that to her.

"Is he married?" Ava questioned.

"I can't discuss that," Zara said. She knew she had to be careful about what she told Ava. According to Rose, the press still hadn't gotten wind of Allison leaving him and the girls and his political advisors wanted to keep it that way. Zara had signed the disclosure stating she would not talk about Aiden or his family to anyone and she was sure that included her best friend.

"What do you mean by that? It's a simple question to answer, Z. Either he is or he isn't," Ava sassed.

"It's not that I can't answer the question because I don't know the answer, Ava. I signed something saying I can't discuss Aiden or his family with anyone—including you. Had I known it was Aiden, I wouldn't have signed that damn form because I need to talk to someone about all of this. I feel as if I'm going to lose my mind if I don't, but I need to make sure I'm not breaking my contract if I tell you everything."

"So you came all the way over here just to tell me you're working for Aiden Bentley and you can't spill any of the details?" Ava asked.

"Right," Zara agreed. "And, I need to ask you not to talk to anyone about anything I've told you prior to today about Aiden. I didn't work for him when our night together happened, but I'm sure that will fall under the agreement I signed, now that I am his girls' nanny." Ava gave a look that told her she found the whole thing as crazy as Zara did. She still wasn't sure how the hell this all happened but it had and she needed to protect herself and the girls. They were both innocent in all of this and that was the main reason she agreed to stay on.

"You can't continue to work for him. You know that right Z?" Ava questioned. The logical side of her knew it was an awful idea to continue to work for Aiden but her heart was the one leading the stampede right over the cliff. She had already developed a soft spot for Lucy and Laney over the past half a week. Every time they talked about their mother, she felt the same pangs of sadness remembering what losing her own mother felt like. Leaving them now would hurt the girls and she wouldn't do that to them.

"Aiden and I have an agreement. I'll stay on for the girls and he'll keep his distance," she said.

Ava barked out her laugh, "You know that sounds completely nuts, right?" she asked. Zara did, especially after hearing herself say it out loud.

"I know," she admitted. "I have no good explanation for any of this other than I can't leave the girls—they need me. They deserve someone stable in their lives and I might just be their only hope."

Ava pulled her in for another hug, "You are such a good person, Z," she whispered. "Just don't go and lose your heart to a bastard like Aiden Bentley. Remember how he treated you that night at the club? You deserve better than a man who could so easily cast you aside based on the status of your virginity." Ava was right and Zara knew she deserved a man who would love her no matter what but that wasn't what Aiden had agreed to. When he met her at the club, she made him the offer of her body—not her heart but she'd never share that information with Ava. She hated that was all she was willing to give to any man right now—her body. Zara needed her heart intact for now and she didn't have time for anything as silly as romance or love. She had to finish college and keep her head on straight or else everything she had worked so hard for would be for nothing.

"Don't worry, Ava. I can handle myself with Aiden," she promised. Zara just hoped she wasn't fooling both of them because her next stop was the sexy Dom's office and with the way he looked at her last night they were both going to have trouble keeping their distance from each other.

❄

Ava helped Zara finish packing up her things and promised to keep her room open and ready for Zara's return. They said a tearful goodbye, which was completely unnecessary given the fact she was only going to be ten minutes across town, and Zara left for her meeting with Aiden. She hoped he'd be in a better mood today than he was last night after finding her using his personal bathroom. Zara needed to get a few things off her chest and it would be easier to do if Aiden was the suave, sweet man she met when she first entered the club.

She stepped off the elevator and was greeted by Rose's smiling face as soon as the doors opened. "Hey there, Zara," she said.

"Rose," Zara greeted. "Is he in?" She looked around the top floor where she had her interview a few days prior and wondered just how much had changed in such a short time.

"He is," Rose said. "Listen, Zara, I had no idea you knew Aiden when I hired you." Zara was worried Aiden had come to his senses and sent Rose to fire her. It made sense; Rose was the one to hire her so why not let her be the one to fire her too?

"Please don't fire me," Zara begged. She knew she sounded desperate but she was. Not only did she need this job to finish college but she wanted to stay on for Lucy and Laney. "I didn't know Aiden was going to be my boss when you hired me," she admitted.

"I know you didn't and no one is getting fired," Rose soothed. She started down the hallway and stopped in front of what Zara assumed was Aiden's office door.

"Um, how much do you know?" Zara questioned.

"Know?" Rose asked.

"Yeah, about me?" Zara hesitantly asked. "What has Aiden told you?" She almost didn't want to know but she wouldn't hide from the truth. Zara wasn't ashamed of what happened but she hoped Aiden didn't share all the details of their night together. "You said you were close to him, like a mother figure," Zara reminded her.

"It's true that Aiden is like a son to me but he doesn't share his personal life easily. He told me you and he went on one date together but that was about it," Rose said. Hearing that Aiden didn't share all the sorted details about the club and the way he took control of her body, taking care of her every need; that had to count for something.

"If something happened between the two of you, it's none of my business. My only concern here is that you take care of Lucy and Laney. Aiden has been working so hard lately, he really needs the help," Rose admitted.

"Well, I will do my very best," she promised. "Thank you, Rose," Zara awkwardly pulled the older woman in for a quick hug.

"He said to send you in when you got here," Rose said. "I've cleared his schedule for the rest of the day and I'll make sure you're not interrupted." Zara nodded and took a deep breath, trying to steady her nerves before having to face her new boss.

"It's now or never," she breathed and turned the doorknob to walk into his office.

"Good luck, Dear," Rose whispered. Zara had a feeling she was going to need a whole hell of a lot more than luck. She was going to need a damn miracle to get through her meeting with Aiden.

AIDEN

Aiden looked up to find Zara walking into his office and he knew his time for hiding was over. He had been waiting all morning for their meeting. He'd like to say he was patiently waiting for his new nanny but that would be a complete lie. When he demanded the meeting, it was to lay down some house rules and hopefully set some boundaries—mostly for himself but partially for Zara. If this thing was going to work, the two of them would have to come to some understanding. His girls were too important not to try to work through the baggage between him and Zara, but seeing her last night naked in his tub made him want her all over again. Zara was a beautiful woman but there was something else —something that inexplicably drew him to her. They needed to get everything out into the open and hopefully find a way forward for Lucy and Laney's sake.

"I hope it's okay I just came in. Rose said you were waiting for me," Zara said. She seemed so unsure of herself and he hated making her feel that way. He stood and crossed his office to meet her, wanting to soothe her, and make her feel some ease around him.

"No, it's fine," he offered, shutting the door behind her. "Please come in." He put his hand on the small of her back ushering her into his office, loving the way she shivered at his touch. He needed to keep his focus because eliciting any reaction from her wasn't what their meeting was about.

"Please have a seat," he said, nodding to the leather sectional that took up most of the corner of his office. "Can I get you something to drink?" he asked.

"No, thank you," she said. "I just came from my townhome, picking up the last of my things. I need to get back to your house, unpack and pick the girls up from school."

"Right," he whispered. So, she wanted to get right down to it and that worked for him. He didn't want to draw this out and make things worse than they needed to be. He was already nervous enough about this little chat. "I'm sorry about walking in on you last night. I didn't know you were naked; you know—when I came home."

Zara shrugged, "How could you? I didn't expect anyone home for two more nights," she admitted. "The girls wanted bubble baths in the big tub and I didn't know it would be such a big deal. It won't happen again," she promised.

"No, it's not a problem. The girls love my tub. They call it their swimming pool," he admitted. Zara giggled and it sounded like magic.

"That must have been what they were talking about when they told me to watch out for the shark," she teased.

"Yeah," he laughed. "They both have big imaginations," he said. "Once, they told me they were mermaids, and the mean pirates were trying to get them. I was trying to figure out what they were talking about and then I realized their grandmother, Connie was reading Peter Pan to them."

"I met her," Zara said. "She seems nice."

Aiden nodded, "She's been great. I wouldn't have been able to make it through the past half a year without her," he admitted.

Zara sat back against the back of the sofa, seeming a little more comfortable with him. "What are we going to do about our night at the club?" she asked.

"What do you mean by, 'do'?" he questioned.

"Well, do we just forget it happened or what?" she asked. The last fucking thing he wanted to do was forget it happened. He wanted her still and forgetting about their night together wasn't something he thought he'd ever be able to do.

"No," he breathed. "I don't want to forget that night," he admitted.

"Good," she said. "Me either. But I don't want it to affect my working for you. It happened and I don't regret making the decision to go back to your room with you. I am sorry I wasn't completely truthful though. I should have told you I was a virgin." She looked down at her hands that were fidgeting with her jacket, and he hated they were back to her being nervous around him again.

"Look at me, Zara," he commanded. He knew he was taking a chance demanding anything from her but he couldn't help it. There was something about Zara that made him want to slip into full Dom mode. Her gorgeous blue eyes darted up to meet his own as she obeyed his order.

"I shouldn't have gotten so angry," he whispered. "I hate the way we left things and I shouldn't have yelled at you."

"But—" she stuttered.

"But nothing," he said. "You did nothing wrong. I should have asked more questions and gotten to know you a little more. I went about things all wrong and that's on me. You didn't do anything wrong. You were perfect," he whispered, pulling her body against his own. "You are perfect," he murmured against her lips. He didn't ask permission because he wasn't willing to wait for her answer. He needed her—now and waiting wasn't an option. He kissed her with all the pent-up desire he had felt for her over the past few weeks and Zara didn't seem to hold back with him either.

Aiden broke the kiss, leaving them both breathless and he wondered if he had just made a mistake, but judging from the desire he saw staring back at him in Zara's eyes, he hadn't. She seemed just as turned on by what was happening between the two of them as he was. Still, he waited, almost as if he was holding his breath, waiting for her to respond to him being so forward. Zara gave him no indication whether she was pissed but he knew better than to push.

"Tell me I overstepped, Zara," he demanded. "Slap me, get mad at me but for God's sake, do something. I need a sign here," he admitted, running his fingers through his own hair.

"I'm not angry with you, Aiden. I know I should be but I'm not. I'm not ashamed of what happened between us at the club. I wanted you then and I want you now, even if it is an awful idea. I mean, I'm your nanny—your employee." Hearing Zara call herself his employee made him want to laugh. He'd never slept with any of his employees, ever. It was just a personal rule that saved him a lot of trouble and probably kept his HR department happy. Corbin kept them busy enough with the way he seemed to like to sleep his way through his private assistants. He couldn't seem to keep his hands off them and Aiden had even threatened to give him Rose as his assistant, just to keep him in line. That always won him a round of groans from both Corbin and Rose, but he was at his wits end with his business partner not keeping it in his pants. He wondered if breaking his policy of no sex with employees was risky or if it was crazy enough to work. Aiden knew his wanting Zara wasn't going to just disappear. The past three weeks had proven that.

"The employee problem is only the tip of the iceberg for me. As far as the political world is concerned, I'm still happily married to Allison. My campaign manager has put on quite a show and I've agreed to stick with the ruse until the primaries are over. After that, I can make an announcement we split, but I've been given strict orders not to rock the boat. If news about whatever this is between us gets out, I can kiss my run for the

Senate goodbye," he admitted. Aiden knew he sounded like a complete ass and maybe he was. He worked too hard and sacrificed everything to get where he was. He had hired the best team to get him into the office and not listening to them might be career suicide.

"So, you are telling me anything that would happen between us would be a secret?" she questioned.

"I would never ask you to be my secret, Zara," he whispered.

"I appreciate that, Aiden. I want you and if that is the only way I can have you; I'll take it." Zara sat back as if waiting him out and he knew what his answer was going to be before he even gave it. He wanted her and there would be no way to deny that. Not having her felt like a denial and he was sick and tired of not having anything his way. Zara would be the one thing he could do for himself.

"You need to be sure about this, Zara. If this doesn't work out between us, my girls will be the one to pay the price," Aiden whispered. "I can't let that happen."

"No, you are right, Aiden. We can't let the girls get caught up in the middle of whatever this is or will become," she agreed. "How do we keep them safe?" Aiden stood and paced the floor. He must have looked as if he was having a debate with himself. When Zara looked as if she wanted to chuckle, he shot her a look that had her thinking better of it.

"One of the reasons I was going to the club was for anonymity. But that's becoming harder to assure as my campaign grows. My ex didn't share my need for kink. Hell, she was as straight-laced as they came when it came to sex. I guess that's why I started going to the club in the first place—you know to explore that side of myself after the divorce." Zara nodded. He wasn't really sure where he was going with all of this. He was probably just spilling his guts, but he wanted to know if he and Zara were even on the same page, before asking her for what he wanted.

"I'm sorry, Aiden. The divorce must have been hard on you, especially if you weren't allowed to talk about it with anyone," she said.

"I've had Rose and her son, Corbin is my best friend and business partner. They know and I can tell them anything. But yes, having only a handful of people to talk to has been hard on me and the girls. That's why I have to be careful with our next move. Did you like everything you saw that night at the club?" he questioned.

Zara didn't even hesitate with her answer. "Yes," she breathed.

"Was that your first time—you know in a BDSM club?" he asked. He knew it was her first time having sex, but he wondered if she had ever experienced any part of the kinky lifestyle or if their night together was one of many firsts for her. She shyly nodded her head.

"Yes," she whispered.

He couldn't help himself, he had to ask the next question even if he might not like her answer. "Did you like what we did together?"

Zara sighed and nodded. "I loved everything up until the point where—well, you know," she said.

"To the point where I acted like an ass and got mad at you?" he asked. Zara nodded again and he wasn't sure what his next move should be. He knew what he wanted to do—push her down onto his sofa and strip her bare but that wouldn't get them to the place where they needed to be. If she was going to be his girls' nanny, he had to tread lightly and not bully his way through this part with Zara.

"I'm sorry for that, Zara. What I guess I want to know is if you'd be willing to explore that lifestyle with me. Again, everything that happens will have to be kept in confidence and we have to protect the girls at all costs. Would you be willing to try?" Aiden sat back down next to her and waited her out. He wanted her to agree but only if it was something she wanted.

"What are you proposing exactly?" she asked.

"Be my sub," he asked. Hell, it sounded more like a command, but he didn't care. He wanted her to agree but he wouldn't push her.

"Your sub?" she questioned.

"Yes," he said. "It would play out like many of the scenes in the club. We would play and when you are in my bed, you will obey my commands." Just the thought of having complete control of Zara's body made him instantly hard.

"What about when we aren't in your bedroom, Aiden?" she asked.

"You will strictly be my employee, nothing more." He knew that sounded harsh but it was all he could give her right now. "As far as the rest of the world will know, you are just my girls' nanny and I'm still happily married to Allison. That can't change until things settle down with my campaign and then we can re-evaluate things."

"If I agree to this, I won't be able to tell anyone, will I?" Zara questioned.

"No," he confirmed. "No one will be able to know about us," he said.

"Can I think about it?" she whispered. His heart sank when she didn't agree with his requests. Aiden wasn't used to people telling him no. He needed to remember Zara wasn't outright turning him down, just asking for time to get her head straight. It was a good thing, really. He wanted her to enter this arrangement with both eyes open.

"Fine," he said. "But just know if you agree to this, you agree to everything. I can't jeopardize my run for office, or my company and I won't hurt my daughters. This stays between us, and I won't go easy on you, Zara. I'm a demanding ass when I want to be, both in and out of the bedroom. You should know exactly what you are signing up for before you tell me yes," he said.

Zara's giggle filled his office, "You're so sure I will tell you yes, aren't you Aiden?" she asked. He couldn't help his smile.

"Yes, Zara. I'm used to getting my way and I love a challenge," he said.

"Good to know," she said. Zara stood to leave his office and he suddenly felt flustered. He worried if he let her walk out of there, she might disappear or worse, disappoint him by saying no.

"Where are you going?" he asked. He stood, crossing the room behind her, and stopped dead when she turned to face him.

"I'm going to pick up your daughters from school and then we have a date at the playground. I'm assuming we will see you for dinner?" she asked, cocking an eyebrow at him as if daring him to tell her no.

"Yes," he agreed. "I'll be home by six."

"Good. After I put the girls to bed, I will give you my answer." Zara kissed his cheek and turned to leave without any further fanfare and Aiden wondered just how much control she'd be willing to give up for him. His new nanny seemed to be as bossy as she was capable and Aiden worried he had just bitten off more than he could chew.

ZARA

Zara spent the rest of the afternoon playing with the girls and watching them take endless turns down the sliding board. Honestly, she spent most of her time at the playground trying to figure out just how to answer Aiden's question. Would she really be able to give him what he wanted? She wanted to tell him yes, that she would be his sub and obey his every command in his bedroom but wouldn't that be selling out? She knew she'd eventually want more than just sex—she would want it all, but Aiden was adamant he couldn't give her what she had been dreaming of. Right now, she was concentrating on earning her degree but after she graduated, Zara planned on having some semblance of a normal dating life. He wasn't offering to be her boyfriend and take her out to dinner or a movie. He wasn't asking to date her—he wanted to fuck her and she needed to decide if that was going to be enough for her.

It wasn't as if she had guys beating down her door offering her anything better but she never thought she'd be someone's sub. Hell, up until a couple of weeks ago, she had no idea what a sub even was. Ava daring her to go to that BDSM club was an eye-opening experience for her and she knew once she saw inside that world, she wouldn't want anything less. She was intrigued to learn more and to be honest, experience more. Aiden could give that to her, but she was going to have to let go of her silly schoolgirl ideology of a knight riding in on a white horse with an armful of roses, asking her if she'd go to the dance with him. Aiden wasn't that man and he might never be for her.

After the girls were good and tired, she decided to take them home and give them an early bath. Zara cooked dinner and was just about to give up on Aiden joining them when he came racing through the front door.

"Sorry I'm late, ladies," he said, sounding a little out of breath. "I had a last-minute meeting that couldn't wait until morning."

"Do you have to go out again, Daddy?" Lucy questioned. Zara didn't miss the sadness in the little girl's voice.

"Nope," Aiden said. Lucy's face lit up with excitement and she got down from her chair and went over to where the craft supplies were stored. "Good, cause I need help with a card for Rose. It's her birthday soon."

"Right, thanks for the reminder, Lucy. You really keep me on my game. How do you remember Rose's birthday better than I do?" Aiden asked. He pulled Lucy onto his lap and tickled her, making her squirm and giggle.

"Rose says it's cause she doesn't put it on your calendar, and you're lost without her," Lucy mock whispered making Aiden chuckle.

"Well, she's not wrong about that, baby. I am lost without Rose. So, I'm guessing she told you it's her birthday soon?" he questioned.

"Nope. She told Zara and I was spying on them," Lucy admitted. She loved to spy on adults, even though Zara had caught her and told her it wasn't nice to listen to other people's conversations. "Rose came over to check on us while you were on your trip. I heard her tell Zara she is going to have a big birthday soon. Can I go to her party?"

Aiden shot Zara a sexy smirk that nearly had her girl parts feel like they might burst. "I'm not sure Rose is going to want a party, Lucy," he said.

"But she said it's a big birthday. I always have birthday parties." Lucy pouted, crossing her arms over her tiny body.

"Rose isn't as excited about her special day as you are for your birthday. It's different for adults," Aiden said.

"How about we bake her some cupcakes and take them by the office? I'm pretty sure her birthday isn't for a few more months, Lucy." Zara interrupted.

Aiden nodded, "See, that sounds like a great idea."

Lucy looked at Laney who sat quietly eating her pasta and they both nodded their agreement. "Fine," Lucy said. "But can we get cupcakes tomorrow too? A few months is a really long time to wait." Zara couldn't help her giggle. Lucy was a tough negotiator, and she was sure to always be a handful.

"Well, that will be up to Zara," Aiden said. "And I'm sure it will also depend on both of your behavior."

"I can be good," Laney finally piped up.

"Me too," Lucy promised.

"Well, then, I think we can stop at the bakery for a treat," Zara agreed. The girls cheered and celebrated.

"How about you two eat your dinner and then we can play a game before bedtime?" Aiden asked. "If you'd like to play with us, you are welcome to. Or, you can take some downtime." Aiden watched her and she thought about taking him up on his offer of some free time. A bubble bath sounded like heaven but the pleading looks on the girls' faces had her changing her mind.

"I'd love to play a game," Zara fibbed. The girls both cheered again and went to work eating their dinner. Aiden went into the kitchen to make himself a plate and then joined them at the table again.

"This looks great," he said.

"It's nothing really. I like to cook and try new things. I didn't have much time to make anything special tonight since we spent a little extra time at the park." Zara wasn't sure why she suddenly felt so nervous around him but she did. She could hear it in her own voice and she worried Aiden would be able to pick up on her sudden case of the jitters. He looked across the table at her and smiled.

"Well, I appreciate you making us all dinner. The girls and I usually do takeout, so this is quite a treat," he admitted. Zara smiled and shyly nodded at him, not quite sure how to react. She was used to making dinner for the kids she worked for, it was part of the services she provided. Plus the families she worked for usually had top-of-the-line kitchens and it was a dream to cook in them.

They finished their dinner listening to Lucy tell the same two stories over and over and Laney even chimed in a few times, when it got to the part where she pushed Lucy on the swings. They were two of the cutest kids Zara had ever seen and she knew getting attached to the families she nannied for was a huge mistake, but there was just something about Lucy and Laney that immediately drew her in—even before she knew Aiden was their father. Maybe it was the little signs of vulnerability Laney showed or the way Lucy overcompensated for her mother's loss by seeking attention. Zara could see herself in both of the girls and it made her want to be there for them, and help them in any way she could. Most of the foster families she was with showed her the same kindness and she knew being a nanny was her way of giving back.

"So, what did you do today, Zara?" Aiden asked, drawing her back to the here and now. He smiled at her and gave a knowing wink. He knew damn well what she did today. First, she packed up her stuff, all the while dreaming about their night together, and moved everything to his house and then she had a meeting with him to discuss becoming his sub. All things she could not say in front of the girls.

"Um, well," she stammered. Aiden chuckled and she groused at him. "I got my stuff all moved into my room. I think I'm going to like sleeping in there—night after night," she sassed. There, she could give as good as he could and it was about time she showed him that. Aiden stopped mid-chuckle and shot her a displeasing look, telling her that she hit her mark.

"Well, I'm sure you will be very comfortable no matter where you sleep," he said.

"Zara can sleep with me," Lucy piped up. "My bed is super comfortable," she added for good measure.

"Me too," Laney added. "Sleep in my bed, Z," she said, calling Zara by the nickname she had given her. It was what Ava called her too and that thought made her miss her best friend. It was one of the things holding her back from outright accepting Aiden's offer. She knew keeping her relationship a secret from the one person in the world she trusted the most wasn't going to be easy. Ava would demand answers and Zara knew her best friend well enough to know she'd have plenty of questions.

"Thank you both for the kind offers to share your beds but I'm afraid I can't accept," she said to a chorus of both girls' groans of displeasure. "You see," she continued, "I snore something awful and I'd just keep the two of you up all night."

"Daddy snores too," Lucy offered. "Sometimes, at night, I hear him and he sounds like a bear," she said. Laney growled and snarled, causing them all to laugh at the girl's theatrics.

"Now come on girls, you're making Daddy look bad in front of your new nanny. How about we change the subject?" Zara loved that idea. Thinking too much about which bed she wanted to end up in wasn't something she wanted to do. Especially not now in front of both of the girls.

"You both look like you've already had baths," Aiden said.

He stood and started clearing the table. "How about I give Zara a hand with the clean-up and you two pick out a game to play? And, no Monopoly—I want to get to bed sometime this century." Lucy agreed to pick a game that wouldn't take all night to play and helped Laney down from her chair. Lucy was used to doing so much for herself and Zara didn't want to stifle her independence, but she wished Lucy would learn to lean on her a little more. She had only been there a week and knew it would take some time for both of the girls to fully trust her, but she was hopeful it wouldn't take too long.

Zara carried her dish into the kitchen and grabbed the rag to dry the dishes Aiden had started washing. "I wash and you dry?" he asked. She nodded, hoping he'd wait to ask her what she knew he was dying to ask. Honestly, she hadn't made up her mind about his offer yet and she was hoping playing a game might give her some more time to think things through.

"So really, how was the rest of your day?" Aiden asked, handing her another plate. She could tell he was a little nervous and she found the whole domestic scene endearing. The least she could do was meet him halfway since he was trying so hard.

"After I left your office, I picked up the girls and we spent the afternoon at the park. They sure do love the playground," she said.

Aiden laughed, "Yep. I usually have to bribe them with ice cream to get them to leave."

"Yeah well, we had ice cream cones on the way home," she admitted. "Negotiating with Lucy is like trying to talk down a terrorist. She knows exactly how to get what she wants and goes to great lengths to make things happen. She even got Laney in on her scheme to make me stop for ice cream."

"Lucy can be ruthless when it comes to snacks," he said.

"When we got home, I made them take their baths since they were covered in dirt and chocolate ice cream. I sat in the bathroom with them while they played in the bubble bath and signed up for the last college class I need to graduate. I will need Tuesday and Thursday mornings off this fall, but Rose said that shouldn't be a problem when she hired me. I hope that is still true." Zara waited him out, worried that might be a deal breaker for Aiden. She could see how busy he was with his company and the campaign. Having her take off twice a week, for a few hours might not suit him.

"No, it's fine. Of course, your education should come first. You take the time you need and I'll take the girls to school on those mornings. I promise to give you study time too," he said.

"I won't need to take too much time away from the girls," she admitted. "I will try to get ahead on my Sunday off."

Aiden shrugged, "Whatever works for you, Zara. What happens after you graduate?" She really hadn't given that much thought. Her plan was to get a job teaching and move on with life but telling him that seemed harsh. She knew she couldn't just leave him high and dry. Walking away from the girls might hurt them more than she planned, knowing how their mother so easily left them.

"I haven't given that much thought," she admitted. "I promise to work things out with you and do what's best for Lucy and Laney though. I won't just leave if that is what you are worried about," she said.

"I appreciate that, Zara," Aiden said. He handed her the last dish and when his fingers brushed hers, she looked up at him to find him watching her. His piercing blue eyes seemed to look right through her, and she couldn't help her shiver. "Tell me you've thought about my offer," he demanded.

Zara wanted to lie and say she hadn't really given it much thought but she was sure he'd be able to see right through her. She sighed and nodded, "I have," she admitted.

"And," Aiden asked. He wasn't going to give her a pass on this. He was going to demand an answer and she wasn't sure she had one to give yet.

"It's all I've been able to think about, Aiden," she said. "I just don't—"

"Daddy, we want to play Candy Land," Lucy shouted, running into the kitchen to find them. Zara realized she was standing so close to Aiden she could feel his breath on her face. She took a step back, not wanting to confuse the girls, and handed the dried plate back to him. Aiden looked as frustrated as she felt and she shot him an apologetic smile.

"We will pick this up later," he promised, gifting her with his sexy smirk. Zara wasn't sure if she was looking forward to his promise or if she wanted to run and hide away until he forgot he made her the offer in the first place. Becoming his sub was something she wanted more and more with each passing minute, but she also knew wanting something wasn't always a good enough reason to dive into the deep end. Zara was worried she was going to need to learn to sink or swim because Aiden was going to demand his answer and the time was ticking away quickly.

❄

Zara watched as Aiden read to the girls not just one but four bedtime stories until he told them they had enough and tucked them into their beds. She knew both girls usually ended up in one or the other's bed together and Lucy would be up about fourteen times, asking for water and saying she had to use the bathroom; all the while just checking to make sure someone was still there. It broke her heart knowing Lucy felt the need to check to make sure she hadn't been abandoned. Zara wished she could take that uncertainty away from the little girl, but she knew only time could do that. All she could do was show Lucy patience and that she wasn't going anywhere.

She thought about hiding away in her room, but she knew Aiden would search for her and sooner or later she'd have to face him. Zara sat in the family room after putting away all the girls' toys and getting their school bags ready for the next day. When she worked for other families, this was the time she would either go home or to her own room to unwind for the day. But nothing was normal working for Aiden. The fact that she had already slept with her boss was a major difference from her past employment history. She had a feeling working for Aiden was going to be anything but normal and she wasn't sure how she felt about that.

"Hey," he whispered, finding her in the family room. "I thought you might have headed to bed. Sorry, Lucy put up quite the fight tonight," he said.

"I heard," she admitted. "You got out after only four books. That's pretty good. Last night, I had to read six to them before she gave up the fight." Aiden chuckled and sat down next to her on the big sectional sofa. His thigh touched hers and she could feel those same damn sparks as she had every time he touched her body. She wondered if he felt them too but that wasn't something she was ready to ask him. He wrapped his arm around her shoulder and she leaned into him, almost on instinct.

"Zara," he whispered. She squinched her eyes closed and took a deep breath. She knew he was going to ask for her answer and she was no closer to having one to give to him. "Please look at me," he asked.

"I can't," she admitted.

"Why not?" he asked. Aiden rubbed his thumb over her bare shoulder and she shivered.

"Because if I open my eyes and look at you I'm going to see that same hope I saw earlier. You want me to tell you yes and I'm afraid if I do, it won't be enough," she admitted.

"What won't be enough?" he asked. She could feel his breath on her face, his lips were mere inches from hers and she wanted to open her eyes but knew better.

"Any of it," she said. "I don't want to be a secret, but I know why you can't tell the world about your wife."

"Ex-wife," he amended.

"Right," she said, her eyes still tightly closed. "Listen, I know I was just some woman you picked up at the club, and things didn't end well. That doesn't mean we should end up together, Aiden. Maybe we should just leave well enough alone and move forward—me as your daughters' nanny and you as my employer."

"What if that's not enough for me, Zara?" Aiden whispered. She couldn't help herself, she peeped one eye open and found just what she expected. He was so close; she didn't dare move for fear of accidentally touching him again. If she did, she knew she would agree to just about anything he wanted.

"What do you want, Aiden?" she questioned.

"You," he admitted. He inched closer to her, his lips brushed against hers and she couldn't help but let him take everything he wanted from her. She snaked her arms around his shoulders as he deepened the kiss, sliding his tongue into her mouth to find hers. It was an all-consuming kiss and Zara wasn't sure where Aiden ended and she began. He kissed her that night at the club but this was something different, something new and raw. Aiden broke their kiss, leaving them both breathless.

"Wow," she whispered.

"Fucking right, wow," he agreed. "You make me crazy, Zara," he admitted.

"Sorry," she said. "I don't mean to."

"No, it's not something you can control. It's just who you are. Since that night in the club, I've been miserable. I've been beating myself up over how we left things. God, I was an ass and all I could think about was the fact I'd never get another chance with you. I'd never get to tell you that you are all I can think about and I haven't been able to be with any other woman since our night together. But then, you show up here in my bathtub and it's like fate is giving me another chance with you. Please, don't deny me another chance to make things right, Zara. Let me show you how good things can be between the two of us. Let me make up for being an ass and not taking care of you. Your first time should have been so much more than I gave you. Give me a chance to make it up to you. Don't tell me no—not yet. Give me tonight to prove to you I can be enough and if I don't, then tell me no tomorrow."

Zara knew telling him no wasn't something she could do, not now. Not when he was offering her everything she ever dreamed of. She didn't want to hope but she couldn't help it. Aiden was saying all the right things and her brain couldn't sort it all out. Her body was in overdrive from just one scorching kiss and she found herself nodding her agreement before she knew what she was doing. Aiden didn't seem to need any other reassurances from her. He stood and lifted her into his arms, making his way back to his bedroom.

He laid her across his bed. "Be sure, Zara," he commanded.

"I'm sure, Aiden," she said, holding out her arms for him. He covered her body with his own and nothing had ever felt so right as being with Aiden. She felt it the first night they were together at the club and tonight was no different.

"Don't move," he commanded. Aiden took his time kissing her, working his way down her body, taking off her clothes as he went. Once he had her fully naked, he stood over her, looking at her. Zara wanted to cover herself and Aiden seemed to be able to tell. "Don't," he warned.

She smiled up at him, "It's like you can read my mind," she teased.

"No, but your expressions give you away, baby. I can see every one of your insecurities looking back at me and there is no reason for any of them. You are so fucking beautiful, Zara," he whispered.

"A girl could get used to hearing those words," she sassed.

"All a girl has to do is agree to be mine and she'll never doubt the validity of those words. I'll prove to you every day just how gorgeous you are, Zara," he promised. "Do you want to play?" he asked.

She wasn't quite sure how to answer him. "Play?" she questioned.

"Yes," he breathed. "Like the night at the club," he said. "Will you give me control over your body tonight?"

Zara nodded, not needing time to think about his request. She loved the way Aiden took care of her at the club and she couldn't wait to see what he had in store for her tonight.

"Good," he said. "Now, get on your knees like a good little girl," he commanded. She hesitated and Aiden waited her out, watching her to see if she'd follow his command. When Zara didn't make a move, he pulled out the big guns, already knowing one of her major weaknesses from their one night together. "I dare you," he amended. Zara felt her breath hitch at his taunt.

"That's not playing fair, Aiden," she pouted.

"No one said I was going to play fair, baby," he said. "What's it going to be, Zara? Are you going to accept my dare and do as I ordered or does this all end here and now?" She thought about getting up and walking out of his bedroom, but she remembered how it felt to walk away from him at the club. It hurt and she had to admit, she spent more than one night awake and restless dreaming of being in his bed again. No, she wouldn't walk away again. This time, Zara would accept his challenge because she wasn't going to take the chance of losing him again. She wanted to be daring and take whatever he had planned for her, even if that meant getting on her knees for him.

She slid to the end of the bed and sank to her knees in front of Aiden, looking up at him through her lashes. Aiden ran his hand down her face and smiled. "Good girl," he praised and her crazy heart did a flip-flop in her chest. What was it about this man that made her into a giddy schoolgirl every time he told her she had pleased him? She wasn't sure what that was all about, but she didn't care. Zara would do whatever it took to hear Aiden call her his "good girl" all night long.

AIDEN

Aiden watched as Zara decided if she wanted to obey his command or not and he knew he was holding his damn breath. She had that effect on him though and his tightly held control would do him no good if he lost his shit and tried to push Zara into something she wasn't ready for. She had the strongest will of any woman he had ever met but their one night together had proven to him she was a natural submissive. She did exactly as he asked of her that night in the club and he hoped she would give him her submission tonight. Hell, if he was being honest, he wanted her submission every night for the foreseeable future but he wouldn't admit that to her for fear of scaring her off.

When Zara sunk to her fucking knees he nearly did the same. He felt himself exhale and when she looked up at him through her long lashes and her tongue softly licked her bottom lip, he couldn't help the moan that escaped his chest. She was his walking wet dream and having her gift him with her submission was everything he could have ever wanted and so much more.

"You are so fucking perfect, baby," Aiden growled his praise and she smiled up at him. His heart felt as if it might beat out of his damn chest and he wasn't sure what to ask for first. He wanted everything from her and all the possibilities played through his mind at once, making it hard to form his next sentence.

Zara waited for his next order and he needed to make a decision. He didn't want to fuck things up with her, but everything he had learned at the club in the last half a year felt like a jumbled mess of information in his head.

"Did I do something wrong?" Zara stuttered. She looked up at him and he could see her uncertainty. That was the last thing he wanted.

"No, baby," he whispered. "You are just so fucking beautiful I needed a minute to get my head together." She gifted him with her shy, sexy smile again and he wasted no time. Aiden stripped out of his clothes, loving the way Zara watched his every move as if she couldn't seem to get enough of his body. When he tugged free from his shirt, Zara's hands darted up to his torso and to his bicep where her fingers traced the outline of his only tattoo.

She softly giggled, "Well, I didn't have you pegged as a shark lover," she teased.

He smiled down at her and shrugged. "That was a very bad decision and a long story," he admitted. "Let's just say I learned not to get drunk with Corbin and let him pick my tattoo." The sound of Zara's laughter filled the room, and it was magical. He couldn't remember the last time he felt so at ease with a woman. Towards the end of his marriage to Allison, everything about their relationship felt forced and wrong. He saw that now that things were officially over, and they were legally divorced. She couldn't give him what he needed and that wasn't anyone's fault. The only thing he could really fault Allison over was she didn't see the girls often. She'd show up for special occasions, but other than that her visits were few and far between.

"Hey, where did you just go?" Zara asked.

"Sorry," he said. "I was just thinking about how easy it is to be with you." Zara's smile faded and he worried he was admitting too much, too quickly. "No, sorry—just forget I said anything," he covered.

"It's all right, Aiden. I feel the same way about being with you. I know we don't know each other—well, at all but I feel like we do. If that makes any sense," she said. Zara looked down at the floor and he hated he was making her feel so unsure of herself again. He crooked his finger under her chin and lifted her face to look up at him.

"It does make sense, Zara. Thank you for that," he praised. "Are you ready to play?" he hopefully asked.

"Yes," she whispered.

"Good," he said. He knew she had little to no experience; their one night together had proven that fact. He needed to take things slowly but he didn't want to hold back with her. "You need to tell me what you like and don't like baby," he said. "We are just getting to know each other and I don't want to push you too far. If you don't like something, just tell me to stop and I will." Zara nodded up at him.

This next part was going to be a little tricky, but he needed to ask her questions to get a feel of what to do with her next. "Have you ever given anyone a blow job before, honey?" he asked. She looked down at the floor again and shook her head.

"Eyes on me, baby," he prompted. Zara did as he asked, looking back up at him.

"You must think I'm a complete freak," she admitted. "Honestly, I just concentrated on work and college. I've dated but that was about it." God, she was apologizing for not having any experience with another man and he found that to be the sexiest fucking thing he had ever heard. She didn't realize what a gift she was giving him but he was about to clue her in.

"There is nothing for you to fucking apologize for, Zara. You not being with any other men is hot as fuck. You are letting me be your first for everything and I can't tell you what that does to me. Look at me," he commanded, palming his own cock. He was hard and ready for her attention. He stroked his dick, and she couldn't seem to take her eyes off him. "Look at what you do to me, baby," he demanded. Zara licked her lips and moaned.

"Can I," she hesitated, "may I touch you?" she asked.

"Yes," he hissed. "I want you to touch me and taste me," he admitted. The thought of having her lips wrapped around his cock made him even harder if that was possible. Zara wrapped her small hands around his shaft, taking his directions and pumping his cock. She leaned forward and tentatively licked the head of his dick, gently sucking him into her mouth. It took every ounce of his control not to take over and pump into her hot mouth. He wanted to give her time to adjust to him and explore what he liked and didn't like.

"That's it, baby," he hissed. "Just like that." Aiden wrapped his hands into her long blonde hair and thrust a little deeper into her mouth. She didn't seem to mind when he pushed her a little further, sliding to the back of her throat. When she swallowed around his dick, he nearly came down her throat. Aiden pulled free from her swollen lips and she mewled out her protest.

"I know, baby but if I let you keep doing that to me, this will be over way too quickly," he said.

She smiled up at him, "So, I did it right?" she eagerly asked.

"You were perfect, baby," he praised. "I want inside of you though," he admitted. "Get up on the bed, Zara."

"Will you tie me up again?" she questioned.

"Did you like that, Zara?" he asked.

"Yes," she whispered. "I feel crazy for saying it, but I did. I liked everything you did to me that night at the club."

"Good to know, honey. How about tonight we try something a little different?" Zara's enthusiastic nod made him chuckle. "Stand and hold onto the footboard," he ordered. He had a four-poster bed in his room and the thought of Zara being handcuffed to the post made him crazy with lust. He watched as she did as he commanded and wrapped her hands around the post, waiting for him to tell her what to do next.

"Perfect, baby," he whispered and slapped her ass. "I'm going to get the handcuffs and then I want to take you from behind," he said. Zara shyly nodded and flexed her fingers on the wooden post, telling him she was just as turned on by his suggestion as he was.

Aiden grabbed the fur-lined handcuffs from his nightstand and secured her wrists around the post. He stood behind her and ran his hand down her back to her curvy backside, cupping her ass in his hands. She moaned and thrust back into his hold, seeming to need more.

"Are you ready for me, baby?" he questioned. He didn't wait for her to respond, running his fingers down the seam of her ass and into her slick folds. Aiden moaned at finding her more than wet and ready for him. "Mmm, you're ready for me, aren't you baby?"

"Yes, Aiden, please," she begged. He lined the head of his cock up to her wet folds and Zara instinctively pushed back against him, allowing the head of his shaft to slide into her slick opening.

"Fuck, baby," he hissed. She was so tight, she nearly milked him. He needed to remember this was all new to her, but she felt too good to hold back. He wanted her, all of her and he planned on taking exactly what he needed.

"This is going to be fast, I'm sorry," he said. He pumped in and out of her body, taking what he needed from her and when he knew he was close, he snaked his hand around her body and stroked her clit until she was grinding against him, screaming out his name. Aiden wasn't sure why hearing her shout his name felt so satisfying but it was. He followed her over, finding his own release, and pulled her against his body, loving the way she seemed to melt into his hold.

"That was—" she breathlessly stuttered.

"Amazing," he finished for her. Aiden unlocked the handcuffs and pulled her into his arms, depositing her onto the bed. "Wait here, honey," he whispered into her ear, gently kissing her cheek. Zara closed her eyes and hummed incoherently. Aiden went into his bathroom to get a wet washcloth and climbed back into his bed and Zara cuddled into him.

"I'm going to clean you up, honey," he whispered. She opened her eyes and looked at him as if he lost his mind.

"What?" she asked, suspiciously eyeing the washcloth.

"I'm going to take care of you, baby. If you agree to be my sub, this will be part of my responsibilities to you. It will be my job to give you aftercare and make sure you are all right. Like this," he said. He tried to spread her legs, but Zara seemed to want nothing to do with his idea of aftercare.

"No," she protested. "I can take care of that myself," she insisted.

"Zara," he warned. "Do I need to go over what punishments are and why you might need them or are you going to let me do my job?" Aiden waited her out.

"Fine," she spat. Zara hesitantly spread her legs and covered her eyes with her hands, as if trying to hide. Aiden didn't hide his amused chuckle and when he finished washing her, he pulled her back against his body so she was facing him.

"Look at me, Zara," he commanded. She sighed against his skin and peeped one eye open. "Both eyes, baby," he said. She finally did what he asked, although he could tell she wasn't happy about having to face him. "I'm done playing games, baby. I need to know what you want—I need your answer," he whispered.

Zara smiled at him and his whole world seemed to spin a little faster. "I'll have to follow your every order—you know if I agree to be your sub?" she questioned. He wondered if she was actually considering his offer or if she was just toying with him. Either way, Zara had his full attention. She snuggled into his body, wiggling her sexy little ass against his hands and he flexed his fingers into her fleshy cheeks. He was going to love controlling her every need and desire if she agreed to be his. Aiden was also going to enjoy doling out her punishments and spanking her curvy ass red when she gave him sass like she currently was. Zara knew exactly what she was doing to him, and he had a feeling she'd be trouble at every turn.

"Yep," he said. "After the girls go to bed, you become mine and I like complete control over what is mine," he growled. Zara gasped when he gave her wiggling ass a sharp slap. "Hold still, baby," he ordered. A part of him was surprised when she stopped moving about, proving his original point she was a natural submissive.

"You like it when I spank you, don't you baby?" he questioned. Zara didn't hesitate this time, nodding her agreement.

"I like it when you do just about anything to me, Aiden," she breathlessly admitted.

"So," he coaxed. "Does that mean you will agree to be my sub?"

Again, she showed no sign of hesitation. "Yes," she said. "I will be your sub, Aiden. But we need ground rules if this is going to work out."

He cocked an eyebrow at her and smirked, "What kind of ground rules?" he questioned.

"Well, for one, we can't let the girls know we are—you know sleeping together. No kissing, touching, hugging, or any of that type of stuff around them. I know they are your daughters, but I don't want them confused about what is happening between us. Explaining to them what's going on between the two of us might prove difficult since I really have no clue as to what we are doing here," she admitted.

"Well, I think we are two consenting adults having some wicked hot sex if that helps in way of explanation," he teased. Zara slapped him and giggled.

"No, Aiden," she chided. He could seriously get used to her stern nanny tone; it turned him on. "This thing between us would be confusing to two little girls. They've been through so much, they don't need to worry about what their father is doing with their nanny," she said.

"Deal," he agreed. "And thank you for caring enough about my daughters to instill such a rule," he said. "It means a lot to me."

"Of course," she said. "I told you I've come to care for your girls and that wasn't a lie. They are two very special little girls."

"Any other rules?" he asked.

Zara wrinkled her nose and nodded, "Yes—sorry," she admitted.

"How about we sit down tomorrow and go over these ground rules of yours?" he asked.

"That works for me," she agreed.

Aiden wondered how he had gotten so lucky with Rose finding Zara. She really was the perfect nanny for his girls and now, she was going to be his. "Remind me to give Rose a raise," he said. "It couldn't have been easy to find the perfect woman," he whispered.

"Hmm," Zara hummed. "You keep saying things like that to me and I might agree to just about anything you'd like Mr. Bentley," she said. Aiden didn't want to push his luck but having Zara in his bed was already like a dream come true. He wasn't sure if he deserved to ask her for anything else at this point but he wasn't done with her—not by a long shot.

"Well, then Miss Joy, you should settle in and get ready for a very long night because I'm about to sing your praises and before you know it you will be my love slave," he teased.

"Deal," she promised. "I'm yours for the rest of the night then." Aiden wanted to remind her she had agreed to be his for every night after this one since agreeing to be his sub, but he didn't want to push. Taking things one night at a time was the best for both of them even if his heart did stutter at the idea of having Zara Joy in his bed for good.

ZARA

Zara woke early the next morning and snuck back to her bed before the sun even came up. She managed to get a couple more hours of sleep in before her alarm went off. The girls were early risers and she had to get them breakfast and off to school. Plus, the idea of either of the girls wandering into Aiden's room to find them in bed together didn't sit well with her. It would be breaking rule number one and she couldn't have that happen. Her and Aiden's relationship—or whatever it was they were doing together—couldn't touch the girls. Lucy and Laney deserved to be blissfully ignorant of their nanny being their dad's sub.

She brushed her teeth and pulled her hair back, pulling on her robe to pad out to the kitchen to make coffee. Zara wondered if Aiden drank coffee and realized there was so much she didn't know about him. She made a full pot, betting a man with so much on his plate would need some form of caffeine. Although, judging by the way his body looked, he constantly worked out and took excellent care of himself, maybe he didn't need coffee.

"Morning," he whispered and kissed her cheek. He was

already showered and dressed for the day and Zara wondered if Aiden ever got any downtime.

"Hey," she whispered back. "You're up early."

"I've been up since you left my bed," he said. "So, I grabbed a shower and decided to get an early start."

Zara smiled and shook her head. "Do you drink coffee?" she questioned.

He looked at her as if she lost her mind. "That is quite a change of topic," he teased.

"I was just thinking I don't really know much about you. You know—likes and dislikes, that sort of thing," she whispered.

He pulled her against his body and a part of her wanted to protest with the girls about to be awake at any moment, but he looked at her as if he wouldn't allow her to raise a fuss about what he was about to do. Aiden pulled her up his body and kissed his way into her mouth, igniting all the same fires that burned during the night when he took her over and over. When he finally broke the kiss, she felt hot and completely out of breath.

"Yes," he said. "I like coffee." Aiden stepped away from her and made his way across the kitchen to pour them both a mug of coffee and all Zara seemed capable of was staring at him with her mouth open.

"Do you have a busy day today?" he asked, handing her a mug.

"Not really. Just running a few errands while the girls are in pre-school and then they have dance class today." She had only been working for Aiden for a little over a week now but had found herself fitting right into the girls' schedules. As far as family schedules went, theirs was easy for her to handle and Zara counted herself lucky.

"Will you have time for lunch?" he asked. Zara noticed Aiden seemed a little shy suddenly and she wondered what that was all about. He was usually so in control—so dominant.

Seeing him a little unsure of himself did strange things to her heart and she wasn't sure why.

"Lunch?" she questioned.

"Yes," he breathed. "It's the meal between breakfast and dinner," he teased.

Zara quietly giggled and rolled her eyes at him. "Yeah, I have a firm grasp of what lunch is, Aiden. I'm just wondering why you're asking me if I will have time to eat lunch today." It was Aiden's turn to roll his eyes and he set his mug of coffee down and pulled her back into his arms. Zara could easily get used to being held by him, but she didn't want to get her hopes up this was going to be the norm. She needed to remember her own ground rules and once the girls were awake he wouldn't be able to so freely touch her.

"Well," he said, kissing down the column of her neck. "I was thinking you could come to my office and we can order lunch in —just the two of us." Zara wasn't sure what to make of his offer. Wouldn't that be breaking some of the rules? He was supposed to be keeping up the appearance he was happily married for his campaign.

"What if someone sees me?" she questioned. "What about your campaign?"

"No one will see you, Zara," he promised. "Rose is like the crypt keeper when it comes to letting people in and out of my office. She holds the keys tightly and protects me from any unwanted guests."

"She is very protective of you, Aiden," Zara agreed. "But don't you worry about her knowing about us?" she questioned.

Aiden shrugged, "She already knows about us," he admitted. "Well, she knows I met a woman, and that woman has been all I can think about these past few weeks. I'm sure Rose is smart enough to put two and two together," he said.

"I was all you could think about—really?" she questioned. Her heart felt about ready to race out of her chest at the way he talked about her. For a man who claimed to only want a sub to play with, he was sure pouring on the romance a bit thick. Zara knew she could be setting her heart up to be broken but she didn't care. Hearing Aiden admit that she was all he could think about made her want things she wasn't sure could even exist for them.

"Yes," he whispered, nuzzling her neck. "It seems I still have that problem—not being able to think about anything but you," he admitted.

"Aiden," she murmured.

"Say you'll have lunch with me, Zara," he asked. "Please."

"Yes," she agreed. "I'd love to have lunch with you. I have an hour between errands and picking up the girls. It will have to be an early lunch though," she said.

"Deal," he said, kissing his way up her jaw and taking her lips in a scorching kiss that had her throwing all her rules out the window.

"Daddy," Laney said, standing in the corner of the kitchen, wiping sleep from her eyes. Aiden quickly released Zara and took a step back from her. She knew she was being silly, but Aiden pulling away from her felt like a punishment; as if she had done something wrong. It was crazy, really. She was the one who insisted they have ground rules and the very first one was the girls could not know of their arrangement. They were going to have to be more vigilant in the PDA around the house if they were going to stick with the rules.

"Hey, peanut," Aiden said, crossing the kitchen to scoop up the two-year-old. "How did you sleep?" he asked.

"Good," Laney said with a yawn. "Lucy's in my bed and she snores." Aiden chuckled and tickled Laney's belly causing her to giggle.

"How about some breakfast?" he asked. "I think Zara's making us pancakes this morning." Laney immediately seemed to perk up at the mention of pancakes.

"Chocolate chips too?" she asked, looking over to where Zara was throwing together the ingredients for breakfast.

"Yep, Squirt," she agreed. "You girls do love your pancakes."

"Well, they get that from me," Aiden admitted. "They are my favorite breakfast food."

Zara smiled, "Well, that's the second thing I've learned about you this morning."

"Second, what was the first?" he asked.

"You like coffee," she reminded him.

"Oh, yes. But I think you learned a little more than just two things about me since you've been here, Zara," he teased, winking at her across the kitchen as if she needed the not-so-subtle hint he was kidding.

She rolled her eyes and got back to stirring the batter for the pancakes. "Can you wake Lucy?" she asked. Laney squirmed in his arms, trying to get down.

"I can do it," she said. Aiden put the rambunctious toddler down and watched as she ran back upstairs to wake her sister.

"You know she likes to torment Lucy to wake her up, right?" Zara asked.

"Yeah, but I think Lucy gets her back during the day. She is a little bossy towards Laney," Aiden said.

"A little is an understatement," Zara agreed. "Do you think she saw us together?" She knew she was worrying over something that was probably nothing, but she couldn't help it.

"No," Aiden said. "And if she did, she's too little to understand what she saw. Lucy is another story. If she caught us, we'd never hear the end of her questions."

"We need to be more careful," Zara whispered.

"How about we discuss all of your rules over our lunch today?" he asked. Zara nodded. She wasn't sure what other rules they should have but she had time to come up with a few. She told Aiden the girls not finding out was her number one rule, but if she was being honest her first rule was to make sure that her heart knew the score. She was his sub and she needed to remember that was all he was offering her. Getting carried away and falling for Aiden Bentley wasn't an option and she needed to remember that rule or she'd walk away from him with one very broken heart.

❄

Zara spent the morning running around town, trying to make sure she got her list of errands finished before having to meet with Aiden. She wasn't sure what to make of his request to have lunch at his office, but she was hoping it was more of a date and less business. Zara didn't date her employers, ever. Finding the fine line not to cross between business and pleasure was proving to be tricky. Aiden had seen to her every need and given her plenty of pleasure the night before, but today they would be in his office and anyone might see them together. That thought scared her but not enough to cancel their lunch plans.

She showed up a few minutes early and Rose greeted her at the elevator again. "Hi, Zara," she said. Zara smiled and nodded, not sure how she was supposed to react. Rose had always been gracious and welcoming, but that was before she possibly knew Zara was the woman from the club Aiden had met.

"Hey, Rose," she said. Zara looked at Aiden's closed door and worried he had forgotten about their lunch date—if that was what this was. "Um, is he in?" she asked, nodding to his office.

"Yep and lunch just arrived," Rose said. "He said for you to go right in." Rose went back to her desk leaving Zara standing in the hallway, worried about going into Aiden's office. She wasn't sure if crossing the line between seeing each other in the privacy of his home and the public space of his office was such a good idea but she was about to find out.

"Who do we have here?" A man the size of a mountain was walking straight toward her and she wanted to jump out of his way. Zara looked around, trying to figure out who the man was talking about. "Please tell me you are here to see me?" he questioned, stopping so close to her, Zara had to take a step back from him to look up at his face.

"I'm, um—I'm here to see Mr. Bentley," she squeaked. "Aiden—he's waiting for me," she stuttered. The man took another step towards her again, completely invading her personal space, and smiled down at her.

"You shouldn't waste your time on Aiden," he dramatically whispered. "I'm a whole lot more fun," Corbin wrapped an arm around her waist and winked down at her. Zara tried to slap him away but he was a lot bigger than she was.

"Corbin James, let that poor woman go," Rose demanded.

"Oh Mother, you never let me have any fun," Corbin teased. "Besides, I was just about to make my move," he said.

Zara gasped and he had the nerve to laugh. "Get your fucking hands off of my woman." Zara looked around the big man to find Aiden standing just behind him and the expression on his face was murderous.

"Your woman?" Corbin and Rose said in unison. God, Zara wanted to hide but there was nowhere for her to go. Besides, the big guy still had his arm around her waist and she knew there was no use in struggling.

"Yes, this is Zara," Aiden said. He wasn't really introducing them. It was more like he was issuing a warning and the big guy seemed to take the hint.

"Fuck, Aiden. Why didn't you warn me? When a woman walks into our office looking like Zara here, you know what my first reaction is. A little heads-up would have been nice." He reached a hand out between them for Zara to shake. "I'm Corbin Eklund. Aiden's best friend and business partner," he said. Zara placed her hand in his and he had the nerve to kiss the back of it.

"Zara," she squeaked. She looked him up and down, noticing he was just as handsome as Aiden, about the same age but Corbin had more of an edge to him. His persona screamed bad boy and his outrageous attitude seemed to fit the bill. Aiden seemed to notice her perusal of his business partner, judging by the angry growl that escaped him.

"Well, it's nice to finally meet you, Zara. Aiden has droned on and on about you, so it's nice to put a face to the name," Corbin released her hand and took a step away from her, giving her a full view of Aiden. He didn't look very happy and she was starting to rethink being at his office.

"This was a mistake," she said. "I'm sorry. I should just go," she offered. Zara turned to leave and another frustrated growl ripped through Aiden's chest, stopping her in her tracks. Corbin chuckled and Rose cleared her throat, as if in warning.

"How about we give you two some privacy?" Rose asked. "Corbin take me out to lunch," she ordered.

"Sure, Mom," Corbin agreed. "But listen, Zara, if things don't work out with the caveman who has obviously taken over my friend; feel free to look me up. I'm in the office right next to this Neanderthal." Corbin brushed past Aiden and slapped him on the back. Aiden shot him a look that would have frightened most men but Zara had a feeling Corbin Eklund wasn't like most other men.

"I'll be gone for an hour, Aiden," Rose said. "And for goodness sake, stop growling at poor Zara," she chided. "See you again soon, Zara," Rose said and pulled her in for a quick side hug and then joined Corbin in the elevator. He smiled and waved at her as the doors closed and she was left alone with Aiden. She turned to face him, not knowing what he was going to do or say next but she was done hiding. If Aiden changed his mind about wanting her there, he was going to have to just tell her that himself. It would hurt to hear he had a change of heart about wanting her, but Zara had lived through worse and she'd get through this—but she wouldn't run away scared, she was done with being afraid.

AIDEN

Aiden watched as Zara slowly turned to face him and he hated he had acted so badly. But seeing Corbin with his arms around her made him half crazy. There was no way he'd let another man touch her—not now that she had agreed to be his. Zara wanted ground rules and he was about to give her them and then some.

"Why were you allowing Corbin to hold you?" he asked.

"Allowing?" Zara questioned. "I wasn't allowing any such thing."

"Then why did I just walk out of my office to find my best friend with his arms around you?" Aiden questioned. He wasn't sure why he was so angry, but seeing Zara in another man's arms made his inner caveman roar to life.

"I'm not sure why you are mad at me, Aiden but you have no right to be. I came here, as you requested, for lunch. I have no idea why your friend thought he should touch me and when I tried to get away, he seemed to think it was a game. He didn't even know who I was until you stepped in and cleared things up." Zara raised a shaky hand to her face and brushed back a strand of hair that had fallen from her ponytail. He was being an ass and seeing how he had shaken her up made him feel every bit as bad as he should.

"I'm sorry," Aiden sighed. "I'm an ass," he admitted.

"Yes, you are," Zara quickly agreed.

He couldn't help his smile. "You know you could lie and tell me I'm not acting like a jealous asshole," he teased. "Just seeing another man touching you set me off, I guess—I don't know." He tried to shrug it off as if the whole scene wasn't a big deal but it was. He had blown things completely out of proportion and then when he had a chance to make things right, he blew that too. He needed to get his unruly temper under control or this thing between him and Zara would be over before it even had a chance to begin.

"Well, I'm not a liar. Telling you that you weren't acting like a jealous asshole would be lying," she sassed. "I think now would be a good time for us to go over those ground rules, Aiden." He nodded, knowing she was right. They would have to find some way to navigate through his crazy political agenda and her being his girls' nanny. The odds were already against them succeeding, but that didn't make him want to give up. Quite the opposite—he wanted Zara now more than ever.

"Yes," he agreed. "After this." Aiden closed the space between the two of them and pulled Zara into his arms, sealing his mouth over hers. When she hesitated to let him in, he swatted her ass, and she gave a surprised gasp that allowed his tongue access to hers. By the time he finished kissing her, she was breathless and needy, a combination he could work with. After their little discussion and lunch, he planned on taking her on his desk. Hell, if he had his way, he'd take Zara on every surface in his office, but there probably wouldn't be time for that with her having to pick up the girls and Rose returning from lunch.

"When you look at me like that, I worry," Zara whispered.

"Worry?" he questioned.

"Yes. I worry that you are going to eat me alive," she admitted.

Aiden smirked and winked, causing her to turn an adorable shade of pink. "Well, that's not such a bad idea, baby," he teased. "Let's go over the rules first and then we can talk about me eating you." Zara shook her head and giggled, and Aiden felt himself relax for the first time since they had coffee that morning. She just had that effect on him.

※

Aiden sat on the sectional that took up the corner of his office and pulled Zara down onto his lap. "Rose picked us up some lunch. I hope deli sandwiches are okay?" he questioned. "I wasn't sure what you'd like," he admitted.

"Sandwiches sound great," she said. "We really don't know each other, do we?" she asked. They didn't but if Zara gave him a chance, he'd make sure to change that. He wanted to know everything about her but he also knew that would lead to her being more than just his sub. Aiden didn't know if either of them were ready for that. How would he navigate a relationship that had to be hidden from the public eye? He told Zara before that he wouldn't keep her as his dirty little secret and he meant it. If they could just keep things quiet until after the primaries were over, he could somehow come clean with the press and introduce Zara as his—but would she want that?

"So," she said around a mouthful of sandwich. "Ground rules."

"Yes," he agreed. "We have rule number one already down— no letting the girls in on our little secret."

"Right, and you almost blew that rule right out of the water this morning. We have to be more careful, Aiden," she chided.

"You're right and it was totally my fault," he admitted. "I just can't seem to keep my hands or lips off you," he teased. Zara giggled as he gave her neck little butterfly kisses. She shivered against him and damn if he didn't want to skip to the part where he took her on his fucking desk.

"The rules, Aiden," she reminded.

"Sorry," he said, even though he wasn't. "So, what should rule number two be?" he asked.

"Um, well I guess you touched on rule number two already—we can't be seen together in public," she said. Yeah—he fucking hated rule number two. Aiden wanted to be able to take Zara out and show her off. Hell, he wanted to go to dinner with her and take her to a movie, but even those simple pleasures would instill a media frenzy.

"For now," he amended. "As soon as these primaries are over, I would like to take you out—you know, on a real date," he said.

Zara smiled and nodded. "I'd like that, Aiden," she agreed.

"Let's add an addendum to rule number two," he said. "How about you let me take you to the club?" he asked. "The one we met at has rules in place for anonymity and as you know, I have a private room."

"But what if someone sees us going into that place together?" she challenged.

"We will just have to take extra precautions," he said. "I had Corbin sneak me in the few times I went, to avoid the press. I'm sure we can work something out. We don't have to do anything you don't want to do, Zara," he said. "As my sub, you will have all the say-so, all the power. I can ask but you have the right to say no," he added.

"This is all so new to me," she said. "I have very little experience and this whole Dom/sub thing is completely out of my league."

"I know, baby. That's why we are going to take things nice and slow. I thought the club would get us out of my house on occasion. Plus, it will be like research for you. We can watch other couples play and you can tell me what you'd like to try and what you are against experimenting with."

Zara seemed to mull over his words and then slowly nodded her agreement. "I think I'd like that. I definitely liked watching some of the couples when we were there. I already know I liked when you spanked me," she whispered. Her cheeks turned that cute shade of pink again from her admission.

"Judging by how wet you were after I finished spanking your ass red, I'd say you loved me spanking you, honey," he said. Zara's tongue darted out and licked her bottom lip and he wanted to moan at the memory of Zara sucking his cock to the back of her throat.

"I liked when you let me taste you," she admitted. "I would like to do that again, Aiden."

"Fuck, baby, when you look at me like that I worry," he teased, giving her own words back to her.

"Worry?" she asked, seeming a little confused.

"Yeah, you look like you want to eat me alive," he joked. Zara's laughter filled his office and he decided the rest of the rules could wait. Two was a good even number to stop at and he had plans for her sassy little mouth. "Up, baby," he commanded.

Zara didn't hesitate; she stood and took his extended hand. "I'm going to give you what you asked for and then I'm going to make a meal of you and fuck you over my desk," he said. Aiden sat down in his chair and Zara sunk to her knees without even being told to.

"Is this okay?" she shyly asked.

"It's more than fucking okay," he said. "You are so sexy, Zara." She gifted him with her shy smile and unzipped his pants, letting his cock spring free.

"Mmm," Zara moaned. She ran her small hands over the head of his shaft and he thought for sure he was going to lose it right then and there. Zara leaned forward and sucked him into her mouth, taking most of him and Aiden wrapped her long blonde ponytail around his hand, taking her control from her. He worked his dick in and out of Zara's willing mouth, loving the popping and sucking noises she made every time he pulled his cock free from her lips.

"That feels so fucking good, baby," he moaned. "I'm going to come, Zara," he warned. He tried to pull free from her mouth but she wouldn't allow it. She sucked him to the back of her throat and swallowed around his cock and Aiden couldn't stand it anymore. He came in hot spurts down her throat and Zara took all of him, even licking his cock clean when he finished.

"You taste good, Aiden," she said breathlessly.

He leaned back into his chair, catching his own breath and trying to remember how to form words. "God, baby," he whispered. "That was incredible." Again, her radiant smile lit up the room when he praised her. She was such a perfect submissive—from the way she took direction to the way she soaked up his praise; he couldn't ask for more. Well, he shouldn't ask her for more, but he was a greedy bastard.

"Up on my desk, honey," he ordered. Zara hopped on top of his desk and he helped her out of her leggings and panties, leaving her bare for him, from the waist down to do with as he pleased. "My turn," he insisted, spreading her legs further apart. He sat back down in his chair and was the perfect height to feast on her pussy. She was already wet for him and she tasted so fucking good.

He ran two fingers down through Zara's wet folds and licked her clit into his mouth. She moaned and just about bucked off his desk. "Hold still, baby or I'll tie you down." Zara moaned again as if telling him that idea made her hot. His girl was definitely into kink, he just wondered how far she'd let him push her.

Aiden pumped his two fingers in and out of her wet core, hitting her special spot while he licked and sucked her clit. It didn't take long for Zara to find her orgasm and he loved hearing her shout out his name.

He couldn't stop himself, he stood and let his pants drop to the ground. He was hard again and ready to play, anxious to get inside Zara. "This is going to be hard and fast, baby," he said. "Rose will be back any minute." Zara whimpered and nodded.

Aiden thrust into her wet pussy and he had to stop and give himself a minute to adjust to the sensation of her tight core gripping his cock like a glove. She spasmed around him and he just about lost it. "Touch yourself, Zara," he commanded. She looked up at him and he could see she wanted to tell him no.

"I—I don't know what to do, Aiden," she whispered.

"Give me your hand," he said. She reached up for him and Aiden took her hand and guided it between where their bodies were joined. "Right here," he said, taking her finger and running the pad over her sensitive nub. She moaned and ground her pussy against his cock. "See, you like that, don't you?" he asked.

She shyly nodded and when he removed his hand from hers, she continued to work her clit. He could feel her orgasm growing and Aiden knew she would be finding her release in no time. He wanted to be with her so he pumped harder into her body, setting a punishing pace.

"Aiden," she shouted.

"Come for me, baby," he whispered, leaning over her body and pumping into her a few more times before finding his own release right along with Zara. She was gorgeous to watch and he wasn't sure what the hell he was going to do about his perfect, secret submissive who was stealing his heart every time she entered the same room as him. Aiden was sure of one thing—rule number three was going to be not to lose his fucking heart to his daughter's nanny.

ZARA

Zara was late picking up the girls and when she ran into their preschool claiming to have been stuck in traffic, their teacher gave her a knowing look. Sure, she probably looked as if she just had a handful of orgasms and her just fucked hair and swollen lips didn't help her case, but spending an hour wrapped up in Aiden was well worth the dirty looks.

"Can we still go to the park?" Lucy asked as she buckled them in the car.

"I'm sorry but not today. You both have dance class and then we have to go home to make dinner. Would you two like to be my little chefs and help me cook tonight?" she asked. They both perked up at the mention of helping her in the kitchen despite not being able to play at the park today.

"Will you stay at dance class?" Lucy asked. "Mommy used to watch us dance," she almost whispered.

Zara was taken aback at Lucy's mention of her mother. The two little girls didn't talk about their mom much. In fact, she didn't realize just how little Allison was brought up until Lucy said her name. "Of course, I'll stay to watch my two favorite girls dance," Zara said. "I wouldn't want to be anywhere else."

Laney smiled and clapped, and Lucy nodded as if she was satisfied. Lucy was the smartest kid she had ever met, and she was sure half of what the little girl did was to test Zara. She worried she had failed most of Lucy's inquiries but she was trying her best. She wanted to be there for the girls, especially since their own mother didn't seem interested in them or anything they were doing.

Aiden had mentioned that his ex only came around for holidays and special occasions, but she was missing out on two pretty fantastic kids. Sure the day-to-day routine could become a little boring, but what mother would want to skip out on any part of her kids' lives? Zara tried to remember it wasn't her place to judge Aiden's ex-wife but the more time she spent with him and the girls, the more she seemed to question Allison Bentley's motives.

They pulled up to dance class two minutes after it started and the instructor shot Zara the same dirty look the girls' teacher had as the three of them raced through the door. What was wrong with people today? It was as if the excuse of being caught in traffic wasn't still a viable one.

Zara sat in the corner of the room, watching the girls spin and twirl, waving to them each time they passed by her. Her phone chimed and she was once again on the receiving end of some very dirty looks, this time from the mothers in the class. Zara mouthed the word, "Sorry," and dug her phone from her purse to silence it. She opened the text from Ava and read her best friend's overly dramatic SOS message. It was the code they used when they had a problem that required immediate attention. Ava was prone to use the SOS message due to a shoe emergency and Zara thought about waiting to call her back, but her phone vibrated with another message, and she was sure Ava wasn't going to be ignored. She opened the new message to find Ava's face pop up on her phone screen, her expression dire and Zara stifled her giggle.

She decided to call Ava back, knowing that her friend hated

being ignored, it would be her best bet if she wanted any kind of peace. Ava was still angry at her for moving into Aiden's, especially after she told Ava who she was working for. She dialed Ava and held the phone to her ear, hoping whatever crisis her friend was having would be a quick fix.

"You can't make calls in the room during class, Miss," the instructor snapped. Lucy looked completely mortified. Zara didn't know the rules and she apologized and stood to go into the hallway. The way Lucy watched her told her she was going to have to do a whole lot of groveling later if she wanted any peace with the little girl.

"Zara," Ava answered.

"Ava, this better be good and no, a shoe emergency is not a real thing," Zara said.

"This has nothing to do with shoes," Ava said. "I just sent you a link. Put me on speaker and go look at it." Zara decided to humor her friend. She was already in deep water with Lucy and would have to probably bribe her with ice cream on the way home. She opened the link and gasped at the pictures that appeared on her phone screen.

"What the fuck?" she whispered.

"Exactly what I was thinking," Ava agreed. "Tell me the article isn't true, Zara. Tell me you aren't a home wrecker," Ava asked.

"No," she breathed. "How can you even ask me that?" Zara quickly scanned the article that followed the scandalous headline, "New Nanny Breaks up Candidate Bentley's Marriage." The article was full of lies about their relationship and said she had everything to do with Allison Bentley leaving both Aiden and her girls. It spewed some bullshit that Aiden was following Zara's request and keeping the girls from their mother.

"I had to ask, babe. I'm so sorry to be the one to tell you all of this," Ava said.

"What do I do now?" Zara asked. She wasn't really asking

Ava; more like trying to figure out her next move. "It all makes sense now," she muttered.

"What does?" Ava asked.

"Why the girls' teachers looked at me as if I was the devil incarnate for being just a few minutes late and why all of the dance moms are spying on me through the windows as if they are trying to read my lips or something." She turned her back on her audience and worried about any of the hateful lies from the article getting back to either of the girls.

"What if the girls find out?" she whispered.

"Where are you now?" Ava asked.

"The girls' dance class," she said. "They are almost finished."

"When they are done, take them straight home. Do you want me to come over?" Ava asked. She wanted to tell her yes, but Zara worried Aiden would find her best friend at his house to be a breach of confidence. Zara needed a friend right now and there was no way she'd want to turn to anyone else.

"Yes," she whispered. "I'll text you the address and you can meet us there. But not a word in front of the girls."

"Of course not," Ava agreed. "I'll meet you there in thirty minutes." Zara ended the call and turned to go back into the classroom, running straight into a solid wall of muscles. She almost had to strain her neck to see who she had bumped into and the smiling, handsome face looking down at her wasn't quite what she expected.

"You," she said, squinting her eyes at Corbin. "Why are you at the girls' dance class? Wait—don't tell me—you've come here to hit on all the hot, single moms who might be desperate enough to fall for your whole caveman routine." Corbin threw back his head and laughed but Zara found nothing about the situation funny.

"Nope, sorry princess, but I'm here to run a little interference for Aiden and to make sure you and his adorable brats get home safely," he said.

"They aren't brats," she corrected.

"Honey, I've known both of them since birth, and let me tell you they are two of the best kids I know, but anything that small and whiney is what I consider a brat." Corbin looked her up and down as if waiting for her to challenge him but she didn't. Honestly, she just wanted to get home and figure out her next move. The whole news article had her head spinning and a glass of wine with her best friend sounded like the start of a great plan.

"I take it you've seen the article then?" she asked.

"Yep," Corbin confirmed.

"And Aiden," she questioned.

"Has seen and read every lie that was printed about the two of you," he said.

"Well, shit," she whispered.

Corbin chuckled again. "Not the same choice words Aiden used but close," he teased. "That's why I'm here. His team thinks if you're seen out and about town with yours truly, it will take some of the validation out of the lies they printed."

"Or, everyone in town will start talking about how I'm a two-timing whore," she offered. Honestly, she wasn't sure what to do. "Aiden sent you?" she questioned.

"Yep," he said, "he told me to tell you it's going to be all right. He said you'd worry and probably give me a little fight but I reminded him I like my women a little feisty," he teased.

"I'm not your woman," she demanded. Corbin shrugged and smiled down at her as if he didn't hear a word she was saying. Of course, he had but he just didn't care. Zara trusted Aiden and if he sent the giant caveman to take her and the girls home, she would go with him.

"Here come the girls," he whispered. "We'll take my car and Aiden will send someone for your SUV," he ordered.

"Uncle Corbin," Laney cheered. The toddler ran to him and held up her arms to be picked up. Lucy on the other hand came out of the classroom with her arms crossed over her chest, wearing a scowl that was directed at Zara.

"Hey, sour puss," Corbin teased; only making Lucy angrier, if that was even possible.

"You said you were going to watch our class," she chided Zara.

"I'm sorry Lucy but I had an important call I had to take," Zara said. The little girl's anger didn't seem to deflate any with Zara's explanation.

"Cut it out, squirt," Corbin said. "Zara had something important come up and sometimes us adults have to do adulty things." Lucy stared Corbin down and Zara almost wanted to laugh. Most grown women would have a hard time eyeballing a man the size of Corbin Eklund, but the five-year-old had no trouble giving him the stink eye.

"She broke her promise," Lucy grumbled.

"Well, I guess you're really mad," Corbin said. "It looks like even ice cream won't make your sister feel any better," Corbin said to Laney. The toddler seemed to play along until she heard the words ice cream and started squirming in Corbin's arms.

"I like ice cream," Laney chanted.

"I know you do short stuff but your sister is just too upset to eat ice cream right now. Looks like I wasted a trip over here to take you girls for ice cream for nothing," he teased.

Lucy dropped her arms to her side, her scowl still in place. "Fine, I'll have some ice cream but I'm still mad at you, Zara. You said you would stay and you lied." Lucy turned around, letting her dance bag hit Corbin's leg, and started for the door.

"Lucy," Corbin said, stopping her in her tracks. "You come back here and apologize or we forget about the whole ice cream deal."

"No, it's fine, Corbin. She's right—I let her down and didn't keep my promise." Zara faced Lucy and crouched to be eye level with the stubborn little girl. "I'm so sorry, Lucy. Can you please give me another chance?" Lucy seemed to mull over her decision and Zara found the whole thing adorable, although she wouldn't tell Lucy that. She knew the little girl was still trying to be upset, but Zara could tell she was letting some of her anger go.

"Will you play a game with me tonight and read me two bedtime stories?" Lucy asked, ever the shrewd negotiator.

Zara smiled, "Of course. But doesn't your dad usually read to you when he's home?"

Lucy nodded, "Yes, but I like the way you do the princess's voice." Zara giggled. "How about if you can be the princess and Daddy can be the prince?" Lucy hopefully asked. Corbin barked out his laugh and Zara shot him a warning glance. He held up his big hands, almost as if in defense.

"Well, that sounds perfect," Zara said. "It's a deal." She held out her hand to shake on it and Lucy did the same.

"I'm sorry I was mean to you, Zara," Lucy offered. She turned to Corbin and smiled. "We're good," she said. "Can we go for ice cream now?" Zara didn't hide her giggle. Lucy was always on top of her game and that worried her. She seemed to even have the big guy a little tongue-tied.

"Fine," he agreed, scooping Laney back up. "Let's hit the road, girls. Your dad will be home soon and I know he's going to want to talk to Zara. How about I take you girls out for ice cream, just the three of us, while they have their chat?" The girls both cheered and agreed to a special date with Corbin. Zara shuddered at the thought of having to have a private conversation with Aiden about the news article. She was sure he was going to tell her whatever was developing between the two of them was now over before it even had a chance to get started.

AIDEN

Aiden sat in four boring-as-hell meetings with his advisors and all he could think about was getting home to Zara. She must have been beside herself when she found out about the news article. Sending Corbin to take care of her and the girls might not have been his finest decision but it was all he had. As soon as the story broke, his campaign manager called him to tell him the news. He was furious someone could print so many ruthless lies about him but it was his own fault really. Aiden was the one who agreed to lie about he and Allison still being together and now, he was going to have to come clean publicly about his whole messy divorce. He hated that this now involved the new woman in his life—Zara. He was developing feelings for her and he wasn't sure how she was going to respond to the breaking story. Hell, he wouldn't blame her for taking off much like his ex-wife had but he hoped she'd agree to stick around.

His campaign manager begged him not to go public with his divorce but he didn't see any other way. Pictures of him and Zara had leaked and the worst bit was they were taken right in front of his home. Someone had taken picture of him with Zara and the girls leaving earlier that morning. His manager wanted him to, "Clear up the confusion," by telling everyone Zara was nothing more than his daughter's nanny. But, when he explained that was just not the case, he was told to lie about his new relationship or forfeit his candidacy. Aiden was sure there had to be some in-between place where they could all meet and find common ground. He just didn't want to believe he'd have to give up one or the other. Zara was quickly becoming an important fixture in his life. The campaign was something he had worked so hard for, giving it up now seemed like failing and that was something Aiden didn't like to do. There had to be a way to have it all, he just needed to figure everything out.

He pulled up to his house and spotted the strange car in his driveway. If another reporter had gotten to Zara or his girls, there'd be hell to pay. He stormed into the house to find Corbin playing Candyland with the girls and no sign of Zara.

"Where is she?" he questioned.

"She's in her room with her friend, Ava," Corbin said, bobbing his eyebrows at Aiden. "You didn't tell me your new nanny had a hot best friend," Corbin said.

"That's because I didn't know about this friend," Aiden complained. "Why the hell is she in my house?" he asked.

Corbin shrugged, "Beats me. She was here when we pulled up and the two of them disappeared up to Zara's room and I've been watching the rugrats." Lucy and Laney were giggling about something or other and Aiden was happy they were distracted. The last thing he wanted was for either of them to be dragged into his drama.

"Can you stick around for a bit?" Aiden asked. "I need to speak with Zara and straighten this whole mess out—if that's even possible," he said.

"Sure, man," Corbin said. "But don't be hard on Zara. She needed someone to talk to and her friend seemed to be on the up and up."

Aiden nodded, "I'm assuming this friend is hot and that's also part of why you're defending her?" Aiden questioned.

Corbin shrugged, "Well, yeah. But your girl has been through a hell of a lot in the past couple of days. Just go easy on her."

Aiden kissed the girls on his way upstairs telling them to behave for Uncle Corbin, but Lucy looked to be in rare form tonight, so he was betting that might be challenging for her. "We'll probably go out for ice cream," Corbin called after him, but he wasn't paying much attention. His only thought was to get to Zara and make sure she was all right.

"Sounds good," Aiden called back over his shoulder. "Don't be too late—it's a school night."

Aiden found Zara's door shut and he wondered if he should knock. Sure, it was his home but Zara was a grown woman entitled to her own privacy. She had also agreed to be his sub which gave him the authority to enter her room when he pleased and right now, he needed to be with her.

Aiden lightly tapped on the door. "Zara, let me in," he demanded. "We need to talk," he said. He winced at his own words, knowing he sounded like a complete dick. He heard her fumbling around her room and then her door slowly opened to reveal one very pissed-off woman whom he assumed to be Zara's best friend.

"Hello," he said. "I'm Aiden—" he wasn't able to get out the rest because Zara's sassy friend held up her hand.

"I know exactly who you are, Mr. Bentley. My best friend is in here crying her eyes out because she feels as though she's done something wrong. But, she hasn't. You, on the other hand, have fucked up royally. How could you let the public believe my girl is a home wrecker? You should have had your people on this already dispelling those vicious rumors and restoring her good name," the woman insisted. Aiden decided immediately he liked her, and he was happy Zara had someone so fierce in her corner, fighting for her. He wanted to be that for Zara but at this point, he wasn't sure she'd allow that.

Zara stood from where she was sitting on her bed and crossed the room to face Aiden. He could tell she had been crying and it nearly tore his heart in two. "Baby," he whispered reaching for her. Zara took a step towards him and then hesitated.

"Ava's right, Aiden. Why are you letting this happen?" she questioned.

"I was a fool for listening to my campaign manager. I should have never let the public believe Allison and I are still married. Hell, it's been over half a year since she left me, and we've been divorced for a while now. I shouldn't have let it go on but I did and I can't take that back. What I can do is fix everything. I've scheduled a press conference for first thing tomorrow morning and I'll be announcing my withdrawal from the race. I'll also be explaining that Allison and I are legally divorced and you are not a home wrecker but someone I am seeing and care for very much," he all but whispered the last part.

"Really?" she squeaked.

"Yes, really," he confirmed. "I was wrong to believe I could run my campaign based on a lie. I could stand here and blame everything on my campaign manager, but this was my fault. I take full responsibility and I promise to make everything right," he said. Aiden turned to leave, knowing he had said everything he had to. It was clear Zara's friend, Ava, wasn't going to let him pass and he wouldn't push his way into Zara's room or life.

"Wait," she commanded. Zara turned to her friend and whispered something into her ear and all Aiden could do was stand and watch them, holding his breath, hoping she'd give him another chance. After what seemed like a whispered heated debate, Ava nodded and started past him down the hall.

"You fucking hurt her again and you'll have me to answer to, Mr. Bentley," she promised.

"Duly noted," he said and watched Zara's protective friend

disappear down the stairs. He wanted to go to Zara, pull her into his arms and tell her everything was going to be all right but he couldn't make her that promise.

"Please know that if I could change all of this, I would," he said.

"You would want to change everything?" Zara questioned. "Even everything that has happened between the two of us?" He took two steps towards her, closing the space between them, and hesitantly reached for her. When she didn't flinch or step away, he took that as his green light to pull her into his arms.

"Never, baby," he whispered. "I'm so fucking lucky you walked into that club. I wouldn't change one thing about us. I just wish this news article would disappear." Aiden's phone chimed and he pulled it from his pocket to read the text from Corbin.

"Apparently, Corbin and your friend—Ava was it?" Aiden asked. Zara nodded. "Well, they are taking the girls for some ice cream Corbin promised Lucy." He smiled at the thought of his daughter's negotiating skills. She was quite ruthless.

"I think Corbin has a thing for Avalon," Zara said.

"Corbin has a thing for just about every woman in the female species. Did he put the moves on your friend?" Aiden asked. Corbin flirted with every woman he had ever met. It was just who his best friend was and he came to accept it long ago.

"No," Zara said. "Just the opposite. You know how forward he was with me earlier?" Aiden nodded, remembering how Corbin couldn't seem to keep his hands to himself at the office earlier that day. He walked out and found his friend with his arms wrapped around his woman and Aiden wanted to pound him.

"Yeah, I remember," he dryly admitted.

Zara giggled, "Well, when I introduced Ava he just stood there, speechless. Since I met him, earlier today, he hasn't shut up and then Avalon walked in, and boom—Corbin hasn't spoken a coherent sentence to either of us since. I'm thinking he's either broken or smitten but I don't know him well enough to make that call."

Aiden chuckled at the thought of Corbin being tongue-tied. It would be a first, for sure. "I'd pay good money to see Corbin speechless," he admitted. "This is going to be fun to watch. Apparently, the big guy was able to get himself together and ask Ava if she wanted to go for ice cream."

"I'm sure Lucy helped him with that. Your daughter is a force when she wants something. I'm guessing she gets that from you?" Zara asked.

"So I've been told," Aiden agreed. "Listen," he started, needing to get back to the topic at hand. "I will do everything in my power to fix everything for you, baby. I'm so sorry you had to read that trash."

Zara sobbed and it gutted him. Aiden wrapped his arms around her a little tighter and let her cry into his shirt. "The girls' teachers looked at me as if I had done something wrong," she cried.

"Oh baby, you did nothing wrong," he soothed.

"How did someone get those pictures of us this morning?" she questioned.

"I have no idea, but I have my security team working on finding out who took them and where. I've also increased security for us and the girls. You won't be going anywhere without your guard, understand?" he asked.

Zara slowly nodded. "Is that really necessary?"

Aiden sighed, not wanting to admit this next part. He hoped to avoid painting a picture for her of just how crazy his life could be. "Allison left me for good reason," he admitted. "Can we sit down and talk about this?" he asked.

"You don't have to tell me about your ex-wife or your life prior to meeting me, Aiden. That's not part of the deal we have in place. I'm assuming it isn't a sub's place to know all the gory details from her Doms past," Zara said.

"Fuck the deal, Zara. I want you for more than just my sub. God baby, I want you for—everything. But once I tell you why Allison left me, you might want to pack your shit and run too," he admitted. He hated the thought of Zara walking away from him and the girls. He knew it was crazy and he had only known her a few weeks now but he couldn't imagine his life without her in it.

"Fine, we can talk but I don't think you are giving me enough credit, Aiden. I'm not your ex-wife and I'm sure you aren't fully to blame for what happened between the two of you." Zara took his hand and led him down the stairs to the kitchen. She opened the oven and checked what had been baking, smiling back over her shoulder to where he stood.

"I hope you like lasagna. I made a big pan this morning and stuck it in the oven when we got home from dance class. Although, I'm pretty sure Corbin is going to ruin the girls' appetites with ice cream, we can still eat." Zara pulled down two plates and found a bowl of salad in the refrigerator. He could tell she was avoiding having their talk but Aiden would give her a few minutes.

"I'm starving, thank you," he said, taking the plate she handed him. "This looks great," he said. He helped Zara with her plate and then into her chair, at the kitchen table.

"Thanks," she said, scooting up to the table.

Aiden sat next to her and took a deep breath. It was now or never, and Zara deserved to know the truth. "Allison left me because she couldn't deal with my crazy schedule or the extra crap that comes with me owning a multi-million-dollar corporation." Aiden sat back in his chair, impressed with himself he was able to get that out all in one breath.

Zara looked around his house and smiled, "Yes, I'm sure she hated having to live in a big, fancy house. That poor woman must have been beside herself," she teased.

"I'm serious, Zara," he said. She took a bite of her food and he decided he was going to have to dig a little deeper to show her just how crazy his life could be. "We received four death threats before I left for home tonight," he whispered.

Zara stopped eating and dropped her fork onto her plate. "What do you mean by 'we,' Aiden?" she asked. Yeah, now she was beginning to catch on.

"I mean us—you and me. Just before I left, my head of security met with me to go over the new detail assignments and he informed me you and I have had four death threats since this new story broke. It's nothing new for me, but I know this must be terrifying for you. Allison hated that part of our lives. It's why we chose a private preschool and why there is so much security around here and the office," he said.

"You must hate it," she whispered. "Living under a microscope and having to constantly worry about your girls."

"Yeah, it's a part of who I am and what I do. It got worse after I agreed to run for the Senate seat. That's about the time Allison had enough and left us," he confessed.

"Wait—you're telling me you have been carrying around the blame for your ex-wife leaving you all this time? Even Connie says her daughter was a fool for walking out on you guys," Zara said.

"Connie?" he questioned. "She told you about my divorce?"

Zara winced, "Yeah, she's kind of an over-sharer."

"Remind me to have a talk with my ex-mother-in-law," he said.

Zara reached across the table and took his hand in hers. "She loves you and the girls, Aiden. She feels awful her daughter so carelessly threw away everything and left you three. She worries about you and the girls," Zara said. "Cut her a break. I don't think you realize how many people in your life truly care about you."

Aiden pulled her from her chair and into his lap. "Are you one of those people, Zara?" he asked.

She shyly nodded and wrapped her arms around his neck. "Yes," she admitted. "I am. Is that okay?" she asked.

"It's more than okay—it's fucking amazing," he said. "But you have to know the good and the bad that comes with me and the girls. We have a lot of baggage, and I don't want you to get in so deep you can't find your way out if you need to."

"I'm not looking for a way out, Aiden," she whispered. "Just let me in, let me show you I can handle all of you, even the bad stuff."

Zara was almost too good to be true, but he wouldn't take such a gift for granted. "All right, but you have to tell me if my crazy life gets to be too much," he said, making her promise.

"Now, let's discuss this crappy idea you have about stepping down from your run for the Senate seat," Zara said.

"It's the only way to keep your name out of the mud they continuously try to drag me through," Aiden offered. "If I continue to run, the press will eat you alive and I can't let that happen."

Zara readjusted her body to straddle his lap and softly kissed his lips. "How about you let me worry about myself and you just worry about your campaign?" she asked.

"You have no idea what you are asking," he said. "The press can be ruthless."

"Well, I've worked for some pretty high-profile clients. That's why Rose hired me to be your girls' nanny. Plus, Avalon's family was in politics and I'm sure she can give me some pointers. But you have to let me talk to her. I know I signed a gag order saying I couldn't discuss you or your family with anyone, but that was before this thing between us happened."

Aiden knew she was right. Corbin warned him that keeping her from being able to talk to her best friend was a mistake and he was right. Zara needed an outlet to vent, especially if she was going to be a part of his life and Aiden wanted that more than anything.

"Fine," he agreed. "I will have Rose shred the agreement as long as you promise to use discretion in whom you talk to. Avalon might be the only person you can truly trust. You have to assume everyone else is out for a story and they won't hesitate to profit from whatever piece of juicy gossip they can extract from you."

Zara squealed and squirmed around on his lap and his cock sprang to life. He didn't miss her surprised gasp when she realized what she was doing to him. Her sexy smirk was almost his undoing. "You know, the girls will probably talk Corbin and Ava into a trip to the park," he said. "I think we might have a little time on our hands if you want to skip the rest of dinner."

He kissed his way down Zara's jaw and watched as she tugged her shirt over her head. "No bra?" he asked, making a tsking noise. Zara shook her head and palmed her own breasts as if offering them to him. "That's sexy as fuck, baby," he said.

Aiden didn't want to waste any time, he stood with her legs still wrapped around his waist and made his way over to the family room, laying her across the sectional. He pulled her yoga pants down her body along with her panties, leaving her completely bare to his gaze.

"You are so fucking hot, baby," he praised. Zara gifted him with her shy smile as he quickly stripped out of his suit. He loved the way she watched him, her heated gaze wondering his body. She lay on the sofa as if waiting for him to tell her what to do, ever the obedient submissive.

"Up," he ordered. She did as he commanded, and he sat down on the velvet sofa and pulled her back onto his lap. Zara straddled his cock and when she slid her wet core over his shaft, taking all of him, they both moaned from the pleasure of it all.

"You feel so good, Aiden," she whispered against his lips. He devoured her mouth, not able to think of anything more than making her completely his.

"You too, baby," he said. Aiden grabbed handfuls of her ass, spreading her cheeks over his cock, opening her further. "I'm going to take your ass," he growled. "Would you like that baby?"

he asked. Zara whimpered and nodded her agreement. "Good girl. We will start training your ass soon."

The thought of sliding a plug into Zara's tight, virgin hole nearly had him coming. He needed to make sure she was taken care of first. He ran a finger through her slick folds and then back to her ass, gently probing her hole. She hissed out her breath and threw her head back.

"Yes, Aiden, more," she begged. She rode his cock with wild abandon. It was as if she couldn't get enough of him, and he loved the way she took what she needed from him. "I'm going to come," she shouted. That was all he needed to hear. He found his release with Zara and when she slumped breathlessly onto his chest, his whole world felt completely right for the first time in a very long time.

"Zara," he whispered. "I think—"

"Hey guys, whoa," Corbin had walked through the front door and turned to quickly usher the girls and Ava back out, closing and locking it, despite their protests. Zara squealed and jumped up, grabbing her clothes to cover her body but it was too late. Judging by his friend's goofy lopsided grin, he had seen every inch of his woman. The big oaf had the nerve to keep staring at her. Aiden stood and covered Zara with his own body but that didn't seem to matter to Corbin.

"Can you please get them out of here and give us a minute?" Aiden questioned.

"Don't worry about the girls and Ava—they didn't see a thing. I forgot Laney's bear and she refused to get ice cream without him," Corbin explained.

"Can you just turn around for a minute, man? Just pretend you are a decent human being and turn your back," Aiden insisted. Zara stood behind him and the string of whispered curses had him smiling. Apparently, Corbin heard her too and laughed.

"You forgot a few choice words, honey," Corbin teased. Zara finished pulling on her shirt and stepped around Aiden, walking straight for Corbin. Aiden pulled on his pants and shirt, preparing for the show he was sure his girl was about to give them. Zara was pissed, reminding him of the way she left the club on their first night together. He knew from experience his woman was a spitfire when she was angry and judging by the way she poked her sexy little finger into Corbin's broad chest, she was good and pissed.

"I'm not your honey, Corbin Eklund. You need to knock before you just barge into a room or at least tie a bell around your neck to let us know you're entering." Aiden chuckled and she turned to face him, her expression murderous.

"And you—" she spat.

"Hey, wait a minute. I'm innocent here," he defended.

"You are most certainly not innocent here," she charged. "You knew we agreed to keep this thing between us under wraps. You agreed the girls wouldn't find out and then you took off all of my clothes and looked at me with your sexy eyes and now this—" she yelled, flailing her arms wildly about as if they were helping to prove her point.

"You're right," Aiden conceded. "I fucked up and I'm sorry. We'll just sit the girls down and tell them we're a couple."

"We will do no such thing," Zara shouted.

"Listen, guys," Corbin interrupted. "I'm just going to grab Barry the bear and be on my way." He found Laney's teddy bear sitting on the bench by the front door and gave a wave over his shoulder on his way back out the door. Aiden wasn't sure if he was happy or worried about being alone with Zara again.

"We can't just announce to those little girls I'm your sub and that their Daddy likes to tie their new nanny to his bed," she said. Zara's anger seemed to dissipate some and he had to admit he was glad. She was so much easier to talk to when she wasn't screaming at him and waving her hands around like a crazy person. But, she was right, he fucked up—again. He needed to get his head on straight, but there was something about her that made him want to throw caution out the window and live in the moment. Fucking her on the sofa might not have been his finest decision but it sure felt right at the time.

"Well, we wouldn't tell them any of that, baby. First—I thought we covered the part where you are more than just my sub," he said. "You admitted you care for me and I told you I feel the same way. We might have a Dom/sub relationship in the bedroom but this 'thing,' as you keep calling it, has evolved into so much more than that for me." Aiden hoped he wasn't saying too much or pushing her too quickly but he wouldn't hide the truth from her. He was falling for her and it wasn't something he planned on doing—it just happened and it felt right.

Aiden reached for Zara and was thankful she let him pull her into his body. "We'll just tell the girls I'm falling in love with their nanny," he whispered.

ZARA

Zara wasn't sure if she had heard Aiden correctly or if it was her heart interfering with her hearing. "Did you just say you're falling in love with me?" she asked.

"I did," he admitted, without hesitation. "Is it too soon?" he asked. She wanted to tell him it was too fucking fast to be talking about feelings and love. It had only been a couple of days since he found her soaking in his bathtub. But they had their night in the club and if she was being honest, she couldn't stop thinking about him these past few weeks either. There was something about Aiden that had drawn her to him that night in the club and it kept her coming back for more. When he asked her to be his sub she wanted to ask for so much more from him, but she was too afraid of him telling her no. Now, he was offering her his world, his heart, and everything she had ever dreamed of and she wasn't sure what to say next.

"Tell me I'm not alone in the way I'm feeling, Zara," he begged. "For fuck's sake, say something," he ordered.

Zara wasn't sure if she was being foolish by admitting it but she didn't care anymore. "You're not alone," she admitted. "I feel the same way but I was too afraid to tell you. I wanted so much more than to just be your sub but I didn't know how to ask," she whispered.

"Thank you for saying that, baby." Aiden wrapped his arms around her and she felt like her whole world was right again. The entire day had been chaotic except for the parts when she was with Aiden. There was something about him that just made her feel as if she was finally home.

"So, we have to tell the girls then?" she asked.

Aiden chuckled, "Yeah, I don't think we have a way around that," he said. "I'm pretty sure I won't be able to keep my hands off you and they are both smart enough to figure this all out for themselves. We need to tell them before someone else does." Zara knew Aiden was right but she worried about upsetting the girls. It hadn't been very long since their mother left and she worried telling them she and Aiden were together might just confuse them. On the other hand, if they heard the news from the whispered rumors that were sure to be circulating about her and Aiden, that would be far worse.

"Fine," she said. "We can tell them when they get home from having ice cream. I promised I'd read Lucy two bedtime stories."

"And how did you get roped into that deal?" Aiden teased.

"I missed watching the last ten minutes of their dance class because Ava called to tell me about the story," she complained. Aiden laughed and she winced. "Yeah, you'll stop laughing when I tell you I promised to do the princess's voice but you have to do the prince's." She was right, Aiden stopped laughing when she told him about his end of the bargain she made with his daughter.

"How did I get sucked into your deal?" he asked.

"Well, it is only fair since the news article was about both of us and it's the main reason I missed watching the end of the dance class." Aiden's pout was adorable and reminded her so much of Laney. Zara took his hand and led him back to the kitchen. "How about I warm our dinners and we can eat before the kids get home?"

Aiden sat down in his chair and pulled her down for a quick kiss. "Deal," he said and then released her. "After we tell them our news, we'll read them their stories and tuck them in, and then I get you all to myself again," he said. She nodded and grabbed his plate. "I think I'd like to tie my little sub up and do all kinds of naughty things tonight," he said. Zara could hear every dirty promise Aiden was making in his gravelly voice and she honestly couldn't wait.

❄

Corbin and Ava didn't get back home with the girls until it was almost their bedtime. Little Laney looked about ready to drop and she wanted to tell Aiden they could talk to the girls another time. Judging by the determined look on his face, he wasn't about to agree to that.

When Zara asked if they had a good time, Corbin mumbled something about them not having as good a time as she and Aiden, and Ava looked about ready to punch him. She loved her best friend for wanting to stick up for her, but she had a feeling Ava's reaction had more to do with liking Corbin and less to do with wanting to protect Zara. Aiden was right, it was going to be fun to watch the two of them dance around each other. She had a sneaky feeling it wouldn't take time for them to fall into bed together and a part of her felt bad for Corbin. Avalon was a force and she knew from experience once her friend set her mind to something, there was no stopping her. From the way Ava was staring down Corbin, she more than wanted him and he wasn't going to even know what hit him.

They said their goodnights and Aiden took the girls up for a quick bath while she finished cleaning up the kitchen. By the time she got upstairs, both girls were sitting in Lucy's bed anxiously waiting with their favorite princess books in hand.

"Before we read your stories to you, Zara and I have something we need to talk to you about," Aiden said. Lucy stared him down as if she was ready to negotiate the terms of how long she was going to have to wait for her story. Laney sat back, sucking her thumb, ever the patient one of the two.

"Is this about you and Zara kissing?" Lucy asked.

"Kissing?" Aiden questioned. "When did you see us kissing?"

"This morning," Lucy admitted. "I came down for breakfast and you were kissing in the kitchen," she said, squinching up her nose as if she found the whole idea of kissing utterly disgusting.

"Um, okay—yes. This has to do with Zara and I kissing," Aiden said. He looked over to where she stood in the doorway and motioned for her to get in there and give him a hand. Honestly, she had no idea what to tell the girls. This could completely change her relationship with both of them and she hated that was even a possibility.

Zara sat down on Lucy's bed and pushed back a strand of her wet hair. "Why didn't you say something this morning when you saw your dad and me kissing in the kitchen?" Zara asked.

Lucy shrugged and Zara wasn't sure if she was going to give her an answer or not. "Daddy used to kiss Mommy like that and then she left. I don't want you to leave now." Zara pulled Lucy onto her lap.

"Oh Lucy, I'm not going to leave. Your Daddy kissing your Mommy had nothing to do with why she left. Just because he kissed me doesn't mean I'm going to leave either," Zara said.

"Then why did Mommy leave?" Lucy asked. Zara looked back to Aiden, hoping he'd field that question. She didn't even know Allison, so answering why she left shouldn't be up to her.

"Mommy and Daddy just couldn't stay married anymore, honey. Remember we talked about that when we were on vacation? Mommy decided she needed to live somewhere else and she comes to see you girls when she can." Laney nodded her little head as if she understood every word, but Zara wasn't so sure that was the case. How could someone so small understand such a big problem?

"I remember," Lucy said. "Is Zara going to be our new Mommy?"

Aiden smiled over at her and for just a minute, Zara was sure her entire world had stopped spinning. They were nowhere near that point in their relationship. Hell, as of just two days ago, she was agreeing to be his sub and now he was smiling at her like a loon at the mention of her being the girls' new Mommy.

"No, honey," Aiden said. "Daddy and Zara are dating. Do you know what that means?" he asked.

"Yes," Lucy said excitedly. "I have a boyfriend at school, and he said I'm his date." Zara stifled her giggle and it was a good thing, judging from the murderous expression on Aiden's face.

"Well, we can talk about you dating and having a boyfriend when you are much older. The rule is you have to be sixteen before you can date, young lady," Aiden chided. "So you tell this boyfriend of yours you aren't allowed to be his date." Zara cleared her throat, hoping Aiden would take the hint he had gone off course with their little talk. This was supposed to be them explaining to the girls they were together and not him grounding his five-year-old for seeing a boy behind his back.

"Right," he said. "Do either of you have any questions about Zara and me?"

"I have one," Lucy said, raising her hand as if she was in school. "Will you do the wizard's voice too? Zara should only do girl voices since she's a girl."

Aiden looked at Zara and smiled, "Yep, I think they are just fine with everything," he said. "And yes, Lucy. I would be happy to do all boy voices if that makes my little princess happy."

Aiden sat forward and tickled both girls until they were giggling uncontrollably.

"Okay, girls. Let's get these bedtime stories done because Daddy is ready for bed." He winked at Zara and she could feel her cheeks heat. Honestly, she was counting down the minutes until she could have Aiden all to herself again, especially with the way he was looking at her like she was his next meal.

AIDEN

Aiden shut off Lucy's light and took one last glance back at his two sleeping daughters. He couldn't believe he was so worried about telling them about him and Zara. They took the news in stride and Lucy didn't seem to miss a beat. His girls were so strong and resilient, he should have known they would be fine with this latest change in their lives.

The house was so quiet, he thought maybe Zara had fallen asleep, but when he walked into his bedroom to find her kneeling in the middle of the floor, completely naked and waiting for him, he felt like the luckiest man on the planet.

"You are so fucking gorgeous, baby," he growled, circling her body. He let his fingers lightly brush her skin and loved the way she shivered with anticipation. "You disappeared after story time," he whispered.

"I wanted to give you and the girls some alone time, in case they had questions they wanted to ask. I worried they might be too shy to ask certain questions in front of me. I'm still so new to them," Zara admitted. Aiden knew Zara cared for his daughters, but hearing just how much made him appreciate her even more.

She looked up at him and paused. "I hope that's okay," she said.

"It's more than okay, honey," he agreed. "I'm just trying to figure out how we got so lucky in finding you," he said. "And now—here you are in my room, kneeling and ready for me—I'm the luckiest fucker on earth."

She gifted him with her shy smile, "Well, you did say I was still your sub and I've done a little research and I think this is right." Zara assumed the kneeling position and put her hands on her thighs, probably having seen pictures of other subs on the internet.

"Baby, you don't have to kneel for me but I have to admit I like it. Seeing you here like this makes me crazy," Aiden whispered. "Come here, Zara," he ordered. He reached a hand down and she didn't hesitate to take it, allowing him to help her up from the floor. Aiden pressed her against his body and kissed her mouth as if he hadn't just taken her hours earlier in his family room. He couldn't get enough of her and he had a feeling he never would.

"I have a surprise for you, honey," he whispered into her ear, loving the way she shivered against him.

"A surprise?" she asked.

"Yep," he almost boasted. Aiden dug into his nightstand drawer and pulled out a blue velvet drawstring bag. "This is for you," he said, handing her the present he ordered for her. Zara hesitantly took the bag and smiled up at him.

"What is it?" she questioned.

"Well, you have to open it to find out," he teased. Honestly, he was a little nervous about giving her something so daring but she did say she wanted to try anal. Zara pulled the little strings and opened the bag letting the three heavy, silver, bullet-shaped butt plugs slide into her dainty hands and looked up at him, questions clouding her beautiful features.

"My question stands. What is it?" she asked. Aiden chuckled and took the anal plugs from her, turning them over in his hand.

"These, my lovely sub, are butt plugs," he whispered the last part.

Zara's gasp was almost comical but he knew better than to laugh at her right now. This was another new toy he was hoping she'd agree to; so there was no place for humor. "You have all the power here, baby. You say the word and I put these back in the bag and we forget the whole idea," he offered.

Zara squinched up her nose and took the anal plugs back from him. She looked over each one carefully and help up the smallest one. "I wouldn't mind this one," she said, handing it over to him.

"That's my girl," he praised. "And yes, it's always best to start small and go up in size to train your ass." He gently pulled her along to his bed and sat on the edge, patting his thighs. "Over you go," he ordered.

Zara did as he asked, laying over his lap with her ass up and ready for him. "I'm going to spank your ass red and then I'll put this in," he said. "I want you to put it into your mouth and suck on it until I finish spanking you," he ordered. She took the plug and looked at it as if it offended her.

"Like a pacifier?" she questioned.

"Yes," he said. "I've already cleaned it, and your saliva will act like a lube, along with your arousal. Plus, your mouth will help warm the metal and that will be a lot more comfortable for you, honey." Zara nodded and took the plug from him and gingerly sucked it into her mouth. Watching her do what he asked always made him hot, but knowing she agreed to let him train her ass was over-the-top sexy.

"Fuck, that's hot, honey," he said. She settled on his lap squirming against his cock, and he was sorry he had decided to spank her first. He knew she liked to be spanked but he wasn't sure if his cock liked the fact he was going to have to patiently wait his turn.

"I'll count since your mouth is full," he teased. She squirmed about and he gave her fleshy ass a good swat, knowing the first blow had to sting the most. "One," he whispered, rubbing where he landed the first slap. He alternated cheeks, never landing in the same place twice, and worked her up to twenty and stopped. Her pussy was soaked; he could feel just what his spanking did to her every time he'd dip his fingers through her folds and back to her ass.

Aiden knew Zara was fully in the zone when he asked her for the plug and she seemed to ignore him. He gently pulled the metal piece from her mouth and she moaned her protest. "Sorry, honey but I need in that tight little pussy of yours now. We can play some more later." Aiden parted her ass cheeks and ran the warm metal plug through her drenched pussy, gathering her natural lube to help the plug slide into her ass. Zara whimpered and bucked on his lap and he landed another sharp slap to her ass.

"Hold still, Zara," he ordered. "I will tie you up if you can't be a good girl for me," he threatened. From the moan that ripped from her chest, she like the idea of him having to tie her to the bed. He worked the smallest plug into her ass and she seemed to fight it at first.

"Just relax, Zara," he ordered. "This will be so much easier if you don't fight it, baby." Zara took a deep breath, and he could feel her whole body relax across his lap. He worked the plug past her tight ring and when he had it fully inserted he inspected his handy work, loving the way the little blue jewel peeked back out at him.

He helped her off his lap and onto the bed. Aiden quickly stripped out of his clothes, loving the way she shamelessly watched him. "Spread your legs for me, honey," he ordered. Zara did and he could see the plug was still firmly inserted into her virgin hole. The thought of being able to take her ass had him nearly coming into his hand. Aiden grabbed her legs and shoved his cock into her pussy with one thrust, causing her to cry out.

He stilled inside of her worried he hurt her. "Tell me you're okay, baby," he said through gritted teeth. It was taking all his willpower not to move.

"I'm good, Aiden," she purred. "I just feel so full with both holes filled," she admitted.

"You feel tighter, honey," he agreed. "This is going to be fast." He pulled his dick free from Zara's drenched folds and slammed back into her, repeating that move over and over until she cried out his name. Aiden pumped into her body a few more times and lost himself deep inside of her and collapsed on the bed next to Zara.

"Well, that was different," she teased. "I think I like my new gift."

"I'm happy to hear that, baby because you have to leave it in all night," he taunted.

"All night?" she asked. "Yep, and I'll be checking in the morning to make sure it's still there. If not, I'll have to come up with another punishment for tomorrow night." Zara groaned and rolled over to cuddle into his side. He chuckled and kissed the top of her head. "Now you're getting it, honey."

ZARA

Zara woke the next morning to Aiden standing over her gently spreading her ass cheeks, to check to see if the plug was still in. "Good girl," he praised and she heaved out her sigh of relief. She hadn't slept much during the night, worried she would relax and let it fall out. She rolled over to face him and Aiden's face turned from amused to worried.

"You look awful, honey. Are you all right?" he asked.

"Gee, thanks for that," she teased and got out of his bed. "I didn't sleep well," she admitted.

"Is my bed uncomfortable?" he asked.

"No," she stretched and yawned, loving the way Aiden's gaze roamed her naked body. "Your butt plug was uncomfortable. Every time I started to let myself fully relax and drift off, I was afraid that damn thing would fall out."

"Fuck," he swore. "I didn't think about that. How about we train your ass during the day, so we don't interrupt your sleep. I'm sorry," he said. He turned her around and bent her over the bed, so her ass was once again presented to him.

"What are you doing?" she squeaked. She had learned not to

question Aiden, knowing that nine out of ten times she loved every kinky thing he did to her.

"I'm taking the plug out and you can wear it some tomorrow. Let's give this sexy ass a break," he said. He gave her a smack and pulled the plug free. Her entire core spasmed and she wasn't sure if she felt relief it was out or if she already missed the weight of it filling her.

"Let's get you into the shower," he ordered. "We need to get a move on if I'm going to make my meeting this morning and fire my campaign manager," he said.

"So, you're really going to do it then? Fire her and quit your campaign?" Zara hated the idea of him giving up his dream because of her. She wanted him to be happy and Zara worried quitting his run for the Senate would be a huge mistake.

"I think it's for the best," he whispered. "I won't have you hurt by all of this." Zara turned and wrapped her arms around his neck.

"I'm fine, Aiden. You do what is right for you and I'll find a way to deal with the press and the gossip. No matter what you do today, I'll be all right," she promised. And she would be. That was who she was and it wasn't going to stop now just because some vicious lies were circulating about her and Aiden.

"How did I get so lucky?" he questioned. "I think I've waited all my life for you, Zara Joy. You are the perfect woman and the perfect submissive." Hearing him say those words did crazy things to her heart. She wanted to tell him she felt the same way but he didn't give her the chance to.

"Come on," he insisted. "We're going to have a shower and then breakfast. I'm sure my munchkins will be up and demanding pancakes before we can get our clothes on." He turned on the shower and cleaned her plug while they waited for the water to heat up.

"What's on your mind, Zara?" he asked.

"Um, nothing really," she squeaked. But that wasn't the truth. She had questions that were probably none of her business but she still wanted to ask them. Zara knew she might be a little pushy asking him about his ex-wife but she felt as though she needed to know.

"Out with it," he demanded, pulling her into the shower with him. The hot spray felt like heaven and she almost forgot about wanting to play twenty questions with Aiden. He cleared his throat, staring her down and Zara knew she wasn't going to get out of asking.

"You said that you and your ex didn't really do the whole Dom/sub thing," she said.

"Right," he confirmed. "Allison wasn't into the whole scene. Maybe that was why she ended up leaving or maybe I unknowingly pushed her away. Either way, I'm happy with the way things worked out. I would have never met you if she didn't leave me." Aiden soaped up her body with his hands and kissed the column of her neck. She leaned back against his big body, loving the way he took care of her.

"You keep this up and you definitely won't make your meeting," she sassed. He chuckled and thrust her body under the spray, grabbing her shampoo.

"Get your hair wet and turn around," he ordered. He worked the shampoo through her long blonde hair and his fingers felt like magic massaging her scalp.

"Mmm, You're good at this, Aiden." Zara was pretty sure she'd like to start each day this way.

"Rinse," he ordered, turning her into the spray of water again. She rinsed her hair, watching him as he lathered up his own body. Everything about the man was sexy and she wasn't sure if she'd ever get enough of him or his bossy nature.

"Did you ever ask Allison for this?" She gestured between their bodies and Aiden shyly nodded, making her instantly regret her question. He was usually so confident and in control, but now she could see his self-doubt.

"I did," he confirmed. "She told me I was a freak." He

laughed at what he said as if he had told Zara a joke. "I believe the term she used was 'sexual deviant,'" he said.

Zara reached up to frame his face with her hands. "You are not a sexual deviant, Aiden. You are Dominant and there is nothing wrong with you."

Aiden nodded and smiled. "And you are my beautiful submissive. You're pretty perfect yourself, baby," he said, causing her heart to feel as if it might beat right out of her damn chest again. Zara wasn't sure what they were doing together or where this thing between them was headed but she was ready to find out. Being with Aiden was like having all her dreams fulfilled and she wasn't ready to let that go—not yet at least.

※

Aiden agreed to talk with the press at his office and Rose set up the conference scheduled for ten in the morning. That gave Zara just enough time to get the girls to school and run over to his building. He told her she didn't have to be there but it didn't feel right not to be.

He had gone in early that morning to meet with his campaign manager. After their meeting, he ominously texted Zara, "It is done" and she wasn't sure if she wanted to cry or giggle. She hated how her being in his life was costing Aiden so much, even if he told her she was wrong every time she brought it up.

Zara texted Rose she was going to come to the conference and Rose told her to come up to Aiden's office using the private elevators for staff to avoid the growing number of members of the press that had gathered in the building's lobby. Rose met Zara at the elevator as usual and smiled at her.

"He's going to be so happy you made it," Rose said.

"I don't know about that," Zara admitted. "This morning he told me not to worry about coming over but how could I not?

This mess is because of me and I feel as if I need to be here for him, even if I'm hiding behind the scenes like a coward."

"The press is watching for you, Zara. It's best you don't give them what they want and stay out of sight. They are like a pack of hungry wolves, but this media frenzy will die down—it always does." Zara wished she could be as positive as Rose, but she had been a bundle of nerves since Aiden left the house this morning.

Rose tapped on Aiden's door and he barked for her to come in. Zara shot Rose a look, probably something akin to terror and Rose just shook her head and smiled. "Aiden, Zara is here to see you," Rose shouted back. She opened the door and let Zara pass into the office. Aiden stood and met her halfway.

"Why are you here, baby? Is everything all right?" He pulled her into his arms, not waiting for her to answer. She sighed against his chest, wrapping her arms around his waist.

"Now it is," she admitted.

"Did the press see you come in? Did they say something to upset you?" he asked.

"No," she said. "Rose had me use the employee entrance and elevator and they don't even know I'm here."

"Good," he said. "I don't want them bothering you and after this conference, I'm pretty sure they'll leave us both alone."

"Aiden, I—" she wasn't sure what to say next. How did she tell him she thought it was a huge mistake to give up his run for the Senate seat? Was it her place to tell him to run? "You shouldn't quit," she whispered.

"We've been over this already," he said. "I won't jeopardize you or the girls to further my political career."

"I appreciate that I really do. But the girls and I aren't in jeopardy," she said. "You can't let them win like this. If you quit now, you'll be playing right into their hands."

"What do you suggest I do then?" he asked. Aiden released her and paced his spacious office. "I can't let the press hound you at every turn," he growled in frustration.

"You've already increased security and you've fired your campaign manager. Don't make any more hasty decisions until you have time to think things through and hire a new manager." She hoped Aiden saw her point of view. It was getting to be time for the conference and she hated to see him throw everything away.

Rose popped her head into his office, "It's time, Aiden," she said.

He gave a curt nod. "I'll be right there," he said. She left the office again and Aiden pulled Zara against his body and crushed her mouth with his own. When he broke their kiss, she was panting—not sure if it was due to lack of oxygen or desire.

"Will you be here when I get done?" he asked.

"Of course," she whispered. "I'm not going anywhere. I'll be watching on your television."

Aiden smiled and walked out of his office and she wanted to stop him, worried she was letting him go off to make the biggest mistake of his life, but she had already done all she could. The rest was up to Aiden now.

AIDEN

Aiden faced down the noisy mob that had gathered in his office's lobby and for the first time in a long time, he wasn't sure what to do next. He stood at the podium and waited for the unruly crowd to settle and when they were finally quiet, he cleared his throat to begin. He pulled the notes he made from his suit pocket and nodded to the crowd.

"Thank you all for coming today. I wish it was under better circumstances," he admitted. "The other day, a story leaked that my new nanny, Miss Zara Joy, and I are engaged in an affair. That news is true." He once again had to wait for the crowd to quiet in order to continue.

"Please, let me finish," he ordered. Aiden looked up the atrium as if he would possibly be able to see Zara watching him from over one hundred floors up but that would be impossible. Just knowing she was in the same building gave him the courage to continue.

"I wouldn't exactly call it an affair since neither of us is married," he said. "Allison Bentley and I have been estranged for almost half a year now. I did not meet Miss Joy until a few weeks ago and she has only been my daughters' nanny for a couple of weeks. I was under the misconception that I needed to keep my divorce a secret or risk ruining my campaign," he admitted. "The person who made that advisement is no longer with my campaign and from this point on, I will tirelessly work to keep an open dialogue with the press. All I ask in return is for you to give my family the courtesy of some privacy. My daughters and Miss Joy are not running for office—I am. I ask that you leave them out of this campaign and I, in return, will have an open-door policy with a promise of no more secrets."

Aiden looked around the room and paused. This was the point in his speech when he was going to announce he was dropping out of the race but the words felt like they were stuck in his throat. He wondered if Zara might be right and he might be making the biggest mistake of his life by dropping out of the race. He could at least wait until he found another advisor, as she suggested. A few weeks wouldn't hurt.

"Thank you for your time," he said and turned to go back upstairs to where Zara was waiting for him. Corbin flanked his side, wearing a goofy grin. "Don't," Aiden ordered. The crowd erupted into a frenzy of questions and Aiden ignored them, stepping into the elevator with Corbin. He watched as his security team tried to keep the crowd at bay and he worried he had just made a crucial mistake.

"What have I just done?" he whispered as the elevator doors closed, shutting out the chaos.

"You just took your chance, man. I have to say, I'm pretty fucking proud of you," Corbin said, slapping him on the back.

"Thanks, man. I just hope I didn't make things worse," he said. He thought about how the hell he was going to keep the girls and Zara safe and Aiden worried he'd never be able to. He might have taken a chance, but at what cost? Playing with Zara and his daughter's safety wasn't a part of the plan.

❄

A month had passed and Aiden was no closer to finding a new campaign manager. For now, he was winging it but he wasn't sure how much longer that would work. Zara and the girls seemed to be adjusting to life as the family unit they were quickly becoming. They didn't even hide the fact he and Zara were sleeping in the same room anymore. The girls seemed fine with it all and he had to admit that took a huge weight off his shoulders.

Zara was about to start her last class to finish up her degree and they had worked out a nice rhythm that suited all of them. While Zara was in class or studying, he tried to pick up the slack, and when he couldn't Rose or Connie helped out. It was nice to feel like part of a team again and it was damn nice to feel like he had a partner in life.

Zara stormed into his office and slammed the door behind her. She was beautiful when she was angry and she seemed to be pretty damn pissed about something and he was sure her ire was directed at him. Rose opened his office door, popped her head in to mouth "sorry" to him, and quickly retreated—being the smart coward she was.

Aiden sat back in his chair and crossed his arms over his chest. Zara looked him over and seemed to lose a little of her anger. "You can't do that," she grouched.

"Do what, baby?" he asked but he knew exactly what he was doing. He usually tried to deflect her foul mood with sex and now was no different.

"You are using your body to try to make me forget how mad I am at you," she shouted.

Aiden chuckled and put his feet up on his desk and she actually growled at him. "This isn't funny, Aiden," she yelled.

"Okay, how about you start out by telling me why you are so angry with me," he asked. Zara threw a piece of paper onto his desk and pointed at it as if it offended her in some way.

"That," she said. Aiden picked it up and looked it over, grimacing when he read the part, "Paid in full." He had found her college bill laying on the kitchen counter a few weeks prior and decided to pay it for her. He knew Zara had struggled to pay her college tuition each semester and her bill was nothing for him. Aiden wasn't one to ever flaunt his money, but he had enough to take care of his family for generations to come. He considered Zara a part of his family now, but he worried pointing all that out might move her from pissed to ready to inflict bodily harm. He needed to tread carefully if he was going to get through this conversation with her and come out unscathed.

"Let me just explain," he said.

"Yes, I would love to hear how you went behind my back and paid my college tuition for the semester," she shouted. "You have no right, Aiden."

"You're right," he agreed. "I went behind your back and paid your bill for the semester. Where you are a little fuzzy is the part where you say I had no right to do it. I had every right, Zara because you are mine and I take care of what's mine." He stood and rounded his desk, slipping in between it and where Zara stood so she was facing him. She wouldn't be able to escape looking at him and that was just fine with him. He needed her to completely understand how he felt about her. Aiden wasn't a fool—he knew telling Zara he had fallen in love with her would probably send her running for the hills, but he needed her to understand he'd always take care of her. He wanted forever with her, but he'd keep that little piece of information to himself for now.

"You can't just go around throwing money at my problems to make them go away, Aiden. You and I live very different lives." He wrapped his arms around her and pulled Zara against his body.

"No," he disagreed. "You and I are now living the same life. You are mine and if I want to give you a gift, I will. If I want to do something to make your life a little easier—I will and if I want to take care of you, I will. You need to accept the fact that you are a part of my life now, Zara, and I am a very rich man. I haven't always been, so I know where you are coming from but I won't hide who I am now."

"But—" she tried to protest but he stole her next words with his kiss. He kissed her until he could feel all the hostility she had worked up against him leave her tightly wound body. Zara relaxed into his arms and he chanced breaking their kiss.

"But nothing, baby. You either want me or you don't," he said, holding his arms wide as if challenging her to tell him she wasn't interested.

Zara sighed and finally gifted him with her shy smile. "I want you," she agreed. "God help me, I want all of you."

Aiden didn't hide his smirk, "Thank fuck, baby. I want all of you too. Can we put this behind us?" he asked.

Zara hesitantly nodded. "Yes, as long as you promise from now on before you do something to help make my life easier, we talk about it first. I don't want to feel blindsided again."

"Of course," Aiden agreed. "Any other stipulations?" he asked.

"No, and thank you," she whispered. "I'd offer to pay you back but I'm pretty sure that will piss you off," Zara said.

"Damn straight it will. And you're welcome," he said, wrapping her in his arms again. "Now can we get to the part where I distract you with my body?"

Zara giggled, "I have just over an hour before I pick up the girls from school," she said. "Will that be enough time?" she asked, giving him an exaggerated wink.

Aiden laughed, "Challenge accepted," he agreed and started stripping Zara out of her clothes. He always loved a good challenge and Zara gave him one at every turn.

ZARA

One Month Later

Zara ran into the school hating that she was once again late. The girls' teachers already thought the worst of her and she wasn't helping her case, but her doctor's appointment had run over since the nurse couldn't seem to find her damn vein. They poked her twice before getting blood and then she had to wait in line to pay her bill but what choice did she have? She had been feeling sick and rundown for weeks now and had put off going to find out what the problem was. Honestly, she had always been a little afraid of needles and doctors and everything that went along with them. Today was just not her day and being ten minutes late to pick up Lucy and Laney was just the icing on the cake. She knew the little negotiators were going to talk her into ice cream. Tonight was the big fundraiser for Aiden and their sort of coming out as a couple of party, to test the waters. Since he hired a new campaign manager a few weeks prior, she felt more at ease attending functions with Aiden. Still, it took some coaxing on his part to convince her to go with him. There would always be haters and if she wanted to be the woman on his arm, Zara was going to have to suck it up and deal with them.

"I'm so sorry I'm late," she said, breathless from her run-in from the SUV.

"You're not late," Lucy's teacher said. She had a fake smile plastered on her face and Zara was sure she wasn't going to like whatever the woman planned to say next.

"But I am," she admitted, checking her watch. "I'm ten minutes late. I got stuck at the doctor's but that's no excuse."

"No, you're not late because the girls were already picked up," the teacher said.

"Picked up?" Zara questioned. "By whom?" She knew for a fact Aiden had back-to-back meetings all afternoon and Connie was feeling a bit under the weather.

"Mrs. Bentley came to pick up her daughters," the teacher said. She almost seemed happy about delivering the news to Zara, as if it gave her some perverse pleasure.

"Allison's not supposed to have them. She didn't let Aiden know she was going to get the girls." Every one of Zara's red flags was flapping in the wind and she worried the worst.

"Well, Mrs. Bentley is still the girls' mother and Mr. Bentley hasn't removed her from the list of possible people allowed to pick the girls up. You'll have to talk to him about that, but we had no reason to keep her from her daughters." The teacher looked her up and down as if mentally sizing her up and then turned on her heel to go back to cleaning up the classroom, effectively dismissing her.

Zara pulled her cell from her bag on the way out of the school. She needed to tell Aiden that Allison had the girls. A part of her hoped he knew about it but had forgotten to tell her, but deep down she knew something was wrong.

"Rose," Zara shouted into the phone before Rose had a chance to even get the company name out. "Allison picked the girls up from school today. She took them," Zara choked back her sob with her last statement. She needed to keep her calm or she'd be no good to anyone, especially not the girls.

"What?" Rose questioned. "Hold on, let me grab Aiden," Rose said and put the call on hold.

Within seconds, Aiden was on the other end of the call. "Zara, tell me where you are," he ordered.

"I'm standing outside the girls' school," she said.

"Get in the fucking SUV and stay there. I'm on my way. Allison has kidnapped the girls and I have my team on it," Aiden said.

This time, she didn't hide her sob. "Oh my God, Aiden. How do you know she took them?" she asked. Zara looked around the parking lot as if making sure she wasn't being watched.

"She left a note with her mother. She visited Connie this morning and when she took a nap, Allison was gone. She left a note saying she wouldn't sit back and let me be happy with someone else. It said she wouldn't let the girls be raised by any woman but herself." Aiden's voice cracked and it was nearly her undoing.

"I'm so sorry, Aiden. This is all my fault—I was late picking them up," she sobbed.

"Where the hell were you, Zara?" he growled.

"I wasn't feeling well and ran to the doctor," she admitted. "I'm going to go to your house to see if maybe she's there." It was worth a shot. Allison might have had a change of heart and decided to take them back home.

"No," Aiden barked. "If she's there and you show up, she could be provoked to anger. I don't want her to lose her temper around the girls or you. Get in your car and stay put." Zara could tell he wasn't in the mood to be questioned.

"Fine," she agreed. "But find them, Aiden," she begged.

"I will honey, don't worry about that," he promised and

ended the call. Zara didn't care if she was sitting in the middle of the girls' school parking lot or the fact that any reporter could come along and take her picture. She covered her face and this time, she didn't muffle her sob. If she would have just waited to go to the doctor, she wouldn't have been late to pick up the girls and they never would have gone with Allison. She worried they would never see Lucy or Laney again and the thought of Aiden losing his girls tore her heart apart. Zara was sure he'd never forgive her.

She knew if she sat in the parking lot and obeyed Aiden's orders she might be risking losing the girls forever. Zara was closer to the house than Aiden was and with traffic this late in the day, she'd be able to beat him there by almost thirty minutes. That was precious time they might not get back and she knew she had to at least try to look for them.

"I'm sorry, Aiden," she whispered and put the car in drive. Zara was going to go back to the house and hopefully, she'd find Allison and the girls there and she wouldn't let her take them anywhere if she could help it.

※

Zara pulled into the driveway and parked behind the white car she assumed to be Allison's. "Got you," she whispered. She thought about calling Aiden, but she didn't have time to argue with him about whether or not she should go in. She already knew what his answer would be, so she decided to text him instead.

At the house and her car is here. Going in, she texted.

Zara sent the text and turned off her phone and tossed it into her purse, not wanting to take the chance Aiden would call her back to talk her out of going into the house. If the girls were in there, nothing would stop her from getting to them.

The front door was open, and Zara stuck her head in,

worried she was too late. It was unusually quiet; too quiet for both girls to be home. "Come all the way in—Zara is it?" A tall, thin woman stood in the corner of the family room with her arms crossed over her chest. Zara knew from the pictures Aiden kept in the girls' rooms that she was Allison; though she looked thinner than her pictures portrayed her to be and with the dark circles under her eyes, she didn't look like herself much at all.

"Where are the girls?" Zara asked.

"Do you mean MY girls?" Allison shouted. "My girls are safely tucked away so you and I can have a little chat."

Zara wasn't sure if she was relieved or worried the girls weren't at the house. That meant she and Allison were all alone and Aiden had warned that might not end well for her. "You knew I'd come here looking for them, didn't you?" Zara questioned.

"Yep," Allison said, seeming almost proud of herself. "You are predictable. Poor Aiden. I know he likes things a little spicy and you must completely bore him," Allison taunted. Zara refused to answer, not wanting to give in to the woman's provoking jabs. She didn't owe Aiden's ex-wife any explanation.

"What do you want?" Zara asked.

"Well, that's a simple question. I'll give you a very simple answer. I want you to leave," Allison spat.

"Why now? You've been gone for almost a year and you and Aiden aren't even married anymore," Zara said. She knew she was poking the bear so to speak, but she couldn't help herself.

"I've heard all about you, Zara. You're disgusting the way you swooped in here to take my husband and girls. The media had you pegged from the beginning—you're a home wrecker, nothing more. Once I realized what you were doing here, I had to step up and save my family. You left me no choice."

"So, this is a selfless act on your part and has nothing to do with the fact that you look like you've been living on the streets and most likely hooked on either drugs or booze," Zara spat. She was done letting everyone think she was a home wrecker. She met Aiden after his divorce was final and she wasn't about to stand there and let Allison spew lies about her. Connie had hinted to her she was afraid her daughter was caught up with the wrong people and possibly hooked on drugs. She said Allison's boyfriend had kicked her out when she ran out of money and she had shown up a few times at Connie's begging for cash.

"How dare you," Allison yelled. "You have no right to judge me. You, along with your self-righteous attitude, can go fuck yourself. I've been through hell since leaving here and I'm ready for my life back. You'll just have to step aside, sweetheart because I'm taking back what's mine and that includes Aiden." Zara barked out her laugh and took a step towards Allison.

"You don't get to come waltzing back in here to demand your life back, Allison. You walked away from the best man I've ever met, and your daughters deserved more from their mother. How could you just throw them all away? No, you won't be taking anyone back—it's too late for any of that," Zara said. She turned to leave, knowing she had said everything she needed to. Allison would never concede and they had reached a stalemate. She'd never convince Allison she wasn't right for Aiden and the girls and really, why would she bother?

"Stop," Allison shouted. "Stop or I'll shoot." Zara's blood ran cold at the sound of the gun cocking and she slowly turned to find Allison holding a handgun that was pointed right at her. "You stupid bitch," Allison yelled. "You are making me do this, aren't you?"

Zara held up her hands, not wanting to give Allison any reason to pull the trigger. "I'm not making you do anything, Allison," she said. "Please just let me go and no one will know I saw you here. No one will know we even had this conversation," she begged.

"I'm supposed to just let you walk out of here and then what?" Allison asked. That was a good question. Zara wouldn't let Allison take the girls—Aiden would never forgive her. But, she needed her to believe she would.

"You let me go and then you can pick up the girls and disappear. I'm sure I can convince Aiden they are better off with you. It will give you a fresh start and I know they miss you," Zara lied.

"They do?" the woman questioned. Zara almost felt bad for lying to her; Allison looked so hopeful when she mentioned the girls.

"Of course they do," she said. "You're their mother."

"That's right, I am," Allison shouted. "And you're trying to take that all away from me. You're just a low-rent whore," she yelled.

Zara could feel her hot tears streaming down her face blurring the world around her. She noticed movement out on the patio and her eyes must have given her away. Allison turned, training her gun on the French doors that led to the outside space. "Who's there?" she yelled. Zara wasn't sure if her eyes were playing tricks on her or not, but she could have sworn she saw Aiden pass by the window and she knew if he barged in on the two of them, it would only piss Allison off further. It was now or never and she had to take her chance. Zara turned and ran towards the open door, knowing if she could make it just a few more steps, she would be clear of Allison's threat and hopefully be able to warn Aiden his ex was armed and dangerous.

The shot rang out and Zara wasn't sure who was shouting— a woman or a man—they both sounded the same. The ringing in her ears was almost as painful as the searing, hot, pain that ran down her thigh and into her left leg. She was falling and there was nothing she could do to stop it, but instead of hitting the ground, she looked up to see Aiden's intense blue eyes looking back at her. He had caught her and she was sure he always would.

"Zara, baby, stay with me," Aiden ordered. She wanted to tell him she would stay with him for the rest of her life if he'd ask her to, but when she opened her mouth to speak, no words came out. The world around her seem like a dream and the last thing she remembered hearing was a woman's voice screaming Aiden's name. Just before her world faded to black, she realized that woman was her and she was sure she had just looked at the man she loved for the very last time—Aiden.

AIDEN

After Aiden got off the phone with Zara, Connie called him to tell him Allison had doubled back to drop the girls off at her house and said something about finding Zara. She mentioned having to set her straight and Connie worried her daughter was about to do something stupid. She was sure Allison was on something and he knew if given the chance, she'd hurt Zara. He couldn't let that happen. Corbin was with him and they headed for Aiden's house, believing Allison would look for Zara there first.

Zara texted she had found Allison's car in his driveway and he panicked. Aiden knew it was a trap, but he couldn't reach Zara to tell her what was happening. He called in his security team and he and Corbin decided not to wait for back-up. There was no way he'd let Allison hurt Zara—she was his whole world.

Peeking in the patio windows hadn't afforded much insight as to what was going on inside his home, but judging by the way Zara stood with her hands in the air, Allison had a gun pointed at her. Aiden motioned to Corbin he was going around the house and through the front door and his friend agreed to take care of his ex-wife. He knew Corbin would get some secret personal satisfaction from taking Allison down and that was fine with him. All he could think about was getting to Zara and keeping her safe, at any cost. But he was too late. By the time he reached the front door, Aiden found Zara running towards him and just before she got to him, Allison shot her in the thigh. Zara stumbled towards him and fell into his arms screaming his name and he felt completely helpless. She passed out and he removed his belt, making a tourniquet for Zara's leg to help stop the bleeding.

Aiden heard a commotion in the house and from the sounds of Allison's protest, Corbin had secured her and the gun. "You good out there, Aiden?" Corbin shouted. He emerged from the house dragging Allison along with him, her gun in his other hand.

"Fuck," Corbin swore, looking at Zara.

"She shot Zara," Aiden choked. Corbin slipped the gun into the waistband of his pants and pulled his cell phone from his jacket pocket.

"Don't worry man, I'll get help here before you know it. Just keep pressure on the wound," Corbin ordered. Aiden felt as if his world was moving in slow motion as he sat on the ground holding Zara against his body. There was blood everywhere and he worried she had already lost too much.

"Why, Allison?" he shouted. She stood next to Corbin, her arms pinned behind her back by his friend, looking down at him as if he had some nerve to ask her why she'd shot Zara.

"You had no right being with her," she answered. "She wasn't good for my daughters or you."

"You don't get to decide that anymore, Allison," he yelled. "You divorced me. You're the one who chose to leave us. Zara came into our lives and took care of the girls. She loved me without questioning who I am or telling me there is something wrong with me for what I liked."

"You're a pervert, Aiden. I wouldn't give in to your disgusting needs so you pushed me away. Maybe you were with her this whole time, who knows? But you stopped wanting me the day I told you I wouldn't play your disgusting kinky games," Allison said. She looked down her nose at him with a self-righteous look on her smug face and he wanted to tell her she was wrong but he wasn't sure he could. Allison and he grew apart towards the end of their marriage and even though he didn't turn to anyone else, as she had, he did push her away.

"You're not right about everything, Allison. In fact, you've twisted a few of the facts around. You were the one who cheated in our relationship. What was I supposed to do, look the other way while you dated other men? Our marriage was one of convenience for you, wasn't it Allison? You married me because you were pregnant and then you got too comfortable to leave. My only fault was not seeing it sooner. I let things go on for too long and when you left I was angry at myself because I felt as if I let the girls down. But you know what really ate me up with guilt?" He paused as if waiting for her to answer but he really didn't care if she did or not.

"I felt relieved you finally left me," he whispered. "I beat myself up over that for so long but now I see I shouldn't have."

Corbin ended his call, "They'll be here in less than five minutes now. I'll meet our security team with Alli here."

Allison thrashed and bucked, trying to get free from his hold and Corbin seemed to be enjoying the fact she couldn't. "Not going to happen, sweetheart," Corbin growled.

"You can't hold me against my will," she complained. "Aiden and I are talking."

"You're done talking, Alli," Corbin said. He turned to Aiden, "Man, she's high and no amount of reasoning will get through to her. She shot the woman you love, Aiden."

Aiden knew Corbin was right. The woman who stood before him now wasn't the same woman who he fell in love with all those years ago. He could see that now. "Take her," he spat. "We're done talking."

"No," She screamed, panicked. "You can't do this, Aiden.

She deserved it. She's nothing. You can't love her." Corbin pulled her along down Aiden's driveway, leaving him alone with Zara to wait for the ambulance to get there.

"She's wrong," he whispered to Zara. "I do love you—more than anything. Please be okay, baby."

❄

Aiden felt about ready to go out of his mind. It had been two days of hospitals, doctors, and nurses giving him polite stares and endless worry Zara wasn't going to wake up. He was allowed to ride with her to the hospital in the ambulance, but when they got her into the emergency room, they took her from him and he wasn't allowed to see much of her. A few of the nice nurses bent the rules and let him into Zara's room but he wasn't always so lucky. No one would give him any answers and it was starting to piss him off. All the doctors would tell him was she was doing well, was stable and still hadn't woken up from surgery. They asked if Zara had any family they could call and according to Avalon, she didn't. He knew her parents had died when she was just a girl, but hearing Zara had been completely alone in the world made his heart hurt. She was lucky to have Ava in her life, but he wondered just how lucky she'd consider herself to have Aiden as part of it. He was the one who dragged her into his mess. He was the one who asked her to keep their relationship a secret as if she was someone he was embarrassed by. He was the one who put her in danger, not realizing just how messed up his ex-wife was.

The local authorities had arrested Allison and were holding her without bail since she was considered a flight risk. They had sent her to a local rehab facility and Aiden hoped she'd get the help she needed. Allison wouldn't be a part of their lives again but he had loved her and she gave him two precious girls. If Lucy and Laney decided to know their mother when they were older he wouldn't stop them, but he just hoped Allison would be clean for such an occasion. He would never want his girls to see their mother like she was the day she broke into his house and tried to kill Zara. She wasn't the same woman he remembered and he knew the drugs had changed her. He was just not ready for how much of her they had taken; she was just a shell of her former self and that made Aiden sad for her.

Corbin and Rose had been stopping by daily to check on Zara. Corbin had picked up the slack around the office because there was no way Aiden was going to leave Zara if he could help it. He had made sure the girls got to where they needed to go and had spent just enough time at home to shower and change. Other than that, he had taken up residence in the hospital waiting room and prayed someone would give him some good news.

Corbin strolled into the waiting area with Lucy and Laney. He picked them up earlier from Connie's so Aiden wouldn't have to run across town again. "Daddy," Laney squealed, running to jump into his arms.

"Hey, Laney girl. How was school?" he asked.

"Good," she said, nodding her little head.

"How about you, Lucy?" he questioned.

"I got in trouble for telling the new kid there was a rule she had to push me on the swing during free time," she admitted. Corbin laughed and Aiden shot him a look to cut it out.

"We've been over this before, Lucy. You can't force people to play with you and lying isn't something that is allowed in our family," Aiden chided. His daughter dutifully nodded her head, but he could tell she really wasn't paying much attention to him. She was too busy looking around the hospital probably seeing what she could get herself into.

"My teacher wants to talk to you," she muttered.

Aiden sighed, knowing the routine all too well. His daughter had acted out just like this when Allison left them. Now, with Zara all but disappearing from her life, she was back to her old tricks. Lucy loved to tell other kids what to do—it was a gift. She even would go as far as lying to them to get them to do her bidding. Sure, she was probably an evil genius, but he was getting sick of being called into a parent-teacher conference to discuss his little angel's behavior.

"I will talk to her tomorrow when I drop you off. You will have to be punished for what you did, Lucy. I'll decide that after I talk to your teacher." Lucy looked down at the floor and nodded and he almost wanted to let her slide this time. Aiden knew he couldn't, otherwise, she'd be back up to her tricks in no time.

"Any word on Zara?" Corbin asked.

"No, man. It's driving me nuts not knowing what's going on with her," Aiden said.

One of the doctors who usually gave him vague updates on Zara popped his head into the waiting room. "Mr. Bentley, Miss Joy is awake and asking to see you," he said.

"I want to see Zara," Lucy demanded.

"Me too," Laney quickly agreed.

"You two peanuts are going to stay with me," Corbin said. "Let your dad check on Z and when she's feeling up to it, you can have a visit with her." Aiden nodded his thanks to Corbin and started for the door, anxious to get back to her.

"Thanks, man. I owe you," Aiden said.

"Damn straight you do," Corbin agreed. "This is probably going to cost me another trip for ice cream."

Aiden didn't care what it cost him. Hearing Zara was awake and wanted him was the best thing he had heard in over two days. He'd make sure she was all right and then he was going to convince Zara she needed a family and if he had his way, he'd do everything in his power to make sure his own family fit the bill.

ZARA

Zara felt groggy and her entire body hurt. The nurse said that was normal for someone who had been in a coma for the past two days. The last thing she remembered was Aiden catching her after Allison shot her and judging from the cast on her leg, she hadn't missed. Even small movements sent shooting pains up her leg and when she asked for pain medication, the nurse smiled and nodded, telling her the doctor would have to talk to her about that before she could give her something and she didn't have the energy to argue with her. Honestly, she just wanted to see Aiden to make sure he and the girls were safe. She had so many questions to ask him but they could wait.

"Hey," Aiden stood in her doorway and she wondered how long he had been standing there.

"Hey yourself," she croaked and cleared her throat. Zara wasn't able to hold her sob in and Aiden was immediately by her side. He carefully sat on her bed and gently pulled her against his body.

"You scared the shit out of me," he whispered, kissing her

forehead. "I'm so happy you are awake; they wouldn't let me back to see you and I worried—" his voice broke and Zara could hear his pent-up fear. She hated how she made him worry that way.

"I'm so sorry," she murmured against his chest. "This was all my fault. If I had just listened to you and stayed in my car, none of this would have happened. I was just worried you wouldn't have gotten there in time and Allison would take the girls. I couldn't allow that."

"I know, honey. When it comes to loving my girls, you are as fierce as they come. I'm so happy they have you," Aiden admitted.

"I love them, Aiden. I can't imagine my life without Lucy or Laney," she said. Zara wondered if Aiden would want to know she felt the same way about him because she did. She was just too afraid to tell him she had fallen in love with him. They hadn't said those words to each other, and she worried about being the first to come right out with them.

"I know, baby." Aiden seemed to hesitate and she worried she had said too much. "How do you feel about their dad?" he whispered. It was almost as if he could read her mind. She could feel his heart beating and could tell he was just as nervous about this as she was. But not giving him the words; not being completely honest with him felt wrong.

"Um," she squeaked. "I feel the same way about him as I do his girls," she admitted.

"Thank fuck," he exhaled. "When I thought I lost you, Zara —God, my whole world collapsed. I sat in that fucking waiting room for two days, worried I'd never see you again. I worried I'd never be able to tell you I've fallen completely in love with you, baby."

"You have?" she interrupted.

"Yes," he said. "Look at me, baby," he demanded. Zara was afraid to look at him for fear she'd burst into tears but really that ship had already sailed. Since Aiden had walked into her room, she was a sobbing mess. She chanced a look up at him, his blue eyes looking back at her with so much promise and love, she wasn't sure how she had missed it before.

"Hi," he whispered. Aiden leaned in to gently brush her lips with his own and she thought it was the sweetest gesture. "Marry me, Zara," he said.

Zara gasped and covered her mouth with her shaking hand. "Aiden," she sobbed. "You can't mean it."

"I can and I do," he said. "When you stumbled into that club, I thought you were the most beautiful woman I had ever seen. Then, you agreed to be mine and I thought you were the perfect submissive. I was sure I couldn't ask for anything more, but I was wrong, Zara. I want more from you. I need you to be my wife, honey. I want you to be the woman who I come home to every night and the person I wake up next to every morning. Be mine, Zara—marry me."

Zara wasted no time answering his command. She was already his—body, mind, and spirit. Agreeing to marry him wasn't something she needed to think about. It was what she had always wanted but never let herself hope for.

"Yes," she breathed. "I'm already yours, Aiden and I'd love to marry you." Aiden gently kissed her lips and Zara knew in an instant her entire life had changed. She wasn't sure what she had done to deserve the man sitting next to her, but she wasn't about to try to figure it out.

"Um, I'm sorry to interrupt." The doctor who had been in earlier after she woke up pushed the door open, letting himself into the room. "How are you feeling, Miss Joy?" he asked.

Zara nodded and winced, "My leg is killing me. Can I get some pain medication? The nurse who was in here earlier told me you would have to approve it." The doctor nodded and looked nervously between her and Aiden.

"Yes," he said. "Um, I'd like to talk to you privately, Miss

Joy." Aiden's frustrated growl seemed to startle the poor doctor. She wanted to giggle but knew better than to poke Aiden when he was angry.

"Aiden can stay," she offered.

"Well, I need to go over a few things having to do with your medical history. He's not your family member, so maybe it would be best to discuss everything, just the two of us." The doctor winced as if he was expecting Aiden to fly off the bed and attack.

Zara worried the same thing, placing a hand on Aiden's thigh, trying to calm him. "Aiden has just asked me to marry him, so technically, he's about to be family. You can discuss anything you need to with me and my fiancé."

The doctor nodded and smiled. Aiden seemed to relax a little beside her and Zara wondered if he was always going to be so protective of her. "Is something wrong?" she asked.

"That depends on what your definition of wrong might be," the doctor said. "You're pregnant, Miss Joy." The doctor crossed the small room and pushed a button on a machine that sat by her bed. Suddenly, a swooshing sound filled the room and she looked at Aiden and back to the doctor.

"Is that sound coming from my body?" she asked.

The doctor smiled and nodded again. "Well, technically yes. It's your baby's heartbeat. We've been monitoring everything since your surgery, and he or she has a very strong heartbeat. We estimate you're about two months along," he said.

"That's impossible," she said. "We were careful."

"No contraceptive is one hundred percent effective," the doctor said. "I will order some pain medication that will be safe for you and your baby, but it won't fully relieve your pain. I'm sorry." He turned to leave the room and a part of Zara wanted to yell for him to come back. She had a million questions she wanted to ask and the thought of having to face Aiden alone frightened her. He had been so quiet since the doctor announced she was pregnant, she worried he would be angry or worse, disappointed in her news.

"Aiden," she said. Zara wished he would look at her, but he seemed distracted by the baby's heartbeat monitor. Aiden stood and walked over to where the machine was measuring the baby's heartbeats per minute and it was as if he didn't even hear her call his name.

"I didn't mean for this to happen," she admitted. Zara hated thinking Aiden might believe she had trapped him. She knew Allison was pregnant with Lucy when they got married and she would never want him to marry her just because she was pregnant.

"If you've changed your mind about marrying me, I won't blame you," she almost whispered. Aiden turned to face her, and she could tell he was angry.

"Why would I change my mind about marrying you?" he questioned. She shrugged, not knowing how to answer him.

"You didn't plan for this," she pointed to the machine and then back to her still flat tummy. "I wouldn't blame you if you wanted to rethink your proposal. Maybe we should just take some time and rethink all of this. I just need time, Aiden. Please, can you do that for me?" Aiden nodded and opened his mouth to say something, closing it again. He turned and walked out of her hospital room without another word. She wanted to get out of that damn bed and chase him down the hallway to tell him she was wrong but that was impossible. She didn't want to push Aiden into something he didn't want and from the way he so easily walked out of her room, the baby wasn't something he wanted.

❄

Zara had taken the pain medication and the doctor once again assured her it was safe for the baby. She already felt a strong protective nature when she thought about the life growing inside of her. Her doctor said it was a miracle she didn't lose the baby with all the stress and trauma of having to deal with being shot and undergoing surgery. They removed the bullet and had to put a metal rod and screws in where it had spliced her bone, but the doctor was confident she would make a full recovery in a few months. Zara wasn't so sure about her broken heart though.

She spent the rest of the day after Aiden left sleeping and even dozed in and out most of the next day. Every time she woke, she would question the nurses if he had been back to see her and their sympathetic looks gave her their answer before they even opened their mouths. Ava had been by to visit her a couple of times and she gave Zara the same look of pity every time she'd ask about Aiden.

"He'll come around, Z," Avalon promised. "He's just dealing with a lot right now—give him time." She wanted to childishly point out she was dealing with a lot too, but she didn't. Zara just hoped Ava was right and Aiden would come to accept the baby, even if he didn't want her anymore. Her son or daughter had the right to have him as part of their life but she wouldn't force him to take part. Zara just hated the idea of her baby not having both parents' love. Aiden was a fantastic father. She didn't want her baby to miss out on having him as a dad.

The hospital kept her for two more weeks and when she was released, Zara wasn't sure where she was supposed to go. All her stuff was at Aiden's house but she wasn't going to just show up there. She made arrangements to stay at Ava's and the nurse told her that her health care would cover a visiting nurse for her therapy and recovery. She didn't want to be a burden on anyone. Zara wished she could say she was finding a way to get over the loss of not having Aiden and the girls in her life but she wasn't. Each passing day was harder and harder. She missed them so much, she wasn't sure she would ever be able to move on, but for the sake of her child she was going to have to find a way.

Ava picked her up at the hospital and helped her into her SUV. "I'm so happy to be out of that place," she whispered after getting settled in her seat. "Thanks for doing this, Ava," she said.

"No problem, Z. I just have one quick stop to make and then we'll get you settled," Avalon said. Zara would go anywhere if it meant she didn't have to spend another minute in that hospital.

They started driving and Zara tried to lay back and relax but getting comfortable was nearly impossible. The pain medication had made her a little fuzzy and she must have dozed off because when she woke up, she was sitting in Aiden's driveway. Ava turned off her vehicle and shot her a guilty look.

"Sorry, Z but he made me promise not to spill the beans," she said.

"Spill the beans? What beans?" Zara asked, confused about the whole situation until Aiden stepped from the front door dressed in a tux. Lucy and Laney sprang out from behind him, both dressed in long flowery dresses and she wondered if they were interrupting one of Aiden's fundraisers.

"What the hell is going on here?" Zara questioned.

"Well, you are about to marry that man—right there," Ava explained, pointing to Aiden.

"He walked out on me. He left me to sit in that hospital room for almost two weeks, believing he wasn't ever coming back," Zara sobbed.

"I know, Z. He was a complete asshole and he feels bad. Just let him explain," she said nodding to the passenger side window where Aiden stood. The girls had gone back into the house and Ava got out of her SUV to follow them in, leaving Zara and Aiden completely alone.

She crossed her arms over her chest and looked straight ahead. "You left me and now you expect for me to just marry you?" She said, summarizing what Ava had just explained.

"I know and I'm so sorry," he admitted. "It was a fucked-up

thing to do and I didn't know how to make it up to you. I was afraid of messing things up with you like I had Allison and when you told me you didn't want to marry me and you needed time, I freaked out."

"So what, I'm supposed to just forgive you and say that I'll marry you?" she questioned.

"Well, that would be nice but judging from your tone, I don't think that is going to happen," he teased. "Please, Zara," he begged. Aiden opened her car door and gently pulled her into his arms, careful of her leg. "Please let me show you we can make this work. I want you and our baby. I want you to be my wife. I knew I wanted more children with you, we're just having the first one sooner rather than later. Say you'll marry me," he begged. "I've arranged everything. All you have to do is say yes and come with me into the backyard."

"You mean now, as in today? You want me to marry you in the backyard, right now?" she questioned.

"Yes," he simply said. "Ava picked a dress out for you, and I have everything arranged. Tell me you still want to spend the rest of your life with me," he asked. Zara wasn't sure what the hell to do. But she knew if she told him no, she'd be making the biggest mistake of her life. She wanted Aiden and the girls and telling him no wasn't an option.

"You just left me at the hospital, Aiden. I thought you didn't want me or our baby," she whispered. Zara thought she had lost him for good when he didn't return and it broke her heart. She didn't want to risk losing him again—this time possibly for good.

"I know and I'm so sorry," he said. "Your doctor told me any upset could possibly hurt you and the baby. I couldn't chance losing either of you," he admitted. "Tell me you'll marry me, honey. Let me make it all up to you," he begged.

She nodded and Aiden lifted her into his arms, crushing her against his body. "What are you doing?" she asked. "I have crutches and can walk."

"I know that baby. I'm just not giving you a chance to change your mind again," he admitted. She wasn't about to tell him that wouldn't happen. She was his, now and forever. Nothing would ever change that for her, even her own stubbornness.

AIDEN

Aiden paced outside the master bedroom, wearing a path in the hallway's floor boards, waiting for Zara to finish dressing. He wasn't taking any chances with letting her get away from him again, even blocking the damn entrance so she couldn't change her mind. Hearing her tell him she needed time just about ripped his damn heart out of his chest but he wanted to give that to her. Aiden wanted her to be sure about marrying him and if he was being honest, he was too stubborn and too hurt to go back to that hospital. He wanted to barge into her room and demand she take him back but he wouldn't chance upsetting her. On his way out of her room, her doctor explained she needed complete calm and rest or she could possibly lose the baby. He received the doctor's message loud and clear and left Zara to get the sleep she needed to recover. But waiting for her one minute past her release from that hospital was damn near impossible for him. He wanted to pick her up from there, but Ava convinced him it would be best if she did it, so as not to cause a scene. She was right but he wouldn't tell Avalon that.

Begging Zara to marry him was easier than he thought it would be. He was ready to grovel for as long and hard as it took, but she agreed and now, the only thing he wanted to do was carry her back down the steps and out onto his patio where he had a pastor waiting to marry them. She was finally going to be his and he was starting to feel like the luckiest man on the planet.

The door creaked open and Avalon slipped out into the hallway. "Um," she whispered. "I think she's a little nervous. She asked to talk to you." Aiden felt his heart drop and he worried he had pushed her too much for her first day out of the hospital.

"Is she all right?" he questioned. "Has she changed her mind?" Ava didn't answer him and that made him even more nervous. Zara's best friend was usually a chatterbox and not at all afraid to speak her mind.

"Just go in and talk to her," she insisted. Aiden pushed the door open and slid past her to find Zara standing in front of the full-length mirror in the dress Ava picked out for her and she took his breath away.

"You look beautiful, baby," he said. Zara didn't turn to face him, but looked at him through her reflection and her worried frown nearly sank every last hope he had of Zara becoming his today. "Ava said you were having second thoughts," he whispered.

"I can't," she sobbed. He couldn't let her finish her sentence. He crossed the room and pulled her into his arms.

"Please don't tell me you can't marry me, Zara. I feel like I've waited my whole life for you and now, this baby. The girls are so excited you are going to be their mom and when I told them about the baby, they were thrilled. Although, they both want a girl and would like to name her Princess," he said, making a face. Zara giggled through her tears and he hoped he was making some headway with her.

"I would like to veto that name, although I'm thrilled they

are happy," she said. Zara carefully wiped at her eyes as if trying to avoid smearing her makeup. "And no, I'm not having second thoughts about marrying you, Aiden. It's this," she said, sobbing all over again.

Zara used her one crutch to balance herself on her good leg to carefully turn in his arms. The gown she was wearing was unzipped and from the looks of it, she was going to have trouble getting it closed. "I can't zip it up," she cried. "Ava didn't account for my expanding belly and I guess I'm not the same size now," she sniffled. He wanted to laugh but knew better than to find a hysterical pregnant woman funny.

"I don't care if you marry me in your pajamas, baby. I just want to marry you—today, right now." Aiden looked around the room and tried to come up with a plan.

"Will any of your clothes fit you, honey?" he asked. She sniffled again and nodded.

"I have jeans that will probably fit," she admitted.

"How about we make a deal," he said. Aiden slipped from his tuxedo jacket and undid his tie.

"Aiden, we cannot have sex right now. I know you think it fixes everything but it's what got us into this mess," she said, cupping her little belly.

Aiden chuckled, "No, I think we can save sex for the honeymoon portion."

"Honeymoon?" she asked.

"Yep. When you get the all clear from your doctor and can travel, I'm taking you and the girls on a little tropical getaway. Ava and Corbin are coming along too, to help watch the girls so we can have some alone time." He waggled his eyebrows at her, causing her to giggle again. "There's my girl," he praised.

"So, what's the plan then?" she asked.

"We get married in jeans and t shirts," he offered. From the look on her face, he wasn't sure she was going to agree, but then Zara's brilliant smile lit up the room and she nodded.

"I'd marry you in anything, Aiden. How about you help me change and then I'll let you carry me to the altar," she offered.

"Now, that sounds like a plan, my beautiful secret submissive," he teased.

"Hey," she grouched. "That's soon to be Mrs. Secret Submissive." Aiden wasn't sure how he had gotten so lucky finding Zara standing in that BDSM club but he wasn't going to question fate. She was his now and that was all that mattered.

❄

Four Months Later

Aiden carried Zara over the threshold of their little bungalow. "I'm too heavy," she said. "Put me down."

"Baby, you are not too heavy," he countered. He eyed her expanding belly and she giggled.

"See, your mouth is saying all the right things but your eyes give you away, Aiden Bentley," she teased. He shut the door behind them and crossed the room to lay her on the bed. Zara looked around the room. "This is gorgeous Aiden."

He smiled down at her and wondered if wanting sex made him an ass. They had spent the better part of a day traveling to the island and he was sure his pregnant wife would be exhausted. "How about I show you what else my mouth does right," he said. Zara's eyes flared with need and he knew she was on board with his plan to get them both naked.

"Are you sure the girls will be all right with Ava and Corbin?" she asked. He loved the way she worried about his girls. They had become a family and he knew his girls loved Zara.

"I'm sure, honey. I got them a nice bungalow with plenty of space for everyone. I'm pretty sure the girls will drive Corbin half-crazy and if they don't, the sight of Avalon prancing around in her bikini will finish him off."

Zara giggled and moaned, "Ugg, don't remind me about Ava and her perfect body."

He looked her up and down, "You don't have anything to worry about, baby. You're the most perfect woman on the planet," he whispered against her lips. "You're mine," he growled.

"I am," she agreed. "Forever."

"I know we've been taking it easy with your recovery, but I'd like to try something new tonight, if you're up to it," he asked. Aiden didn't want to get his hopes up, but they already were.

"Yes, Aiden," she purred. "Please."

That was all the confirmation he needed. "Clothes off and get on your knees, baby," he ordered. Zara squealed and clapped, making him chuckle. "Oh, you like my command?"

"Yes," she said, breathlessly stripping out of her sundress to reveal her naked, sexy curves. He had to admit seeing Zara naked and pregnant with his baby always did crazy things to him. Lately he couldn't seem to get enough of her, but he refused to push her too much. He had to squelch his dominance to just a burning ember when it came to making love to his new wife, for fear of hurting her. Now that she was medically cleared and more than willing, his inner caveman could come out to play.

Aiden ran his hands over her belly and up to cup both of her breasts. "I like these," he teased.

"Yes, well they are pretty hard to miss now that I'm pregnant. Unfortunately, my ass is twice the size it was pre-pregnancy too." She rubbed her hands over her fleshy globes, thrusting her breasts into his hands. She more than filled his palms and he couldn't wait to get his hands on her ass next.

"I think you and I see your ass very differently," he teased. "I find every sexy new curve of yours drives me completely crazy," he admitted.

"You're supposed to say that," she said. "Isn't it in the husband handbook?"

"No wife, it isn't," he said, reaching back to give her ass a playful swat. "I think I need to give that sexy mouth of yours something to keep it occupied."

She got down on her knees and smiled up at him, playfully batting her eyes. "I'm ready, Sir," she said. Aiden shucked out of his clothes, possibly setting a record for getting naked.

"Open," he ordered. He stroked his cock and loved the way her eyes seemed to follow his hand's movement up and down his staff. Zara was just as turned on by this as he was. He let her suck the tip of his cock in and nearly swallowed his own damn tongue at just how good her mouth felt. He moaned his pleasure and shoved further in, needing for her to take all of him. Aiden pulled her hair back into his hand giving him better access to watch her sucking him in and out of her mouth. He gave a little tug when she tried to take control and he set the pace, letting her know just what he wanted. He pumped in and out of her sexy mouth until he was on edge. Aiden knew if he didn't stop, he wouldn't be able to and he didn't want to finish in her mouth this time. No, he had special plans for her new curvy ass, and he just hoped Zara was on board.

He pulled his cock free from her swollen lips and she mewled her protest. Aiden chuckled, "Sorry honey, but you need to catch up," he said. He helped her from her kneeling position. "Get up on the bed and spread your legs as wide as you can. I won't tie you up tonight as long as you hold still, baby. Can you do that for me?"

Zara climbed onto the bed and nodded. "Yes, Aiden. I will try." He loved her obedience, even craved it and Zara seemed to need it as much as he did. She really was the perfect woman for him. She spread her legs open, gifting him with the view of her drenched pussy. "Like this?" she questioned.

"Yes, just like that," he said, his voice hoarse with need. "Fuck, your sexy," he swore. Aiden wasted no time settling between her legs, running two fingers through her wet folds, and stuffing them deep inside her. Zara cried out from the pleasure of his sudden invasion and then stilled, seeming to remember his orders. "Good girl, baby," he praised.

"Please," she whimpered. "I need to have an orgasm," she begged.

"I'm going to take good care of you, Zara," he promised. Aiden dipped his head and ran his tongue through her slick pussy, loving her taste. His girl held so still; he knew he was driving her crazy, but she was being so well behaved. Aiden decided to give her exactly what she asked for. "I'm going to eat your pussy, baby and I want you to come for me," he ordered. She whimpered and nodded her head.

He lapped and sucked her sensitive folds until she couldn't seem to control her body any longer. She bucked and writhed against his mouth, taking over, finding her release. Aiden loved when she got so wild she couldn't seem to stop herself and he especially loved knowing he was the one giving her that pleasure. Zara shouted out his name as she came on his mouth and he knew it was time to tell her what he was going to do with her tonight.

Aiden kissed his way up over her belly and up the rest of the way to her mouth. He let his tongue leisurely dart into her mouth, knowing Zara would be able to taste her own release from his kiss always made him wild. "Roll over and get on your hands and knees, baby," he ordered. Zara didn't hesitate, doing exactly what he asked. He slipped from the bed to find his surprise for her he had stowed in his suitcase.

"You were such a good girl, I thought you might like another reward," he said. He pulled the purple vibrator from his bag and showed it to her. She wrinkled up her nose at it and he couldn't help his chuckle.

"A vibrator?" she questioned.

"Yes," he said. "I'm going to shove this into your pussy and then I'm going to lube up that sexy ass of yours and take your virgin hole," he said. Zara gasped and moaned and he knew he was on the right track. "You like that, baby?" he asked.

"Yes," she hissed. "I've been waiting for you to take my ass, Aiden," she admitted. He had started training her ass before the accident and then he didn't want to push her, so he stopped. Now that he knew she was willing and ready, there would be no stopping him. He grabbed the lube from his bag and got back onto the bed with her, letting it dip with his weight.

"Up on your knees again and lean back against my body, baby." Zara did as ordered. "Wrap your arms back around my neck," he said. She did, laying her head to rest on his shoulder. Zara looked up at him and smiled. Aiden settled behind her and ran his hands down her body, tweaking and plucking her taut nipples. He knew she had to be ready for him, but he wanted to drive her a little crazy.

"Have you ever used one of these before?" he asked. Zara studied the vibrator and shyly shook her head.

"No," she admitted. "I only used my fingers to masturbate." The thought of Zara giving herself pleasure made him nearly come up her back. He rubbed his cock against her ass and knew if he didn't get inside of her soon it would be over much too quickly.

"Um, I'd like to watch you do that sometime," he admitted. "But now, we're going to try something new."

"Okay," she said, her voice a little shaky from need or nerves. Either way, she'd forget both once he got the vibrator inside of her and turned it on. He gently guided the vibe into her pussy, and she was so wet and ready for him. He turned it on and she moaned and thrust back against his body at the new sensations.

"You like that, don't you, honey?" he asked.

"Yes," she hissed.

"Good, now get on all fours again. I'm going to lube your ass and make it mine," he growled. Zara did as ordered and he squirted lube on his finger, working it into her tight opening. She was going to feel amazing. He worked his finger in and out of her ass as she rode out her first orgasm. Aiden lubed up his cock and spread her cheeks, gently nudging his way into her body. His unruly cock hated having to take his time but he wanted Zara's first experience with anal to be pleasant.

"Fuck," Zara swore, "please Aiden, hurry. I'm going to come again," she cried. He pushed into her ass a little further and his impatient girl push back against him, taking him completely into her body. She spasmed around his dick and Aiden knew he wouldn't last long.

"Move please," she begged.

Aiden slid in and out of her ass, popping almost completely free before slamming back into her. Zara didn't protest as he dug his fingers into her hips, pumping in and out of her body. She quickly came again, shouting out his name. Aiden pulled her back against his body, loving the way she fit him. He held her so tight, he knew she was going to wear his marks in the morning.

"I'm going to come, Zara," he panted. "I can feel the vibrator inside of you." He felt every wave and pulse from the vibe he had inserted inside of Zara for her pleasure. But it was rubbing against his cock through the thin membrane that separated her ass and her pussy and he felt about ready to explode.

"Fuck," he swore, pumping into her body twice more and then losing himself in her ass. Aiden pulled the vibrator free from her slick folds and collapsed with Zara onto the bed. "Tell me that was okay," he asked.

"That was better than okay," she said. She wrapped her arms around his neck and pulled him in for a kiss. "That was fucking fantastic," she admitted with a smile.

"Mrs. Bentley," he feigned shock. "I think your cursing has gotten worse since you married me. I must be a bad influence."

"I swear it's this pregnancy," she said, rubbing her belly. "Either that or I'm turning into a sailor. Will you still love me if I turn into a swearing pirate?" she asked.

"Baby, I'd love you if you had a wooden leg and rocked an

eye patch." Zara's laughter filled the room and Aiden was sure he'd never heard a sound more magical. He had waited his whole life to meet someone like her. She was his other half, the woman who owned his body, mind and soul—his secret submissive, and she was his.

HIS RELUCTANT SUBMISSIVE

AVALON
PROLOGUE

Avalon Michaels knew that being summoned to her father's house wasn't a good thing—it never was. She and her father tried to have as little to do with each other as possible, so being called to stop by at her earliest convenience made her nervous. Plus, she had consumed way too much coffee to be calm about anything.

She rang the bell which to most people might seem strange but it didn't feel right to just barge into her father's home anymore. She hadn't lived with him in some time and the familiarity of just waltzing into his home felt wrong. Surprisingly, her father answered the door himself and seemed downright chipper for a change.

"Ah, Avalon. I'm glad you could make it on such short notice," he said. "Come in." Ava did as he requested, filing past him and into the grand foyer. Every time she stepped foot into her childhood home, it made her a little sad. She thought about all the people who used to live there that were lost to her—her mother and brother. She hated how empty the big old house now seemed and she almost felt sorry for her father for having to live there alone. He must be haunted by the same ghosts as she was but he never let on.

"What's up, Dad? You said it was urgent so I'm here on my lunch break. I do need to be getting back to the office though," she lied. After meeting with her father, she really had no other plans for the day and hoped to head home early. There was a bubble bath and a glass of wine with her name all over them.

"This shouldn't take too long," he promised. "Can I get you anything?" He asked.

"Nope," she said. Ava made a show of checking her watch and her dad sighed and handed her a sealed envelope.

"What is this?" she asked. Ava hadn't received mail at her father's house in years.

"It's from the lawyers. I've been meaning to give this to you for a while now but I haven't seen you. My lawyer has been hounding me for weeks to get these to you and well, I guess time is running out," her father said. He wasn't making much sense but Ava tried to keep up.

"Time's running out for what?" she questioned.

"Until your birthday," he said. "It's a big one this year, right? The big three zero," he teased. Honestly, Ava wasn't sure what her birthday had to do with anything. Her father hadn't recognized her birthday in years. Usually, she and Zara did something together to celebrate but that was about it. Her father hadn't called to wish her a happy birthday in years—why would he all the sudden be bringing it up?

"Well, go on, open it," he said. Ava cautiously did as she was told, carefully pulling the edges of the sealed envelope open as if she was afraid something was going to pop out at her.

When she finally got it open, she pulled free some papers that looked suspiciously like legal documents. "Will I need my lawyer to go over these?" she asked, still not sure what the papers were.

"There really isn't a need," her father said. "Everything is in order and completely legal, trust me. I'm sure you won't listen to me and you will have your lawyers combing through them despite my assurances." Her father was right; she didn't trust one word that came out of his mouth and if he expected her to sign some legal documents without having her lawyer look them over first, he was crazy.

She flipped through the papers and shoved them back into the envelope, deciding that she really didn't have the time or patience to read them over in her father's foyer. That's why she kept a lawyer on retainer.

"You're not even going to ask what they are?" her father asked. Ava could tell from his tone that he was disappointed.

"Like I said, I have to get back to work. I'm sure my lawyer will be able to clarify everything for me later," she offered. Ava turned to leave and her father growled in frustration. She didn't bother to turn around, knowing that if she did, he'd expect her to engage with him and that was the last thing she wanted. When her dad didn't get his way, he tended to get a little nasty and she didn't want to deal with that side of him.

"You won't be keeping the money your grandfather left you," he shouted after her. Ava stopped dead in her tracks. Her father hated that her grandfather had left her the majority of his fortune when he passed. She was closer to her grandfather than her father was and when the will was read and she walked away with most of the inheritance, her father refused to even speak to her. That went on for months, but ever since then he had been finding little ways to weasel back into her life.

"It's already a done deal, Dad. Grandpa left me almost everything and there isn't anything you can do about it."

His smile was mean and Ava knew she wasn't going to like what he had to say next. "There was a clause," he spat. "A marriage stipulation, if you will."

"What?" she questioned. "As in I have to be married to keep the money? How in the hell did you do that, Dad?" Ava accused.

"I didn't do anything except convince an old, dying man

that it might be smart to ensure that his line of succession be in place. You want to keep your inheritance—you have to marry by your thirtieth birthday." Her father seemed almost pleased with himself and Ava knew that arguing with him would get her nowhere.

"Grandpa would have never willingly put that kind of stipulation on me," she said. "You had to have done something to convince him to do it."

"Either way, it's done. How much more time do you have until your special day?" He asked, already knowing full well that there were only two months until her birthday.

"Two months," she whispered.

"Well, you better get busy trying to find your better half then, my dear. Time is a wasting," he said.

"What happens if I don't get married by my thirtieth birthday?" she asked.

"That's the best part," he said. "It all goes to his next closest living heir—me." Ava didn't hide her gasp. The thought of her father getting all her grandfather's money made her sick. She knew for a fact it wasn't what her grandpa would have wanted either.

Ava couldn't stand there in that stuffy old house for a moment longer. She turned to leave and her father laughed. "In a hurry to leave, Ava?" he called after her.

"Yes," she said over her shoulder. She stopped at the front door and turned back to face him. "Like you said, Daddy, I have two months to find my better half. I better get cracking because there is no way I'm going to just let you walk away with grandpa's money." Ava noticed the subtle look of disapproval in her father's eyes, and she knew she had hit a nerve with her empty threat. There was really no way to keep him from getting his hands on her inheritance because finding a man and convincing him to marry her in two months, was going to prove damn near impossible.

❄

Two Weeks Later

Avalon sat in the corner of the club and watched the couples and a few threesomes who had gathered around the room. She thought about running out of there as quickly as possible, but the thought of not facing Corbin's stupid dare head on made her feel like a coward.

She spied him as soon as he walked into the BDSM club and wasn't sure if she was worried he'd see her or if he'd find someone else more interesting and forget all about her. Corbin Eklund was a tease and she'd do well to remember that before she lost her heart to the serial player. She watched him for a few minutes and could tell the exact moment he saw her. His sexy smirk told her all she needed to know—he didn't believe she would actually take him up on his bet to show up at the club. He made his way across the crowded club and towered over her.

"I didn't think you'd show, Darlin,'" he drawled. "What made you decide to go through with it?" Ava smiled up at him, trying not to let on what the little nickname he called her did to her girl parts. Every damn time he called her Darlin,' she had to bite back her moan. Frankly, everything Corbin did made her a little crazy but telling him that could never happen. He had asked her to the club because he thought she wouldn't take him up on his bet and then she'd lose at the little game they had been playing. Losing wasn't an option for her. Ava was competitive but losing to Corbin Eklund felt worse than forfeiting to the devil himself. He was the sexiest devil she had ever met but keeping that to herself was for the best. The man already had a serious problem with humility—he had none. He was the most confident, self-possessed, arrogant man she'd ever met and for some reason, that wasn't enough for Ava to stay away from him.

"Well, a bet is a bet—so here I am. Now what are you planning on doing with me, Corbin?" she asked. Honestly, she tried not to think about the possibilities leading up to tonight. She had two very long nights to think about what she wanted him to do to her. Ava had spent the past two nights restlessly tossing and turning trying to figure out how to get through this evening with her heart intact and the answer wasn't one she easily entertained—she wouldn't.

She had met Corbin a few months prior, when her best friend, Zara hooked up with Corbin's best friend, Aiden. They stood up for their friends at their quicky wedding a few months ago, when they got married. She was happy for her friend; Zara deserved every happiness she had found with Aiden and his two little girls. But now, Ava felt more alone than ever. It wasn't as if Zara was moving away but being the new Senator's wife was going to take up a good deal of her time. Well, that and the fact she was a new step-mother to two of the cutest little girls Ava had ever seen and Zara was pregnant with her first baby. There would be little to no time for the two of them to hang out or stay up all night talking about life and guys. Those days were over and it was time for Ava to grow up and move on.

He smiled down at her and winked. Ava rolled her eyes at just how cheesy he was, but she smiled back at him. She couldn't help it—his carefree nature was infectious. She needed to relax and just enjoy tonight because it had been a damn long time since she had any fun with a man. Hell, she lost count of how many months it had been since she had sex. This night was about finding her mojo and getting back in the saddle again, nothing more. Corbin had made her no promises and she wouldn't ask for any.

"I have no idea what to do with you, Avalon," he admitted. "You showing up here caught me completely off guard."

Her smile turned quickly into a frown at his admission. She stood from her seat. "Hey, if this wasn't something you wanted to happen, I can just leave. No hard feelings or anything," she sassed. Ava turned to leave, and Corbin caught her by the arm.

"Stop," he commanded.

"Really Corbin, it's fine if you aren't interested," she said. Actually, it hurt like hell knowing he didn't want her, but she wasn't going to stand in that damn club and cry all over him. She was stronger than that and sobbing all over a guy just wasn't her scene.

"Who the fuck says I don't want you, Darlin'?" he asked. He took her hand and led it to his bulging erection, letting her feel every impressive inch of his arousal. "Does this feel like I don't want you?" Ava let her shaking fingers aimlessly run over his shaft and he groaned and leaned into her touch.

He watched her; a hungry look in his eyes and she knew he was going to give her exactly what she had been needing. She tried for coy, even asking, "Is that all for me?" but Corbin didn't seem to be buying her blasé question.

"Don't play with me, Ava," he whispered. "I've wanted this for too long." Hearing him admit he wanted her did strange things to her girl parts. She felt a new wetness coat her thighs and she was sure one touch from Corbin would set her off.

"How long, Corbin?" she almost whispered. Ava cleared her throat, "How long have you wanted me?" she questioned.

Corbin looked her up and down as if taking in every inch of her curvy body. "I've wanted you since the first night I saw you —at Aiden's place the day the news story broke about him and Zara. You were so fucking beautiful and the way you fiercely stuck up for your friend made me hot." She had no idea Corbin even noticed her that night. She thought back to their trip to take the girls for ice cream and then the park, and as far as she knew, Corbin found her annoying more than anything. Boy, had she misread the situation.

"Wow," Ava whispered.

"Yeah, wow," Corbin confirmed. "So, now that we've cleared that up, I'll ask again. What made you decide to accept my little bet and show up here?" Corbin had finally come clean with her and now it was her turn to give him some truths. She wasn't a coward but Ava knew telling him she wanted him just as much was going to sting a little. She had spent months trying to act nonchalant about anything having to do with the big guy but seeing him now, towering over her, made Ava want to take a chance.

She went up on her tiptoes and brushed back a strand of Corbin's overly long, dark hair back from his eyes. He had the most soulful brown eyes she had ever seen. Whenever he looked at her she felt as if he could see straight into her soul. "I showed up here tonight for the same reason you did, Corbin. I want you just as much as you want me. I won't lie about that or hide behind my own insecurities."

Corbin wrapped an arm around her waist and pulled her up his body, kissing his way into her mouth. God, he tasted like bottled sunshine and she couldn't seem to get enough of him. "Thank fuck," he whispered against her lips. She wrapped her legs around his waist and he walked back to the hallway that led from the public playroom to the private rooms for exclusive members. She had only been to the club a handful of times before but Ava remembered her way around.

He opened a door and walked in, setting her on the bed that took up most of the room. "This is my private room," he said. "I thought we could do a quiet setting tonight unless you would like to try the playroom," he offered. Ava didn't want to get into the fact she had been a guest at the club before accepting his dare tonight. Truthfully, she loved the kinky lifestyle and was training to be a sub, but telling Corbin that didn't exactly feel like "first date" material.

"This works for me," she admitted, sitting back on the bed. She didn't hide the fact she was checking Corbin out, looking his body up and down. She loved that he was dressed like a total badass tonight. Usually, he was impeccably dressed in a suit. Ava guessed that matched his whole CEO business owner day gig but tonight he was dressed to fit who he really was. Corbin filled out his black tee, showing off all his muscles and his full sleeves of tattoos. She knew he had quite a few of them hiding under his dress shirt but not full sleeves. And the way his erection pressed against his jeans almost looked painful.

"You keep looking at me like that, Darlin', and this won't last very long," he growled.

"Sorry," she said. "I was just trying to figure out just how far up your tattoos go." Corbin gave her a wolfish grin and she knew she was in trouble.

"Well, I can help you figure that out, honey," he said, yanking his black t-shirt up over his head. She gasped when he revealed most of his upper torso was covered in tats. She had always thought Corbin was hot, but seeing him in only his jeans, she realized he was downright beautiful.

"Corbin," she whispered. It was all Ava could manage because he literally took her breath away.

CORBIN

He watched Avalon as she looked over his upper body and when she whispered his name, all Corbin could think about was getting inside of her. He wanted her more than he wanted his next breath, but he also knew this might be his only shot with her and he needed to take his time. Tonight was a fluke, a bet he thought he was going to lose but instead he had won the woman he was dreaming about for months now. Avalon Michaels hadn't agreed to be his but gifting him with one night of her time was more than he could have ever hoped for.

After they all returned from Aiden and Zara's honeymoon, he convinced Ava to go out for a drink with him. At first, she protested, saying she was already behind at work and making some excuse about having to get caught up with laundry. Just when he thought she was going to walk away from him, she turned back and agreed to just one drink.

He took her to his favorite little bar that had live music loud enough they had to sit incredibly close to each other just to have a conversation. One drink turned into three and then four and before he knew it, they were both drunk and he was betting her she wouldn't go to the BDSM club where he was a member. It was the same club where Aiden met Zara, so he was hoping lightning would strike twice and somehow Ava would end up in his bed.

The next day he texted her reminding Ava about the dare she boldly accepted with the help of alcohol. He was sure her return text would tell him to go fuck himself but she didn't. Instead, she confirmed she would be at the club at nine sharp and even told him not to be late. Like he would show up even a second past nine and chance her leaving. Corbin had waited too long for something like this to fall into his lap with Ava. He wasn't about to fuck it up.

Now, they were finally in his private room, and he was wondering just how much kink Avalon would allow. They really never discussed sexual likes and dislikes, and this was uncharted territory for him. As a Dom, he knew communication was key and neither of them would get what they needed if he didn't ask questions. Still, he worried asking Avalon what she liked in bed was going to send her running from his room and that was the last thing he wanted.

"Hey," she said, kneeling on the bed in front of him. "Where did you just go?" she questioned. Knowing Ava knew him well enough to pick up on the fact he was worried about this next part did crazy things to his heart. She ran her hands down his face and he pulled them back up to his mouth to gently kiss her fingers and then let them rest on his chest. He liked the way she flexed them into his flesh as if she already needed more from him, and they hadn't even gotten started yet.

"I was trying to decide how to ask you what you like—you know in bed," he said. She giggled and he took a step back from her, letting her hands fall back to her side. "That wasn't quite the response I was hoping for, Avalon," he said.

"No Corbin, I'm sorry," she said, reaching for him. "I was just laughing because I was worried about telling you what I like—you know kink-wise," she admitted. He took a deep breath and stepped back towards her.

"What kind of kink do you like, Avalon?" he asked. She gasped when he ran his hands through her short dark hair, grabbing a handful and giving it a yank, forcing her to look up at him. She moaned and closed her eyes, telling him she liked it a little rough.

"Eyes open, Darlin,'" he commanded. Ava did exactly as he asked and he knew she was going to be a perfect sub. "You've done this before, haven't you honey?" he questioned. She shyly nodded her answer.

"I'm going to need more than head nods, Ava. Give me the words," he demanded. He knew he could be a little overbearing, but Avalon seemed to take everything he was throwing at her and giving him back everything in return.

"Yes, Corbin," she hissed when he tightened his grip on her hair.

"Sir," he corrected. "In here, you will call me Sir."

Avalon smiled up at him, "Yes, Sir," she corrected. "I have done this before. I've had training to be a sub, here at the club." The thought of any other Dom taking Ava on as a sub made his inner caveman roar to life and he was pissed. There was nothing he could do about the past but if another Dom tried to touch her, he'd break the guy in two.

"How long ago?" he questioned. He knew he was torturing himself with the details of her time at the club, but he couldn't help it. Corbin needed to know before he moved forward with her.

"About a year ago, I wanted to explore this life—you know see if it was for me." He released her hair and sat down on the bed next to her. Corbin pulled Ava's small body onto his lap, loving the way she so eagerly straddled him.

"Is it?" he whispered, "the life for you?" She framed his face with her small hands again and loved the way she seemed to need to touch him.

"Yes, Sir," she whispered against his lips.

He let out his pent-up breath, not realizing he had been holding it, waiting for her answer. "I'm so fucking happy to hear you say that, Ava," he admitted.

"I take it you like it kinky then too?" she asked.

"I do," he said. "I'm a Dom and God, I've dreamed of what I want to do to you, Darlin'," he said. Corbin rolled Ava under his body and pressed her into the mattress. "You're going to need a safe word, Avalon," he ordered. "I plan on taking you to the very edge of your limits and since this is our first time together, I want to be sure you are with me."

Ava smiled up at him and seemed to think for a minute. "Ice cream," she whispered. "For the first time we met," she said.

He kissed his way into her mouth, loving the breathy little sighs and moans she gave him. He wasn't sure how he had gotten so lucky, but he really didn't want to think about that right now. All Corbin wanted to do was concentrate on making Avalon his. The rest of his worries could wait until tomorrow. She hadn't made him any promises beyond the here and now and he planned on soaking up every second with her.

AVALON

"Ice cream it is then," Corbin growled. "I'm going to push you to your limits, Darlin'." Ava nodded, wanting to let him know she was with him. She knew how important communication was within the Dom/sub relationship from her training.

"Yes, Sir. I want that too, please," she smiled up at him.

"If you use your safe word, this all stops and we can talk about what you didn't like," Corbin said. Ava nodded again and Corbin gave a sharp yank to her short hair. "The words, baby," he ordered.

"I understand," she said, dramatically rolling her eyes. "I'm with you, Corbin—completely," she sassed. Corbin's expression turned from turned on to pissed in a matter of seconds.

"I'm not playing games here, Ava. I just told you that I've waited too long for you to not take this seriously. If you don't feel the same, just tell me now and we can forget this ever happened," he threatened. Ava instantly regretted her sass. She knew better than to be a brat, but she was a work in progress when it came to being a submissive. She wanted to at least try to give Corbin what he was asking for; otherwise, she might never get another chance with him.

"I'm sorry, Corbin. I suck at this submissive thing sometimes. I will try to do better—I promise," she swore, crossing her heart with her hand for good measure. She almost forgot that she still had her clothes on until her fingers lightly brushed her t-shirt causing her nipple to pucker from the sensation. Judging by the way Corbin looked her over, he noticed the same thing.

"Sir," he whispered into her ear. Corbin grabbed the hem of her white t-shirt that barely covered her belly and tugged it up over her head. Ava obligingly lifted both arms, letting him pull her shirt from her body, leaving her breasts completely bare for him.

How he expected her to follow their conversation now was a mystery. "Um, sorry?" she questioned. Corbin's eyes flared with need as he looked over her body.

"I'm sorry, Sir," he said correcting her. "You called me by my name and that isn't what we are doing here tonight, Ava. You are my submissive for the night and if you want to address me, you will call me Sir," Corbin ordered.

Ava didn't hide her smile, "Yes, Sir," she hissed the last word, adding emphasis to show Corbin she was capable of playing things his way. Corbin stood, shaking his head at her; his smile playing with his lips as if he was amused by Ava's sassy spirit. When he took a step back and crossed his arms over his massive tattooed chest, it was her turn to ogle him.

"I hear you saying the correct words, Darlin' but I'm not sure you mean them. You are a brat, Ava," he said.

"I've been told," she sassed. When Corbin stood at his full height in all his angry glory, he was quite a sight. Most people would be intimidated by just his size alone, but Ava was taught the bigger they were, the harder they fell, by her grandfather. She was never the type of person to back down from a challenge and now was no different.

Ava crossed her arms over her own bare chest and Corbin let his eyes dip to follow her movement. She knew that standing her ground might land her in some trouble with the big Dom, but she was curious to see just how far he'd let her push him. Plus, she had a sneaky feeling that Corbin would end up punishing her and the thought of that made her pussy wet. Ava squeezed her thighs together, trying to hide the fact that she was wet and ready for him. Her short schoolgirl skirt barely covered her ample ass and she worried that Corbin would be able to see her arousal.

"I think you could use a few reminder lessons, Ava," he said. "For one, I'd like to teach you to control that sassy mouth of yours and then we can move on to your fidgeting," he said. She knew he was trying to go for threatening and maybe even a little menacing, judging by his tone, but all Ava could hear were the promises he was making her.

"Yes, Sir," she whispered.

"On your knees, Darlin," he drawled. Ava felt downright giddy at his command and she immediately sunk to her knees. "Thank you, Avalon," he said. His gravely tone gave him away and Ava could tell that Corbin was on edge. He was just as turned on by this whole scene as she was. She licked her lips and looked up at him through her lashes, using every trick she was taught last year about pleasing her Dom. Corbin moaned as he unzipped his pants and let his cock spring free.

Avalon's breath hitched and he smiled down at her, even giving her a saucy wink. She watched as Corbin pulled his pants off and tossed them in the corner of the room. He liked showing off for her, palming his own cock to let her know exactly what he was going to give her.

"You're big, Sir," she whispered. Corbin's chuckle resonated through the room, and she worried that whatever he planned next might have her safe word out of her mouth before they even got started.

"Ready?" He looked her over and she wasn't sure how to

answer his question. Was she ready for Corbin Eklund to make her his—hell yeah! But would she be able to take all of him and his dominance? She wished she could enthusiastically answer the same to that question but she wasn't sure that she'd be able to.

"Yes," she stuttered, "Sir, I believe I'm ready."

"Let's talk about what you like and don't like. If you haven't done something I'm asking you to do, then just speak up," he offered.

"Okay, Sir," she agreed.

"So, I'm guessing that you have had sex before?" Corbin started. Ava giggled and nodded.

"Yes, I've had sex before, Sir," she said.

"Well, I had to ask. We wouldn't want a fuck up like Aiden and Zara had, would we?" Ava thought back over the past few months and the roller coaster that her best friend, Zara, seemed to be on. When Ava dared Zara to go to the BDSM club, she met Aiden and lied about her virginity. Well, Zara didn't exactly lie about it, but she didn't come right out and share that she was a virgin. Aiden and Zara seemed to find a way forward though and Ava had to admit she was happy for her best friend.

"No, that wouldn't be good," she agreed.

"Anal?" Corbin asked.

"I've had it a few times, but I can't say I'm a huge fan of anal, Sir," she offered.

"Well, maybe your partner didn't know what he was doing," Corbin teased. He took a step toward her and stood so close she could smell his sexy, musky scent mixed with his cologne. He always smelled like heaven and now was no exception. She wanted to lean forward and suck the head of his cock into her mouth but she waited. Instead, she watched as Corbin stroked his hard shaft, making her mouth water.

"For the rest of these questions, I want you to hum if you have done what I'm asking or if you'd like to try it. Understand?" She must have looked at him like he was crazy and Corbin laughed.

"Why do I need to hum? Can't I just say yes, or no?" she questioned.

"It's going to be hard to form words from this point on, since I plan on having my cock shoved down that pretty throat of yours, Darlin'." Ava gifted him with her sly smile and nodded. She opened her mouth as if offering him what he wanted and he rested the tip of his cock on her bottom lip. "Take as much of me as you can, Ava," he ordered.

Really it was no easy feat to take all of Corbin, but she managed to take most of him, greedily sucking him to the back of her throat and swallowing around his massive shaft.

"Fuck, baby," he hissed. "When you do that, I can't think straight." Ava felt her inner goddess spring to life with Corbin's praise and she knew she'd give him anything he wanted.

Corbin ran a hand down her cheek and Ava looked up at him. It was such a soft, caring gesture; it almost threw her off guard. "You are so fucking beautiful, Avalon," he whispered. Ava moaned and sucked him to the back of her throat again. If she wasn't careful, she was going to forget that Corbin wanted her for just one night. This wasn't a date or even leading to the possibility of one. This was sex between a Dom and a submissive. She wasn't his and never would be. It wasn't the way Corbin worked.

Ava knew guys like Corbin—hell, she only dated guys like him. It was easier that way. She didn't want a messy relationship that got in the way of her work commitments and personal goals. Ava had so much she wanted to do in life and none of it involved feelings, a boyfriend, or falling in love. All that mushy shit would have to wait until later.

Avalon concentrated on sucking Corbin in and out of her mouth. That was easy—sex could help her forget the things that she told herself she wasn't ready for because when Corbin looked at her the way he was, she was ready to throw all her personal plans out the window and agree to anything he wanted from her.

"How about spanking?" he questioned, bringing her thoughts back to the present. Ava hummed her approval around his cock, feeling her own arousal coating her thighs. Every time Corbin offered another kinky activity, she felt a new surge of wetness between her legs.

"Will you let me tie you up?" Corbin asked, shoving his cock to the back of her throat. She once again hummed, and Corbin moaned. She knew he was close but she didn't want to push him.

"Flogging and other forms of spanking punishments?" He questioned. Avalon hummed and Corbin pumped in and out of her mouth.

"Blindfold, nipple clamps, sex toys, rope play?" He listed them all off and Ava had to admit they all sounded like things she would enjoy. She hummed her agreement.

"Will you let me share you with another man?" He asked. Ava didn't make a sound, not sure how she felt about that idea. Would she want to let Corbin give her to another Dom to use? A part of her thought it was hot, but there was a little voice inside of her that was telling her that if he could share her so easily, she must not be worth much. Plus, if she only had tonight with him, she wanted Corbin all to herself.

Corbin pulled free from her mouth, causing Ava to mewl in protest. He chuckled, "Sorry, Darlin'," he said. "I don't want to finish in your sexy mouth. I want in that pussy of yours but first, we need to talk about my last question."

Ava shrugged. "I'm not sure I'd like to be shared," she admitted. "I only have you for tonight and I don't want to waste any time," she said, giving him an honest answer.

Corbin pulled her up his body, from her kneeling position, to stand in front of him. Ava looked down at her bare feet and Corbin crooked a finger under her chin, raising her face to look at him. "What if I wanted this to be more than just one night?" he asked.

Ava shook her head. "I don't know if I'd be able to give you more," she admitted. "I didn't say anything earlier, but I'm leaving tomorrow for France, and I don't know when I'll be back."

Corbin dropped his hand from her chin. "Why didn't you say so before now?" Corbin grumbled.

"Because it wouldn't have mattered. We agreed to one night, Corbin. I have to go on a business trip. I'm sure your company requires you to leave town and you don't tell everyone else your business," she said.

"No, you're right. And, we did say that this was a one-night deal. Fine, no sharing," he said. Ava could tell that he was trying to change the subject and she had to admit she was thankful he did. "Any other hard limits?" he asked.

"I don't like electric or fire play," she admitted. Ava tried to remember her training and all the different things she had to experience as a submissive. "I think that about covers it though," she said.

Corbin nodded, "Noted," he said. Ava could tell that he was shorter with her and she worried that telling him about her trip might have been a mistake. Really, she didn't think it was a big deal but judging from Corbin's sour mood, it was.

He crossed the room to sit on the bed. "Come here," he ordered, patting his bare legs. His cock jetted out from between his legs and Ava hoped that the talking portion of their evening was just about over. She stood in front of Corbin as if waiting for further instruction. "I'm going to spank your ass red and then I'm going to tie you up and fuck you until you can't remember your name."

"Yes, Sir," she said.

"Good girl," he praised. "Lay over my lap with your ass up for me, Darlin'," he ordered. Ava did as asked and when he landed the first blow without warning, she yelped.

"This is going to go fast and hard, Ava," he said. "If it's too much for you, use your safe word." It almost sounded like he was issuing her a dare. She knew that she had pissed him off and Ava worried that he'd try to push her to use her safe word. She loved a good challenge and from his tone, Corbin was issuing her one.

"Am I being punished, Sir?" she asked.

Corbin didn't answer, just rubbed his big palm over her ass where the first smack probably left a welt. When more than a few minutes passed, she turned to her side to look back at him.

"Corbin?" She asked. He turned away from her, so she couldn't see his expression and Ava knew that something was wrong. "Please tell me if I did something wrong," she begged.

"No," he breathed. "I'm mad at myself for letting this get so out of hand. I am mad and I can't do this—not now. I wouldn't ever touch you while I'm angry with you, Ava."

"What did I do to make you so upset?" she asked, standing from his lap. She righted her skirt and sat down on the bed next to him. "Please talk to me, Corbin," she asked.

"I'm mad that you are going to France and didn't tell me. But I'm mainly angry at myself because you are right—it's none of my business. I guess I was just hoping for more with you, Ava, and I was too much of a chicken to ask."

Hearing that Corbin wanted more with her did crazy things to her heart. She just wasn't ready to give him more of herself. Her company was sending her to France for a few weeks to do some buying. She was a fashion acquisitions manager for a major department store in town and part owner of a clothing design company. They wanted her to stay in Europe until she was finished, and Ava had no idea when she'd be back in town. Honestly, she needed some time away from home and her family. She had seen her father earlier that week and he had dropped a bomb that had an expiration date ticking down on it. Ava needed some time away to think over what her next step would be. Dealing with her father was always like that, playing a game of chess and she had to carefully consider her next move or chance of losing the game to him, and losing wasn't something she liked to do. Being sent to France could not have come at a better time, even if the sexiest man she had ever seen wanted her to stick around.

"I'm sorry that I didn't tell you sooner, Corbin. Maybe we can pick this up when I get back to town?" she asked.

Corbin gifted her with his shy, sexy smile. "I'd like that, Ava," he said. Ava decided to take a chance, straddling his lap, and letting his cock slide through her slick folds.

"What's this?" Corbin asked, cocking an eyebrow at her.

"This is me trying to make peace with you. Forgive me?" Ava watched him, almost holding her breath waiting for him to answer.

"Yes," he whispered. Corbin kissed his way into her mouth, lifting her body from his lap and sliding her back down onto his cock. Ava moaned at the pleasure of being so full. He was big but they still fit and all she could think about was moving on him, riding him, and giving them both all the pleasure they seemed to need. That was what she would concentrate on tonight—making Corbin remember every sinful detail of their time together and then when she got back to town, she'd give him another night. Maybe it was time to let a little romance into her busy schedule and Ava couldn't think of any other man she'd want to do that with more than Corbin Eklund.

CORBIN

Corbin had spent the better part of a week in meetings, putting out fires and feeling consumed by his memories of Avalon. She was everything he thought she would be and so much more. When he met Zara's sassy little friend, he couldn't work her out of his mind and he had tried. He spent countless nights at the club finding a sub to try to take his mind off Ava but nothing seemed to work. When she finally agreed to meet him at the club and give him one night, he wasn't sure if he was happy or upset about the whole deal. He was sure of one thing though, one night with Avalon wasn't enough and he worried he'd never be able to get her out of his mind.

After their night together, Avalon and he made each other the promise to make no promises. It was strange but he wanted so many fucking reassurances from her, but he wasn't ready to ask her for any of them. Ava made it clear that their night was just about sex and while she was away, she wouldn't fault him for enjoying the company of other subs at the club. He almost wanted to laugh in her face when she said it but he knew better than to piss her off. The thought of being with anyone else at the club made him cringe. He wanted one woman right now and she was thousands of miles away in France.

He asked her if the whole no promises thing was more for her, so she could see other men while she was away and Ava tried to assure him that she would be too busy to even notice another man. But, she never really gave him a straight answer and that really burned his ass.

"Hey," Aiden said, letting himself into Corbin's office. Aiden Bentley was his best friend and his business partner, but more than that he was like the brother Corbin never had.

"What's up?" Corbin asked, looking up from his computer screen.

"I haven't seen you around the office much this week. In fact, the only time I've seen your ugly mug was during meetings. Want to tell me what's going on with you?" Aiden said. He knew that his best friend could always tell when something was off with him and vice versa. They were a team and he'd expect no less from Aiden.

"It's a woman," Corbin said.

"Shit," Aiden cursed. "Please don't tell me this has anything to do with Avalon because if my wife finds out that you are screwing around with her best friend, she'll have my balls," Aiden grouched.

Corbin didn't hide his amusement. "Man, Zara already has your balls. I'm pretty sure she keeps them in a jar on her bedside table to remind you that she's in charge."

Aiden seemed to find the whole thing less funny than Corbin. Aiden was a Dom like him and he had found his perfect submissive in his new wife, Zara. Corbin often wondered if he'd ever find someone as perfect for him as Aiden had. Avalon was far from being a perfect submissive. In fact, the idea of her not giving him grief was a foreign one. Ava liked to question and give him sass around every corner and the thought of spanking her ass red for being a brat turned him completely on.

"Okay, I won't tell you about Ava and I spending a night together at the club and then the way she packed her shit and took off for France the next morning," Corbin complained.

"Dear God," Aiden growled. "Fuck, now I'm going to have to hear about how my best friend is fucking up Zara's best friend's life. I'll never hear the end of this."

"Calm down, man. I'm not fucking up anyone's life. I wanted more but Ava shot me down. She just left and made me promise that we'd make no promises," Corbin said.

"What the fuck does that even mean?" Aiden questioned.

"Hell if I know," Corbin grouched. "But all I can think about is Ava and some French asshole hooking up while I'm sitting here acting like a complete pussy about the whole thing," Corbin admitted.

"So, what are you going to do about it, man?" Aiden questioned.

"It's not that simple, Aiden," Corbin grouched.

"What's not simple? Do you want Ava?" Aiden asked.

"Yes," Corbin confirmed.

"All right—then what are you going to do about it?" Aiden asked again. Corbin paused. The last thing he needed was to dive into his feelings with his best friend. Aiden liked to jump in with both feet and not really think about the consequences. His friend always led with his heart and that wasn't who Corbin was. He was an over thinker, even a worrier, and the idea of just jumping into the water feet first and to hell with the consequences, made him half crazy.

"I don't know, man. A part of me wants to have the jet fueled and go to France to set that woman straight and the other part of me wants to sit here and mope," Corbin grumbled. Aiden chuckled and Corbin knew he shot him a dirty look. He held up his hands as if in defense and took a step back from Corbin's desk.

"Sorry, man but if you want my two cents—" Aiden started.

"I don't," Corbin admitted.

Aiden chuckled again, "Well, I don't really give a fuck. I say call down to the runway and get the jet ready. Isn't that why we have all of this?" Aiden said motioning around Corbin's office. His friend wasn't wrong, although he'd never tell Aiden he was right. They had built a multi-million dollar company from nothing and they had a jet waiting to take them anywhere they pleased. What would it hurt to run to France and surprise Ava? He knew exactly what was holding him back, but saying the words out loud made him sound like a complete coward.

"What if she doesn't want me to chase after her? What happens if I get there and she tells me to get lost?" Corbin all but whispered his question.

Aiden sat down on one of the chairs that were in front of Corbin's massive desk. "I guess you'll never know how she'll react unless you get on that fucking plane and go find her. I'm betting I can get her address from Zara—just give it some thought." Corbin nodded and Aiden stood to leave his office.

"Thanks, man," Corbin called after him.

"Always," Aiden said and shut his office door. He knew he was being a coward, but the thought of flying halfway around the world only to be turned down scared the shit out of him. He was usually so self-assured and confident when it came to women and what he wanted and didn't want. He usually just picked up subs at the BDSM club and played with them until he grew tired or found someone better to play with.

Ava was the first woman to make him feel things he had never felt before. She had him so twisted up inside he wasn't sure which end was up. Maybe it was time to put on his big boy pants and go to France to talk to Ava. What did he have to lose?

"Everything," Corbin whispered to himself, picking up his cell to call his pilot.

AVALON

Ava tried to bury herself in her job and it had worked for the most part, but she found France a great deal less interesting since having to leave Corbin's bed at the club. Thoughts of their night together consumed her waking hours and left her restless and needy all night long. All she wanted to do was cut her trip short and head back home but that wasn't who she was. Her boss would understand; hell, she owned a large percentage of the company so she could get away with just about anything. Ava knew better than the throw around her last name and money to get what she wanted though and living up to her boss's expectations was part of what drove her to stay put and finish her job there.

Her grandfather and father had both been heavily involved in local politics back home. They had both been popular Senators and she grew up very privileged. Some might say she was born with a silver spoon in her mouth, but she never wanted people to assume that she wasn't also a hard worker. Her family came from old money, but she didn't want to sit back on her inheritance and do nothing with her life. Ava decided at a very early age that she wanted to go into the fashion industry and after she got her Masters' in fashion design and marketing, she invested a good deal of money into a few of her favorite local designers. She liked the idea of helping a local struggling artist that might not have a chance without her money. She became friends with her current boss, Peter, and when he offered her forty-nine percent of his company and a job that she loved doing, she jumped at the chance. He was already established and honestly didn't really need her investment, but he liked what she was doing in the fashion community and made her the offer.

Now, with the possibility of losing her inheritance because of some crazy stipulation her father demanded her grandfather put into place, she was happy to have her little piece of the company to fall back on. That was also part of the reason why when Peter asked if she could go to France, she jumped at the chance. Ava needed to get away from town for a while and decide what to do about the little bomb her father dropped on her. He was all too happy to share the fact that he had convinced her grandfather to put a stipulation on the money she inherited from him. If she wasn't married by the age of thirty, she would lose everything—her townhouse, her car, her monthly allowance, bank accounts, and assets—everything. Honestly, she was fine with having to make her own way, but when she found out that it would all revert to her dear old dad, she just about threw a tantrum. But she wouldn't give him that satisfaction. Really, it would be playing right into her father's plans. She still had time—one and a half months to be exact and who knew what could happen in that time? Maybe she'd meet Mr. Right and he'd whisk her down the aisle and her father wouldn't get a penny of her money. Given that Corbin was her only prospect and the man seemed to be allergic to even the word "commitment," she was going to have to make some hard and fast decisions. The first being where she was going to live once she got back home. The second would be what the hell to do about Corbin Eklund.

Ava decided to call back home and check on everyone and if Corbin's name casually came up, she wouldn't mind. She picked up her cell and called her best friend Zara, hoping she'd be willing to listen and give her some advice.

"Hey, girl," she said, trying for casual.

"Don't 'hey girl' me, Avalon Michaels," Zara spat into the other end of the phone call. Her friend was very pregnant and Ava wasn't ever sure which person she was going to get when she called—her nice best friend or "I'm ready to murder someone" Zara. Tonight, she apparently was talking to the latter.

"Okay, what is going on now?" Ava asked.

"You are going on," Zara said. "You went to the club with Corbin and didn't tell me?" Ava sighed into the phone. She knew that sooner or later word would get around and if she had to guess, Corbin had talked to Aiden and now the cat was out of the bag.

"Corbin told Aiden?" She knew she was asking a question but honestly, she already knew the answer.

"Yes!" Zara's temper was sounding more heated by the minute. "Care to explain to me why I had to hear the news from my husband and not my best friend who may or may not be my daughter's Godmother now?"

"Hey, you can't hold my Godmother status over me like that. Either I'm in or I'm out but don't use my Goddaughter against me like that, Z," Ava ordered.

There was a pause on the other end of the line and Ava worried that she had lost the call. Zara sobbed into the other end and she instantly regretted her words. "Aww, Z," she crooned. "Don't cry."

"I can't help it," Zara cried. "I'm hormonal." Ava wasn't sure what to do or say. She wasn't a crier and having a best friend that currently cried over everything wasn't a picnic.

"Listen, if you'd rather I call later—" Ava started.

"No," Zara sniffled. "I'll get it together, I promise," she swore. "So, why are you calling me all the way from France?

Isn't it the middle of the night there?" Zara was right—it was two in the morning, not that it mattered since she couldn't sleep.

"Yeah, I guess my body and brain are still on home time." Ava suddenly felt like a complete chicken. The last thing she wanted to do was involve her pregnant best friend in her problems but she really had no one else to turn to. "Listen, I'll call you another time and we can talk," Ava offered.

"I'm assuming you called me to ask about him?" Zara taunted. There would be no lying to her. Zara seemed to know her inside and out and not being completely honest went against their strict girl code.

"Yeah," Ava admitted. "What do I do about him?"

"Well, I'm assuming that you like him. You know like him, like him." Ava rolled her eyes and giggled.

"Are we back in middle school, Z?" she questioned.

"No," Zara defended. "I'm just trying to get a feel of where the two of you stand since this was the first I've heard of you liking him—you know directly from the horse's mouth." Ava winced at Zara's slight.

"Please don't call me a horse, Z," Ava teased. "And God help me, I like him, like him. I just have no clue what to do about it."

"You're going to have to make a decision fast," Zara said. "He took the jet and rumor has it he's heading for France."

"What?" Ava questioned.

"Yep," Zara confirmed.

"Why the hell didn't you call to tell me this earlier?" Ava sounded as panicked as she currently felt. "When will he get here? Oh my God, what do I wear or say or even do?"

Zara's laughter filled the other end of the line. "Yeah, this sounds exactly like middle school," she teased. "I'm sure you'll figure it all out. You might want to hurry though. He left yesterday."

"Fuck," Ava swore. Zara giggled and ended the call. Ava

looked at her phone as if it somehow personally offended her and thought about throwing the damn thing across the room. She let an angry growl rip from her chest and looked around her hotel room in a panic.

"What the hell do I do now?" She shouted into the air, half expecting someone to answer her. Really, there was only one thing to do—run. She'd find another hotel or at least change rooms. Avoiding Corbin was her only hope for eventually forgetting him. Until she could figure out her shit, that was her only option.

Ava grabbed her suitcase, shoving everything she had brought with her into it, not taking the time to neatly pack her things as she usually did. She found her purse and her jacket and did one last check of her room before heading out. Ava pulled her door shut and headed to the elevators, jamming her thumb into the lit button as if that would help it ascend any faster.

She breathed a sigh of relief when her floor number lit up above the elevator doors and tried to patiently wait while the doors opened. The ding of the elevator doors gave her a sense of relief that she hadn't had in days and when the doors slowly opened to reveal the sexy Dom standing on the other side, her heart sank.

Corbin smiled at her and stepped off the elevator and practically bumped into her allowing others to exit. "Ava," he whispered.

"Why are you here?" she asked. She looked up his big body and made the mistake of looking him in the eyes. Corbin's expressions always gave him away and the sadness and confusion she saw in his eyes was nearly her undoing.

"I came to find you," he admitted. "Were you leaving?" he asked.

"No," she said. He looked down at the suitcase in her hand and back up at her, his sexy smirk firmly in place. "Well, not now," she admitted.

"Let me guess—you talked to Z and she told you I was on my way to find you and you panicked. You do know I have the resources to find you, even in a city this size, right?" He looked her up and down again and Zara could feel her blush. What was it about this man that made her act like a giddy schoolgirl at prom?

"And you know that I have the resources to never be found again—by anyone, right?" Ava didn't usually flaunt her money but she wouldn't let Corbin's wealth intimidate her. She could probably match him dollar for dollar if he wanted to go toe-to-toe with her.

Corbin sighed and put his hands on his hips. "This isn't going like I planned," he admitted.

"What was the plan here, Corbin?" Ava waited him out. She wasn't sure if she wanted to tell him to go the fuck away or jump into his arms and tell him to take her.

"I was hoping that we could talk," he said.

Ava's laugh sounded more like a cackle and she turned to walk back to her room. There would be no running or hiding now, so she might as well kick off her heels and drop her belongings if she was going to have to a come to Jesus meeting with the sexy alpha who was currently staring her down. She looked back over her shoulder to where Corbin seemed frozen to his spot.

"You coming or not?" she asked.

"Yeah," Corbin said, chasing after her to keep up.

Ava opened her door and tossed her bags in the corner of the room. She took off her heels and put them by the door and pulled off her jacket. Ava could feel Corbin's eyes on her, watching her as if he was just as clueless in all of this as she was.

"Make yourself at home," she offered. "The mini bar is in the other room and I'll be in soon. I just need to change." Corbin nodded and found his way into the adjoining sitting room. She could hear him rummaging through her bar as she opened her suitcase to find her pajamas. She was going to be comfortable while dealing with Corbin—she owed herself at least that. She found her favorite set; the ones covered in polar bears and went into her bathroom to change. By the time she had found her way to the sitting room, Corbin was lounging on her settee, a drink in his hand and another for her waiting on the table in front of him.

"I thought you might like a drink," he said, motioning to where her glass sat on the coffee table. "Rum and pineapple juice, right?" he asked. She was surprised he remembered her drink order from their one night together. She nodded, taking the drink and sitting across the room from him, giving herself some much needed space.

"Cute pajamas," Corbin teased.

"Thanks," Ava said, taking a sip of her drink. "So, what would you like to talk about?" she asked. Ava knew she sounded like a bitch but she was tired and confused. The man she couldn't stop thinking about over the past week was finally sitting in front of her. She was confused and worried that she would assume or say the wrong thing, so letting Corbin get his story out first seemed like a good enough plan.

"I missed you, Ava," he said. "I know you wanted to keep things between us casual, but I don't know if that's an option for me," he admitted. Ava could feel her heart beating and worried that Corbin would be able to hear it across the small space that separated the two of them.

"Tell me you missed me, Ava," he ordered. "Fuck, tell me I'm not a complete lunatic for coming all this way to track you down."

Ava took another sip of her drink, not sure what to say. He was telling her everything she wanted to hear, but she also knew the truth about Corbin—he was not a man who dated. He met women at the club, and he fucked. She knew from just their one night together that wasn't going to be enough for her. God help her, she wanted more than that from him and Ava knew she couldn't expect him to be able to give her that.

"I missed you too, Corbin," she admitted. "But, I don't see how this thing between us will work out. I know you well enough to know you don't date. I don't want to be a fuck buddy, so that leaves us at a bypass in our relationship. I'd rather end things then jeopardize our friendship. It would kill Z and Aiden if we couldn't be in the same room together. It wouldn't be fair to do that to them. This way, we can part ways and still remain friends."

"I don't want to be friends," Corbin growled. "I don't want to be your fuck buddy, as you so colorfully called what is happening between the two of us. I want you, Ava. Is it so hard to believe that I may have changed and am looking for something more than just casual hookups at the club?"

Ava looked him over and every part of her wanted to believe him—except her heart. She worried that if she trusted what he was telling her, she'd end up losing that to him and there might not be any coming back from that.

Ava set her drink down and covered her face with her hands. "Fuck, don't cry," Corbin soothed. Ava pulled her hands free from her face and looked over at him. She almost wanted to laugh at the concern she saw etched in his brown eyes.

"I'm not crying," she corrected. "In fact, I rarely cry—just for future reference."

Corbin sat back and crossed his ankle over his knee, "Good to know, Darlin'." He smiled at her and winked; his mask firmly back in place. This was the Corbin she knew—not the kind, caring man who worried about making her cry. This Corbin was the big, badass Dom who told her what to do and expected her to do it. This was the Corbin she understood.

"Listen, I'm tired and I have a long day ahead of me tomorrow. How about you get back on your plane and go home and we can catch up and chat once I get back?" She stood, effectively dismissing him but he didn't seem to take the hint.

"I thought you might say that but you see, I don't do well with other people giving me orders," he said, standing to tower over her. "How about this—I'll let you get some sleep and you let me take you to dinner tomorrow night?"

"And how will you possibly take me to dinner if you are back home and I'm here in France?" she sassed.

Corbin set his drink down next to hers and pulled her against his body, not giving her any chance to object. "It will be possible because I'm staying in the room right next door to you, baby." Corbin crushed his lips against hers, taking what he wanted and giving her no room for objections. It seemed to be his go-to move.

He broke the kiss leaving her breathless and a little off kilter. "Tell me you'll have dinner with me," he ordered.

"Yes," she breathed. Corbin released her, gave her a curt nod, and before Ava even knew what happened, was gone from her hotel room. He left her standing there confused and backtracking in her mind, trying to figure out what the hell just happened. If she was remembering the last few seconds correctly, she had just agreed to not only go to dinner with Corbin Eklund but to give him a chance to completely destroy her life and break her heart.

"Fuck," Ava whispered.

CORBIN

The next day, Corbin had woken before the sun, still trying to adapt to his jet lag. With all the traveling he did, he should be used to the time differences but he wasn't. Plus, he chalked up some of his insomnia to the fact that he couldn't wait for his date with Ava. He knew she was probably getting ready for work but he didn't want to check on her. He would just wait to see her tonight for their date. Besides, he had a lot of prep work to do if he was going to make it as magical as possible for Ava. He wanted to sweep her off her feet and convince Avalon to give him a chance and judging by her cold reception of him last night, he had his work cut out for him.

He had settled into the room next to Ava's and found where the staff had put his luggage. Last night hadn't gone exactly how he planned but he was counting it as a win. If he had his way, they would have ended up in one of their beds, but judging from the skepticism he saw every time he looked at Ava, she wouldn't allow that. Getting her to agree to a date was a major victory for him and one that he wouldn't let fall flat. His first order of business would be to book the best table in town. He had a few favorite restaurants in France but one stuck out as the clear choice for their date. It was elegant and perfect, just like Ava and he was sure she'd love it.

Corbin would spend the day planning an unforgettable evening for Ava and then he'd talk her into spending the night with him. She had given him his chance and there was no way he was going to blow it again. This time, he'd do things the right way.

❄

After spending the day making arrangements, he knocked on Ava's hotel door promptly at six, as she requested. She answered after his second knock and when she pulled the door open to reveal that she was in just a white fluffy bathrobe, he nearly swallowed his tongue.

"Um—you look hot, honey but I think you might be a little underdressed for dinner," he teased.

Ava smirked at him and ushered him into her room. "Well, I got stuck in an afternoon meeting that didn't feel like it was ever going to end. I decided to take a quick bath and then realized that I might have misjudged my time in the tub. Sorry," she offered. The thought of Ava naked and soaking in a tub full of bubbles had his cock springing to life and he wasn't sure he would be able to make it through the rest of the evening if she didn't put some clothes on fast. He silently pleaded with himself to remember that he didn't want to fuck up tonight and taking her to dinner and not just fucking her was a major part of his plan.

"I'll be ready in ten," she promised, grabbing her dress from her bed and sauntering off to the bathroom. She left the door open a crack and Corbin knew he was going to need a distraction in order to keep from peeking in on her.

"Take your time," he offered. "Our reservations aren't for another thirty minutes."

"Reservations?" she asked. "Wow, you've been busy today," she said. "By the way, the flowers you sent were lovely." Ava came out of the bathroom wearing a sapphire blue cocktail dress and she nearly took his breath away.

"You look gorgeous, honey," he said. Ava suddenly seemed nervous, smoothing her hands down her curves and he wished they were his hands feeling her every outline.

"Thanks," she said. "I picked this up today. I really wasn't planning on having many fancy dinners out while I was here. I have to admit, I was unprepared, but working in the fashion industry affords some luxuries."

"So, no special dinners out then?" he asked.

Ava shook her head. "No," she whispered. "Honestly, when I'm in France, it's all business. I don't have time for fancy dinners and usually just get room service and catch up on work." Hearing that Ava wasn't dating her way through the French male population as he feared while he was sitting back home, gave him hope.

Ava giggled, "You look as if you're relieved, Corbin," she teased.

"Well, it's just good to know that your whole stance on no promises didn't mean that you were running off to France to go out with other guys," he said.

"Is that what you thought? That I made that statement so I could come here and sleep with every man I met?" Her tone was teasing but Corbin could tell from the hint of anger that she was testing him.

"Yes, and no," he admitted. "My imagination got the best of me and all I could think about was you with another man. Fuck, just that thought alone drove me insane, honey," he admitted. He wasn't sure if his honesty would earn him any points but he wouldn't give her anything less than the truth.

"I said what I did for your benefit, Corbin. I didn't want you to think that our one night together had me believing that you were making me any promises," she said. "I know the score

—it was just one night and you like to hang out at the club. I said that we would make each other no promises for your benefit, not mine." He nodded and took a step towards her, wanting to close some of the distance between them.

"You keep saying that you know the score, Ava but I'm not sure you do. What if I want to make you some promises?" he asked. She looked him up and down, silently questioning him. Corbin knew he was throwing a wrench in their "keep it casual" mantra, but he just didn't care anymore. It was time he laid all his cards on the table and let Avalon know just where he stood.

Ava looked just as nervous about their little date as he felt. Honestly, this was all new to him—taking a woman out to dinner and having to make conversation.

"So," Ava stuttered. Corbin reached down to take her hand into his, trying to help steady her nerves.

"So," he whispered back. "You don't have to be nervous, Ava. It's just me," he offered.

"I know but this is starting to feel suspiciously like a date and I am usually a bundle of nerves on a first date," she admitted.

"Well, I'm glad this feels like a date because that is exactly what I want it to be. I hope that's all right with you?" he said, waiting for her to give her agreement. Ava slowly nodded her head, her brown curls played in her eyes and he reached down to gently brush them back from her face. He liked the way Ava leaned into his touch, as if she craved it.

"As for the first date jitters; you can just forget them because this isn't our first date—not really," he said.

"You can't seriously consider the night in the club to be our first date. We didn't do much dating, as I recall," she teased.

"Nope," he said. He smiled at her and squeezed her hand into his. "Our first date was the first night we met—at Aiden's. As I recall, you went out to have ice cream with the girls and me." He remembered that night as if it was just yesterday. The news story leaked about Zara and Aiden and he met the most beautiful woman he had ever seen in his life—Ava. She took care of her best friend like a fierce mother hen and everything about her seemed to do it for him. If he remembered correctly, he was the one feeling like he had a million butterflies take up residence in his tummy and to say he was tongue-tied was an understatement. He forgot his own damn name every time Ava even looked in his direction. If he was being honest with himself, it was at that moment that his world started to spin off kilter and the only time it he felt any peace was when she was near.

"That doesn't count," she countered.

"It certainly does. I treated and you even shared that your favorite ice cream was chocolate chip. I think that definitely counts as a first date," he said.

"Why'd you wait so long to ask me on a second date then?" she asked. That was a good question. Their ice cream date happened months ago and so much had happened since, but that had nothing to do with his reason for not asking her out again.

"I was a coward," he admitted. "I was afraid you'd say no. Hell, the only way I got you to the club and into my bed was to basically dare you."

"Well, a bet is something I never renege on," she said. "I wouldn't have said no, by the way," she whispered. Corbin ran his thumb over her palm, eliciting a shiver from her.

"Thank you for telling me that, Ava," he said. "I'd like to get to know you a little better," he admitted.

Ava nodded, "Sure, I'm an open book. What would you like to know, Corbin?" He sat down on the side of her bed, trying for casual but kept a hold of her hand, needing their connection.

"Tell me about your family," he asked.

"What about our reservations?" she questioned.

"We have a little time," he lied, pulling her down to sit on his lap.

"Okay well, my grandfather was a Senator. In fact, Aiden now occupies his old Senate seat," she started.

"Yes, I'm aware," Corbin said. "I was sorry to hear about your grandfather's passing. It was all over the news. That must have been tough for you and your family, having it thrown in your face that way."

Ava shrugged, "Not really. I was taught that having power and money is nice but it comes with some drawbacks—like always being in the public eye. That's probably why I like traveling abroad so much. Here, no one really knows my family and I'm free to just be me. That must sound silly," she said.

"No, not at all," Corbin admitted. "After our company started growing, Aiden and I had to get used to people thinking that they should have the freedom to look into our private lives. Hell, once Aiden started his run for your grandfather's vacant Senate seat, things got crazy. I can't leave work without being hounded by cameras and reporters screaming questions at me about my best friend."

"Yeah well, welcome to my everyday life," she sassed.

"I'm sorry," he offered. "Are you close with your parents?"

"No," Ava said without hesitation. "My mother died when I was just five and my father was left to raise me. Well, him and an army of nannies," she said.

"Army?" Corbin questioned.

"Yes," Ava said. "Unfortunately, my father used my nannies as his personal dating service. After my current nanny agreed to have sex with him, he moved her out and called the agency for another to be sent over. Honestly, I don't know how many he went through. I lost count after a while."

"Jesus, baby. I'm so sorry that you had to live that way," he said.

"It wasn't all bad. My dear father was too busy making his conquests to notice me and he occupied my nannies so I could do as I pleased, for the most part. If it wasn't for my grandfather, I would have been all alone in the world. My favorite memories were of the two of us just hanging out in his big old house when I spent the weekends with him." She shrugged, "At least I have Zara now, so I'm not completely alone."

Corbin hated the sadness that he saw in her eyes. He wished he could tell her that she wasn't alone, that he was there for her, but he also knew that things between them were still too new for such declarations.

"No brothers or sisters?" Corbin asked.

"I had a brother. He was older than me by ten years and we weren't close. He went away to college and that's when he disappeared. No one knows what happened to him," she whispered. Corbin remembered hearing something about the disappearance of the rich frat boy who was the Senator's son. He had no idea the kid was Avalon's brother.

"I remember that," Corbin said. "I was a teenager at the time it happened but I recall hearing the news stories about his disappearance. That must have been horrible for you."

"I know this makes me sound like a fucking awful person, but like I said, we weren't very close. After my mother died, our family kind of fell apart. I had a very lonely childhood, except the time I had with Grandpa. I guess that's why I nabbed Zara up as soon as we met. She had no family and my own was broken. She used to come home with me on semester breaks from college. We'd celebrate Christmas with my Grandfather and she would tell me how lucky I was. I never had the nerve to tell her that my life wasn't as picture perfect as it seemed. I've never told anyone this—well, until now."

Corbin's heart beat a little faster and he wasn't sure how to respond to her admission. Hearing that she trusted him with her sad past made him want her even more—if that was possible. Still, a part of him wondered if it was futile for him to get his hopes up.

"Why tell me? Why now?" Corbin questioned.

"I'm not really sure," Ava admitted. "Talking to you is easier than I thought it would be. Maybe it's that I feel safe with you—I don't know," she said.

"Thank you, Ava," Corbin whispered. "I'm glad you feel safe with me. I'd never do anything to hurt you," he offered.

"Well, now, that remains to be seen, Corbin," she said. "Trusting you with my past is one thing, but I'm still not so sure I can trust you with my heart."

Corbin hated that she wouldn't trust him with everything but he understood that he had to earn that from her. "How about we just take this nice and slow?" he asked. "You know get to really know each other before we decide what we can and can't be."

"I think I'd like that," Avalon agreed. "How slow are we talking here?"

"Well," he thought. Corbin hated the idea of not ending up in bed with her again tonight. Every time he was near her, his body hummed to life and all he could think about was making her his again. But rushing Avalon into anything might be a giant mistake and one that could lose him his chance with her.

"How slow do you need me to go, Darlin'?" he asked.

AVALON

They had a quiet ride to the restaurant and all Ava could think about was Corbin's questions. Ava wasn't quite sure how to answer. She wanted to tell him to take her back to her room—or his for that matter and fuck her until she forgot everything but his name. Ava worried that might be more than he was planning for them tonight and she decided to just play things the way he wanted.

Plus, there was the whole subject she didn't share with Corbin when he was asking her questions about her past and her family. How did she just blurt out that she had to get married in the next month and a half or lose everything her beloved grandfather had left her? She had no problem telling Corbin what an ass her father was, but she conveniently left out the part where he conned her grandfather into putting a marriage clause in his will to try to trick her out of her money. Hell, the whole thing sounded crazy to her and maybe that was why she didn't share with Corbin. Ava hated she was going to have to come clean with him but there was really no other way. Time was ticking and she had less than six weeks before her thirtieth birthday to find a man who wanted to marry her so she could claim her inheritance, keeping it out of her father's hands. It was the least she could do for her grandfather. She knew he wouldn't want any of his money going to his son. Ava remembered just how much her grandfather disliked her father and that made this whole thing so surreal. Why would her grandfather allow her dad to manipulate him into changing his will to add the marriage clause? It was something she planned on getting to the bottom to once she got back home. But for now, she had a very large, sexy problem that followed her to France and she needed to figure him out first.

They were seated in a private corner of the small Italian restaurant and Corbin seemed to have planned their evening down to the very expensive bottle of wine waiting for them on the small table. He helped her into her seat and sat so close to her, she was sure that they would elicit stares from other diners, but no one even glanced their direction.

The waiter poured them both a glass of wine, told them the specials and disappeared with a nod, promising to return soon to take their orders. Ava felt flustered and nervous suddenly being alone with Corbin again.

"You seem nervous again, honey," he chided, taking her hand in his own. Just that simple gesture had her relaxing some.

"I was just thinking about how I should answer your question," she admitted.

"My question?" he asked.

"Yes, the one about how slowly I'd like us to take this—well, whatever this is between us," she said.

"Don't think about your answer," he prompted. "Just tell me what you want, Ava," he said.

"How about we see how tonight goes and take our cue from there?" she questioned.

"I'd like that," he admitted. The waiter reappeared and Corbin asked if she'd mind if he ordered for the both of them. Honestly, she was happy to let him make that decision for her. Corbin threw her for a loop when he ordered in Italian and his shy smile after the waiter left just about made her swoon like a love struck teenage girl.

"I just realized that I know nothing about you, Corbin," she said. "You speak Italian?"

"Yes, Spanish, French and a little Russian too," he admitted.

"Wow," she breathed.

He shrugged, "It's not a big deal, really," he said, playing off his impressive talent.

"I'd like to know more about you," she said.

He held his arms wide, "I'm an open book, ask away," he offered, throwing her earlier words back at her.

"Tell me about your childhood," she asked.

Corbin chuckled, "Geeze honey, you should look into becoming a therapist," he teased. Ava knew he was avoiding her question but she was willing to wait him out. She sat back in her seat and smiled at him until Corbin seemed to take the hint that she wasn't going to let him off the hook so easily.

"Well, you met my mother at Aiden and Zara's wedding," he started.

"Yes, Rose is lovely. She seems too young to be your mother though," she said.

Corbin's laughter filled the small room. "She loves to tell people I'm her brother. Honestly, she was way too young to have me. My mother got pregnant with me when she was just sixteen. It was a huge scandal in her little town and her parents all but disowned her for it. They tried to get her to abort the pregnancy but Mom refused and well, here I am," Corbin said motioning to himself.

"That's awful," Ava whispered.

"Yeah, my grandparents aren't the nicest people. They are still around but I don't see them much. My mother tries, she really does, but they treat her like crap still. All I have to say is my mother should be sainted for putting up with their bullshit." Corbin sipped his wine and when he didn't seem as if he was going to share anymore, Ava decided to pry a little deeper.

"And your dad?" she hesitantly asked. "Are you close with him?"

"No," Corbin said. "When my mom told him she was pregnant, he took off. He was quite a bit older and he didn't want to deal with the possibility of going to jail. When my grandparents threatened to press charges, he ran and the last my mother heard about him, he had ended up in prison for fraud and tax evasion."

"Wow," Ava breathed, "your poor mother."

Corbin shrugged, "She did just fine without the bastard if you ask me. She raised me and let me tell you, that was no easy feat. When Aiden's mother took off and his father started drinking, mom took him in too."

"Have you known Aiden your whole life?" Ava asked.

"Since we were ten. He became my best friend and once my mother decided to basically take him in, he became like a brother to me," Corbin admitted.

"Kind of like Zara and me," Ava said.

"Exactly," Corbin confirmed.

"So, no brothers or sisters either?" she asked.

"Nope," he said. "Mom never really even dated when I was growing up. I guess she had her hands full with me and then Aiden."

"She had to have been lonely," Ava said. "How about now that you are both grown?"

"God no," Corbin growled. "The last thing I want to even think about is my mother out with a man." Corbin made a face and she giggled.

"It wouldn't be as bad as that, Corbin. She's a beautiful woman and still young. Maybe she'll meet someone nice. Don't you want your mom to be happy?" Ava asked.

"Not like that," Corbin admitted. "Mom has Aiden and she loves his girls as if they were her own grandchildren. I'd say her life is pretty full." Ava could tell that Corbin wasn't about to budge on the matter and she gave up trying to push the topic.

Besides, it wasn't really her place to question whether or not Corbin's mother should or shouldn't be hitting the dating scene.

"So, you are pretty much up to speed on my childhood," he teased. Ava giggled. There was still so much she felt like she wanted to ask but Corbin seemed to be finished talking about himself.

"How long do you plan on staying in France?" Ava asked, changing the subject.

"That depends," he said.

"On?" she asked.

"On how long you will be in France. I came all this way, Ava and I don't plan on returning home without you," he admitted. Ava wanted to protest that Corbin couldn't just sit around and wait for her to finish her business all the while putting his life on hold, but judging from his determined look, he wasn't going to budge an inch on the subject.

"So that's your plan?" Ava asked. "You're just going to sit in your hotel room day in and day out waiting for me to finish up at work?"

"Naw, Darlin'," he said. "I have plenty of work to keep me busy and I was hoping to get you to agree to come back to my house and we could both get out of that cramped hotel," he said.

"Wait," Ava always felt as if she had to be on her toes around Corbin. He seemed to move at lightning speed and now was no exception. "You have a house here—in France?"

"Yep," he said. The waiter brought their food and Corbin waited for him to leave before filling her in on all the details. "It's not far from here. I'd love to take you by and give you a tour after dinner," he said.

Ava nodded, "I'd love to see your house," she admitted.

"Great," Corbin said. "Eat up and we can head out."

"You are full of surprises, Corbin," she admitted. Ava knew she was going to have to drop one major surprise of her own, but she also knew that timing was everything. She wanted one last night with Corbin and then she'd find a way to walk away. It was time for her to get her head on straight and either find a way around her father's latest scheme or come up with one damn good plan. One thing she knew for sure, she wouldn't drag Corbin into her family's drama or this mess with her father.

"Oh honey, I'm just getting started," he insisted. Ava wasn't sure if she should be excited or afraid of just how true he made that statement sound.

CORBIN

Corbin was having trouble reading Avalon. One minute she seemed to be on board with the possibilities of them testing the waters to see where this thing between the two of them was heading and other times she was cold and distant. It was almost as if she was trying to push him away.

He decided to show her his place just outside of town and hopefully convince her to spend the rest of her time with him while she was in France. If not, he'd be keeping his room right next to hers at the hotel. Either way, he didn't have any plans on letting sexy little Avalon out of his sight.

They finished dinner and he decided to let his driver go for the night. He drove the two of them out to his place and when they pulled in, he didn't miss the way Ava looked at his house. He took the fact that she was smiling as a good thing and when she got out of his car and practically ran up the steps to go into the front foyer, he knew she liked it.

"This is your place?" she questioned. "I pass this house on the way out of town, heading to the airport. I love this place.

Doesn't it have a garden on the side with a little gazebo?" Corbin slyly nodded. He wasn't one to put much stock in where he lived. He still thought of the little shit hole that he and Aiden shared in college as his favorite home. But seeing the way his place brought out such excitement in Ava made him happy.

"How do you keep up with a place this big? You must come here a lot," she continued, spinning around the grand foyer as if checking over every square inch of the entryway.

"I have a housekeeper and a gardener who is also quite handy. Mr. and Mrs. Bisset are married and they take care of this place when I can't be here. I do like to spend most of my free time in France though," he admitted.

"Hmm," she hummed. "I never pegged you as a guy who'd vacation in France much less own a house here. I'm here a good bit of the year too—for work. It's almost crazy that we never ran into each other here since it's such a small town." Corbin had to admit he wondered the same thing.

He shrugged, "Well, you said you don't go out when you are here and I like to hit the clubs and do the whole French night life thing." Avalon wrinkled her nose, almost as if she smelled something bad.

"Yeah," she said. "I don't really care for the night clubs or bars in town. When I'm here, it's all business."

"We should do something about that," Corbin offered. "How about you let me take you out to some of the area clubs tomorrow night?" He didn't want to feel so nervous about asking her out again, but he was. Corbin felt as though he was holding his breath waiting for her answer.

"I don't know," she whispered. "I have a busy day tomorrow —lots of meetings."

Corbin nodded, not wanting to let her off so easily. He wanted more time with her and letting Ava come up with any excuse to avoid him, didn't play into his plans. "Then a quiet dinner in?" He asked, still hopeful.

"How about you give me a tour of your place and then we can talk about tomorrow," Ava offered.

"What's going on here, honey?" Corbin asked.

"I thought you were showing me your house," Ava said, resting her hands on her hips. It was her telltale sign that she was going to get shouty about something and it usually involved her stomping her little feet and making Corbin completely hot in the process.

"Sure, I'll show you around and then what?" Corbin asked. "I'm starting to get the feeling that you are going to give me the brush off and I have to tell you that won't work for me, Darlin'." Corbin pulled Ava against his body, but she refused to lower her arms that she had perched on her hips, making it damn near impossible to get close to her. The whole scene was almost comical but he knew better than to laugh judging from her very serious expression.

"I'm not sure what you want from me, Corbin," she sternly warned. "I thought we were just having fun and not making any promises."

"Fuck, Ava," he growled. "Are we seriously back to the whole 'no promises' thing?" he asked. "I thought I was pretty clear when I explained that I want to make you some fucking promises," he shouted. Avalon pulled free from his hold and he instantly regretted his tone.

"You can't make me the kind of promises I need from you, Corbin. You're not ready for what I need right now and you might never be. I'm running out of time," she whispered.

Corbin wasn't sure why they suddenly had to worry about a time limit and he was pissed that Ava had already weighed and measured him. He wanted a fucking chance to prove himself, but she wasn't willing to even meet him halfway.

"I knew the score when I hopped into bed with you, Corbin. I told you it's fine. You like to play with subs at the club and I was one of them. You don't own me anything and I'm fine with that," she said.

"Well, I'm not fucking fine with any of it," he grumbled. "How many times do I have to tell you that I want more with you, Ava? You are the most stubborn woman on the planet."

"Gee, thanks for that," she teased.

"Really, Ava. How about you tell me what it is you don't think I'm willing to give you? What is it you need that I can't do or be for you?" he asked. Ava sat down on the small settee and looked up at him, almost as if pleading for him to take back his questions, but he wouldn't. It was time that they both laid their cards on the table and he was done with dancing around the truth.

"I want to get married," she whispered.

"And you don't think that I can give you that? I told you that I'm not playing at the club. Hell, I followed you all the way to France to tell you that I don't want anyone else but you. I was so afraid that you wouldn't make me any promises when you left because you wanted to date other men while you were here."

Ava barked out her laugh. "While I appreciate your grand gesture of showing up here to make sure I wasn't dating my way through the French male population, it's still not enough."

"Then tell me what else it is that I have to do to convince you that I'm ready to take a chance here, Ava," he said.

"Marry me," she offered.

Now it was Corbin's turn to laugh. "I'm flattered but don't you think we should go on a few more dates first?" he teased.

"How many more dates are we talking?" she asked.

Corbin crossed the room to sit down next to her on the small sofa. Red flags were waving like crazy and he knew that he was missing something but she wasn't giving any hints as to what it might be. He pulled Ava onto his lap and was surprised that she actually allowed him to hold her.

"Talk to me, Ava," he ordered. "Tell me what the hell is going on with you, please," he begged.

"I can't," she whispered. "You'll think I'm insane," she admitted.

"I already think that," he teased. "All I can piece together is that I'm crazy about you and I'd like to think you feel the same way about me," he said.

"I do," she whispered.

"Great, then why do you keep pushing me away and shooting me down at every turn? One minute, you seem to be happy and we're having fun and the next you can't even commit to another dinner."

"Tonight was going to be our last night together," she admitted. Before he could protest, Ava covered his mouth with her hand. "Please just let me finish," she demanded. Corbin nodded and sat back. He asked her to come clean with him and the least he could do was hear her out.

"Thank you," she said. "I need to get married and I know that isn't what you are looking for right now." Corbin opened his mouth to contradict her but quickly shut it again when she shot him a stern warning look.

"I know you say you want me and you'd like to see where this is going between us but I honestly don't have time to do that. About two weeks before you dared me to show up at the club, my father dropped a bomb that my inheritance, that I received from my grandfather, had a few strings and stipulations tied to the money."

"Marriage strings?" he asked.

"Yes," she said. "I have about six weeks to get married or my money goes to my father."

Corbin whistled, "Why would your grandfather do that to you?" he asked.

"I'm not really sure," she said. "My father said something about convincing him that by ensuring that I was married by thirty, it would also help make sure the family line continues. But, I don't buy that for a minute. I think my father had something he could use to blackmail my grandfather and that's how he got him to amend his will. Either way, I had my lawyers look at it and he's right. I now have just weeks before I either have to find a man and get married or lose everything."

Corbin wasn't sure if he wanted to ask his next question but he also had to know. "That night at the club—was that about this whole marriage deal?" God, that sounded worse out loud than it did in his head, if that was possible.

"No!" Ava shouted. "I'd never try to trap you or anyone else into marrying me, Corbin." She tugged his arms free and stood from his lap. "I'd rather lose my fortune than spend the rest of my life trapped in an unhappy marriage. Besides, you said it yourself—I've been pushing you away because I don't want to hurt you. That would be the last thing I want," she admitted.

Corbin felt like a complete louse for even asking his question. "I'm sorry but I had to know," he said. "But, what's the plan here, Ava? You push me away and then what? How were you planning on finding some guy to agree to marry you?"

"It's more complicated than that," she said. "Not only do I have to find some 'guy,' as you put it, to marry me but we have to prove that we are committed and in love."

"What the fuck?" Corbin asked. "How will you prove that?"

"My father has hired a team of people to follow my new husband and I around to make sure we are truly as happy as we will hopefully portray. We would have to submit to questions and pass tests along the way. After our six-month anniversary, if my father can't prove that I've married for convenience and money, rather than love, I walk away with my money and he gets nothing."

"That sounds fucking awful," Corbin admitted. "How can your dad do that to you?" he asked.

"I told you we don't get along. My father has always been jealous of the relationship my grandfather and I had. I guess this is just his way of getting back at me," she admitted.

"Threats and interrogation seem like one hell of a way to go about getting back at someone, honey," he said.

"Yeah, but that's just a normal day for my family. It's one of the reasons why I try to steer clear of my father but now I don't really have a choice in the matter." Corbin could feel his wheels spinning and a plan forming. If he played his cards right, he'd be able to convince Avalon to give him a chance and be able to help her out with her situation.

"Okay," he agreed. Ava stopped pacing for a moment to look down to where he still sat.

"Sorry, okay what?" she questioned.

"Okay, I'll marry you," he said.

AVALON

Ava wasn't sure if she had heard Corbin correctly or if the exhaustion of traveling and work accompanied by the drama her father heaped on her, was all starting to catch up with her. She couldn't have heard him correctly, could she? Had Corbin Eklund just agreed to marry her?

"You can't be serious," she chided.

"Why the hell not?" he asked. Ava hated that she made him feel the need to defend himself but he couldn't mean what he said.

"Because you and I barely know each other. Did you not just hear a single word I said? I have to prove that my new husband and I are married for love and not convenience or money. You and I would have to submit to vigorous questioning and constantly being watched. We wouldn't ever be able to let our guards down for the next six months. I can't ask you to live like that, Corbin," she said.

"Fine, then don't ask. I'm offering, Avalon," he said.

"And what will you get out of the deal?" she questioned. Ava knew that Corbin was a shrewd businessman and he would want something in return.

"You." He shrugged. "I'd get you."

Ava giggled, "I think you're getting the raw end of the deal," she admitted.

"Not at all," he said. "Be my submissive," he offered. "You get a husband and I get a sub. We can get married and spend the next few weeks getting to know each other while we're in France. Then, by the time we go home, it won't be difficult to convince everyone that we are anything but a happily married couple, madly in love with each other."

"And at the end of six months, you'll be free to move on. You'll have to stick it out with me until the deadline," she said. Ava wanted to ask him for more but she really had no right to. He was offering her so much more than she ever hoped for and that would have to be enough for now.

"How about we just get through the next half of the year and then we can decide where we go from there?" he asked. Corbin held out his hand for her to shake, almost as if he were brokering a business deal.

"You'll be my submissive both in and out of the bedroom, Ava. In return, I'll be your husband and you get to keep your inheritance," he said.

Ava hesitated taking his hand. "You know first-hand that I'm a lousy sub," Ava said. "What happens if I disobey you?" She had a pretty good idea what his answer was going to be but she wanted to hear it for herself.

"I will come up with creative ways to punish that sexy ass of yours, honey," he admitted. "But, I will also reward you when you please me," he offered. The thought of having Corbin do anything to her made her skin feel warm and tingly all over. She couldn't seem to get the picture of him spanking her ass red out of her head and she started thinking of all the naughty things she could come up with to make that happen.

"I can see from the mischievous glint in your eye that I'm going to have my hands full with you, aren't I, Ava?" Corbin asked. She smiled and nodded.

"I won't lie," she said. "I like the idea of you spanking me when I misbehave," she sassed.

"I'll also withhold your release," he promised. "Only good girls get orgasms," he said. Ava pouted and he laughed. "Yeah, now you're getting it, honey."

"Do we have a deal?" he asked, still holding out his hand.

"Yes," she said, placing her hand into his and giving a firm shake. Corbin scooped her up into his arms causing her to squeal. "What are you doing?" she asked.

"I'm taking my new sub up to my bedroom and tying her to my bed," he said.

"But we need to talk about the wedding," she insisted.

"We can get married tomorrow as far as I'm concerned," he said. "Tonight, you are mine," he growled and Ava shivered from the promise she heard in his voice. She didn't want to admit that she would be his every night if he wanted her. She kept that bit of information to herself.

Corbin carried her up the stairs as if she weighed nothing and when he got to his master suite, he turned on the lights, causing Ava to blink against the brightness. "Are you going to leave those on?" she questioned.

"Yes," he said, pushing her up against the wall. Ava wrapped her legs around his waist and could feel his erection pushing into her core. Suddenly the idea of having the lights on seemed to frighten her a little less, especially with the way he was looking at her as if she was his next meal.

"Corbin, please," she whimpered, rubbing herself against him.

"Hold still, Ava," he demanded. "I'll take care of you but I won't allow you to top from the bottom."

Ava was still so new to this whole Dom/sub thing. She was sure that asking what topping from the bottom meant might get her into trouble but her curiosity got the better of her.

"Um," she squeaked as Corbin kissed his way down her jaw to her neck. "What exactly does that mean?" Ava wasn't sure if his heated gaze turned her on or scared the shit out of her.

"It means, Little One, that you are trying to take the upper hand. You are claiming to be submissive but trying to remain in control," he growled. She shot him a sheepish grin, not really trying to hide the fact that he was correct.

"Do you know what happens to pretty little subs who try to hold onto their control, Ava?"

She shook her head, "No," she admitted.

"No what?" Corbin demanded. Ava liked the way he pushed her for more; it made her want to give him everything.

"No, Sir," she stuttered as he stared her down.

"Well, my beautiful submissive, why don't I just show you?" He lowered her to the floor and Ava reluctantly released her legs from his waist. Corbin pulled her along with him to his bed and he sat down on the end of the mattress. "Strip," he commanded.

"You want me to take my clothes off?" Avalon asked. She swallowed past the lump in her throat, not sure if she wanted to laugh or cry.

"Yes," he barked. "Slowly—take them off slowly. You remember your safe word?"

Ava remembered it and she worried that she was going to have to use it tonight, judging by the heat in Corbin's eyes, he wasn't going to go easy on her. "Yes," she said. "Ice cream."

"Good girl," he praised. "Now, strip," he said, reminding her of his original order. She had never taken her clothes off for a man while he watched before and she had to admit it made her downright uncomfortable. Ava tried to pull her zipper down but she was too nervous to get it to work.

"Turn around," Corbin ordered. She didn't hesitate, doing exactly as he asked. He slowly pulled the zipper down her back, letting his fingertips brush her skin as they went, eliciting shivers from her overly sensitive body.

As soon as he finished, he turned her back around so she

was once again facing him. "Go on," he said. Ava smiled and let her cocktail dress slide down her body to reveal that she was wearing nothing underneath. She loved the way Corbin's breath hitched as he looked her bare body up and down.

"Fuck, if I had known you weren't wearing anything under that skimpy little dress all night, we wouldn't have made it through dinner," he admitted.

"So, you like?" she questioned, spinning slowly around. Corbin gave a sharp slap to her ass and she yelped.

"Do you like, Sir?" he corrected.

"Sorry," she hissed. "Do you like, Sir?"

"Yes," he confirmed. "You are so fucking hot, Avalon. Now, it's time to get onto your punishment for topping from the bottom. You ready?" He looked at her as if he was staring her down waiting for her to safe word him already. Ava always loved a good challenge. If he was going to marry her, he would learn that fact soon enough.

"Yes, Sir," she agreed. "I'm ready." Corbin chuckled and pulled her across his lap. Ava had tried spanking for pleasure during her training as a sub at the club back home. She had never been spanked as a punishment and she wondered if it would feel the same. She had to admit that she liked being spanked and she was hoping that Corbin wouldn't figure out that little fact until she was wet, completely turned on and getting off on his thigh.

"You will need to keep count," he ordered. "We are going to twenty and then we'll see how you feel from there."

"Yes, Sir," she said. Corbin didn't give any warning, just brought his palm down to land a firm slap on her right cheek. She yelped from the sting of his hand and choked out, "One."

He didn't bother with niceties like gently rubbing each blow to help her acclimate to his palm meeting her flesh. He wasn't sugar coating her punishment and God help her, Ava wanted to use her safe word but that would mean admitting defeat and that wasn't who she was. She kept count with him, blow for blow, just as he ordered.

"Eighteen," she finally cried out. Ava realized that her face was wet from her own tears and she wondered if Corbin would be able to tell that she had been crying. She hated the thought of giving him that satisfaction.

"Nineteen," she growled through her gritted teeth. The last blow was the hardest and nearly took her breath away, "Twenty," she sobbed. Corbin rubbed her ass and just the touch of his skin against her hot flesh was almost too much to bear. Ava was sure she wouldn't be able to sit down the next day and if she did, she would remember every single time Corbin's palm made contact with her ass.

Her heart was racing from the excitement of the whole scene and she wondered how she had gone her whole life without feeling this way with any other man. Her spanking made her feel things beyond just the physical pain and that scared the shit out of her. It was as if her world was spinning too quickly and all she wanted to do was make it stop so she could catch her breath for just a second.

Corbin helped her to stand and when he saw that she had been crying, he stood and pulled her against his body. She didn't make a move to relax in his arms as he wrapped his own around her. "I didn't mean to make you cry, Ava," he said. "Tell me that you're all right," he demanded.

"You want me to lie then?" Ava choked. How could she tell him she was okay when she clearly wasn't? How did she explain to him that she wasn't hurt or upset about the punishment, but that it had quite the opposite effect, making her want things with Corbin and from him that she had never wanted with any other man?

"No, never," he said. He released her and she took a step away from him. The way he looked at her as if she had hurt him, nearly did her in. "Ava," he said, reaching for her but she took yet another step back. She couldn't look at him anymore.

It was all too much and she wasn't sure why she was having such a reaction to his punishment. "I just want to hold you, please," he begged.

Ava needed a minute to pull herself together and figure out what she wanted next. It was as if she couldn't think with him watching her the way he was, as if she was fragile and might break from what he had just done to her.

"I can't—I just need a few minutes," she begged.

"No, let me in, Ava," he said. "Just talk to me. Say something—anything."

"Ice cream," she said and turned to go into the adjoining master bathroom. Her mistake was looking back as she shut the door and seeing the hurt and confusion in Corbin's eyes. She just needed to get her shit together and hurting him wasn't part of the plan but it was too late for that. She had given him her safe word because she was a coward. He had made her feel too much, too fast, and left her no other choice. Ava shut the bathroom door, effectively closing out the man who was beginning to own a piece of her heart and that was enough to make her want to scream her safe word from the rooftops.

CORBIN

A half hour had passed since Avalon used her safe word to hide from him in his bathroom. Corbin refused to leave his bedroom, taking up camp on his bed, waiting for her to come to her senses and come out of the bathroom. He could see all her raw emotions looking back at him through her tears and it gutted him. He knew that her spanking had release so much more than her disobedience. He could hear it in her voice every time she choked out her count and God help him; he could see it in her tear-stained cheeks when he finally released her body from his lap and she pushed him away. He felt the same hurt and panic he saw on her beautiful face and all he wanted to do was hold her and tell her that everything was going to be all right—but she wouldn't allow that. She said the only thing that would stop him from demanding that she obey him—her safe word.

He hated how she wasn't letting him in and talking about what had just happened between the two of them but he wouldn't force her to talk to him. Avalon's past with her father and lack of family support had to instill trust issues and he knew from his own experiences that breaking through those barriers would take time. Ava was worth the wait and effort he was going to have to give, but there would be no walking away from her—not now.

When she told him about the way her father had twisted and manipulated her grandfather to change his will, his heart ached for her. His father at least did him the favor of walking out on him and his mother before he could fuck them both up. Ava had to endure living with a dad who obviously didn't care what happened to her. He wanted to show her that not all men hurt women and that he especially would never do anything to hurt Ava. He wanted to be the person she turned to when things got rough and he was hopeful that someday she'd let him be that for her, but then she ran to hide in the bathroom, taking all his hope for their future together.

It was really a no-brainer when he had agreed to marry Ava. Hell, she was the first woman that he had ever entertained the possibility of marriage with. Avalon brought something out in him that he wasn't sure existed until they spent their one night together. He had no idea how they were going to make this whole thing work, but Corbin knew that he couldn't just let her walk out of his life and give some other asshole a chance to make her happy. Ava seemed determined to find a husband to beat her father's marriage clause and keep her inheritance. She seemed to be the type of woman who loved a good challenge and he knew from experience she wouldn't back down from her own father when he threw down the flag and challenged her to find a husband.

Ava cracked the bathroom door open and peeked out; not retreating into the dark bathroom after she found him sprawled across the bed. Corbin took that as a good sign and hoped that she was finally ready to talk. He just wanted a chance with her, but that wouldn't happen if Avalon continued to shut him out both metaphorically and physically.

"Hi," she whispered. He could tell by her tear-stained face that she had been crying in the bathroom and every one of his instincts were screaming at him to go to her and pull her into his arms but Corbin wanted Ava to come to him. She needed to meet him halfway if they were going to find a way to make this thing work.

"Hi," he said back, not moving from his spot on the bed.

"I—I'm sorry," she squeaked. "I freaked out and I ran. I'm sorry," she buried her face in her hands and sobbed. That was all he could take and Corbin was quickly by her side, pulling her into his chest to wrap his arms around her body.

"You have nothing to apologize for, honey," Corbin whispered into her hair. They stood there like that, Ava letting him hold her and he thought that might be the end of it. He wanted to talk about what had just happened between them but he didn't want to push.

"Want to talk about it?" He offered, trying to sound casual about his offer. Ava wasn't the type of woman who liked to feel pressured into anything.

She shrugged and pulled free from his arms, grabbing the blanket that sat on the end of his bed, wrapping it around her bare body. "I told you that I had done some training as a sub?" she asked. Corbin nodded and sat on the chair across the room from where she stood. He knew she would need a little space and he was willing to give it to her, for now.

"Well, I did most of my training at the club but not all of it. Some I did here in France," she admitted. Corbin could tell by her expression that he might not like what she was about to say.

"Did someone hurt you?" he growled.

"No," she quickly admitted. "Not really. I like a little pain, or at least I thought I did."

"So, you're telling me you didn't like the spanking, but it wasn't for your pleasure," Corbin said. "Listen, if this is all too much for you—"

"It's not," she shouted. "Please, let me finish, Corbin." Ava was right to be mad at him, he was acting like an overbearing ass and that wasn't going to help things between them.

"Sorry," he grumbled. "You're right." He waved his hand at her to continue and she rolled her eyes at him.

"Thanks," she sassed. "I never really gave the whole BDSM thing a fair try. I would go into the club to work with a Dom here and there, but I never liked giving up that much control of myself. I had a few Doms tell me that I just wasn't submissive and that I should maybe look into becoming a Domme, but that never felt quite right either. I tried, really tried to do what they asked of me, but I didn't seem to get as much pleasure as they thought I should have from trying to meet their demands. I stopped training, believing that I just wasn't a submissive."

"Bullshit," Corbin interrupted and Ava shot him a look. He held up his hands in defense. "It's a fair statement, Ava. From everything you've shown me at the club and tonight, I would bet money you are submissive. Hell, I'd stake my life on it."

"That's the thing," she said. Ava paced the floor in front of him, letting the blanket fall around her shoulders and Corbin's palms itched to touch her bare skin again. "I thought I wasn't, and I gave up entertaining the idea of ever having a Dom/sub relationship—until I met you. Our first night together opened up a whole new world for me and now, tonight I just can't explain it—I loved it."

Corbin let out his pent-up breath, not realizing he was even holding it. Hearing Ava admit that she liked what they had done so far made him want to demand more from her—he wanted everything, all of her, but he also needed to let Ava finish getting out whatever was bothering her. He didn't want to chance a repeat of her using her safe word to run to the bathroom to hide again.

"I wasn't sure what to expect from tonight. I've never been spanked as a punishment," she admitted. "I've been spanked for pleasure but tonight—what you did to me—it made me feel things I was never sure were possible."

"Like?" Corbin pushed. He was hoping they were at the same place, maybe even on the same page.

"Like, um—well, I might be falling for you," Ava admitted.

Corbin stood and closed the space between them, pulling her against his body again. "Yeah?" he questioned.

"Yes," she whispered. Corbin brazenly pushed the blanket from her body, leaving her completely naked.

"Well, you did agree to be my wife, so falling for me is a good thing, right?" Corbin asked.

"I said I might be falling for you and we both know you are marrying me just to help me out of a jam, Corbin," she said. Maybe it was time that he did some confessing, just as Ava was brave enough to do.

"What if I told you that I might be falling for you too and me asking you to be my wife was purely a selfish gesture?" Ava looked him up and down as if she was trying to decide if she wanted to believe him or not.

"No," she breathed.

"Yep," he admitted. "So, no more hiding?" Corbin waited her out and when she nodded her agreement, he couldn't wait anymore. He crushed his lips against hers, kissing and licking his way into her mouth. He loved her little breathy sighs and moans. Corbin was sure that he wasn't ever going to get enough of them or Ava, but he didn't give a fuck anymore. She was finally going to let him in and that was more than he could have ever asked for.

Ava was panting by the time he broke the kiss and smiled up at him. "I won't promise to be the perfect submissive. Hell, I'm probably going to fuck it up at every turn, but I want to try Corbin," she said.

"Sir," he growled, giving her hair a light tug.

"Sir," she corrected.

"Maybe we should go over some ground rules and training,

Ava," he said. She didn't exactly look thrilled about the prospect of him telling her what he expected from her, and he almost wanted to laugh as she groaned and nodded her agreement.

"Fine," she agreed. "Just as long as you promise that we are going to get to the part where you take your clothes off and we get to actually have sex." Corbin swatted her ass, causing her to yelp. He knew she had to still be sore from her spanking. He didn't go easy on her, and he wouldn't ever promise to. It was just who he was and the sooner Ava learned that, the better.

"First step of your training is going to be learning not to top from the bottom, Baby Girl," he said.

"I told you that I suck at being a submissive," she said, rubbing her ass with her hands.

He grinned, knowing she didn't pick up on her pun but it wasn't a bad idea. "Let's see just how well you can suck as my submissive," he said. Corbin pushed her body down until Ava took the hint and sunk to her knees before him. He unzipped his pants, letting his cock spring free and Avalon hissed out her breath.

"Finally," she almost cheered.

"That remark just earned you another punishment," he said.

Ava covered her ass with her hands, "Please no," she begged. "My ass is already raw."

"I know, honey," Corbin soothed, running his hand down her soft face. "But I have other lovely ways of punishing you without hurting that sweet ass of yours any further." He thought of all the wicked ways he could teach Ava obedience and he had to admit that he hoped she was as mouthy and spunky as he knew she could be. It would give him plenty of opportunity to do every naughty thing he was thinking and then some.

"I don't think I like the sound of that and I definitely don't like that look on your face," she whined. Corbin chuckled. His

Ava was definitely submissive but she was the most reluctant sub he had ever had. Corbin wasn't sure how he was going to tame her and maybe he'd never be able to, but he was going to have a fucking fantastic time trying.

"Oh honey, I'm just getting started," he admitted. "Now open that sweet, sassy mouth of yours," he ordered.

AVALON

Ava wasn't sure if she felt giddy or scared kneeling in front of Corbin as he stroked his heavy shaft waiting for her to comply. She wanted everything he was offering her; that wasn't a question. Ava worried that if she fell completely for Corbin Eklund, her heart wouldn't survive.

He stroked a hand down her face, forcing her to look up at him. "You don't have to do anything you don't want to, honey." She knew that as a submissive, she had the power to make her own decisions. Ava just worried that she was making the right one. She smiled up at him and opened her mouth.

"I want this," she said. She reached for his cock, wrapping her hands around his shaft, and helped to place the head into her open mouth.

"Thank fuck," Corbin exclaimed and thrust himself a little further in. He caressed her face again and her heart was nearly undone by his gentleness. "That's so good, baby," he praised. "Yes, just like that," he moaned as she sucked him to the back of her throat and swallowed around him. Corbin stroked in and out of her willing mouth a few more times and then pulled free. Ava didn't hide her frustrated groan and he chuckled.

"I know, honey," he soothed. "But I want to be inside of you when I come," he said. Corbin helped Avalon from her kneeling position and ordered her up onto his bed.

"I'm going to handcuff you to my bed and then I'm going to fuck you until neither of us has any strength left." Ava whimpered at his promise, not sure she was still capable of making coherent words. She watched as Corbin secured first her wrists and then her ankles to his bedposts using handcuffs. She was completely sprawled out and vulnerable to whatever he wanted to do with her.

Corbin stood back from the bed and looked her over as if admiring his own handy work. "Fuck, baby," he growled. "You look good enough to eat." Ava smiled up at him and he shook his head. "Later, baby. Right now, I need to fuck you," he admitted.

Ava felt the bed dip with his weight and Corbin ran two big fingers through her drenched pussy, checking to see if she was ready for him. She knew that he'd find her more than ready to take him. She tried to rub herself against his fingers, needing more, bucking against her restraints.

"Hold still, Ava," he ordered. "You will hurt yourself if you keep thrashing about." He was right; the bite of the metal handcuffs was more than uncomfortable.

"Please, Corbin," she moaned.

"Sir," he reminded.

"Please, Sir," Ava corrected. "I need you."

"It's okay, baby. I'm going to take good care of you," he promised. He knelt between Ava's legs and thrust balls deep into her body, not giving any warning. Corbin pumped in and out of her drenched pussy, using her body and giving her so much pleasure in return. Ava began to lose track of her orgasms and she didn't remember him unlocking her cuffs and pulling her onto his lap to straddle his cock. He ruthlessly pumped in and out of her body and just when she thought she wouldn't be able to take anymore, he snaked his hand down between their bodies and stroked her sensitive clit, sending her soaring.

"That's right, baby," he crooned. "Come with me," he said. He pumped into her body a few more times and shouted her name when he came.

"Thank you," she whispered, lying limp in his arms.

"Never thank me for that," he said. "It's my pleasure." Corbin rolled them to the mattress and pulled her against his body, wrapping her in his arms. Ava was sure she had never felt more secure or protected in her life and dare she ever dream it possible—loved.

※

The next morning Avalon woke and found the bed empty, but the smell of bacon and coffee wafting down the hall from Corbin's kitchen was enough to wake her up. She found his shirt from the night before lying on the chair in the corner of the room and she pulled it onto her bare body.

Ava wasn't quite sure where his kitchen was, not really having a full tour of his house the night before, but she followed the smell and the racket Corbin was making. She found him standing at his stove, flipping pancakes in just his boxers and Ava suddenly forgot that she was hungry or in dire need of coffee.

"Morning," she said, seeming to startle him. His big body jumped, and she love the way his muscles bunched and flexed, really giving her a good view of his tattoos. He was even more gorgeous in the morning light if that was possible.

"Hey," he said. "Sleep well, beautiful?" Corbin turned off the stove and poured her a cup of coffee, handing it to her, and then carefully pulled her into his arms for a kiss.

"I did," she admitted. "Best sleep I've had in a long time. In fact, I woke up wondering just where I was and that hasn't happened for quite some time."

"Well, I hope you don't make a rule of waking up at strange men's homes in France and forgetting where you are," he teased. She swatted at him and when he let her go, she sat down at his kitchen table and gulped down half her coffee.

"You're up early," she said.

"Yeah, jet lag," he admitted. "I don't sleep well when I'm not at home," he said.

"You should have woken me up," Ava offered. "I'm sure we could have found something to do together to make you tired again," she said and giggled.

"Hmm," he hummed. "You might just be a decent submissive after all," he joked.

"Speaking of being submissive," she said. "Don't we have some rules to go over or something?" She hated the idea of putting rules in place to govern what she hoped was a relationship between the two of them, but Corbin was right last night when he said she could use some more training.

"How about we discuss those tonight?" Corbin offered. "I don't want you to be late for work. I can pick you up and we can have a quiet dinner here if you'd like." Ava's heart seemed to beat a little faster when she heard him mention them going back to his place again. Honestly, she loved his house, and staying there was so much nicer than her hotel, but she didn't want to read into the situation or get her hopes up, only to have them dashed.

Corbin chuckled, "You are way overthinking all of this, Darlin'. I'd like to have dinner with you tonight and if you're okay with the idea, I'd like for you to move out of your hotel and in here with me," he offered.

Ava didn't take any time to think his offer over. Honestly, she didn't need to. After last night, she was willing to do just about anything the gorgeous man sitting next to her wanted, although she'd never admit that to him.

"I'd like that," she said. "I can have the hotel send my things over and that way I won't have to waste time packing later." Ava didn't miss the guilty grimace on Corbin's face and she sighed, "I'm not going to like what you are about to tell me, so just spill it," she ordered.

"I kind of already had the hotel send your belongings over and they are in the foyer." Corbin held up his hands as if in defense and gave her his sexy smirk. "Before you get angry with me, I did it, so you'd be able to get dressed this morning; not because I assumed you'd say yes to my offer."

"But you had a hunch?" She questioned.

"Well, not so much a hunch as I was hopeful," he admitted.

"Fine," she said around a mouthful of pancake. "But we are going over some ground rules tonight—for both of us." She pointed her finger at him, for good measure and Corbin smiled and nodded.

"Deal," he agreed. "Finish eating your breakfast and I'll run you a bubble bath. We have just enough time for one if you hurry," he said. Ava shoved a few bites of bacon into her mouth and Corbin laughed again.

"What?" she asked. "I love a good bubble bath. I'm assuming you will be joining me?"

"Only if you behave yourself," he teased. "I have a meeting this morning and I can't be distracted by your feminine charms."

Ava smiled up at him, "A girl can try," she said, watching as Corbin stacked some dishes in the sink and then disappeared down the hall to his master bedroom.

"A girl can try," she whispered again to herself.

❄

Avalon felt as if her meetings would never end. Her day seemed to drag on with no end in sight and she had a feeling that had everything to do with the sexy man who texted her every hour to tell her how much he missed her. Honestly, she felt the same way and was counting down the minutes until he was supposed to pick her up.

Ava told Corbin that she'd find her own way home, but he insisted that he had business in town and would be around at six to pick her up and he was. She walked out of her office building to find her sexy as-sin Dom standing by the back door of his SUV, arms crossed over his massive chest, waiting for her. She couldn't read his expression behind his dark sunglasses, but judging by the sexy smirk on his face, he was happy to see her.

"You brought your driver?" she asked, hating that he went to any fuss over her. "I could have called for a car and met you back at your place."

Corbin sighed and opened the back door. "I brought my driver so that you and I can talk about our days and God, I've wanted to do this since dropping you off this morning—" Corbin pulled her into his arms and sealed his mouth over hers, kissing her as if he hadn't seen her in months and not just hours. She felt as if he was touching every inch of her body, being pressed up against his and she could think of nothing she wanted more than for Corbin to take her home and strip her bare.

"There," he panted. "That's so much better." He let Ava slide down his body and when she felt his erection jutting into her belly she gasped. Corbin's wolfish grin told her everything she needed to know—he had the same plans as she had for their evening together.

"Wow," she stuttered. "You really missed me," she teased. Ava daringly snaked a hand down between their bodies and cupped his erection through his pants, loving the way his breath hissed out and he leaned into her touch.

"That feels so fucking good, baby," he said. "But this isn't the time or place." He pulled her hand into his own and kissed her fingers, as if trying to ease his rejection. She knew she was pouting but she didn't care. There was just something about

Corbin Eklund that made her feel daring and want to take risks.

"I promise honey, as soon as we get into my car, you can have free reign," he said. Ava wasted no time, pushing past him to eagerly climb into the back of his SUV. Corbin chuckled and slid into the back seat next to her. "You seem pretty determined to have your way with me, Darlin'," he drawled.

"Well, I'm sure you offering free reign over your body isn't going to happen very often. I want to take advantage of your generosity while it lasts," she said. Corbin threw back his head and laughed and Ava was sure she had never seen a more beautiful man in her life.

Corbin raised the privacy partition, separating them from his driver, and pulled her onto his lap. Avalon straddled his thighs and framed his face with her hands.

"Hi," he whispered, palming her ass through her clothing.

"Hey," she said. "I missed you today," she admitted. Ava almost felt silly saying those words out loud. Really they hadn't been in each other's lives for very long and the time they did spend together was because their two best friends sort of threw them at each other. But now, since their one night together at the club, she was beginning to see another side to Corbin and she had to admit, she liked it. Sure, she loved his dominance—craved it even but there was more to him than that.

He pulled her down and sealed his lips over hers, licking his way into her mouth. He broke their kiss long enough to whisper that he missed her too and Ava was sure that she had just lost another piece of her heart to him. She needed to be careful with those pieces because if she didn't keep them safely guarded, Corbin Eklund would end up with her whole heart and she wasn't sure how she felt about that.

CORBIN

Corbin wanted to get Ava naked and beneath him more than he wanted his next breath but they needed to go over a few things first—namely rules to govern their relationship. She wasn't going to like all of them, but they were necessary to protect them both and he hoped Ava knew enough about Dom/sub relationships to understand their necessity.

When Ava seemed determined to get them both naked again, as fast as humanly possible, he tugged on her hair and she sat back, seeming to take his subtle hint that she was topping from the bottom again. He liked that she was a quick study, but he was pretty sure that his new little sub was going to give him more trouble sooner or later and she'd be right back over his knee taking her punishment.

"Rules," he breathed.

"What about them?" Ava sassed. He swatted her ass and she yelped.

"We need to go over them to make sure you are comfortable with what's about to happen between us," he said.

"I'm pretty sure that what is about to happen between the two of us is already happening, Corbin," she teased. Ava ran her hand over his erection which was still trapped in his pants, and he groaned. All he wanted to do was let her have her way but he knew that would get them no closer to having rules in place. He was a Dom down to his core and he needed order and rules to make sense of any of what was going on between them. This was all so new for him; Corbin needed some familiarity to get himself feeling back on track again, but he was pretty sure that being tangled up with sexy Ava would never afford him such comforts.

"You keep giving me reasons to want to punish you, baby," he warned. Corbin didn't miss the way Ava's eyes seemed to flare with need every time he mentioned punishment. He knew his little vixen liked it a little rough in the bedroom.

"What kind of punishment are we talking, Corbin?" she playfully asked.

He swatted her ass again but this time instead of her surprised yelp, he was gifted a sultry moan as her reaction. "You are trying to get me to spank your ass, aren't you, baby?" He asked. She slyly nodded and smiled, rubbing her hot core all over his lap. Even through all their clothing, he could feel her wet heat.

"You don't have to misbehave for me to spank you, Darlin'," he promised. "I'll gladly spank your ass red if that's what you'd like for me to do. All you have to do is ask."

"Please," she begged. "Please spank me, Sir," she said. He loved the way he didn't have to remind her to call him that when they were roleplaying or having sex. She seemed to slip into her part with ease in just the short time that they had been together.

"Good girl," he praised. Ava all but purred and rubbed herself against him, seeming to need the contact. "Lie over my lap and pull your skirt up over your hips, honey," Corbin ordered. "I think we have time for a spanking and a few rules, if we multitask. You up for a game?" He asked. Ava nodded and inched her black skirt up over her hips, just as he asked, gifting him with the view of her bare pussy. He loved that she went sans panties all day. He liked to think that she spent her day wet and thinking about him every time she shifted in her seat, especially after the spanking he gave her the night before.

"Yes, Sir," she agreed. Ava lay across his lap with her curvy little ass up and he moaned and caressed each cheek, giving them each a light smack.

"I'm going to give you a rule and if you agree to it, you get a smack. If you don't, then nothing." Corbin knew his game wasn't fair and when Ava practically tried to sit up on his lap to protest, he wanted to laugh. She really was going to give him trouble at every turn. Corbin pushed her back down and ordered her to obey or use her safe word. Although, after what happened the night before, he hoped like hell she wouldn't ever have to use her safety net again.

"That's not fair, Corbin," she complained. "You can't force me to agree to your rules by offering to give me what I want."

"Sir," he growled.

"Okay—that's not fair, Sir," she corrected. He smacked her ass and she moaned and rubbed her wet folds against his thigh.

"Hey, you tricked me," she said. "This game is rigged," she accused. Corbin planned on using every trick he could to get her to comply.

"Maybe so, Darlin'," he agreed. "But I'm going to teach you that I always get my way and after you learn that little lesson, I'm going to fuck you until I'm sure the driver can hear you screaming my name." He picked up his cell phone and ordered his chauffeur to drive for another hour—he didn't care where. When he ended his call, he looked down to find Avalon looking up at him and he knew she wasn't going to easily agree to any of this, but that was something he could fix. Corbin always liked a challenge and Ava sure did give him one.

"First rule," he said. "When we are together, in this way—" He palmed her bare backside and she thrust her ass into his hands. "You will obey me and call me Sir." Corbin took a breath before saying the next part. This was where his little Avalon might give him some trouble.

"Agree or disagree?" he asked.

She smiled up at him and for a split second, he worried that she was going to disagree. "Agree," she said. Corbin wasted no time landing the first blow on her ass and she moaned and thrust back against his palm, anticipating the sharp smack.

"Rule number two," he continued. "You will wear what I pick out for you when it's just the two of us—you know, like around the house and when we go to dinner."

Ava started to sit up again, and Corbin pushed her back down onto his lap. "Corbin," she protested.

"Rule number one," he shouted.

"Fine—Sir," she said. "You can't dictate what I wear out in public, when we go to dinner. I'm part owner of a fashion company and I can't wear a competitor's brand. I agree to wear whatever you like when we are in the privacy of your home," she said.

Corbin thought about her offer. He knew her job was important to her, and she was right, wearing a competitor's clothing brand wouldn't be good for her business. He could also show Avalon that he wasn't being an asshole just for the sake of it.

"All right," he agreed. "We can take me dressing you to go out in public off the table as long as you're willing to add that when we go to a club, I get to pick your outfit."

"Club?" Ava questioned. "Like a night club?"

"No," he said. "Like the BDSM club, when we go to play."

Ava smiled up at him and nodded. "I agree," she said. Corbin raised his hand and let his palm fall to meet her ass with a hard slap. Ava moaned and wiggled on his lap as he caressed her skin where he landed the blow.

"You do like this, don't you baby?" he asked.

"Yes," she admitted.

"I can feel how wet you are and you smell so fucking good,"

he whispered, dipping two fingers into Ava's wet folds and running them through her pussy. He liked the way she writhed against his fingers, seeming to need more. "Not quite yet, baby," he teased. Ava mewled her protest, causing him to chuckle.

"Rule three," he said, running the pad of his thumb over her sensitive clit, giving her just a taste of what her impending orgasm was going to feel like once he let her get off. "I want to take you to a club to play at least a few times a month, if not more. Even after we're married, I'd like to continue to play with you at the club," he said.

Ava didn't even look up at him this time. She simply nodded, "Agreed," she said. Corbin landed another blow to her ass liking the way it was starting to turn a pinkish shade.

"Rule Four," he continued. "I control all of your orgasms. You will not touch yourself unless I tell you to and you don't come until I allow it," he said.

"Fine," she said. "I don't really like to do that anyway," Ava admitted.

Corbin stilled, "You don't like to touch yourself?" he asked. Ava looked back at him and shook her head, scrunching up her nose at the thought of it. Honestly, he had the exact opposite reaction when he thought of her touching her wet pussy to get herself off.

"Fuck, honey." He smacked her ass and ordered her to sit up on his lap. She did as he asked, and he spread her legs wide over his own. "I need to see you touch yourself now," he ordered.

"But you just said—" she started to protest. Corbin pinched her taut nipple between his fingers and she yelped.

"I don't need to be reminded of what I just said, Avalon. I told you that you wouldn't touch yourself until I ordered it. I'm telling you to slide those sexy fingers down your thighs and run them over your wet pussy, nice and slow so I can watch," he ordered.

Ava hesitated and he wasn't sure if she was going to follow his orders, but when she finally slid her hands down her thighs, he thought for sure he was going to come in his own fucking pants—she was so hot. He looked down her body as he held her to his own and watched as her fingers easily glided through her slick folds and when she pulled them free, all he could think about was tasting her.

"Show me, Ava," he growled. She held her wet fingers up, as if allowing him to inspect them and he pulled them to his mouth and sucked them in, humming his approval around her fingers.

"That's so fucking hot," she whispered.

"Yes, it was," he agreed, guiding her hand back down her body. "Do it again but this time, don't stop until I tell you to." He knew he was going to test her but it was time to see what his girl was made of. "And Ava—don't come," he added. She groaned and slid her fingers through her pussy and it was all he could do to concentrate on what rule number he was on.

"Rule five," he whispered into her ear. Corbin couldn't keep his hands to himself, running them up and down her sensitive nipples. She bucked on his lap and he grabbed her thighs, spreading them further apart and holding them down on his own. He kissed a path up and down her neck and gently bit into her shoulder, causing her to cry out his name. He knew she was close but he didn't want to let her come yet.

"Five," she almost shouted, she was so on edge.

"This thing between us is exclusive. You won't be with anyone else unless I feel we need to bring a third in for our roleplaying at the club," he said. Although the thought of someone else touching Ava both turned him on and pissed him off all at the same time. He'd have to figure all that out later—for now, she was his and only his.

"Agreed," she moaned. "But you too," she amended. "No one but me," she panted. That was an agreement he could honor.

"Yes," he said. "You are so fucking beautiful right now," he praised. Corbin watched as Ava worked her fingers in and out of her pussy, trying to stay off her impending orgasm.

"Please," she whimpered. He wanted to give her what she needed. Hell, he wanted to give her the whole fucking world, if she'd let him.

"Come for me, my beautiful girl," he ordered and that seemed to be all she was waiting for. Ava had obeyed his every command and agreed to most of what he wanted. She was his; body, mind and soul and Corbin wasn't sure which he wanted to command first. All he knew was his once reluctant submissive was finally becoming everything he ever could have dreamed of in a partner and Corbin knew he was holding his entire world in his arms.

AVALON

Ava felt as if her body was floating on a cloud and hearing the sweet praises from Corbin made her heart feel as though it was soaring along with her. As far as rules went, Corbin's demands weren't completely unreasonable and she had to admit, she was happy they were in place. They both knew exactly where the other stood except she wasn't ready to admit that she was falling in love with him. Her feelings had nothing to do with his rules and their relationship and it was time she remembered that and kept them separate.

"That was—" Ava wasn't sure how to finish her sentence. Saying that it was wonderful wasn't quite right. Hell, it was everything but that sounded downright sappy.

"Yeah," Corbin agreed. "I need you," he said. Ava realized that she had been completely greedy and forgot to take care of him and judging from the erection practically bulging out of his pants, Corbin looked about ready to explode.

"Yes," she agreed. "You do need me." Ava ran her hands over his cock, and he hissed out his breath.

"Clothes off," he ordered. Ava hesitantly looked out the window and he growled. "No one can see us, Ava. The windows are heavily tinted, and your hesitation might just earn you a punishment."

"What kind of punishment, exactly?" Ava asked. She watched as Corbin unzipped his pants, letting his cock spring free. He let his hands glide over his shaft and Ava licked her lips, wanting nothing more than to taste him.

"No, baby. If I let you get your sexy lips on my cock, I'll be coming down your throat in seconds. Besides, I promised that you can ride my cock until I have you screaming out my name," he reminded. Avalon smiled and nodded. She quickly tugged her shirt up over her head and Corbin helped her out of her skirt. He looked her over like a wolf would look at its prey and Ava shivered. He was always so intense, from the way he watched her to the way he made love to her and she was sure she'd never get tired of his demands.

"Straddle me," he ordered. She did as he asked and Corbin held her hips, lowering her onto his cock until she was fully seated. He pulled her down and sealed his mouth over hers, pumping into her, taking what he needed.

"You feel so fucking good," he moaned against her neck. "Move for me, Ava," he demanded. Ava threw her head back and rode his cock, taking every ounce of pleasure he was offering her. "Yes," he groaned. "Don't stop, I'm going to come." Corbin pumped into her a few more times and just when she thought she couldn't take anymore pleasure from him, another orgasm slammed through her core and she shouted out his name. Corbin followed her over and pulled her down on top of his body.

"See," he said. "I told you I'd have you screaming out my name before we got back home." Ava giggled against his chest and he tightened his arms around her body.

"I think I could get used to this," Ava whispered.

"Me too, honey," he admitted.

"Tomorrow's Saturday," Corbin reminded. "Do you have to go into work?"

Ava knew that she really should go in for at least a few hours but the thought of having to spend the day away from Corbin again felt pointless. She would just spend the time in her office wondering what he was doing and if he missed her, as she had today.

"No," she lied. "I have the whole day free."

Corbin's smile nearly made her heart stutter. "Good," he said. "I thought we could get married," he said.

"Married?" Ava asked. He offered to marry her when she told him about her dilemma with her grandfather's will, but a part of her didn't believe that he would follow through. She should have known that when Corbin Eklund made an offer, he lived up to his promise.

"You'll really marry me tomorrow?" She asked. She had been marking off the days until her time was up—her thirtieth birthday was only weeks away and it felt as if she was going to lose everything just because of a stupid stipulation. Ava hated that her father might win and take away everything her grandfather worked so hard for.

"Honey, I'd marry you any day of the week. I meant it when I said that I want to help you out. Your father won't even know what hit him," Corbin said. Ava didn't want to admit she was hurt by the fact that he wanted to marry her to help her win a legal battle. She was a fool to believe this thing between them was anything more to him.

Ava sat up and found her clothes, pulling them back on and sliding into her seat. "Yes, thank you," she said. Her voice sounded a little colder than she planned but she didn't care. "I'd be happy to marry you tomorrow."

"I've scheduled an appointment for two o'clock," he said. Ava looked out the window at the passing landscape, refusing to look at Corbin. She wouldn't let him see her hurt or disappointment.

"Ava," Corbin said. "Please look at me," he asked.

When she shook her head and wiped at the hot tears that

now spilled down her face, his frustrated growl filled the cabin of his SUV. "Fuck, Ava," he shouted. "Stop hiding from me and tell me what's going on," he ordered.

Ava chanced a look at him and the anger and concern she saw on his handsome face nearly took her breath away. "Is this what you want to see?" she spat. "Me crying over something that will never be. Me getting upset about something you never offered me but my stupid mind believed to be a possibility?"

"I don't think I'm following, honey," he said. "I told you that I'll marry you. I thought that was what you wanted."

"It is," she groaned. "But I thought that when I got married, it would be to a man who wanted to be with me. Not to someone who was doing me a favor to keep my money. You said it yourself, Corbin; you're doing this to help me out."

"No," he breathed. "I'm doing this because you are all I can fucking think about anymore, Ava. Ever since I met you, I've been looking for a way into your life—a way to get you to agree to even give me a chance and now that you have, there is no fucking way I'm letting you walk away from me. I want to marry you because I want you—all of you. I think I'm falling in love with you, Avalon," he admitted.

Ava's breath hitched and she wasn't sure what she should do next. She felt like cheering and fist pumping the air but she was sure that wasn't the right reaction.

"Tell me you feel the same way," Corbin ordered. "Fuck, just say something."

Ava climbed back onto Corbin's lap and snuggled against his body. "I'm falling in love with you too," she admitted. "And I will gladly marry you tomorrow or any other day of the week," she said, giving him back his own words. "I can't wait to be your wife."

❄

Corbin had thought about everything, right down to having her partner meet her at his house to help her throw together a dress for their special day. They practically made a wedding dress from scratch, staying up half the night to do it but Ava wouldn't have changed a thing. When she found Corbin standing at the bottom of the steps waiting for her in his black suit, she couldn't help but feel like the luckiest woman on the planet.

"Wow," he said as she walked down the long staircase in the dress she helped to design. The front was cut just below the knees but the back had a train that trailed behind her on the floor, covered in sequence and beads that she had hand sewn onto the dress.

"You look fantastic," he said, taking her hand to help her down the last few steps.

"Thanks and you look pretty fantastic yourself," she said back. "Are you sure you want to do this today?" Ava had heard Corbin on the phone with his mother, Rose, who was back in the States. He was trying to find a way around the major snowstorm that had grounded his private jet and every other plane on the East Coast, effectively trapping his mother and Aiden from making the trip over to France for their ceremony. Ava was sad that Zara was too pregnant to travel, but there was no way she'd chance her best friend's health or that of her god child. She told Zara that she and Corbin would plan a special ceremony for friends and family when they got back to the States. Ava kept the fact that the clock was ticking and they were racing time to get hitched to herself. Her best friend might not be too happy to hear that Corbin was marrying her to help her keep her inheritance. Zara wouldn't understand. Hell, Ava didn't really understand this whole mess but she wasn't going to overthink it too much. She wanted Corbin, anyway she could get him and if that meant marrying him without any promise in place for their future together then so be it. Sure, he had admitted that he was falling for her but that really didn't mean anything. He didn't come out and say that he was in love with her and maybe he wasn't. And, for now, that was okay with her.

She could see the sadness in Corbin's eyes at the reminder of his mom and best friend not being able to make it. "It's like you told Z, we can just have another ceremony for our friends and family when we get home. Mom is already planning it and hopes that you'll let her help."

"Of course," Ava agreed. "I love Rose." She meant it too. Corbin's mom was one of the nicest people she had ever met. She loved the way Rose took care of Zara when she and Aiden were just starting out. She'd always be grateful to Rose for the way she helped her best friend.

"Then today can be just for us," Corbin whispered. She nodded and Corbin wrapped his arms around her body. He smelled as good as he looked and from the way he was watching her, he was ready to get to the honeymoon portion of their evening. "Good, I've made us an appointment at the courthouse. We will be married in an hour—any regrets?" He seemed to be waiting her out as if she would protest marrying the sexiest man she'd ever met. Sure, she wished the circumstances were different, but he did admit that he was falling for her and if she wasn't such a coward, she'd fully admit that she was already in love with him. But she was too afraid to let herself hope that what had started as a scheme for her to keep her money could possibly lead to her finding her happily ever after.

❋

The drive to the courthouse took less than five minutes, but it was long enough to give her time to rethink everything that had happened over the past couple weeks.

"Nervous?" Corbin questioned. She shook her head and he laughed. "Liar," he accused. "You look like you are about to open that fucking door and run from this car as fast as those sexy heels will carry you."

"Well, the thought has crossed my mind," she admitted.

"Don't," he barked. "I'm not sure what is going through that pretty little head of yours but just cut it the fuck out," he ordered. "I want to do this, Avalon. I wouldn't have offered otherwise. You need to stop overthinking all of this and just let it happen."

"But—" she tried to protest but Corbin wasn't having it. He sealed his mouth over hers and by the time he let her up for air, she completely forgot what she was going to say.

"But nothing," he said. "Ready?" Corbin asked, reaching out his hand for hers. This time, Ava didn't hesitate. She took his hand and allowed him to help her from his SUV and she didn't let go until the judge pronounced them husband and wife and told Corbin to kiss his bride.

He pulled her against his body and kissed her as if they weren't standing in the middle of a courthouse surrounded by about fifty strangers. It wasn't what Ava had dreamed about when she thought of her wedding day. In fact, it was probably the exact opposite of what she planned but it was perfect. She even got a little choked up when the judge asked her to recite her vows after him. They were lucky that he spoke English because her French was a little rusty. Of course, Corbin spoke perfect French and even said his vows in it. She barely understood him, but when he got to the part where he had to say, "I do," he said it in English, gifting her with a sexy wink. She giggled at his theatrics and judging by the swoon of the women in the crowd, they were buying into his performance too.

And when he was finally allowed to kiss her, she could feel her own heart beating wildly in her chest and Ava knew right then and there that she was a goner. Her heart was his whether he knew it or not and when or even if this thing between them ended, she would never find another man that made her feel the way Corbin Eklund did.

"Well, Mrs. Eklund," he whispered into her ear. "You ready to get the honeymoon portion of this marriage thing started?" Corbin asked.

"Yep," she agreed. "As long as I report back to work Monday morning, I'm all yours until then." He smiled a wolfish grin down at her and she didn't hide the shiver that ran up the length of her spine. He knew exactly the effect he had on her and she was pretty sure that he was going to live up to every silent promise he was making her.

"That works," he agreed. "I have a little wedding present I'm hoping you like," he said. Corbin beat a path out of the courthouse like a man on a mission and pulled her along behind. Ava could barely keep up between tripping over her dress and falling over her heels.

"Corbin," she complained. "You can't just drag me along. I need to slow down," she insisted.

"Can't," he said. Corbin turned and lifted her into his arms despite her squealing protests and picked up the pace to his waiting SUV. He all but tossed her into the back seat and slid in next to her, pulling her to practically sit on his lap.

"Thank you for doing this for me," she whispered against his neck.

Corbin wrapped his arms around her body. "Honey, you never have to thank me for anything. I did this because I want you in every way possible, Avalon." His voice dripped with innuendo and Ava suddenly felt too hot.

"Where are you taking me?" she questioned.

"Mmm," he hummed. "Remember I told you about a little club in town that I used to go to?" Ava nodded. She remembered thinking that she would kill any sub he took on after her and even having extreme feelings of jealousy that were foreign to her.

Corbin chuckled, "From your murderous expression, you remember it," he said.

"I think I do," she smirked. "You want to go to the club and play with other subs?" Ava asked. She didn't want to admit that she was holding her breath, waiting for him to answer, but she was.

"No," he immediately spat. "I want to go to the club and play with my wife. I might have left out the part about me owning the club," he admitted.

"You own a BDSM club here—in France?" she asked. She sounded more like she was accusing him of something but honestly, she was more shocked than anything else.

"Yep, and as for me wanting to play with other subs, Ava, that isn't going to happen. I only want to play with you. You good with that?" Ava shyly nodded her head.

"Good to know," she teased.

"Now you're just begging to be spanked, aren't you? Between thinking that I'd put my hands on another woman after marrying you and then giving me your sassy backtalk, I think I'm going to need to remind you of rule number five," he said.

"Rule five?" She questioned. Honestly, she had forgotten most of the rules they had made. Corbin told them to her while spanking her ass red and then fucking her. The last thing she remembered from that scene was the rules.

He made a disapproving tsking sound and Ava stifled her giggle. "Yes, rule five—this thing between us is exclusive. I won't touch another woman and you don't get to be with any other man, unless I give permission first." Ava smiled at the thought of being between Corbin and another man. Honestly, she thought the whole thing sounded hot.

"You'd like for me to put you between another Dom and myself, wouldn't you?" he asked.

"I don't know," she stuttered. "Really, I've never done anything like that before but the thought of you doing that with me—to me, makes me hot." She felt crazy admitting something like that to him, but he was her husband now and Ava knew full well Corbin would never let her hide from him.

"Good to know," he teased, giving her own words back to her.

"Any other rules I need to be reminded of?" she sassed.

Corbin reached up under her dress and swatted her bare ass. She intentionally wore no panties because she knew he liked her pussy bare and ready for him. She gasped at the sensation of his big hand rubbing over her sensitive folds.

"I think we should revisit rule number four," he growled.

"Four?" she whispered.

"Yes," he said. "That's the one about me controlling all of your orgasms," he hissed. "It's going to be a damn long time before I give you one," he teased.

"Shit," Ava breathed.

"Yeah, now you're getting the big picture, Wife." He pulled her down for a kiss and Ava knew that she was in for a whole lot of sexual frustration before her new husband finally gave her a release, but it was going to be a hell of a lot of fun in the meantime.

CORBIN

Corbin wasn't sure how he got so lucky with finding Avalon. She was his perfect match and there was no way that he was going to willingly give her up. Sure, the idea of sharing her with another man might be a turn on for them both, but there was no way he was going to let her forget she belonged to him. In fact, tonight he was going to prove that to the whole damn club and if his new wife wanted a third, he knew just the guy to join them. His friend Eric was someone he could trust and Corbin knew he'd be on board for a little fun. He and Eric had played with women before and his friend was fine with being told what to do, usually letting Corbin take lead with everything.

"You have that devilish look on your face that scares me," Ava warned. "Should I be afraid?" That was a very good question and one that Corbin wasn't sure how to answer. Their relationship was so new, he worried that playing with a third might be too much for them.

"Do you trust me?" Corbin questioned.

Ava didn't hesitate, "Yes," she breathed, "with my life."

Corbin wasn't sure what he had done to earn her complete trust, but he was sure as hell not going to do anything to hurt what they had built together in such a short amount of time.

"Thank you for that, baby," he said. When the car stopped in front of his club, he got out of the back seat and helped Ava to step free. "If tonight gets to be too much for you, I need you to promise me that you'll use your safe word."

Ava nodded, "Yes, I remember it," she said. Corbin slipped a jewelry box from his jacket pocket. He was going to wait to give it to her but this seemed as good a time as any. "What's this?" Avalon questioned when he handed her the box.

"It's something I'd like you to wear whenever we come to the club to play," he said, suddenly feeling shy. Ava took the box from him and hesitated.

"You've already given me my beautiful wedding ring," she said, holding her hand out to admire the diamond band he had gifted her. Ava opened the jewelry box and gasped. "Ice cream," she whispered. "You gave me my safe word on a collar?"

Corbin nodded, "I had it and your ring both made yesterday, after you agreed to marry me today. I have a local jeweler that does work for me, and he was willing to put a rush on the order, for the right price." Corbin pulled the silver choker chain free from the black velvet box and admired the little diamond pendant of an ice cream cone that dangled from the center.

"May I?" He asked.

"Well, it is beautiful," Ava said. "And I did promise to let you dress me when we go to clubs," she teased, looking up at the massive building that housed his BDSM club. "So, yes," she said, turning away from him to give him better access to her bare neck. He couldn't help himself; Corbin kissed his way down her neck loving the way she shivered against his body and the sexy little sighs she gave him.

"This and your wedding band will be all you wear tonight, Avalon," he whispered into her ear. Her gasp told him that she fully understood his command. She was going to be completely naked while in his club. She was his and it was about time that he showed her and everyone else exactly what that meant.

Corbin fastened the collar around her throat, loving the way it seemed to pinch her skin a little. He knew she had to feel the constraint of the silver chain around her neck and he liked that it would be a constant reminder to Ava who she belonged to.

"Too tight?" he asked.

Ava pressed her fingers against the metal and looked up at him. "No," she said.

"Good, let's go in then," he ordered, holding out his hand for hers. Ava reached for him to let him take her into his club. He nodded to the new woman that sat behind the desk in the lobby. To anyone just happening into the club, it looked like any other business office, but once he led Ava into the main playroom through the heavy wooden doors, it screamed sex club, right down to the velvet red wallpaper.

Ava looked around the room at the various couples that had found quiet corners to play in. "Wow," she breathed. "It's beautiful, Corbin," she said. He shot her a stern look and Ava smiled up at him. "I mean, Sir. It's beautiful, Sir," she corrected.

"Thank you," he said. "It's time to have some fun with my beautiful wife," he said. "You're wearing too many clothes—strip," he ordered. Ava kept her eyes on him and he silently waited her out, ready to dare her to comply, but he watched as Ava did as he asked and by the time she finished stepping free from her wedding gown, all she wore was a sexy smirk that let him know she understood his challenge and she was up for it.

"Good girl," he praised. She bent to remove her heels and he stopped her. "Don't," he ordered. "Leave those on. You will need the height for what I have planned." Ava stood and nodded. She was completely naked; wearing only her new collar, her wedding ring and her sexy, fuck me heels. Corbin was so hard he wasn't sure he was going to be able to keep his promise and hold back her release. He wanted to make tonight last and the only way he was going to be able to do that would be to find his own release.

"On your knees," he commanded. Ava never took her eyes off him, even after they had drawn a small crowd of onlookers to admire her beautiful body. She seemed oblivious to everyone else around them except him. The way she watched him made him even hotter and she knelt in front of him, silently waiting for his next orders.

Corbin pulled his zipper down and let his cock spring free, loving the way Ava licked her lips in anticipation of what he was going to have her do next. "Open," he ordered, and she complied. "I need to have an orgasm, baby. It's the only way I will be able to last and make this good for you. I've wanted to fuck you since we left the courthouse," he admitted.

"Yes, Sir," Ava said. She wrapped her hands around his shaft and Corbin let her have that control. He loved it when she touched him, seeming to need more of what he was giving her. It was as if she needed all of him and he wanted to give Ava that but he worried that he didn't know how. He watched as her tongue darted out of her mouth and licked the head of his cock, causing it to jump.

"Fuck," he spat. "Stop playing with me, Ava. Get me off," he ordered. She smiled and sucked him into her mouth, knowing exactly what she was doing to him and how she was driving him to the edge. Corbin took control of her mouth, pulling her hair back so he could watch his cock as he used her mouth to pump in and out. He took what he needed from her and when she let him slide to the back of her throat and swallowed around him, he lost himself into her mouth. Ava took everything he gave her and licked his cock clean. When she finished, she sat back on her heels and looked up at him, a proud smile on her face.

"Vixen," he taunted. Ava giggled and took the hand he offered to help her off the floor.

"I just did as you asked, Sir," she teased.

"You never do as I ask, Wife," he said. "But you will." Corbin spotted Eric in the corner of the room, surrounded by a few women he didn't seem much interested in and nodded for him to join them.

"Up on the bench," Corbin ordered.

Ava climbed up onto the spanking bench gifting him with a glorious view of her ass. "That's perfect, honey," he praised. Corbin stripped out of his shirt and jacket, wearing just his trousers, and turned to find Eric eyeing Ava. Corbin shook his friend's hand and nodded to where Ava was perched on the bench, still assuming the position he ordered her into.

"My wife," he said, nodding to her. "You want to give us a hand tonight?"

"Wife?" Eric asked. "Congrats, man," he offered. Eric was always a big draw to the local French BDSM scene. The women really loved American men and Eric Balthazar was as American as they came. The French women fell for his long blond hair and baby blue eyes that fit perfectly with his Southern California appeal.

Corbin could tell that Ava was listening to everything they were saying and judging by the look of panic in her eyes, he was going to have to do some convincing and fast if they were going to get their chance to play with Eric.

"You trust me, baby?" Corbin asked again. This time, he could feel Ava's hesitation. "You say your safe word and this all ends, here and now," he promised. He meant it too. Corbin wouldn't do anything to push Ava into something she wasn't ready for. "If you don't want to play with a third, then we don't." Ava looked over her shoulder to Eric, as if sizing him up.

"Hi," Eric said, giving a little wave.

"Hey," Ava whispered. She looked back up at Corbin and sighed. "Who do I take orders from?" she asked.

Corbin stroked a hand down her face and cupped her jaw. "Me and only me. I'm your Dom and your husband. You will never take orders from anyone else, understand?" Corbin knew he sounded like a possessive ass but he didn't care.

"Yes, Sir," she stuttered. "I want to play," she said.

"We will take this slow tonight," he offered. Ava nodded and he tossed Eric a leather flogger. "She likes it rough," Corbin said. "Just her ass," he added. Eric nodded, knowing just what to do. That was the main reason Corbin had chosen him to play—he knew, and trusted Eric and he wouldn't let just anyone touch his wife.

Corbin sat in front of Avalon, watching her beautiful face as his friend marked her ass with the leather flogger. She was so expressive and he could tell the exact moment she started to slip into sub space. She was gorgeous to watch and the very last thing he wanted to do was deny her the release she so desperately needed.

Eric landed the final blow and Ava cried out and moaned. "Please," she whimpered.

"Roll over and let your legs spill over the sides of the bench," Corbin ordered. "I want to see how wet your pussy is, baby and then I'm going to let Eric have a taste of just what his spanking did to you." Ava whimpered and Corbin waited her out, hoping like hell she didn't use her safe word. She nodded and did as he asked.

"Like this?" she questioned.

"Yes, my beautiful wife, just like that," Corbin praised. He nodded over to Eric who seemed to be eagerly waiting for his next set of instructions. From the erection he was sporting, Corbin could tell his friend needed to get off.

"You can taste her but that will be it for tonight," Corbin said. Eric nodded and smiled down at Ava, spreading her legs further open to inspect her drenched folds.

"She's so fucking wet, man," Eric groaned. Corbin had

called one of Eric's groupies over and whispered into her ear. The little blonde smiled and nodded and went to stand beside Eric, just as Corbin had ordered.

"Steph wants to give you a blow job while you eat my wife's pussy," Corbin offered. The little blonde vixen coyly smiled and nodded. When she sank to her knees and sucked Eric into her mouth, Corbin knew his friend wouldn't last long.

He stood over Ava and watched as Eric licked his way into her pussy, causing her to buck and squirm on the small leather bench. "Hold still, honey," Corbin ordered. "Let Eric taste you and then I'm going to fuck you until you are shouting my name," he promised.

"Yes, Sir," she breathed. "I need you, Corbin," she begged. He kissed his way down her body, giving each one of her breasts special attention, knowing that she was on edge from what he and Eric were working together to do to her.

Corbin worked his way back up her body and kissed his way into her mouth and when he knew she couldn't take anymore, he told her to come for him and she did. She squirmed and thrashed against Eric's mouth and Corbin was sure he had never seen anything so beautiful in his life.

Eric finished lapping up Ava's release and stood, pulling his cock free from Steph's mouth and jerking himself off onto the blonde sub's pretty breasts. Steph smiled up at Eric triumphantly and he helped her to stand. "Get a room with me?" he asked and the blonde nodded. He nodded at Corbin on his way out of the playroom and gave one last look back at Ava.

"Was that all right?" Ava stood and nervously tried to cover her body with her arms.

Corbin tugged her against his body. "It was more than all right," he admitted. "I loved watching you and sharing you with another man. I liked knowing that he wanted what is mine, but he could never really have you because I own you, Ava—body, mind and soul."

Ava nodded and Corbin worried that he had pushed her too hard. "Tell me you are all right," he ordered.

"I think I am," she admitted and gave him her sweet smile. "I liked it too, knowing that you were in complete control and wouldn't let anything go too far."

"Always," he promised.

AVALON

They spent the next week in France and most of that time was spent in bed or at the club. Ava was beginning to get the full gist of just how demanding Corbin was going to be and she had to admit, she loved every minute.

Her business partner had given her some much needed time off to spend with her new husband as a wedding gift. Today was her first full day back at work on the new line and she used her time to daydream about her husband. Her blissfully happy mood lasted until Zara called to say she was in labor and heading to the hospital. As soon as she hung up with her best friend, Corbin called to tell her that Aiden had phoned to tell him the baby was on the way. He had sent word to his pilot to have his jet ready for them and with any luck, they would get home in time to welcome the new addition to their little makeshift family.

A part of her was worried about what their lives were going to look like once they got back to the States. They really hadn't made plans and were basically living day to day, but going home was going to prove challenging, especially since they hadn't even discussed where they were going to live.

Corbin rushed into the bedroom where she was packing her bags for their trip home and he looked just as frazzled and excited as she felt. He kissed her cheek and grabbed his own suitcase.

"You ready to be an aunt?" Corbin questioned.

Honestly, she was. Ava had been excited about Zara's little one since the day she announced she was pregnant. What she wouldn't admit to was the fact that every time she saw her best friend, she felt a pang of jealousy and a strange longing for something she thought she never wanted. When she was growing up, the thought of someday meeting a man, falling in love and having a family never crossed her mind. After her mother died and her brother disappeared, she decided to follow her dreams and go into fashion. Her grandfather convinced her to take the leap and invested in her company and she was able to make him proud of all her achievements before he passed away. That was enough for her until she met Corbin.

He made her feel things she didn't plan on feeling and want things she never would have guessed were possible. "I am," she admitted. "I already love Zara's baby, so much," she said.

"I know how you feel. When Lucy and Laney were born, I wasn't very impressed by the little people taking my best friend away from me. But spending time with them—well, let's just say that I've had a change of heart. Those little girls are pretty damn awesome," he admitted. Ava watched as Corbin threw his clothes into his suitcase, not bothering to fold them and shook her head.

"What?" he asked.

"You really are a crappy packer," she teased. "Here, let me help." She took his shirt from his hands and took over packing for him, neatly folding his now wrinkled clothing.

Corbin wrapped his arms around her from behind and kissed her neck. "You know, I could get used to my wife taking care of me," he admitted.

Ava giggled, "I'm pretty sure that was a part of our vows," she teased.

"You mean you vowed to pack for me?" he asked. Ava swatted him away and tried to pretend to be upset by the idea of having to pack for him even though she wasn't.

"Have you ever thought about having kids of your own?" Ava questioned.

"No," Corbin said. He didn't seem to hesitate with his answer and Ava didn't try to hide her disappointment. "I never thought about having kids before," he added. "Well, before I met you. Now, it's all I can think about and everything I want for us." Ava smiled up at him and he pulled her into his arms.

"Really?" she asked.

Corbin smiled, "How about you? You ever thought of having a few rugrats?"

Ava nodded, "I always put my career first, but ever since Zara told me that she was pregnant, it's been in the back of my mind. I think I'd like to have kids—someday." She knew that they were nowhere near ready to talk about having a baby, but she liked the idea of them revisiting the whole subject when things calmed down.

"Someday it is then," Corbin agreed. "Now get a move on, Wife. We have a plane to catch and a new baby to meet." Ava hesitated and Corbin seemed to notice. "What's wrong?" he asked.

Ava shrugged, "I'm just worried about what happens next," she admitted.

"I thought we just covered that," Corbin said.

"Sure," she agreed. "But I'm talking about after we fly home and meet the baby. What happens then? Where will we live?" Corbin gently kissed her lips and she snuggled into his hold. What was it about this man that made her feel that everything was going to be all right no matter how messed up things were?

"Honey, we can live wherever you'd like. Your townhouse,

my penthouse—hell, I'll buy you a new house and we can live there." Ava rolled her eyes and giggled.

"I think we can make do with one of our houses, Corbin."

"Great, then move in with me. My penthouse is bigger and closer to both of our offices." The thought of giving up her beloved townhouse made her heart ache a little. That place was home for both her and Zara for so many years. They got through college together in that house. They had parties, movie marathons, and stayed up all night to talk about boys in that little townhome. Sure, Zara wasn't moving back in, and Ava was left to live alone but it was still hers.

"You're making this more difficult than it is, baby," Corbin said. "I'll move into your place, if that will make you happy. What do you want, Ava?" That was a good question and one that she didn't want to think too long on. She already had what she really wanted—him. He was right, where they lived didn't matter.

"I'll move into your place and put my townhouse on the market," she said. "You're right—it doesn't matter where we live and your penthouse has more space than my tiny townhouse."

"Say that again," he prompted.

"Your place has more room?" Ava questioned.

"No, the part about me being right," he teased.

Ava giggled. "Fine—you're right, Corbin," she said. He practically gloated, smiling down at her as if he had just won a contest.

"You'll find that I'm right a lot of the time, Ava," he boasted. She rolled her eyes and finished throwing the last of her things into her suitcase.

"Ready?" Corbin asked, holding out his hand for her.

"Yep," she said, taking it. Ava knew she was being silly but she felt sadness about having to leave France. It was as if she and Corbin had built their own personal little world and they were leaving it to return to what was certain to be utter chaos. But there would be no hiding from reality—it was waiting for them and it was time to face it but this time, she wouldn't be alone. This time, she'd have Corbin by her side.

CORBIN

They got home just in time to meet their niece and Corbin had to admit that watching Ava holding a newborn did strange things to his heart. It made him feel things he wasn't sure he'd ever feel and that made him a little nervous.

As soon as Ava agreed to move into his place, he set the wheels in motion, calling his mother to enlist her help. Rose was all too happy to lend a hand in planning the move and even had the moving company at Ava's place before their plane landed the next morning. He knew he was rushing things but he wouldn't take the chance that she would change her mind. Besides, that seemed to be how this whole thing between the two of them worked—fast. Ever since their first night together at the club, he couldn't seem to slow things down and honestly, he didn't want to.

As soon as they landed, he called Aiden to get an update and he told them that they had a little girl and were naming her Lexi Avalon. Corbin didn't miss the way Ava teared up hearing that they named the baby after her.

When they finally got to the hospital, she and Zara acted as if they hadn't spoken every day on the phone or video chatted every chance they got. Ava gushed about how perfect the newest addition was and Corbin had to agree that she was pretty awesome. But when Ava took the baby from Zara, his heart stuttered and all their talk about having kids "someday" went right out the window. All he wanted was to convince his new wife that they should start working on expanding their family now, but he worried that she wasn't ready for that big of a step.

First, he needed to get her settled in his penthouse and then they could sort out this mess with her father. Ava's birthday was just around the corner and it was about time he met the man who was trying to hurt the woman he loved. They needed to get a few things straight and then he was going to take great pleasure in watching as Ava gave him the news that she was married and would be keeping her inheritance. Not that any of that mattered to him. Corbin didn't marry Ava for her to be able to keep her money. He didn't give one fuck about how much money she had. Hell, she now had access to everything he had and that was enough for them both and their future generations. He married Ava because he was in love with her and the thought of her walking away from him, to marry someone else, just pissed him off. He couldn't let that happen.

By the time they got back to his place, he knew Ava had to be exhausted but the movers were there, bringing in the last of her things. Rose was bossing them around, just like she had him when he was a little boy. God, he missed his mother while he was away.

As soon as they walked into the penthouse, Rose shooed them right back out the front door. "Out," she shouted.

"Ma," he protested. "What the hell?"

"Don't you Ma me," she shot back. "You carry your new bride over the threshold of your first home together or you'll have bad luck," she insisted. Ava giggled and looked at him expectantly. Corbin dropped both of their suitcases in the front hallway and lifted her into his arms. She breathlessly looked up at him and he couldn't help himself, he kissed her and by the time he finished, he was feeling a little breathless himself. Rose cleared her throat, reminding him that she was still waiting on him to follow tradition and carry Ava across the threshold.

He stepped into his foyer, holding Ava against his chest and shot his mother a condescending look. "How about now, Ma?" Corbin questioned. "Will we have better luck now?"

His mother shook her head at him. "It's like someone else raised you, Corbin James," she teased. He put Ava down and pulled his mom in for a quick hug.

"You raised me, Mom and you did a fantastic job, even if I do say so myself," Corbin boasted. Ava and Rose both broke down in fits of laughter and he didn't hide his smile. He loved to hear them both laughing together; he wanted so much for them to get along. They were the two most important women in his life and the fact that they seemed to like each other helped him to relax some.

Rose hugged Ava and welcomed her into the family. They talked about where the movers had put most of her stuff and then slid right into chatting about the ceremony and France. After a good thirty minutes had passed, Corbin gave up trying to find a place in their conversation and went to find a takeout menu for his favorite Asian place. He ordered them all dinner and found a bottle of wine to go with their meal. When he returned to the family room to find them, Rose and Ava were huddled together on his sectional, still gabbing about their trip.

"So, you liked the house in France then?" Rose questioned when Ava told her that Corbin had moved her into his French home. It was silly that it mattered to him, but he was curious to hear her answer. He wanted her to feel at home in all his places.

"I loved it," she gushed. Corbin found himself breathing a sigh of relief and his mother looked up at him, her smile seemed to be permanently plastered on her beautiful face. He knew that Rose always wanted him to settle down, but every time she brought up the topic of him finding a nice girl, he'd quickly change the subject. His poor mother must have thought he wasn't ever going to settle down and find someone, yet here they were, talking about houses and surprise weddings.

"I hope you don't mind me taking the initiative to move you in here so quickly," Rose said. Ava reached across the seat and took Rose's hand.

"Of course not," she said. "I appreciate everything you are doing for me, Rose," Ava said.

Rose nodded, "How about you call me Mom?" she asked. Ava didn't answer at first and Corbin worried that his mother's request had been too much for her. He knew that Ava's own mother passed away when she was little and maybe calling her that would bring back bad memories.

"No, never mind," Rose said, probably picking up on Ava's indecision. "Forget I mentioned it. I guess I'm just so happy to have you in our little family," Rose admitted. "I just got carried away."

"It's all right," Ava said. "It's just that I haven't called anyone that for a long time. My own mother died when I was very young and well—I'd love to call you 'Mom,' Rose," she said. Rose pulled Ava in for a side hug and Corbin moaned.

"You all right, son?" Rose questioned.

"You two are mushier than a sappy card commercial," he grumbled, causing them both to laugh.

"Well, I feel very fortunate that my son has finally taken my advice and found someone to settle down and be happy with," Rose said. "I'm just hoping that I don't have to wait too long to be a grandma," she admitted.

"Don't push, Ma," Corbin warned. "How about you practice on Aiden's three girls and let me, and Ava get adjusted to married life first?"

Rose nodded. "Sorry," she said more to Ava than to him. "I guess I have baby fever after getting to meet little Lexi today."

"Oh—I feel the same way. She's beautiful, isn't she?" Ava asked.

"Yeah, thank God she looks like Zara and not Aiden," Corbin butted in.

"Corbin James," Rose chided. "Aiden is a good-looking man and your best friend."

"I haven't forgotten that Ma," Corbin said. "But he'd make one ugly girl."

"So, what's next for you two newlyweds?" Rose questioned. "Have you met Ava's family yet, Corbin?" Ava shot him a pleading look and he smiled and winked.

"Nope, but I have a feeling that I will be meeting her dad real soon," he admitted. Ava rolled her eyes and he laughed.

"Well, I'm sure he will be just as thrilled about the two of you getting married as I am," Rose said.

"I doubt that, but thanks, Ma," Corbin said. The doorbell rang and he thanked his lucky stars for the interruption. The last thing he wanted to do was explain to his mother about the stipulations of Ava's inheritance or the fact that she had to get married. She was his now and nothing else mattered.

AVALON

Ava walked into the kitchen and flopped down into a chair. She hated that she was going to have to face her father so soon after returning home but there would be no avoiding him. Ava counted herself lucky that her father had waited at least a few days to demand her presence, after she and Corbin had returned home to the States. But, he wasn't about to let her birthday pass without seeing for himself if she was truly married or not. Ava told her father that she had 'news' to share with him but left it at that. And now, she had been summoned to his home. Her dear old dad was sure to add the fact that he was quite willing to call in his team of lawyers to force her to accept his invitation, if necessary. He could do it too and that thought alone had Ava seeing red.

When her grandfather gave her dad permission to alter his will, to add the stipulation that Avalon would have to forfeit her inheritance if she wasn't married by age thirty, he also allowed for her father to be made executor of his estate. That meant her father could challenge her marriage to Corbin and there would be nothing she could do about it. There were built in safety nets in her grandfather's will that also permitted both

Ava and her new husband to be extensively questioned if there was any plausibility of their marriage not being legal. The document was legal—iron-clad in fact. Corbin had his personal lawyers go over the will, but she knew that whoever was going to be investigating them, on her father's behalf, would be sticking his or her nose into their business. They would be asking private questions that Ava would rather not have to answer and the thought of putting Corbin through any of this infuriated her. A family reunion was the very last thing she wanted on her birthday. Honestly, she wanted to spend her thirtieth birthday cuddled up with Corbin in bed but now that plan was shot to hell.

"What has you in such a lovely mood, Princess?" Corbin teased. Ava huffed out her breath and shot him a look to let him know she was not in the mood for his teasing. "Whoa, honey," he said, holding up his hands as if in surrender. "It was just a question. Geeze Ava, what's going on?"

"My father is what's going on," she admitted. "I received a phone call this afternoon and I have been summoned to his home for dinner tonight," she moaned. "I just wanted a quiet evening with you for my birthday and now we have to see my father."

"I think you mean to say that 'we' have been summoned because we're a team now—remember? I can tell you I don't really do well with taking orders. I'm more of a give the orders type of guy," Corbin said, bobbing his eyebrows at her. Ava couldn't help but giggle. He was always doing that for her—making bad situations better and taking care of her, even when she was acting like a miserable cow. "But I'm sure I can think of a few ways to salvage your birthday, baby. How about we go to dinner after our visit and then come back here so I can worship that sexy birthday suit of yours." Ava giggled again, loving the way he couldn't seem to keep his mind or hands off her body.

"Thanks," she said.

"For?" he asked.

"For always making me feel better." Ava stood and crossed the room to where Corbin sat. She didn't wait or even hesitate, just crawled into his lap and snuggled against his body.

"We have to go. It's part of the stipulation with my grandfather's will. We will need to not only prove that we are legally married, but we will most likely have to answer questions that will be personal or even private. My father will leave no stone unturned when it comes to trying to prove that we aren't legally married. If he can prove that we are married just so I can collect the rest of my inheritance, I'm screwed."

"Except he won't be able to prove that because it isn't true—right, Ava?" Corbin questioned. He looked downright angry and Ava thought back over her words trying to figure out where she had gone wrong.

"That's not what I meant, Corbin," she defended.

"We might have started out that way but you have to know that isn't how I feel about you or our marriage now," Corbin said. "This isn't a marriage of convenience for me, Ava. I didn't marry you for you to be able to keep your damn money. Hell, I have enough of my own and now, what's mine is yours."

"No, Corbin," she whispered. "I don't want your money. I want what is mine and I won't just let my father waltz into my life and take it away from me. I appreciate that you want to take care of me but that isn't necessary. We just need to get through this next part and then I'll have my inheritance back and won't need your money."

"Is that all this is to you, Ava?" Corbin asked. "Am I just a way for you to get your money back? Is our marriage just one big scam to you?" He sounded as if he was accusing her of something awful but he wasn't completely wrong. This thing between the two of them might have started as a way for her to keep her inheritance but it ended up being so much more.

"No," she admitted. "At first, I took you up on your offer so I'd be able to keep my money, but it's turned into so much more, Corbin." Ava took a deep breath. It was now or never, and she had always been a rip-the-band-aid-off quickly, kind of girl.

"I've told you that I'm falling for you but what if that isn't completely true?" she asked.

"So this has all been a ruse? You don't have feelings for me?" Ava wasn't sure which hurt more—Corbin's anger or the hurt she could hear in his voice.

"No. I guess I'm not explaining any of this right," she mumbled. "I'm in love with you, Corbin," she admitted. He opened his mouth as if he wanted to say something and then seemed to decide against it and quickly pressed his lips together. They sat in silence for what felt like forever. Ava hated that she just blurted out how she felt about him with no warning or pretense.

"Say something," she begged. "Anything."

"What do you want for me to say here, Ava?" Corbin asked. "Do you want me to say that I'm in love with you too and I've been waiting to hear you admit how you felt for weeks now?"

"Only if that is what you are really feeling," she said.

Corbin nodded and smiled. "It is," he said. "I'm in love with you too, Ava. Hell, maybe I have been since we took Laney and Lucy for ice cream, all those months ago—I don't know. What I do know is that I'm head over heels for you and that isn't going to ever change."

"But, my father," she started to protest, but Corbin put his big hand over her mouth, effectively stopping her from saying anything else.

"Your father can come for us and we'll be ready. We know the basics and we'll just have to learn the rest. For now, we'll get dressed and go see what your father wants, but we won't be having dinner with him. I've already planned a birthday dinner for my new wife. If your dad decides to pursue questioning us, he'll have to do it another day," he assured. Ava just wished she could bottle some of his enthusiasm because she wasn't quite so sure of everything. What she was sure of was that her father was probably up to no good and she was madly in love with her new husband.

※

Corbin had his driver bring the car around to pick them up and Ava was glad that he wasn't driving them to her father's house. This way he could sit in the back seat with her and offer her the comfort she so desperately needed. As usual, he seemed to sense just what she needed and as soon as he slid into the back seat, Corbin pulled her onto his lap.

"You know we don't have to do this. I can have my lawyers deal with this whole mess and we can avoid your father altogether," Corbin offered. Ava wished that could be true but she knew her father—he'd find a way to get to her. He seemed to take some sick pleasure in making her squirm and Ava knew the sooner they got this visit over with, the better.

"No, I can handle this. Besides, I have my birthday dinner to look forward to after this is all over," she said. Corbin had promised her a night out at her favorite restaurant in town and then they'd spend the rest of the night in bed if she had any say in the matter.

"And, don't forget the part about me taking you home and the whole matter of body worshipping," he teased. Ava wrapped her arms around his broad shoulders and pulled him in for a kiss.

"I don't think I could forget that part," she admitted. "In fact, it's all I can think about."

Corbin kissed his way down the column of her neck. "How long will it take us to get to your father's house?" He whispered into her ear, causing her to shiver. God, she wished she could lie and tell him that they had enough time to do everything that his sexy voice told her he wanted to do with her, but they didn't. Her two worlds were about to collide. Honestly, she was shocked that Corbin and her father lived so close to each other but had never run into each other. They even ran in the same elite circles, but knowing her father, he wouldn't have given Corbin Eklund a second glance knowing that he wasn't from old money.

Her father used to like to remind her that there were two types of rich men—those from old money like him and those that made their fortune on their own. For some reason, her father looked down on the men who worked hard for every penny—men like Corbin. Maybe it was because he was simply handed everything in life but she had a deep respect for people who worked for what they had. She appreciated the money she had made on her own in the fashion industry so much more than the money her family had given her.

"Not far," she answered. "My father lives just around the corner from your building."

Corbin groaned his frustration and she giggled. "Then let's get this fucking meeting over with so we can go to dinner, and I can get you home," he said. "I want to play." Hearing Corbin admit that he wanted her made her feel as though she might self-combust.

"Deal," she quickly agreed just as the car pulled up in front of her father's place. She looked at the house that she once thought of as home and felt nothing. It was crazy that she once happily lived there with her mother, brother, and father and now they were all gone—well except her dad but he wasn't the same man she once knew. She felt a deep sadness every time she had to go to that house now and Ava hated that she was dragging Corbin into this mess with her.

"You don't have to do this," she offered. "You can back out now and no one will ever have to know that you married me." Ava looked up at Corbin and saw every ounce of his anger staring back at her.

"Now I think you're just trying to piss me off, honey. I've already told you that I didn't marry you to save your inheritance. I'm in love with you and if you try to give me a fucking out again, I'll spank your ass red and you won't be able to sit down for weeks." She nodded, knowing that her bossy husband meant every word of his threat.

"Okay," she whispered. "I just feel like I'm piling a lot on you and we're still technically newlyweds."

"Then let's start acting like fucking newlyweds," he growled, pulling Ava down onto his body and sealing his lips over hers. He kissed her for so long, she forgot all about being parked in front of her father's house until a sharp rapping sound on the back window got their attention. Corbin rolled down the window and looked out at her very angry father who was standing on the curb, watching them.

"What the hell is going on here?" he asked.

"Dad," Ava coldly greeted him.

"You want to explain what you are doing making out in the back of a car while parked in front of my house, Avalon?" Her father seemed more than angry; he was downright pissed. She hadn't gotten around to telling her dad that she was married. Really, Ava wanted to see the look on his face when she broke the news. All she disclosed was that she was seeing someone and that she wanted to bring him by to meet her father. Of course, he reluctantly agreed and demanded that she come over to sign the final papers from her grandfather's will. If she was a betting woman, she'd put money on her father already believing that he had won in this whole game he was playing. What he didn't know was that she was holding a trump card and she was about to play it.

"Well, Dad," she started but before she could get the rest out, Corbin squeezed her hand to let her know that he had it. She looked up at him, smiled, and nodded, giving him the go-ahead.

"I was kissing my wife," Corbin said.

"Your wife?" her father stuttered.

"Yes, Dad," Ava confirmed. "Corbin and I have been married for a few weeks now." The look on his face was almost comical and she was doing everything in her power not to burst out into fits of laughter.

"Married," her father said again.

"Yep," Corbin said. "Married."

"I'm assuming that's why you summoned me here, Dad," Ava asked. "Did you find out that I had a new boyfriend and never assumed that we'd taken the next step? What did you have planned? Were you going to rub it in my face that I didn't meet my deadline? Did you want to size up the man that I am with—because he's quite impressive," she admitted.

"Aw, thanks, babe," Corbin said, giving her another quick kiss.

"So, which was it going to be, Dad?" she asked again. Her father didn't answer and she knew that her hunch was correct. He had already taken a victory lap and now he was clueless as to what to do next. She almost felt bad for her father—almost.

"Were you going to even wish me a happy birthday?" Ava questioned.

"As you've already guessed, this wasn't about your birthday —this is business, Avalon and you know how I handle business." She knew exactly how her father handled his business and the people he considered threats to him and his interests. She and Corbin's challenge now presented a threat to him and Ava knew to watch her back.

"How about we go into the house and discuss this like civilized adults," Corbin offered.

"Really, there isn't much more to talk about, Mr.—" Her father looked at him as if he was trying to size Corbin up.

"Corbin Eklund," he said, opening his door to stand. Corbin held out his hand for her father and she could tell by his wide-eyed expression that he wasn't planning on her new husband being quite so big. Again, Ava had to fight the urge to giggle.

"Ronald Michaels," her father said, shaking Corbin's extended hand. "You know this changes nothing, right Avalon?" he said, looking around Corbin to where she still sat in the back of the car. "You will have to prove that your marriage isn't a sham and I will make sure that my lawyers leave no rock unturned in the process of proving you a liar."

Corbin stepped in front of her father's sight line to her and squared his shoulders. Ava was behind him, but she knew what her husband looked like when he was pissed off and she also knew her father might be afraid of him but he'd never back down.

"From now on, Mr. Michaels, when you have something to say to my wife, it will go through me or my lawyers. You will find that I have just as many resources as you do and I will protect what's mine. Avalon is now mine and you will do well to remember that," Corbin growled. He turned and slid back into the car and pulled her against his body, shutting his window. Corbin gave the driver directions to the restaurant and they left —just like that. There were no further arguments or fanfare that usually occurred when she tried to put her foot down with her father. They simply pulled away from the curb and she didn't even bother to look back to where they had left her dad. She knew all too well that she'd find him watching them drive off, a mean scowl on his face. But this time, she didn't worry about what he could do to her or what her next move should be. She had Corbin by her side, holding her protectively against his body, and that was all she needed.

CORBIN

After a quiet dinner, Corbin took Avalon home and had plans to tie her to their bed, but as soon as they entered the building, he and Ava were immediately ushered into a small office by the head of his security.

"You mind telling me what the hell is going on here, Rob?" Corbin questioned. "It's Ava's birthday and I'd like to get on with celebrating with my new wife."

"Sorry Mr. Eklund, Mrs. Eklund," Rob nodded at Ava and tried to smile, but Corbin could see the concern behind the older man's eyes. "We've had a security breach and our team hasn't finished sweeping the penthouse yet," Rob said.

"What the fuck do you mean by security breach?" Corbin growled.

"Housekeeping saw a man in the elevator on their way out and he got away before they could report him. He apparently gained access to your penthouse and we're not sure how. We were given a good description and the team is working on pulling up video footage to see if we can get a picture of him. Don't worry, Sir, we will find him and figure out why he was here."

"Make sure you do," Corbin said. "I won't have my wife put in danger. We are going to stay elsewhere tonight. I'll be in touch and have one of the guys bring us some things we will need." The idea of staying at the penthouse while someone was lurking outside their front door made him half crazy. Ava had been through enough crap with her father; he couldn't let someone else completely ruin her birthday.

"We can go back to my townhouse," she offered. "It's still on the market and there is enough furniture there that we would be comfortable."

"Your security is basically non-existent, Mrs. Eklund," Rob cut in before Corbin could veto her idea. His head of security was right, she had awful security measures in place and there would be no way to keep her safe there.

"Okay, then what are our options?" Ava asked. Corbin hated the defeat in her voice.

"I own a hotel on the outskirts of town. It has fantastic security and I'll be able to keep you safe there," Corbin said. He wrapped his arms around her and she shivered. "I'm sorry about all of this, baby. I hate that this is ruining your birthday."

"Corbin, no," she said. "You aren't responsible for any of this. Being with you has only made my birthday all that more special."

"I'm sure I can do better once we get to my suite at the hotel," he whispered into her ear.

"Keep this between us and the team, Rob. I don't want this leaking to the press," Corbin ordered. His head of security nodded and promised to keep him updated when they had more information.

"I'll contact you as soon as we have a clear image of the guy," Rob agreed. Corbin nodded and ushered Ava out of the security office and into his private elevator that would take them back down to the garage.

"Are we safe?" Ava stuttered. "You know without your security?"

Corbin hated the fear he heard in her voice. "Yeah, baby," he said. "I have two guys waiting for us in the garage and my driver. They will tail us to my hotel to make sure we aren't being followed. I won't let anyone touch you, Ava." He wrapped a protective arm around her body and she snuggled into his side, seeming to need his comfort.

"Thank you, Corbin," she whispered. The elevator doors opened and they were immediately flanked by two of his security detail. He wasn't taking any chances with his wife. When Aiden was running for the Senate, they decided to up their security measures for both of their families and that included Rose. Corbin and Aiden weren't going to take any chances with the people they loved. They quickly found out that there were a lot of people in the world who wanted to get to them just because of who they were and the company they built. Now that Ava was in his life, he appreciated the security team even more. He'd do just about anything to keep his wife safe.

They stepped out of the elevator, his arm still protectively around Ava's body and he didn't miss her little gasp when she realized that his security team was by their sides. "Is this all really necessary?" she asked.

"Yep," he said. "I won't take chances with you, honey. Once we are at the hotel and I go over the security plans with my team there, I'll make this all up to you." He playfully bobbed his eyebrows at her, hoping to alleviate some of the stress he himself was feeling. He knew that people would try to get to them—they were one powerful couple with his money and her name, but he didn't like the fact that someone was actually in their home. That was the last straw for him and he would make sure that never happened again.

"I'm sure you will," she whispered. Corbin helped her slip into the back seat of the waiting SUV and slid in next to her. "How long until we are at the hotel?" she nervously asked.

"Not too long," he said. "You just relax and let me worry about everything."

"I just think that it's a crazy coincidence that this guy broke into our home after we had our meeting with my father today," she whispered.

"Are you accusing your dad of breaking into our place, Ava?" Corbin asked. Honestly, he had the same suspicions, but he didn't want to outright accuse her father or anything like that. He wouldn't put it past the guy though. From their earlier exchange, her father wasn't too happy with Ava and her decision to marry him. Corbin wasn't sure how a man could have so much contempt for his own child but that was always something that haunted him. His own father walked away from him and his mother before he was even born and he always wondered how a man could do that. He had thought about Ava pregnant with his child a half dozen times, since getting back and meeting Aiden and Zara's little one, and each and every time his damn heart felt as if it would burst in his chest. If he was ever given the privilege of having kids with Ava, he wouldn't fuck it up.

"I think it's a good possibility that he had something to do with the break-in. But why would he go to such lengths to get to me? Was anything taken?" she asked. That was the part that had Corbin stumped—nothing seemed to be touched.

"No," he breathed. "It was as if he didn't touch anything. He must have been wearing gloves too because my team found no trace of prints." Corbin wished he had more information, but he knew his security team was the best his money could buy and if there was something to be found, they'd find it.

"Then, why go to the trouble of breaking into our place?" Ava asked. Corbin shrugged, not really having an answer to give her.

"We'll know more soon, honey," he promised.

"I need for you to tell me what you find, Corbin," she insisted. He worried that she'd ask that of him. He was hoping to keep her safe from this mess. If there was an issue with her father, he wanted to handle it for her, but he also knew his wife and Ava would give him hell for keeping her in the dark. "Corbin," she warned, when he didn't immediately give her an answer.

"Fine," he reluctantly agreed. "I'll keep you up to speed, but you won't be getting involved in this, Ava. If something needs to be handled—even something involving your father, I'll be the one doing it. Agreed?" Corbin waited her out, knowing that she wanted to give him some fight just from the expression on her beautiful face.

"Fine," she said.

"Thank you for that, honey," he said, kissing the top of her head. Ava snuggled into his body, and he wrapped an arm around Ava's waist. She yawned and he knew it had been a long day for her. "Get some shut eye," he ordered. "I'll wake you when we get to the hotel."

Ava nodded and yawned again and before he knew it, his girl was softly snoring on his shoulder. Corbin smiled to himself, loving the fact that she felt so comfortable around him, letting him see all of her and he had to admit, he loved every part of Avalon Eklund—especially her new last name.

※

They spent two long days cooped up in his suite at the hotel he owned across town. He had kept Ava occupied in his bed, but he could tell that his new wife was getting a little antsy. If he was being honest, he was starting to feel the exact same way, but there was no way Ava would let him leave the hotel without her and taking her out into public without knowing who or what the threat was yet, wasn't acceptable.

Corbin had called Aiden to warn him about what was going on. They couldn't rule out the possibility that whoever was in his penthouse, two nights prior, wasn't there for Avalon but for him. He and Aiden had faced a few security breaches in their time, especially owning a multi-billion dollar business. Hell, he had faced his share of surprise visits from women admirers who wanted a piece of him, but this was different. He couldn't explain it, but this time his gut was screaming at him that Ava was the target and he would do everything in his power to keep his wife safe.

Aiden agreed with him, but also took measures to protect his family. Zara kept the girls home from school and Aiden had taken up residence in his family room, turning it into a makeshift office. Corbin had done the same at his hotel and even had Ava's business partner send over her laptop and some work she could do from the hotel. She was supposed to travel back to France in a week, but there was no way he was going to let that happen—not until they knew who or what was after them.

Corbin looked across the room to find Ava hard at work on her computer and the way she was biting her bottom lip into her sexy mouth, as if deep in thought, was completely turning him on. "I can feel you looking at me," she said, not looking up from her laptop. "And I can't. I'm working."

"You could, if I ordered you to," he countered. Ava shot him a sexy smile and rolled her eyes.

"I'll make you a deal. You let me go to France next week and I'll stop working to meet your demands," she sassed. It was a tempting offer but he also knew that letting Ava out of his sight wasn't an option. There was no way he would agree to let her go to France next week.

"No," he said, pointing a finger in her direction. She made a humphing noise and stuck her nose back into her computer screen. Her adorable, sultry pout was nearly his undoing. "It's just not safe, Ava," he amended.

"How am I any safer here, trapped in this hotel room with you and your security team stationed outside in the hallway? We can just bring them along and they can guard the house in France," she offered. They had already been over all of this though and he had a feeling that his wife would continue to push until she got her way.

"I told you I don't have time to go to France and you're not going without me," Corbin grumbled. "I won't change my mind on this, Ava." She crossed her arms over her impressive cleavage, and it was all he could do to keep his wits about him.

"I need to get out of this hotel room, Corbin. Take me to the club—we'd be safe there and we can play," she offered. Now, that sounded like a fucking fantastic idea but he also knew it was a bad one.

"You know that your father is a member there and he has friends in high places. If he's the one trying to get to us, we would be giving him easy access." Corbin had done a little digging around at the club and he had found that Ronald Michaels' reach was far and wide in town. He practically owned everything, including a piece of the BDSM club where he and Ava met up. There would be no way he would be taking her back there any time soon.

"We don't even know that my father was behind the break-in," she said. Corbin looked at her as if she had to be crazy. Sure, they didn't have concrete proof, but what other explanation was there for a strange man showing up at their home the same night she told her father that she had beat him at his own game and gotten married. "Well, it's true," she said, defensively. "What if it was just some guy looking for a payday and he just so happens to break into your penthouse?"

Corbin rolled his eyes, "It's our penthouse and that might be a plausible explanation if something had been taken, but nothing was. Hell, he could have had quite a payday with everything I had just laying around but he took nothing. It just doesn't add up."

"When will we know more?" Ava asked. He had been waiting to tell her this next part. Corbin didn't want to get her hopes up and honestly, he was hoping to sneak down to his office in the lobby while she was working. He had promised to keep her in the loop, but until he had firsthand information to give her, he wanted to try to handle things himself.

"In about an hour," he admitted. "Rob called to tell me he had a clean picture from the video footage and he was bringing it over personally." He could feel her heated stare and Corbin knew that keeping that bit of information to himself was a shitty idea.

"And you were going to tell me this when?" she questioned.

"After the meeting," he admitted. Corbin knew better than to lie to Ava—she'd have his balls and he had grown rather fond of them.

She growled and stood from the sofa, all but throwing her laptop down onto the coffee table. "Corbin James Eklund," she shouted. He winced at the use of his middle name. His mother was the only other person in his life that ever middle named him and he had to admit, when Ava said it, it didn't seem to have the same effect as when his mom did. Honestly, it made him kind of hot, but he knew to keep that part to himself—at least for now.

He stood and crossed the room, standing over her body, loving the way his fierce wife didn't even stammer. Backing down wasn't her thing and he loved how she stood up not just for her friends, but also for herself. "Ava," he whispered.

"Don't you Ava me," she yelled, pressing her little finger into his chest. God, everything she was doing was having the opposite effect on him of what she was probably hoping for. He found the whole scene hot and he wondered just how she'd feel about him stripping her bare and sinking into her body.

"Is this our first official fight?" he whispered. Ava leaned into his body and he had his answer—she was just as hot and bothered by him as he was her.

"Don't try to distract me," she insisted, pressing both of her palms into his bare chest. Ava was wearing just his dress shirt and he knew from watching her get dressed earlier, that she had nothing on underneath it. They had spent most of the past two days completely naked and if he had his way, they'd be that way again in the next few minutes.

"Am I?" he taunted.

"Are you what?" she whispered.

"Distracting you?" he asked.

"Yes," she said, her lips so close to his he could almost feel them brush against his own.

A sharp knock at the door had Ava almost jumping into his arms. "Fuck," he swore. "Hold that thought, baby," he ordered. Corbin crossed the hotel suite and pulled the door open, ready to murder whoever had interrupted them.

"This better be good," he growled. His head of security stood on the other side of the door and looked Corbin up and down and smirked. Rob nodded and strode past him into the room as if Corbin wasn't a threat to him. It was one of the things he liked best about the guy—nothing seemed to faze him, not even a man Corbin's size with an even bigger attitude problem.

"Sorry to interrupt, Mrs. Eklund," Rob said. Corbin suddenly realized what his wife was wearing and growled his frustration.

"For the love of fuck, Rob," Corbin shouted." At least turn around until my wife can put some clothes on," Rob turned to face him, giving Ava some privacy, and had the nerve to smile at him, as if he enjoyed the whole song and dance, they had going on between them. Ava giggled and pulled a blanket from the back of the sofa and wrapped it around her body.

"All clear," she said.

"Sorry, Mrs. Eklund," Rob said but Corbin knew he didn't mean a damn word of his apology.

"It's not a big deal, Rob. My husband is just a bit on edge. You have news?" Ava asked, as if taking charge of their little meeting. Rob nodded and sat down on the sofa, waiting for the two of them to join him.

"I do and I'm not sure you're going to like it, Mrs. Eklund," he said. Corbin sat down in an armchair and pulled Ava onto his lap. If it was news she wasn't going to like, he was going to damn well be there for her to help her through it.

"All right," she stuttered. Corbin was sure he could feel her heart beating and he hated that they were going to have to face the possibility that whoever was in their penthouse was there to hurt his wife. "Just say it," she ordered. "I'm ready."

Rob took a deep breath and let it out. "It's your brother," he said. "Ashton Michaels."

Ava gasped, "No—it can't be," she said. "We haven't heard from him in over twenty years. He disappeared and my family believed him dead." Ava reached a shaking hand to her mouth, to muffle her sob, and it nearly broke Corbin's heart.

"What's he fucking want?" Corbin questioned.

"I'm not really sure yet," Rob admitted. "But, as soon as I have any more information, I'll be in touch." He stood and handed Corbin an envelope which he assumed had Ava's brother's picture in it.

"Thanks, Rob," he said, giving a curt nod. Rob turned and left the suite, pulling the door shut behind him and Ava's soft sobs filled the room. Corbin felt helpless in knowing what to do for her, but he knew one thing—there would be no fucking way that her brother or anyone else in her damn family was ever going to get close enough to hurt his wife again.

AVALON

"Pack your fucking bags," Corbin growled. "We're going to France."

"But, I thought you just said we weren't going," Ava said. "We can't run from this mess, Corbin. If Ashton is alive and he was the guy in our apartment, I need to find out why. Let me talk to him." She could tell by the expression on his face that Corbin wasn't going to agree to her request before he even opened his mouth.

"No," he said. Corbin crossed his arms over his massive chest and she knew that he had already made up his mind. "Getting you out of town is the best option."

"But you said," she tried arguing, but he covered her mouth with his big hand.

"I know what I said, honey. I also know that until we know for sure why your brother is back and was in our home; I can't take any chances with you. I'll call to have my jet fueled and ready to leave within the hour. Pack your stuff but don't tell your partner we are leaving yet. You can call him when we get there and fill him in. I don't want any loose ends." Corbin waited her out as if he expected her to give him an argument.

Ava nodded and pulled his hand from her mouth. "Fine," she agreed. "But for the record, I think that running and hiding is an awful idea. I don't know why Ash was in our home but he's still my brother. I don't believe he was there to hurt me. The sooner we get answers the sooner we can put this mess behind us."

"It's too much of a coincidence, Ava. He showed up the same night we announce to your father that we're married. What if the two of them are working together? Do you trust your father?" Corbin asked. He already knew her answer and Ava hated that he was playing that card.

"No," she said. "You know I don't trust him and with good reason. But, that doesn't mean that Ash is bad too. It could just be a coincidence." Corbin shot her a disbelieving look and she sighed, knowing she had lost the fight. Really, she shouldn't be too upset—she was getting what she originally wanted, to go to France. That was before she found out that Ashton was the man in their penthouse. It was before she found out that her long lost brother was back from the dead. Going to France was the last thing she wanted to do now. But, convincing her husband not to run wasn't an option he seemed willing to explore.

※

Corbin rushed Ava through packing and ushered her down to the lobby, surrounded by his security team. She was sure that even an armored tank wouldn't be able to reach her through the army he had amassed to keep her safe.

"Is this all really necessary?" Ava asked.

"You are mine and I will protect you how I want to, Ava," Corbin growled. He stayed close to her side and she had to admit that Corbin having her back through all this mess gave her comfort. Just knowing that he meant every one of his promises made her feel safer.

"I appreciate that, I really do, Corbin. But, I think this is all a little overkill. If Ashton is the one who is after me, he won't hurt me. I'm his sister." She knew she had no real proof that her brother wouldn't hurt her. Hell, her own father wanted to hurt her for just marrying the man she had fallen in love with. Of course, her dad didn't know that part. As far as her father was concerned, she had married Corbin out of spite, to keep her grandfather's money. Could that be the reason Ash had come back? She didn't want to believe the worst of him, but she really had no other information to go on.

Corbin helped her into the waiting SUV and slid in next to her. As soon as they were both in the car, it pulled off from the curb and Corbin had slung his arm protectively around her shoulder. "Tell me about your brother, honey," he ordered. Since finding out that Ashton was the one in their home, she had been racking her brain trying to remember every detail of her older brother. Sadly, he left when she was still so young that she had forgotten a good deal about him.

"He disappeared when I was about nine. He had gone away to college and even pledged a fraternity. He seemed happy every time he came home on break, and I honestly hated him for it. Our mother died about four years prior, and I was miserable being left at home with my father and nannies," she said.

"Yes, you told me about how your father liked to work his way through your nannies. That must have been hard—not having any real stability at home," Corbin offered.

"Yeah, I had my grandpa and I got to go over to his house on weekends, but my father wasn't around a whole lot. He split his time between Washington, D.C. and here. I was lonely, besides the time that I spent with my grandfather. I learned early on not to get attached to my nannies and self-reliance became my refuge," Ava admitted. It wasn't until Ava got to college and met Zara that she started to come out of her shell. Zara saved her in more ways than one and she knew her best friend felt the same. They became each other's family and Ava even considered Zara her sister.

"Zara was the person who eventually helped to pull me from my shell. I guess that's why I'm so fierce when it comes to anyone or anything trying to hurt her. That's why I gave Aiden such a hard time when we all first met." Corbin laughed.

"You were pretty fantastic at giving Aiden crap, honey," he said. Corbin kissed her cheek and she smiled up at him. "Tell me more about Ashton," he prompted.

She thought back to the time after her brother seemed to disappear from the face of the earth and frowned. "The night we got news that he disappeared was so chaotic. I was at home alone with the nanny of the month and we were woken in the middle of the night by the cops banging at our front door. She tried to tell me to go back to sleep—that everything would be all right, but she was wrong. I went back upstairs, but hid at the end of the hallway, out of sight, to eavesdrop. I heard the cops ask where my brother was and she told them that he should be in his dormitory at school. They kept asking questions," Ava remembered.

"What kind of questions?" Corbin asked.

"Um—stuff like what kind of car he drove and if he had a girlfriend or boyfriend. The nanny kept telling them she had no idea and the cop accused her of being uncooperative. They threatened to take her down to the station to answer questions if she refused to cooperate. That's about the time that my grandfather showed up. He told my nanny to go back to her room and called me down from my hiding spot in the hallway."

Corbin chuckled, "He knew you were there, listening?"

"Yep," she said. "He knew me inside and out. I couldn't get away with anything when he was around." Ava giggled at the memory. He always knew what she was up to and usually called her on her shit. If it wasn't for him, Ava would have been allowed to get away with just about anything and there was no telling the person she would have turned out to be.

"I think I would have liked your Grandpa, Ava," Corbin admitted.

"I know he would have liked you, Corbin," she said. She had thought about that a few times since meeting Corbin, whether her Grandpa would have approved of her marrying a man like Corbin Eklund. He was never so stuffy to buy into that new and old money business that her father had. Ava was sure that her grandfather would have wholeheartedly approved of her choice of Corbin and that thought made her happy.

"Did you get into trouble?" he asked.

"Nope." She smiled at him triumphantly and Corbin chuckled, shaking his head at her. "He told me that it wasn't polite to spy on people and to go to my room. I didn't dare disobey him and try to listen in on the rest of the conversation." Ava shivered against Corbin. Her grandfather was a fair man, but if crossed he wasn't pleasant to deal with.

"Was that when you found out Ashton was missing?" Corbin asked.

"No, not that night. I woke up the next morning full of questions, but my grandpa was gone. The nanny pretended that nothing had happened the night before. She even had the nerve to brush off my questions about the cops showing up at my house as me having bad dreams. But, I knew what I saw," she said.

"Shit," Corbin swore. "What did you do?"

"I waited until that next weekend. I knew the only person who would give me an honest answer would be my grandfather. I pretended to forget all about the cop's visit but as soon as I got to my grandpa's house, it was as if everything I was holding in that whole week exploded out of me." Corbin laughed again. "Yeah, that was the same reaction my grandfather had too," Ava admitted.

"I bet. You do have a way with words, baby," he teased. Ava slapped at his chest and giggled.

"Well, it didn't do me any good. He told me nothing except

that Ashton was missing. They didn't know where he was or when he'd be back." Ava felt the same sadness she had when her Grandpa told her about her brother all over again. She remembered how upset he seemed when he told her and if she wasn't mistaken, he even shed a tear as he told her about Ash.

"I'm sorry, honey," Corbin said, cuddling her into his side. "But, why did you believe he was dead?"

"After a few years, I just assumed it to be true. My father didn't allow any talk of Ashton in our home. It was the same way when my mother died—we weren't allowed to even bring up her name." Ava remembered wanting to talk to anyone who'd listen about her mother, but that wasn't allowed. Her father even went so far as to forbid her nannies to talk to her about her mom. It was a very confusing time for her.

"I wanted to remember them both, but it wasn't allowed," she admitted.

"You were just a little girl, honey. Of course you just wanted to talk about your mom and brother," Corbin soothed. Ava thought her father was just upset about losing them both, but after time she came to realize that it was a form of control for him. He started to control everything about her—from what she said and thought to who she hung out with. It was one of the main reasons she had no real friends in high school. She shut herself off from the world and that girl was someone she never wanted to be again.

"Somewhere along the way, I just started believing that Ashton was dead like my mother. No one corrected me and that was that. Now—" Her voice cracked, and Ava hated feeling so helpless. Corbin wrapped his arms around her tighter.

"Now," he said. "We find out just where the hell your brother has been all this time and figure out why he was in our home. You have me now, honey and I'll be by your side the whole time and we'll figure it out together." Ava nodded, not sure she could speak passed the lump of emotion in her throat.

"Thank you, Corbin," she whispered.

"No need to ever thank me, honey. You're my wife and we do all of this together from now on."

"Deal," she said, smiling up at him. Corbin gently kissed her lips and Ava wondered just what she had done to deserve such a man in her life. She wasn't going to question it though because he was hers now and there wasn't anything she'd want to do to change that.

※

Corbin gave instructions to his pilot and Ava hated that they were going to France. Sure, she had all but begged him to take her there just that morning, but now it felt more like they were running away from their problems. She wanted to start facing down her demons and going to France now felt wrong; not that there would be any way for her to change her husband's mind on the matter. He had seemed to make his decision just as soon as his head of security showed up at the hotel with news about Ashton.

He ushered her onto the waiting jet that his and Aiden's company owned and went to find the pilot. Ava sent Zara a quick text telling her that she was fine but they had a change in plans. Hell, her entire life was starting to feel like one giant change of plans and she wondered if or when that would ever be different.

Corbin made quite a ruckus entering the plane and she didn't bother to look up from her phone. She needed a few minutes to get herself together and if pretending to talk to Zara bought her time, she'd use it to her advantage.

"Avalon." Ava heard his voice and knew exactly who was talking to her, but she worried that when she looked up, she wouldn't find her brother standing in front of her. She tightly closed her eyes, like when she was a child and wanted to hide from whoever was trying to talk to her. Ava always foolishly believed that if she couldn't see someone, they wouldn't be able to see her.

"Ava, please look at me," Ash whispered.

"No," she said. "You aren't here, and this isn't real. You're supposed to be dead." Her brother barked out his laugh, causing her to jump in her seat. Ava opened her eyes and stood. There would be no hiding from the person who was now mere inches away from her. If her brother was there to do her harm, she'd find a way to get to Corbin.

"What the fuck?" Corbin growled from the door. "Ava, tell me you are all right," he ordered.

She nodded, "I'm fine, Corbin."

"Come here," he said. She didn't hesitate, brushing passed Ashton to stand by Corbin. He pulled her protectively against his side and she swore she could hear his heart beating.

"Ava, please," her brother begged. "Just talk to me."

"Ashton," Ava squeaked and cleared her throat. She wasn't going to let him know how much he had upset her. Ash owed her explanations and she was going to keep her wits about her and ask him for those answers. "How are you here?" Corbin tugged at her arm, as if he wanted to get her the hell out of there, but the way her brother was watching her, he looked just as upset about the whole situation as she felt. "I'm okay, Corbin," she lied. "This is my brother, Ashton. Or at least I think he's my brother." Ava looked him up and down and honestly, she wasn't quite sure if the man standing in front of her was the same boy who had left them years ago. Ash looked so different now but she knew firsthand how time could change people.

"Hey Sis," he whispered. "It's been a while."

"That's what you say to me after not having any contact for over twenty years? God, Ash—I thought you were dead. How could you just leave with no word? Do you know what losing you did to Grandpa?"

"Please believe that if there was any other way, I would have done everything differently. But there wasn't," Ashton said.

"I'm sorry if I don't buy that you had no choice but to leave our family, and especially our grandfather, completely broken-hearted, Ash," Ava spat.

"Grandpa was the one who came up with the idea for me to leave," Ashton admitted. Ava belted out her laugh and shook her head, as if she was trying to shake the image of her beloved grandfather forcing her brother to leave town.

"You said you had no other choice," Corbin interrupted. "Mind telling us what you mean by that?" Ava shot him a look as if he had lost his mind and he just shrugged it off.

Ash nodded, "I did something that would have ruined our family and I was sent away. Honestly, it was the best decision for everyone."

Avalon bravely took a step towards Ash. "It wasn't the best decision for me, Ash," Ava shouted. "You left me with a monster and after Grandpa died, I had no one."

"I know, Sis and if I could take back any of your pain and suffering, I would." Ashton reached for her and she took a step away from him, backing right into Corbin's body. He wrapped his arms around her and she had to admit, she was thankful for his support.

"Why did you break into our home?" Corbin growled.

"To warn you, Ava," Ashton said, looking directly at her. "Dad will stop at nothing to keep you from getting all of Grandpa's money. He's lost everything and you were his last hope of holding onto the family fortune."

"Tell me why Grandpa would send you away like that, Ash," she demanded. "Make me understand why you left." She sounded like she was begging him and hell, maybe she was, but Ava didn't care.

"It's a long story," he said.

"We've got time," Corbin said. "And, if you think about trying to leave, you should know that I have two armed guards waiting just outside the plane to take you into custody."

"I don't want any trouble," Ashton admitted. "I just want to warn my sister—keep her safe."

"Then we are in agreement because I will do whatever it takes to keep my wife safe," Corbin said.

Ash smiled, "I like him." He crossed the fuselage to the jet's mini bar and pulled a bottle of scotch down, pouring himself a generous portion. He swallowed it back in one and turned to face Avalon. "Sorry," he said. "I needed a little liquid courage. This isn't going to be pretty, and you aren't going to like any of it, Ava," he admitted.

"If you can't tell," Ava said, holding her arms wide, "I'm all grown up now."

"I see that and you turned out good, baby sister," Ash said, smiling over at her. Ava could see the sadness behind his eyes and worried that he was right about one thing, she wasn't going to like what he was about to tell her.

"Just tell me, Ash," she begged.

He sat down in one of the leather seats, leaning back into the plush cushions. "My freshman year in college, I killed someone," he said. Avalon gasped, covering her mouth with her hands.

"Fuck," Corbin swore. Ava shot him a sideways glance and he held up his hands, as if telling her he'd back down and let her handle things with her brother. Ava knew that Corbin wouldn't let her have the floor for long. He liked his control, but he also seemed to know that she needed to get to the bottom of what was going on with Ashton.

"How?" she asked.

"Hit and run," Ashton said. "I went to one of those stupid fraternity parties and I was a fool. I was pledging the fraternity and got way too drunk; apparently that didn't stop me from getting behind the wheel and trying to drive home. I hit a woman who was walking home from a bus stop and killed her, instantly. I woke up in our driveway. Apparently, I blacked out and don't remember the accident, which is my only saving grace. When I realized what I had done, I was a coward and I ran—straight to Grandpa and he told me he'd fix everything."

"You didn't go to the police?" Corbin questioned.

"No," Ash whispered. "It would have ended both Dad and Grandpa's careers. They wouldn't allow it. I begged Grandpa to let me turn myself in. Days after the accident, I felt so much guilt I wanted to do the right thing but he refused. He didn't tell Dad at first and by the time it was all over, I was picking up with a new life across the country and no one was the wiser. You were just a kid, but I have to admit leaving you was the hardest part."

"You left without a word," she cried, and Corbin tightened his arms around her.

"I said goodbye to you, Sis. You were sleeping at the time," Ashton said. "The night I left, I snuck into your room and kissed your forehead and told you how sorry I was. It was just before the police showed up at the door and Grandpa shooed them away."

"You were there that night?" Ava asked. "Why didn't you say something?"

"I couldn't. He made me promise that I'd do exactly as he wanted. Hell, he didn't even know I showed up at the house until the next day. I just couldn't leave without seeing you one last time. So, I snuck out of Grandpa's house and by the time I got to Dad's, you were sound asleep. I hid in your closet when the police showed up and woke you and your nanny up. I snuck out the back of the house when Grandpa caught you eavesdropping and didn't look back. The next day, he told me that he knew that I had left his house and gone to see you. He was furious that I disobeyed him and I was so worried that he might change his mind about helping me, I panicked," Ash admitted. "I promised to do whatever he wanted and he sent me away."

"Why come back now?" Corbin asked. "You obviously got away with it, so why risk coming back now?"

"Because Dad is completely off his rocker and if you're not careful, he'll use whatever means necessary to keep you from getting your hands on Grandpa's money. Dad must have found out about what I did and how Grandpa helped me. That was how he got his old man to put the marriage stipulation into his will. He basically blackmailed him to add that fucking clause, never expecting you to settle down."

"Well, that explains everything. I wondered how Dad got Grandpa to agree to that crazy clause. He would have never willingly handed over control to Dad unless he had no choice," Avalon said.

"You're right. They hated each other and I'm betting Dad pulled out all the stops when he stuck it to Grandpa," Ash said.

"How is your father out of money?" Corbin asked. That was a good question. Even without her grandfather's fortune, her father would have inherited enough money, to keep him in the lifestyle he was accustomed to, from his mother. Both of her grandparents came from well-to-do families and old money. That was part of the reason why her grandpa didn't want her dad getting his hands on his money. Her grandmother had doted on her father and made sure that he'd never want for anything. Maybe that was the reason her father and grandfather never really got along. Ava didn't personally know her grandmother, but from what she had gathered, she wasn't a very nice person.

"You know Dad has a problem with keeping his pants zipped up. He made a few bad decisions in his personal life and with the few businesses that he bought into. He's broke, Ava," Ashton said. "Grandpa's money is his last hope and you're the only thing standing between him and that fortune."

"Correction," Corbin barked. "We're the only thing standing between your father and Ava's money. If I have a say in all of this, and I do now that Ava is my wife, your dad won't touch a penny of it."

Ashton smiled again, reminding Ava of the young boy she used to know. "Yep, I like him."

"So, now what?" Ava asked. "You just disappear into the shadows again and I'm supposed to pretend that you're dead?"

"No," Ash breathed. "I'm turning myself in. It's the right thing to do. It's time I paid for my crimes and made things right. Besides, Grandpa's gone and I don't give a fuck about Dad's non-existent political career."

Ava hated thinking about her brother being locked away but he was right. He committed a crime and their family had kept his secret for long enough. "You said you have guards outside?" Ash asked Corbin. Her husband reluctantly nodded. "Good, tell them that I'm in here and I wish to surrender." Corbin looked down at Ava and she nodded.

"He's right," she said. "It's for the best."

"I'll be right back," he promised, turning to leave the plane.

"Will you come visit me?" Ash almost whispered his question.

"Of course," she promised. "Whenever I can." Ava crossed the plane's small cabin and wrapped her arms around her brother. "You're my brother, Ash and I love you."

"Love you too, squirt," he choked. Corbin walked back onto the jet with his two security guards and Ava watched as they took her brother into custody. She was proud of herself for keeping it together until they removed him from the plane and then she broke down in Corbin's arms. She allowed herself to fall apart knowing that he'd be there to catch her.

CORBIN

Corbin listened to his wife's sobs and they nearly broke his heart. It was almost too much but he knew she needed him now more than ever. "We're going to be okay, honey," he soothed.

"I know but it just doesn't feel that way at the moment," she admitted. "We can't go to France right now, Corbin. I need to be here for Ashton. He'll need a lawyer and someone in his corner." He hated the idea of sticking around and giving her father a chance to make good on his threats. Her dad had hired a team of lawyers to poke into their marriage and try to prove that they had married for her inheritance. He worried that the truth would come out and he hated that Ava might lose everything. They might have started out getting hitched as a way for her to keep her grandfather's money, but it had turned into so much more. He was completely in love with her and he knew she felt the same way about him.

The fact remained that she had married him as a way to keep her money and if her father's lawyers could prove that fact in a court of law, she'd lose everything she was fighting so hard to keep. "But your father," he protested.

"Can go straight to hell. I'm done running and hiding from him. If he wants to come at me, let him. What he's going to find is a woman who's willing and ready to fight for what she wants now," Ava said.

"And a man who's completely in love with her, who's also willing to fight alongside of her." Ava turned to face him and smiled.

"I love you too, Corbin. Let's fight this—together," she said, holding out her hand, waiting for him to take her up on her offer. Corbin didn't feel even the slightest hesitancy, reaching for her hand and taking it in his own.

"Together," he agreed.

"So, what do we do first?" Ava asked and he laughed. God, he loved his woman.

"First, we go home and take our lives back. No more running and no more hiding. Then, I think we need to use our resources and get some people in high places involved. I think that once your father sees that he can't bully his way out of this, he might back down." Ava shot him a look that told him she didn't believe him, but she would.

"We have friends in high places?" she asked.

"Sure—I happen to even know a Senator," Corbin teased. "It's time to come clean with our friends and tell Aiden and Zara what's really been going on between us. They'll understand."

"I doubt that Zara will be so understanding, but you're right. It's time to stop going it alone. I've done that for so long, I've forgotten what it's like to have someone in my life that has my back."

"Baby, I'll always have your back—and your front," Corbin teased, bobbing his eyebrows at her to drive his point home. Ava's giggle filled the jet's cabin and for the first time in days, Corbin felt as if everything might be all right.

"Let's go home," Ava said and he had to admit, that sounded like one hell of a plan.

❄

"You want to say that again?" Zara shouted. She handed her daughter to Aiden as she rounded the sofa to confront Corbin and he had to admit, he was scared of what she planned on doing next. Not too many women scared the shit out of him, but Zara was one of them.

"He married me to help me keep my money," Ava said. They had already been through all this a couple times, but Zara refused to just accept what they were telling her.

"You just settled?" Zara growled at Ava. Corbin tried to tuck her behind his body, but Ava wouldn't have it. She stepped out from behind him and faced her friend head on.

"I did not settle," Ava spat. "I love Corbin and he loves me. It just started out as a way for me to keep my grandfather's money, but it turned into more."

Zara pointed her finger into Corbin's chest, and he knew she was far from finished giving him the run around. "You did this," she accused. "You fed on my best friend's moment of weakness. You saw your in with her and took it." She poked her boney little finger into his chest with just about every word, as if accenting her point.

"No, he didn't," Ava defended, stepping between him and Zara's offensive finger. "I was the one who took advantage of him. I wanted him to marry me and he said yes."

"How about I put Lexi in her crib and the four of us sit down like adults to discuss this?" Aiden asked. "The girls will be home soon, and I don't want them to see us fighting."

"You're right," Zara agreed. "Then Corbin can explain to us how he plans on making this all right with Ava. You can't just use her and dump her."

"Woah," Corbin protested. "Now that's going too far, Zara. You can yell at me and berate me all you'd like but don't ever accuse me of using Ava. I'd never do that and there is no fucking way I'm going to ever dump her." The idea of losing

Ava scared the crap out of him and he wouldn't let Zara imply that was even a possibility.

"Zara, honey, let's just hear them out before we start accusing any one of anything," Aiden insisted. Corbin nodded his thanks and his friend disappeared upstairs with the baby.

"How about you help me with some food, Ava," Zara insisted. Ava looked back at him as her best friend pulled her into the kitchen and he smiled and shrugged. Corbin needed a reprieve and maybe that made him a complete fucking chicken, but he didn't give a shit.

Aiden came jogging back down the stairs and peeked into the kitchen to where the two girls were talking, probably about him. "Geeze man, why would you go and open up a whole can of worms like that? You had to know that Zara would react to your news that way. What were you thinking?"

"That I need your help," Corbin admitted. He hadn't gotten to that part. Zara hadn't given him or Ava the chance to get to the part where they believed that her father would stop at nothing to get his hands on her money.

"My help?" Aiden asked. "You know you never even have to ask for that. Whatever you need, I'm here for you, man." Corbin breathed a sigh of relief. He knew that Aiden was true to his word and that he could always count on his best friend to have his back, but hearing him say the words felt as if a burden had been lifted off Corbin's chest.

"Thanks for that, Aiden," he said. "I think Ava's in trouble."

"In trouble how?" Aiden asked.

"I think that her father realizes that he's about to lose at this little game he has been playing and he's flat broke. He won't let her walk away with her grandfather's money and I won't let him anywhere near my wife," Corbin admitted.

"Okay, let's get the women back in here and we can talk this through. I think you should start at the beginning and we'll figure things out from there," Aiden promised. As if on cue, Zara and Ava returned with their arms full of food and it was as if things weren't vamped up and heated between them just moments before. But that was the way things were with them. It was the way things worked in a family and Corbin was damn happy that he had both Aiden and Zara behind them. They needed all the help they could get at this point.

"First, we eat," Zara insisted, setting the plates down on the table. "Then, we plot. There is no way Ava's father is going to touch one cent of her grandfather's money," she said. "Not if I have anything to say about it."

AVALON

"I'm going to take a quick shower and then I will come back, and we can veg out and watch some television, if you'd like," Corbin offered. He had been so quiet the whole car ride home from Zara and Aiden's, she was starting to worry that she had done something wrong. What she really wanted from her husband was the chance to show him how much she needed his dominance. It had been days since Corbin had commanded her body, mind and soul and it was about time she reminded him how well they worked together.

Ava slyly nodded and watched as he walked back to their master bathroom. As soon as she heard the water turn on, she tugged her clothes off and stood naked in the middle of their bedroom. The urge to touch herself made her half-crazy with lust. She knew it was one of Corbin's hard and fast BDSM rules —he liked to control all her orgasms, but she was already topping from the bottom, and she was pretty sure that act alone was going to earn her a few spankings.

Ava snaked her hand down her body and found her already wet, throbbing clit and hesitantly ran her fingers over it. She moaned at just how good that felt. She sunk to her knees and palmed her breasts, needing more. Ava worked two of her fingers in and out of her pussy, wishing they were her husband's cock, needing more pleasure than she could ever give herself. She had just about found her release when Corbin emerged still wet from the shower, to find her kneeling on their bedroom floor, masturbating.

"Well, I see someone has thrown all of my rules right out the window," he growled. She looked up at him through her lust fueled haze and wondered if she was going to be punished before or after she found her release. Her husband was quite ruthless when it came to withholding her orgasms when she broke his rules.

"Corbin, please," she whimpered, not bothering to remove her fingers from her drenched folds. "I need you so much."

He barked out his laugh, dropping his towel to show off his already impressive erection. "Looks like you're doing pretty good there all by yourself, sweetheart." He stroked his heavy shaft through his hands and threw back his head, his sexy lips parted on a moan.

"Fuck," Ava swore. "That's so fucking hot, Corbin. Please can I taste you?" she begged.

"Sure, baby," he said, staring her down. "Just as soon as you tell me what this little show is all about."

Ava pouted and he chuckled, not letting go of his cock. She couldn't take her eyes off him, and she worried that he was going to leave her wet and needy in the middle of their bedroom floor while he found his release. He was stubborn enough to wait her out and knowing that left her no choice but to admit to her feelings.

"Fine," she said, sitting back on her heels, gifting him with the perfect view of her pussy. "I miss you."

"So you said," he teased. "But what you're doing has nothing to do with me. In fact, it's breaking one of my rules," he said.

"Two actually," she whispered, inwardly cursing herself for saying anything that would get her in deeper trouble.

"Sorry?" Aiden questioned. "You broke two rules?" he asked.

"Yeah, although it's technically not a rule. I'm topping from the bottom," she said.

"Hmm," he hummed and just that little sound had a fresh wave of wetness coating her thighs. "Looks like you're right," he said. "So, I take it this is your way of telling me you don't want to watch a movie cuddled up in bed tonight?" he teased.

"No," Ava breathed. "I need you, Corbin—all of you. Ever since this thing with the break-in happened and the whole mess with Ash, you haven't touched me."

"That's not exactly true," he defended. "We've made love since finding out about your brother." He wasn't wrong. They had sex a few times a day but he was always so careful not to push her. She could tell he was holding back with her and Ava hated that.

"I need all of you, Corbin," she said. Ava fought to hold back her tears. She needed to get through this without crying. Corbin seemed to pick up on her distress and crossed the room to stand in front of her.

"Tell me what's going on, Ava," he ordered.

"I can tell that you're holding back from me. You aren't giving me your full dominance and I need that from you right now, Corbin. Especially now," she sobbed.

Corbin grabbed handfuls of her hair and gave a sharp yank, getting her attention. "Open," he ordered. "You want my dominance and I'll give it to you, baby. When we are done here, I'll be giving you your punishment and I'm pretty sure you won't be able to sit down on that sexy, curvy ass of yours for days." Ava's body hummed to life with his promise and she willingly opened her mouth, letting him slide his cock all the way in to the back of her throat. Ava loved the way Corbin took control, pumping himself in and out of her mouth.

"Touch yourself," he ordered. "Finish being naughty for me, honey." Ava looked up his body to find him watching her and she knew better than to disobey him again. She reached back down and let her fingers glide through her slick pussy and moaned around his cock. "God, Ava," he growled. "I'm not going to last much longer if you keep doing shit like that. I want you with me. Get yourself off," he ordered.

She bucked and writhed on her fingers as they slid in and out of her wet folds. When Corbin reached down to pinch her taut nipple between his thumb and finger, she couldn't take anymore. She felt as though she was flying and when Corbin threw his head back and moaned her name, she knew he was just about ready to lose himself down her throat. He pumped in and out of her mouth a few more times, until he shot his seed into her willing mouth. Ava took everything he was giving her and licked his cock clean.

"Good girl," he hoarsely praised. "Now, for your punishment," he taunted.

Ava smiled up at him, not hiding how much she was looking forward to everything his sinful voice promised. "Yes, Sir," she enthusiastically said. Corbin chuckled and ran his hand down her jaw to cup her chin.

"Don't play games with me," he said. "If you want or need something from me, all you have to do is tell me, Ava. I'm sorry I've been holding back with you lately. You were right—I was worried about how you were holding up with everything that was happening, and I should have known my tough girl would be able to take just about anything life threw her way." Ava soaked up his praise, not quite sure how she had gotten so lucky in the husband department but she wasn't about to start questioning things now. Corbin was hers and that was all that mattered.

"Now, up on the bed and show me that ass," he ordered. "I'm going to spank it red and then fuck you from behind, Wife," he said.

"Yes, sir," she agreed because what else could she do? Her Dom gave her a command and Ava was nothing but obedient.

"You will keep count for me, Ava," he ordered. "This isn't

for your pleasure, and I won't go easy on you." She felt almost giddy with anticipation at Corbin's promise. This was exactly what she had been craving. He was everything she needed and so much more—she just needed all of him, no holding back.

"Yes, sir," she said. She crawled onto the bed and laid face down on the soft comforter, her knees bent under her and her ass up in the air for Corbin, just as he demanded. He groaned and ran his big hand down her bare ass, cupping her sex.

"This is mine after we are finished with your punishment, Avalon," he said.

"Yes, sir," she stuttered. "Everything I have is yours." She meant it too; Corbin owned every inch of her, including her heart.

"Count," he growled. Corbin landed the first blow on her left cheek, and she whimpered from the after sting that seemed to burn her skin. Honestly, it took her breath away and she was having trouble being able to count out loud. "Ava," he warned.

"One," she sobbed.

"Baby, if this is too much, you know your safe word," he soothed. She knew her safe word all right, but she was determined not to use it. This was what she had asked him for, and he was finally giving her all of himself. She could handle all of Corbin—there would be no backing down from his challenge.

"I'm fine, Sir," she said.

"We'll go to ten," he said, landing the second blow on her right cheek.

"Two," she said, gritting her teeth to get through the sting of pain. Corbin set a punishing rhythm, not giving Ava much time to recover between blows. By the time he got to ten, she was sobbing, tears rolling down her face and she was sure her ass was marked with red welts.

"Ten," she whispered.

"Tell me you're okay," Corbin said. Ava could hear the raw emotion in his voice, and she wanted to reassure him that she was fine. She kneeled in front of him and put her arms around his neck.

"I am," she said. "This is us, Corbin. You are what I need and not giving this to me—holding yourself back from me—it hurts."

"I promise that won't happen again, honey," he said. "I just got so caught up with keeping you safe and making sure that you were emotionally coping with all of the shit being thrown at you, that I forgot what you needed from me."

"Well, I didn't really mind having to remind you," she teased.

"That was quite a display you put on for me, baby. You sure do know how to get my attention," he said. "I promise to find a balance, for us both, but you have to know that keeping you safe in all of this will be my top priority."

"I understand," she said. "I just need for things to go back to normal, Corbin. Not just between the two of us but in our everyday lives. We weren't away for that long, but I have work piling up for me at the office. My partner can only take so many more days of me calling in to tell him that I won't be able to make it in again. I need normal." Corbin was quiet and she knew that he was mentally trying to figure out her request. She was quickly learning that her husband always had a plan and right now, he seemed to be executing their new "normal" lives in his mind.

Ava giggled, "I think you might be overthinking things more than I usually do if that's even possible," she teased.

"I'm trying to figure out just how 'normal' we can be when your father is still a threat. We got another package of questionnaires from his lawyers today at work. That makes three big envelopes of questions they are legally allowed to ask us about our marriage because of that damn stipulation your grandfather put in his will. Is it all really worth it, Ava?"

"Are you asking if it's worth all the trouble we're being put through, to keep my grandfather's money from my dad?

Because my answer will always be yes. If my father needs that money, like Ash said he does, then my answer is hell yes!" The thought of her father blowing through the money he got from his mother and then going after Ava's inheritance infuriated her. He was a greedy, selfish bastard and she would answer every question thrown at them if that's what it took to keep her father from her grandfather's money.

"Are the questions very personal?" she asked. Ava had a feeling that she already knew the answer and judging by the angry expression her sexy husband wore, she was correct.

"They want to know about our sex life," he grumbled.

"No," she breathed. "That's not any of my father's or anyone else's business. We just need to find a way to answer their questions without getting into specifics." Ava knew that would be easier said than done. Her father was going to try to break them down, to prove that their marriage was a sham. The problem for her dear old dad was that her marriage was as real as they came and there would be no way for him to prove otherwise. Not now, at least.

"All right," he agreed. "We will need to sit down with our lawyers soon then and come up with answers that don't give all the personal details of our relationship away. I won't allow that, Ava. This," he said, motioning between their two bodies. "This is just between the two of us and is no one else's business."

"Agreed," she said. "Now, please make me yours," she begged.

"Deal," Corbin said, rolling her under his big body.

CORBIN

Corbin headed into the office for the first time in weeks and he wasn't sure that leaving Avalon was his best decision. The night before, he made Ava a promise that he would let life go back to normal and that meant they would both go back to their jobs. He loved that Aiden was willing to hold down the fort at work, but his wife was right, it was time for them to resume their regular schedules.

"Corbin," Rose said, meeting him at the private elevator that he and Aiden used before he could even step free from the closing doors. She threw herself against him and wrapped her arms around his neck.

"Easy, Ma," he chided. "Let me get off the fucking elevator," he teased.

"Language, Corbin James," she chided. "I didn't raise you to be a caveman. I've missed you," she said.

"You just saw me a couple of weeks ago, when Ava and I got back from France," he said.

"Yeah, but you haven't been around much and Aiden told

me what was going on with Ava and her brother. I'm so sorry," Rose said. "How's she holding up?"

"She's tough," Corbin praised. He knew his girl would be able to get through whatever she'd have to in order to be by her brother's side in all this mess.

"Yes, she is," Rose agreed. He knew his mother liked his wife and he had to admit, he was thankful for that. It made his life so much easier knowing that the two women he loved most in the world, actually liked each other.

"Sorry that I wasn't the one to tell you about the crap going on with her family, Mom," Corbin said.

"No problem," Rose said. "As long as I'm kept in the loop, I don't care which one of my boys gives me the four-one-one," Corbin laughed at his mother's use of modern slang.

"Do not use that saying again, Ma," he begged.

"And why not? I'm young," she teased. "I've got it going on." Corbin groaned and started passed her, almost making it to his office when Aiden stopped him.

"She is, you know," Aiden agreed with Rose, feeding her ego. "Rose still has it going on, even if you refuse to see it, Corbin."

"Don't suck up to her. Lying to Mom only ends badly for both of us," Corbin said. Rose giggled and returned to her desk that sat between their two offices. Corbin liked knowing that his mom was so close. Most days, they had lunch together and he worried that sooner or later, she'd find a reason to leave them. She was always threatening to quit, but Corbin worried that if she did, he and Aiden would fall apart. She was their glue, but he'd never admit that to her.

"Can I talk to you for a minute?" Aiden asked. From the concern in his friend's eyes, he knew that it was something that couldn't wait. All the work that had piled up on his desk for the past two weeks would be there after they talked.

"Oh, Ma," he said, stopping at her desk on the way past, to Aiden's office. "Ava said to tell you that she wants you to come to dinner one night this week. Just call her and make the plans," he offered.

"That would be nice," Rose said.

Corbin joined Aiden in his office and turned to face him. "Okay, spill it. What has you looking like complete doom and gloom?" Corbin asked.

"I think you should sit down before I just spit it out," Aiden offered, nodding to the sofa that sat in front of his big desk.

"Fine." Corbin did as his friend asked, knowing that when Aiden got in one of his bossy moods, nothing would stop him from getting what he wanted. Corbin settled on the sofa and looked up at Aiden, expectantly.

"I talked to two of the fraternity brothers who were there the night of the party Ash attended." Corbin whistled at Aiden's news. "That was fast, man," he said. "You found them in less than a day."

"Well, they go to my club and when I was there this morning to work out, I ran into them. They told me that Ash was there, and he was near blackout drunk, but he didn't drive home that night," Aiden said.

Corbin sat on the edge of the sofa. "What the hell?" he said.

Ash held up his hands as if trying to rein Corbin's temper in. "Just hear me out, man, and then your head can explode." He sat back, wanting to hear the rest but he felt about ready to jump out of his own damn skin.

"Sorry," he offered.

"No problem. Anyway," he continued, "they said that Ava's grandfather was never called. In fact, her father was the one who showed up at the house that night. He and Ash had a huge fight and he accused his son of trying to ruin their family. He demanded that Ashton leave with him and took his car keys from him. He was the one driving that night, not Ash."

"Fuck," Corbin swore.

"It gets better," Aiden said. "The guys were never questioned about that night. The officer in charge of the case never pursued the matter and it was just presumed that Ash was the one who was at fault since he took off just after the accident."

"So, now what do we do?" Corbin asked. He wasn't sure what the next step was, but knowing Ava the way he did, she'd want Ashton out of that prison as soon as humanly possible. His only thought was how to keep his wife safe. If her father had gone to so much trouble to hide the truth all those years, Corbin was pretty sure he'd do much worse to keep them quiet.

"Let me do a little more digging. I'll use my resources to get to the bottom of this. Are you going to tell Ava?" Aiden asked.

Corbin barked out his laugh. There would never be a secret he could keep from his wife. "Yeah, I'm pretty sure if she finds out that I kept a secret from her, she'd have my balls," Corbin said.

Aiden laughed, "Welcome to the club, man. We might think we're dominant but our wives keep our balls in their very expensive handbags." Corbin grimaced at the thought of Ava having him by the balls but in all honesty, he wouldn't want it any other way.

"My wife can do just about anything she wants to with my balls, man," Corbin teased. "But, I'm still going to tell her what you found out. She has a right to know." Aiden nodded. "Thanks for this, man," Corbin said. "I owe you one."

"You owe me a hell of a lot more than one, but we can call it even," Aiden teased. "You are my best friend," he said.

"Brother," Corbin corrected and walked out of his office.

❄

Corbin spent the rest of the day worrying about having to tell Ava about Aiden's news. She wasn't going to be happy about the fact that her own father cared so little about his family that he all but destroyed both Ava and her brother. But, he wasn't a coward and he wouldn't hide from his own wife.

He had his driver drop him off at the front of the building.

He rode his private elevator up to their penthouse and smiled at the sound of Ava singing off-key from their kitchen. His wife had taken to trying to cook for him and honestly, it was a toss-up as to which was worse—her singing or her cooking.

"Hey," he said, turning the corner to find her dancing around in her pajamas, singing into a spoon. "I see you got home early today," he said. Ava put down her spoon and crossed the kitchen to jump into his arms.

"Yep," she said. "It was an easy day in the office, and I decided to knock off early and come home to make my husband dinner." Corbin eyed the half-burnt concoction she was cooking up and laughed.

"Well, it's definitely your cooking, then," he said.

"What's my cooking?" Ava asked, seeming confused by his random remark.

"I was trying to decide which is worse, your singing or your cooking. That confirms it," he said pointing to the boiling pot. "Your cooking is."

"Well, it could have been good," she defended, eyeing the pot. "But you came home early and ruined the surprise."

"Sure, honey," he teased. "Let's go with that. How about I help you clean up this mess and then we can order takeout?"

"Asian?" she questioned, causing Corbin to chuckle. His girl sure did love Asian takeout.

"Sure," he agreed. "I'm assuming you want your normal noodles with the sauce on the side and steamed vegetables?"

Ava enthusiastically nodded, "And, spring rolls and oh—that meat on a stick thing you get sometimes, get two of those for me. Also, don't forget the fortune cookies this time. In fact, order extra."

"Wow," he breathed. "You worked up an appetite today."

"I have been hungry all day and unfortunately—I've been eating all day, too. I guess I'm stress eating, but that's easier than punching everyone who annoys me or makes me mad." Corbin knew Ava had been going through a lot of crap with her brother's return. He hated that she was so stressed, but if Asian takeout helped, he'd do that and so much more for her.

"I have a few ideas of how we could work off some of your stress, honey," he said. Ava swatted at him and giggled.

"First food, then you can give me some stress management tips." Ava winked at him and turned to start to clean up the mess in the kitchen. Corbin placed the order for delivery and by the time he got back to the kitchen to help Ava, she was just about finished.

"Perfect timing," she teased. "You missed the whole gory mess."

"Well, I was hunting and foraging to bring home food for my woman," Corbin growled, giving her his best caveman imitation, even thumping his chest for good measure.

"My hero," she sassed, batting her eyelashes at him.

"Let's just hope you feel that way after I tell you about the news Aiden gave me today," he said. Corbin took the pot she was drying from her and the towel. "I'll finish the last of these up and you pour us some wine. I think you'll need it for this conversation."

"Well, shit," she mumbled. Corbin finished up the few dishes she had washed, drying them and putting them away. Ava had poured them both some wine and was waiting for him at the center island. He could tell that her worry had amped up and he again wished they didn't have to discuss what Aiden had learned about her father, but there was no getting around the news. He just needed to get it out and be by her side while she processed everything.

"Your father was the one driving the car the night of Ash's accident," he blurted out. Ava sat her wine glass down so hard, he worried that she broke it.

"What?" she asked. "How is that possible? He was in D.C. at the time of the accident. I remember the police showing up at my house that night. It was just me and the nanny until my grandpa showed up."

"I don't know all the details yet, but Aiden found two of the fraternity brothers who were at the party that night. Your grandfather was never called about Ashton. In fact, they said your father showed up and insisted that your brother leave with him. Made a big show of taking his keys away from him, saying he'd drive."

"So, Ash is really innocent? Why would he willingly turn himself in to the police for a crime he didn't commit?" That was a very good question and one that he had been mulling over all day.

"All I can come up with is that Ashton believes that he did it. Why else would he have run and then showed up all these years later to turn himself in? Someone told your brother that he hit and killed that woman," Corbin said.

"And, he's lived with that guilt all these years," Ava whispered. "We've got to get him out of that place," she insisted. This was what Corbin was most afraid of. He worried that telling Ava the news would spark a fire in her and she'd go off half-crazy and do something dangerous.

"We will, honey," he promised. "But, you have to let Aiden and I handle this. He's got the resources we need to get to your father and we need to let them play out."

"But, if we could just get him to confess," she interrupted.

"No," Corbin barked.

"But—" Ava tried to protest but he covered her mouth with his hand.

"I said no," Corbin growled. "You will not try to see your father to get a confession out of him. If he finds out that we know the truth, he'll do whatever it takes to stop you from telling the world." Corbin hesitantly removed his hand from her pouty lips when she nodded her head. "He let your brother go to prison for a crime that he didn't commit. What do you think he'd do to you if he found out that you know the truth?"

Ava sighed, "You're right," she grumbled.

"Tell me you'll let Aiden and I handle this," he insisted.

"I promise," she said, holding up her right hand as if swearing an oath.

"Good girl," he praised. "I'll get the door," he offered when the doorbell sounded. "Our food is here." Ava squealed and pulled some plates and forks from the cupboards. Corbin knew that the distraction of food would only last so long and Ava would be back on the hunt to find the truth. It was just who she was, promise or no promise, his girl was probably going to stick her nose in where it didn't belong and he just hoped like hell he'd be there to keep her safe.

AVALON

Ava sat in her car in front of her father's house. She had done the exact opposite of what Corbin asked her to do and snuck away to confront her dad. She had basically fulfilled her end of the bargain she made with Corbin a few weeks prior, but she was done waiting. Ava gave Aiden and Corbin time to come up with answers and they still had nothing but theories to go on. Time was running out for her brother and she had to do something—for Ash's sake. So, Ava ditched her guard and convinced Zara to help her come up with a plan to record her conversation with her father. She'd do it all again if it meant saving her brother from that God-awful place, even if it meant pissing off her husband. She had been in to see Ashton every day in the last three weeks he had been in that prison, and each time, he looked worse. He went in strong and capable and now; she saw him as a broken shell of a man who might not make it back out of that place alive. Ava hadn't told him about what Aiden found either. She couldn't give Ashton hope, not while he was locked away. It wasn't fair to build him up for something that might not possibly happen.

"Stop being a chicken," she whispered to herself, looking at the big stone house that stoically stared back at her. She wondered if Zara was listening on the other end. They had done a few mic checks before she left, but that was no guarantee that her best friend could still hear her. Zara had reluctantly promised not to tell Aiden or Corbin where she was going or what she was up to. She also warned that if things went south, she'd be calling in the cavalry as back up and that would mean being found by one very angry husband.

Coming up with a plan to ditch her security wasn't easy but she did. Telling them that she had a doctor's appointment wasn't a stretch. She had one scheduled for that afternoon. Her personal guard told her that it would be no problem to accompany her to her appointment and he'd be happy to pick her up from work and take her. When Ava filled him in on the fact that she was seeing her OBGYN because she suspected she was pregnant, his expression was priceless. His face turned the cutest shade of red and the way he stood in front of her, rendered speechless by her news, was a perfect distraction. He agreed to not only keep her secret from her husband, claiming she wanted to surprise him, but he told her that it would be perfectly fine for her to go to her "girly doctor" by herself and to just check in when she was done. That was something she could do and hopefully, she and Corbin would have more than just news of a baby to celebrate tonight. She wanted to be able to share her good news with her brother too, but Ava wanted to wait until he was free from prison to do it. If today went well, she'd be celebrating two things tonight. Sure, Corbin would spank her ass bright red for defying him yet again, but what choice did she have? Ashton was her brother and she couldn't let her father get away with his lie for another day longer.

"Here goes nothing," she whispered to herself. Ava opened her car door and walked up the path to the big, red front door. Her mother had painted that door red, much to her father's protest and it was the only thing from her mom still left in place. When he'd have it repainted, she'd hold her breath as if worried he would choose a different color, but he always had it done bright red, just as her mom chose.

Her father pulled the door open before she could even raise her hand to knock. "Avalon," he hissed.

"Dad," she coldly returned. "I think we need to talk." Her father poked his head out the front door and looked around as if he expected to find the entourage that usually accompanied her, at Corbin's insistence.

"I see you left your Neanderthal husband and guards at home," he said. Ava nodded and he grabbed her arm and pulled her into the front foyer, slamming the door shut behind her. "Now," he said. "This is so much better. We can talk in private and not air our differences out in public. I take it you're here about my lawyer's questions?" he asked.

Ava smirked at him and shook her head. His team of lawyers had been hounding both her and Corbin since she told her father they were married. He made it his personal business to poke at their marriage and she almost wanted to laugh at the irony. Her father would never allow anyone poking their noses into his business and now she knew why—they'd find his skeletons.

"No, Dad," she said. "I'm here because I wanted to tell you about some information that I've come across that might help Ashton's case," she said. She knew she was teasing him, only feeding him small bits of information, but she couldn't help herself. Ava almost felt like savoring this moment. "Not that you've seemed overly concerned about your son, since he's been back."

"That boy has been nothing but trouble," he hissed. "He did the crime, now he can serve his time. This family has a long, proud lineage of men who did the right thing. I'm sure they would all be ashamed of what Ashton has done to the Michaels name," her father said.

Again, Ava had to refrain from laughing in his smug face. "Did you know Ash was alive this whole time?" she questioned.

Her father shrugged as if it wasn't a big deal and she had her answer. "I assumed he wasn't dead," he offered. "You were the one who conjured up that story."

"Because it was easier than the truth. I was a little girl whose mother died and her brother took off. It was easier to think he died rather than believe that he didn't want to be around us." Ava bit the side of her cheeks, trying to stop her threatening tears. The last thing she wanted was to give him the satisfaction of seeing her cry.

"Well, that was on you. I had nothing to do with your overly active imagination," he said.

"But, you did have something to do with Ashton leaving, didn't you Dad?" She knew she was rushing the point but it was time for this show to begin.

"Just what are you hinting at, Avalon?" he asked. Her father crossed his arms over his chest, just as he used to do when she was a kid and she knew she was in trouble. Seeing him do this now only made her want to burst into fits of giggles.

"Nothing, really," she lied. "I've just started running with a very different circle of friends lately, Daddy. They've had some things to tell me about the night that Ash disappeared, although I'm not sure you'd be surprise by most of it."

Her father waved his hand through the air. "People gossip especially about men like me," he offered as an excuse.

"Men like you?" Ava questioned.

"Sure. Rich, powerful men," he said. "Always trying to bring us down but only the weak fall, Avalon. I taught you that." He had taught her that but now, she was going to be able to prove him wrong. Ava took great satisfaction knowing that she was going to be the one to topple her father's empire, once and for all.

"You sure about that, Dad?" she taunted. "They were two of the guys at the fraternity party, where you found Ashton that night." Ava could see the panic behind his eyes. Her father's smile was easy but his eyes always gave him away.

"Absolutely," he said. "Besides, who would believe some fraternity boys instead of me—a former Senator?"

"I don't know, Dad, they were pretty convincing," she said. "They did grow up, you know. Those fraternity boys are now a prize winning journalist with a national television syndicate and a decorated police detective who also happens to be a veteran. I'm thinking that the two of them combined trump a former Senator."

Her father barked out his laugh and Ava knew she had him right where she wanted him. It was his tell, his nervous tick and all she had to do now was reel him in. "What exactly are these frat boys saying about me, Ava?" he questioned.

She knew her smile was mean; she could feel it. "Oh, just that you showed up to the party that night and had an argument with Ash. You forced him to give you his keys and leave with you. And, my favorite part—you were the one driving that night. You hit that woman, didn't you, Daddy? You were the one who left her for dead in the middle of that road, not Ash." Ava felt as if she had run a marathon, lobbing accusations at her father but she didn't stop.

"You can't prove that—no one can," he spat. "You and your brother never understood all of the sacrifices I made for you." Ava wanted to laugh at just how untrue that was. Her father never did one unselfish thing in his life.

"Please, tell me how unselfish you are, Dad. What exactly did you do for us? Ash is in jail now because of something you did." She knew she was pushing but she was running out of time. If she didn't get her father to say the words and admit what he did, she might never be able to prove her brother's innocence.

"Ash was collateral damage," he said. "Just like you will be, Avalon." Her father pulled a gun from his jacket pocket and pointed it at her. Ava made a move for the door, but he shouted for her to stop and she had no choice. Her father would have shot her. He had all but proven that he didn't give a shit about her or Ashton.

Ava turned to face him and she could see the determination in his eyes. "You can't just shoot me, Dad," she said. "How will you cover that up? It won't be so easy this time. People know where I am. They know the truth."

"Who knows, Avalon? Your husband and some former frat boys?" he asked.

"Sure," she said. "Them and the new Senator who won Grandpa's seat. Aiden and a few of his friends on the police force know. In fact, they're on their way here now," she lied. "It's over, Dad."

"Why did you have to go and stick your nose into this, Ava? It didn't have to end like this," her father said. He almost looked upset about having to kill her—almost.

"So, how's this going to end, Dad?" she asked, not hiding her bitter tone. "You are just going to shoot me and then what? Bury me in the backyard under Mom's rose bushes?"

He chuckled, "Don't be silly, Avalon. I got rid of your mother's rose bushes a long time ago," he taunted. "I thought we could sit down and write a suicide note and then you could swallow a bottle of pills. Not too messy that way and I'm sure a whole lot less painful. You can just fall asleep and forget this whole ugly mess."

"I won't," she choked. "I think I'm pregnant and I won't do that to my child. You might be a monster who can do that kind of thing to your kids but I'm not."

"Really, Avalon," he said. His tone was dry and condescending and she knew he didn't care if she was carrying his grandchild or not. "I would be doing the world a favor. Anything that you and that caveman husband of yours created won't be an asset to our family."

"At least tell me what really happened that night," she pleaded. Ava knew that if Zara was listening, keeping her father talking might be her only plan for staying alive. She would have called in the cavalry by now, or at least that was what Ava had hoped.

"I'm not sure what you want from me, Ava. Do you want me to admit my guilt and profess my deep sorrow for what I had done? That woman practically jumped out in front of that fucking car and there was no way for me to avoid her. I knew she was dead as soon as I saw her lying in the middle of the road. Your dumb ass brother had passed out as soon as we left the party, so he had no clue as to what had just happened." Her father's laugh was mean.

"You ran that poor woman down and left her for dead," she sobbed. "And, then you pinned it all on Ash. He was just a kid and you let him take the fall for what you did."

"He wasn't a kid. He acted like a fucking kid but he was a grown man. He should have acted more responsibly. If he was more like me and less like your mother, none of this would have happened. I would have never found your brother at that party, drunk and trying to drag our family's name through the mud. He would have destroyed my political career if he wasn't stopped. I just turned the circumstances around and took care of two problems. I had a dead woman on my hands and your brother needed to grow the hell up and stop all of his partying."

"So, you dumped him off at Grandpa's? Did he help you? Was my grandfather a part of your scheme?" she asked. Ava wasn't sure if she wanted to know the answer but she had no other way around it. She had put her grandfather up on a metaphorical pedestal and she worried that she was wrong about the man who she loved so very much.

"No," her father breathed. "My father would have never helped me. He would have protected Ashton with his life and he did. He kept Ash's secret and sent him away rather than watch his grandson face jail time. He protected you both."

"That's how you got him to put my marriage clause in his will, isn't it?" Ava asked. "You blackmailed him."

"Very good," her father praised. "Look at you figuring things out." She hated that he was smugly taunting her but she had no choice but to play along. "I told him that I found out about what Ashton had done. I threatened to use my money and resources to find Ash and drag him home to face his punishment, if he didn't put that clause into place. He knew I'd do it too, so he agreed. But, you found your way past that clause, didn't you, Avalon?"

He was right, she had, and thinking about Corbin now made her regret going against his orders and running to confront her father. If she had just obeyed him, none of this would be happening and she would be safely at work. Ava had to remember that she was doing all of this for Ashton, though. Her brother never had anyone besides her grandfather in his corner. Now that her Grandpa was gone, sticking up for Ash was her responsibility and one she didn't take lightly.

"Sorry I went and found the man of my dreams and fell in love, Dad," she sassed.

"You fucked everything up, Ava. My father's money should have been mine, but he chose to give it to you—a spoiled brat who didn't deserve it."

"You have more money than you should have been able to spend in your lifetime," she yelled. "But, you managed to do just that, didn't you Dad? You lost it all and now, you want what is mine. That was your plan all along, right?"

"No, but I have to admit, things did work out pretty perfectly. I couldn't have planned it any better—well, until you went and got married. I guess we can call that decision the beginning of your end," he said.

"You still haven't told me how you convinced Ashton that he was guilty of hit and run," she said, trying to buy more time.

"Like I said earlier, he passed out and missed all the excitement. I drove back here and moved him to the driver seat, with the keys still in the ignition. I took my jet and flew to Washington, D.C. and even paid off my maid to back my story of being in the Capital the whole time, if it came down to that. Your brother woke up and found the damaged front end of his car and put two and two together himself, after the news broke of the hit and run accident, leaving that woman dead. It was almost too easy with the way he stitched it all together for me. I didn't have to lift a finger and your grandfather stepping in, to keep Ashton out of prison, was the icing on the cake. All I had to do was sit back and wait for it all to happen." Her father looked almost proud of himself. He destroyed their whole family and stood there to boast about it?

"You're a monster," she shouted.

"Maybe," he agreed. "But the good news is you won't have to deal with me for much longer. Let's go on up to your mother's old sitting room. That might be a fitting place for you to take your last breath, since it was where she took her own."

"No," Ava protested. "You won't get away with any of this," she insisted.

"Oh, Ava," he said. She hated the way he looked like he pitied her. "I already have." He walked towards her, pushing the gun into her side and she sobbed. "Move, Ava," he demanded. "Upstairs." Ava wasn't sure what other options she had. She turned to walk up the grand staircase, feeling the gun barrel in her back with every step.

"You could just let me go," she begged. "I won't tell anyone about this."

"Sorry Ava, but your word isn't good with me. Not anymore," he said. She was to the top step when his front door swung open, Corbin and Aiden stood on the other side.

"Corbin," Ava screamed. Her only thought was to warn her husband. "He's got a gun." Her father spun around on the second to last step, training his gun on Corbin and she did the only thing she could think of. Ava pushed him in the back as hard as she could, hoping that it would be enough to make him lose his balance.

Her father looked back over his shoulder, as if trying to figure out just what had happened and before he started falling forward, he fired the gun. It was as if her entire world suddenly started moving in slow motion and all she could do was watch her father falling down the staircase.

"Ava," Corbin yelled, but she didn't look at him, worried that he wasn't really there. At some point, he had started up the stairs to her and before she could even take a breath, he had her wrapped in his arms. "Tell me you're all right, honey," he whispered into her ear.

"You're here?" she said, still too afraid to let herself hope.

"I'm here," he confirmed. "You got him, Aiden?" Corbin yelled down the stairs and it echoed throughout the foyer.

"Yeah, but he's in pretty rough shape," Aiden said. "He's knocked out cold and it looks like he broke his leg in the fall. The paramedics are about five minutes out. You're girl good?"

"I'm not sure," Corbin said. "Open your eyes and look at me, baby," he commanded. Ava squinted one eye open, and Corbin laughed. "That's a start at least," he teased. "I need for you to tell me you're okay," he demanded.

Ava took a step back from him and looked herself up and down, as if accessing her current situation. Was she all right? That was a good question. Ava wasn't sure she'd ever be okay again, not after she found out just what kind of person her father was—what he was capable of.

"I—I think I am," she stuttered. "He shot you?" she asked. She heard the gun go off and worried that her father had shot Corbin, in his fall.

"Naw," Corbin drawled. "He shot at me, Darlin'," he said. "Thank fuck your father has awful aim. I'm sure it didn't hurt that he was tumbling down a flight of steps at the time."

"How did you know where I'd be?" she questioned. Honestly, her brain felt as if it wasn't all caught up yet.

"You mean after you went behind my back and against my wishes to sneak over here?" He asked. Ava shrugged and Corbin cocked his eyebrow at her which was never a good sign. That usually meant that he was going to wait her out for her answer, but not believe a word that came out of her mouth anyway. That look usually landed her bare-assed, over his lap, getting her ass spanked red.

"I just couldn't sit by and not do anything, Corbin. Ashton is my brother and seeing him day in and day out, rotting away in that awful place—I just couldn't take anymore. I had no other choice," she said.

"Yeah, you did, honey. You could have trusted that Aiden and I were working on things on our end. I told you that I'd have your and your brother's backs and I meant it. Instead of obeying me, you just went out on your own and almost got yourself killed." Corbin stroked his big hand down his beard and she could tell that she had completely stressed him out. It was his tell-tale sign that he was at his wits end and she was responsible for driving her poor husband there this time.

"I'm sorry," she whispered. "You're right."

"Damn straight, I'm right," he growled. "Thank God Zara had the good sense to tell Aiden about your crazy ass plan. Really, honey—you wore a wire?" Ava shrugged again. She seemed to be doing a lot of that since Corbin showed up to save her ass.

"Zara told you where to find me?" she asked.

"She did one better than just tell me where I'd be able to find my wife. She gave me the bug you wore, so I could hear exactly what was going on here while I was driving," Corbin said. Ava cringed at the idea that Corbin heard every sorted detail, including the part where she thought she was pregnant. It wasn't the way she wanted to tell him, but from the beautiful, furious frown he wore, he had heard it all.

"Was the part about you being pregnant a lie to throw your father off, honey?" he whispered. Ava shook her head, too overcome to find her voice.

"Say something," she begged. "Anything, Corbin. Just please don't be mad at me because I'm not sure if I'm pregnant and if I am, I don't want you to be upset."

CORBIN

"Upset?" he asked. "Why the hell would I be upset about a baby?" He wouldn't be either. The thought of Avalon pregnant with his child did crazy things to his heart.

"Because you don't seem happy," she said.

"I'm not happy about the rest of this," he said, wildly waving his arms around, as if trying to prove his point. "Do you have any idea how crazy it made me to hear your father talk about his plan to kill you? If anything would have happened to you, honey—" Corbin's voice broke, and he hated showing any weakness around Ava. He wanted to be her rock, her solitude and the person she knew she could turn to for anything. But she was his weakness. Ava was the only thing that could break him and losing her would have left him broken.

"I'm still here, Corbin," she said. "You haven't lost me."

"But I almost did," he growled. "When Zara admitted what you two were up to, Aiden and I left the office immediately. Do you know what I went through when I heard that your father had a gun pointed at you?" His voice cracked again with emotion and Ava reached for him, but he couldn't let her touch him. He'd never get the rest out if he did.

He hated feeling so completely out of control and not being there to protect his wife made him feel exactly that way. "You ditched your guards," he shouted. "Did you even have a doctor's appointment today?"

"Yes," she whispered. "At two."

"And when were you fucking going to tell me about the possibility of a baby?" he yelled.

Ava jumped, startled by his question. "I was going to surprise you, Corbin," she whispered.

"The EMT's are here, guys. How about you take this down a notch? I'll handle everything down here," Aiden said.

"Thanks, man." Corbin nodded.

"I have a feeling the police are going to want to talk to Ava, too," Aiden finished.

"That's fine," Corbin said. "I'm done talking for now. I can't do this anymore, honey. I need some time to think things through." He turned and walked down the steps and all Ava could do was watch him leave. Corbin disappeared out the big, red front door and the last thing he saw was his best friend's disappointment, as he passed Aiden on his way out.

❄

It had been five hours since he walked away from Ava. Well, five hours, thirteen minutes and forty-two seconds, to be exact, but who was counting? In that time, Zara had tried to call him twelve times and Aiden, four. Even his mother called a few times and when he texted that he was fine but wanted some space, Rose told him to stop being a fucking baby and deal with his shit like a grown-up. He had to admit, his mother's messages were the bright spot in his whole fucking day and who knew, maybe she was right. But up until about thirteen minutes ago, he wasn't ready to deal with any of this mess and sulking felt like his best option. So, he locked himself away in his office and ignored the constant texts, phone calls and his mother's persistent, annoying nagging through his door.

Thirteen minutes ago, the entire universe changed and he realized that if he didn't take his mother's advice, he'd lose the best thing in his life. Technically, the best two things, given the news Ava had sent him via text. It was time for him to get over the possibility of losing his wife and move forward with his plan to keep her. He acted like an ass; he panicked and now, he hoped like hell his wife would forgive him.

Where are you? Corbin texted her after receiving a picture of the sonogram of their baby. He missed his kid's first milestone and he hated that. He had a father who missed everything, and he wouldn't be anything like his dad. He owed it to this kid to be more for him or her.

Home. Ava texted back. He packed up his briefcase and made a beeline for the elevator, ignoring his mother's pleas for him to stop. His only thought was getting home to his wife and groveling for forgiveness.

"Sorry, Ma," he said. "Got to go and beg my wife to forgive me for being an ass." The elevator doors closed but the last thing he saw was his mother's triumphant, goofy grin.

He sped home, not wanting to waste a minute and when he got to the penthouse, he worried that he wouldn't find Ava still there. His panic gave way when he found her soaking in a bubble bath in the master bedroom. She was completely covered in bubbles, just her head sticking out of the water, her eyes closed.

"Hey," he breathed. Ava peeped one eye open and quickly closed it again. "I'm sorry," he whispered.

"For?" she asked. He wanted to laugh, but judging from her icy reception, she wasn't in the mood to find anything he said funny.

"You aren't going to make this easy on me, are you, honey?"

he teased. She opened her eyes and looked at him and Corbin wished he hadn't just said what he did.

"This isn't a joke, Corbin," she said. "I had to go to our baby's first doctor visit alone. I had to face the police alone and I had to deal with everything my father told me—alone."

"In all fairness, Ava," he said, sitting on the edge of the tub, "you did go off this morning to face your father, alone. You were going to go to the doctor by yourself and I'm pretty sure that if you didn't get Zara in on your crazy plan, you would have died today—alone," his voice broke and he knew that he needed to calm the fuck down. The last time they had a shouting match, he ended up walking away from the only woman he had ever loved.

"I know that Corbin. That's why I'm mad at myself, not you. I'm the one who should be telling you how sorry I am." Ava stood from the tub, the soapy bubbles running down her body and he didn't hesitate to pull her into his arms. "I'm all wet," she complained.

"Mmm, that's my favorite way for you to be, honey," he teased. "How about we both agree to forgive the other and move forward from there?" he asked.

"How do we move forward, Corbin?" she asked.

That was something he had given a lot of thought to over the past few hours. "We have to trash all of our old rules and just have one new rule between the two of us."

"Trash the rules?" Ava said. "But, why?"

"Because you aren't my submissive anymore, Ava. You're more than that now—you're my wife. When this thing started out between the two of us, I planned on making you mine slowly. What started out as you being my reluctant submissive ended up with me falling madly in love with you." Ava framed his face with her wet hands. "I feel the same way, Corbin. But I need your dominance. I'm not sure that this thing works between the two of us without it," she whispered.

"Thank fuck, honey," he growled. "Because, I have no idea

how to be anything but dominant with you. How about our one rule be that we are just completely honest with each other from here on out?" Ava pretended to weigh her pros and cons and he swatted her bare, wet ass, causing her to yelp.

"Okay," she said. "Complete honesty. But, I think we need to amend your one rule policy."

"How's that?" he asked.

Ava smiled at him, and it nearly took his breath away, she was so fucking beautiful. "All your prior rules stand and we add the honesty one to the mix." He palmed her ass and she wiggled against his body.

"I think you just like having the extra rules in place so you have more chances of breaking them," he said. Her giggle told him he was right on track.

"Well, I do like when you spank me," she sassed. "Do you think you can handle that?" she asked.

"I think I can work with the rules, Mrs. Eklund," he said.

"That's good to hear, Mr. Eklund because I've broken a few of them just today," she teased.

"Well, then, Wife, I think it's time for me to take you off to our bed and spank your ass a pretty shade of pink."

Ava squealed and clapped her hands together and he hauled her over his shoulder, carrying her to their room. Corbin felt like the luckiest man on earth, holding his entire future against his body and he wasn't sure how he deserved such a perfect submissive, but Ava was his and that was all that mattered.

AVALON
EPILOGUE

Three Months Later

Ava waited for Corbin at her office, and she was starting to get a little edgy. Being five months pregnant really didn't lend to her patience and it wasn't her strong suit to begin with. She paced the front lobby like a lioness watching for her prey, keeping an eye out for Corbin's black SUV.

"Hey beautiful," he said, startling her from behind.

"Corbin," she screeched. "You scared the shit out of me."

"Language," he said, covering her barely there baby bump. This was the first week that she was beginning to look like she was pregnant and he was having trouble keeping his hands to himself. "We don't want his first words being a curse word."

"I'm sure it won't be and what if it's a she?" Ava reached down to put her hands over his, loving being able to share this new experience with Corbin.

Corbin palmed her belly and smiled. "I'm sure she will be the best first girl quarterback on her high school football team," he teased.

"Or a ballerina," Ava quickly added.

"Sure," Corbin said. "Although, she'll look silly hiking the ball in a tutu." Ava giggled and Corbin pulled her in for a quick kiss. "Ready?" he asked. "I had my driver park around the back. Traffic is crazy tonight."

"Are you going to tell me where we are going and what all this secrecy is about?" Corbin told her to be ready to leave work at five on the dot because he had something he wanted to show her. Her husband forgot the fact that she really hated surprises or secrets and when she begged him to give her a hint, he reminded her who was in charge. Ava knew he was distracting her, but she had to admit, he was pretty good at the art of diversion.

"We will be there in less than ten minutes, but if you can't be patient and behave, Wife, I'm sure I can get our driver to circle around town while I remind you how to be a good girl." Corbin's devilish grin made her girl parts want his undivided attention and she was always up for car sex, but Ava was too curious to give in to her overly active libido.

"Fine," she said. "I'll play nice." Ava pouted and took his hand, following him out to his waiting car.

"You only have to play nice for a few minutes, honey. And then, you can play as dirty as you'd like." His words dripped with innuendo and it took all of Ava's will power not to ask him to make good on his promise to punish her in the back of his car.

The ride felt like it took forever and the touching and kissing didn't seem to help her body to cool down any. Ava just hoped that whatever it was he wanted to show her didn't take long. She was anxious to get back to their penthouse and show Corbin just how dirty she liked to play.

The car pulled up in front of the club where she and Corbin met, to spend their very first night together. "Um, I thought we couldn't come here anymore because you were worried about our privacy?" she asked. After her father went to prison, Ava hoped that Corbin would want to take her back to her favorite BDSM club but he told her that they wouldn't have any privacy there. They had gone to France a few times since and played at his club there, but she wondered if they'd ever find a place to play in the States.

"I was worried about our privacy," he agreed. "That's why I bought this place and renamed it." Corbin pointed up to a giant black sign with red letters that spelled out her name.

"Avalon," she read her name and smiled. "You named your new BDSM club after me?" Ava wasn't sure if that was the weirdest or sweetest thing she had ever heard.

"Yep," he proudly said. "You okay with all of this?"

Honestly, Ava was more than just all right with Corbin owning the club—she was ecstatic. This hopefully meant they would be able to go out to play and that idea had her body's need amping up to new levels. "Does this mean we can play?" she questioned.

"I'd like to, but only if you're ready for this. I know that some of your father's old friends might be in there from time to time. Hell, Aiden and Zara might even come over to play. You have to know that we will not have the same privacy we do when we go to play at my club in France. You good with that?"

Ava wrinkled up her nose at the thought of seeing Zara and Aiden at the club. She knew her friend and her husband liked kink but that was something she didn't want to see. "How about on nights when it's less private, we go back to our own room?" she asked. "I'm not sure that seeing Aiden and Zara playing at the club is something I'm looking forward to. Can we keep your private room for ourselves—as a secret retreat? We'll just have to work out a schedule."

"Sure," Corbin offered. "I think that sounds fair."

"Besides," she said, knowing this next part might just piss him off. "Your mother might show up one night to play and then you'll want to hide away in our private room."

"No," Corbin growled pointing his finger at her. "Take that back," he ordered.

"Oh, come on, Corbin. You have to know that Rose is into kink. You didn't invent it," she teased.

"It's just not going to happen," he insisted. "Ever," he added. "I don't want to talk about my mother anymore. How about I take you into our new club and show you one more surprise I got for you."

"Another surprise?" she asked. "Wow, I must have been a very good girl," she teased.

"You have and I've checked with your doctor and we are clear to play." Corbin wagged his eyebrows at her and she giggled. Ava loved how protective Corbin was with their baby already. She knew that he would take extra precautions to keep both her and the baby safe but calling her doctor was the sweetest.

"Well, then, show me your club," she said.

"Our club," he corrected. "You remember your safe word?" he asked.

"Yep—ice cream," she said.

"Good girl," he praised. "Let's play."

※

Corbin had remodeled the playroom and his special surprise for her was a Saint Andrew's cross that Ava couldn't wait to use. "It's beautiful," she gushed. "All of it, Sir."

"I'm glad you like it," Corbin whispered against her ear. "Now strip and get your ass over to that cross." She did just as he ordered, loving the way he never took his eyes off her. He helped Ava up against the cross and made sure that the wood wasn't touching her belly. He secured her ankles and wrists to the beams, leaving her spread eagle, her front to the wood, gifting him with a glorious view of her ass.

He gave her ass a smack, "This is mine," he growled.

"Yes, Sir," she agreed. "Everything I have is yours." Ava could feel his possessiveness in his every touch, as he let his big hands glide down her bare body.

Corbin walked around to the back of the cross to stand in front of her and smirked. He held up a flogger in one hand, with what looked to be a soft leather tip and a leather paddle in the other. The paddle looked like something that, if used properly, could leave a mark. "Well," he challenged. "Which one would my wife like for me to use tonight?" he asked.

"I get to pick?" she questioned.

Corbin shrugged, "This is for your pleasure tonight, so sure," he agreed. Ava smiled at the possibilities but suddenly felt very unsure of which to choose. "Tick-tock," he pushed.

"Um, the paddle?" she said. It sounded more like a question than an answer and Corbin chuckled.

"You asking or telling me, baby?" he teased.

"Telling," she said with a nod of her head. "The paddle."

"You do like a little bit of a bite, don't you, honey?" he asked. He ran the soft leather of the flogger down her body and lightly tapped her already wet pussy with the pad. Her husband knew just what his little show was doing to her, but he wanted to see for himself, firsthand. He raised the flogger back up to inspect it and hummed his approval.

"You're so fucking ready, aren't you, Ava?" he asked.

"Yes, Sir," she agreed.

"Then let's get this show started. Once I'm done working your ass over, I'm going to take you like this. Do you like the idea of being bound to the cross while I'm fucking you from behind, Ava?"

"Yes," she hissed. Corbin landed a hard slap on her ass with the paddle and she yelped.

"Yes?" he questioned.

"Yes, Sir," she corrected.

"Better," he praised. "Count for me, Avalon," he ordered. She loved to be spanked, but when it was for her pleasure and not a punishment, Corbin always played with her a little more. Tonight was no different. He dipped his fingers through her folds and back, using the paddle to spank her ass. Avalon kept count and when he got to twenty, she felt as though she could literally fly. She loved this feeling—Corbin called it sub-space, but it felt more like heaven. Ava never wanted to come back down once she got there.

At some point, she must have stopped counting because every time the paddle met one of her fleshy globes, Corbin growled out the number they were on. "Twenty-five," he hoarsely shouted. Corbin tossed the paddle to the side of the cross and she could hear him lower his zipper. He was behind her, filling her and rubbing up against her raw skin from the spankings and it was almost too much for her. Ava cried out his name when she was close, and Corbin picked up the pace, pumping in and out of her body.

He snaked his arms around her, sealing himself up against her backside, reaching around to palm her sensitive nipples and just that extra friction was all she needed. Ava soared and Corbin followed her over, whispering praises of love into her ear as he helped her down from the cross. "Beautiful," he praised. "You are so fucking beautiful, Ava."

"I'm yours, Sir," she whispered. "I'm still your submissive, right?"

"Yes," he agreed. "You are so much more than that though, my wife. You are my reluctant submissive and you are mine."

HIS COUGAR SUBMISSIVE

ROSE

Rose Eklund sat at the end of the large mahogany bar and tossed back her shot of vodka. She usually didn't drink the hard stuff but if she had to celebrate her fiftieth birthday, she'd do it in epic proportions. At least she figured that the hangover she was sure to have tomorrow would be pretty damn epic. She might be another year older but that didn't mean she had to slip into her new year quietly or willingly. She was going to go down fighting and angry as piss about turning a half a century old.

Her son, Corbin, had offered to throw her a party but that was the very last thing she wanted. As far as she was concerned, fifty could come in quietly and no one had to be the wiser. Then, come morning, she was going to march right into her son and his best friend's offices and announce that she was retiring. Sure, it was a little early but why not? Rose had spent her entire life taking care of everyone else and it was time for her to take care of herself for a change.

She had Corbin just shy of her seventeenth birthday and against her parents' wishes. They had begged her to terminate her pregnancy when she found out she was going to have a baby. Her son's father was almost ten years older than she was and when he found out she was expecting, he took off. Her parents had threatened to press charges and throw him in jail for getting a minor pregnant and he didn't bother to stick around to meet his kid.

Rose was forced to grow up quickly out in the world on her own as a single mom. She had a baby who was depending on her and parents who wanted nothing to do with her. She moved into a little efficiency apartment and didn't once allow herself to wallow in self-pity—there just wasn't time for it. She got her GED, finishing up her senior year at night and working at a local convenience store during the day. She relied on the kindness of friends and neighbors to help watch Corbin and after she graduated and could get a better paying job, she decided to pay back the kindness that was shown to her any way she could.

When her ten-year-old son brought home a new friend from school, she instantly took a liking to Aiden Bentley. He was scrawny and shy and for the life of her, Rose couldn't figure out how the two had become friends. Her son was loud and outgoing and usually the biggest kid in his class but he and Aiden seemed to hit it off from the start. Aiden's mother left him when he was little and his father was a drunk who couldn't seem to get his shit together, even for his only son. So, when she saw that Aiden was struggling to get by, she stepped up and lent a hand. Before long, he was spending nights at her house and just about every waking minute too. He had practically moved in with her and Corbin and that was just fine with her. She considered him her son and she could tell he loved her like a mother.

When the boys went away to college, Rose panicked, worrying about what her next stage in life was going to be. She was only thirty-five years old, and she wasn't quite sure what she was supposed to do with herself. She took a few college classes and got her AA degree in business management, which came in handy when the guys graduated from college and announced that they were opening their own company. Rose agreed to help out in her spare time and they jokingly called her their assistant. They set up shop in her basement and Rose felt more like a babysitter than an assistant, at first. But the guys seemed to find their niche and grew the small start-up into a multi-million dollar company. She was proud of them and thankful that they kept her around.

She became Aiden's assistant and honestly, that worked for them all. She got to see her two favorite guys and Aiden's kids all she wanted, and Rose was sure she couldn't be any happier. But turning fifty had thrown her for a loop and she wasn't sure which end was up. It was time for her to get off the ride and slow down some. She wanted to travel and explore the world while she was still somewhat young and it was about time she took a chance on life. She didn't want to wait another twenty birthdays to find out that she didn't live her life and was too old to do anything about it.

"This one is from the gentleman at the other end of the bar," the bartender loudly whispered over the bad honky-tonk music. Rose nodded to the handsome man who was facing her at the other end of the bar and swallowed back the shot of vodka, giving him a mock salute when she finished it.

He smiled at her and nodded, sipping his beer. He was probably younger than her, but almost everyone in the bar was except the bartender and he wasn't her type. Rose wasn't much of a dater and the idea of being brazen enough to talk to a stranger at a bar made her nervous. Honestly, she could count on one hand the number of men she had been with since having Corbin and that was fine with her. She had a son to take care of and dating just never seemed a priority. When Corbin was a toddler, her best friend had tried to fix her up with a guy but he wasn't interested in a twenty-year-old with a toddler in tow. Most guys weren't into single mothers at that age and Rose decided to save herself some heartache and time by deciding to stay out of the dating pool. Sure, she was lonely, but she had Corbin and Aiden and a whole drawer full of vibrators.

"Hi," a sexy, deep voice whispered into her ear. Rose turned to find the man who was formerly sitting at the end of the bar, now perched on the seat next to her. "I'm Clayton Nash," he said, holding his hand out for her to shake. "But everyone calls me Clay."

"Um," she stuttered, cursing herself for having the fourth shot. She knew her limit was three but when he sent her the drink, she didn't want to seem rude and refuse. "Rose," she said, placing her hand in his and gently shaking it.

"Nice to meet you, Rose," he said. She couldn't stop staring at him. He was younger than she was and probably the most handsome man she had seen in some time. Honestly, he looked more like one of her son's friends than someone who'd be buying her drinks at a bar. His dirty blond hair was pushed back as if he had been wearing a hat and had taken it off and his blue eyes matched the plaid blue shirt he was wearing. He reminded her of one of those cowboys she had seen in a western movie.

"Tell me you can ride a horse," she whispered. Rose wasn't sure she had even said those words out loud until he threw his head back and laughed at her. She smiled back but was internally kicking herself for saying something so stupid.

"I can, in fact, ride a horse," he said. "It's kind of a prerequisite for owning a ranch." Rose nearly swallowed her tongue thinking about him fulfilling her dirty cowboy fantasies that she loved so much. They were honestly her favorite romance books to read—the ones with the sexy cowboys but meeting one in real life wasn't something she planned on.

"So what is a beautiful woman like you doing in a bar like this?" he asked.

Now it was Roses turn to laugh. "That is the cheesiest pick-up line ever invented," she giggled.

"Well, I don't know about that," he drawled. "I got to see

that pretty smile of yours now, didn't I?" Rose wasn't sure if she successfully rolled her eyes, but she knew she was trying to.

"I'm here drowning my sorrows," she said.

"Please don't tell me that I'm going to have to find and beat the shit out of some asshole for breaking your heart, Rose," Clayton said.

"Oh God, no," Rose almost yelled. "No, no man or boyfriend to speak of," she said, holding up her hand and pointing to her empty ring finger. "It's my birthday," she said.

"Really?" Clay asked.

"Yep, and not a good one at that," she added. Rose sipped the water the bartender handed her, and she nodded her thanks.

"What happened to make your day such a bad one?" Clay asked.

"I turned fifty," she admitted with a grimace.

"No fucking way," he said. Clay sounded almost as upset about her age as she felt.

"Fucking way," she said.

"Well, if it makes you feel any better, you don't look it," he said. As sweet as it was of him to say, it didn't make her feel any better. Rose knew that she didn't look fifty and had good genes and night cream to thank for that but she also didn't need anyone to blow smoke up her ass. She knew how old she was and there was nothing she could do about it.

"Thanks," she dryly said. "But it doesn't soften the blow of that number."

"I get it," Clay said. "I'm here for the same reason."

"You're turning fifty today?" Rose questioned.

"Close—forty," Clay said.

Rose groaned and called the bartender back over. "I'll take a Moscow Mule and another beer for my ancient friend here," she teased.

"Hey," Clay complained.

"How about you come talk to me in another ten years and then you can properly complain about my slight," Rose teased.

"How about we help each other forget that we're turning another year older, Rose?" Clayton asked. Rose wasn't sure if the sexy stranger was asking her what she thought he was, but she sure wanted to find out.

"Um, what?" she asked. Clayton smiled up at her and from the devilish grin he gave her, she was sure she had heard him correctly. The question was, would she be a coward and bail or finally do something she wanted and take him up on his offer?

CLAYTON

Clay had a shit day and since it was also his fortieth birthday, his obvious choice for ending his day was at his favorite bar. But tonight, instead of finding all the same prospects, he was happy to find a sexy little blond in a business suit that made him completely hot and bothered. She was wearing sexy high heels that made him want to wrap her long legs around his neck and make her scream out his name. Even her name was pretty and Clay was sure that spending a night over or under her, for that matter, would help him forget about turning forty.

There was no other way he would forget about his milestone birthday. His brother and business partner, Tyler, gave him a good deal of shit about being older and now that he was forty, his brother's propensity for making fun of him only seemed to grow. Of course, it didn't help that his brother was younger than him by eight years. He was still a baby and Clay hated that he was starting to have trouble keeping up with him around their ranch. He didn't dare bitch about his back hurting or any of his new aches and pains otherwise, Ty would never let him live it down.

Now, he was sitting at his favorite bar in town, trying to forget the shit day he had by asking a pretty woman to spend the night with him. Sure, he was probably losing his mind and maybe even his grip on reality, but if he was going down, he wanted it to be with the sexy blond who looked as though she could give just as good as she got.

"So, how about it, Rose?" he whispered close to her ear. He liked the way she shivered as his warm breath brushed over her skin. God, her skin looked soft. "Want to come home with me?" He asked. Rose gasped and turned an adorable shade of pink, making him chuckle. It was refreshing to meet a woman who seemed a little put-off by such an offer. Most of the women he met were usually pasted up against him by this point of the conversation and it was nice to know that women like Rose still existed.

"I appreciate your offer," she stammered. "But I don't think that would be a good idea. I'm a little older than you and we both know that come morning, you'll sober up and forget that you even met me tonight." She was wrong. Clay was only on his second beer, and he was about ready to call it a night when he spotted Rose across the bar. Honestly, she looked about as sad and depressed as he felt and there would be no way he'd forget her.

"I hate to break it to you, but this here," he said, holding up his glass, "is my second beer. I'm not drunk, although I'd give my left nut to be. I'm alone and celebrating a milestone birthday, just like you. I thought we could commiserate together. And I can assure you, Honey, there would be no fucking way I'd be able to forget you, drunk or not," he admitted. Rose turned that adorable shade of red again and he was sure that he was going to be in a perpetual hard state if he didn't get her to agree to go back to his ranch with him.

"So, why are you here alone tonight?" Rose asked, not so subtly changing the subject. Clay could tell that she had a little more to drink than he had but he was hoping that the waiter would bring her more water and less of those Moscow Mules she was drinking. If he was going to convince her to go home with him, he wanted her to be sober or as close to it as possible.

"I didn't want to celebrate my birthday with anyone," he admitted. "I've never been one for big celebrations or blowing out candles to mark another passing year, so here I am." He held his arms wide as if trying to prove his point.

"What about your wife or girlfriend?" she pried.

He laughed, "Subtle," he teased. "Like you, I don't have either of those. I have a thirteen-year-old daughter but she is conveniently on vacation with her mother right now."

"That's awful," Rose said. "Your ex took her on vacation during your birthday?"

"Yep," he said. "It's fine really. What thirteen-year-old girl wants to hang out with her father for his fortieth birthday? My younger brother, Ty, offered to hang out with me tonight but there was no way I wanted to spend my night hearing about how old I am from my thirty-two-year-old little brother."

"No," Rose agreed, sipping her water. "I think that would be an awful way to spend your birthday."

"Well, I can think of at least one way I'd like to spend both of our birthdays, but you would have to say yes," he said. He knew he was pushing a little and hell, maybe Rose thought he was a total creep, but he didn't care. He wanted a chance with her and if he had to beg for it that is exactly what he was going to do.

Rose sighed and he braced himself to be let down. "I want to," she admitted, surprising the hell out of him.

"Really?" Clay knew he sounded surprised, but Rose had caught him off guard.

"Really," she confirmed. "But I have a list," she said.

"A list?" he questioned. "What kind of list are we talking here, Rose?" Clay asked. "Grocery, laundry, chores, demands?"

He chuckled at his joke, but Rose seemed to find him a lot less funny.

"No, smart ass. A list of things I want and don't want in a man," she said.

Clay whistled his surprise, "So, it is a list of demands then," he said. "I'm guessing it's a long one?"

Rose rolled her eyes and nodded. "According to my son and well, his best friend, I'm a very picky dater. If you could call being out on five dates in the last thirty-three years dating at all."

Clay choked on his beer and set his bottle back on the bar. "You have only been out on five dates in thirty-three years? Shit, Rose," he said.

"Yeah," she whispered. "So, thanks for the offer but I understand if you'd like to take it back now." Clay knew he had to play the rest of his hand smart otherwise he was going to spend his evening alone and the thought of having to watch Rose walk out of that bar and his life stung a little.

"What's number one?" he asked.

"Sorry," she said, seeming confused by his question.

"The first thing on your list of what you want and don't want in a man?" Clay asked. He knew he might be asking for trouble, but he had to know. "If you're going to flat out reject me, I'd like to know the reason why."

"Um," Rose squeaked, "number one would be the guy had to be older than me," she said. Her frown said it all and he knew that arguing would get him nowhere.

Clayton stood and laid down cash for both of their drinks. He nodded at Rose, "Thanks for your honesty," he said, tipping his hat to her. "At least you gave me that. Happy birthday, Rose." Clay turned to walk away, and he was just about to the door when he felt a hand on his shoulder. He turned to find Rose looking up at him and the pleading look in her eyes nearly did him in. The country music was so loud that there would be no way he'd be able to hear anything she had to say. He could see her lips moving but that was about it. He pointed to his ear and shook his head as if trying to signal to her that he couldn't hear her.

Clay could see her sigh even though he couldn't hear it. Rose went up on her tiptoes and wrapped her arms around his shoulders, taking him completely by surprise and gently brushed her lips against his. He wasn't sure if Rose was agreeing to everything that he wanted or just telling him goodbye, but either way, he was going to take full advantage of having her pressed up against his body. Clay wrapped his arms around her and pulled her in closer loving the way she seemed to fit up against him and deepened their kiss. When she finally pulled free from him, she was panting and he could tell that he left her just as needy as she did him.

Rose smiled up at him and nodded and he was almost afraid to hope that she was giving her agreement for him to take her home. She didn't give him much time to think about anything, taking his hand into hers and yanking him along to the door. He followed her because honestly, the thought of going home alone sucked. If Rose was offering to spend their birthdays together, he'd make it one neither of them would ever forget—he deserved at least one happy fucking birthday.

ROSE

"Um, so where are you taking me?" Rose asked. He had convinced her to leave her car at the bar and let him drive her home. He was sober and she was—well, less than sober. Hell, she was full-on drunk but still had enough of her good sense to know that agreeing to Clay's private birthday celebration might have been the worst mistake she'd ever made. This wasn't who she was but God, she wanted to be this woman for just one night. Rose was always so sure and steady. It made her a good mom and a good office assistant, but she wanted more. She turned fifty and was sure that she was too old to try new things but her old, boring ways were making her feel stale and lacking. Meeting a stranger, albeit—sexy as hell and a cowboy to boot—and agreeing to go back to his place, wasn't on her playlist.

"Well," he said clearing his throat, "we can go to my place if you'd like." She wasn't sure that was such a good idea. "Or," he said when she didn't immediately accept his plan. "We can get a hotel room."

Rose tried to think past the muddled confusion clouding her brain. It would be silly for them to get a hotel room. Plus,

Corbin and Aiden had a lot of friends around town and having her son or his best friend find out that she was spending the night with a stranger wasn't something she wanted.

"Your place is fine," she said. "If that's what you would like." Clay took her hand into his own and pulled hers up to his lips, gently kissing her knuckles.

"You always this compliant, Rose?" he asked.

"No," she breathed. Every mile that passed she sobered just a little more and instead of finding this whole idea to be a really bad one, she only wanted it more.

"You don't have to do anything you don't want to, Honey," he said. "If you've changed your mind—"

"No," she almost shouted. "I want this."

"You sure you haven't had too much to drink?" he questioned.

"Oh, I've had way too much to drink," she said. "But I'm sobering up. I want this, Clay. It's about time I do something for myself, list be damned."

Clay chuckled. "About this list, Rose," he started. "You want to tell me just what I'm up against. I mean, what if my age isn't the only thing playing against me here?" She knew he was teasing but she was sure he was right. If she told him her list, there would be quite a few "drawbacks" to dating him. But that wasn't what this was. They weren't dating. Hell, they were just having sex and that was number five on her list—no one nightstands.

"Come on, Rose," he pushed. "It can't be that bad."

"It's not good," she admitted. "I made the list when my son was born, and I started to think about dating again."

"How old is your son?" he asked.

"Almost thirty-three," she said, cringing at the realization that Corbin was only seven years younger than Clay. But he didn't even seem to blink at his and her son's age difference.

"Well, I know that number one is the guy has to be older

than you. We're kind of blowing rule one out of the water tonight. What's number two?" Clay asked.

Rose squinched up her nose and took a deep breath. "No tattoos," she said.

Clay barked out his laugh and she instantly knew that rule number two was also blown to hell. "How many do you have?" she almost whispered.

"A full sleeve on my left arm and one that covers most of my right side and shoulder," he admitted. "That okay?"

"I guess," she grumbled. "As you said, we've already blown past rule one." Clay laughed again and kissed her hand.

"Rule number three," he said. "Let's have it."

"The guy has to have a job," she said. Rose closed her eyes as if silently praying that he wouldn't tell her that rule number three was a no go too.

"Well, today is your lucky day, Rose. I do have a job. In fact, I own a ranch—well, co-own with my brother Tyler. But you already knew that." Rose thought back to their conversation at the bar, her brain still a little foggy. Yeah, he had mentioned something about owning a ranch when she made a big deal about him looking like a cowboy.

"So, rule number three is safe," she mumbled. "Rule four is probably safe too," she admitted. "I like for the guy to be taller than me. I'm about five-eleven," she admitted.

"Yep, rule four is safe," he agreed. "I'm six-three."

"Wow," she breathed. "That's pretty impressive." Rose tried not to think about what else might be impressive about the sexy cowboy sitting next to her.

"Thanks, but I had nothing to do with that. Just the luck of good genes and all. Rule Five?" he asked.

"Rule five is a doozy," she admitted. "We haven't broken it yet, but we are about to."

"I'm almost afraid to ask," he said.

"No one-night stands," she dramatically whispered.

Clay glanced over at her and smiled. "Here's your chance to

save rule number five, Rose," he offered. "Just tell me no and I'll take you home." Rose wasn't about to tell him no. The longer they drove, the more determined she was to have this whole thing happen between them. She wanted it all—one night of kinky sex. At least, she was hoping that was what she was getting herself into.

"How kinky do you like things?" she asked, ignoring his offer to back out of their deal. "Sex wise I mean." Clay choked and she worried that she had overstepped. "Never mind," she said. "Pretend I didn't ask."

"Well, that's going to be a pretty tough question to ignore, Rose," he said. "Honestly, I like things kinky—sex-wise," he said, giving her back her words. "Is that okay with you?"

Rose smiled over at him and nodded. "I've always liked kink, not that I've had a whole lot of sexual partners," she admitted. Rose wanted to put her entire fist into her mouth to shut herself up. What was it about Clay that made her want to share her entire life's story with him?

"How many partners have you had, Rose?" Clay asked.

"Um—two," she said.

"I'm not sure if you're asking or telling me," he teased.

"Telling," Rose said firmly, nodding her head for good measure. "Two, definitely two. My son's father and then one other guy before him. We were in high school together," she admitted.

Clay pulled his pick-up onto the side of a gravel road, out in the middle of nowhere and she worried that he was going to tell her to get out of his truck and walk the hell home. "You mean to tell me that you haven't had sex since you had your son?"

Rose didn't look at him, too embarrassed by that truth. She shook her head, looking out the passenger window into the darkness. "And, your son is almost thirty-three years old," he added. God, when he said it like that, she sounded as pathetic as she currently felt.

"Right," she said, clearing her throat. "I was kind of busy

raising my son and his best friend when he needed a place to stay after his mom died. When you're busy raising two boys, there isn't much time to go out and have sex," she defended.

"Thirty-three years though, Rose," he said. "That's a damn long time." He didn't need to tell her how long it had been since she was with a man. There were some nights that her whole body ached to be touched, loved, even held. But there was no one.

"I had my vibrator and my imagination," she said. Clay chuckled and she tried to open her door. "Please unlock my door," she said. "I'd like to get out."

"No," he breathed. "If you don't want this, I'll take you home, but you can't get out here. We're in the middle of nowhere. I should know, it's my ranch. You'll be attacked by a coyote or worse if you try to find your way back to town from here in the dark."

"I'll take my chances," she said. Rose fought to keep her tears at bay, not wanting to sit next to a stranger and cry. "I won't let you judge me for my past decisions, Clay." She couldn't stop the sob that bubbled up from her chest and she hid her face in her hands and cried.

"Oh, now Rose, don't do that," he begged. "I'm sorry, Honey. You're right—I have no right to judge you." Clay unbuckled her seatbelt and pulled her across the seat onto his lap. Rose didn't fight him, just cuddled into his chest and God, he felt right. "If I'm being completely honest here, Baby," he said. "I think it's kind of hot that you haven't been with a man for so long. I'm just worried that I might be the wrong kind of man for you," he said.

Rose wasn't sure if she heard him correctly. She sniffled and wiped her eyes, knowing that she probably had smeared her makeup and looked like a hot mess. "Why aren't you the right man for me?" she stuttered.

"Because I'm a demanding asshole, Rose," he admitted. "I wasn't lying when I told you I like kink. Hell, I like a whole lot of kink—I'm a Dom," he said. Rose knew exactly what a Dom was. She had overheard her daughter-in-law, Ava, and Aiden's wife, Zara talking about her son and Aiden being Doms. They even talked about a BDSM club that they all liked to go to. She wasn't blind or stupid—Rose knew exactly who her son and Aiden were but that was their lives and she tried to keep her nose out of their sex lives. Plus, what mother wanted to hear about her grown son having sex or what he liked in bed? Still, Rose would often think about what that lifestyle would entail and even had fantasies of someday trying some of the stuff she had looked up online.

"I've Googled some BDSM stuff," she admitted.

"Googled?" Clay asked. "As in you researched it online?"

"Yes," she said.

"And what did you think?" he asked.

"I think I'd like to try some of the things I saw," she admitted. Clay slid her back over to her seat and reached across her body, buckling her back in. Rose thought for sure that she had said the wrong thing and he was taking her home.

"Hold that thought, Baby," he ordered. They drove the rest of the gravel path back to his house in silence. Rose watched as he quickly put the truck in park, jumped out and rounded his pick-up to open her door.

"Ready?" he asked, holding his arms up to her.

"For?" she questioned.

"For me to show you a few of the things you looked up online. Let me introduce you to my world, Rose," he offered. Rose didn't hesitate; she let him wrap his arms around her body and practically carried her into his home.

"And, about your list Rose," he breathed.

"What about it," she asked.

"I'm about to give you a whole new list, Honey," he whispered in her ear. Rose shivered, causing him to laugh. "Now you're getting the idea, Baby."

CLAYTON

Clay carried Rose up to his master bedroom and laid her across the bed. What he wanted to do was take her down to his playroom and show her exactly what he was about, but he didn't want to scare her away. He wanted his night with her and then, if she agreed to be his submissive, he'd introduce her to all his kinks.

Rose sat up on the bed and watched him. He could tell that she was waiting for him to tell her what to do next and God, he loved that.

"You ready for this?" he asked. Rose sat forward and he couldn't help himself he had to touch her. Clay ran his hand down her cheek, cupping her jaw. When he ran his thumb over her bottom lip, her tongue darted out and he couldn't help his groan. All Clay could think about was how her tongue would feel against his cock, just before she sucked him into her mouth.

"Yes," she agreed. "I'm ready. I'm just a little out of practice —as you well know. I need you to tell me what to do next. It's like riding a bike, right?" she teased.

Clay laughed, "God, I hope not," he said. "How about we

take this slowly—you know one step at a time. You don't like something, just say so."

"Will I need a safe word?" she asked. "I um, well, I Googled that."

Clay smiled down at her, "Do you want a safe word, Rose? I won't push you too hard tonight but if it would make you feel better, we can come up with one."

"Oh," she breathed. Rose sounded a little disappointed and he worried that he had said something wrong.

"Tell me why you're frowning, Honey," he demanded.

"Well, I was hoping to be pushed a little," she admitted. "Actually, a lot. I wanted you to show me what I've been missing. I won't break, Clay."

"Okay," he said. "Tell me what you'd like to try, and we can go from there."

"Um, everything," she said, sitting up on the edge of the bed. "Do you like to spank women?" she asked. He sat down next to her and pulled her onto his lap. He suspected that telling her, "Fuck yes," as his answer might scare her off.

"Yeah," he said, shrugging, going for casual. Rose smiled and nodded.

"I'd like to try spanking," she admitted.

"Do you want me to use my hand, flogger, paddle—" Rose reached up and covered his mouth with her hand.

"Yes," she said. "All of them." Clay liked where this discussion was heading. It was giving him the in he was looking for with Rose.

"Well, If you want to try all of them, we will need more than just one night. You up for that, Rose?" he asked.

"You mean you want to see me past tonight?" she questioned.

"Yeah," Clay admitted. "I do. Are you okay with that?"

"I—I think so," she said. "If you're all right with that."

"We'll need rules," Clay said. "You okay with replacing your rules about who you'll date with new ones?"

"What are we talking here, Clay?" she asked.

"Nothing out of the ordinary. You'll agree to be my sub and I will give you rules that you will need to follow, or you'll be punished." Rose tried to scramble off his lap and he banded his arms around her waist. "Just give me a chance to explain before you run off," he said.

Rose stilled on his lap and his cock wanted to complain. "Fine," she said. "What do you mean by having to punish me?" she asked.

"Oh, you know—waterboarding, bamboo shoots up your fingernails, electric shock therapy. I'm sure you saw all of that in your Google search, right?" Clay teased.

"What?" Rose questioned. She started to squirm around on his lap again and his cock sprang to life.

Clay chuckled, "I'm teasing, Rose. Punishment can be whatever you agree to. I like to spank with a paddle when my sub doesn't follow the rules."

"Have you had many submissives?" she asked.

"A few," Clay admitted. "I'm a member of a local BDSM club and I like to go there to play. My ex wasn't into the lifestyle and when I admitted that I wanted to try adding some kink into our sex life, she started losing interest. Honestly, it was the beginning of the end, looking back."

"I'm sorry," Rose offered. "If I agree to be your submissive, will you still go to the club to play with other subs?" There was no way he'd want another woman if Rose agreed to be his.

"No," he breathed. "I'm a one-woman kind of guy. But I'd like to take you to the club to play." Rose smiled up at him and shyly nodded her agreement.

"So, rule number one," he said. "You agree to be my submissive and we both agree to an exclusive arrangement."

"I agree to rule number one," she said. "Is it that easy or will I need to sign something?"

Clay laughed. "No, I don't think we'll need a formal contract," he said.

"How many rules will there be?" Rose asked. "You know I like rules."

"Yeah," he breathed. "But your rules were limiting you, holding you back. My rules are supposed to free you; help you to experience something new and exciting. You think you can handle that?"

"Yes," she said without hesitation. "I think I might like that."

"Good, Baby," he said. Rose squinched up her nose and he thought it had to be the cutest thing he'd ever seen. "Why the face?" he asked.

"Well, you keep calling me, 'baby,'" she said.

"You don't like nicknames?" he questioned.

Rose shook her head, "I like them but it seems funny for you to call me that since I'm a full ten years older than you."

"I don't give a fuck about our ages, Rose," he growled. "When we're here, just the two of us, you are mine and I'll call you whatever I'd like. I use 'baby' as a term of endearment and that has nothing to do with our ages—got it?"

"Yes," she said. "So, rule number two is fuck our ages?"

Clay barked out his laugh, "Yep," he agreed. "Rule number two is that there is no age difference between us and I'll call you, 'baby,' 'honey,' or anything else I'd like to."

"I think I'm going to like rule number two most of all," Rose said.

"You haven't heard rule number three yet," he teased. Clay rolled her under his body and kissed his way down the column of her neck.

"What's rule three?" she squeaked.

"Number three is that you are mine—body, mind, and soul. You will do what I want when I want," he growled against her neck. Clay unbuttoned her white silky blouse and let it slide across her body, leaving Rose in just her lacy bra. God, she was sexy as fuck. Rose had no idea just how much she turned him on but she was about to find out. The rest of the rules were going to have to wait because he needed to make her his.

"What about the rest of the rules?" she stuttered as he sucked her nipple into his mouth through the lace of her bra. He gently bit down and she yelped, writhing against his body. He could feel the heat of her core through her sensible business skirt. He had to admit, the whole hot businesswoman thing did it for him. Clay grabbed a handful of her hair and gave it a sharp tug, causing Rose to hiss out her breath. Yeah, she liked a little bit of pain with her pleasure. Training Rose was going to be a whole lot of fucking fun.

"We can finish going over the rules later," he said. "Right now, you should choose a safe word."

"I thought you said I won't need one for tonight," she whispered.

"Plans changed," he murmured against her skin. "I'm going to give you a little taste of what I plan on doing with you and you might need to use your safe word if it gets to be too much."

"O-Oh," she stuttered when he bit into her flesh. He waited for Rose to give him her word and when she smiled down at him and said the word, "Walrus," he couldn't help but laugh.

"Walrus?" he asked.

Rose looked up at him and batted her eyelashes, gifting him with her sexy smile. "Well, I read online that I should choose a word that I wouldn't use during sex. I would not use the word 'walrus' during sex," she defended.

"Fair enough, Baby," he said. "Walrus it is. If you don't like something I'm doing, I want you to tell me. If you want me to stop, use your safe word. Got it?"

"Got it," she breathed. "What will you do with me, Clay?" she asked.

"Sir," he corrected. "When we're together like this, you call me 'Sir'."

"Sir," Rose purred, rubbing her body against his.

"Thank you, Honey. I'm going to spank your ass red and

then I plan on spending the rest of the night making you mine. Spend the night with me, Rose?" he asked. Clay didn't want to sound like he was giving her an order when he asked her to spend the night with him. He needed that to be something that Rose wanted to give him.

"Yes," she whispered. "I'd like that." Clay let out his pent-up breath and she wrapped her arms around his neck. "Thank you for asking, Sir."

"Up," he ordered, helping Rose from his bed. "Strip for me, Honey." She looked shyly down her body and back up at him. Clay sat back and waited her out, watching the indecision cross her features. This was the moment he had been waiting for—the moment she would have to decide what she wanted from him. He just hoped that she would decide that she wanted what he was asking for because letting sexy, little Rose go now wouldn't be easy.

ROSE

"What's it going to be, Baby?" he asked. He had been waiting her out, watching her and Rose could see the hope in his eyes when he asked her for her decision. Rose reached up and unsnapped her bra and slipped it down her arms, letting it fall to the floor. Clay looked her over and she loved the sexy smirk he wore as he blatantly watched her. Clay nodded to her skirt, and she unzipped the back and let it fall to the ground around her ankles. She had already slipped off her heels when they got to his place.

Rose Looked down her body and said a little silent prayer that she was wearing her good lacy panties and was relieved to see that was the case. She had on thigh highs with garters that attached to her pink lacy panties. Rose looked back over to where clay sat on his bed and worried that she had done something wrong. He was so still and quiet, she knew that she must have messed up at some point during her pathetic strip tease.

"I'm sorry," she whispered. Clay stood and pulled her down to his lap.

"What the hell for?" he questioned.

"I've obviously done something to displease you, Clay. You

haven't said a word since I started taking my clothes off." Rose looked down her body and back up at him.

"You're fucking perfect, Baby," he praised. "I was quiet because I was afraid that if I said anything, I'd end up swallowing my damn tongue. I especially love these," he said, running his hands down her thigh-high stockings. "How about we leave this for now?" Rose shyly nodded her agreement.

"Will you take off your clothes?" she asked. She felt so out of her element with Clay. It had been so long since she had been with a man and Clay seemed to have so much more experience than she had.

"Sure," he agreed. Clay unbuttoned his plaid shirt and tugged it free from his body and she couldn't help but let her eyes greedily roam his torso.

"You work out," she said. God, it sounded more like she was accusing him of something rather than praising him.

"A little," he admitted. "It's mostly from working around here—you know dealing with the ins and outs of the ranch. I build a lot of fences." Clay shrugged and she watched as his muscles bunched and moved. He was beautiful. Clay helped her to sit down on the bed next to him and stood to shuck out of his jeans. He stood in front of her in just his boxer briefs, making her mouth water with what she hoped would be next. His erection practically jutted out at her, and she wanted to reach for his cock but he hadn't given her permission yet. Rose knew enough about a Dom/sub relationship to know that she had to wait for him to give her the order to touch him. She ran her hands up and down her thighs, eager to have him give the order.

"You want something, Honey?" he asked. She knew he was taunting her; testing her but she looked up at him and smiled.

"I do," she said, nodding. "Please."

"Please what, Honey?" he questioned. Clay seemed to know exactly what she was asking for, but he wasn't going to make any of this easy on her. Rose felt tongue-tied and saying the words, "I want to give you a blow job," seemed foreign to her. It wasn't something she had ever felt comfortable doing, being forward when it came to sex. Maybe that's why she sat on the sidelines for so long, coming up with one excuse after another to avoid the male population.

"How about I give you time to think about what you want? How about a distraction?" he asked. Rose shyly nodded and he chuckled. Clay sat down next to her on the bed, and he pulled her across his lap, his erection jutting into her belly. Rose looked down at the floor and closed her eyes when he ran his big hand over her silky panties. He cupped a handful of her ass and squeezed and Rose just about wanted to run and hide. She wasn't used to anyone paying her ass so much attention.

"How does this make you feel, Honey?" he asked, running his hand over her other cheek and down her thigh.

"Um," Rose squeaked. "Embarrassed." She sounded more like she was asking a question rather than telling Clay how his touching her ass made her feel. Clay gave her ass a sharp swat and it felt like a fire had spread from the top of her thigh, where he had spanked her, up her cheek. Clay rubbed the spot where he had landed the first blow and the sharp, hot pain turned to intense pleasure. Rose moaned and writhed against his hand.

"You like that, Baby?" he asked.

"Yes," she hissed. "More, please."

"More please, Sir," he corrected, gifting her other ass cheek with the same attention. She ground her drenched pussy against his thigh and Clay swatted her ass again.

"Hold still, Honey," he ordered. "The more you move, the longer it's going to take me to give you what you want. What do you want, Rose?" he asked. Again, she didn't answer. If she had, she would have told him that she wanted him to help her find her release. Her entire body was screaming for it but asking for something so intimate, so personal, felt wrong.

"You don't like to talk dirty, do you, Rose?" he asked. She

kept her eyes trained on the floor, trying not to think about her ass perched in the air, waiting for his attention. He saw her at her most vulnerable. She was completely out of her element, giving him complete control of her body and Rose wasn't sure she liked it. Sure, it was nice not to have to make any decisions but Clay was a stranger to her and letting go and giving him her complete submission wasn't an easy task for her.

"No," she said. "I don't like to talk about sex—you know ask for what I want."

"Did you ever like to talk about what you wanted sexually," he asked. "You know, with your son's father?"

"No," she said. "He was older than I was, and I was just a young girl. I didn't know anything about sex back then."

"Oh Rose," he said. Clay helped her to sit up and she was horrified that her admission had him changing his mind about having sex with her tonight. Rose quickly scurried off his lap and covered herself with the blanket he had tossed over the foot of the bed.

"It's okay, Clay," she whispered. "I get it if you're not interested anymore. I'm not what you were expecting. Heck, I'm not what I was expecting either. I guess the alcohol was making me braver than I really am and now—well, I'm just pathetic." She stood to find her clothes. Rose would call an Uber and head back to the bar to pick up her car and try to put this whole horrific birthday behind her.

"Stop," Clay ordered. "Come here, Rose." She wasn't sure why, but she did as he commanded, standing in front of him, almost naked. He took her hand into his and led it to his bulging erection. She playfully let her fingers trace it's impressive outline through his boxer briefs and loved the breathy little groans she elicited from him.

"That feels so good, Honey," he hissed. "Does it feel like I don't want you?" he challenged.

"N-no," she stuttered. Clay held her hand in his, not letting her take her fingers from his cock. "Don't stop," he commanded. Rose felt a surge of courage that gave her the confidence to dip her hands into his briefs and let them freely roam his cock. Clay moaned and threw his head back. It was the hottest thing Rose had ever been a part of.

"Was this what you wanted to ask me, Rose?" he asked. "Did you want to touch me?"

"Yes," she admitted. "I wanted to touch you and taste you, Clay. I still do." That was possibly the dirtiest thing Rose had ever said out loud and a part of her wanted to run and hide.

"I want that too, Rose," Clay said. He laid back on the bed, letting her have full access to his body. "Do whatever you want to me, Baby," he ordered. Rose shyly smiled down at him and nodded. Her tongue darted out and she licked her lips. "Fuck, that's hot, Honey," he said. Rose loved the way Clay challenged her, talking dirty to her like it was nothing. This world was so new to her, but Rose was sure she was going to like it.

She leaned over his body and licked his cock from base to tip, cupping his balls with her hand. He moaned and thrust himself at her, as if he needed more from her greedy mouth. "You like that?" she questioned.

"I fucking love it, Baby. More," he ordered. "I need more, Rose. Suck me into your mouth." Rose was not very experienced with blow jobs. Hell, she had only given a few in her lifetime but Clay made her want to try.

She firmly grasped the base of his cock with her hand and wrapped her lips around the tip, letting him push his way into her mouth. "Yes," Clay hissed. "Just relax your throat and let me take over." Rose did just that, loving the way he grabbed her hair to hold her steady. He bobbed in and out of her mouth, hitting the back of her throat and Rose did her best to breathe through her nose. He pushed a few more times to the back of her mouth and tried to pull free from her lips.

"I'm going to come, Rose," he said. That was exactly what she wanted but she wouldn't let him free to give him the words. She sucked him back into her mouth and pressed her fingers into his thighs, holding him in place. "Fuck, Rose," Clay shouted. He pumped in and out of her mouth and before she knew it, he was coming down her throat in hot spurts. She took all of him and licked him clean, pretty proud of her efforts. Rose let him pop free from her mouth and licked her lips.

"Was that okay?" she questioned, suddenly unsure of herself. Clay didn't make a move from the bed, panting as if trying to get air in and out of his lungs.

"Okay?" he asked. "It was fucking perfect," he growled. "Are you okay? Was I too rough with you?"

She smiled down at him, running her fingers over his jawline. He leaned into her caress. "I'm fine," she whispered. "You taste good, Sir." Clay pinned her to the mattress and rolled on top of her.

"Minx," he teased. "Let's see how good you taste," he said. Clay kissed a path down Rose's body, giving her breasts special attention. Her whole body felt as though it was on fire. It consumed her and made her want more. She wanted him to stoke the fires that were always burning in her.

Clay popped her garters loose and made quite a show of working her thigh highs down her legs, kissing, and nipping her sensitive skin with each and every inch that he exposed. He finished pulling her panties down her body and settled between her legs.

"You smell good, Honey," he teased. Rose wanted to die from embarrassment but the raw need that consumed her was winning out. Clay didn't give her any time to think or hide. He ran two fingers through her wet folds and she moaned and laid back on the bed.

"Tell me what you want me to do, Rose. Give me the words," he ordered. She sat back up and looked at him like he had lost his mind. Was he really going to make her beg him? Was he going to make her say the words? "Rose," he prompted. "What do you want me to do to your sweet pussy?" he asked.

Rose covered her eyes with both hands, refusing to look at him. "Lick it," her muffled voice commanded.

Clay chuckled and ran the pad of his thumb over her sensitive clit. "Look at me and tell me what you want, Honey," he ordered. Rose knew that disobeying him wouldn't get her what she wanted.

Rose slowly lowered her hands and stared down at him. "Lick it," she squeaked, repeating herself.

"Gladly," he said. Clay smiled and gave her an outrageous wink, making her giggle. Her laughter quickly faded when his tongue slid through her slick pussy.

"Not so funny now, Honey, is it?" Rose lay back again and waited for him to continue. "Rose," he whispered against her pussy. She couldn't help but squirm against his mouth, needing more. "Hold still or I'll tie you down," Clay growled.

Rose tried to hold as still as possible but gave some honest thought about disobeying him. She always wondered what it would feel like to be tied to a man's bed, completely at his mercy, letting him do whatever he pleased with her body.

"You'd like that wouldn't you, Baby?" Clay questioned. He looked up her body, waiting for her answer.

"I'm not sure," She admitted. "I think I might like to be tied up."

Clay smiled up at her. "I think that can be arranged but right now, I'm going to make you scream my name."

"Oh God," Rose moaned. "Yes, please." Clay licked her pussy, and she held her breath, trying to hold as still as possible.

"Breathe, Honey," he ordered. Rose let out her pent-up breath. She was so close to finding her release and when he sucked her clit into her mouth, she couldn't stay off her orgasm. She shouted out Clay's name and when he finally finished with her, she felt like a lifeless rag doll.

"Thank you," she whispered.

"Don't thank me yet, Honey," he said. "We're not done yet." He drug her limp body to the end of the bed and spread her open. Clay didn't give her a warning; he just sunk into her body, balls deep.

"You feel so fucking good, Baby," he groaned.

Rose reached up and ran her hands down his chiseled chest. "You feel good too, Clay." It had been so long since Rose felt the weight of a man's body against her own or the thrust of a man's cock deep inside of her core. She had forgotten just how good it all felt. Sure, her vibrator was nice but everything Clay was doing to her was a million times better. Rose wasn't sure where she ended and Clay began.

"Tell me you're close," Clay begged.

"I am," she said. "I just need—more." Clay seemed to know exactly what she was asking for, snaking a hand between their bodies and rubbing his thumb over her sensitive nub. "Yes," she hissed. Rose rode out her orgasm, taking what she needed from Clay. He quickly followed her over and when he came, he shouted out her name and Rose thought it was the most beautiful thing she had ever heard.

Clay collapsed with her onto the bed and she curled into his body. Rose had never been a very touchy, feely person but snuggling into his body just felt right, especially given what they had just shared.

"You still want me to spend the night," she asked.

"Absolutely," he said. "I can't imagine anyone else I'd rather spend the rest of my birthday with."

Rose smiled and nodded, "Agreed," she breathed. As far as birthdays went, her fiftieth was one for the books and not something she'd be able to forget for a very long time.

CLAYTON

Clay woke up the next morning before the sun and carefully extracted himself from Rose's body to get out of bed. He found his jeans, slipped them on, and decided to start some coffee. It was the only way he was going to get through his morning chores since he had spent most of the night making Rose shout out his name. He turned back to look her over and then made his way to his kitchen.

His house was the original main house for the ranch. The place had been in his family for six generations now and he and his brother, Tyler were the current caretakers of the ranch. Ty lived just down the road in a little house that he, Ty, and their dad built ten years back, just before his dad passed. Now, the ranch depended on the two of them if they were going to pass it on to future generations. Ty didn't have kids yet—or a woman for that matter and Clay had one daughter, Paisley. His thirteen-year-old daughter seemed to have no desire to run the ranch. She spent as little time as possible helping out around the homestead since he and her mother, Abilene divorced. They split up when Paisley was just little and they had been divorced for five years now. His daughter still came to spend weekends with him but she was spending less time out at the barn and refused to do anything around the ranch, including riding her favorite horse—unicorn. Their only hope for passing down the ranch was falling on his brother's shoulders and that had him worried. Tyler was too busy playing the field and reliving his glory days as a quarterback on the high school football team to find a nice woman and settle down. They were fucked but Clay would worry about all that another day.

Now, he had bigger things to worry about—namely the sexy blond who spent the night with him last night. He needed to figure out how to convince Rose that what they did last night wasn't a mistake. Clay was pretty sure that would be her argument when she woke up this morning, given her lengthy list of whom she should and shouldn't date. Her ridiculous list read more like a ransom note rather than a list of what she wanted in a man. Who the hell made lists like that? He had a feeling that once Rose woke up and overthought their night together, she would be rushing out of his house and his life. His only saving grace was that Rose left her car back at the bar and she'd need for him to take her back to pick it up. That would buy him some time so he could figure out a way to convince Rose to see him again tonight.

"Hey," Ty said, walking in through the back door.

"What are you doing here?" Clay whispered.

Ty walked over to the cabinet where Clay kept the coffee mugs and helped himself. "I'm out of coffee and I need my fix," Tyler grumbled. "What's got your panties in a bunch this morning?" Clay looked him over and frowned. "You look like shit, by the way."

Clay took his brother's mug of coffee from him after he got done pouring it. He took a sip of the coffee and scowled. "Thanks for that," he whispered.

"Want to tell me why you're whispering?" Ty asked. "You sick or something?" Clay wasn't sure how he wanted to answer his brother. He thought about lying and telling him he was sick.

Maybe that would get him the day off and he could persuade Rose to spend the day in bed with him. But, that wouldn't be fair to his brother. Especially today when they were mending fence. It was a grueling job and he'd be pissed if Ty bailed on him.

"If you have to know," Clay started. Ty's attention was quickly turned by Rose walking into the kitchen, yawning, and stretching, wearing just his plaid shirt from the night before. "Shit," Clay cursed.

"Oh my God," Rose shouted. She tried to cover herself with her arms and watching her flail around was almost comical. Clay set his coffee mug on the kitchen counter and crossed the room to stand in front of Rose.

"Morning, Baby," he said, pulling her up his body to kiss her. Rose protested and slapped at his chest until he finally put her down.

"Clay," she breathed. "You could have warned me that you had company."

Clay chuckled, "He's not company, Honey. He's my little brother, Tyler. Ty, this is Rose." His brother crossed the room to offer Rose his hand. She quickly reached around Clay's body and shook Ty's offered hand.

"Nice to meet you, Tyler," Rose said.

"You too, Rose. I didn't know my brother was entertaining. I'm sorry to barge in on you so early."

"It's fine. I should be going anyway," Rose said. She turned to walk back to his bedroom and Clay shouted at her to stop. She did and he followed her into the hallway. It was now or never—he needed her to give him some promise that their one night together wasn't going to be their only night.

"I have to take you for your car," he reminded.

"No, it's fine, Clay," she said. "I can call an Uber. I don't want to put you out."

He chuckled. Rose was so peculiar and so refreshing from

the women that he usually dated or played with at his club. "Not at all," he said. "I insist."

Rose seemed to mull it over and then she smiled up at him and nodded. "I'd appreciate the lift," she said. "It will give me time to get home, grab a quick shower, and head into the office."

Clay worried that he was losing his chance at asking her out again. The thought of what happened between the two of them being only a one-night thing wasn't acceptable to him. "What are your plans for dinner tonight?" he asked. Rose looked at him as if he had lost his mind.

"Dinner," she questioned. "I haven't thought that far ahead yet. Why?"

"Have dinner with me," he said. "Go on a real date with me."

"Last night didn't count as a real date?" she challenged.

"No," he breathed. "Last night was wonderful but hooking up at a bar and bringing you back here doesn't count as a real date. Have dinner with me, Rose?" This time she didn't hesitate or take time to think his proposal over. Rose smiled and nodded her agreement.

"Okay," she agreed. "Will I need to pack my toothbrush or is this offer just for dinner?"

"That depends on what you want, Rose. It's your call," Clay said, although he wanted to tell her to pack more than just her toothbrush.

"I'd like to spend the night again, Clay," Rose whispered. She went up on her tiptoes and gently brushed his lips with hers. Clay needed more and he didn't give a fuck that his brother was standing in his kitchen probably listening to every word they were saying. He pushed Rose up against the hallway wall, pressing her between it and his body. Clay loved the way she wrapped her arms around his neck and moaned into his mouth. When he finally broke the kiss, they were both panting for air.

"That was just a little teaser of what's to come tonight," he said. "I also have a surprise for you and I think you'll like it."

"I'm not much for surprises, Clay," Rose admitted. "But, I'll try to keep an open mind. As long as it's not a surprise birthday party, we'll get along just fine." Clay must have made a face at her mention of a surprise party. It was something he never had and never wanted—a big birthday bash. Honestly, a party like that sounded more like torture than fun.

"Deal," he agreed. "No surprise birthday party for either of us. But I think you'll like what I have in store for you tonight."

"Mind if I use your bathroom to freshen up?" Rose asked.

"Not at all. You want some coffee?" he asked.

"Please," Rose said. "Cream and sugar if you have it, too," she said.

"Sure. I'll have it ready for you when you're done getting ready," he said. Clay watched Rose walk down the hallway and back to his master suite. He turned to go back into the kitchen and just about ran into his brother.

"Fuck, Ty," he grumbled. "Why are you still here?"

"Well, I thought about heading out to the barn, but I wouldn't be able to hear your conversation from there. So, I stuck with eavesdropping from the kitchen," his brother teased.

"You hear enough or do you need for me to recap our private conversation?" Clay spat.

"I got the gist," Tyler said, his stupid smirk in place. "You like this woman, don't you? Usually, you pick a woman up from the club and play with her until you get bored. What's different about this sub?" Clay shot his little brother a look and Tyler shrugged. "I know more than I let on," he admitted. He didn't know Ty was so well versed in the BDSM world. It wasn't something that they discussed but his brother was right, he didn't like to keep a sub for more than a night or two but Rose wasn't just his sub.

"I didn't pick her up at the club," Clay admitted. "I went to

Shooters and had a few drinks for my birthday and well, Rose was there drinking for the same reason."

"To celebrate your birthday?" Ty asked.

Clay sighed, "Try to keep up, Ty," he teased. "Rose and I have the same birthday." Clay conveniently left out the part about their age differences because honestly, it didn't matter and it wasn't his brother's business.

"So, you were both sitting at Shooters and commiserating over turning the big four-zero?" Tyler asked.

"Well, one of us was upset about turning forty." Clay chugged down his lukewarm coffee and put his mug in the sink.

Tyler looked him up and down and smiled. "You're baiting me to ask how old Rose is but a true gentleman never asks," Ty said.

"That works for me because a true gentleman doesn't tell a woman's age either," Clay said.

"And," Rose said, standing in the doorway to the kitchen. "A real woman doesn't give a fig about her age because it's just a number. I turned fifty yesterday, Tyler." Clay had to give him credit, his little brother didn't even flinch at Rose's mention of turning fifty. Clay finished making her coffee and handed Rose the mug. She took a sip and hummed her approval.

"Good?" Clay asked.

"Perfect," she agreed. It was strange spending their first morning together with his brother watching on. There were so many things he wanted to ask Rose to get to know her better but having Ty looking on made that nearly impossible.

"I'm going to drive Rose to pick up her car," Clay said.

"That works," Ty agreed. "I'll eat some breakfast and then get started on the fencing. You have any eggs and toast?" Tyler asked.

"Sure, just help yourself why don't you?" Clay grumbled.

"Thanks, man," Ty said. "I appreciate that." Clay shook his head at his brother.

"I just have to run back to the bedroom, grab a shirt and

brush my teeth," Clay said to Rose. "You good?" He shot Ty a look telling him to behave himself.

"Yep," she said. "I'll finish my coffee and be ready to go by the time you're done." Clay kissed her cheek and brushed past his brother on his way out of the kitchen.

"Don't worry," Ty said. "I'm sure Rose and I will find something to talk about while you are gone."

"That's exactly what I'm afraid of," Clay admitted and disappeared down the hall. After he had worked so hard to get Rose to agree to another night with him, the last thing he needed was for Tyler to fuck that all up for him. Yeah, he'd just have to hurry and give Ty as little time alone with Rose as humanly possible. That way he'd have less chance to fuck things up with her.

ROSE

Rose played twenty questions with Tyler and she had to admit, she kind of liked the guy. He reminded her a lot of Corbin and Aiden and that thought made her feel ancient. She needed to remember the rules that Clay had set into place for them. Especially the one about age being just a number and not coming into play between the two of them. It was still pretty hard to forget their drastic age difference, no matter how much Clay said it didn't matter to him. Rose just hoped like hell that she'd be able to work past that or this thing with Clay wouldn't work.

The car ride back to Shooters with Clay was about the same as her game of twenty questions with Tyler. He sure did ask a lot of questions but it was nice to have someone take an interest in her that way. When they finally made it back to Shooters, Clay walked her to her car and gave her a scorching kiss in the empty parking lot, promising her that they would pick things up tonight. Clay told her to be ready at six and she promised to text him her home address so he could pick her up. Rose wanted to insist that she just drive over to his place, so she'd have her car in the morning but Clay was hell-bent on picking her up properly for their date. She had to admit, it was nice to be treated like a lady for a change and not like someone's mom, office assistant, or even grandmother, even though she wouldn't trade any of those titles for anything.

By the time Rose showered, changed, and got into the office, she was over thirty minutes late. She stepped off the elevator and almost ran right into Corbin. "Why the fuck are you so late today?" her son questioned.

Rose tried to breeze past him and he stepped in her path. "Corbin James," she chided, knowing how much he hated when she middle named him. "I had something come up and I'm a little late—no big deal." The more she tried to brush off her being late, the more he seemed to press her for answers.

Aiden poked his head out of his office. "What the hell is going on out here?" he asked. "I'm pretty sure they can hear you two arguing down the street."

"Mom was late today and now she's avoiding giving me an answer about why," Corbin said, catching Aiden up.

"There, now you have all the news and we can get on with our day," Rose sassed.

"Mother, you've been acting strangely since last week. I know that turning fifty has hit you hard but you don't have to go through all of this alone," Corbin said. If he only knew how not alone she was while she celebrated her birthday.

"My being late had nothing to do with me turning fifty," she lied. It kind of did since she met Clay while commiserating about turning another year older. Telling her boys about her night with some guy who picked her up at a bar wasn't what she wanted to do this morning.

"Then why were you late, Rose?" Aiden asked. "We just want to make sure that you're all right."

"I'm fine," she said, tossing her bags down onto her desk. "Now, if you both don't mind, I'd like to get on with my day. I have to leave here tonight on time."

"What, why?" Corbin questioned.

"No reason, I just have plans. Geeze son, maybe you should take up a new hobby if you have so much time to wonder what I'm doing with my free time." Rose laughed at her statement. "Maybe take up knitting."

Corbin smirked at her, and Aiden barked out his laugh. "I'm going to leave you two to resolve this. I have a meeting in ten minutes," Aiden said. He kissed Rose's cheek. "I hope you had a nice birthday and if you need anything, you know where you can find me."

"Thank you, Aiden," she said. "I did have a nice birthday. I appreciate you keeping your nose out of my business, too." Rose looked at Corbin and he huffed out his breath.

"Subtle, mother," Corbin said. Aiden laughed and walked back into his office, shutting the door behind him. "I stopped by your house last night and you weren't there," he said. Corbin sounded as if he was accusing her of something, but she refused to feel guilty about what happened between her and Clay.

Rose turned and stared him down. "I think you are confused about who the parent is here, Son," she said. "While I appreciate you stopping by to visit it doesn't mean I owe you an explanation about why I wasn't home."

"If you wanted to go out for your birthday you could have come over and celebrated with us," Corbin said.

"Again, I appreciate that, but I had other plans," Rose said. She was beginning to see that she wasn't going to get away with not spilling the beans about where she spent the night last night. Honestly, she didn't know what she was worried about. She was a grown woman and what she did in her spare time wasn't her son's business.

"The thing is, when I went out on my run this morning, I stopped by your house and you weren't home then either." Corbin crossed his arms over his massive chest and stared her down. Rose almost wanted to laugh at how much he looked like the same angry little boy who used to try the same tactics when he was younger.

"Again, it's none of your business, Corbin. I was out and that's all you need to know." Rose turned back around and busied herself with the pile of folders that Aiden had left on her desk for her. She was hoping that her son would take the hint and get lost but she also knew how stubborn he could be. Corbin was like a dog with a bone when he wanted answers. Rose knew he'd dig down as deep as he could to get to the answers he wanted.

"Were you with someone?" he asked, cutting right to the chase. Rose shot him a look that told him to tread lightly. She was pretty good with her mom faces and if she was doing it right still, she was giving him the, "Don't mess with me" face. "Shit," Corbin grumbled. "You were with someone. You met a man and have been keeping it from me? How long have you been seeing him?"

"It's not like that," Rose admitted. She wanted to cover her face and hide; she was mortified she was going to have to tell him that she picked up a guy at a bar and went home with him. That wasn't the person she was but she wouldn't change a thing about her night with Clay.

"Then tell me what it's like, Mom," he prompted.

Rose sighed, "I met a man last night and well, one thing led to another. The rest is none of—"

Corbin didn't let her finish her sentence. "Yeah, I get it—it's none of my business. But it is, Mom. You're my business and if you're meeting strange men and spending the night with them, I have a right to know."

"You make it sound like I've done this before," Rose whispered. "I don't meet strange men in bars. It was one man and one night."

"In a bar?" Corbin questioned. "You picked up a guy in a bar and stayed with him. Tell me you didn't tell him where you live or give him any personal information about you or our company."

"You make him sound like a corporate spy or something. This man wants nothing to do with your company," Rose said.

"You can't know that, Mom. You don't know him, do you? He could work for a competitor or something." Corbin paced the floor in front of her like he always did when he was upset or worried.

Rose barked out her laugh. The thought of Clay being out to bring down her son's company was crazy. "I think you're overreacting," she said. "He owns a ranch just outside of town and we were both at the bar for our birthdays."

"You two have the same birthdays?" Corbin asked.

"Yeah," she said. "And we were both miserable about turning another year older. And, I guess I had a little bit too much to drink."

Corbin stopped pacing and looked her over, "Tell me he didn't take advantage of you, Mom," he demanded.

"No, of course not," she said. "He's nice, actually."

"Well, that's terrific," Corbin said. "If he's nice then that's all that matters, right?"

"I was having a shit day, upset overturning fifty and well, he bought me a drink and made me feel special. And, he was just as miserable about turning forty, so we gave each other comfort."

"Okay, first off—eww," Corbin said, squinching up his nose. "Wait—did you say he was upset about turning forty? He's ten years younger than you, Mom?"

Rose looked back down at her desk and nodded. "Yes," she said. "I'm older than him and he's fine with it. Honestly, age is just a number." Rose wished she believed her own words but she didn't. Being with Clay felt right but getting past his first rule of "age doesn't matter," didn't feel like one she'd be able to follow.

"Geeze, Mom," he said. "You get that he's closer to my age than yours?"

"Are you telling me you want to date him?" Rose teased.

"Very funny," Corbin said. "You telling me that's what's going on between the two of you? You're dating now? I thought you said it was just a one-night thing."

"It is—it was," Rose slumped into her chair, suddenly feeling very tired.

"I'm not sure what's going on between Clay and me but I want to find out. He's asked to see me again tonight and I've agreed. I think I like him," she admitted.

"Will I be meeting this younger rancher that you think you like, Mom?" Corbin asked. Rose's first instinct was to tell him no but she also knew Corbin would use his vast resources to figure out who Clay was and go out of his way to meet him.

"At some point," she said. "Let me get my mind around all of this first and then I'm sure I can arrange a meeting."

"What do you know about him, Mom?" Corbin almost whispered.

"I've already told you most of what I know. He's been divorced for five years now and he has a thirteen-year-old daughter. He and his brother, Tyler, run the ranch together. There, now you're all caught up. That's about all I know—unless you want personal details about our activities."

"Fuck no," Corbin growled. "I'd prefer not hearing about my mother's sex life, thank you."

"So, we have a deal then? You let me work out a few things with Clay and when the time's right, you can meet him," Rose promised.

"Yeah," Corbin agreed. "It's a deal. Just take things slow and if you need me, just yell." Rose stood and wrapped her arms around her son's middle. He wrapped her in a bear hug and squeezed her.

"Thanks, Son," she whispered. "Let me go. I can't breathe." Corbin chuckled and released her. "Now, get lost. I have a ton of work to do if I'm going to leave here on time tonight for my big date."

CLAYTON

Clay had spent the day fixing the fencing around the farm. They had a rough winter and now that the weather was breaking, he wanted to get a jump start on patching some of the holes in the fence. His herd would be itching to stretch their legs and allowing them to roam in the southern pasture would be a nice change for his cattle.

He and Tyler had worked opposite ends of the field and that worked for him. Clay knew that his brother probably had a ton of questions about Rose but Clay didn't want to answer any of them. Ty had gotten the gist of what was happening between him and Rose. The rest wasn't any of his brother's business.

"Hey—I just finished up the back corner of the fence. I'm about ready to call it a day, man," Ty said. Clay checked his watch and realized that it was already four in the afternoon. He needed to finish up and get ready for his evening with Rose. He had called and booked a reservation at his favorite restaurant and then, he was hoping Rose would let him take her home. He wanted to show her his playroom and maybe try out some new things with her. What Clay wanted to do was take her by his BDSM club and have some fun with her but they weren't to that point of their relationship yet. She had barely agreed to be his submissive and he wanted to lead her into his lifestyle as easy as possible.

"Yeah, I need to knock off soon myself," Clay admitted. Tyler jumped up onto the back of his pick-up and started unloading the extra posts and equipment that they didn't use.

"You going to see Rose tonight again?" Ty asked.

"If I say yes, are you going to give me a bunch of shit?" Clay questioned.

Ty shrugged and smiled, "Probably," he admitted. "You know that's my job, right? I'm your little brother and it's my duty to give you as much shit as possible, man."

"Well, mission accomplished," Clay said. "You've always been damn good at your job then."

"Thanks," Ty said and chuckled. "Before we call it quits for the day, I do have something I'd like to talk over with you."

"Sure," Clay agreed. "Shoot."

"I'm just spit balling here, but I think I'd like to strike out on my own. Our neighbor is selling off a good chunk of land that butts up to ours. I'd like to buy it and build my own place."

"This is your place," Clay argued. "Grandpa and Dad left the ranch to us."

"I appreciate that, Clay. I really do. But I also know that someday Paisley and her family might want to take this over. That's how this generational thing works in ranching. I want to have something to pass on to my kids someday." Ty tossed the last fence post down onto the pile from his pick-up and jumped down.

"So, does that mean that you're planning on having kids then?" Clay teased. He had always hated that Paisley was an only child. He wanted to give her a brother or sister but that was out of the question. He and his ex, Abi had tried for years to get pregnant again but they never did. Abi blamed herself but he insisted on them going to a fertility doctor. That's when he found out that he was the problem. He had a low sperm count and the doctor said he would probably never father any more children. Clay beat himself up for years, even feeling like less of a man. Abi and he grew apart and by the time he picked himself up and put himself back together again, it was too late. Their relationship was over, and Abi filed for divorce. He couldn't blame her but it stung like a bitch all the same.

They had lived apart for six months and Clay was miserable. He convinced Abi to give him another chance and that's when he finally admitted that he wanted to try a little kink in the bedroom. He wanted to spice up their sex life. Hell, he wanted complete dominance over her and Abi wanted nothing to do with him. It was the final nail in his coffin and when she left him again, this time, he let her go. It was for the best. She deserved to find someone who wanted the same things she wanted—namely more kids and a vanilla sex life. He also deserved to find someone who might be into the same kinks he was, and he had to admit, meeting Rose was a nice surprise.

"I'd like to have kids," Ty admitted. "I'm pretty sure I'll need to find a woman first though."

Clay chuckled and slapped Ty on the back. "Times a wasting," Clay teased. "You might need to leave your house if you plan on finding a willing woman to have your kids, Brother."

"Ha, Ha," Ty dryly snarked. "You think Rose has a younger sister?"

"No," Clay breathed.

"Okay, then how about getting me into your club?" Clay had always suspected that his little brother liked kink, but they never really discussed stuff like that. Some things were just off-limits, even with his brother.

"My club?" Clay questioned, playing dumb.

"Sure, that BDSM club you belong to in town. I know you go there, man. I've heard the rumors about what you're into. This is still a small town, you know." Clay knew better than most how small their town was. When he and Abi divorced, he heard nasty rumors flying around that he had cheated on her.

Someone had seen him coming out of the club and word got out that he was meeting women there and having sex with them. That part was true but he and Abi had been separated for over a year by the time he first stepped foot in the club.

"I guess I'm just surprised that you're into that kind of thing, Ty," Clay said.

His brother shrugged and gave him a goofy grin. "Yeah well, I don't go around advertising what I like to do behind closed doors. I've always liked a little kink. I just haven't met a woman who was into all of that. Was Abi up for that part of you?"

Clay moaned and hung his head. "You want to get into all of this, man?"

"Sure, why not? I mean, you are my brother and well, we didn't invent this stuff. I'm sure we're not the first men who liked a little kink, Clay." Ty had a point but discussing his sex life with his little brother wasn't something he thought he'd ever do.

"No, Abi wasn't into what I like. It was just the final straw, you could say. That and my not being able to give her another baby. I guess she just couldn't handle all of it and I can't say that I blame her. We had a lot of good years together and Paisley," Clay said.

Ty smiled, "Yeah, she is a pretty fucking fantastic kid, Clay." His daughter was an awesome person and honestly one of his best friends.

"She is," Clay agreed.

"Does Rose know what you like?" Ty asked.

"Yep," Clay smirked back at his brother. "She seems to be up for all of my kinks and I'm hoping that she'll want to go to the club with me. I'm seeing her tonight for dinner and then I plan on bringing her back to the house and showing her my playroom in the basement."

"Wait, you have a playroom in the basement of the house we grew up in? How the fuck did you manage that?" Ty asked.

"I had it built a little over a year ago. I wasn't sure that I wanted to keep going to the club—privacy issues and all that shit. I had a run-in with a few subs who wanted more than just some playtime and I needed a break from the club." Honestly, Clay was hoping that he would find someone—someone like Rose who wanted to be more than just a fun time at a club. He was looking for a sub and since Rose agreed to be that for him, he was glad that he put that playroom in. Rose was so new to his world she was probably going to need a little coaxing to go to the club with him.

"Lowdown Ranch will never be the same, Clay," Ty teased. "You've taken the place to new levels of class." Clay chuckled at Ty's assessment.

"Shut the fuck up, asshole," Clay grumbled. "You keep giving me shit, I won't get you into my club."

Ty sobered, "Fine—sorry," he said. "So, you'll get me in?"

"Sure," Clay agreed. "But you and I will have to have open communication. I don't need you showing up when I'm there. That would be the last thing I want to see my little brother doing."

"Deal," Ty agreed. "And, thanks, man."

"No problem. Now, I've got to go and get ready for my date. You good with finishing up here?" Clay asked.

"Yep," Ty said. "You go and get all pretty for your date. Have fun." That was exactly what Clay planned on doing with Rose tonight. He planned on having a hell of a lot of fun.

※

Clay picked Rose up at her townhome and smiled at the crafty way she tried to hide her overnight bag under her jacket. She shyly looked around to make sure that no one saw her as she handed it to Clay, and he helped her into the cab of his pick-up truck. He leaned into the cab of his truck and gently kissed her lips.

"Hey," he whispered. "You look beautiful." She did too. Rose wore a black cocktail dress that hugged her every curve and didn't leave too much to the imagination. Her high heels just about made him want to swallow his damn tongue. Clay shut her door and rounded his pick-up to get into the driver's seat.

"Thanks," she said. "You look very handsome too." He had taken time to shower and even get a little dressed up if you could call throwing on a blazer over his white dress shirt and jeans, dressed up.

"Thanks," he said. "I hope you like steak," he said.

"I do," she admitted.

"Great. We're going to a little place in town that I'm part owner of," Clay said.

"You own part of a restaurant?" Rose questioned.

"Yeah," he said. "A few years back my best friend from college asked me for pricing for my cattle. He wanted to source local beef and when I found out he needed a partner, I jumped at the chance. It's one of the businesses I've invested in to help when times are tough around the ranch. We have our good years and our lean years. Having stock in some local area businesses helps me through the lean years."

"I'd love to have dinner at your restaurant, Clay," Rose said.

"Partially own," Clay corrected. "And thank you, Honey. I take it from your overnight bag that you will be spending the night with me too."

Rose turned the cutest shade of pink and shyly nodded. "I'd like to if that's still okay," she said.

"It's more than okay," Clay agreed. "I'd like to try a few things—if you're up to it."

"Like what?" Rose asked.

"Well, I'd like to tie you up, if you think it's something you might like." Clay wished they weren't having this conversation while driving. He was hoping to go over all these details at dinner. Instead, he couldn't really gage how Rose felt about what he was suggesting, not able to see her expressions.

"I um, I think I'd like that," Rose stuttered. Clay nodded

and pulled into the parking lot to the steak house. He parked around back, turned off his truck and unbuckled her seat belt, pulling her onto his lap.

"This is so much better," he whispered. "I'd like to spank you over my saddle," he said. He didn't mean to just blurt that out, but there it was.

"Over your saddle," she said. "Like out in your barn?"

"No," he said. "I have a saddle in my playroom and God, I'd like to see you sprawled over it while I spank your ass red." Clay ran his hands down over her body to cup her perfect ass. "Would you like that?" he asked squeezing her fleshy globes in his hands.

"Oh," Rose breathed, "I think I would like that, Clay."

"Sir," he corrected.

"I thought I only had to call you that when we are in the bedroom," Rose said.

"When we're together like this you call me Sir and I'll call you mine," Clay growled.

"Yes, Sir," Rose agreed. "What else do you want to do with me tonight?" she asked. A million things ran through his mind, and he gave her a wolfish grin. He wanted to do so much with her but he needed to remember that she was new to his world. He was introducing her to his lifestyle and needed to go slowly to let Rose get acclimated to all his needs and desires.

"Well, let's recap," he teased. Clay kissed his way up her neck, over her jawline and when he got to her lips, he paused just a hair from taking them. He liked the way her breath hitched in anticipation and he knew that he had her full attention. "You said you'd like to try being tied up. Is that right?"

"Yes," she breathed.

"And, you seem to like the idea of having me spank your ass while you straddle my riding saddle. Am I correct?"

"Yes," she moaned. Rose wiggled on his lap, doing nothing to help relieve his growing erection. Clay wished he wasn't trapped in his pick-up but he refused to skip any of the date night activities that he had planned for the two of them. Rose deserved a nice night out, a real date, and not just him having his way with her, taking what he needed.

"Rose," he whispered her name against her lips. Clay couldn't help himself; he ran his hand up under her tight skirt and could feel the heat from her core before he even ran his fingers through her drenched folds. "You're wet for me, Honey," he said hoarsely. He wanted to take her right there in the cab of his pick-up but he also knew that there were people in and out of the busy restaurant's parking lot.

"Clay," she whimpered. "Please, Sir."

He wanted desperately to give her what she was begging him for, but he also knew that getting caught was too much chance to take with her. "I promise to give you everything you need, as soon as we get back to my ranch," Clay said. "For now," he plunged two fingers deep into her pussy, loving the way her breath hissed from her lips. "I'm going to give you a taste of everything you have to look forward to once I get you back to my playroom."

"Oh God," Rose moaned and threw her head back. "Yes, please." He loved the way she shamelessly rode his busy fingers and when he let the pad of his thumb leisurely stroke over her clit, she just about bucked off his lap. Rose whimpered and rode out her orgasm and when she came, it was his name she whispered on her lips like a prayer. She was beautiful to watch and everything he'd been looking for and God help him—Rose was his. Every minute he spent with her made him more and more aware that Rose Eklund was the woman he'd been searching for. He wouldn't tell her that. Not yet at least. There was no way that he'd want to spook her and give up his chance at showing Rose that they could work together.

Rose slumped against him, breathing hard and flushed from her release. "You are so fucking beautiful, Baby," he praised. Clay righted her skirt and helped her back to her seat. Rose reached for him, and he chuckled.

"What about you, Clay?" she protested, running her hands over his erection. "I want to—" Clay covered her mouth with his hand, not letting Rose finish her sentence. If he allowed that, he would take her up on her offer and let her have her way with him. That would lead to him high tailing it out of that fucking parking lot and dragging her back to his ranch and willingly down to his playroom.

"Honey," he said. "I think we need to have a nice dinner and then we can get to the part where I let you do exactly what you want with me." Rose pouted and he chuckled again. "While that's pretty damn adorable, Baby, I want tonight to be perfect. Dinner and then we can play," he ordered.

"Fine," she said, pout still firmly in place. "But you haven't finished telling me what you want to do with me when we get back to your ranch." Clay knew that if he finished telling her what he wanted from her that dinner would be pretty uncomfortable for him to sit through.

"How about we discuss it over steak?" he asked. "I've got a secluded little corner reserved for us and we'll have plenty of privacy to talk the rest of it over."

"All right," she agreed. Clay didn't give her time to change her mind. He got out of his truck and rounded to her side to help her out. She cuddled into his side and he felt like the luckiest man in the world with her on his arm.

ROSE

Rose was shocked at her behavior. Making out in a pick-up truck wasn't something she'd ever thought she'd do. But, there she was, letting Clay give her an incredible orgasm and leaving her carelessly throwing caution to the wind and not caring if anyone saw them. For some reason she couldn't explain, Clay made her want to try new things and be more daring. Maybe it was just time for her to take a chance on life and hope that Clay would want to take a chance on her.

The hostess led them back to a quiet, dark corner in the back of the steakhouse and Rose knew that Clay had arranged for them to have privacy and she had to admit, she liked the idea of having him all to herself. Clay ordered a bottle of wine and some appetizers and she was happy to let him take charge of that for her.

"I hope this is all right," he whispered across the table.

"It's perfect," Rose gushed. "I have to admit that I usually just go home after work and have a sandwich or a salad for dinner. This is a treat."

"I'm no better," Clay said. "By the time I get done around

the ranch, I'm so tired when we knock off for the night that I sometimes don't even eat dinner."

"Well, aren't we a pair?" Rose teased.

"What about your son? Are you very close?" he asked. "If you don't mind me asking personal questions."

Rose giggled and shook her head. "I think we're past the whole no asking personal questions thing, Clay. I mean, you have seen me naked and all." Rose cringed and rolled her eyes.

"Yeah, I guess you're right. I just don't want you to feel like I'm prying," he offered.

"Not at all," Rose said. "We are close. We kind of grew up together. I was just a teenager when I had him and we leaned on each other when things got tough. We have a good relationship. I work for both of my boys."

"Both?" Clay asked. "I thought you said you only have one son."

"Well, that's a long story," Rose said.

Clay held his arms wide, "I'm not going anywhere and I'm pretty sure we can order a second bottle of wine if we need to."

Rose laughed. "All right," she said. "Well, I was raising Corbin on my own. My parents didn't want anything to do with me once I got pregnant and refused to have an abortion."

"What about Corbin's father? Was he in the picture?" Clay asked.

"No," Rose breathed. "He was almost ten years older than me and well, I was a minor. When I told him I was pregnant, he took off. It didn't help that my parents told him that they would have him arrested if he stuck around. So, he left and I had to make some hard and fast decisions. I decided to raise my son on my own and it was the best choice I've ever made. He became my reason for hanging in there and he kept me going even when I didn't think I could."

"Kids have a way of doing that for us, don't they? Whenever I'm having a bad day, I talk to my daughter, Paisley and it instantly becomes better. She's my reason for being the best person I can be," Clay admitted.

"I always wanted a daughter but I'm afraid I wouldn't know what to do with one, having two boys. When my son brought home his best friend and told me that his mom had just died, it broke my heart. Aiden started staying with us more and more after that. His dad went through a tough time. He lost his wife and was lost trying to figure out how to take care of his son. He started drinking and when he just couldn't take care of Aiden anymore, I took him in and finished raising him." Rose smiled at the memory of Corbin and Aiden being young. It sometimes surprised her that her boys were grown and had kids of their own. It felt like just yesterday that they were arguing over who was going to be Superman and who was going to be Batman when they were playing superheroes.

"You're amazing," Clay whispered, taking her hand into his. "You did all of that on your own?"

"Yeah," she said. "Sometimes it was a breeze and I thought I had it all together. You know, like I could take on the whole world and do just about anything. But most days I felt like a complete failure and wondered if I was screwing everything up." Rose shrugged. "I'm guessing that I did an okay job. They both turned out pretty fantastic. Both are married now and I'm a grandmother." Rose winced at admitting that last part.

"You made a face," Clay said.

"Well, when I say things like that, it reminds me that there is quite an age difference between us. I know that I'm not supposed to say that and it's one of our rules but it's just a fact." Rose sipped the wine that Clay had poured for her. "I'm fifty years old, Clay. You making a rule to forget about our age difference won't change the fact that you're only forty."

Clay chuckled, "Only forty sounds like an oxymoron to me. It's all relative, Honey. When I look at you, I don't see a fifty-year-old grandmother. I see a sexy as fuck woman who I can't wait to get all to myself tonight." Rose felt her cheeks heat and she shyly nodded at Clay.

"Thank you for that, Clay," she said. "I guess I'll just need to work on all of that," she admitted. The waiter brought their appetizers and Clay asked if he could order dinner for her. She gladly accepted his offer and by the time dinner was over, she realized that they had spent nearly three hours talking about everything from her job to his life on the ranch and their kids. Every moment she spent with Clay only made her realize that she liked him. Hell, she was practically falling for the guy but she wouldn't ever admit that. What kind of woman lost her heart to a man she picked up in a bar and only knew for two nights? Clay was supposed to be a one time, one-night thing but he was surprisingly turning out to be so much more to her.

"How about we head back to my place," he whispered into her ear. Rose felt a shiver run down her spine at the promise she heard in his sultry voice.

"Yes," she whispered. "I'd like that."

※

It didn't take long to drive from the restaurant to Clay's ranch and when he pulled into his garage, she suddenly felt shy again. This world was so new to her, Rose worried that she was going to do or say something wrong and Clay would call this whole thing off between them. She so desperately wanted more of a taste of his world and she was hoping he'd give it to her.

"You know, we didn't finish our discussion about what you want to try tonight, Rose," Clay said.

"You distracted me with food, wine, and excellent conversation," Rose teased.

"How about you let me distract you with sex now?" he countered. Rose nodded and took his offered hand, following him down to the finished basement. It looked like a giant family room, complete with a bar in the corner and even a pool table. Clay tugged her along down a hallway to a room with a locked door. He pulled the key from his pocket and unlocked the door.

"Why do you keep this room locked?" she asked.

"Mainly to keep my nosey brother and my teenage daughter out. I wouldn't want Paisley stumbling across my playroom by accident. Her mother would never let me see her again if she knew I built this place." Clay turned on the lights to the room and Rose blinked, letting her eyes adjust.

"You said your wife wasn't submissive?" Rose asked.

"Ex-wife and no, she wasn't. We had other problems, too. I couldn't give her any more children and she wanted more. That was when our marriage started to turn. My telling Abi that I wanted a sub was just the last straw. She told me she couldn't live the life that I wanted and we agreed to go our separate ways. I play at a local club but built this place for more privacy."

Rose walked into the room and suddenly wanted to run and hide. "Do you bring many women down here, Clay?" she asked. Why she worried about his answer was beyond her. This thing between them wasn't a relationship—it was for fun. He wanted a sub and Rose wanted to try something new. She was up for some excitement and a whole lot of fun. She deserved it.

Rose could feel Clay standing behind her. His body was so close to hers; she could feel the heat of his breath on her neck. "No," he breathed. "I just got done this room and honestly—you're the first woman I've brought down here."

Rose turned to face him, "Really?" she questioned.

"Yeah," he admitted. Clay turned the cutest shade of pink and Rose ran her hand up over his shoulders and leaned into his body.

"It's okay, Clay. You can be honest with me. I know the score—this is just for fun. I don't need pretty promises and for you to tell me that I'm the only one." Rose meant it too but the last thing she wanted to do was listen to how many women he had brought back to his ranch to have sex with.

"Rose," he whispered. "What if I want to make you pretty promises?" Rose felt as though her heart was going to beat out of her chest. "I won't lie to you—ever. There have been other women since my divorce. I told you that I like to play at the local club and have taken on subs there. But, you're the first woman I've ever brought back to my place and the first woman to use this room with me." Rose wanted to beg him to be the last woman he'd use the room with but that would be a promise he wouldn't be able to make her. She wasn't lying when she said she didn't want him to make her pretty promises—not unless he could keep them.

"I appreciate you telling me that, Clay," she said.

"Sir," he growled. "You will call me, Sir in here, Rose,"

She smiled up at him and nodded. "Sir," she corrected. Rose looked around the room.

"Good," he whispered against her neck. "You ready to play?"

"I think so," she stuttered. "I'm not going to lie, Sir, I'm feeling a little out of my element here," she admitted.

Clay wrapped his arms around her from behind and tugged her tighter against his body. "I've got you, Honey," he said. "We can take this as slow as you need," he drawled. Her cowboy had a way of making her knees feel week and her heart flutter with just one sentence and Rose felt like a giddy schoolgirl.

"Thank you, Sir," she whispered. "I think I'd like to try that saddle," she said pointing to the corner of the room where a riding saddle was perched over the arm of a sofa. Clay chuckled in her ear. "You do like to be spanked, don't you, Rose?"

"Yes," she said. "I liked the way you spanked me last night. I wanted more."

"Oh Honey, I can give you so much more," he agreed. Clay unzipped the back of her dress and let it fall down her body. She said a little prayer of thanks that she was wearing a pair of lacy black panties and a strapless lacy bra that matched. He let his fingers trail down her body and she leaned into his touch, craving more.

"Up on the saddle, Baby," he ordered. She turned and did as he asked, gifting him with a view of her ass. It was as if all her insecurities just melted away. Clay made her feel like a goddess and Rose knew that he'd worship her body—all she had to do was let go.

Clay unhooked her bra and she gasped when he reached around her body to cup her ample breasts. "I'm going to put some nipple clamps on these," he said, tweaking her taut nipples between his fingers. Rose moaned and writhed against the saddle.

"Yes," she hissed.

"Have you ever had nipple clamps on before, Honey?" he asked.

"No," she whispered. Rose rubbed her pussy on the saddle. She was so wet and ready for him, she needed to find her release, but Clay seemed to have other ideas for her.

Rose felt his loss as soon as he removed his hands from her sensitive nipples and crossed the room to a large storage cabinet. He rummaged through the open drawer; his handsome face so stern with concentration that she almost wanted to giggle. She sat up in the saddle and watched him and when he returned to her wearing a triumphant grin and holding up something that looked more like jewelry than clamps, she couldn't help but smile back at him.

"Those are nipple clamps?" she asked.

"Yep," Clay said. He held them out for her, and she ran her fingers over the pretty blue jewels that decorated the ends. "Hold your finger out," he ordered. Rose did as he asked and he clamped the little jewel onto her finger. "I can make them as tight as you like," he said. Clay tightened the clamp on her finger, making her hiss.

"I think I'll like that," she admitted.

"When I take them off," he said, pulling the clamp free

from her finger. "All the blood will rush back to your nipples giving you the most wonderful pain and pleasure, all at the same time. Want to try them?"

Rose wiggled her tingling finger and smiled up at him. "Yes," she agreed. Honestly, she wanted to try everything. She looked down her body as Clay fitted the pretty little clamps to her nipples, wincing at the tingling sensation that almost felt as if it was too much. She had to admit that once she got used to the pinching weight of the clamps, she liked it. They gave just enough of a bit of pain and Rose was starting to realize that she liked the discomfort.

Clay pushed her down over the saddle, so her belly was almost flat with the leather. "We're going to twenty," he ordered. "You will keep count, Rose."

"All right," she whispered. Clay praised her, rubbing his big hand over her ass. Her lacy panties did nothing to hide her desire from him. He dipped his fingers down and rubbed her wet pussy, moaning as he pulled them back up to her ass and gave it a firm smack. Rose loved the way he didn't hold back with her even knowing how new this all was to her.

"One," she moaned. Clay peppered her ass with terse smacks and in between each one, he'd rub her fleshy globes, while she kept count. They got to twenty rather quickly and Rose wasn't sure if she was happy or sad about Clay being done spanking her. He ran his fingers back down through her wet folds and she moaned, rubbing shamelessly on the saddle, trying to gain the friction she needed to get herself off.

"Fuck, Honey," he growled. "You're so wet and ready for me. Hold still and let me take care of you, Rose," he ordered. She tried to hold as still as humanly possible and was probably failing miserably. Clay pulled her from the saddle and onto the nearby sofa, shucking out of his jeans as quickly as humanly possible. Just before he pulled her on top of his body, he helped her out of her panties, and Rose eagerly straddled his cock.

"Please," she whimpered. Rose could tell that Clay was just

as on edge as she was, but he just seemed to control it a little better than she did.

"Please what, Honey," he taunted. Clay knew that she wasn't a fan of asking for what she wanted—especially not in bed.

"I need you in me," she whispered against his lips. That seemed to be all Clay needed to give her what she wanted. He lifted her onto his erection, lowering her inch by delicious inch until she was fully seated on his cock.

"So fucking good," he moaned. Rose agreed with him. She was so close to finding her release, she couldn't help but move. She rode him like she was on fire and couldn't get enough. She couldn't. Rose was sure she'd never get enough of Clay and that thought scared the crap out of her.

She cried out his name as her orgasm ripped through her and Clay pulled the nipple clamps from her sensitive breasts. It felt like a fire ripped through her and Rose shouted out once again. She loved the way Clay followed her over, pumping himself deeper inside of her and pulling her down to kiss her. His hands were everywhere as he peppered her face and lips with kisses. Rose soaked up his whispered praises and collapsed onto his chest, her quickly beating heart matching his beat.

"Perfect," he whispered and kissed her head. He was right—everything about the two of them together was perfect.

CLAYTON

They spent the whole next morning in bed and Clay had to admit, Saturday was quickly becoming his favorite day of the week. He had texted his brother and begged him to fill in for him for the day. He told Rose that he had nothing pressing that he had to get to but that was only because Ty had called in the calvary and asked some of their ranch hands to help him out for the day. Clay was for whatever worked because he didn't have any plans of getting out of bed and going out to work.

"You know, if you have to go out to the barn, I'll understand," Rose offered.

"Nope," Clay said. "I'm good right here."

"Do you usually take Saturdays off?" she asked. He wanted to tell her that he usually did but that would be a lie.

"No," he admitted. "I usually don't take a whole lot of days off. When Paisley is here, I don't work as many hours. I try to spend as much time with her as possible but she also comes out to the barn with me and hangs out while I do my chores."

"If you need, I can do the same," Rose offered.

Clay kissed the top of her head, "Thanks for that, Honey," he said.

"When will Paisley be back?" Rose asked. That was the million-dollar question because once that happened, his worlds would collide, and Clay worried that he'd have to choose between spending time with Paisley and spending time with Rose. How could he do that? The circumstance hadn't happened yet but he was feeling the panic of having to make that choice.

"She's with my ex for another week," he said. "She'll be home late next weekend."

Rose snuggled into his side, "So, we have another week?" she asked. Clay wanted to tell her that they were going to have a lot longer than just a fucking week. Hell, he wanted to tell her that they didn't have an expiration date but after just two nights together, that might not be the type of declaration he should make.

"Yeah," he breathed. "Spend the week with me and let's see where this all goes," he asked. Hell, he sounded more like he was telling her what to do and maybe he was, but he didn't give a fuck. He wanted time with her and if he had to demand it or even beg for it, he would.

"Are you sure?" Rose asked.

"I've never been so sure of anything in my life, Honey. I like spending time with you. I want to do more of it," he admitted.

"Me too," she agreed. "I'd love to spend the week with you, Clay. I can stop over to my townhome after work each night and grab a change of clothes." He wanted to tell her to bring over her entire closet, for all he cared, but that might be a bit too pushy for just two days in.

"Sounds good, Baby," he said. "How about I make us some breakfast and then I'll take you out to the barn and we can go for a ride?"

Rose grimaced and he thought it was probably the cutest

thing he'd ever seen. "I haven't been on a horse in about twenty-five years," she admitted.

"We can take it slow," he promised.

"I'd love to go riding with you then, Clay."

"Perfect. I'll pack us a lunch and we can turn it into a day," he said. Clay swatted her bare ass, "Up and at em', Honey." He loved the way Rose's giggle filled his bedroom. Clay was quickly getting used to having her in his space and he wasn't sure if that was a good or bad thing.

※

Clay saddled up his horse and decided to let Rose ride Lulu. She was his gentlest horse, and he was hoping that Rose would be able to handle her. Rose had pulled her long blond hair back in the sexy bun that she usually opted to wear to work. Every time she pulled her hair up like that, he wanted to unpin it and mess her up a little.

"Here, Honey," he offered, linking his hands together for Rose to step into for a boost.

"You don't have to help me up," Rose countered.

"It's not as easy as it looks. Besides, it gives me a chance to put my hands on that fantastic ass of yours," Clay teased. Rose gifted him with her shy smile, looking around the empty barn to make sure that no one was watching them.

"Fine," she said. Rose put her hands on his shoulders and hooked her boot in his palms, letting him give her a hand up onto Lulu. And yeah, his favorite part was running his hands all over her ass to help her up into the saddle. Flashes of the night before bombarded his overly active brain and Rose looked down at him and giggled.

"I know exactly what you're thinking," Rose almost whispered and gave him an outrageous wink.

"Yeah, it's kind of hard to forget how fucking sexy you were in my playroom last night." Clay mounted his horse Rebel and grabbed the reigns from Rose to help lead Lulu out of the barn. "You think you can remember how to hold the reigns?" he asked.

"Yep," she said. "It's like riding a bike, right?"

Clay chuckled, "That's the second time you've asked me that, Honey. No, riding a horse is a little trickier than riding a bike. Just take it slow and if you have any questions, let me know. Follow my lead."

"Yes, Sir," Rose teased. Clay started slowly and led her out to the South meadow. It had a pond and was probably his favorite place on the ranch. They had been riding for almost thirty minutes and he could tell that Rose had just about had enough. He hadn't gone easy on her ass the night before and taking her riding today might not have been the best idea.

"How about we stop here and have our picnic?" he asked. Rose nodded her agreement and he jumped down, helping Rose down from Lulu and pulling her into his arms. "You know, we have some things to talk about still," he said. Rose looked up at him like he had lost his mind.

"Like?" she asked.

"Well, your likes and dislikes about what we've done so far. And we need to talk about what you'd like to try," he said.

"You mean sexually?" she squeaked.

Clay chuckled, "Yeah—I mean sexually. How about we get comfortable and then we can talk."

"You know, I'm starting to see a pattern with you, Clay. I've never been a prude," she said. "But, you talk about sex more than any other man I've ever met."

"I'm going to take that as a compliment, Baby," he said. "I just want to make sure that we're on the same page. The most important bond between a Dom and his submissive is trust and communication," Clay said. He had seen it one too many times, a Dom who didn't know what the hell he was doing, who ended up hurting his sub. He wouldn't do that to Rose. She deserved more from him both as her Dom and her lover.

Rose giggled, "You should," she teased. "It's quite impressive, Clay." He spread out the blanket that he brought along with him and helped her to set out the food that he had packed into a basket.

"This looks great," she said.

"It's just some sandwiches and salad," he said. "And" Clay reached into the basket and pulled out two wine glasses and a bottle of wine. He wasn't a wine drinker but he had a feeling that beer wasn't in Rose's wheelhouse and he wanted their little makeshift picnic to be perfect.

"Wine," Rose said. "Well, that is a nice surprise."

"I wasn't sure if you liked wine," he said. "I know you like vodka." Rose made a face and groaned. "Still not something you want to remember?"

"No," she breathed. "Honestly, I wasn't that sick the next day but let's just say that birthday drinks didn't love me as much as I loved them. I don't drink hard liquor and that night wasn't my finest. Wine is a much safer choice for me."

"Well, it's good that I stuck with my first choice then." Clay poured her a glass and handed it to her. He poured himself one and held his glass up to toast. "To us," he said.

"Us?" Rose asked. Clay worried that he had overstepped and wanted to play it cool but the look on her face had him panicking.

"Um, sure," he said. "I mean, you agreed to move in with me," Clay said.

"Temporarily," Rose corrected. "I agreed to spend the week with you to see where this thing between us is heading."

"Sure," Clay said. Her correcting him felt like a slap. "Temporarily. I won't lie, I'm hoping you'll want to stick around though." Clay smiled at her, and she rolled her eyes.

"I just need to take things slowly," Rose said. "If that's not okay—"

Clay pulled her onto his lap and wrapped his free arm around her. "I never said that," he said. "We can work this anyway you need, Honey. Hell, you can call all the shots here, Rose. We can go slowly and you can put whatever stipulations you need to on whatever this is between us. But, I'm hoping you'll give us a chance to become an 'us,'" Clay admitted.

"I'd like that," Rose said.

"Great," Clay said. "Now, let's talk about sex." Rose moaned and Clay playfully bit her shoulder. "You said you've Googled a few things, right?"

"Yes," she whispered.

"Is there anything you would like to try next?" he asked. The possibilities ran through his mind, and he had no problem coming up with a few things he'd like to try with Rose.

She chugged her glass of wine and held it out for a refill. Clay laughed and filled it up. Rose clearly needed liquid courage for what they were about to discuss. "Thanks," she said. "I saw this thing that looked like a wooden cross and the woman was strapped to it."

"Mmm," Clay hummed his approval. "The St. Andrew's cross. Did you like it?"

"I think so," Rose agreed. "The woman was facing her Dom, and he was flogging her." Rose almost whispered the last part and he had to admit, the thought of flogging Rose made him damn near want to swallow his tongue.

"Where did he flog her, Rose?" Clay hoarsely asked.

"Um, her breasts," Rose admitted.

"And where else?" Clay asked. Rose looked down at her empty glass and he took it from her. "Tell me," he ordered.

Clay watched her, waiting for her to give him his answer. He thought for sure that Rose wasn't going to do it when she opened her mouth and squeaked, "Her pussy."

"Fuck," Clay swore. He set their empty glasses in the basket and rolled Rose under his body. "I need you, Honey."

ROSE

"Out here?" Rose asked, looking around the empty pasture. "Won't someone see us?"

"No," Clay growled. He was working her tight t-shirt over her head, exposing the lacy white bra Rose wore. "I love this," he said, biting the fabric. She gasped and moaned when he sucked her taut nipple into his mouth through the fabric that stood in his way of having all of her.

"Up," he ordered. Rose stood and looked down at where Clay sat, panting, trying to catch his breath. "Strip," he commanded. Rose had learned that disobeying him would earn her a spanking but that wouldn't be so bad. Clay laughed. "I can see your wheels spinning, Baby," he said. "You think I'll spank your ass red if you disobey me but there are other punishments I can come up with."

"Such as?" Rose asked. She had to admit that all the possibilities made her more and more breathless.

"Well, I could work you up, get you wet and on the verge of finding your release," he said. Rose felt as if her heart was going to beat right out of her chest with every word he said. She was already wet and ready for whatever he had planned for her.

"And," she prompted.

"And, then I'll stop," Clay said. He sat back, leaning leisurely on his elbows and Rose looked him up and down.

"Stop?" she asked.

"Yep," Clay agreed. Rose moaned and unbuttoned her jeans, slowly pulling them down her long legs. "See, I knew you'd see things my way," Clay teased. He even dared to wink at her, causing Rose to giggle.

"What next, Sir?" she asked.

"Bra and panties too, Honey," Clay ordered.

Rose shyly looked around and hesitantly nodded. "All right," she stuttered.

"No one comes out here, Rose. I promise you're safe. Trust me?" Rose did, even after just a few days together, she trusted Clay.

"I do," she admitted.

"Thank you for that, Honey," he said. Clay didn't make a move to sit up and after Rose removed her bra and panties, as he ordered, and took the initiative to crawl naked onto his lap. Rose shamelessly rubbed her wet folds on his jean-clad erection as he kissed his way up her neck.

"What's this?" he questioned.

"I thought you wouldn't mind," Rose squeaked as he palmed her bare ass.

"Well, I do like what you have in mind, Honey." Before Rose could make her next move, he had her on her back and was settled between her legs. "But, I have other plans for you, Rose." Clay licked her pussy, causing her to buck and writhe from the pleasure of his mouth on her core. She needed more, but begging wasn't something she was used to doing. Rose panted out his name and when he chuckled against her pussy, his hot breath caressing her clit, she came. Rose didn't care that they were out in the middle of a field where anyone could see them. As her orgasm ripped through her, she was suddenly freed from all her inhibitions, shouting out Clay's name, begging him for everything she never knew she wanted.

"Fuck, Baby," he growled. "That was sexy as hell." Clay hovered over her, quickly pulling off his shirt and tugging his jeans down to free his erection. He lined Rose's core up with his jutting cock and thrust into her balls deep, moaning out her name.

"Clay," she whimpered. Rose was still experiencing the aftershocks of the earth-shattering orgasm he had just given her, and every movement made her want to come all over again.

"You're so tight, Honey," he said. Clay pulled her limp body up to his, seating her on his thighs. Rose felt like a rag doll, completely rung out from what he had just done to her. She wrapped her arms around his shoulders and loved the way he didn't go easy on her. He was just as demanding as when he laid her out on their picnic blanket, making a meal of her body. Rose loved that he never let her hide and the way he shamelessly took exactly what he needed from her.

Clay kissed her like he would devour her mouth, licking and sucking his way in. He roughly pumped in and out of her pussy and she couldn't hold back anymore. Rose's second orgasm felt like a wave crashing over her and she couldn't do anything but hold onto Clay and ride it out. He thrust into her body, just about lifting them both off the ground, and when he came, he whispered her name like a prayer on his sexy, full lips.

"You're mine," he growled.

"Yes," she whispered because she was, whether her mind knew it or not, her heart was his and there was nothing she could do about that, even if she wanted to.

※

They spent the next few days out at his ranch. Rose had gone into the office late and left early every day and she could tell that Aiden and Corbin were starting to worry about her. It was strange having their roles reversed. Usually, it was her worrying about the two of them and not the other way around. She had been the stable force in both of their lives since they were little boys and now that she was seeing Clay, that wasn't the case anymore. Rose understood the worry that she saw in both their eyes but that didn't mean she'd stop seeing her cowboy. No, she had a taste of his dominance and there would be no turning back for her. In the half a week she had spent with him, she knew that she wouldn't be able to walk away from him anytime soon. She wanted Clay—all of him and if her boys didn't understand that, well, it was just too bad.

"Mom," Corbin interrupted her daydreams about Clay, bringing her attention back to the here and now. He stood over her desk, judgmental scowl in place, Aiden by his side. Rose knew that they were both going to give her some trouble, but she didn't care. It was nearly quitting time and all she wanted to do was stop by her townhome, pick up her mail and head out to Clay's ranch.

"Boys," she countered, staring them both down. "What can I do for you?"

"We're worried about you, Rose," Aiden said. He was always the one to take lead when they were trying to present a united front. He might not be her biological son but Aiden was most like her when it came to the way he handled himself and others around him—always so practical.

"And, why's that, Aiden?" she asked. Rose stood and rounded her desk, sitting on the corner to square off with the two of them properly.

"Because you aren't acting yourself, Mom," Corbin chimed in. "Ever since your birthday, you've been acting strangely."

Rose knew what her son meant to say. "You mean, ever since I met Clay?" she retorted.

Corbin shrugged, "Well, I didn't want to make it sound like

I was blaming the guy for anything. I'll save that for after you introduce us to him."

"And, that's exactly why she doesn't want to," Aiden groaned. "You can't even give the guy a fair shake and we haven't even met him yet."

"I'll judge him fairly once I have something more concrete to go off of, man," Corbin shouted. "How do we know this guy isn't just using her, Aiden?"

Rose stood between them and felt dwarfed by their size. "She is standing right here," she challenged. "And, she doesn't like when you talk about her as if she's not in the room. I'm not being used, Corbin James. I've met a very nice man and I am enjoying his company."

"You are spending every night at his place," Corbin said.

"Are you spying on me, Son?" Rose asked.

"No," he lied. She could always tell when her boys were lying to her and now was no different. Corbin nudged Aiden, "He is," Corbin said, throwing his best friend under the bus.

"Thanks, asshole," Aiden growled. "I've stopped by your townhouse a few times and you haven't been home."

"At eleven o'clock at night, Mom," Corbin added. "He stopped by at eleven and you weren't home. You go to bed at like eight every night. What are we supposed to think?"

"First of all, you don't need to think at all about me, boys," Rose said. She felt mad enough to put them both in time out and take away all their electronics, just like when they were little. But she was dealing with grown men who should both know better than to stick their noses in her business.

"Second—who's to say that I'm not still in bed by eight?" she taunted. Rose almost giggled at the groans and disgusted faces they both made.

"Seriously, Rose," Aiden moaned. "We don't need the mental picture of what you're doing with your mystery man."

"Well, then don't stick your nose where it doesn't belong, Aiden," she challenged. "What I'm doing, where I am, and who

I'm with is neither of your business. To quote you both, 'I'm a grown-ass woman who doesn't need you in my business,'" Rose laughed at the shocked expressions they both wore. "Isn't that what you two like to tell me?"

"Yeah," Aiden breathed. Corbin shot him a look and he shrugged. "Well, she's got us up against the ropes, man. We do tell her that all the time. Maybe it's time to let your mom fly the nest and find her way," Aiden said. Rose giggled at the way he threw her words back at her. She always told them that they needed to do that whenever they asked her for her advice. Sure, she'd willingly give them her two cents but she also wanted her boys to find their ways. It's why they had been so successful in business and how they found the perfect women and were in loving relationships with beautiful kids. They were given the chance to find their ways and she was so proud of them both.

"I love you both, so much," she whispered. "But, now it's my time to find some happiness. Clay makes me happy," she admitted.

"Are you in love with him?" Corbin asked. He sounded more like he was accusing her of something than asking her a question.

"It's much too early in our relationship for something like that, Corbin," she lied. She had already fallen in deep with Clay and if she was being completely honest with herself and her boys, she had fallen in love with him. But, admitting that out loud would only make her sound like a lunatic.

"I think we're just curious about the guy you're spending your time with, Rose," Aiden offered.

"Younger guy," Corbin chimed in.

Rose sighed in frustration. "His age has nothing to do with any of this," Rose countered. "This is going nowhere and if you both don't mind; I'd like to close down my computer for today and call it. I have some errands to run before—" She almost said before she went home to Clay's ranch but then she'd have to admit that she had temporarily moved in with him and that wasn't something she planned on telling them. At least, not until things became more permanent in her living situation.

"Before you go spend the night at your boyfriends?" Corbin taunted. She refused to go another round with her son. Rose knew that was exactly what he wanted.

"Look," Aiden cut in. "How about you just let us meet the guy and then we'll back off some."

"Some?" Rose asked. "How about you back off completely?"

"That's not going to happen, Mom. I've told you this before and I meant it. You're my business. You're both of our business and we'll check in on you whether you like it or not," Corbin said.

"He's right, Rose," Aiden agreed. "Even though he could use some work on his delivery, I agree with Corbin. We love you and will always keep an eye on you. That's all we're getting at. Just let us meet the guy to see for ourselves that he's not some crazed killer that wants to drag you off to the woods to murder you," Aiden teased. Rose smiled but Corbin seemed less amused by Aiden's theatrics. He groaned, running his hands through his blond hair, making it stand on end. Rose went up on her tiptoes and smoothed his hair back into place.

"If I agree to let you meet him, will you two agree to give me some space. I like this man and I'd like to see where this thing between us is going. I can't do that with you two hovering over me like two mother hens." Rose framed her son's face with her hands, forcing him to look her in her eyes. "Please," she asked.

Corbin closed his blue eyes, shutting her out and when he opened them again, she could see his resolve. Her son wasn't going to easily back down, but he'd let her win this battle.

"Fine," he conceded. "If we get to meet him and he checks out, I promise to give you some space, Mom," he agreed.

Rose turned to face Aiden and he smiled and nodded his agreement before she even asked her question. "Me too," he said. "But I will probably still check in on you from time to time," he amended.

"Fair enough," she said, kissing Aiden's cheek. "I love you boys but I need to get going." Rose scurried around her work area, turning things off and shutting down for the day. "How does Saturday sound—you know, to meet Clay?"

"I'll check with Zara, but I think I can make it. You just want me and Corbin or the whole crew?" God, the thought of Corbin and Aiden bringing their wives and all their kids to meet Clay was a scary one.

"How about just you and Corbin this time and then we can get everyone involved once I have a clearer understanding of what's happening between the two of us?" Rose asked. Corbin and Aiden both agreed. "Good, and you'll have a chance to meet Clay's daughter, Paisley. She'll be home from her mother's that night and I'll be meeting her for the first time." Clay had sprung that little surprise on her that morning, just before she left for work and she had been a nervous wreck all day.

"How old is his daughter?" Corbin asked.

"Thirteen," Rose squeaked. "And, from what I understand, she's a handful. I don't know that I agree with Clay on this but he's not telling Paisley about me until we meet, face to face. I think he's afraid his daughter won't come home if she knows what she's walking into." Aiden's long whistle rang through the small office.

"This is going to be a shit show," he said.

Corbin laughed and shook his head. "I think you just bit off more than you'll be able to chew, Mom," he teased. "I'll be there Saturday. I wouldn't miss this show for anything." Rose grabbed her things and headed for the elevator.

"I'll be out tomorrow," she said. "Your calendar isn't too busy, Aiden and you and Zara are taking my grandson to the park for the day," she told Corbin. "I'll text you both Clay's address. Let's say you boys get there by six and I'll have a little something for dinner," Rose said. She knew that food always made Corbin and Aiden more agreeable.

"See you Saturday," Aiden called as the elevator doors closed. Rose wasn't sure what she had just agreed to but one thing was perfectly clear—Aiden was right. Saturday was going to be a complete shit show.

CLAYTON

Clay worried that they were rushing things introducing their kids into the equation. He and Rose had only known each other for a week now but he already knew how he felt about her. He was in love with her but telling her that wasn't going to fly. No, his Rose was too practical to hear him say the words out loud. He hoped that she could feel the way he felt about her every time he touched her and see it in his eyes every time he looked at her. God, he wished that they were at the point that he could make some sweeping declaration and not have his woman freak out but that would just take time. He could be patient if that's what it took because Rose was worth it. Clay wanted to spend the rest of his life with her and he'd wait forever, if that's what it would take.

"Corbin and Aiden will be here any minute," Rose said. She was scurrying around his kitchen and he loved the way she looked in his home. She hadn't gone back to her place since their second night together. She had stopped by her townhome to pick up essentials like clothing and personal items. Other than those few trips home, she was staying at his place twenty-four, seven and he loved that she was so comfortable with him and his ranch. If tonight went as planned, Clay wanted to ask her to make it official and just move in with him.

"Well, this is quite a spread you put on for the kids, Honey," Clay teased.

"I am fierce when it comes to ordering out," she said. Rose giggled and he couldn't help his smile. Her good mood was infectious.

"What's so funny?" he asked.

"You calling my boys, 'kids,'" she said. "They're almost as old as you are." They had already been over everyone's ages a few times and he hated how she kept reminding him of their age difference. It didn't matter to him—none of that crap did.

"You know it doesn't bother me, right?" Clay questioned. He caged Rose against the counter, effectively trapping her. "You keep breaking our new rule number one," he whispered into her ear.

"I know," she said. Rose leaned back against his body and sighed. "It's just hard not to think about our age difference. I'm just hoping that my boys can see past it. I'm worried that this is a bad idea," she admitted.

"If we're being completely honest here, Baby, I'm worried too. I've never introduced Paisley to any of my women friends," he said. There wasn't any other woman that he felt this way about besides his ex, but he'd keep that bit of information to himself. "I'm worried she won't be very receptive to meeting the new woman in my life."

"Have you had many women friends that you would have wanted to introduce your daughter to?" Rose asked. He could hear the uncertainty in her question and he hated that he made her feel that way.

"No," he honestly admitted. "You know that I played at the local club, even took on a few subs but there was never a woman I cared enough about to introduce to Paisley—that is until now. You're so much more than a friend, Honey."

"You care about me?" she asked. It pissed Clay off that Rose didn't already know that.

"I more than care about you, Rose," he said. "I think I'm falling for you." He was a coward. Clay was taking the chicken's way out and he owed her so much more than that. He had made her a promise to give him only her honesty and here he was hiding behind half-truths, lurking in the shadows of his fear.

The knock at the door startled them both back to reality and she turned to face him, finally looking him in the eyes. "That must be the boys," she whispered. He wanted to tell her to let them wait. Clay wanted to convince her that they were good for each other and that he was more than falling for her—he was already in love with her. He wanted to ask her if she felt the same way about him and demand that she share her feelings with him, but he knew that pushing Rose wouldn't end well for either of them.

Rose crossed the family room and opened the front door to let Aiden and Corbin into his house. Clay watched as they hugged Rose and protectively flanked her sides as they walked back to the kitchen. "Boys," she said. "This is Clay." He rounded the center island and held out his hand.

"Aiden Bentley." He shook Clay's extended hand and smiled. "Good to meet you," Aiden said.

"You too," Clay said. He turned to Corbin and held out his hand noting the indifferent scowl Rose's son wore compared to Aiden. Clay stood there for what felt like forever before Rose cleared her throat. It was a clear warning and her son backed down. He reluctantly shook Clay's hand and grumbled his name.

"Corbin Eklund." Clay noticed that his handshake was more like a tug of war than a handshake. The guy was as big as a mountain and if he wasn't Rose's son, he'd be weary of crossing paths with him.

"It's nice to meet you, Corbin," Clay said. "Your mom has told me so much about you—both of you."

"Well, I hope she hasn't told you everything about us. I mean, we've done some pretty questionable things over the years," Aiden joked. Clay had to admit, he liked the guy. He was at least trying to lighten the mood whereas Corbin seemed to want to rip Clay apart and ask questions after.

Rose giggled, "You boys were the worst growing up. You still cause me trouble, but I wouldn't change a thing because you both turned out to be pretty fantastic."

"You're not wrong. I am pretty fantastic," Aiden teased. Corbin still hadn't said more than his name to Clay and he was wondering if the big guy would ever chime in. They followed Rose to the kitchen and she pulled out two beers and handed them across the counter to the guys and one to Clay.

"Thanks, Honey," he said, taking the bottle from her.

"I have questions," Corbin grumbled.

"Shit, man," Aiden complained. "You couldn't wait until we have dinner or something? You agreed not to fuck this up for Rose."

"Language," Rose chided. "Clay's daughter will be here in about thirty minutes and I can't have you talking like that, Aiden."

"Sorry," Aiden grumbled.

"And you," Rose said, pointing her finger into Corbin's massive chest. "Whatever you want to ask, do it now because once Paisley gets here, I won't have you causing trouble."

Corbin nodded and turned to Clay, staring him down. "Why are you with my mother?" Corbin asked, jumping right to the heart of it all.

Clay took a swig of his beer and wrapped his arm around Rose's waist. "Because your mom is a fantastic person. I care for your mom, very much," he admitted.

Corbin barked out his laugh and set his bottle down on the

counter with a thud. "In just a week?" he asked. "You care about my mother, very much, in just one week?"

Clay shrugged, "I know that sounds crazy but yes," Clay said. "The night we met; I was wallowing in self-pity. I was turning forty and feeling bad for myself. When I met your mom, she was going through the same thing and—"

"No," Corbin all but shouted. "She wasn't going through the same thing. My mother turned fifty, not forty. You do realize that, right?" Clay wanted to deck the guy for being such an ass. He hated the shame and embarrassment that he saw in Rose's eyes.

"Corbin," Aiden said. "That's not fair."

"If you're asking if I know that Rose is ten years older than I am—sure. She was upfront with me about everything. But, our age difference isn't something that we've chosen to focus on. Just because you choose not to understand our relationship doesn't mean that it won't work for us. I personally don't give a fuck about how old your mom is. If you have a problem with it then that's on you." He tugged Rose closer and kissed her forehead.

"What are your intentions with my mom?" Corbin asked. Man, the guy wasn't going to quit. He didn't seem happy with any of Clay's answers. He hated how badly this evening was going but he wouldn't let Rose's son ruin their plans. He still had to get through introducing his daughter to Rose and he worried that Paisley was going to have the same reaction to the new woman in his life as Corbin had about him.

"That's enough, Corbin," Rose chided. "I asked you both to come here tonight to meet Clay, not to have you tear him down for wanting to be a part of my life."

"I'm just saying that this has all happened a little fast, Mom," Corbin countered.

"Well, as you so politely pointed out, Son, I'm fifty years old. I don't have much time left to waste." Aiden tried to muffle his laugh and failed. Corbin shot him a look like he wanted to tear him apart and Aiden had the good sense to back down, even holding his hands up as if in surrender.

"She's got you there, man," Aiden said.

"Your mom and I haven't figured out what our intentions are. We're feeling this out as we go," Clay admitted. "All I know is I like spending time with your mom, Corbin. I hope you can come to understand that I have no bad intentions or plan on hurting your mother in any way."

Rose shrugged, "We're just having fun," she added. Clay wanted to protest and tell them that she wasn't just someone he was having fun with. Rose was quickly becoming so much more to him but that was something he might want to share with her first.

Paisley came running in through the front door and Rose shot Corbin a look. "Behave yourself. Clay's daughter is just a kid," she reminded. "Act like the grown men you are."

Aiden crossed his heart and smiled, "Promise," he agreed.

"You're such a suck up," Corbin groaned. Clay released Rose and met Paisley in the family room to pull her in for a big hug. It had been a week and a half since he saw his daughter and he had to admit—he missed the hell out of her.

"I missed you, Squirt," he said, squeezing her extra tight.

"Dad," Paisley moaned. "I can't breathe." Clay chuckled and released his daughter.

"Sorry, Squirt. How was your Mom's?" he asked.

"Good," Paisley said.

She never really elaborated on what she did at her mom's house. It was almost as if she was afraid to talk about her mother in front of him no matter how many times he insisted that he didn't mind. He wanted to hear about all parts of his daughter's life, not just the time she spent under his roof.

"Did Daisy have her baby yet?" she asked. Daisy was Paisley's favorite horse on the farm and she had been ready to drop her foal for days now.

"Nope," he said. "But it should be any day now."

"I'm glad I didn't miss it," Paisley said.

"Come on in the kitchen," Clay said. "I've got some people I want you to meet." He had run Paisley meeting Rose past Abi. It was something they always agreed to do but this was the first time he had an occasion to talk to his ex about their daughter meeting a new woman in his life. His ex seemed fine with it all but told him to call her if Paisley needed to talk. He knew their daughter was closer with her mom. She was a thirteen-year-old girl and that just seemed par for the course. Still, it stung a little that Paisley would need to turn to her mom when she got upset. He wanted to be there for his daughter too but he somehow felt ill equipped to do so.

"Paisley, this is Corbin and Aiden." His daughter shook both of their offered hands and smiled.

"Nice to meet you, Paisley," Aiden said.

"What's up, kid?" Corbin casually asked.

"Not much," she answered. "Do you two work with my dad?" Corbin shot Clay a look and shook his head.

"Nope," he said. Clay could tell from Corbin's smart assed smirk that he was going to enjoy this next part. "Your dad and my mom are dating," he said. Clay wanted to curse inwardly but kept his cool. Now was not the time to start a fight with Corbin. He needed to keep his head and they would all get through this fucked up evening.

"Dating?" Paisley looked at him as if he had lost his mind. "What's he talking about, Dad?" she asked.

"Well," Clay said, clearing his throat. "I was getting to that part." He glared at Corbin and the big guy had the nerve to smile back at him, crossing his arms over his massive chest. Yeah, Corbin didn't give a fuck that he had just messed up their plans.

"I'm Rose." She held out her hand for Paisley to shake and his daughter just stood there, looking at her offered hand as if she didn't understand what to do next.

"Paisley, this is the woman I'm seeing. This is Rose," Clay

said. Paisley took a step back from Rose's hand and when she realized that his daughter wasn't going to shake her hand, she dropped it back to her side.

"What about mom?" Paisley asked.

"You know that your mom and I aren't together anymore, Paisley," Clay said. "We haven't been for a long time."

"So, you're just going to replace her?" Paisley challenged.

"Maybe we should give you both some privacy," Rose asked. "That way you can talk through all of this."

"No," Clay said. "Paisley, you know that your mother and I are no longer together. Rose is going to be around here a lot and you'll need to get used to that fact. She's a part of my life now."

"Well, if she's going to be staying here, then I won't be," Paisley picked up her backpack and stomped off to her bedroom. Clay wanted to go after her and tell her to go back into the kitchen and apologize but he also knew his daughter well enough to know that would do him no good. Paisley was a lot like him and when she lost her temper, it was best to let her work through some of her anger and give her time to cool off.

"Should you go after her?" Rose asked.

"No," he said. "I'm so sorry," he whispered.

"Well, this has been fun. I can't say that I'm surprised at how things have turned out," Corbin said. "Honestly, mom, you've known him for a week and you expected us to all just be okay with this?" Corbin waved his arms around like a crazy person as if trying to drive his point home.

"That's not fair, Corbin," Aiden challenged. "Rose has given up so much for us, maybe you should try to meet her halfway."

Rose held up her hand, effectively stopping Aiden from saying more. "While I appreciate you trying to help, Aiden, it's not necessary. Sink or swim, I'll take care of myself and clean up my own messes. I'll be taking a week's vacation, effective immediately. I need some time to think about a few things." Clay worried that he was one of the things Rose needed to think about. "If you need me, I'll be right here." She linked her fingers with his, giving him some comfort.

Paisley stomped back out to the kitchen from her room, another bag slung over her shoulder. "Mom is coming to pick me back up. I won't stay here as long as that woman is in our house," she said, pointing her little finger at Rose for good measure. "I'll stay at Mom's—she said it's all right with her."

"That isn't for you to decide, Paisley. Your mother and I discuss this stuff together," Clay shouted. He knew he was letting his anger at the way their night had blown up, get the better of him. He didn't mean to take it out on his daughter but she was acting like a complete brat.

"If you need me to go," Rose whispered.

"No," he said, not letting her even finish her thought. "My daughter needs to learn some manners, as does your son. They should be the ones to leave. As for you, Paisley, I'll be calling your mom and we'll be discussing a punishment for the way you've acted tonight. You might not like the fact that I'm dating but you don't get to be rude to guests in our home. I'm disappointed. We raised you to be better than this." Paisley stared him down, challenge bright in her hazel eyes.

A car honked out in the driveway and Paisley turned to leave. "That's mom," she said over her shoulder. She was leaving without even saying goodbye to him. "Let me know when she's gone, and I'll come home. Take care of Daisy for me." Paisley walked out the front door and before he heard Abi's truck even leave the driveway, his phone chimed. He pulled it from his pocket and saw that his ex had tried to call him three times.

"I need to call Abi and work this out," he said to Rose. "It was nice to meet you both," he lied, nodding to Aiden and Corbin.

"You too, Clay," Aiden said. "Good luck with everything." Corbin didn't say a word, just stared him down as he left the room. The last thing Clay heard was Corbin's muddled curses after Rose slapped him and he couldn't help but smile to himself. It had been a complete cluster fuck of a night but the one thing that got him through was having Rose by his side. They might all be right—it might be too soon for him to feel the way he did about Rose but Clay didn't give a fuck. She was his and there was no way he was going to let either of their kids come between them.

ROSE

"What the hell is wrong with you?" Rose whispered to her son. "I can't believe I'm saying this, but you acted worse than a thirteen-year-old girl tonight, Corbin." Aiden laughed and Rose slapped his arm. "And you," she said. "You should have warned me that Corbin was acting like an ass before you got here. A head's up would have been nice, Aiden. How many times a day do I save your ass?"

"Geeze," Aiden grumbled. "A thousand times a day. You're right," he offered. "I'm sorry but I had no idea he was going to be this bad."

"What's going on with you that you acted out like this, Corbin?" Rose asked.

"I'm not a child, Mom and I wasn't 'acting out,' as you like to call it. I guess when I saw how young your new boy toy is, I lost my shit. You do realize he's closer to my age than he is yours, right?" Corbin taunted. She was well aware of that fact but she was also trying to forget their age difference, as Clay ordered.

"He's not my 'boy toy,' Corbin," she chided. "Age has

nothing to do with what's happening here. You acted like an overbearing ass," Rose said.

"You know when she cusses that you're in deep shit," Aiden teased.

"I know," Corbin said. "I just don't want you to get hurt, Ma," he said. Rose wrapped her arms around her son's waist.

"I'm finally having some fun, living the life I want to live. If you can't be happy for me, Corbin, then just be civil. That's all I ask," Rose said.

"So, get on the Clay bandwagon or stay the fuck out of your way?" Corbin asked.

"Basically," Rose agreed. "It's finally my time to be happy. Raising you boys brought me so much joy and you've turned out to be such good men. I love you both, so much. I love the women you've chosen to build your lives and families with. I just want a chance to find that same happiness."

"You're right, Rose," Aiden said. "You do deserve your shot at happiness. I'm team Clay all the way," he agreed.

Rose hugged him, "Thanks, Aiden," she said. They both turned to look at Corbin and he dramatically threw his arms in the air.

"Fine," he grumbled. "I'll give him a chance. I won't pretend to be happy about any of this or to like him, but I'll try."

"Thank you, Son," Rose said. "That's all I ask."

"We need to get going," Aiden said, checking his watch. "Sorry about dinner," he said.

Rose looked at the untouched food and sighed. "It's fine," she said. "I'll wrap it up for later. You guys go home to your families." Rose walked them out.

"You still taking the week off?" Aiden asked.

"Yes," she said. "I just need some time to think things over. Is that okay?"

"Sure," Aiden said. "I'll get a temp for the week and we'll muddle through." Rose giggled when he made a face and kissed them both goodnight. She watched as their headlights disappeared down the long drive and turned to walk back into the house. She could hear Clay still on his call and wanted to give him some privacy, so she started to put away all the food she had ordered.

"Fine," she heard him bark. "I'll let you know." Clay ended his call and tossed his cell onto the counter.

"Everything all right?" Rose asked.

"No," Clay said. "Paisley is really upset and now Abilene wants to meet you. Apparently, my daughter fed my ex some bullshit that you were mean to her. I told her you didn't have a mean bone in your body, but—"

Rose giggled and covered her hand over her chest, "Your ex-wife didn't believe you?"

"No," Clay breathed. "She said our daughter wouldn't be this upset over nothing."

"Well, this is hardly nothing. You introduced your thirteen-year-old daughter to the first woman you've been dating. I'm sure it was a complete shock to her."

"I don't know that I'd call what we've been doing, 'dating,' Rose," Clay said. She thought it was cute the way he used air quotes around the word, "Dating". She wouldn't necessarily call what they had been doing dating either but she wasn't sure what the correct term was.

"What would you call it, then?" she asked.

"Um," Clay stalled. He even tapped his finger to his chin and Rose smiled. She wrapped her arms around his waist, and he pulled her tighter against his body. "Well, there's been a heck of a lot of sex," he teased.

"Yes," she agreed. "There has been quite a bit of that. And we did go out to your favorite steak house for our second night together," she offered.

"Yep," he said. "I think it's time to take this thing to the next level," he whispered.

"Next level?" Rose questioned. "We've known each other

for seven days now. Don't you think we're jumping ahead of ourselves?"

"Well, we did just introduce our kids to each other," Clay reminded. "I'd say that you moving in with me is just the next natural step."

"Moving in with you?" Rose repeated.

"You know, you're repeating what I say an awful lot," Clay said. "I stand by what I told your son, Rose. I don't give a fuck how long we've known each other or what our age difference is. What's happening between us just feels right and I don't want to wait to be with you just because that's what other people think we should do. I want to move forward with what's next. Move in with me—permanently?" he asked. Rose took a step back from him, not missing the disappointment in his eyes as she did.

"I—I just don't know if that's a good idea," she said. "What happens if you change your mind in a month?"

"Won't happen," Clay assured her. She looked at him like he lost his mind. If she gave up her townhome to move in with him and this thing between them didn't work out, she'd be homeless. Rose was too old to be so reckless. No—old wasn't the correct word. Mature—she was too mature to just jump in feet first and not think about the consequences.

"Okay—let's compromise," Clay offered.

"That sounds fair," Rose agreed. "I love a good meeting of the minds. What are you thinking?"

"Well, how about you move enough stuff here, to stay with me on my ranch and not have to run back to your townhouse every few days? That way we can take what's happening between us for a test drive—what do you think?" Clay watched her and God, he looked so hopeful, she couldn't tell him no. Plus, she kind of liked the idea of a test run. She could save some time every day not having to run by her place and she'd have more time to spend with Clay when his day was done on the ranch.

"I'd say we could live at your townhome but then I'd have to find someone to take over my early morning and evening chores around here. Ty already does more than his share around here. But, if that's what it takes to get you to agree to live with me, I'll gladly move my shit over to your townhome." Rose smiled up at him and shook her head.

"Nope," she said. "I know how much you love your ranch, and it would be silly for us to cram into my tiny townhome. Your place is so much bigger," she said. "I'll move some of my stuff over this weekend," she offered.

Clay picked her up and spun her around his kitchen, making her squeal. "You've made me so happy, Baby," he said. "Thank you."

"Let's see how you feel after spending the next week with me. I have a week off from work, don't forget," Rose said.

"So, you aren't going in to work this week?" Clay asked.

"No," Rose breathed. "I think it's for the best. Corbin needs to calm down and honestly, I could use a little breathing room myself."

"Well, then, I have another proposition for you," Clay offered.

"Wow," Rose teased, "I'm not sure I can handle more, Clay."

He chuckled and kissed the side of her neck, right on her ticklish spot. She giggled and swatted at him. "Go with me to Texas," he said.

"Texas?" she asked.

"Yeah, I have two auctions for my cattle in Austin this week and I'd love to show you my home away from home." Rose knew that getting out of town might not be such a bad idea. She'd let things calm down and then they could come back fresh and deal with their kids and whatever this was that was happening between them.

"When do we leave?" Rose asked.

"You mean, you'll go with me?" Clay asked. Rose smiled and nodded.

"I just need to pack up my stuff and move it over here and then I should run by the office and let the boys know I'm going out of town for a few days."

"You sure that's a good idea?" he asked.

"Yeah, it's the right thing to do. I need to at least tell Aiden where I'll be. Just in case I'm needed while we're gone." Rose finished putting away the rest of the dinner that no one touched and turned to face him. "That just leaves us with what to do about me meeting your ex-wife."

Clay looked like he wanted to say something but closed his mouth. "You sure you're up for that too?" he asked. Rose crossed the kitchen and wrapped her arms around Clay.

"I'm up for just about anything with you by my side," she said.

"Well, that's good because Abi just messaged me that she dropped Paisley off at her mom's house and was stopping by here in a few minutes. Now's your chance to run," he teased although Rose was pretty sure he wasn't joking.

"I'm good," she lied. "How about I give you guys a few minutes to talk things over and then I'll join you after my shower?" Rose knew that meeting his ex-wife at the front door, presenting a united front might make Abi feel as though they are ganging up on her and that was the last thing Rose wanted.

"I think that might be a good idea," Clay admitted. "Just don't take too long—I'd like to get this over with and celebrate the fact that you've agreed to move in with me."

"Deal," Rose agreed.

❋

She had spent a good thirty minutes in the shower, hiding from having to meet Clay's ex-wife. Having to face the woman he spent so much of his life with; the woman who gave him a child, made Rose want to run and hide. But she agreed to meet with Abi and talk through what happened tonight. She just hoped that she had wasted enough time showering and drying her hair to give Clay time to smooth things over. Rose pulled on her robe and walked back out to the kitchen. As soon as she heard Abi shouting at Clay, she wanted to turn back around and go back to the bedroom to hide.

"You let her walk right into an ambush," Abi yelled.

"I know and maybe that wasn't the best way to handle all of this. I was worried that if I told Paisley about Rose, she wouldn't come home. Plus, Roses boys were here and I thought it would help soften the blow, meeting them too."

"Boys—she has kids? How old are they?" Abi asked.

"Thirty-three," Rose said, turning the corner to walk into the kitchen. "I have a son who's thirty-three and I also raised his best friend, whom I consider a son. He's the same age." Rose held her hand out to Abi who seemed too shocked to do anything but openly stare at her with her mouth gaped open. "I'm Rose Eklund."

When Rose realized that Abi wasn't going to shake her hand, she dropped it back to her side. Clay cleared his throat and pulled Rose against his side, wrapping his arm protectively around her.

"This is my ex-wife, Abilene," he said.

Abi seemed to find her tongue and stuck her hand out in Rose's direction. "Abi Nash," she said, putting special emphasis on her last name. Rose knew that the other woman was marking her territory. Clay had already admitted to her that he had never brought another woman around Abi or Paisley—she was the first. This all had to be so new and disturbing for his ex, Rose almost felt sorry for the woman. She shook Abi's hand and plastered her best fake smile on her face.

"It's good to meet you, Abi," Rose said. "I'm sorry about what happened here tonight. Clay and I were just trying to introduce our kids to each other and it seems to have backfired. My son wasn't very receptive to meeting Clay either."

Abi sneered at her and Rose knew she wasn't going to like

what she said even before she said it. "I can understand where your son is coming from. I mean, he and Clay are practically the same age. Isn't Ty about thirty-three?" Yeah—her question was laced with what felt like a slap in the face.

Clay flexed his fingers in Rose's side and smiled down at her. "Tyler is thirty-two," he said, shrugging as if it wasn't any big deal. "They might have all gone to school together," he said. Rose hadn't thought about that, but it was probably true.

"You weren't far in front of them," Abi continued. "In school that is."

"Don't Abi," Clay all but shouted. "I know what you're hinting at and Rose being older than me has nothing to do with any of this. What the three of us are here to discuss is what happened with Paisley tonight. Our daughter was rude to both Rose and me and she has to know she can't treat adults that way."

"Our daughter is a matter for you and me to discuss, Clay. Rose has no business in what we decide to do about Paisley's rudeness." Abi countered. Rose pulled free from Clay's side and nodded.

"It was good to meet you, Abi. I hope to see you again," Rose said, turning to go back to Clay's bedroom. She wouldn't insert herself into their private conversation no matter how bad it felt to be dismissed by his ex.

"Rose, wait," he ordered. She stopped short and Abi gasped.

"It all makes sense now," Abi whispered. "She's what you wanted me to become. Oh—what did you call it again? Submissive, right?" Clay shot Abi a look and Rose stared him down.

"Yes, Clay?" Rose questioned.

"Dear God, I'm right, aren't I?" Abi went on. "Women aren't meant to be pathetic, meek little mice, obeying their masters. You've set our cause back by at least a hundred years, Rose."

"Don't talk to her that way. You have no right to stand in my home and question me about my relationship with Rose. It has nothing to do with you," Clay spat.

"This used to be my home too and it's still our daughter's if she chooses to ever come back here," Abi said, standing her ground. Abi was so different from what she expected. Rose thought that Clay was exaggerating when he said that his ex didn't have a submissive bone in her body, but he wasn't. Knowing how dominant Clay was with her made Rose's heart ached for him, knowing that he had to hide who he was for so long.

"You have no right to treat Rose like she's done something wrong because of who she is. She gives me what I never got from you. Rose has made me realize what I've been missing all these years," Clay said.

"Clay," Rose whispered. "It's all right. You're right, Abi. I am submissive and I do take orders from Clay. But, it's not because I'm a meek mouse, as you put it. I don't bow to his dominance or take power away from myself or any other woman, for that matter. Being Clay's submissive gives me all the power in our relationship. He might call the shots, but I get to decide what I want to give and not give in our relationship. You wouldn't understand that, though because you aren't submissive. That's okay too. We're all different and Clay just found someone he can be himself with."

"What the hell does that mean? Are you saying that my husband couldn't be himself with me?" Abi asked.

"Clay's your ex-husband, Abi. And yes. He had to hide a part of who he was with you and that makes me sad for you both. You both deserve to find people who make you happy and give you what you need." Rose boldly walked back across the kitchen to kiss Clay. She could feel Abi's eyes boring into her like laser beams and she almost wanted to laugh.

"I'll be waiting for you in our bedroom," Rose said. She knew she wasn't playing fairly, but she didn't care anymore.

"So, she's living here now?" Abi started back in as soon as

Rose turned the corner to go down the hallway. She smiled to herself when she heard Clay's simple answer.

"Yep," he said. "And if I have my way, it will be a permanent situation."

Rose heard Abi's gasp as she shut herself away in the master suite. She trusted Clay to handle his ex and now that they all knew exactly where each other stood, she had no doubt he'd be coming to find her in his bed, sooner than later. She'd give him a little surprise and be waiting for him naked. It was what he told her he'd like from her every night that she slept in his bed —her completely naked and ready for him. It was the least Rose could do for Clay, after all—he was her Dom.

CLAYTON

Clay booked an extra plane ticket for Rose to go with him on his business trip to Austin and then turned off the lights in his office and trudged back to bed. It had been a long ass day and he was ready to wrap his arms around Rose and sleep for days.

He and Abi had worked out that Paisley would be grounded from her electronics for a week for her rude behavior. He was happy that his ex at least saw the way their daughter treated Rose and him as unacceptable behavior and agreed to discipline her. Unfortunately, her compliance came at a cost to him—Paisley would be staying at her mom's house until they could work this whole mess out. He agreed that forcing her to be at the ranch with Rose when she didn't want to be, wasn't the answer.

Abi left shortly after Rose went back to their bedroom. His ex realized that there was nothing left to say to him to convince Clay that he was making a mistake. Rose wasn't a mistake. She was the best fucking thing to ever happen to him, besides his daughter. They both came up with a punishment for Paisley, agreed to all the terms of her staying with Abi and he showed his ex-wife out. The only thing left to do was to buy Rose's plane ticket before she could change her mind about going with him to Texas on business. She had already told her boys that she was taking next week off, so there wasn't anything to stand in her way but self-doubt and fear that Abi was right. Clay wouldn't allow that to happen and booking her ticket was the only sure-fire way to make sure Rose followed through with their plans.

He crept into their room, the lights were all out and he could hear Rose's gentle breathing from her side of the bed. She had fallen asleep waiting for him. Clay quickly brushed his teeth and decided to take a shower before crawling into bed. He had just stepped into the hot spray of the shower when Rose sleepily walked into his master bathroom, blinking against the light. She wore nothing but a smile and when he opened the shower door, in invitation for her to join him, she immediately took him up on his offer.

"Hey," she whispered, as he pulled her against his wet body.

"Hey yourself," he said back. "You okay, Baby?" Clay worried that Abi's criticisms were a bit harsh for Rose.

"Yeah," she breathed. "Sorry I fell asleep. I was trying to wait up for you."

"It's fine," he said. "Abi left a bit ago and I had to buy your plane ticket for Austin." Rose smiled up at him and snuggled against his body.

"When do we leave?" she asked.

"How does tomorrow sound?" he asked. "I'd like to get out of here and put today as far behind us as possible."

"That sounds like heaven," Rose agreed. "I'll just need to tell the boys that I'm heading out of town. And well, I need to check in on Corbin."

Clay wanted to tell her that her son could use a time-out like Paisley, but things were a little different with Corbin being a grown man.

"All right," he agreed. "You want me to go with you?"

"No," she said. "I think it would be best if I sat down with my son and we had a little heart to heart. He can't treat you like he did tonight—I won't allow it."

"Thanks for that, Honey," Clay said. "Abi and I agreed that Paisley should stay with her for a bit. You know, until she gets used to us being an us. She's grounded though."

"I'm sorry, Clay," Rose said. "I hate that it's come to this."

"She'll come around," he offered. "My daughter's stubborn, but she's also fair."

"Gee, I wonder if she gets that from you or your ex," Rose teased. She had a point, both of them were pretty damn stubborn.

"Funny," he said, swatting her ass.

"Well, the apple didn't fall far from either tree," Rose teased. "I wish I could just ground Corbin for acting like an ass but I'm not sure that will work. He'll come around too. If he doesn't, I'll get his wife, Ava involved and she'll set him straight." Clay chuckled, "It's hard to believe that anyone could set your son straight. He's a big guy."

"He is," Rose agreed. "But, he's a big teddy bear."

"Well, the bear part is probably right," Clay teased.

"How about I get up early tomorrow and go over to Corbin's and deal with my ferocious bear?" Rose said. "Then, I'll meet you back here and we can head to Austin."

"Now, that sounds like a deal to me," Clay agreed. He pushed Rose through the hot spray of the shower and up against the cold tile of the shower wall. "How about we negotiate another deal, my beautiful sub?" he asked. Clay kissed down her neck and back up to her mouth giving her hot, wet kisses. Rose daringly wrapped her hands around his erection, eliciting a hiss from his parted lips.

"Fuck," Clay swore.

Rose giggled and ran her hands over his wet shaft. "Now, that sounds like a deal to me," she teased, giving him back his words.

"On your knees, Honey," Clay ordered. Rose gave him a sexy little smirk and sunk to her knees, letting the water fall over her body. He palmed his cock, loving the way she seemed almost greedy to taste him.

"Open," he ordered. He didn't have to wait for Rose to comply. She leaned back on her heels and opened her mouth, looking up at him as if waiting for him to give her what she needed. Clay shoved his cock in past her willing lips and into the back of her throat. He loved the way she took over, letting him slide in and out of her mouth. Her tongue teasing the head every time he slipped out and then back into her hot mouth. He was so close but he didn't want to find his release down her throat. No, Clay wanted in her tight pussy.

Clay pulled his dick free from her mouth, loving the groan of displeasure she gave. "I know, Baby. I need in your pussy."

"Oh," Rose said, smiling up at him. Clay helped her to her feet and pressed her back up against the wall, lifting her so she could wrap her legs around his waist. His cock pushed through her wet folds allowing him to completely to sink into her body. Every time he took her felt like he was coming home and now was no different.

"You feel so fucking good, Honey," he breathed against her neck. Rose held onto his shoulders like he was her lifeline.

"You do too, Clay," she whimpered.

"This is going to be fast," he admitted. "I was so close when I was in your mouth, I almost came down your throat."

Rose groaned and nodded. "Please, Clay," she begged. Clay wasn't about to make her wait another minute.

"I've got you, Baby," he said. He pumped harder into her core and felt her tighten around his cock. She was close and he wanted Rose with him when he found his release. Clay flexed his fingers into her fleshy ass, kissing his way up to her mouth.

"I need you with me, Honey. I want you to touch yourself," he ordered. Rose seemed to hesitate at his command. "Rose," he warned. She closed her eyes as if trying to hide from him and nodded.

"Al-alright," she stuttered. Rose hesitantly snaked her hand down between their bodies and he could feel her fingers as they fumbled around to find her clit.

"You don't like to touch yourself?" he asked.

"I—I usually use a vibrator," she admitted. The thought of Rose getting herself off with a vibrator made him hot as hell. Clay moaned against her mouth and pumped furiously in and out of her pussy. He was so close.

"Tell me you're close," he growled.

"I am," she moaned. Rose's pussy clenched around his cock as she found her release and that was all Clay could stand. He pumped in and out of her body twice more and followed her over.

"Rose," he whispered her name like a prayer. He wanted to say so much more—tell her that he was falling for her. Hell, he had already fallen for her but saying those words out loud wasn't something she was ready to hear. Instead, he closed his eyes, pressing his forehead to hers. I love you, he thought, wishing he could say those words out loud. Someday, he would —when they were both ready to accept the truth.

ROSE

Rose stopped by her townhome to pick up her suitcase and a few things she needed for her trip and then called Ava to let her know that she would be stopping by. Her daughter-in-law would be her best ally in making Corbin listen to reason and right now, Rose needed all the help she could get. Ava told her that Corbin went into the office earlier that morning and as far as sulking went, he was going for the gold medal in that event. Rose almost wanted to laugh at just how far her son could take sulking when he was in the mood. Ava warned her that he wasn't in any better mood now that he had met Clay but Rose was done pussyfooting around. Corbin needed to hear from her how much his bad behavior and treatment towards Clay hurt her. It was time for her son to stop acting like a giant man child and luckily for her, Ava agreed. By the time she and her daughter-in-law came up with a plan, she had driven to the office and was ready to do her part.

Rose was waived through security and got on the private elevator she and the boys used to access their penthouse office suites. She took a deep breath when the elevator stopped on the top floor, just before the doors opened. Rose knew what or who, in this case, would be waiting for her on the other side of the closed doors. Ava was supposed to call Corbin to warn him that his mom would be stopping by, giving him just enough time to meet her at the elevator.

The doors slid open and Corbin stared her down, arms crossed over his massive chest. Rose stepped out of the elevator and nodded to him, walking straight past him to her office.

"Mother," Corbin said, trailing behind her.

"Son," she returned.

"What are you doing here? Not only is it a weekend but you said you were taking next week off," Corbin reminded.

"It is and I did," Rose agreed. "I just needed a few things before I head off on my trip," she lied. She didn't need to stop by the office at all but if Corbin knew she was there to read him the riot act, she'd get nowhere.

"Trip," he asked. "Where are you going?"

"Austin, Texas," she said. "With Clay." Corbin's groan filled the empty office, and she was happy that they were alone. She was a private person and spilling her dirty laundry for everyone in the office wasn't something she usually did.

"You just met the guy and now you're going on vacation with him?" Corbin questioned. Yeah, he wasn't going to like this next part but it was time for her to spell out her relationship with Clay for her son.

"I know you think things are going a little fast between Clay and me but it's none of your business." Corbin started to talk over her and she held up her hand, effectively stopping his tirade. "Before you say something stupid like I'm your mom and your business, let me remind you that I'm a grown woman and while I appreciate your concern, I won't let you bully me. I'm going on Clay's business trip with him and when we get back, I'm moving in with him."

"Moving in with him?" Corbin yelled.

"Lower your voice, Corbin. I won't stand here and let you shout at me. Yes, I'm moving in with him. I told him that I'd move to his ranch and give this relationship a chance to play out."

"Are you going to marry him?" Corbin asked. That was a question she hadn't given much thought to. Clay hadn't asked and things between them were so new, marriage hadn't even crossed her mind.

"I haven't thought about marriage, Corbin. I'm enjoying the time I spend with him and whether you think so or not, I'm taking things slowly. I like Clay and he treats me well—that's all you need to know. My happiness should be enough for you."

Corbin exhaled and sat in one of the chairs she kept in front of her desk. "It is," he breathed. "I just don't want you to get hurt."

"I'm a big girl, Corbin. I think I can handle myself," she teased. Corbin refused to look at her and Rose knew that he wasn't telling her something. "What am I missing here, Son?" she asked.

"I didn't tell you because I didn't want to worry you. My father reached out and he wants to meet with me." Corbin still refused to look her in the eyes and Rose was fine with that. She didn't want to have the reaction she did about her ex. She thought she was past all the anger of being left pregnant and alone at seventeen, but she wasn't.

"Brock contacted you?" she whispered.

"Yeah," Corbin said. He stood, pacing in front of her and Rose knew he was worried about telling her. She didn't want to tell him that he shouldn't see the man who left them both so long ago. It wasn't her place to make that decision for him. "I think that's why I responded to meeting Clay as I did. Brock reached out a couple of days ago and I guess his message just set me on edge. I'm sorry, Mom."

"Well, that's understandable, Corbin. You're a grown man and he's never even bothered to get to know you. It had to be a shock," Rose said, trying to be as understanding as possible.

"It was," he agreed. "He said that he has been following my success and he found out about Brody and wants to meet his grandson." Corbin slunk back into the chair and looked up at her. "What the hell should I do, Mom?"

"I can't tell you that, Son. What did Ava say?" Rose asked.

"Nothing, really. She gets the whole, 'crazy father' thing. Ava said it's up to me and I'm not sure what to do. I don't know that I want him to be a part of my life. What happens if I let him in, Brody gets to know him and then he takes off again? I never had him in my life—why let him be a part of it now?"

"Again, I can't make that decision for you, Corbin. This is your decision to make, not mine." Rose said, sitting down in the chair next to him. Corbin shot her a sheepish grin and took her hand into his.

"It kind of is your decision, Mom. He's asked to see you too but he didn't have your contact information. He asked me to give you the message," Corbin almost whispered.

"Well, shit," Rose grumbled.

Corbin chuckled, "Mother," he teased. "Such a potty mouth." Rose tried not to curse; it was just who she was. In the office, she was constantly telling Aiden and Corbin to watch their language. Their wives had banned them from cursing around their homes with the kids listening on, so the boys had been using more swear words than normal lately. It took a lot for Rose to curse and the prospect of having to face her ex after more than thirty years pushed her over the edge of polite conversation.

Rose stood and nodded, "Thank you for delivering the message, Corbin. I don't have anything to say to Brock after all these years though."

Corbin stood, facing her. "I was hoping we could go

together. You know, strength in numbers," he said. Corbin shrugged as if it was not a big deal, but Rose could tell that it was to him.

"So, you've made up your mind then? You're going to see him?" Rose asked.

Corbin groaned and ran his hands through his already unruly hair. "I don't know," he moaned. "You go on your trip and I'll think about what I want to do. I don't want to just jump into a decision and end up regretting it."

Corbin pulled her in for a quick hug, "Thanks, Mom. I'll try to give Clay a chance. Just make me a promise that if you need me, for any reason, you'll ask for my help."

"I promise," she said. "Thank you for giving Clay a chance."

"I said I'd try," Corbin corrected. "But, if he hurts you, I'll tear him apart."

Rose giggled, "I have a plane to catch. Walk me to the elevator?"

"Sure," Corbin said. "You tell Aiden you're going to Texas?"

"Not yet. I'll call him on my way home," Rose said. She pushed the button to call the elevator just as the doors opened and Aiden stepped off.

"I'm so glad you're still here," Aiden breathed. "I went by your house and Ava told me you were here and that Rose was stopping by."

"What's up, man?" Corbin asked. Rose knew that Aiden was a little high strung, but this was next level, even for him.

"We have a problem," Aiden said. "The merger we've been working on these past few months—it might fall through." Rose knew the boys had been working non-stop to make sure the merger happened. It was the company's biggest deal so far and important to their companies future.

"Fuck," Corbin swore. "What the hell happened?"

"Our rival company happened," Aiden said.

"Newman and Sons?" Corbin asked.

"Yeah—apparently, one of the sons stuck his nose into our deal and now, the merger is being questioned," Aiden said.

"Which son?" Corbin growled. "If it's fucking Evan Newman, I'm going to tear him apart."

Rose put her hand on Corbin's arm. "You can't just go around threatening to tear people apart, Corbin."

Aiden chuckled, "It's Evan, and Rose is right. If you tear him apart, I won't be able to run this company while you're in prison. How about we sit down and come up with a solution that doesn't involve physical violence?" Aiden looked between Rose and Corbin and she hated that she was going to have to break the news about her trip to Aiden this way.

"I'm going out of town," Rose whispered.

"Wait—what?" Aiden questioned. "I thought you were just going to take some time off next week. Now, you're going away?"

Rose nodded, "Yes, sorry. I'm going to Texas with Clay."

"Can't you postpone that? We need you here, Mom. If this deal falls through, we could be facing some end of year layoffs. Please," Corbin begged.

Rose looked at Aiden and he shrugged and nodded. "He's right," Aiden agreed. "A lot is riding on this merger. We need you, Rose." She hated the idea of having to break the news to Clay that she wouldn't be going with him to Texas. He seemed so excited about their trip and even purchased her ticket last night before coming to bed.

"We wouldn't ask if it wasn't important, Rose," Aiden added. God, she couldn't say no to her boys, especially when they needed her help around the office. She knew how important this deal was for them and telling them no might send the whole merger down the toilet. She couldn't let that happen.

"Fine," she agreed. "I'll need to go home and break the news to Clay but I can be back here in a couple of hours to help." Aiden and Corbin both kissed her cheeks and she giggled. "But, when this merger goes through, I'm taking a week off—no questions asked."

"You got it," Aiden said. Rose stepped into the elevator and waved at them as the doors closed. She would have to run back to the ranch and break the news to Clay. Rose just hoped that he'd be okay with her backing out of their little trip—she'd just find a way to make it up to him, somehow.

CLAYTON

Clay spent four long days without Rose and he hated how much he missed her. It was unexpected and he found that instead of concentrating on the meetings and auctions he had to attend, he was daydreaming about the woman waiting for him back at home.

When Rose broke the news to him that she wasn't going to be able to go to Austin, he insisted that she stay out at his ranch while he was gone. She balked at the idea but then he told her it would make him hurry home faster knowing that a sexy as fuck, willing woman was waiting in his bed for him to return. He just didn't realize how true his words were because she was all he could think about while he was in Austin.

They talked on the phone every night like they were both high school sweethearts and she'd fill him in on what was going on around the ranch and how busy she was at work. The good news was that the merger had gone through, despite the hiccups and she was going to be able to take a few days off to spend with him. That news made Clay even more anxious to get home to Rose.

He dropped his bags in the front foyer and went into the

kitchen, hoping to find Rose. Instead, he found his brother, Tyler. "Hey stranger. How was your trip?" Ty asked. He was rummaging through Clay's refrigerator and didn't stop building himself a monster sandwich to even look in his direction.

"Good," Clay said. "Where's Rose?"

Ty shrugged. "She hasn't been around."

"What?" Clay asked. "She told me she was staying here while I was away."

"Calm down, man. She was here last night but she said something about meeting her son about having to see someone. She seemed a little at odds. You know her son and I went to high school together, right?"

Clay sighed. He was tired of everyone reminding him about the age difference between him and Rose. It wasn't anyone else's business. "Yeah, I guessed that was the case. You and Corbin are about the same age. Does it really matter? I mean, does me being with an older woman bother you, Ty?"

Tyler stopped piling ham on his sandwich to look up at him. "No, why are you asking me that?"

"Because you keep bringing up our age difference. I mean, not outright but you drop subtle little hints and I want you to know that it doesn't bother me. Rose makes me happy."

"Then I'm happy for you," Ty admitted. "You deserve to be with someone who makes you smile, man. I see the difference she's made in your life in just a few weeks. I think it's great, Clay."

"Thanks, Ty," Clay said. "I appreciate that." Rose came in through the side door and dropped her stuff on the bench next to the door. She looked as though she had a tough day, and all Clay could think about was helping her to forget her bad day.

"Hey Honey," Clay said. He pulled her against his body and kissed her. "You look like you had a bad day."

"I did. But it's better now that you're here. How was your trip home?" Rose asked, subtly changing the subject.

"Uneventful. How about you let me take you out to dinner?"

he asked. Clay shot Ty a dirty look and laughed when his brother didn't seem to even notice. "My brother seems to have eaten us out of house and home." Clay teased.

"Hey," Ty said around a mouthful of sandwich.

"I'd love to," Rose said. "But we need to talk first." Clay looked her up and down, not missing the worry in her eyes.

"You're worrying me, Honey," he admitted. "What's up?"

"It's just something has come up and I need to fill you in." Rose looked down at her fidgeting hands and he took them into his own. "It's Corbin's father. Well, if that's what you'd call a man who created a new life with me and then just took off, not bothering to look back."

"I thought he wasn't a part of your or Corbin's life?" Clay questioned.

"He's not," she said. "He's never met my son." Ty stopped eating his sandwich, setting it down on the counter and joining them in the foyer. Rose stopped talking and looked over at Ty.

"Really, Ty," Clay said. "You don't have anything better to do?"

"Nope," Tyler admitted.

"It's all right," Rose said. "This isn't something that's a secret, really."

"Thanks, Rose," Tyler said. "So, this guy just shows up out of nowhere and wants to see you and Corbin?"

"Yep," Rose said. "I met him when I was only fifteen. He was ten years older than me, and I thought he was honestly my knight in shining armor. But there's no such thing. Boy, was that a hard lesson to learn." Rose barked out her laugh and Clay wanted to protest, telling her that he'd ride in to save her from just about anything.

"What happened?" Tyler asked. Clay knew some of the story but he always wondered if there was more to it.

"I got pregnant," she admitted. "Brock was in my father's class at the university. My dad was a professor there and one night, he brought Brock home to introduce him to my mother. He was my dad's most promising student and he had such high hopes for Brock. One thing led to another and I started seeing Brock behind their backs. He convinced me that they wouldn't understand our relationship, given our age difference."

Tyler nodded, "Kind of like you and Clay," he said.

"Shut the fuck up, Ty," Clay growled.

"No, he's right. Maybe that's why I've had such a tough time with our age difference. But, in our case, I'm the one who's ten years older," Rose said.

"It's not the same," Clay said. "None of this has anything to do with us. I wouldn't have walked away from you, Rose—ever." He meant it too. They were past the point of pregnancy scares and doing the right thing, but he knew with every fiber of his being that he would have stepped up if he was in that situation with Rose.

"I appreciate that, Clay. I know you aren't Brock, but it took me a long time to get over being left like that. I told him I was pregnant and my parents threatened to have him arrested for having sex with a minor. Brock bolted leaving me pregnant and alone. My parents shut me out when I refused to have an abortion. They told me that if I choose not to terminate my pregnancy, they didn't want to have anything to do with me or my child. I just couldn't do it," Rose whispered. Clay pulled her into his body, needing contact with her.

"Of course you couldn't," Clay agreed. "You're such a good mom, Rose. I can see how much you love both Corbin and Aiden. Hell, you took in your son's best friend and raised him as your own. Not many people would do that."

"I do love those boys," she said. "I just had no idea how hard it was going to be—being a single mother, finishing high school, and getting my diploma so I could get a crap job to keep us afloat. But I did it. I'd do it all again, too. My son was worth every sacrifice I made."

"Why does your ex want to meet after all these years?" Clay asked.

"I have no idea, really," Rose admitted. "He got in touch with Corbin, saying he followed his career all these years and that he wanted to meet his grandson. Corbin's worried that if he lets that happen, he'll be setting Brody up for the same heartache he faced growing up without a father. I can't blame him, really."

"No one will blame Corbin if he decides not to meet with his father. But, why would you have to see him?"

"He asked to see me. Brock told Corbin that he didn't have any contact information for me and to give me the message. Truth is, I'm worried that Brock is up to no good but I'm just not sure what it is. I'd heard that he settled down and even got married. Last I heard, he and his wife had two kids and were happy. It hurt to hear that he found happiness with another woman, raising kids and having the family I should have had." Hearing Rose say that she wanted a family with another man-made Clay half-crazy with jealousy.

"No family is perfect," Ty said. "You probably dodged a bullet when he walked away from you. Why would you want to be with a man who could do that to you?"

Rose shook her head, "I don't know," she whispered. "I guess it was the fantasy of it all—you know that perfect little family, cute house, and white picket fence. The whole nine yards. I was a foolish girl. I had to grow up fast once Corbin got here, and I never really looked back. I was too busy raising a kid."

"Are you going to see him," Clay asked.

"I don't know," Rose admitted. "I told Corbin that if he chose to see Brock, I'd go with him—you know for moral support. I don't really have any desire to have a reunion with the man who left me so easily."

"I get it," Ty said, still listening in. "What would you even say to him?"

"Okay Tyler, how about you take off and go check in at the barn," Clay ordered. Having his brother stick around for such a personal story probably made Rose feel uneasy. She was a very private person.

"Fine," Ty grumbled. "Good luck with your ex, Rose." Ty smirked at Clay, and he honestly wanted to punch his brother.

"Thank you, Tyler," Rose said. Clay watched his brother leave and even locked the side door behind him.

"Sorry about him," Clay said.

"No, it's fine. I'm beginning to get used to Ty being around so much. It's his place too, really. He checked on me while you were gone—it was sweet the way he seemed to care."

"Well, he's never been accused of being sweet before. My brother has quite the reputation for being an ass when he wants to be," Clay said.

"Corbin said as much when he not so kindly reminded me that he and your brother went to school together. My son has a knack for pointing out the fact that I'm ancient compared to you." Clay nodded. He hated that most of their conversations came back to the fact that there was an age gap between them. He really wished people would quit reminding him and Rose about it. It felt like every step forward with Rose on the topic of their ages, led to two steps back.

"Does Corbin know if he's going to meet with Brock?" Clay asked.

"He decided this morning," Rose whispered.

"I'm assuming that you brought this up today because he agreed to see his father," Clay said. "And you're going to go with him, aren't you?"

Rose nodded her head, "Yes," she said. "Corbin set up a dinner meeting for this coming Tuesday," Rose admitted.

"Would you have told me all of this if Corbin didn't agree to see him?" Clay asked. He wanted to believe that Rose would share all aspects of her life with him.

"Of course." Rose defiantly held her chin up as if challenging him to call her a liar. "You've been away, Clay. I found out about this the day you left for Texas and telling you over the phone didn't feel right. This was much too personal to just blurt out while you were hundreds of miles away. I wanted to tell you face to face. Heck, as soon as you walked through the door tonight, I spilled my guts to you." Rose was right and he felt like an ass for even asking her his question.

Clay pulled her against his body and Rose reluctantly let him. "I'm sorry, Honey. Forgive me for being such an ass?"

"You are an ass, Clay." Rose pouted and it was just about the cutest damn thing he'd ever seen. Clay tipped his hat back and kissed her full, pouty bottom lip, nipping it with his teeth.

"I missed you, Rose," he whispered against her mouth.

Rose sighed, "I missed you too," she said, seeming to give up some of her fight.

Clay smiled down at her, "How about you show me how much you missed me, Honey and I can make it up to you for being an ass?"

"You are going to have to do a whole lot of groveling to make up for being an ass, Clay," Rose teased. She freed herself from his arms, giggling and running down the hallway to the master bedroom. Clay reached for her, grabbing a handful of her shirt, and pulled her back against his body.

"I want to play, Baby," he whispered into her ear. Rose's shiver told him she was up for a little fun too. He just hoped that his idea wouldn't fall flat. "Let me take you to my club," he asked.

"Your club?" Rose questioned.

"Yeah, I told you that I belong to a little BDSM club in town. I want to take you there and show you off a little. You up for that?" Clay asked. He felt as though he was holding his damn breath waiting for her to respond.

"People will see me?" she asked.

"Only if you want them too. I can get us a private room if you'd like to play behind closed doors." Rose didn't respond and

Clay was about to give up. "Come on, Rose. Let me show you my world," he begged.

"Okay," she whispered. "We can try it."

Clay kissed her neck, "Thank you, Baby. If you don't like it or want to leave, just say the word."

"Walrus?" Rose asked. Clay was confused for a minute and then barked out his laugh.

"Yep, your safe word will work just fine," he agreed. "Now, go pick out your sexiest, skimpiest outfit and be ready to leave in twenty minutes," he ordered. Rose nodded and ran back to the bedroom. He was going to show Rose his world tonight—all of it and hopefully, she'd be ready for it. There would be no turning back now.

❊

Clay loved the sexy little black dress that Rose picked out to wear for him. It hugged every one of her curves and he knew for a fact that she wasn't wearing panties or a bra underneath it. He had teased her to the point of almost having an orgasm on the ride over, letting his fingers leisurely slide through her drenched pussy. Clay loved her breathy sighs and gasps that told him she was close and her frustrated growls that erupted from her throat every time he removed his fingers.

By the time they got to the club, Rose was about ready to self-combust and completely relaxed—just how Clay wanted her. The more relaxed Rose was, the more things she'd be willing to try in the club.

"You remember your safe word?" he questioned.

"Walrus," Rose breathed. "Will I need to use it tonight?" she asked. Her voice still sounded raspy, needy, and completely sexy.

"Only if you don't like something we're trying. You have all the say here, Honey," Clay said. "We won't do anything you don't want to tonight."

"All right," she said.

"Good," Clay said. "Stay put," he ordered. He got out of the truck and rounded to the passenger side to grab her door for her. "Did I mention you look beautiful tonight?" he asked. He offered his hand to her, and Rose took it, stepping down from his truck and straightened her dress.

"Yep," she breathed. "Just before you slipped your hand up my skirt and ran your fingers through my—" Rose didn't finish her sentence, smiling up at him. Clay liked that she was sometimes too shy to tell him the dirty parts of what she wanted. He considered it a challenge that she refused to say certain words. He hoped that more time in his playroom would have her saying all the dirty words.

She shot him a disgruntled look and he shrugged. "Don't expect me to apologize for the drive over here, Honey. I'm not one bit sorry." Rose shook her head at him and laughed.

"Fine," she said. "I'm sure you'll make it up to me."

"Oh—that's a promise, Baby." Clay pulled the door to the club opened and ushered Rose through. This wasn't his first time at the club but it was his first time bringing a woman with him. Usually, he hooked up with subs at the club and went back to his ranch alone. Not tonight. Tonight he was sure that he was entering the club with the prettiest woman there. All eyes were on him and Rose and he could just about feel her heart beating as she pressed her body up against his.

"You all right, Honey?" he whispered in her ear. Rose nodded and looked around the room. He could tell that the St. Andrews cross drew her attention. She had told him that she wanted to try it sometime and he took that as his cue to order one for his playroom. He was waiting to surprise Rose with the new addition to his room but tonight would be a perfect night to try it just to see if she liked it.

"You want to try the cross?" he questioned.

"Yes," she breathed. "Can we?" He nodded and looked

around the room. The club wasn't very busy tonight and the smaller crowd would help get Rose over her shyness.

"Sure," he agreed. The cross was empty and Clay led Rose over to the corner of the room. "Strip," he commanded. Rose hesitated and he worried that she was reconsidering using her safe word. He wouldn't push but a part of him was secretly hoping that she'd agree to all his demands.

"I'm not wearing anything under this dress," she admitted.

Clay feigned shock and Rose rolled her eyes at him. "The point of this is for everyone to see my beautiful sub," he said. "Again, this is all your decision," Clay reminded.

"I want to do this," Rose said. He could almost see her resolve and courage and God; he was so proud of her. Rose stripped out of her dress standing completely bare in front of him. She shyly covered her breasts and Clay shook his head at her.

"I want to see all of you, Honey," he ordered. "I've got you." He blocked Rose from the few people who had gathered to watch her. Rose did as he asked and dropped her arms to her side. "Up against the cross, Rose. I'm thinking I'd like to flog your sweet ass tonight so face the cross."

Rose quickly turned and pressed her body up against the wooden cross, gifting him with a view of her glorious ass. "Perfect, Honey," he said slapping her fleshy globe. Clay worked quickly to secure her wrists and ankles, leaving Rose completely vulnerable and open for him to play with. Clay grabbed a flogger from the rack and ran the soft leather tip up her thighs, teasing every inch of her. Clay's cock protested that it had to wait for its turn.

"You're perfect, Honey," he said. Clay ran the flogger over her ass, giving it a sharp slap that rang through the playroom. They had drawn quite a crowd but Rose had no clue since she was facing away from the club members who were looking on. He gave her a few more sharp slaps with the flogger, loving her breathy little sighs and moans. Rose strained against her bindings and Clay was sure that he had found the perfect woman for himself. He dipped the tip of the flogger between her parted thighs again and rubbed it through her wet folds. Rose moaned and tried to thrust back, needing the release that he had been withholding from her.

"Please, Clay," she begged.

"Please, Sir," he reminded.

"Sir, I need to come," she cried.

"Fuck," Clay heard a man swore and turned to find Rose's very pissed off hulk of a son standing behind him. "What the fuck are you doing to my mother?" Corbin shouted over the hum of the crowd.

"Shit," Clay cursed. He covered Rose's body with his own.

"Oh my God," Rose whispered. "My son is here?"

"Yeah, Honey. I'm so sorry. I didn't know that he's a member here," Clay whispered into her ear. "Could you maybe give her some privacy to slip her dress back on?" he asked Corbin.

"Sure," Corbin said. "And then how about you meet me outside so I can beat the shit out of you?" Corbin turned to make his way back through the crowd. He took the hand of a pretty woman who Clay assumed was his wife, Avalon. He needed to get Rose dressed and grovel for her to forgive him and then he'd face her son.

Clay undid her bindings and found her dress, helping her back into it and shielding her body from the onlookers. "You have to know I didn't know he comes here, Rose. I'm so sorry. I didn't plan any of this."

"Of course you didn't," Rose said. "I'm sorry that he saw me like that but I won't apologize for what we're doing here. Let's go sort this out." Clay followed Rose out of the club and they found Corbin and his wife standing by his pick-up.

"I guess he figured out which truck is mine," Clay grumbled.

"Well, you do have your ranch's logo on the side of your truck," Rose said.

Corbin started for them and Rose stood between him and Clay. "Move Mom," Corbin shouted.

"No," she yelled back. "You will not lay a finger on Clay. This wasn't his fault. I wanted this, Corbin." Her son took a step back from her as if Rose slapped him.

"You wanted this?" he yelled. "You wanted to be taken into a BDSM club and have your ass flogged in front of all of those people?" Ava caught up to Corbin and smiled at Rose.

"I'm Ava," she said, nodding to Clay. "I've heard a lot about you, Clay."

"Sorry to have to meet like this," Clay said.

Ava smiled and nodded at Clay and then turned to face her very pissed off husband. "Honey, you're forgetting that I like to be taken to a BDSM club and have you flog my ass. You didn't invent kink," Ava said. "What your mom was doing in there was completely normal and none of your business." God love Ava, she seemed to be the voice of reason when it came to calming Corbin.

"But," Corbin tried to argue. Ava cocked her eyebrow at him and magically silenced him.

"Not our business," she repeated. "It was good to meet you, Clay," Ava said. She pulled Rose in for a quick hug and grabbed Corbin's hand. "Time to head home," Ava insisted. Corbin reluctantly followed his wife back to his SUV and slid into the driver's seat after helping her into the vehicle. He never took his eyes off Clay and if looks could kill, he'd be dead a few times over.

"Well, that was a shit show," Clay whispered.

"I'm sorry," Rose said. "Are we good?"

"I should be the one asking you that, Honey," Clay said. He wrapped an arm around Rose and walked her to his truck.

"We're good," she promised. "Now, take me home and finish what you started," she said.

"You sure?" Clay questioned. "We can just call it a night if you'd rather."

"Nope," Rose said, smiling up at him. "I'd like to see how close you can get to working me up to use my safe word." Clay chuckled and started his truck.

"Well, all right then," he said.

ROSE

The next morning, Rose headed into the office early hoping to avoid another scene with Corbin. Unfortunately, he and Aiden were both waiting for her at her desk.

"Well, you two are early birds this morning. Everything all right?" Rose wasn't going to bring up the club unless Corbin did first. As far as she was concerned, that was behind them and didn't need to be rehashed.

"You're here awfully early yourself," Aiden taunted. She could tell from the shit-eating grin he wore that Corbin had filled him in already. "Especially after the eventful night you had last night."

"Oh—" Rose looked between Aiden and Corbin as if daring either of them to call her out for being at the club. "What events are you referring to, Aiden?" she questioned already knowing the answer.

"Cut the shit, Mom," Corbin growled. "You know exactly what he's talking about. What the fuck were you thinking?"

"I was thinking that I wanted a fun night out with a man that I care deeply for. I'm also thinking that what I do with my time and whom I do it with is none of your damn business," she shouted, pointing her finger into her son's massive chest. "We've already been over this, Corbin."

Aiden chuckled and shook his head. "What so funny?" Rose asked.

"You and your caveman son," Aiden said. "And, for the record, you are correct—it's none of our business but you have to understand that Corbin and I both go there with the girls. Our wives are both into kink," Aiden said, bobbing his eyebrows at her. Rose made a disgusted sound in the back of her throat.

"See, now you know how I feel," Corbin chimed in. "I had to see parts of you that I didn't ever want to see, Mom."

"Oh, don't be so dramatic, Corbin," Rose chided. "You'll be fine. You have plenty of money—why not go see a therapist and tell him how your mother failed you."

"Now who's being dramatic, Mother?" Corbin asked.

"Before this gets into a shouting match and takes up the rest of our already busy day," Aiden said. "How about we work out a schedule, so this doesn't happen again?"

"A schedule?" Rose asked.

"Yes," Aiden said. "Corbin and I have worked out a schedule for when we can go to the club so Ava and Zara don't have to feel embarrassed if the other just happens to pop up—like what happened with you and Lug Head here." Corbin shot daggers at Aiden and Rose quickly piped up.

"A schedule sounds perfect," she said. "What nights do you guys have?"

"I have Tuesdays with Zara. It's a standing date and we have a regular babysitter that watches the kids," Aiden said.

"Ava and I take Saturdays. It's the only day that neither of us is crazy with work," Corbin said.

"Um, okay," Rose tried to think of Clay's schedule. "How about if I take Fridays?" she asked.

"Sounds good," Aiden agreed. "See this wasn't so hard."

"Fine," Corbin grumbled. "And it was easy for you because you didn't have to see mom naked, strapped to the cross, and getting her ass flogged."

"Not cool, Man. Now I won't be able to shake that image from my brain. Not cool at all," Aiden mumbled as he made his way to his office.

"We good?" Rose asked her son.

"Yep," he said. Rose noticed how he refused to look her in the eyes and worried that he had just lied to her. "No," he corrected. "But we will be. I just need a little time and space, Mom." Rose nodded. That wasn't going to be a problem for her because honestly, she felt the same way. Corbin walked back to his office and shut the door and Rose slunk into her office chair. She was exhausted and it was only eight in the morning. Yeah, it was going to be a hell of a long day.

❄

It had been a day since their incredibly awkward conversation about her son finding her in the club. Rose had laid low and Corbin seemed to forget the whole thing. At least, that was what she was hoping. Tonight, they were going to meet up with Corbin's biological father and she could tell he was nervous about the meeting. He had spent most of his day locked away in his office while Aiden and Rose attended meeting after meeting, putting out small fires as they popped up.

They drove in complete silence to the meeting and when they got to the restaurant, Corbin grabbed her hand and squeezed it; a telltale sign that her son was just as nervous about this dinner meeting with her ex as she was.

"We'll be fine," she whispered. Honestly, she worried that it was a total lie. Nothing about seeing the man who left her pregnant and alone to raise her son felt "fine" to her. She promised Corbin that she'd be by his side for the meeting and that was exactly what she planned to do.

Clay had offered to join them but that would be the last thing her son would want. He had promised to give Clay a chance but they were still taking baby steps in their relationship. Plus, she didn't want Clay to be tainted by the bad choices of her past. Corbin's biological father was one of her worst choices. The only good thing that came out of their relationship was her son. She needed to remember that when she looked into her ex's eyes and felt only contempt.

They got into the little Italian restaurant that she knew was her son's favorite and she looked around, trying to see if she could spot Brock after all these years. He was sitting in a corner booth in a dark corner and stood to wave them over as soon as he saw them.

"He's over there," Rose whispered to her son. She had forgotten how much Corbin resembled his father. He got his size from Brock and his good looks. She remembered just how much she wanted to be with him when she was younger but now, when she looked him over, all Rose felt was sadness. Not for herself. More for her son who had to miss out on having a father in his life. She tried to fill the voids for him but a boy needed a male influence no matter how good she got at throwing a baseball.

"Rose," Brock said. He looked unsure of what to do next. She could tell that he wanted to hug her but that was unacceptable.

"Brock," she said. Rose nodded at him and crossed her arms over her chest, letting him know in no uncertain terms that touching her was not an option. "This is my son, Corbin," she said. Sure, she was hitting a little below the belt, introducing him that way but she didn't care.

"Corbin," Brock said, holding out his hand. Corbin shook his hand and nodded.

"Good to meet you," he said. Corbin ushered her into the opposite side of the booth from where her ex was sitting and slid in next to her.

"This is a nice little place," Brock said. Rose could tell he was trying to break the ice but exchanging pleasantries wasn't why they were there.

"Why did you ask to meet with us, Brock?" she asked, getting right down to business.

"Yes, I guess we'll just get right to it then," Brock breathed. "I wanted to meet my son." He simply said it as if that would explain everything after all these years.

"Well, that explains everything," Rose grumbled. "You just woke up one day and decided it was time? He's thirty-three years old, Brock. It wasn't time to meet him when he was born? How about when he was ten and had to have his appendix out and was scared to death. Maybe when he graduated from high school or college—wouldn't that have been the right time? Instead, you waited until he was grown and had a multi-billion dollar company under his belt and then you crawl out from whatever rock you were hiding under."

"Mom," Corbin whispered.

"Maybe this was a mistake," Brock said. "I shouldn't have asked you to join us."

"She's the only reason I'm here," Corbin said. "If my mother didn't agree to come with me, this meeting wouldn't be happening. So, I'll ask you one last time before we leave. Why did you want to see us?" Corbin stared Brock down and Rose had never felt prouder of her son.

Brock heaved out a sigh and shook his head. "I have cancer," he said. "I'm dying."

Corbin sat back in the booth and looked Brock over. "You look pretty healthy to me," he countered.

"I've been doing my chemo but the doctors said that this period of feeling good won't last," Brock said. "Unless I can get a bone marrow transplant, I won't make it another six months."

Rose barked out her laugh. "Ah—now we're getting somewhere. You wanted to meet your biological son to see if you two are a match. Am I getting it right, Brock?"

"No," he protested. "I wanted to meet him to tell him that I don't have long to live."

"Then why bring up the whole bone marrow topic," Rose challenged.

"Because it's the truth. A bone marrow donor match is the only way I'll beat this thing," Brock admitted.

"And you think I'll be a match?" Corbin asked. Rose hated that her son was being put in this situation. He had such a big heart; Corbin would go out of his way to help just about anyone if it were within his power. She just hoped he didn't overlook the big picture in his hurry to help a man who probably wouldn't return the favor if the shoe were on the other foot.

"The doctors told me that a blood relative would be my best match. My younger kids weren't matches. You or your son might be though," Brock said.

"No fucking way are you taking anything from my son," Corbin said. He stood and pulled Rose with him out of the booth. "I'll get tested but my son will not be. If I'm a match, I'll donate bone marrow to you. But that's it. You won't contact my mother or me again—ever."

"But," Brock stuttered. He stood and Corbin towered over him.

"But nothing, Brock," he shouted. "There is no room for argument. You didn't come here looking for a relationship with me or to ask forgiveness from the woman you walked away from. What type of man walks away from the woman carrying his child? As a father now myself, I can tell you that's a pretty unforgivable offense. You don't deserve anything from me but I wouldn't be able to live with the fact that I didn't at least get tested. So, I will. But that's where this ends. Take it or leave it." Rose wrapped her arm around Corbin worried that if Brock said the wrong thing, her son would do what she so desperately wanted to and punch the asshole.

"I'll take it," Brock said. He sat back down in the booth and

Corbin didn't say another word. He nodded and turned to leave.

"My attorney will be in touch with the results," Corbin said over his shoulder. "If you have any questions, you can go through my team. We won't be meeting again face to face—ever." He held the door open for Rose and she walked out into the parking lot, blinking against the sun.

"I'm sorry, Son," she whispered, taking Corbin's offered hand.

"Not your fault, Mom," he said. "We're better off without him."

"You can say that now because you don't know what your life could have been like if he had stuck around. You missed out on a father who would have taken you to little league games, taught you to ride a bike, thrown the football with you, and taught you about girls," Rose said.

"Yeah, I did miss out on a father who wanted to teach me those things but I had you, Mom. You did all those things with me. You taught me how to throw a knuckleball and swing a bat. You were the one who taught me how to slow dance with a girl for my seventh-grade dance, so I wouldn't fuck things up too bad. You were the one who sat in the stadium every Friday night during high school to cheer me on when I played football. I've never thanked you for all of that," Corbin said. He opened the car door for her and she slid into her seat, happy for the reprieve as Corbin rounded the front of the car and got into the driver's seat. Rose fought to keep her tears at bay, not wanting to let the emotions of the day overcome her but each passing moment was proving harder and harder to do that.

"Shit, Mom—don't cry," Corbin groaned as she wiped her hot tears from her face.

"It's been a long week," Rose defended. "And, hearing you say nice things was just—well, it was just nice. But son, don't shut Brock out of your life just to spare my feelings. If you want to have a relationship with him, don't let my feelings towards him dissuade you."

Corbin reached across the center console and took her hand into his. "I've made my decision, Mom. It was my own and I won't be changing my mind. I appreciate what you said, though. I'll get tested and then we'll go from there. But, I won't let that man into my life or my son's life. He's just not worth it. Besides, Brody already has the best fucking grandma in the world, what more could the kid want?" Corbin teased.

"I can still throw a mean knuckleball and I'm an excellent cheerleader. Thanks, Son," Rose said.

"Anytime, Mom. Now, let's get something to eat, I'm starving. That was the worst dinner meeting I've ever had." Rose checked her watch and nodded.

"Let me text Clay and tell him that I'm staying at my townhome tonight. I have a feeling he'll be in bed by the time I finally get back to the ranch and I could use a night to myself to decompress," she said.

Corbin chuckled and started his car. "Just as long as he doesn't think I'm the one keeping you from him. I'm trying to make up for my bad behavior."

"Yeah, that's probably a good idea—you are on thin ice, Corbin," she teased.

ROSE

Two Weeks Later

Rose sat down at Clay's big mahogany desk. His whole office was so masculine from the trophy antlers and stuffed deer heads adorning the wood-paneled wall down to the fishing gear he kept stowed in the corner. Of course, her favorite piece in the room was the riding saddle that he perched in the corner on the coffee table. Clay had originally kept the saddle in his playroom but moved it to his office when he had the St. Andrews cross installed, giving them more room to play. She loved that saddle and everything Clay had done to her while she straddled it their second night together. She smiled and shook her head at the way she felt her whole body blush at just the memory of him commanding her every need.

Clay had gone out to the main barn to check on a horse who was foaling and if she hurried she could get Aiden his contracts before the pony was born. Rose wanted to see the little guy enter the world. For a city girl, she was finding every nuance of the ranch fascinating. Clay told her she'd be an old farm hand before long, but she wasn't sure she'd ever get used to life on his ranch.

Rose opened Clay's laptop that he let her borrow and typed in the password he had shared with her. A cute picture of him and Paisley popped up on his main screen that made her smile. Rose hoped that at some point Clay's teenage daughter wouldn't seem to hate her so much. She understood how the girl felt. She was just thirteen years old and a part of her probably lived under the deluded fantasy that her parents would get back together.

Abilene seemed to be warming up to her—slowly. Rose couldn't see her and Clay getting back together. He had told her time and again that he and his ex-wife were just friends determined to make the whole co-parenting thing work for Paisley's sake. Abi was finally letting Clay have some time with Paisley and a part of Rose felt guilty every time the teen stared her down when Clay and Abi handed her off. It was crazy that Paisley blamed Rose for her parents split, especially since they had been divorced for almost five years now. She hadn't been a teenager for a damn long time but she could remember the hormones she had to deal with daily and she worried that her relationship with Paisley might never improve. Teen girls were irrational and emotional and that was the case on their best days.

Rose's phone chimed and she pulled it from her pocket but was sure she knew exactly who it was. Aiden was almost as impatient as Corbin; especially when it came to business contracts. "Yes, Aiden," she answered.

"Were you able to find a laptop?" he asked. "If not, I'd be happy to send yours over via courier." Rose was regretting leaving her laptop at work for her week "off". She had finally decided to take some much-needed vacation days and spend them with Clay around his ranch. In a grand gesture, she told the boys that she was leaving her laptop in her desk, locking the drawer, and throwing away the key. Her freedom lasted all of one day before Aiden was calling her and begging her to help him find some files. When she asked him if they could wait until next week he just about had a meltdown.

"I'm not sure if I should find your offer sweet and charming or bossy and overbearing," Rose teased him. "I love you like you're my son, Aiden. You know how I feel about you but if you don't give me a little faith, my feelings will be hurt."

"You didn't answer my question," he said. "Do you need me to send your laptop to you?"

"No," she breathed. "Clay is letting me borrow his."

"So, I can expect my files?" Aiden asked.

"Yes, Aiden," she moaned. "I'm working on them now. You know what would help me get them to you faster?" she asked.

"Name it," he said.

"You are leaving me alone to do my job and quit micromanaging me. I am, after all, on vacation," Rose chided.

Aiden chuckled into the other end of the phone and she knew that asking Aiden to back off was like asking a cheetah to change its spots. Relaxing and letting someone else take some of his load wasn't in his wheelhouse.

"I'll be here in my office watching for the files to come through, Rose," he said. "Talk soon." He ended his call and she shook her head at her cell phone.

"Bossy," she whispered, returning her attention to Clay's laptop. Rose logged into the companies secure website and pulled up her files. This deal was going to be huge for the company and Corbin and Aiden had been on edge for months now. She was looking forward to the deal being done and the contracts signed. They would all be able to breathe a little easier once this deal was behind them. Rose attached the contracts onto an email and hit send, smiling from ear to ear like a loon.

"Done," she said. "Now, time for some wine." She planned on making Clay her famous buttered chicken for dinner and then she was hoping he'd take her to his playroom for some fun.

She missed going to the club with him but a promise was a promise. Corbin made her swear on her grandson's life that she'd not show her face in the club he and his wife frequented unless it was her appointed night. Clay had been working so many long hours around the ranch that asking him to take her to the club on a Friday evening, after he had worked all day, didn't seem fair. Still, it was an easy promise to keep once Clay took her to her favorite room in the house. His secret playroom was equipped for more pleasure than she could handle.

Rose logged out of the company's website and was just about to turn off Clay's laptop when a private message popped up on the screen. She was going to downsize it until she read who it was sent by—Clay's ex-wife Abilene. Rose wondered why she wouldn't just contact him by his cell and worried that Clay wasn't getting his messages out in the barn. Abi had Paisley and Rose worried that something might have happened and she'd need to get the message to Clay. Plus, there was that small part of her that was curious about the message. She trusted Clay completely but she was only human and as her son liked to point out—nosey.

Rose sat back in Clay's big leather office chair and studied the computer screen. "Shit," she whispered to herself. "I really shouldn't do this," she huffed. Rose ran her finger over the keyboard and opened the message; sitting forward to read Abi's PM.

Hey—we still on for Saturday night? I can't wait to see you again. Honestly, last Tuesday was one of the best nights of my life. Don't worry, I will keep this our little secret until you can figure out how to get rid of Rose.

Rose read the message four more times, trying to figure out what it meant exactly. Clay was seeing his ex? That just couldn't be. Rose pulled her cell phone from her pocket and scrolled through her apps, trying to find her calendar with her shaky fingers. She wiped the hot tears that were freely falling down her cheeks and pulled up her schedule from last Tuesday. She and Clay had spent almost every evening together since they met. Hell, she was beginning to forget what her little townhome even looked like since they usually stayed at his ranch. It was easier that way with his early mornings and late nights. Rose had even accepted his offer of moving in with him so why would he start seeing his ex-wife again?

She looked over the entire day from last Tuesday, remembering each hour as if it had just happened yesterday. They had meeting after meeting at work that day and then she and Corbin met her ex for their dinner meeting. It turned out to be a late-night and rather than driving back out to the ranch and waking Clay, she spent the night at her townhouse. That night she realized that missing Clay sucked and it wasn't something she wanted to do often.

The fact remained, he could have spent the night with his ex-wife and Rose would have never known. The question was, would Clay do that to her? He told her he was falling for her but they hadn't given each other the words. There were no grand sweeping declarations of love made yet, although he did ask her to move in with him. He was a free man and ten years her junior. If he was seeing his ex, she wanted to know. It was going to hurt like hell to walk away from him but she'd never been with a man who could sneak around behind her back and cheat on her. Clay had her heart, whether he knew that fact or not but Rose still had a death grip on her pride—for now.

Rose closed the laptop and neatly tucked everything back into place, sliding his office chair back under his desk. She turned off the lights to his office and padded to the kitchen. She'd wait for him to come back from the barn and then she'd confront him about Abi's message. She looked around the spacious room and sobbed at the thought of confronting him. Rose wasn't a coward but having to face the man she loved and ask him such a darkly disturbing question scared the crap out of her. She ran through the scenarios of what she'd say and how she would respond to his denials. Rose even considered finding the bottle of wine she had been saving for their dinner but thought twice about drinking before their conversation.

Fifteen minutes passed and it felt as if it had been hours. With every passing minute, Rose's nerve deteriorated and she felt the strength she prided herself for, slowly slipping away. She found her purse and her car keys, deciding that what she needed was time to think and she couldn't do that at Clay's ranch. She needed to be at her townhome, in her own space, so she could get her head on straight. Then, she'd find a way to face Clay when she was stronger and calmer.

Rose was just about to her car when Clay rounded the corner into the garage. He parked his truck in its bay and looked over at her. He jumped down out of the cab of his pick-up and started towards her. Rose could see that he was confused and why wouldn't he be? They had plans tonight. She was going to make them a nice dinner but Rose couldn't think about any of that now. Self-perseverance kicked in and she quickly hopped into the driver's seat of the car and turned on the engine. She chanced one last look over at Clay and instantly regretted it. He was shouting her name and before he could run over to her car, she pulled out of the garage. Rose didn't bother to look back again—she knew what she'd find—him staring back at her and that would be more than she could take. Clay's disappointment was going to tear her heart out and she needed to keep it together long enough to get back to her place. Then, Rose could fall apart and figure out how to pick up the pieces and put herself back together again. That's how she raised her son and Aiden on her own. It's who she was and what she did—broken heart be damned.

CLAYTON

Clay watched as Rose sped out of his garage and down the long drive that led away from him. Where the hell was she running to? They were supposed to have a nice romantic dinner together. He had planned on taking her to his playroom and introducing her to a few new toys he had gotten for her. Then, he planned on telling Rose that he was more than falling for her. He had fallen in love with her and it was about time he gave her the words that were always on the tip of his tongue every time she gave him her submission and the gift of her body. She was so perfect for him and it was past damn time that he told her that.

Clay had waited so long to find someone who wanted the same things he did. He struggled with his dominance, worried that he'd never find a woman who'd want him for who he truly was. His ex-wife never liked his dominant nature. Hell, it's what ended up destroying their marriage. He spent countless nights at the club, sating himself with women who tried to be what he needed but they only got a glimpse of who he was. He was too demanding and ended up scaring off most of the women who promised to be his perfect playmate.

He looked through the house for any sign of what had spooked Rose enough to make her run away as she had. The kitchen was spotless and there were no signs of her making dinner. Maybe she had decided to order out and was just going to pick it up but that wouldn't explain the pain he saw in her eyes when she looked at him.

"This is ridiculous," he breathed. Clay pulled his cell phone from his jeans and tried to call Rose. If she was upset about something he needed to know what it was so he could fix it. His call went straight to voicemail and he cursed under his breath. Rose's cheery voice prompted him to leave her a message and by the time the beep sounded, he was about ready to get back into his damn truck and go looking for her.

"Rose," he growled. "Where the fuck are you?" Clay took a deep breath, trying to reign in his anger. "Listen, just call me and let me know that you are okay. Talk to me, tell me what's wrong. Whatever it is, we'll figure it out together but don't shut me out." Clay ended the call and tossed his cell onto the kitchen counter.

He tried to remember what Rose had planned to do before he left for the barn. She had asked him if she could use his laptop and he, of course, told her yes. Clay walked back through the house to his office and found it just like he found the kitchen—everything in its place and neat as a pin. He flicked on the lights and looked around, walking over to sit behind his desk. He opened his laptop and waited for it to boot up. As soon as it did, he saw that he had a private message from Abi and he wondered why she hadn't just called his cell. He opened the message worried that something was wrong with Paisley and his service was down while he was down in the barn.

He read and re-read the message a least a half dozen times, trying to figure out what his ex's message meant. Maybe she had sent it by mistake. She was seeing some guy, at least that was what Paisley had told her. Maybe Abi sent Clay the message instead of her new boyfriend.

"Shit," he mumbled. "She must have read this." That would explain why Rose sped out of there like her ass was on fire. It would also explain the eye daggers she was shooting him on her way out. The only way he was going to work this out with Rose was to figure out why Abi had sent him the message in the first place.

He walked back to the kitchen to find his cell. He pulled up Abi's number and called her. She answered on the third ring. "Clay," she said.

"Abi," he returned. Their relationship had always remained cordial, but she was always short and to the point with him. "Want to tell me what your message was all about?" His question sounded more like an acquisition and he took a breath and let it out, releasing some of his pent up anger. "Sorry," he said. "I'm just a little on edge."

"No problem." Abi let the silence fill the call and he worried she wasn't going to answer his question. "Um, what message? I just looked through my texts with you and I haven't sent you any new messages."

"It wasn't through text. It came through on my computer as a private message," he said. "Hold on." Clay went back to his office and opened his laptop. As soon as it booted up he copied and pasted the message to send back to Abi. "I just texted you the message you sent me."

Again, there was silence on Abi's end, and he felt like he was holding his damn breath. He needed answers. Hell, he needed to find Rose and tell her that Abi's message wasn't real. He needed to tell her he'd never cheat on her. He was in love with Rose and planned on spending the rest of his life with her but he didn't tell her that. Instead, he was taking things slow and letting her get used to the newness of their relationship. It's what she had asked him for and instead of following his gut instincts, he allowed her to set the pace. Sure, it had only been two months since they met at the bar, on their birthdays, but it had felt like a lifetime that he had known Rose.

"What the hell?" Abi breathed. "I didn't send this to you, Clay."

"Well, whoever you were trying to send it to never got it, Abi and it's messed things up with Rose and me," he said.

"I didn't send this message at all, Clay. Not to you or anyone else. But, I have a sneaky feeling I know who did. Paisley was using my laptop tonight. She said that she left her charger at your place and her battery died. I think our daughter intended for Rose to find that message. I'm sorry, Clay. I know she's become important to you."

"Fuck," he swore. "I'm in love with Rose," he whispered. "Why would Paisley do this? I know she isn't Rose's biggest fan but to hurt her like this is just plain mean. Put her on the phone," he ordered. "I want to talk to her."

Abi barked out her laugh. "You think that yelling at our thirteen-year-old daughter is going to make things any better, Clay? How about I sit her down and try to figure this out and you work things out with Rose. Then, we can all sit down and get to the bottom of why Paisley is acting out like this."

Abi was right—shouting at Paisley would get him nowhere. All he wanted to do was find Rose and explain that he would never cheat on her and that this whole thing was the evil plan of one very grounded thirteen-year-old girl.

"Fine," he agreed. "But she's grounded."

"Agreed," Abi said. "And Clay—good luck with Rose. I know I acted like an ass when I first met her, but I hope everything works out between the two of you. I'm happy that you've found someone." Abi ended the call.

"Thanks," Clay whispered. "Me too."

❇

Clay spent the better part of the night trying to track down Rose. He went by her townhome and pounded on her door only to have it answered by her very angry hulk of a son. Corbin wasn't too happy to see him and from the look in his eyes, about ready to tear him apart.

Clay held up his hands, "Before you go and do something you might regret," he warned.

"Oh, I won't regret a single second of pounding you into a pulp for hurting my mother, Clay," Corbin said.

"I didn't do anything to hurt Rose," Clay defended. "The message was a fake."

"Bullshit," Corbin accused. "You were double-timing my mother and now, you are covering your tracks to save your sorry ass." Corbin was a scary site angry but Clay wouldn't back down, not even if the guy didn't believe him. What did he have to lose if Rose wouldn't give him a second chance?

"It was from my daughter, Paisley," Clay said.

"Your daughter?" Corbin questioned. "I thought the message was from your ex-wife."

"You know that my thirteen-year-old daughter doesn't much care for me seeing your mom," Clay admitted. "My ex didn't send me that message—my teenage daughter did. I'm betting she was hoping that Rose would see it and take off."

"Well, mission accomplished," Corbin said. "My mother doesn't want to see you, Clay. Do you have any idea how badly seeing that message hurt her?"

"Is she all right?" Clay asked. God, the thought of Rose hurting just about tore his damn heart out. "Is she here? I just want to explain."

"I think it would be best for you to give her some time, man," Corbin said. "Let her decide for herself if she thinks you're worth all of this trouble."

"Trouble?" Clay asked. "What the fuck does that mean?" He took a step towards Corbin, going toe to toe with the big guy.

He wouldn't back down from whatever threat Corbin posed—Rose wasn't someone he was willing to let go of.

"It means that you've upset my mother and I won't allow you to do it again," Corbin growled.

"And I told you that message was a fake. I would never hurt your mother," Clay challenged.

"What's stopping your daughter from doing something like this again? What's stopping her from hurting my mother?" Corbin made a good point. Clay couldn't stop Paisley from going after Rose again to hurt her. Sure, this time it was words that did the damage but what would stop her from taking things to the next level? He and Abi were going to have their work cut out with her but he'd make sure Paisley didn't hurt Rose ever again.

"My ex and I are going to have to work through this with our daughter. I won't stand for Paisley hurting Rose again—ever. You just need to believe that," Clay begged.

"I don't need to believe anything, Clay," Corbin said. "My mother's off-limits."

"I appreciate you wanting to protect your mom, Corbin. But, I need the chance to explain what happened. I need to tell her that I've fallen in love with her," Clay almost whispered. He couldn't believe that he was standing on Rose's front porch telling her grown son that he was in love with her. He pictured saying those words out loud going so differently. Sharing his feelings with Corbin wasn't part of that picture. Clay watched as Corbin ducked his head back behind the door. He could hear him whispering, or what he assumed was Corbin's attempt at a whisper. The man honestly had one volume.

"Hold on," Corbin said. He shut the door but Clay could still hear Corbin's voice and who he assumed to be Rose's voice on the other side of the door. After a few minutes of what sounded like a heated debate, Rose opened the door, Corbin standing behind her. Judging from the angry expression he wore; he had lost the fight and reluctantly gave Rose her way.

"Rose," Clay said. She had fresh tears in her eyes and Clay hated that he was the person who made her cry. If it had been someone else who made Rose cry, he'd want to tear that person apart.

"Clay," she whispered, raising her chin defiantly.

"I'm so sorry," he said. "Paisley sent that message, not Abi. Nothing is going on with us. Hell, there's no one else—just you. Tell me you believe me, Rose," he begged.

She held up her hand, stopping him from saying another word, and Clay worried she was going to tell him to leave. "What did you just tell Corbin?" she asked.

"Corbin?" he asked. Clay thought back over what he and Corbin had just discussed and when he realized what she was asking, he couldn't hide his smile.

"Oh, you mean that I love you?" Clay asked. Rose sobbed and covered her mouth with her shaking hand.

"Yeah," she said. "That."

"I do, Rose. I have since the first night I met you. I just needed to get up the nerve to tell you." Clay looked over Rose's shoulder to where Corbin stood, still listening to their private conversation. "Mind giving us a few minutes?" Clay asked.

Corbin shook his head, "That's up to my mom," he said.

"I'm fine, Corbin," Rose said. "Maybe just go to the kitchen and make a snack or something."

"All right," Corbin grumbled. "But, there better be ice cream in your freezer."

Rose waited until her son had disappeared to the back of her house and turned back to face Clay down. "I can't do this," she whispered. "Not now."

"If you want to talk privately, we can go back to my ranch," he offered.

"This has nothing to do with Corbin being here or our lack of privacy. I can't do this at all, Clay."

"Wait, what?" he asked. Here he had just poured out his heart and soul for the woman he loved and she wasn't giving him an inch. "Please, believe me, Rose. I haven't been cheating on you with Abi or anyone else for that matter."

"I do believe that Clay. At first, I had my doubts. You and Abi have a history and a child together. That's a pretty strong bond and I believed you might want another chance at being a family with her. But, I believe that Paisley was the one who sent the email. Your daughter doesn't like me much and that's why this won't work. If I'm in your life it will drive a wedge between you and Paisley. I can't do that to you or her. She needs her father and you need to be there for her to help her through whatever is bothering her."

"No," Clay breathed. "We can all sit down and work this out," he offered. Abi had offered to do just that tomorrow and he was hopeful that they'd be able to come to some truce that would help heal the rift between Paisley and Rose. He wouldn't give up the woman he loved just because his teenage daughter was being a brat.

"Sitting down with Paisley is a good idea," Rose said. Clay took a deep breath and let it out.

"I'm so glad to hear you say that, Honey," Clay said.

"Paisley needs you and Abi to lay down some rules but she also needs your understanding and unconditional love. If I'm in your life, she'll never believe you are giving her either of those things. Go be with your family." Rose turned to shut the door in his face and he stuck his boot-clad foot in the way.

"You're my family, Rose. Don't shut me out," he begged.

"I'm sorry, Clay. This is for the best, really," she said. Rose looked down to where his boot was still holding her door open and back up at him as if expecting him to just comply.

"This isn't over, Rose. I won't give up on you—on us. I'll let you hide away tonight but I'll be back. I love you," he said and pulled his foot free from her door jam. Rose gently shut the door, closing him out and putting up her walls. He wouldn't let her hide for long though. He meant it when he said he'd be back. He planned on spending every waking minute trying to convince Rose that they are made for each other, even if she couldn't see it for herself right now.

ROSE

Rose spent the better part of a week dodging Clay's calls and pretending not to be in her townhome every morning he came over banging on her door, demanding to talk to her. He had even shown up at the office and she had security show him back out. Corbin and Aiden joked that she was abusing her power and authority as their mom and personal assistant. Maybe they were both right but she didn't care. She wasn't ready to face down Clay yet because if she did, she'd give in to everything he wanted from her. She'd spill her guts and tell him she was in love with him too and that would ruin his relationship with his daughter.

Clay had texted that he and Abi had sat Paisley down and talked with her about what she had done. Rose couldn't blame the girl. She wanted her parents to get back together and thought that if Rose was out of the picture, they'd have the chance of rekindling their marriage. Clay's message said that he and Abi explained that would never happen. They had been divorced for so long now, getting back together wasn't something that either of them wanted.

Besides his recap of his discussion with Paisley and Abi, he had messaged her daily begging her to give him another chance. He told her all the things she so desperately wanted to hear and believe but words weren't enough. Words wouldn't fix his daughter's hating her. That would take time and she wasn't a spring chicken. What she and Clay had was very real but giving in to what they both needed wouldn't fix their problems. She couldn't give him anymore—she just didn't have it in her, even if she was completely in love with him.

Rose hurried into Aiden's office and sat down in front of his big desk. Today was the big day they had all been working so hard for. If everything went well, they'd close the biggest deal their company ever had. Corbin and Aiden were about crazy with all the last minute details and she couldn't get her head out of her ass and stop thinking so much about Clay.

Aiden looked up from the pile of papers he was studying and nodded. "Rose," he said. "Thanks for putting in so much overtime. You know that Corbin and I would be lost without you, right?" She smiled and nodded. He wasn't wrong. Aiden was in his second year of office as a Senator and she knew that he had very little time for the company but he made this project his baby and there was no keeping him away from closing the deal.

"How does Zara feel about you spending so much time at the office?" she asked. Rose knew first-hand that Zara was done with the whole "I have to work late" thing. "And the girls must miss you too," Rose added for good measure.

Aiden looked up at her again and smirked. "You know damn well that my wife isn't very happy with me right now. She hasn't been in for lunch all week. I think it's her way of punishing me." Aiden's famous lunches with his wife usually ended up with them both naked in his locked office and Rose trying to pretend she didn't hear Zara's pleas for Aiden to "not stop". Even Corbin noticed the lack of lunch meetings between Zara and Aiden and her son brought the topic up every chance he got to ride Aiden's ass and piss him off. It was nice the way her two boys loved each other more like brothers than best friends. But, that meant they fought like brothers too and this week, with the tensions riding so high about this deal, there was a whole lot of fighting going on in the office.

"I promised to take her and the girls on a family vacation as soon as this deal is finished and I have to head to Washington, DC for this year's session," Aiden said.

"Oh—that sounds great," Rose said. "Where are you guys going?"

Aiden sighed, "Disney—again. But, I'm hoping that a few days there will make the girls happy and then we can head to our beach house." Aiden had a few homes around the country, as did Corbin. Rose had a little condo on the coast but she didn't see the need for a fancy beach house like the boys had. If she wanted to spend a day at the beach with her grandchildren, she could go to their home and that left her condo as her place to sit back and relax.

"Well, you are married to a saint, so I'm sure she'll agree to your plan," Rose teased. Zara was a wonderful woman and she balanced out Aiden's crazy obsessive need for his life to be perfect. She was his chaos and his sanity all rolled up in one person. Clay was that for Rose and she wasn't sure if she'd ever find another person like him to fill that void in her life. She wasn't expecting to find Clay in the first place. She wasn't looking for anyone but once she found him, he seemed to take over the dark crevices of her heart and made them lighter.

"Yeah—Zara's pretty awesome. Especially for putting up with me and my ambitions." Aiden chuckled at his statement. "How are you doing, Rose?"

"Fine," she lied. "I'm good."

"Liar," Aiden accused. "You raised me not to tell lies, Rose. You think that I can't see what's going on with you. You're the closest thing I've ever had to a mom, Rose. I see that you're upset."

"And Corbin told you what happened between Clay and me, right?" she questioned.

Aiden cringed and nodded. "Sorry, but your son can't keep his mouth shut. Hell, if you have a secret you don't want anyone else to know, don't tell Corbin." Aiden was right but it still upset her that her son was spreading the news about her and Clay.

"Crap," Rose groaned. "I wanted to keep this all to myself. You know, work through my problems and not drag everyone else down with me." She was always the one helping everyone around her to pick up the pieces when their lives fell apart. She was the mom in the equation between her, Aiden, and Corbin. Having the tables turned felt plain wrong.

"What are you going to do—you know about Clay?" Aiden asked.

Rose sat back on the sofa and kicked off her heels. "I have no idea," she moaned. "I know what I should do but it doesn't add up to what I want to do."

"What do you think you should do here Rose?" Aiden questioned.

"I think I should let him go. My being in Clay's life will only destroy his relationship with his daughter. Do you remember being thirteen, Aiden?" He nodded and smiled. "I can sure remember you boys at that age. You were so impressionable. I'd never let anyone or anything come between the three of us. How can I stay with him knowing that I'd be hurting that poor girl?"

Aiden chuckled, "That poor girl tried to shove you out of Clay's life by sending a fake message to break the two of you up. I think that 'poor girl' as you call her is going to be just fine if you stay a part of Clay's life. Sure, she'll give you a lot of shit because she is a teenager, but don't let her make your decisions for you."

"I get that, I just hate knowing that whatever decision I make, I'm hurting someone," Rose almost whispered.

"Including yourself," Aiden offered. "You're avoiding the most important point in all this."

"What's that?" she asked.

"Do you love him?" Aiden asked. Rose gasped and covered her mouth to hide her sob. "Oh Rose," Aiden breathed.

"I know," she cried. "I'm pathetic. I do love him and God, that sounds so silly since I've only known him for a couple of months. What am I going to do?" she asked.

Aiden stood and rounded his desk, pulling Rose up from her perch on his sofa and into a bear hug. She smiled and wrapped her arms around him.

"Isn't this supposed to be my job?" she questioned. "You know, comforting you?"

"Sometimes it's all right to let other people take care of you, Rose. I know you don't like us to make a fuss but get over it. I won't pretend to have the answer you need. Don't you think it's time to be happy for yourself? Isn't it about time that you do something for you and stop overthinking everything? Just be happy Rose." Aiden let her go and she wiped at the tears that fell down her face.

"Thanks, Aiden," she said. "Now, I'm going to go to the ladies' room to fix my makeup. You good for the meeting?"

"Yep," he said. "Corbin and I have everything we need. We've got this if you want to knock off a little early," Aiden offered. Rose didn't hide her smile. He knew her too well.

"I would like that," she said. "I think I need to go have a talk with a certain cowboy."

Aiden chuckled, "Good luck," he said.

"You'll tell Corbin for me?" she questioned. Aiden made a face and she giggled.

"Fuck no," he grumbled. "You can do that yourself. I'm not sure who's going to give you more trouble in all of this—the teenage girl or Corbin."

"Well, crap," Rose mumbled. Aiden laughed again and walked her out of his office. She decided to deal with her son later, sneaking off to the ladies' room before he came out of his office. Sure, she was being a coward but she could only deal with one crisis at a time. First, she needed to find Clay and see if he wanted to hear her out. Then, they would need to sit down and figure out what to do about their kids—one problem at a time.

CLAYTON

Clay was trying to stay busy around the ranch but keeping his mind off Rose was nearly impossible for him to do. She was all he could think about. The question was would he be able to persuade her to give him another chance. He had spent the good part of everyday banging on her front door and begging her to just come out and talk to him. He'd gone by her office only to be tossed out on his ear. He was starting to feel that she wasn't ever going to let him back into her life but that wasn't something he could just accept. He needed Rose and sooner or later, she'd come to her senses and realize she needed him just as much.

Clay looked at the foal that had been born just over a week ago and smiled. "What should I do boy?" he asked, patting down the baby's side. The foal whinnied, causing Clay to laugh.

"Yeah, I got it—go talk to her. But what if Rose doesn't listen?" Clay asked.

"Maybe she's ready to give listening a shot," Rose said, standing in the side doorway to the barn.

"Rose," he said, backing away from the pen he had just mucked out. "You're here," he said. Clay was never one to feel tongue-tied but right now, staring down the woman he loved, he was having a hard time coming up with the right words to say.

"I am," she said, a sassy smirk firmly in place. "I'm glad to find you here too."

"I was just finishing up for the night and then I was going to come by your place," he admitted. "To pound on your door and beg you to talk to me."

Rose sighed and looked down at the floor. "I'm sorry about that, Clay. I was being a chicken and well, I didn't want to make the wrong decision. I just needed some time." She had taken a little over a week to come to her senses but Clay wouldn't point that out. Rose was here now and that was all that mattered to him. Well, that and if she was going to give him another chance to prove to her that they were made for each other.

"Did your time help?" he asked.

"Yeah," she agreed. "I think it did."

"Did you come all this way to tell me goodbye again, Rose?" he asked. God, he hated that might be the case, but he wanted her to have a voice in their relationship. He knew that was important for Rose. She had given up so much in life he wanted to give her everything. Her submission was a gift but he wouldn't take her decisions from her.

"No," Rose said. "I didn't come here to tell you goodbye, Clay. I came here to tell you that I love you."

Clay pulled the pen door closed and locked it so the foal wouldn't be able to get loose. He was afraid to cross the barn to where Rose stood. He needed to make sure that he had heard her correctly. "Say that again," he demanded.

"I love you," she said. Her smile nearly lit up the entire barn and he didn't hesitate to go to her.

"I love you too, Rose," he said.

She giggled, "I know," she admitted. "I heard you tell Corbin that you loved me when you were at my house last week. So, you still do—love me—that is?"

"I do, Rose. That night, when you left here, I was going to ask you to marry me."

Rose gasped, "I thought you just wanted me to move in with you," she said.

"Well, sure. But that wasn't enough. I didn't want to spook you, so I waited. I just couldn't wait anymore, Rose." Clay stared her down and he felt his damn heart beating like it was going to pound right out of his chest.

"I'm not a horse, Clay. You won't spook me," she said. Clay reached for her and pulled Rose against his body.

"How about you promise not to run off and I promise to try not fucking things up too badly," Clay offered. Rose giggled.

"Not quite how I was going to put it, but deal," she said.

"Good," Clay said. "Then let's get this part over with." He got down on one knee and reached into his coveralls, pulling out the ring box that he had been keeping in his pocket since she left over a week ago.

"Marry me, Rose," he said. "Spend the rest of our lives with me, please." Rose covered her mouth with a shaking hand and gasped.

"Clay," she whispered.

"Is that a yes or a no, Honey?" he asked. He felt like he was holding his damn breath waiting for Rose to give her answer. "Well?"

"Yes," she whispered, nodding, and crying. Clay took the ring from its box and slipped it on her finger, not giving her time to change her mind. He stood from the ground and pulled her up into his arms.

"It's official now," he whispered. "You can't change your mind now—I put a ring on it," he teased. He started walking to his house with her in his arms and Rose protested that he needed to put her down, squealing and giggling along the way. Clay swatted her ass, making her yelp.

"Clay," she shouted. "Put me down."

"Not until we get to the playroom," he said.

"O-Oh," Rose breathed. "We're going to play?"

"Yep," he said. "And I plan on reminding you of all the rules—including the one where you don't run off without talking things through with me."

"That's not one of the rules," Rose challenged.

Clay swatted her ass again and headed down the stairs into the basement of his home. He turned the corner and opened the door to the playroom. "It is now," he said. "You don't like something; you and I talk it through. Otherwise, this thing between us won't work. Got it?" Rose shyly nodded. "I need the words, Honey," he reminded.

"Yes, Clay. I won't run—promise," she agreed. He lowered her down his body, letting her feel every inch of his erection, loving the way she ground herself against him. She was always his little vixen, taking what she wanted from him.

"You are bad," he said, pointing an accusing finger at her.

"You going to punish me, Sir?" she asked.

"Is that what you want, Rose?" he asked. "You want me to punish you for being naughty?"

"Yes, Sir," she breathed, kissing his neck. She gently bit the sensitive skin just under his ear and he swatted her ass.

"Strip and get on the saddle," he ordered. Rose's breath hitched and he gave her fleshy globe another smack, just for good measure.

"You brought it back into the playroom?" she asked.

"Yep, now do as I asked, Rose," he commanded. Rose quickly stripped out of her skirt and blouse, leaving just her thigh highs that made him half-crazy with lust, her skimpy lace thong, and her lacy, see-through bra. God, she was his walking wet dream.

"Fuck, Baby," he whispered. "Stop there. Leave all that on and keep the heels," he ordered. She nodded and reached for his hand so he could help her up onto the saddle. Rose leaned forward, gifting him with the sight of her perfect ass perched and ready for his attention.

"Like this, Sir?" she taunted. Rose knew exactly how he wanted her, and she also knew what her submission did to him. He needed a minute to get his unruly cock under control.

"Yeah," he said. "Just like that, Baby." He smacked her ass, leaving a red mark where his hand had landed. "Flogger or paddle tonight?" he asked. "I'll leave that decision to you."

"Whichever you want, Sir," Rose said. Clay knew she liked the paddle, so he reached for it, and Rose gifted him with her sexy smile as she watched him over her shoulder.

"I take it you approve?" he asked, holding up the paddle for her to inspect.

"Yes, Sir," she admitted. "I love it when you use the paddle on me."

"Thank you for telling me that, Honey." Clay loved the way Rose had learned to share her likes and dislikes with him. It was an important part of their give and take as Dom and sub.

"I'm going to go to twenty-five and I want for you to count for me, Rose," he ordered.

"Yes, Sir," she stuttered. His Rose always was up for a challenge. He rubbed her ass and gave the right cheek the first smack with the paddle. She hissed out her breath and he waited for her to count for him.

"One," she yelped.

He landed a hard whack on the left cheek, and she cried out. "Two," she shouted.

He kept going, rubbing his big hand over her flesh in between blows, to help her ride out the pain. When he got to twelve, Clay dipped two fingers through her wet folds and loved the way she moaned and pushed back against his hand, as if insisting he give her more.

"You love to play, don't you, Honey?" he asked.

"Yes, Clay," she hissed. "I need more," she said. "Please, Sir."

"I'll take good care of you, Honey," Clay promised. He withdrew his fingers from her drenched pussy, and she mewled her protest, causing him to chuckle. He gave her already welted, red ass another smack and she cried out and moaned. Rose kept count and he watched her, so proud of his sub. When he got to twenty-five, Clay dropped the paddle to the tile floor and undid his jeans. His cock was screaming for attention and he could see Rose's arousal coating her thighs. She was more than ready to take him, and he wanted to get into her pussy more than he wanted his next breath.

"This is going to be hard and fast, Honey," he said. Clay pulled her from the saddle and she cuddled against his body. He carried her over to the leather couch he had in the corner of his playroom and laid her down. Rose hissed when her hot flesh hit the cold leather and he wasted no time. Clay drug her body to the edge of the sofa and plunged balls deep inside of her.

"You feel so fucking good," he groaned. He stilled, getting himself under control. He promised her hard and fast, and he wanted to deliver on both counts, not just the fast part. Clay pumped in and out of her body, loving the breathy little moans he elicited from her parted lips. He dipped down to kiss his way into her mouth, letting his tongue playfully meet her own. She wrapped her arms around his neck, demanding more, and Clay could tell that she was close to finding her orgasm.

He snaked his hand down her body and found her clit, giving it a playful tap. Rose moaned into his mouth and when he let the pad of his thumb stroke over her sensitive nub, she lost control, riding his cock like the wild force he had come to love. His Rose, his life, his sub. Her pussy milked his cock with the spasms as she rode out her orgasm. He couldn't help but lose himself inside of her, quickly finding his release.

"I'm so glad you bought me a drink on our birthday," Rose whispered.

"I'm so glad you agreed to come home with me, despite your very long list of dating do's and don'ts," Clay said.

"Well, you showed me that there is more to life than living by the rules, Clayton Nash," Rose teased.

"Naw," he drawled. "I just introduced you to a whole new

set of rules, my little sub." Rose giggled and they tumbled down onto the sofa together, wrapped up in each other's bodies. Clay wasn't sure how he had gotten so lucky finding her. Rose was the perfect woman for him. The partner he never thought he'd find. The woman he was going to spend the rest of his life with —his cougar submissive.

HIS NERDY SUBMISSIVE

TYLER

Tyler Nash walked into the bank and the very last thing he wanted to do was beg, but that's what he was reduced to. He was going to have to beg for a fucking loan to keep his business afloat. He had always dreamed of owning his own ranch, but he wouldn't take the money from his older brother, Clay. He'd offered time and again but that wasn't how he wanted to start things off. No, begging some bank manager who knew nothing about him to give him the cash he needed to buy the land adjacent to his brother's ranch, was so much more reasonable.

He knew that with no collateral and no real money to put up for the down payment, they'd be turning him down flat. Ty was hoping that his lucky plaid shirt and shined-up cowboy boots would sell his whole, "I'm a rancher" vibe.

He walked into the lobby and removed his cowboy hat and got in line to ask for the manager. He waited for his turn with the only teller on duty, and when he finally got up to the counter, she put up the "This window closed," sign up.

"You're kidding me," he whispered under his breath. "Will someone else be coming to take your place?" he called after the teller. She merely shrugged and walked to the back room, closing the door between them. "Great, just great," he mumbled.

"I'm so sorry, Sir," a woman's voice called from the back corner. "We're short-staffed today and it's Candy's break. I can help you back here, in my office," she offered. Clay turned to find the sexy redhead standing back in the doorway to her very small office. The walls were all glass, reminding him of a fishbowl.

"Thanks," he said, walking back to her office. "I appreciate that. I'm inquiring about a business loan, and I'd like to speak with a manager."

"Well, then it's your lucky day," the woman said. She waved him into her office and pointed to one of the very uncomfortable looking chairs that sat in front of her desk. He waited for her to round her desk and find her chair before sitting. It was ingrained in him to be a gentleman and sitting before a lady was something his Mama would have boxed his ears for.

"What can I do for you, Mr.—" She held out her hand to him and waited for him to take it.

"Tyler Nash but you can call me Ty," he offered.

"It's good to meet you, Mr. Nash," she said, stressing his last name. He smiled and nodded. "I'm Lucinda Dixon, this branch's manager. I think I can help you with your request." Ty wanted to laugh at how proper Lucinda Dixon was, but he dug the whole business vibe she was giving off. She had on a tailored gray pinstripe business pantsuit that hugged her every curve. The blazer was covering up an almost see-through white blouse that had just the right number of buttons undone to make his mouth water. He didn't miss her heels which made him just about lose his mind when he watched her cross her legs and swing her foot around playfully. Ty needed to get his head on straight because that wasn't why he was there today. No, he needed to get pretty little Lucinda Dixon to give him a loan.

"Now, what kind of business are you needing the loan for Mr. Nash?" she asked, getting right down to it.

"Right," he said, clearing his throat. "You're not much into small talk, are you Lucy?" he questioned.

She shot him a look that told him she wasn't. "My name is Lucinda and I'd prefer you to call me Ms. Dixon," she said.

Ty chuckled, "All right, sorry," he said. "You know, you look very familiar, Ms. Dixon," he said. She looked him over, her eyes flaring when they reached his again and he knew he was onto something. She knew him, that much was clear. Hell, everyone seemed to know everyone else in their small town. She looked to be a few years younger than him but if he had to guess, she remembered him from high school or something.

"Were you in my class?" he asked. Lucinda put her pen down and looked across her desk at him.

"No," she breathed.

"Right, you are a lot younger than I am, sorry," he offered.

"Not that much younger," she challenged.

"So, we didn't graduate together, but were we at Milford High at the same time?" he asked. She shyly looked down at her laptop and fiddled with some papers on her desk. Ty tried to think back to his high school years, trying to remember a red-headed beauty, and drew a blank. "Did you always have red hair?"

"Yes," she murmured. "If you don't mind, I have a very busy day. Can we continue with your application?"

He wanted to tell her no, but he needed this loan to buy the land before someone else snatched it up. "All right," he agreed. "You know we could speed this up if you just tell me how we know each other."

Lucinda picked up her pen and cleared her throat. "How about you tell me what you plan on using the loan for?"

"Sure," Ty said. "I want to buy land for a ranch."

"I thought that you and Clay ran Lowdown Ranch together?" she asked.

"Now see, you do know me," Ty said, wagging his finger at her accusingly.

Lucinda shrugged and looked back at her laptop. "So, you'll be starting a new business venture aside from the ranch you run with your brother?"

"It will be a separate entity," he agreed. "Did you go to school with my brother?"

"No," she almost shouted. "He's like ten years older than me. Although he was friends with my older brother."

"So, you have a brother that went to school with Clay?" Ty pushed.

"No," she said. "My brother went to school with you. You both graduated from Milford the same year." Now he was getting somewhere. Not knowing how the hell he knew Lucinda was starting to piss him off.

"Wait—your brother is Ford Dixon?" He remembered Ford, they played on the football team together.

"Yes," she said through her clenched teeth. Ty could tell that she wasn't very happy about his questions. "Can we please get on with this?"

"Sure, sorry," he said. "I didn't mean to upset you, Ms. Dixon."

"It's fine," she lied. "I'd just rather not talk about my personal life while at work. If you are here on business, I'd like to get on with it."

"Sounds good, Ms. Dixon. Next question," he prompted. Lucinda studied her computer screen and chewed on the tip of her pen. The whole scene made him hot, but he was pretty sure that saying so wouldn't be considered business-like, and the last thing he wanted was to piss Lucinda off enough to get him thrown out of her office.

She cleared her throat, "Will you have a co-signer on the loan?" she asked.

"No," he said.

"Not even your brother?" she asked.

"No," he repeated.

"How about a spouse or girlfriend?" she questioned.

"Is a co-signer necessary?" he asked.

"Um, no," she squeaked. "It just makes things easier sometimes. We can move on from that question." Ty nodded. A part of him wanted to tell her that he had no wife or significant other, but that would be crossing the whole business/personal border she had put up. He'd stick with the facts, and his relationship status wasn't her business or a fact that she needed to know. But why did he want to tell her those personal details more than he wanted to do just about anything else?

LUCINDA

Lucy pushed long strands of hair back from her face and tucked them back into the messy bun she usually wore for work. She was so self-conscious about the way Ty Nash was watching her. When she was just a teenager, she would have given just about anything to have him looking at her like he was now. But he was a high school golden boy who didn't give her a second thought when they passed in the hallways day after day. Lucy was two years behind him and her brother, Ford, in high school, and God, she had such a crush on him. Every girl did. He was the quarterback on the football team and girls followed him around like lovesick puppies, her included.

She pushed her glasses up the bridge of her nose, noting the way Tyler's eyes seemed to follow her every movement. Lucy knew he was only studying her to figure out how they knew each other but it still made her hot and somewhat bothered. His blue eyes were always so intense and having them on her now made her girly parts do a happy dance. No—he was just here for a loan, nothing else.

"How much are you looking to borrow, Mr. Nash?" she

asked. She had stopped herself from calling him Ty a few times now. She knew that everyone called him that, but she just couldn't. How many nights had she dreamed of calling him by his nickname while he was holding her in his arms? How many times did she imagine screaming out his name when she got herself off thinking about him? Yeah—it would be one colossal fucking bad idea to call him Ty.

"The land is valued at two-hundred and five thousand but I think I can get it a little lower than that price," he said. "Plus, I'll need to build a barn or two and the main house. All in, I'm thinking five-hundred thousand should do it."

Lucy stopped typing and looked over her laptop at him. He was sitting back in one of the two crappy chairs she had in her little office, ankle resting over his leg like he just hadn't asked her to approve his half-million-dollar loan. He smiled at her and even dared to wink. Lucy rolled her eyes and looked back down at her screen.

"That's an awfully big ask, Mr. Nash. You have any collateral?" She already asked if he had a co-signer, although that was more of a fishing expedition on her part, to find out if he had a wife or girlfriend. Not that it mattered.

"No," he breathed. "Listen," Ty sat forward on his seat, firmly planting both feet on the floor in front of himself. "I've been in ranching my whole life. When our dad died, my brother and I took over his ranch and we've been partners since. Ranching is in my blood and I just know that this property will be perfect for raising cattle. It's been a part of the Phillip's place and now, they are auctioning the land off to the highest bidder. I want to be the person it goes to, but I can't do that without a loan."

She was mesmerized at how passionate he seemed about his work. It made Lucy wonder how passionate he might be about other things he loved in his life. That was a rabbit hole she couldn't go down though. Professional—she needed to remember to be completely professional in this little meeting otherwise, she'd be stamping "approved" on his loan and that would end up getting her fired.

"Do you have anything to put down on the loan?" she asked again.

"I have a small nest egg, but it isn't much—only about twenty-thousand."

"Well, that's at least a start," she said. "Let me get the rest of your personal information and I will see what I can do. It's a large loan, so I will need to run it past my boss before I can make a final decision."

Tyler stood and nodded, "Does that mean you'll consider it, Lucy?"

"Ms. Dixon," she reminded. "And yes. But don't get your hopes up. I'm not sure our little bank can float such a large sum of money."

"Okay," he breathed. "Let's give it a try. What do you need to know about me?"

Everything. "Oh, you know just the usual stuff—date of birth, social security number, address, and relationship status." She wanted to kick herself for slipping that one in. Sure, she would have to put if he was married or single on the form, but it wasn't something she wanted to make a big deal out of.

Ty smiled and sat back down in his seat. "Single," he said. "How about you?"

"Um, my relationship status isn't something we need to fill out on your loan papers, Mr. Nash," she protested. Although, it felt good to have him showing interest in her. She needed to remember that Tyler Nash was a flirt and someone she should steer clear of if she wanted to keep her heart in one piece.

"Come on now, Lucy. Turnabout is fair play. I'll show you mine if you show me yours," Ty teased. God, she wanted to tell him she'd show him anything he wanted to see, but that wouldn't be professional at all. "How about we start with an easier question," he offered.

She wanted to tell him no and ask him the next question on

the loan application but she found herself nodding her agreement like a lunatic. Lucy inwardly chastised herself for being such a fool. "Great," he said, sexy smirk firmly in place. "Will you go out with me on a date?" he asked.

"A date," she squeaked, sure she hadn't heard him correctly.

"Yeah—you know, dinner or a movie. Hell, how about both?" he asked.

"I don't think that's a good idea," she whispered. "You are applying for a loan at my bank."

"All right, to make it fair, how about you work on the loan and get back to me with your answer. Then, we can circle back to my question," he said.

"And, if I deny your loan?" she asked. "You'll still want to go out on a date with me?" She was holding her breath, waiting for him to answer and when he smiled and nodded, she couldn't help but smile. Tyler Nash was asking her out on a date and even though her mind was shouting at her that it was a fucking awful idea, her heart was doing a little butterfly dance in her damn chest.

"It's just a date, Lucy," he said. "Say yes."

"Yes," she whispered. "I'll go on a date with you."

TYLER

Ty signed the loan application and now, he had to play a waiting game—both for the bank's answer and his chance at a date with sexy little Lucinda. He wasn't sure that he remembered Lucy but he sure remembered her brother, Ford. Ty wanted to grab a sandwich and hopefully find a few minutes to dig his old yearbook out to look her up. The problem was his high school crap was stored away out at the main house at Lowdown Ranch—his brother's house. If Clay found out that he was stalking a woman he went to high school with, he'd never hear the end of the shit his brother would give him. He was hoping to slip past his brother and down to the basement to do his snooping in private, but he gave up any hope of that happening when Clay stopped him on his way into the house.

"Hey, little brother," Clay said. "You wake up my woman and I'll beat your ass."

His sister-in-law wasn't feeling the best lately, "She still not feeling better?" Ty asked.

"No," Clay said. "She's got a nasty head cold. The doctor said she needs her rest—so don't you fucking wake her," Clay said, pointing his finger at Ty as if trying to drive home his point.

"Got it," Clay agreed. "Don't wake Rose or you'll kick my ass. Anything else?"

"Yeah—why the hell are you here? I thought you took off early because you had some business in town today," Clay said. He wasn't exactly one-hundred percent honest with Clay about what his business entailed. If he told his brother that he was going to apply for a loan to buy the land that butted up against Lowdown Ranch's land, he'd offer to help him out and that was the last thing he wanted. He wanted to buy the land on his own and Clay would want to run in to save the day, just like he usually did.

"I need a copy of my high school diploma," Tyler lied.

"What the hell for? You've been out of high school for a while now," Clay said.

"It's just something I'm doing and I'd rather not talk about it until it's finished. I don't want to jinx it, you know?" he asked. Ty was hoping that reason would be good enough for his older brother, but Clay usually liked to stick his nose in where it didn't belong. He had a feeling that this was going to be one of those times where Clay's nose got stuck in his business. He wasn't being dishonest; he was worried about even being able to get the loan. Telling his brother about it now would only put more pressure on him and if the loan fell through, he'd have to explain to Clay that he fucked up again. But he wasn't at the ranch to pick up his high school diploma. He was there to find his old yearbook and pathetically look up a woman who he didn't remember. A very hot, feisty redhead that he was hoping to get to know better. Yeah—he'd keep that bit of information to himself though.

"Fine," Clay breathed. "I'll let you keep your secrets, Ty. I don't have time for this anyway. Besides having a sick wife, I have a heifer who's about to calf. Your stuff is in the back of the storage room and most of it is labeled. Good luck." He watched his brother leave through the side door and Ty could tell that he was good and pissed. It wasn't like them to sit and share their deepest, darkest secrets, but they also didn't run to each other with every little thing that popped up in their lives. Clay certainly didn't share when he had met Rose or told Ty that he was dating an older woman. No, that wasn't something that he'd want to discuss with his little brother, and Ty respected Clay's privacy—for the most part. He did love giving him shit for falling in love with an older woman though.

If Clay knew he was trying to buy the old Phillips place, he'd be hurt that Ty didn't go to him for help. Ty was just hoping that his brother hadn't already caught onto his plan and that's why Clay was acting butt hurt. He needed the deal to go through and then he'd tell his brother that they were going to be neighbors. It wasn't a family thing; it was his stubborn pride keeping him from going to his brother for the money. He wanted to do this deal on his own, not to prove to Clay that he was capable but to prove it to himself.

Ty walked down to the storage closet in the basement that held the family treasures. His grandpa's old saddle was stored in the corner and seeing it sitting there always made him smile. He loved the ranch and his grandfather was the backbone of Lowdown Ranch. Ty and Clay spent countless summers working the ranch with their Grandpa and he loved every minute of it. His father and grandfather taught him everything he needed to know about ranching and raising cattle and he liked to believe that they would both be proud of him for trying to branch out on his own and start his own homestead. Ty just wondered if Clay would be as proud of him for making a go of it on his own.

Ty found his boxes in the corner of the room and started looking through them. They were all labeled, "Tyler's things" and he was pretty sure that Rose had organized the storage room when she moved out to the ranch. She was the most organized person he had ever met. He opened a few boxes and was surprised to see that his father had saved old high school mementos for him, such as newspaper clippings with stories of his football team's wins, and even some ribbons and trophies from over the years.

"Wow," Tyler breathed, pulling his old football jersey from one of the boxes and holding it up to himself. He dug through the rest of the box and found his yearbooks, pulling out the one from his senior year.

"Lucinda Dixon," he whispered to himself as he flipped through the pages of the Sophomore class from that year. He ran his pointer finger down the page until he found her name. She looked nothing like the sexy woman who gave him so much sass at the bank today. She had on thick, dark glasses, and her red hair was wildly out of control. Her long curls looked more like an untamed mane and he couldn't help but laugh. She had certainly grown into a fine looking woman but her high school picture told him everything he needed to know about her—he wouldn't have even given Lucinda Dixon a second glance back in the day.

She seemed so different from her older brother. He and Ford used to hang out on weekends after the big game on Friday, usually at someone's party, getting drunk off cheap warm beer from a keg. Lucinda wouldn't have hung around the same crowds as him and Ford, that was for sure. He knew his friend had a younger sister—he just never pictured her to be a giant nerd.

Ty tossed the yearbook back into the box along with his football jersey and closed it back up. He grabbed the box and started back up the stairs to the main level only to come face to face with his sister-in-law, Rose.

"Hey," she whispered. She looked awful and sounded even worse.

"Clay said that you are under the weather. I'm sorry you aren't feeling well," Ty said, taking a step back from her.

"I'm not contagious, Tyler," Rose chided. "I have a sinus infection and I'm on antibiotics."

"Well, I can't be too careful. Clay will have my ass if I don't show up for work because I caught your cold. Plus, he said you were supposed to be in bed." He looked around, making sure that they were alone. The last thing he needed was for Clay to think he purposefully woke Rose. His brother was already grumpy enough around him.

"I needed something to drink, and Clay said he'd be out at the barn," she said. "What's in the box?" she asked, looking him over.

"Just some old high school crap," he admitted. "You know, football jersey, yearbooks, that kind of stuff."

"I reorganized the basement storage space when I moved in. I hope I didn't mix up your stuff too badly," she said.

"Not at all," Tyler said. "I found just what I was looking for and didn't waste time going through generations of shit we have stored down there. I swear—I think we have stuff down there from a few hundred years ago. My dad kept everything."

"There's nothing wrong with a parent who keeps their kid's mementos. I've kept so many little things from Aiden and Corbin's high school years. I'm sure that someday, they'll want them again but for now, I'll hold onto everything for them. You'll see someday when you have kids, Ty," she said. He must have made a face at the mention of him having kids because Rose cracked a smile. Her laughter turned into coughing.

"You should go back to bed, Rose," Ty ordered. "You need your rest. I can tell Clay to check in on you if you'd like."

"No need," she croaked. "I'm going to take my hot tea and go back to bed. By the time he gets in here, I'll be asleep again. These cold meds really throw me for a loop," she said.

"All right," Tyler reluctantly agreed. "I hope you're feeling better soon."

"Thanks," she said. He watched as she padded back to the master bedroom and closed the door. He planned on heading back to his place and doing some much-needed research. He was going to have to work his ass off to prove that he could handle paying back the loan. Otherwise, pretty little Lucinda would toss his ass right out of the bank the next time she saw him, and he couldn't let that happen. His future depended on him getting that loan and the only way to make that happen was to take Lucinda on one fucking great date.

LUCINDA

Luci got home from work a little late, as usual, and fed her very pissed off cat. Mr. Rogers was not okay with her staying late at the office to finish up some of the piles of paperwork that covered her desk.

"You'll be all right, buddy," she offered. The cat looked up from his food bowl at her and glared as if trying to tell her that she was not only late, but she was also wrong.

"I've had a long day," she grumbled. "What did you do all day? I'm betting you napped your day away while I had to see my old high school crush. Do you know how embarrassing that is? I mean, he didn't even remember me." She looked down at Mr. Rogers who had resumed eating as if he didn't give a fig about the embarrassment she had to endure while seeing Tyler Nash again. He looked good but then again, he always did. The fact that he didn't know who she was had her tongue-tied and flustered. At first, he seemed to believe that he knew her from somewhere but that turned out to be a lie. He had no clue who she was until he put two and two together and came up with her being Ford's little sister. And when he asked her to go on a date with him, she caved and agreed. That was something she knew was a big mistake as soon as the words left her lips. He was a client and she needed to remember that and cancel their date. Going out with Tyler might be her dream come true but it would also be her greatest mistake.

Her cell phone chimed and she checked her texts. She groaned when she saw who the message was from—Tyler. She had foolishly given him her cell number after she agreed to the date. She opened the message and gasped at the image he had sent to her—her high school sophomore picture from the yearbook. She looked at the girl staring back at her through the cell phone screen and couldn't decide if she wanted to laugh or cry. She had given herself a home perm and fried her red hair. She had an afro and looked like a clown and had to wait over a year for it to grow out. It was her first and last perm, but she learned a valuable lesson—less was more and she tried to remember that whenever she thought about changing her hair once again.

Her mother was strict about her not wearing make-up but that school picture day she snuck some pink lipstick and a little mascara. Her mom was furious when they got the pictures back from the school. Luci was grounded for a week for disobeying her mom's rules and wearing make-up. Her mother would have made it two weeks had she known that Lucinda had also helped herself to a pair of her heals from her closet that day. She couldn't see them in the school picture since the pose was only of the top half of her body. All in all, it wasn't a horrible picture of herself. Lucinda didn't have any grand delusions about who she was back then. She was a giant nerd and she learned to accept who she was a long time ago. She decided to ignore Tyler's text and relax in a hot bath.

Luci locked up the house and made her way to her master bathroom, finding her favorite bath bomb. She just about had the tub filled when Tyler called her. She thought about ignoring his call but she knew that he wouldn't give up. He didn't like being ignored.

"Hello," Lucinda said.

"Hey," Tyler breathed. "You get my text?" He knew that she did. She was stupid and didn't mark her texts as private so, he could tell that she saw it.

"I got it," she said. She wasn't going to give him much more than that. If she did, she'd be playing right into his game.

"See—I remembered you," he said. She was betting that he didn't remember her at all. He probably ran home to look up her picture in the yearbook to jog his memory.

"Um—well, thanks for letting me know, Tyler," she said. "Now, if you'll excuse me, I have a bath to soak in."

"Wait—you're just dismissing me?" he asked.

"Yep," she said.

"What about our date?" he asked. "I'd still love to take you to dinner, Luci." That was a massively bad idea and the sooner she shut down his plans for their date, the better.

"Listen, Tyler," she said. "I think you're a nice guy, but if I'm going to be working on your loan with my bank, I need to stay neutral. I'm pretty sure that dating you won't be remaining neutral."

"So, you changed your mind, just like that?" he asked.

"No," she lied. "I've been thinking about this all day—since you left my office, really."

"Well, then, if you've given it so much consideration, maybe you're right and we should just forget the whole thing," Tyler grumbled.

"I'm being reasonable, Tyler. I can't remain neutral if I go out with you to dinner," she said. "It wouldn't be right."

"It's just dinner," Tyler said. "How about we turn it into a working dinner? I have to bring you a bunch of paperwork, and we can go over everything while we eat. I'll get my dinner with you, and you'll get your loan documents."

"You can't be serious, Tyler," she said. He was the pushiest person she had ever known. Tyler could give her older brother, Ford, a run for his money with his bossy, overbearing nature.

"I'm very serious about dinner, Luci. I never joke about

food. Plus, I want this loan, so I'd like to make sure that you have all the paperwork that you requested. I'm going to do everything I possibly can to show you and your bank that I'm worthy of this loan," Tyler said. She loved how he had a plan for his life and was stopping at nothing to achieve it. She just hoped that she wouldn't have to let him down or stomp on his dreams.

"Please, Luci," he begged.

"Fine," she reluctantly agreed. "I can meet you Thursday night to go over the loan documents. I'll even eat dinner while we look things over, but that's it, Ty," she said. "And I don't want you calling this a date."

"Why not?" he asked.

"It's not professional. This is a working dinner and that's all," she insisted.

"Got it," Tyler agreed. She held her cell phone from her ear and looked at it, squinting her eyes as if she thought he was lying. "See you Thursday, Luci. I'll text you with the place and time." He ended the call and she once again looked at her cell phone as if it offended her in some way.

"Crap," she whispered to herself. "What have I just agreed to?" Mr. Rogers was sitting on the edge of the tub, watching her as if she just lost her mind while she talked to herself. Who knew, maybe she had lost her ever-loving mind, agreeing to go out with Tyler.

※

Thursday seemed to drag on and by the time she closed the branch, she had just enough time to run back home, shower, and change her clothes. She wanted to look sexy but didn't want to look like she was trying. That was a tall order because she felt like she was putting way too much effort into her hair, make-up, and outfit. By the time she left for the restaurant, she was already fifteen minutes late. She thought about just canceling the dinner, but she didn't want Tyler to think she was a coward.

Ty tried to get her to agree to him picking her up, but she thought that sounded too much like a date. She made up some excuse about coming straight from work and he seemed to buy her lie. She was nervous and excited about what they were calling a working dinner, even if it felt a hell of a lot like a date.

She parked around the back of the restaurant, and walked to the front entrance, cursing her choice of heels. The shoes were sexy as sin but she was sure she was going to break her neck walking around the gravel parking lot to the front.

"Hey," Tyler shouted from the side lot. "Wait up, Luci." No one called her Luci except her brother, and she knew that Tyler was doing it just to piss her off. She pasted on her best smile and turned to face him.

"Hello Tyler," she said, holding out her hand for him to shake. "It's nice to see you again." He looked her over, giving her the exact reaction she was looking for when she picked out the curve-hugging black cocktail dress for dinner.

"You look gorgeous," he said. "You wore that to work?" he asked. She looked down her body and grimaced, knowing that he was about to catch her in a lie.

"No," she breathed. "I got out of work a little early and had time to change." He leaned into her and she could have sworn that he smelled her.

"You smell good too, Darlin'," he drawled.

"Um—yeah, I had time for a shower too," she stuttered. "And I'd appreciate you not smelling me again, Tyler," she chastised.

"Noted," he said, taking a step back from her, giving her some space. "May I help you in the restaurant? I'm no expert but I'm guessing that the gravel is hell on your heals."

She looked down at her black pumps and nodded, "I'd love some help," she agreed, taking his arm. "Thank you, Tyler."

"I wish you'd call me Ty," he said.

"Yes, well, I'd like for you to call me Lucinda," she breathed. "But I have a feeling that's not going to happen."

"You don't go by Luci?" he asked. "If I remember correctly, your brother called you by that name, right?"

"Yes, he still does. He's the only one who's ever called me Luci though," she said.

"Okay, Lucinda," he said. "I'll try to remember that."

"Well, then, I'll try calling you Ty," she agreed.

"See, we're making deals already," he teased.

She couldn't help but giggle, "Did you bring the paperwork I need?" she asked.

"I did," he said, patting his jacket pocket. He had cleaned up well in his dress pants and blazer. She was used to seeing him in jeans and a t-shirt that hugged his biceps but seeing him dressed up was just as good.

"Perfect," she said. "I know it might be a tough sell, but I think you have a real chance of getting this loan. We just need to be able to prove that you should be able to turn a profit in the first two years. If we can do that, I think my bank will go for the loan."

"Really?" he asked. "I know it's a long shot, but this would mean everything to me. I've been wanting something of my own for so long now," he admitted. "I just never thought that my dreams could become a reality."

"Well, I can't make you any promises but I think if we put in a little elbow grease, you'll have a chance." He covered her hand, which was holding onto his forearm, with his hand and squeezed it into his own.

"Thank you so much," he breathed. "You don't know how much that means to me, Lucinda."

She smiled when he got her name right and nodded. "No problem, Ty," she said. "I love helping people fulfill their dreams. It's why I love my job so much. I mean, I'm not curing cancer or rescuing people from burning buildings, but when I close a loan to make a client's dreams come true, I feel like I'm fulfilling my purpose."

He held the door open for her and waited for her to go into the restaurant. "I know what you mean. I feel the same way when I help birth a calf or mend a fence, as crazy as that sounds. It's like I can see my progress and after a hard day's work, I can sit back and look at what I accomplished—really gives me a sense of purpose."

"Exactly," she agreed. Tyler gave his name for the reservation, and they were quickly seated.

"I've always wanted to eat here," she admitted after the host left them to look over the menu. "I was happy that you suggested it." It was one of the newest steakhouses in the area and she knew that they had a waiting list to get a table. "How did you get us in here with such short notice?" she asked.

He smiled at her over his menu. "Well, Clay and I supply this place with beef and well, we both own a percentage of the restaurant. Well, not just this one but all the chains that have opened up—I think there are five now."

"Wait, you own part of this place?" she asked.

He nodded and smiled at her, "Yeah—why?"

"Well, that changes things," she said. "You have collateral. You can use your portion of shares in this place to put up for the loan."

Ty shook his head, "Can't," he said, studying the menu again.

"Tyler, this is a good thing. If you own shares in this place, my bank will approve your loan. All you have to do is put them up as collateral," she said. Lucinda was wondering what he was missing. To her, this was a simple fix but he didn't seem to get it.

He sighed and put his menu on the table. "If I put up my shares, I'd have to tell my brother what I'm doing and I can't do that," he said.

"Why not? Won't Clay be happy for you?" Lucinda asked.

He shrugged, "Don't know," Ty admitted. "I'd like to think he'd be happy for me. I mean, this has always been what I've secretly wanted, but I just never told him about wanting my own ranch. Plus, if I told him I was trying to get a loan, I'd have to put up with him trying to give me the money."

Lucinda rolled her eyes, "Yeah, that sounds awful," she teased. "You seem to have two viable options and you aren't even considering them. What if you let me try to get you approved without telling your brother that you're putting up your restaurant shares? Are they in your name or both of your names?" she asked.

"Just mine," he said. "We each own twenty percent."

"Tyler, that's awesome. It would help your case," she said, feeling more excited by the minute.

"I don't know if that's a good idea," he admitted. "Can I think about it? I just don't want to go behind my brother's back any more than I have to. I already feel that by keeping this secret, I'm lying to him. If I put up my shares and this venture fails, I'll be throwing away the nest egg that he helped me to procure for myself. I'm pretty sure that won't go over well with him. Buying into the restaurant was Clay's idea."

"I get it," she said. "Is it profitable yet?" She was very aware that it took a few years for a business to turn a profit and this place was new on the scene.

"Not really, but we've been told by the owner that should happen sometime next year. This place has only been in business for just over two years now," he said.

"Do you have records from your business partner's accountant?" she asked.

"Yes," Ty said.

"If you let me look them over, I'm sure I can help you with your loan," she offered. "But I understand if you need to give it some thought. It's a good option, Tyler," she said.

"I'll think about it," he promised. Lucinda could tell that he wanted her to drop the topic. She wanted to push; it was her go-to. Her brother, Ford, liked to tell her that just about every time she pushed his limits—which was often, he felt about ready to pull his hair out. She couldn't help herself when it came to bossing around her brother, even though he was older. Their mother passed when they were both just kids and their father raised them both. She assumed the role of a bossy, overbearing mother and he just allowed her to do so. She knew he was just humoring her, putting up with her bossing him around but it worked for them. Ford was one of her closest friends. Honestly, Lucinda didn't have many friends and that was just fine with her.

In high school, she found out fast that girls could be downright mean. She learned to be alone and that worked for her. At least, when she was alone, she didn't have to worry about who was talking behind her back or worse, pretending to be her friend just to get closer to her hot, older brother.

"Do you know what you would like to order?" Tyler asked, changing the subject.

"Not really," she admitted, studying the menu. "You have any recommendations?" she asked.

"Well, sure," he drawled. "The beef is out of this world," he teased. She rolled her eyes and giggled at his boasting. "I like it when you smile, Lucinda," he said.

"How about I let you order for me while I take a look at the paperwork you brought?" she asked. She wondered if the smirk on his face was disappointment or amusement. He pulled some folded papers from his blazer jacket and handed them to her. She started going through them when the waiter reappeared to take their order. She didn't pay much attention to what Tyler was ordering for her because she flipped through his paperwork to find a black and white photo of herself. It was from the yearbook and it looked like he had made a copy of the picture.

She remembered that day as if it were yesterday. It was the pep rally for the big homecoming game her sophomore year and God, she wanted Tyler to notice her and ask her to be his date. She knew that would never happen but it was all she wished for that year. The photo showed her sitting by herself, staring at the back of Tyler's head. He was sitting next to her brother two rows down on the bleachers and didn't even know that she existed, let alone was sitting behind him, pining for him.

She tried to pretend that she hadn't seen the photo but she could feel Tyler watching her. He knew that she found it; the question was what to do about it. There would be no denying that she was staring at the back of his head in the photo or that she had one major crush on him. If she was going for complete honesty, she'd also admit that she still did.

"That was the year your brother won the game for us. We always played our rival's over at South High and if it wasn't for Ford, we would have lost that game by a touchdown," Tyler said, still watching her.

"Why is that photo in with your paperwork?" she asked. Lucinda was pretty sure she already knew the answer to her question though. He was going to make her feel foolish for having a crush on him or tease her for sitting behind him and staring at the back of his head like a fool.

"You were looking at me—in that photo," he said. He wasn't asking a question. It was more like he was stating a fact.

Lucinda defiantly raised her chin and stared him down. "Yes," she admitted. "So what?" she challenged.

"You liked me, didn't you?" he asked. God, she wanted to crawl under the table to hide. This was the most embarrassing conversation that she had ever had.

"So what if I did?" she spat. "It was a stupid school girl crush on one of my brother's older friends. That's all, Tyler," she insisted. His smile was easy, and he nodded.

"I appreciate your honesty," he said. She was far from being completely honest with him but she wasn't about to tell him that.

"I'm not sure what you were trying to accomplish here, Ty," she said.

"Just testing the icy waters, Lucinda," he admitted. She wasn't sure if that was a slight toward her or not but she didn't want to think about it. She wanted to eat her dinner, promise to look over the paperwork he had given her, and pretend that this disastrous date never happened. No—this wasn't a date. She just needed to keep telling herself that because the way Tyler was looking at her made her want to melt into a puddle and that was dangerous. Someone needed to tell her girl parts that she wasn't on a date with her hot high school crush. Otherwise, she was in way over her head.

"I need to run to the restroom," she lied. She stood and Tyler did also, pulling her chair out for her, playing the gentleman. He grabbed her arm and pulled her against his body. He was so close; she could feel his heart beating.

"I'll let you hide, for now, Lucinda. But sooner or later, you won't have anywhere to go and you'll have to admit that you feel what's happening between us too," Tyler whispered in her ear. Tyler released her arm and she practically ran off toward the restrooms. Yeah—she was going to hide but he was wrong about the rest of it—she wouldn't ever admit that she still had a silly crush on him. Pigs would fly and hell would freeze over first.

TYLER

Tyler waited her out and after five minutes passed, he told the waiter to hold their food and he went off to find Luci. She was in the woman's bathroom still and when he was sure that she was all alone, he snuck into the lady's room to find her staring at herself in the mirror.

"You can't get much more perfect than you already are, Honey," he teased. "I say you come on back out to the table. Our food is ready, and we can eat."

She turned to face him, surprise in her big, blue eyes. "You can't be in here, Tyler," she said. She fiercely shook her head at him and a long strand of her red hair escaped her messy bun. He wondered what she would look like with her hair down, spilling over her shoulders. Every time he had seen her, she had her hair pulled back, and while the sexy banker thing did it for him, he wanted to see the fiery redhead that he knew lived deep inside of her. Tyler quickly crossed the small room and reached behind her head, loosening her hair from its tie. She gasped as her hair spilled around her shoulders and he ran his hands through it. He was happy that she responded to him, leaning into his body as if craving more from him. Ty would give her everything and demand nothing less of her if she let him, but he wasn't sure that they were at that point yet.

"I want to kiss you," he whispered. He was standing so close to Luci that he could feel her warm breath on his lips. She gave a slight not and he couldn't help his smile. "I'm going to need the words, Honey," he insisted. Sure, he was being an ass and pushing her for more than she might want to give him, but that was who he was. Tyler liked his dominance and if he was going to persuade sexy, little Lucinda to jump into his bed, she'd learn that fact sooner than later.

"Yes," she breathed. That was all the confirmation that he needed. Tyler dipped his head and took her mouth in a hard kiss he knew would leave her lips swollen, but he didn't care. He took his time kissing her and when he finally let her up for air, she was panting for her next breath.

"Wow," she breathed. "That was—"

"Everything," Ty finished for her. "For the record, Lucinda, I'm flattered that you had a crush on me in high school. If I wasn't such a bone head, I would have noticed you back then. If it matters, I notice you now, Honey." She shyly smiled up at him and his heart melted a little bit more for her.

"You were a bone head," she teased. "But, you wouldn't have paid me much attention. Especially with all the cheerleaders and popular girls throwing themselves at you every day. You had your hands pretty full and I wasn't like the rest of those girls. If you didn't notice, I was a little bit of a nerd." Tyler chuckled. He had noticed but he wasn't about to admit that to his sexy little nerd.

"I didn't notice you because I was a moron," he admitted.

"Um, I'm pretty sure you were a moron—like most of the boys we went to high school with, but I wasn't someone you would have gone out with. I would have ruined your reputation," she said.

"No," Ty breathed. "I'm pretty sure I would have ruined your reputation back then. Girls who went out with guys on the football team were known for being fast and loose. It's why we asked them out and pretty much why we were all morons. I'm noticing you now, Luci," he whispered, leaning in to kiss her again.

Lucinda put her hands on his chest, effectively pushing him back from her. "This is a bad idea still," she whispered.

"Only if you believe that to be true, Honey. How about we agree to be adults about this and keep business and pleasure separate. Hell, I can even draw up a contract for you to sign, if that'll make you happy."

"Don't be ridiculous," she said. "We can't make up a contract for a relationship, Tyler," she said. He wanted to tell her that he usually had his subs sign a non-disclosure statement but she didn't know about that side of his life. He wasn't asking her to be his sub yet. Hell, he was only asking her for one night, but that might be a shitty way of telling her what he was after. No, it might be best if he just lay out what he was looking for and let the chips fall where they may.

"I can and I have," he admitted. "I'm a Dom, Lucinda. I like to play at the local BDSM club and I have my subs sign a non-disclosure statement. It keeps both parties safe and it's not as messy when things end. Usually, it's mutual but sometimes, things get out of hand."

Luci held up her small hand, effectively stopping what he was saying. "You are a Dom?" she asked. "As in—you like to boss women around?" Tyler pulled her hand into his and gently kissed her knuckles.

"As in I like complete control in the bedroom. You'll have the right to say yes or no to what I want but if you tell me no, I have the right to terminate our relationship," he said. Luci was smiling but he knew she wasn't happy about what he was saying to her.

"Um—" she hummed. "So, you'll be able to do what to me, exactly?" she asked. "Tie me up and beat the hell out of me and

I'm supposed to just stand there and take it? Will you expect me to beg you for more?" she sassed.

"It's not like that," Tyler said, releasing her. "And, you'd have a contract protecting you," he breathed.

Her laugh was mean, "Well, that changes everything. If there's going to be a contract protecting me, then sure," she said. Luci didn't mean it; he was at least bright enough to realize that. He was a fool for believing that he should just come clean with her. Now, she was not only going to turn him down flat, but she was also going to walk out of his life and take her loan money with her.

Tyler took a step back from her and dropped his hands to his sides. "Forget I even brought it up, Luci," he whispered. "Let's just have our dinner and go over the paperwork as we agreed to do tonight."

"No, Tyler," she hissed. "You can't just drop a bomb like that and not expect me to just go back to our normal business dinner. I mean, come on—you tell me you want me to sign a contract to be your sub, one that will prohibit me from telling anyone about our relationship, and then tell me to just drop the subject. What exactly are you asking me for, Ty?" she asked.

He knew he was making a giant mistake answering her, but he just couldn't help himself. "I'd like you to be my submissive and in return, I'll make you feel things you never thought possible."

Luci giggled, "Does that line usually work with the ladies, Ty?" she asked. He was careful not to touch her again. If he did, he'd haul her up against his body and show her exactly what he was asking her for.

"Yes," he admitted. "Listen, let's just forget this whole conversation. I'll have your dinner wrapped up and you can just take it home. Obviously, you don't want what I'm asking you for and I'm not looking for anything else." Yeah, he sounded like an asshole.

"So, I agree to be your sub or nothing else. You're just

looking for a quick fuck, someone who obeys your every command and that's all? No, I can't give you that, Tyler. I do appreciate your honesty though." Luci grabbed her purse from the countertop and turned to walk out of the ladies' room. He followed closely behind her and when they got back to the table, he pulled out her chair for her, but Luci kept walking. He watched as she walked past the waiter, who was bringing their food to the table, and out to the parking lot. Luci couldn't seem to get away from him fast enough and he couldn't blame her.

※

Tyler paid for the dinners that they didn't eat and then drove back to his place. He lived just down the road from Lowdown ranch and he loved his little house. But it wasn't where he eventually wanted to end up. He wanted a ranch house like the one they had grown up in; a family and a lifelike he and Clay had growing up. At the rate he was going though, he wasn't going to have any of that. He had probably blown his chances for the loan with Lucinda's bank, but what he regretted even more was blowing his chance with Lucinda.

He decided to wash the entire day away in a nice hot shower and then, he planned on going to bed and hopefully sleeping. The past two nights, he had been so worried about the loan that he barely slept. Now, with the possibility of his loan being approved off the table, he'd be able to hopefully get some rest. The problem was he wouldn't be able to get the sexy redhead, who admitted to having a crush on him in high school, off his damn mind.

Ty quickly showered and dried off, pulling on a pair of boxer briefs to crawl into his bed. He was exhausted and every muscle in his body ached. His phone rang on his nightstand and he rolled over to answer it.

"Lo," he answered.

"Um, hi," Luci whispered into the other end of the call.

"Sorry to call so late." He checked his bedside clock and chuckled when he saw that it was only just after ten at night.

"It's only ten," he challenged. "I don't think that qualifies as late to most people." Tyler wasn't sure why she was even calling him. When she left the restaurant, she couldn't seem to get away from him fast enough.

"Okay then, I'm sorry to call you at all, Tyler," she sassed. He could hear that she had a little more fight now and that was something that turned him completely on. He liked it when she gave him shit and went full-on sassy with him. He wanted to give her smart mouth something better to do, but Luci made it perfectly clear that she wasn't on board with what he wanted from her.

"You still there?" she asked when he didn't say anything.

"Yep," he breathed.

"Were you like this back in high school?" she questioned.

"Like what?" he asked, although he knew exactly what she was asking.

"Dominant," she said. "Were you always dominant?"

"Yes, and no," he said, sitting up on his bed. She was taking an interest in him and his lifestyle and that had to count for something, right? "I liked to be in control, you know during sex, but I didn't go as far as I do now. I didn't have the nerve to spank the girls I dated back then or tie them up."

"You like to tie women up and spank them?" Lucinda asked.

"Yes," he admitted. "I do. Does that upset you, Luci?" he asked.

She didn't answer at first and he worried that her silence was going to be her answer. Luci sighed into the phone and whispered, "No," and he felt like his damn heart might beat out of his chest. "I think I might like those things," she admitted.

"Really?" he asked.

"Yeah, but what if I don't?" she asked. "What if I agreed to submit to you and I end up hating everything you demand of me? Then what happens?" Luci still wasn't getting that she held all the power in a relationship like he was asking her for. Submissives had the power to use their safe word when things got to be too much or even say no, outright.

"You'd have a safe word," he said. "If you don't like something, you would just need to use your safe word and whatever we're doing would stop," he said.

"You would just stop? Just like that, no questions asked?" She sounded confused and excited all at the same time. He wished they could be having this conversation face to face so he could read how she was feeling. It was hard to gauge what she was thinking when he couldn't see her expressions. Luci had a way of letting him know exactly what she was feeling just by her facial expressions alone.

"I'd just stop but I'd want for us to talk about what you liked and didn't like. Communication is a big part of a Dom/sub relationship," he said.

"And the contract—that's a real thing too?" she asked.

"Sometimes, yes," he admitted. "It's for both of our protection. The contract protects both parties. For example, I wouldn't be able to tell people about our relationship or your role as my submissive. That might be useful to someone with a job like yours. I mean, your clients don't need to know the sorted details of your love life, right?" Ty knew he wasn't playing fair, turning the tables back on her but he couldn't help himself. The contract was something that the manager of the BDSM club he frequented, told him about. He told Ty that it was less messy to have a contract in place and even gave him one he could use until he could do some research to write one of his own. He thought it was a good idea, in theory, but he also knew how cold and uncaring it made him sound every time he asked a woman to sign a piece of paper before having sex with him.

"No, I wouldn't want my clients knowing anything about my private life. I like to keep business and pleasure separate and I guess that's why this is so hard for me. Your loan can't have anything to do with this, Tyler," she said. "I need to know that you aren't asking me to do this with you because you hope that it will win me over so that I will give you the loan. I won't do that—it's unethical."

He knew she wasn't that type of person just from the few times they had talked. He would never ask her to compromise her position as bank manager because they had sex. "I'd never do that," he admitted. "The two will remain separate, of course—you have my word."

"I need time to think," she whispered. "I hated leaving the restaurant the way I did. I'm sorry I walked out on you like that but I was confused and upset. I just needed time to decompress. Will you give me some time to think about your offer, Ty?" she asked.

"Of course," Tyler agreed. "I'd tell you to take all the time you need but the greedy bastard in me wants to push you for an answer."

"I just need a day or two, please," she said.

"Deal," he agreed. "I'll call you in two days, Luci. Thank you for calling me and thanks for giving me a chance. It means a lot."

"Good night, Ty," she breathed.

He smiled at the way she was avoiding him. He'd let her hide and think—for now. But in two days, he'd be calling her for her answer. Ty just hoped like hell she'd tell him yes.

"Night, Lucinda," he said and ended the call, tossing it back onto his night table. "Talk to you in two days, Honey," he whispered to himself.

LUCINDA

Lucinda called her best friend, Journey Ross, hoping that she might be able to give her some guidance. She was supposed to give Tyler his answer tonight. He had texted her earlier that morning and asked if she could meet him at the same restaurant they were at just days prior. He wanted to try their "date" again and this time, they would hopefully eat the food that they ordered. She knew he'd also press her for an answer too, but that was going to be a problem since she still did not have one.

Ninety percent of her wanted to tell him yes. Lucinda had been waiting for Ty for so long that denying herself what she wanted, felt wrong. Telling him yes would be easy. She could sign his contract and let him have the control he seemed to crave, but that would mean giving up her own control, and she wasn't sure that was something she could do—no matter how much she wanted Tyler.

Journey answered her phone right away making Luci giggle. "What's the good news?" Journey asked.

"I have no good news," Lucinda grumbled.

"Oh come on, Luci. You have to have some kind of news for

me. I mean, your last text was that you were meeting Tyler Nash for dinner. You have no news about your date?" Journey asked.

"Nothing," Luci lied.

"You are such a bad fucking liar," Journey chided. "I've known you your whole life and I know when you're lying, Luci. What happened?"

"We didn't have dinner. I left before we even got to that point," she said.

"You left before dinner—well, that sounds promising," Journey teased.

"Don't get yourself all excited, Journey," Luci grumbled. "I got scared and ran out of the restaurant like a coward."

"You were scared of what, exactly?" Journey asked.

Lucinda sighed, "I was scared of what Tyler wants from me," she admitted.

"What exactly does he want from you?" Journey pushed. She could tell her friend to butt out and mind her own business but she had already come this far. Plus, knowing Journey the way she did, her best friend would never back down. She'd keep pressing until Luci came clean and answered all her questions.

"He's into kinky shit—you know tying women up and spanking them. He said he likes to go to a BDST club in town," Lucinda said.

"You mean, BDSM club," Journey corrected. "I know the one—I've gone there a few times. It's fun," she said.

"You've gone to a BDSM club?" Lucinda asked.

"Yep," Journey proudly admitted. "So, Tyler Nash is into kink and that scared you?"

"Basically, yes. I mean that and the fact that he wants me to sign a contract before we have sex," Luci admitted.

"A contract?" Journey asked. "Is he selling you something?"

Luci giggled, "No," she said. "At least, I don't think so. He said it would protect both of us. You know, like neither of us would be able to talk about what happens in the bedroom."

Journey laughed, "Kind of like you're doing now? That contract doesn't stand a chance of being upheld on your end, Luci. You can't keep a secret to save your life. I love you like a sister but you know it's true." It was and that sucked. If she signed Ty's contract, she wouldn't be able to talk to or confide in her best friend. She wouldn't be able to talk to anyone about her relationship with Tyler—if that's what she would call what they'd be doing. She knew the score, he was asking her for sex —hot, kinky, ass slapping sex, and that might be something she would need to talk to her best friend about. If she signed Tyler's contract, talking to Journey wouldn't be possible. Would he demand that she keep everything about their time together a secret? Would she even be able to tell people that she was with him or would they have to pretend to be strangers? Lucinda still had so many questions and the only way to answer them was to go to a second dinner with Tyler and ask him.

"Yeah—I think I might suck at this whole non-disclosure thing," she assessed. "I'm meeting with him again tonight and we're supposed to talk about everything. I don't know that I can sign his contract, Journey. I want to do what he's asking. Hell, I've wanted to be with him since high school but I'm afraid that he's asking too much of me. Keeping secrets isn't my strong suit. I don't want to make him promises that I won't be able to keep."

"Wow—I can't believe you might actually turn down the guy you've wanted since you were just a kid. I mean, that's big, Luci," Journey said. "Do you have to give him your answer tonight?" she asked.

"Yes," Luci said. "I've stalled for two days now and I'm betting he won't let me get away with that for much longer. Ty is going to demand my answer tonight and I'm just not sure what I am going to tell him. I mean, he's working to secure a loan through my bank and if I have sex with him, it will look like I am giving him preferential treatment if I give him the loan."

"And if you don't have sex with him, you might just regret it for the rest of your life," Journey said.

"I know. What should I do?" Luci whined. She sunk into the closest chair next to her vanity and looked at her reflection in the mirror. "I'm so confused."

"Go out to dinner with him again and try to stick around until the food gets to the table this time. Hear him out and give it some thought but ultimately, you should follow your heart, Luci." Journey was right, but she wasn't about to tell her that. She should follow her heart and she had a feeling that doing that would lead her right into Tyler Nash's bed—tied up and thoroughly satisfied.

"Thanks, Journey," she whispered into her cell.

"No problem. Just do me a favor and get him to exclude me from that contract. I'm going to need all the gory details," Journey teased. She ended the call after making Luci promise to call her in the morning to let her know that she was alive. Luci checked her reflection one last time in the mirror, powdering her nose before heading out to meet Ty for their date.

"As good as it gets," she whispered to her image. She was going to meet Ty at the restaurant and hopefully, by the time she sat down at the table, she'd have her answer.

※

Tyler was waiting for her in the parking lot, standing by his pick-up, angry scowl firmly in place. He looked sexy—all brooding and stern. She could just imagine how intense he would be in the bedroom, especially knowing what he liked to do with women. If she agreed to what he wanted, she'd be Ty's submissive and she'd have to obey his every command. That thought should scare the shit out of her but instead, it turned her completely on.

Lucinda parked her car and turned off the engine. She sat in her car for a minute, taking a few deep breaths before hesitantly opening her door. Facing Tyler wasn't the issue—she was stalling, trying to make up her mind on what to do.

"Hello, Tyler," she breathed. She stood in front of him and looked him over. He was wearing his jeans and cowboy boots along with a black, muscle-hugging black t-shirt that made her mouth water. He had on a baseball cap that hid his eyes from her and she strained her neck to look up at him. He was big and even at five-ten, she felt petite standing in front of him. Luci pushed her glasses up the bridge of her nose and Ty groaned.

"You make me so fucking hot when you do that, Lucinda," he breathed.

"Um, it makes you hot when I push my glasses up my nose?" she asked.

"You have no idea how fucking sexy you are, do you?" he asked. She had pretty much grown out of her awkward, nerdy phase, but she'd never considered herself sexy or even fucking sexy, for that matter. Whatever Tyler saw in her was foreign to her, but she'd take it.

"No," she whispered. "I don't think I'm sexy at all," she admitted. Ty ran his hand over her cheek, and she leaned into his touch. He stroked his fingers through her long, red hair that she had left down, and gently gave it a little tug, forcing her to look up at him again.

"Look at me, Honey," he ordered. She immediately opened her eyes, wanting to obey his command, and looked up at him. She could see all his desire and pent up need for her, staring back at her in his blue eyes. "Tell me that you came here tonight to say yes to me," he demanded. Luci wouldn't lie to him. She owed him at least that.

"I didn't," she whispered. "I wasn't sure what my answer was going to be. I went back and forth over my decision for the past two days and I have to admit until I pulled into the parking lot, I wasn't sure what I was going to tell you." He released her and took a step back, giving her some space. She didn't want that from him—she wanted his arms around her body, holding her so closely that she could feel his heart beating.

"I see," he breathed.

"No, I don't think you do see, Ty. As soon as I got here, I knew what my answer needed to be. I'm saying yes to you but with stipulations," she said. Luci winced when she whispered the word, "Stipulations," knowing full well that she might piss him off.

"What kind of conditions are we talking about here, Luci?" he asked.

"Um, well, I'd like to be able to talk to my best friend, Journey, about us," she said.

"Journey Ross from high school?" Tyler asked.

"Yes—we've been best friends all these years and well, I told her about you—all of it. I need someone that I can confide in and talk to about things. You know girly things having to do with sex. Journey will be the only one I talk to and if you agree to that, I'll sign your contract and agree to be your submissive."

Tyler paced in front of her, "I don't know about you telling Journey all the details about what I plan on doing with you, Honey. She might not understand a Dom/sub relationship."

"She does. Journey said she even goes to the same club you belong to. At least, I'm assuming it's the same one. Unless there is more than one BDSM club in our little town," she teased.

"There's only one," he said.

"She's the one who talked me into doing this. I wasn't even going to show up tonight until I talked to her and she told me to stop being a coward and tell you yes," Luci admitted.

Tyler's smile nearly lit up the night sky. "You know, I always like Journey," he teased. Luci giggled and he wrapped his arms around her again. "Will you let me take you to the club?" he asked.

That was a very good question. She wasn't quite sure what she wanted him to do with her. Tyler had told her that she held all the power in the relationship. She had the right to veto anything he asked her to do and would even need a safe word for if things got to be too much for her. She wouldn't know if she liked something unless she gave it a try though.

"I think I'd like to try that," she admitted. "This is all so new to me, I'm not sure what I will like and what I will dislike. Can we take things slowly until I feel more comfortable?" she asked.

"Of course," he agreed. "We can take this at whatever speed you'd like, Luci," he promised. "How about we go back to my place, and we can talk?" he asked.

"Talk?" she questioned. Luci was hoping that Tyler would want to do more than just talk. She'd waited so long for a chance to be with him, she felt about ready to self-combust.

"Talk," he said. "We need to have open communication for all of this to work, Honey. I told you that I won't rush you through anything, and I want us both to be on the same page when it comes to what you want to do and don't want to do. Trust me, I'm just as anxious about all of this as you are." Hearing him say that he was anxious about anything they were about to do made her want to laugh. Tyler was the coolest, calmest person she had ever known.

"Okay," she agreed. "Can I follow you back to your place though? I don't want to leave my car here."

"Sure, but first, we're going to have dinner," Tyler said. He grabbed her hand and pulled her along with him. She almost had to jog alongside him to keep up with his pace.

"Tyler, slow down," she demanded.

"Can't," he said. "We need to eat so I can get you back to my place."

"How about we just get the food to go?" she asked, pulling her hand free from his. She stopped to catch her breath and he turned to look at her.

"I wanted to take you out and actually eat our dinners this time," he said.

"I appreciate that, but honestly, I'm too on edge to sit

through dinner in a restaurant. Besides, if we eat our dinners at your place, we'll be able to talk freely without having to worry about anyone overhearing our conversation."

"Right," he said, giving her a curt nod. "Let's order and then we can take the food back to my house."

Luci smiled up at him and nodded, "You're the boss, Ty," she sassed. He laughed and gave her ass a quick swat, making her yelp.

"That sassy mouth is going to get you into trouble, Baby," he teased. "Keep it up and I'll treat you to your first spanking tonight."

"You will?" she breathed. God, she was a complete freak. Why did the thought of Tyler spanking her ass make her so wet?

"You would like that, wouldn't you?" he asked.

"Um, I think I would," she admitted. Tyler spun her around and pushed her back up against the brick building. They were almost to the front entrance, and she wondered if anyone would be able to see the two of them. Tyler pressed his body up against hers and she moaned, shamelessly rubbing herself against him.

"You feel so fucking good, Baby," he whispered in her ear. "I can't wait to get you back to my place and start going over the rules. I want to show you my world, Lucinda." She moaned again and this time, the sound was muffled by his mouth covering hers. He kissed and licked his way into her mouth and when he finished with her, releasing her, her legs felt wobbly. Tyler wrapped a protective arm around her and helped her into the restaurant. Calm, cool, and collected Ty was back as if he didn't just drive her completely crazy, pressed up against the side of the brick wall.

"We'd like to order two dinners to go, please," he said to the hostess. "And we're in a hurry," he quickly added.

TYLER

Luci fidgeted with her jacket and he offered to take it from her. Ty slipped it down her arms, letting his fingers graze her bare skin as he revealed it. They had waited twenty long, excruciating minutes at the restaurant for their meals. Then, he had to be apart from Luci while she followed him back to his place. He couldn't blame her for not wanting to leave her car in the parking lot at the restaurant. He just hoped that she wasn't going to use it to run from him if things got to be too much. He wanted to go over everything that they needed to get out on the table and then, he wanted to persuade her to spend the night with him. That wasn't his usual go-to move, but Luci wasn't the typical girl that he contracted to be his submissive. The more time he spent with her, the more he wished he would have paid better attention in high school. But then, he knew that Luci wasn't his type back then and the teenage prick he used to be wouldn't have given her a second glance.

"Your place is nice," she almost whispered. He was going to have to do something to help loosen Lucinda up. Otherwise, their little chat would go nowhere fast.

"How about a drink?" he asked. "You want red or white wine with your dinner?"

"Um, how about red?" she asked.

"That sounds perfect," he agreed.

"Will I get to continue to make decisions like that?" she asked. He pulled out a chair for her at his kitchen table.

"Of which wine you'd prefer?" he asked. Luci nodded and took the dinner that he handed her. "Yes," he said. "Hang out for just a minute while I grab us some plates and the wine." He disappeared into the back of the kitchen and reappeared a few minutes later. Tyler handed her the plates and she got their meals ready while he opened and poured the wine. It was all very domestic, and he wasn't sure how he felt about that.

"You will always have a say about things in your daily life. When we go out, I won't tell you what you should order or drink. That's not the type of submissive I'm looking for," he said. "I want someone who gives me complete control in the bedroom."

"Only in the bedroom?" she asked.

"Well, no," he breathed. "By bedroom, I mean any time we're having sex. I like complete control over my submissive during sex—no matter what room we're in."

"Oh," Luci breathed. He could tell that she was a little flustered and turned on by what he was telling her, and Tyler counted that as a win. By the time he finished with her she'd be a whole lot flustered and so turned on, she'd be begging him for everything that he wanted with her.

Luci sipped her wine and he nodded to her plate of food. "Eat up," he said. She started eating the pasta she had ordered and with every damn bite, she made sexy little moans and noises that made him hard. Why was it so fucking hard to eat a meal around this woman?

"We should talk about what you would like and want to try, and things that you are a hard pass for," he said. Luci practically choked on her dinner.

"All right," she agreed. "Although I already told you that I'm not sure what I will like. I think I'd like to try spanking." Luci brushed her long, red hair back over her shoulder and all Tyler could think about was how he wanted to be behind her, spanking her ass red, and then, he'd fuck her from behind, pulling her long hair until she screamed out his name and came around his dick. Fuck—he needed to stop thinking about shit like that or they wouldn't get through dinner again.

"Spanking your sexy ass is at the top of my list too," he admitted. She shyly smiled and took another bite of pasta.

"I think I'd like for you to tie me up," she said. He stifled his moan and nodded. "That's about the extent of what I know about kink," she admitted. He'd have his work cut out for him. Not only did Luci not know much about his lifestyle, but she had also never really tried any of the basics. He was going to like being the first man to introduce her to his world.

"How about I run things by you before we do them?" he asked. "You know, like tell you what I'm planning on doing with you and you can give me the green light or the red."

"Will red mean that we stop?" she asked.

"For now, yes," he said. "You won't need a safe word until you trust me enough to give me free rein," he said.

"Okay," she breathed. "Will we start tonight?" she asked. God, she sounded so hopeful he almost wanted to laugh.

"That, again, is up to you, Honey. If you'd like to start tonight, I'm game." He was trying not to sound too eager, but he was failing miserably.

"I think I'd like that. Will I be allowed to spend the night?" she asked. He had never had a woman spend the night before. Hell, he'd never had a woman back to his home before. He usually took them to the club and when they were finished, they parted ways.

"I'd like for you to spend the night, Luci," he admitted.

"I'd like that too," she breathed.

They finished their dinner and Luci helped him clean up. Everything about her felt comfortable. He could get used to having her in his home and that was a dangerous thought. Tyler didn't do relationships. He took on subs and that was what she was—he just needed to remember that.

They didn't do much talking during their meal. Lucinda seemed to be a bundle of nerves and he knew that talking about contracts and submission would only help to intensify her fears. Tyler decided to keep the conversation light and it was nice reminiscing about the old days. They might not have spent any time together in high school, but they knew most of the same people, especially since her brother, Ford, was a part of his friends' circle. They spent most of the dinner laughing about her brother's hijinks that usually landed both him and Ford in the principal's office.

He took her into his family room, deciding to get comfortable on the couch. Tyler thought about taking her up to his bedroom, but they still had so much to discuss, that would be a big mistake. He sat down on the sofa and pulled her down next to him, draping her legs across his lap.

"You know," she almost whispered. "We were in the same Creative Writing class when you were a senior," she said. I sat just behind you. He was an ass for not seeing her back then, but he had no recollection of her in that class. Hell, most of his senior year was a blur because he partied so much. Tyler strained his memory trying to remember a nerdy redhead being in that class.

"Wait—did you wear jean overalls a lot?" he asked. Luci made a sound, deep in her throat, which told him just how disgusted she was by those overalls.

"I did," she groaned. "They were awful but back then, I thought I was so cool. I saw Jenelle O'Conner wearing them and I thought she was the coolest girl in the universe. So, I had my mother go out and buy me a pair and I wore them just about every day." Jenelle O'Conner was one of the popular girls in his senior class. He took her to Homecoming that year but that was about all their "relationship" could stand. He couldn't take her incessant whining about the music and how hot the gymnasium was. All he wanted to do was dance as little as possible, hang out with the guys from the football team, and go to the after-parties to get drunk and make out with his hot date. But all that changed when she insisted that he take her home early and by the time he dropped her off, he decided to call it a night and head back to the ranch. Tyler knew that his grandpa would be getting him up at the butt crack of dawn to work on the ranch, and he'd done enough of that hungover to know it wasn't any fun. Looking back now, he saw that Jenelle wanting to go home early and him heading back to the ranch, instead of going to the after-parties, was his saving grace. Ford got pulled over for driving while intoxicated and was charged for underage drinking. He spent a night in a jail cell before his parents showed up the next morning to bail him out. They hired an expensive lawyer and he got off with just community service hours. If Ty would have gone out that night, he probably would have ended up in the car with Ford or worse, driving his grandpa's pick-up truck home, and his grandpa would have let his ass rot in that jail cell rather than bail him out. He sure in hell wouldn't have hired a high-priced lawyer to save his ass from going to juvie. Nope, his grandpa would have let him pay the price for his fuck-ups and that made him love the old guy all the more. Tyler had to learn to be a grown-up and handle his shit before the rest of his friends. His grandfather used to say, "If you're stupid enough to do the crime, you're sure in hell gonna do the time." When he was seventeen, he thought his grandfather was just a stubborn old ass, lacking any compassion. But now, as a full-grown man, he knew that his grandfather was just trying to instill values in him that he hoped to one day teach his own children and grandchildren.

Luci cleared her throat, bringing him back to the present. "Um—sorry," he said. "I was just trying to think back to that class. I think I remember you."

Lucinda rolled her eyes and giggled. "You remember my awful overalls," she said. "Not me, though."

"No, I think I remember you. Didn't you read a poem in front of the class because you won some award for it?" he asked. Luci gasped and he knew that he had remembered correctly.

"Not just the whole class, but the whole school," she said. "God, I was humiliated in front of everyone. Mrs. Donner insisted that I read that stupid poem for the talent show and I was so nervous that I threw up backstage just before I went on. Everyone called me 'Puke' for weeks after that."

"Shit—that's awful." Tyler wasn't about to admit that he remembered her nickname and how all the kids in school talked about some poor girl who threw up backstage at the talent show. High school kids could be so cruel—he included. In fact, he and Ford were probably the worst when it came to making fun of other kids and taking advantage of their popularity.

"Yeah—it was pretty bad until Lisa Myers passed out during an assembly a few weeks later. Everyone forgot about my awful ordeal and focused on spreading false rumors that she was pregnant, and that's why she passed out. I was happy to have the focus off me but God, I felt bad for Lisa. She was my friend. She had low blood sugar and was starving herself to look good in a new pair of jeans she got. We were pretty dumb back then, but it seemed so important at the time. I thought I was going to die if people kept calling me 'Puke,' yet here I am, alive and well," she said, holding her arms out as if proving her point.

"Well, I'm glad you persevered," he teased.

"Thanks," she giggled. He pulled her against his body, and she snuggled into his hold. "That poem that I wrote was about you," she whispered. He wasn't sure that he had heard her correctly at first.

"Me?" he asked. "You wrote a poem about me in high school?"

"Yep, and it won an award," she reminded.

"Well, I'm an award-winning subject," he teased.

"You were," she agreed. "You still are Ty. I know you still see yourself as that high school jock, living in his brother's shadow but you're so much more. I wish you could see yourself through my eyes."

"Honey, I'm not sure if you want to stick to singing my praises. I didn't even remember you in high school until tonight. Hell, I've been an ass to you and you're still sitting here on my couch with me."

"No, Ty," she said, sitting up to be able to look him in the eyes. She framed his face with her small hands, and the way she looked at him nearly did him in. "When we were in school, some of the mean girls knocked into me and I dropped everything in the hallway. My books, my bag—it all went flying while I lay on the concrete floor trying to hold back my tears. You know who helped me up?" she asked.

He had a vague recollection of that day. He had just found out that if he didn't bring up his math grade in the last month and a half of school that was left, he wasn't going to graduate with his class. He was pissed at himself and he knew that if he didn't graduate on time, he'd disappoint his dad and grandpa and that wasn't acceptable. That was the first time that he realized that he needed to get his act together if he wanted to graduate. He decided that from that point on, he was going to grow the hell up and figure his shit out. He was done being the irresponsible jock that everyone counted on him being. He just about tripped over some poor girl on the verge of tears on his way to his locker and he helped her up.

"That was you?" he asked.

"Yep," she said. "I already had a crush the size of Texas on you. You helping me up that day and gathering my belongings for me, kind of sealed your fate as my knight in shining armor."

He barked out his laugh. "I'm no one's knight, Honey," he grumbled.

"You were mine," she argued. "You helped me when every one of those other assholes just stepped over me and laughed about the stupid nerd laying on the floor crying. I hated myself for crying—for showing them weakness. I allowed them to do that to me and now, if I could go back and change things, I'd stand up to those girls."

"You turned into one kick-ass, sexy woman, Lucinda. Those mean girls from high school wouldn't be able to hold a candle to you now," he praised.

"Thank you for that, Tyler," she breathed. "I've embraced my inner nerd. Heck, I love her. She's a part of who I am. But I'm not that same weak girl who let everyone step all over me."

"No—you're not. And here I've been avoiding the topic of you being my submissive because I didn't know if you were ready to talk about it. You're strong as fuck, Baby, and I underestimated you. I'm sorry," he said.

"I'd like to talk about it, Tyler. I want to be with you." Luci straddled his lap and rested her hands on his shoulders. "What do we need to discuss?" she asked. Right about now, he wasn't sure he'd be able to discuss anything. All the blood rushed to his cock and all he could think about doing was sinking into her body.

"Um," he croaked. "You're likes and dislikes. Can I use my hand to spank you?" he asked. She smiled up at him and nodded. "Paddle?" he asked. Her face turned an adorable shade of pink and she ducked her head to shyly nod her agreement. "Flogger?" he asked.

"I'm not sure what that is," she admitted. Their conversation was going to require some show and tell.

"I was holding off on doing this but we need to go to my

bedroom. It will be easier to show you the items that I'm talking about," he said.

"I bet that line works with all the ladies, Ty," she sassed. "Is that how you get them up to your room?" she asked.

"Actually," he breathed. "You're the first woman I've ever brought back to my home, Luci." The surprise in her eyes was almost comical.

"Really?" she asked.

"Yep," he said. "I told you that I don't date. I take on submissives and meet them at the club to play." Yep—that made him sound like a complete ass.

"Why bring me here then?" she asked.

"Because you're different," he admitted. "At least, I want you to be different from the rest of the women I've been with. You good with that, Luci?" he asked.

"Yes," she breathed. "I'm flattered," she said. "I'd like to go up to your bedroom with you. I want you to show me everything, Tyler." His dick was certainly on board with showing her everything, but he also knew that he needed to take things slowly with Luci. He wanted to give her just a taste of his world and hope to hell that it didn't scare her off. He was being honest with her—he never had another woman to his place and he never made a habit of dating or getting involved personally with a woman. Ty felt like he had a connection with her, outside of her being his loan officer, as someone from his past. She was becoming important to him and that thought terrified him.

Tyler stood and lifted her into his arms. "Tyler," she squealed. "Put me down." She was flailing around and giggling. Ty swatted her ass, and she hissed out her breath. He was pretty sure that she liked the sting of his hand on her ass and that only made him want to strip her down and spank her bare, fleshy globes.

"This is going to be fun," he said. Ty dropped her onto the bed and went to his closet. He kept a bag of new toys and things he liked to take to the club, in there. He liked having his own things when working with submissives. It was his personal preference.

He tossed the black duffel bag on his bed next to her and she sat up, curiously looking into the open bag. "What's all this?" she asked.

"A beginning," Tyler said. "It's some things I'd like to introduce you to and then when we go to the club, we'll broaden your education."

"Oh," she breathed. He pulled out a crop and her eyes widened. "Is that the flogger?" she asked.

"Yep," he said. He ran the tip of the flogger over her lips and when she darted out her tongue to lick it, he nearly came in his pants. "That's hot," he breathed.

"I wouldn't mind you using this on me," she said.

"Noted," he whispered. This whole "talking" thing was starting to take a toll on him. He was hard as a rock and ready to be inside of her, but his cock was going to have to wait.

"Now," she whispered. "Will you try it on me now?" Luci looked up at him and the pleading in her eyes was enough for him to nod his head at her in agreement.

"You sure you're ready? I don't want to rush you, Baby," he said. Luci went up on her knees and wrapped her arms around his neck.

"You aren't rushing me, Tyler," she insisted. "I've been waiting for you since I was fifteen years old. I think we've waited long enough."

"Fuck," he swore. "I'm going to be bossy, Honey," he said.

"So you've told me," she teased. "I think you being bossy is hot, Ty."

"Shit," he cursed.

"You seem to be doing a lot of cussing, Tyler," she chastised.

"You're throwing me for a loop, Baby. I didn't plan on this tonight. I wanted to take things slowly with you and just give you a taste of my world." He tossed down the flogger onto the bed and wrapped his arms around her, palming her ass with his big hands. She was perfect for him. Luci seemed to fit with him and he wondered if she'd fit him in every way.

"I'm fine with all of this, Ty," she said. "As you said, I'll tell you if I don't want to try something or if I don't like something—promise." He didn't need any more time to consider his next move with her. He needed her naked and kneeling, there was no other option.

"Up," he ordered. Tyler took her hand and helped her from the bed. He sat back and stretched out. "Strip for me," he demanded. "Slowly." Her sly smile told him that she was up for the challenge he was giving her. Luci tossed her red hair over her shoulder and started to slowly unbutton her blouse. He watched her, unable to look away from the little show she was putting on for him. God, she was beautiful. He sat up a little straighter on the bed, his hands itching to reach out to touch her, but he didn't. She let the silky blouse fall down her shoulders, revealing her lacy, white bra and he damn near swallowed his tongue.

"You are so fucking beautiful," he praised. She seemed to soak up his words and when she shimmied out of her black slacks, he couldn't help his moan. She stood in front of him in just her lacy bra and matching panties. Luci fidgeted and covered herself with her arms.

"Don't," he ordered. "Don't hide from me, Honey," he said. "Let me look at you." She did as he asked, and Tyler let his eyes roam her body. She was perfect and right now, she was his. "Come here," he ordered.

Luci took the two steps toward the bed, and he reached out, framing his hands on her hips. He let his fingers flex in her flesh, pulling her into his body. "These need to go," he ordered, hooking a finger into the side of her panties. He pulled them down her body and helped her step free from them. "Bra too," he said. He was barely holding his shit together. Watching her remove her bra would probably send him over the edge but he couldn't help himself. He held his breath as she unhooked her bra, and when she pulled it free, he huffed it out.

Tyler let his hands roam her body, paying special attention to her breasts. He cupped her full breasts in his hands and she was more than a handful. "You are so perfect," he whispered. He licked and sucked her nipple into his mouth, and she moaned and thrust herself in his direction.

"Yes," she hissed. "Tyler—that feels so good." He pulled her onto his lap and laid back with her, letting her naked body cover him. He suddenly felt like he was wearing too many clothes and all he wanted to do was remove the barrier between the two of them.

He rolled her to the side and pulled his t-shirt over his head, loving the way her hands roamed his upper body. "You work out, don't you?" she asked. He did but that wasn't something that he wanted to discuss right now. He intentionally left on his jeans because if he didn't he knew he'd never get through what he wanted to do next with her.

Tyler grabbed a handful of her ass and squeezed. "Time to make this mine," he said. He sat up and scooted to the edge of the bed. "Over my lap, Baby—ass up," he ordered. She scurried to the end of the bed and laid across his jean-clad lap, presenting her perfect ass to him. "That's it, Honey. We're going to start easy. If you don't like something or if it gets to be too much for you, all you have to do is say the word, 'red'."

"Got it," she agreed, looking back at him over her shoulder. He grabbed the flogger from the bed and ran it down the seam of her ass, loving the way she squirmed against his cock.

"I'll use this to finish you up but for now, I'd like to start with my hand. I want to feel your warm flesh against my palm. You good with that?" he asked. He ran his hand over her fleshy globes as she continued to squirm.

"Yes, Tyler," she moaned. "Please." He raised his hand and let it fall, landing a sharp slap to her right cheek. She groaned and thrust her ass back against his hand when he rubbed the spot that was already turning a pretty shade of pink.

"You good?" he asked.

"I'm fine, Tyler," she insisted. "I need more."

He gave her left cheek the same attention and when she didn't protest the amount of force he used, he began peppering her ass with smacks, turning her skin bright pink. She'd wear his marks in the morning and that thought turned him completely on. Luci was wet and ready for him. He could feel her heat through his jeans and he could smell her arousal. What he wanted to do was toss her over the bed and eat her pussy until she was screaming out his name, but first, he needed to finish what he started. He helped her from his lap and grabbed the flogger.

"Stand at the side of the bed, bend over the mattress, ass in the air, legs spread," he barked orders like a drill sergeant and she quickly obeyed him. "Perfect," he praised. Ty used the flogger to pepper her ass with little stings, knowing that she'd feel every welt he was leaving on her flesh. Seeing her vulnerable like that; giving herself to him, he needed to be inside of her or he was going to come in his jeans.

He finished flogging her ass and when he knew he couldn't take anymore; he unbuttoned his jeans letting his cock spring free. Ty slid into her body, giving her no warning, and filled her. "Shit," he swore. "I forgot the condom." He was always so careful, but Luci made him crazy with lust.

"I'm clean and on the pill," she said.

"I'm clean too, but this is your call, Honey. I can pull out and suit up." He hoped like hell that she'd give him the green light to continue without a condom because she felt so fucking good.

"I want you like this, Ty," she agreed. He pumped in and out of her body, pressing her face and upper body into the mattress. He wasn't gentle and he knew that every time he slammed into her, his thighs hitting her raw ass, it had to smart a little.

Tyler knew that he wasn't going to last long and when he came, he wanted to see her face and know that she was with him. He pulled out of her body and Luci mewled her protest, causing him to chuckle. "I know, Baby," he crooned. "But I want to see you when we come." He turned her around and helped her up onto the bed, covering her body with his own. She wrapped her arms around him and he stroked her red hair back from her face.

"So much better," he said. Tyler kissed her as he thrust back into her drenched pussy. "You feel so fucking good," he said.

Luci wrapped her legs around him, hooking her ankles behind his ass. "You do too, Ty," she said. "I need to come," she cried out. He could tell that she was close and when he picked up the pace, she was shouting out his name in record time. God, she was beautiful when she came, and the way she milked his cock nearly made him go cross-eyed. He pumped into her body just a few more times and when he lost himself, he shouted out her name, spilling his seed deep inside of her. They laid in his bed for what felt like forever, her body wrapped around his, still joined in the most intimate of ways and all he could do was think about how perfectly she fit him. It was almost as if she was made for him and there was no way he'd ever find a more perfect woman. Lucy was everything he had been waiting for but didn't know it. Everything else faded away in the world and the only thing Tyler could hear was his brain screaming, "She's mine," over and over again. She was his but that was something he'd keep to himself for now.

LUCINDA

Two weeks passed and Luci spent most nights at Ty's house. The last thing she needed was to have her brother stop by while Ty was spending the night at her place. She kept that bit of information to herself but that was her reasoning for spending so much time at his house. She still hadn't told Ford that she was seeing Tyler. And telling her branch supervisor that she was sleeping with the man that they were considering for a very large business loan wasn't an option either. Besides Journey, Luci hadn't told anyone else about her and Tyler's arrangement and she was beginning to feel like he was her dirty little secret. It didn't matter that she had lost her heart to him completely or that she had fallen in love with him. Not telling the world about her and Tyler was beginning to weigh on her.

Tonight was the night that he had promised to take her into his club and she had to admit, she was nervous as hell. He had told her what to expect and she even asked Journey half a dozen questions—mostly about what she should wear and how she should behave. Her best friend jokingly told her that it didn't really matter what she wore because Ty would have her naked in front of every member at that club, for most of the night, and that thought terrified her.

She wanted to please him more than anything. Tyler said that made her a natural submissive and she had to admit, she was really liking the lifestyle he was showing her. Luci had never really heard of BDSM or knew what to expect from what Tyler was asking her for. She would have never guessed that she'd enjoy being spanked, flogged, handcuffed, tied up, gagged, and bossed around so much—but she did. She even liked it when Tyler used hot wax on her body. He said that most subs liked a "bite of pain," as he called it. She had to admit, she got off on the pain that he gave her—especially the spankings.

Journey had lent her some things to wear to the club. She never pictured herself wearing a black leather corset and a catholic school girl, much too short, skirt. But when she looked herself over in her full length mirror, she had to admit—she looked pretty good. Luci just hoped that Tyler liked it too. He was going to pick her up at her apartment and then, they were going to spend the night at his place, after they were done at the club.

Luci reapplied her red lipstick just as her doorbell rang and she squealed and clapped her hands as if a surprise gift had just arrived for her birthday. She slipped on her red pumps and hurried down the stairs to the door, pulling it open to reveal her very sexy outfit. Tyler froze in her doorway and looked her body up and down, checking her out.

"You look so fucking hot, Baby," he said. Ty pushed his way into her house and shut the door behind them. He had his black duffel bag full of toys with him. It was strange that every time she saw that bag, she got wet just knowing that it was full of fun toys and gadgets he'd use to get her off. Tonight was no exception; if she was wearing panties, they'd be soaked.

He pushed her up against the wall and kissed her red lips. She knew he probably smeared her lipstick that she just applied, but she didn't care. Luci loved the way Tyler acted as if he couldn't ever get enough of her. When they first started out, she worried that she wouldn't measure up to the rest of the women he had been with. She had no formal training as a submissive and she knew he liked his women obedient—something that she struggled with. But she found that it was easy to give herself over to him. Her job as a bank manager was very demanding. She had to make decisions that affected people's lives every day. Having someone else be in charge, for a change, was nice. She knew that Tyler would never push her past her limits and he never asked her for more than she was willing to give.

He snaked his hand up underneath her short skirt and hissed out his breath when he realized that she wasn't wearing any panties. "I can't wait until we get to the club, Honey. I need you now. You up for some play before we head out?" he asked. She looked down at his duffel bag and back up at him, smiling and eagerly nodding her head. He chuckled, "Well, okay then." He pulled her into his arms and grabbed the bag on his way into her family room. "This good with you?" he asked.

"Yes," she breathed. Honestly, she didn't care where he took her as long as he gave her a mind-blowing orgasm. He laid her across the oversized ottoman that took up most of her living room.

"I'm going to want you to keep the corset on," he ordered. Hell, you can keep the whole outfit on, Baby, as long as I have access to that pussy. He spread her legs and stood between them. She was so ready for him but she could tell by the mischievous glint in his blue eyes that he wanted to play. Ty reached into the large bag and pulled out what looked like a bar.

"This is a spreader," he said. "I hook one end to each ankle, and it opens, spreading your legs apart. Do you want to try it?" he asked.

She looked at the bar, noting the cuffs on either end. It sounded like fun. "Sure," she agreed. "Will it hurt?" she asked.

"Nope," he said. He made quick work of hooking the bar to both ankles and when he pushed a button, the bar expanded and spread her legs wide apart, leaving her completely open for him. He grabbed the bar and flipped her over to her belly, so she was face down.

"Tyler," she hissed.

He smacked her ass, "Quiet or I'll put a ball gag in that sexy little mouth of yours, Baby," he said.

"Tyler, you can't gag me just because I'm talking," she insisted. He laughed and she heard him rummaging through the bag again. He rounded the ottoman and stood in front of her. She could see his impressive erection straining against the zipper to his jeans and she reached for his fly, wanting to help free him. All she could think about was getting him into her mouth. She licked her lips, and he grabbed her hands.

"Not going to happen, Honey." He slapped cuffs on her wrist, and she whimpered. Before she could protest, he slipped a ball gag into her mouth and fastened it around her head. "There," he said, standing back to admire his handy work. "Just a few more things and I think we'll be ready to play." He walked back behind her to where his bag sat on the floor and she was powerless to turn to see what he had planned next. He pulled a blindfold from the bag and covered her eyes, leaving her completely in the dark, literally, and figuratively. She had to admit—it was hot.

"Let's play," he said, giving her ass a sharp slap. Luci was so wet that she was sure she was dripping onto the ottoman. Tyler ran his fingers through her wet pussy and when she tried to thrust back in his direction for more, he gave her ass another sharp slap.

"Stay still," he ordered. "I'll give you what you need and take good care of you but you need to let me do my job, Luci." She nodded and hung her head, ready to give herself over to him completely. This was part of her training and she wasn't about to disappoint Tyler.

She heard more rustling around and she knew he was going through his bag again. He had also stripped out of his clothing because when he stepped behind her, she could feel his bare legs against her. He helped her to her knees, her legs still spread apart by the spreader, but this gave him perfect access to her pussy. She heard the hum of a vibrator and braced for whatever he planned to do with it. The last time he used a vibrator on her, it ended up in her ass and she wasn't sure she'd ever had an orgasm quite like that one. It felt almost as if she was floating on air by the time he finished with her.

"Hold still now, Luci," he reminded. She whimpered and nodded and that seemed to be all the green light Tyler needed. He ran the vibrator through her wet folds and let it rest on her clit. When she didn't think she could take another second of stimulation, he pulled the vibrator away and let her come down. He did this to her over and over again. Tyler took her to the edge and she was so ready to fall but then, he'd pull the dildo free and he'd have to start all over again. Luci was frustrated and ready to shout, "Red" at him, but then she remembered that she had a ball gag in her mouth. He knew exactly how frustrating he was being too. Every time she moaned in distress; he had the nerve to laugh. Tears were streaming down her face and she knew she wouldn't be able to take much more teasing.

"I'm going to give you what you want now, Baby," he whispered into her ear. He ran the vibrator through her wet folds again and this time, when he pressed it against her clit, he sunk into her body, balls deep, and left the vibrator on her clit. They groaned in unison as he rode her with fury. She came and the moan that ripped from her chest sounded foreign even to her own ears. She sounded like a feral animal and that was exactly how she felt. He did that to her. Tyler made her wild and crazy for everything he wanted to do to her, give her, and even take from her.

"What the fuck are you doing to my sister?" She was sure it was a man's voice who had asked that question, but her brain felt disconnected from her body and she couldn't seem to get it to work.

"Ford," Tyler shouted. He pulled free from her body and turned the vibrator off. "Turn the fuck around man," Ty shouted. Oh God, her brother was in her apartment and he could see her—see them having sex. Shit, shit, shit.

"I'll ask you one more time, Tyler. What the hell are you doing to my sister?" Ty was unbuckling her handcuffs and ankle cuffs and she quickly pulled the ball gag from her mouth, along with the blind fold from her eyes. Tyler pulled the blanket from the sofa and wrapped it around her body. Luci blinked against the light, trying to let her eyes adjust. Ford had turned his back to let them get dressed and Tyler pulled on his jeans, lifting her from the ottoman, holding her against his body as if shielding her from her brother.

"Why are you here, Ford?" she whispered. She hated that she felt ashamed about what he had just walked in to find her doing with Tyler. They had nothing to be embarrassed about. In fact, they were supposed to be at the club right now, doing this exact thing in front of a crowd of people. But something about having her older brother catch her and Ty together made her feel like a little girl again and she was regrettably filled with shame and embarrassment.

"I tried calling you and you didn't answer. I was in the neighborhood, so I thought I'd come over to check on you, Luci," he said.

"Well, that was very nice of you, but I'm fine. So, if you don't mind," she said, making as shooing motion with her hands.

"Yeah, well, I do mind, Sis. I mind that my old high school

buddy is doing nasty shit with my sister in her family room. What the hell do you think you were doing with my little sister, Ty?" he asked.

"He wasn't doing anything to me or with me that I didn't want him to," she admitted. "And, what I do with Tyler in my own home or elsewhere isn't any of your concern, Ford."

"You're my sister and that makes it my concern. How could you let him do that to you, Luci?" Ford asked.

Tyler stepped in front of her as if blocking her from Ford's view. "You won't make her feel ashamed of what we were doing. I know you like kink too, Ford. So, don't stand there and act all high and mighty with us. We weren't doing anything wrong."

"How did you two even meet, Sis?" Ford asked. "You know this guy has a reputation for only playing with subs around the club, right?"

Luci pushed past Tyler and stood in front of him. "We met when Ty came into my branch on business and I'm his submissive, Ford. It's what I want and I won't have you come barging into my home, asking questions and making me feel bad for what I'm doing. You need to give me your key to my place. From now on, if you want to come into my home, you can ring the doorbell like a normal person." Luci held out her hand, carefully holding her blanket around her body, not wanting to give her brother any more of a show than she already had. He sighed and pulled out his keys, separated hers from the ring, and handed it to her.

"He's just going to break your heart, Luci. That's who Tyler is. It's who he has been since high school. I know you had a crush on him but I never thought he'd give you a second look," Ford said. His words felt as though he had physically slapped her.

"And why is that Ford?" she asked.

"Because you're not his type," her brother responded. She knew what type of woman Tyler usually went for and her brother was right—she wasn't his usual type. Luci had been dealing with feelings of insecurity her whole life and being with Ty just compounded those feelings. He was everything she ever wanted and so much more, but did he feel the same way about her or would he get bored with her and dump her for the next pretty submissive he found?

"Who the fuck are you to say what my type is, Ford. I think you're judging me on who I used to be. You haven't talked to me in years and all you know about me now is my reputation around the club. Your sister is who I want and if you or anyone else has an issue with that, you can talk to me privately." Tyler wrapped his arms around her from behind and pulled her back against his body. "I'm in love with your sister and nothing will change that."

"You're what?" she asked, turning to face him.

"I'm in love with you, Luci," he said.

Ford barked out his laugh, reminding her that he was still there. For just a few seconds, she had forgotten everything else but Tyler. Hearing him admit that he was in love with her was more than she could have ever hoped for.

"He's using you, Sis. Whatever business he has with your bank, as soon as it's over, he'll dump you. I just hope you won't expect me to be there as your shoulder to cry on when that happens," Ford warned. She turned back to face her angry brother and pointed her finger at him.

"Get the hell out of my house, Ford. I might not be his type. Hell, I'm a nerd and proud of it, but I'm in love with Tyler too. I won't have you come into my home and tell me that I'm making a mistake by admitting my feelings about him. I want to be with him and if that's not okay with you, then stay the hell out of my life." Ford looked her over as if she had lost her mind, and maybe she had. The hurt in her brother's eyes almost had her recanting her words and begging him to just understand that she wanted to be with Ty. He wasn't going to accept the two of them together though, that much was clear.

"Later, Sis," Ford spat. Luci held back her tears as she watched her brother walk out. A part of her wondered if she'd ever be able to find a way to convince him that she was doing the right thing by being with Tyler, but she was pretty sure she already knew the answer to her question—she wouldn't.

All she really knew was that the man of her dreams had just told her that he was in love with her. "Did you really mean what you just told my brother?" she asked, not turning back to look Tyler in the eyes. She didn't want to know if he had been lying when he told Ford that he loved her. She wanted to live in the fantasy of being his for as long as possible.

"Luci," he whispered, "turn around and look at me, please." She wanted to, really, she did but she felt frozen to the spot where she was standing, unable to physically or mentally face him. She felt his hands on her shoulders and Ty slowly spun her around. She looked up into his blue eyes and she saw the truth—he did love her. How had she missed that look over the past couple weeks? Had he always looked at her like that and she was just too lost in her own fantasy world to notice it before now?

"I can't explain any of this, but I am in love with you. I know this all seems sudden and I know what your brother said probably put doubts in your mind. I don't care about contracts or other submissives. I don't care about the fucking loan. I want a future with you and that's it. I've fallen for you. Did you mean it when you told Ford that you're in love with me?" he asked.

"Yes," she whispered. "I'm in love with you and I want a future with you too, Tyler." He pulled her against his body, and she dropped the blanket she was holding. "And technically, I never signed a contract, but I'm your submissive. I love being yours, Ty." She wrapped her arms around his body and went up on her tip toes to kiss him.

"Thank fuck. I've been trying to figure out a way to tell you how I've been feeling," he whispered against her lips.

"Will you still take me to your club?" she asked.

"Yes—but not tonight. Right now, I want you all to myself, Baby," he said. She nodded and giggled as he lifted her into his arms. Tyler carried her up to her bedroom and made love to her and she knew that she'd be his for as long as he'd ask her to be. She belonged to him—it was just that simple.

TYLER

They spent the next few days together talking about the future and he had to admit, he was pretty damn excited to know that his future would include his fiery, nerdy, redhead. Ty was going to ask her to move into his little house with him tonight over dinner, but then she called and asked if he could meet her down at the bank. He was also going to surprise her with tickets to the local comic con that was coming to town next weekend and if she agreed, he had something even bigger planned.

Luci had been hinting for days now that she wanted to go to comic con, but the tickets had sold out months ago. What she didn't know was that his sister-in-law, Rose, had connections. Well, her son, Corbin, and his best friend, Aiden, had connections. They were able to get him two tickets for the con and he was going to give them to her over dinner tonight. But then, his wheels started spinning and he decided to use the event for something bigger—something he decided he wanted to do with her the day her brother walked in on them. Tyler wanted to ask her to marry him at comic con. He had the ring and the perfect woman to give it to, all she had to do was say yes—first to going to comic con with him and then to his proposal.

Tyler agreed to pick her up a little early, down at the bank, since she had asked him to meet her there. He found her sitting behind her desk and smiled. Luci was really in her element in her little office, wearing her sexy, nerdy glasses and her red hair up in a messy bun. She wore a black business pantsuit, with a white silk blouse underneath, that always turned him on. He loved knowing that he could strip her out of that stuffy suit, and she'd be panting and screaming out his name within minutes. There was no way he'd ever let her go now.

He had dropped Luci off at work that morning and planned on just meeting her at the restaurant. She was going to have a co-worker give her a lift because he wasn't sure how long he would be out at the ranch. But when Luci called him and asked if he could pick her up early, he made an excuse up to his brother and left Clay holding the bag. Really, he was just missing the last leg of feeding the cattle, and his brother seemed fine with him taking off early.

"Hey," Ty breathed, walking into Luci's office.

"Oh good," she said, standing from behind her desk. "I was hoping you'd be able to come in early. I have news for you," she said.

"News?" he asked, feeling a little worried. "It must be pretty serious if you called me into your office," he teased. A part of him felt like he had just been called in by the principal to the office. He thought it might be hot to have her reprimand him and then, he could turn the tables and spank her on her desk. Yeah—her whole hot manager vibe was making him horny.

She rolled her eyes as if she could read every dirty thought that was running through his mind. He grabbed her hand and pulled her into his arms. "Move in with me," he breathed. Ty leaned in to gently kiss her lips, noting the way her eyes widened with the surprise of his question. "Move into my place.

Let's start our forever together now, Luci," he asked again when she made no move to answer him.

"I—I can't move in with you," she stuttered. The disappointment felt like someone was stabbing him in the gut. He thought that they were on the same page. They had just declared their feelings toward each other in front of her very angry brother, no less. But Lucinda turning him down made him question it all.

"I see," he said, dropping his arms to his side. "I'm rushing things, aren't I?" he asked, suddenly feeling foolish for going out to buy an engagement ring for her. He was jumping into their relationship with both feet while Luci was just testing the water, dipping her toes in.

"No—not at all and I'm pretty sure that you don't see, Tyler," she said. "I can't move in with you because you won't have a house to live in for very much longer."

"Wait—what?" he asked.

"You will need to sell your house—it's the only way," Luci insisted.

"The only way?" he questioned.

"Yes, the only way that the bank will approve your loan." She smiled up at him and pulled his hand into hers. "You see, I told my boss about us dating. I came clean about the whole thing and turned your case over to him. I recused myself from making a decision about your loan and he promised me that he would take care of it personally. He took almost a week to look everything over, but he decided that you are a good risk to take. Your experience with ranching gives you a leg up on the competition out there and well, he said he's willing to take a chance on you if you can sell your current home and put the money back into the loan."

"I got the loan?" he whispered. "I'll have my ranch?"

"Yep—and if you're still game, you can move into my place. You know—until the ranch house is done. Then, if you're not sick of me, we can move in there."

He pulled her into his arms and kissed her, not caring that her whole office was watching them through the glass wall. He broke their kiss and framed her face with his hands. "You've figured this whole thing out, haven't you?" he asked.

"Well, you do need a place to live, once your house sells, and you did promise me a future together," she teased.

"I did," he agreed.

"I figured us moving in together was a good start," she said. "Seems like you had the same idea."

"I did," he breathed. "How about you let me take you out to dinner to thank you for your help with my loan and then, I think I can show you just how much I appreciate you by a little shameless worshiping of your body."

"Now that is something I think I can handle," she agreed. "I can be ready to go in a few. How about you sign some loan papers while I finish up here?" she asked. "My boss is expecting you." She pointed him in the right direction and gave him a little push. He was going to sign the papers that could be not only a fresh start for himself but them as a couple. Their future together was looking brighter by the minute.

❄

Ty fidgeted with the table cloth and Luci seemed to notice how nervous he was. Tonight was just the precursor to the big event. First, he had to get her to agree to comic con, and then, he'd have to shake off his nerves and ask her to be his wife. He carried the ring everywhere with him, since picking it up at the jewelry store two days prior. The little black ring box felt as though it was going to burn a hole through his pocket, he wanted to give her the ring so badly.

"You seem nervous, Ty," she whispered across the cozy table. "Are you having second thoughts about us living together?" Luci asked.

"No," he said. "Never—I meant it when I said that I want

to live with you, Honey. I have a surprise for you and well, I guess I'm just nervous about asking you."

Her eyes lit up, "I love surprises," she said.

"I know you do and I think that this is a good one." He reached into his pocket and pulled out the tickets and handed them to her. "How would you like to go to comic con with me?" he asked. She studied the tickets and he noted the hint of disappointment in her eyes.

"Oh—I'd love to," she said. Luci held the tickets against her chest and smiled at him. "The event was sold out. How did you get these?" she asked.

"Clay's wife, Rose, has connections. She got them for me," he said.

"I'd love to thank her. When will I meet your family, Tyler?" That was a very good question. He had been avoiding his brother as much as possible lately, not wanting to tell him about the possibility of getting the loan and leaving Lowdown Ranch. He'd go to work every day, taking on whatever jobs he could do that wouldn't involve a run-in with Clay, and when his day was done, he high tailed it out of there. Clay knew something was up—he had to. Ty usually stuck around to bum dinner off of Rose but lately, he was gone by quitting time.

"How about if we have them over to dinner on Friday?" he asked.

"That's in two days," she said.

"Yes, I'm aware," he teased. "We can order out or I can grill. What do you think?" She squinted her eyes at him, and he smiled his best smile at her.

"You're up to something," she accused. How did she know him so well after just a few weeks together?

"Fine," he breathed. "I have to tell Clay about the loan and my buying the Peterson place. He doesn't know that I've been thinking about leaving and well, I think he'll take it better with you and Rose around. What do you say? Want to help save my ass?"

She looked him over and smirked. "Well, I do love your ass, Tyler," she sassed. He chuckled and grabbed her hand across the table.

"So, you'll help me out and be a buffer between Clay and me?" he asked. She sighed and nodded. "Thanks, Honey," he said. "I'll owe you."

She giggled, "Tonight is going to be a very good night for me," she whispered.

"Topping from the bottom will only get you a red, sore ass, Baby," he said. "You sure you want to do that?" She smiled at him across the table. He knew she would accept his challenge and he had to admit, spanking her ass red sounded like a damn good night to him.

"I want to do that, Tyler," she breathed. "Tell me more about this topping from the bottom thing. I think I need details if it will earn me a spanking." Tyler couldn't help but laugh at her.

"You're going to give me so much trouble, aren't you, Honey?" he asked.

Luci shrugged and nodded, pasting on her best smile, "Yep," she admitted. "Every chance I get."

❄

Clay and Rose were due to arrive at his place any minute and watching Luci rush around his kitchen, fussing over every little detail made him laugh. She had no idea that the next day, he was going to ask her to be his wife while they were at comic con. First, they needed to get through the next few hours, and he had to come clean with his brother. Clay had a right to know that he was leaving, no matter how pissed off he was going to be.

Luci whisked past him with a big bowl of potato salad in her hands and he waited for her to put it onto the table before pulling her into his arms. "Everything looks wonderful, Luci," he said. He could feel her heart beating as if it was going to thump right out of her chest. He hated how nervous she seemed about meeting his family, but he was honestly feeling the same way about telling his brother about leaving the ranch to start his own.

"I just want to make a good impression with your brother and his wife," she admitted. "My own brother won't talk to me since he walked in on us and well, I'd like for one of us to have family that isn't pissed off at us," she teased. He felt awful that Ford wasn't returning any of her calls. It had been a week since he caught the two of them together. Sure, finding your little sister bound, gagged, and being fucked in the family room wasn't the most ideal, but Ford had to talk to her at some point. At least, Ty hoped so for Luci's sake.

"My brother and Rose will love you, Baby. I mean—what's not to love? As for your brother, maybe we should invite him over for dinner at some point—you know, break the ice, and let him see that we're in this thing for more than, um—sex."

He was hoping that once he put a ring on her finger and got her to agree to marry him, her brother would see that he wasn't just using her as his submissive. He wanted forever with Luci and once Ford accepted that he'd start talking to his sister again.

The doorbell rang and Luci took a deep breath. "It's time," she breathed. He laughed at how "doom and gloom" she sounded.

"Just breathe," he said. "I'll answer the door and you finish up in here." He kissed her and went to let his brother and Rose in. He was trying to make her feel comfortable about the whole night, but he was feeling completely on edge himself. He pulled the door open and plastered on his best smile. "Hey guys," he said. Clay's frown was firmly in place and Rose looked worried.

"Why is your house for sale?" she asked.

"What, no hello?" Tyler teased.

"Hello," Clay said. "Why the fuck is your house on the market?" he asked.

"Um, because I'm selling it," he admitted. "Just come in and I'll tell you everything." He stood aside and ushered them into the house. Luci joined him in the front foyer and took the dish that Rose was holding.

"This is Lucinda," Tyler said. "My girlfriend." Honestly, calling her his fiancée was on the tip of his tongue. He wanted to tell his brother that he was going to ask her to marry him. Hell, he wanted to tell the whole world that he wanted to marry her but first, he needed to pop the question to Luci. "This is my brother, Clay, and his wife, Rose," he said. They all shook hands and exchanged pleasantries but he could tell that Clay was chomping at the bit to get to the point where he told him about selling his house.

"Dinner's ready," Luci said. "I hope you like roast."

"Love it," Rose said. "It's one of Clay's favorite meals." Ty knew that and that was why he asked her to make that for dinner—to help butter his brother up.

"Great," Luci said. "Why don't we sit down?" They all followed her to the dining room and he and Clay sat at opposite ends of the table. He could feel his brother staring at him and he knew that it was going to be best if he just ripped off the band-aid and tell his brother all of it.

"The house is for sale because I have to sell it. The bank is making me," Ty said.

"If you needed money, Ty, I'd be happy to lend it to you, but you didn't have to lose your house. How stubborn do you have to be before you give up some of your pride and come to me? You're my brother and I'd always try to help you, Ty," Clay said.

"I know that Clay, and I appreciate it. But, I had to do this on my own. You see, I'm buying the Peterson ranch. I just signed the papers this morning. That's how I met Luci—she's the manager at the bank where I got the loan for the property.

One of the stipulations was that I sell this place to put the money down on the ranch house I'm going to build out there."

"Wait, you're buying the Peterson ranch? What about Lowdown?" Clay asked. This was the part Ty wasn't looking forward to.

"I want a place of my own, Clay," he admitted. Rose reached across the table and took her husband's hand into her own. "Grandpa's ranch has always been yours, Clay. You took it over when Dad died and were kind enough to bring me along with you for the ride. You even treated me as a partner, even though I didn't always act like one. You put up with my rebellion and slacking off when you needed me most, and I appreciate everything. But it's time for me to make my own way. I've always dreamed of having a ranch of my own, I just worried that telling you that would only hurt you. Honestly, I didn't think that it would ever happen. I didn't think that I'd find a bank willing to take a chance on me." Tyler smiled at Luci and reached for her hand. She took it and squeezed his hand into her own, letting him know that he wasn't alone in all of this.

Clay sighed and sat back in his chair. "I get it, Ty," he breathed. "I'm not thrilled that you're leaving Lowdown, but I get it. I hope you know you'll always have a place on the ranch. Grandpa left it to you too," Clay said.

"I appreciate that," Ty said. "Maybe we could work on a few projects together. After all, we will be neighbors."

"I'd like that, man." Clay stood and rounded the table to pull Tyler up from his chair and into a big bear hug. "I'm proud of you, brother—Dad and Grandpa would be too."

Hearing his brother say that choked him up a little. Having Clay's approval meant more to him than he'd ever admitted out loud.

"Thanks, Clay," Tyler choked.

"Of course," he said. "We can talk business later. How about we eat some roast and get to know your girl here," Clay said.

He sat back down and looked at Lucinda. "You look familiar," he said. "Have we met?"

"Actually, we have. You were friends with my brother, Ford Dixon," she said.

"Hey, yeah," Clay said. "Ford was a freshman with Ty when I was a senior. As I remember, you and Ford got yourselves in a whole lot of trouble together. You had Dad and Grandpa running down to that school just about every other day to get you out of the principal's office."

"Yeah—we stirred some shit up in high school. Especially after you graduated," Ty remembered. "And poor Dad and Grandpa bailed me out of sticky situations more times than I care to admit. Lucinda graduated two years after I did and well, I was a dumb ass and didn't pay attention to her in school."

"I was a complete nerd back then," she said. "I hardly think I was Ty's type."

"Well, you're definitely my type now, Baby," he breathed. He winked at her and her giggle filled the dining room.

"So, you two met when you went into the bank for a loan?" Rose asked.

"Yep," Tyler said. "She was my loan manager until she admitted to her boss that she's in love with me and can't live without me. My case was turned over to her supervisor when that happened." Clay choked on his roast and Tyler laughed.

"In love with you?" Clay asked.

"Yes," Luci breathed. "But as I recall, I wasn't alone in my admission. You also said that you're in love with me, Tyler," she chided. Clay dropped his fork onto his plate, drawing attention from the three of them.

"I did," Tyler said, not taking his eyes from Luci. "I do," he whispered. He couldn't wait to say those words to her someday. He just hoped like hell that she agreed to be his wife.

"Can I talk to you in the kitchen for a minute, Ty?" Clay asked.

"Whatever you have to say to me, you can say it in front of Lucinda," Tyler said.

"Well, I just think that this is awfully sudden. I mean, you two have known each other for how long, exactly?" Clay asked.

"Well, since she was fifteen and I was seventeen," Tyler teased.

"That's not exactly true," Luci admitted. "I knew who Ty was in high school. Heck, I had such a crush on him, but he had no idea who I was. We've officially known each other for a little over a month now. I know it sounds crazy and seems way too fast for us to be claiming that we're in love, but it's how we feel." Ty reached under the table and put his hand on her thigh, needing the contact with her.

"I've asked her to move in with me," Tyler said.

"But you're moving," Rose reminded.

"Right, that's why I asked Ty to move in with me. Well, until he builds his new house at the ranch, and then we'll move out there," Luci said.

Clay pushed his half-full plate back from himself and tossed his napkin on the table. "So, that's it? You're just going to build a house together and move in with each other. What happens if this thing between you two doesn't work out? What happens if you get to the two-month mark and decide that it was just a fling?"

Rose gasped and looked at her husband, "Clay, how can you say such awful things to your brother and Luci? I'm happy for you—both of you. It wasn't that long ago that everyone thought that Clay and I were crazy for falling in love so quickly. We didn't know each other very long before I moved to the ranch, Clay," she reminded.

"Sorry, but I won't sit here and pretend to be all right with this, Rose," Clay said.

Tyler stood and threw his napkin down onto the table. "You don't have to be all right with any of this, Clay. If our relationship upsets you—there's the door," he said, pointing to the front door. "But I love Luci and I want to spend the rest of my life with her. I want to marry her."

"Marry her?" Clay asked.

Ty reached into his pocket and pulled out the ring box that he kept on himself since purchasing it. He didn't want Luci to accidentally find it, so he kept it in his pocket. He opened the box and held it out to his brother as if trying to prove a point. "Marry her," Ty repeated. Luci's gasp filled the room, and she covered her mouth with her trembling hand. Tyler realized what he had done. In his anger at Clay, he had fucked up his whole proposal plan.

"Shit," he grumbled.

"Ty," she whispered. He pulled her up to stand and held the ring out to her.

"I'm sorry that I fucked it all up, Luci. I was going to ask you at comic con tomorrow, but I let my anger get the best of me. I know I don't deserve you, Honey," he admitted. "But I want to spend every day, for the rest of my life, trying to earn the right to call you mine. Marry me, Luci," he said. Luci wiped at the tears falling down her face and nodded.

"I'll marry you," she sobbed. He pulled the ring from the box and slipped it onto her finger. It looked right to see his ring on her hand.

"Well, it's about damn time," Clay said. Tyler looked at his brother who was grinning like a loon at the both of them. Rose sat next to him, smiling through her tears.

"Wait—you wanted this to happen?" Tyler asked.

"Yep," Clay said. "I was worried that you two would move in together and wouldn't commit. I wasn't sure if you were serious until you pulled that fucking ring out of your pocket. Congrats, man," his brother said. He and Rose both stood and pulled Luci, and then him in for a hug.

"I think I'm in shock," Luci admitted. "I didn't expect this at all, Ty."

"How about we get out of your hair and let you guys celebrate privately," Rose offered.

"No—you two don't have to leave," Lucinda protested.

"We do, but we'll all get together to celebrate soon," Clay promised. "Hell, between your engagement and Ty's new ranch, we have a lot to celebrate."

"Our new ranch," Tyler said, wrapping his arm around Luci.

LUCINDA

Luci wasn't sure why she was nervous. Ford was her brother but the way she was acting, it was almost like she was waiting for someone important to show up at her favorite little diner. She had asked him to meet her there for coffee and he actually agreed. Luci was surprised when he returned her phone call since she had been trying to reach him for weeks now. Ford called her back and told her that he just needed some time to work through what he had walked in on.

She knew it had to be shocking, the way he found her and Ty together, but she was a grown woman who agreed to everything Tyler was doing to her. Hell, she more than agreed, she loved every minute of it, but that wasn't something she'd tell her brother. She knew he wouldn't want to talk about it—that wasn't his style. In fact, Ford would want to pretend that it never happened, and that was just fine with her. He didn't like to talk about her personal life and she felt the same way about him. Ford didn't share his latest conquests with her and she never discussed who she was dating—not that there had been many guys to tell him about over the years.

She ordered some coffee for herself and sat in the corner

booth that they usually had Sunday brunch in. They were regulars at the diner, and when her brother walked in, she knew it from the way the waitresses fawned over him. Her brother was good looking and Ford knew exactly how to work his charm on the ladies. She smiled at him as he quickly scanned the room for her and waved him over. Ford slid into the booth across from her and ordered a coffee as soon as the waitress came over to take his order.

"We doing breakfast?" he asked.

"God, I hope so, I'm starving," she admitted. Ford laughed and pulled two menus from the next table over, handing her one. She took it and opened the menu, pretending to look it over. They both already knew what they wanted for breakfast. They always ordered the same thing. Ford ordered pancakes and she ordered French toast. They were creatures of habit and they were avoiding what happened between them by pretending not to be.

The waitress came back with Ford's coffee and took their orders, smiling and winking at Ford when he handed her their menus, making Luci roll her eyes at him. They sat in silence until their food came out. "We good?" Ford said around a mouthful of pancakes. She wanted to tell him that was more a question for her to ask him, but she wasn't going to look a gift horse in the mouth. Luci hoped that they were good. She missed him the last few weeks that he was taking his time and ignoring her. It hurt that he could shut her out of his life the way he had.

"Not sure," she answered honestly. "I need to know that you're going to be more accepting of me being with Tyler."

Ford groaned and shoved another bite of pancake into his mouth. "How about we agree to not bring up his name while we're hanging out together, and I'll accept that you're sleeping with him."

"It's more than me sleeping with Tyler, Ford." He pushed another bite into his already full mouth and she almost wanted to giggle. Instead, she used the fact that his mouth was too busy chewing to lecture her about her choice in men. "I'm in love with him and well, he's asked me to marry him." She held out her engagement ring and he studied it, pulling her hand into his own.

"Seriously?" he asked.

"Yep," she said. "He asked me a couple of weeks ago. I wanted to tell you sooner, but you wouldn't return any of my calls," she said.

"Shit—sorry about that," he said. "I took a quick assignment and was out of town for the past two weeks." Ford was in the military—US Army Special Forces, and he was always going on quick, secret missions he couldn't tell anyone about.

"You usually tell me when you're going out," she said. He always called her to let her know that he was going on a mission so she wouldn't worry about him not being in touch. She knew that when he was in the field, he couldn't call her.

"As I said, I needed a little time, Luci," he whispered. "Finding my little sister bound and gagged in her family room wasn't something I ever wanted to see," he hissed.

Luci quickly looked around to make sure that no one heard what her brother had said. "Keep your voice down," she said. "What I do in the privacy of my home isn't your or anyone else's business. You walked into my house and found us. I won't apologize for what Ty and I were doing. We are two consenting adults and we did nothing wrong."

"No," he said, sitting back in the booth. "You didn't and I acted like an ass. I guess finding you with Tyler just threw me for a loop. I haven't seen the guy in years, and when he turns back up in my life, I find him with you—like that," he said.

"I get that it must have been quite a shock," she agreed. "Can you accept the two of us together, Ford, or is this going to be weird?"

"I think I can accept the two of you together," he said.

"You'll just have to give me some time to get used to everything."

"Um, how much time do you think you'll need?" she asked.

"No idea, why?" He wasn't going to like this next part, but she wanted him to give her away when she married Ty.

"Because I'm getting married," she said.

"You said that already," he grumbled.

"I'm getting married in two weeks, Ford. I'd like for you to give me away," she said.

"Two weeks?" he asked. "Why so quickly?"

"Why wait?" she asked. "I mean, we know how we feel and decided that we didn't want to wait."

"Are you pregnant?" he whispered. She giggled and shook her head.

"Not yet but I'd like to be as soon as we're married. Tyler is kind of old-fashioned, in that way. He wants to get married first and I want a baby. We just want a small ceremony and it's going to be on the ranch that Ty and I are buying. We want to start our life on the same land where we'll work together. I'm going to work at the bank for a bit longer, to help get us started, but then I'd like to try my hand at being a wife and mom for a while."

Ford nodded and took her hand from across the table. "You will make an awesome wife and mom, Sis. You were born to be a mom."

"Thanks for that, Ford. So, you'll give me away at my wedding?" she asked.

He didn't even take the time to think about it. "Yes," he breathed. "I'll give you away to Tyler," he agreed.

"Thank you, Ford," she said.

"No problem. Just do me a favor and hang a sock on the door when you guys don't want company, from now on. I don't think I can take another surprise like that last one again."

Luci giggled, "Deal," she said.

She wasn't sure how it had all come together, but she and Ty had pulled it off. Well, their families had chipped in and lent a hand too. Both of their brothers had helped get the gazebo built and they were going to stand under it to exchange their vows. She had found a white dress that was off the shoulders and way too sexy to be considered a traditional wedding dress, but she loved it, and apparently, so did Ty. The way his face lit up when he saw her at the end of the makeshift aisle, holding onto her brother's arm, told her just how much he liked it. She could almost guess every dirty thought that ran through his mind as he watched her walk down the aisle. Tyler looked so happy in his suit, standing up under the gazebo, waiting for her. She had waited her whole life to be with Ty. Luci had come a long way from the girl who used to follow him around high school, lurking in dark corners, lusting after him. The same girl who used to practice writing her first name with his last name would now have that wish come true. She was going to finally be Lucinda Nash and she didn't think it was possible for her to be any happier.

Ford walked her down the aisle and placed her hand into Ty's. "Take care of her, man," Ford said to his old friend.

"Always," Tyler promised. "You have my word, man." Ford kissed her cheek and took a seat next to her best friend Journey. They had only invited a small group of close friends and family since neither she nor Tyler had much family. It was just them, the pastor they found to marry them at the last minute, and their handful of guests, and it was perfect.

"You look beautiful," Ty whispered to her.

"So do you," she said. He chuckled and pulled her against his body, giving her a quick kiss.

"Sorry, I had to," he said to the pastor when he cleared his throat.

"Are we ready to start?" he asked. Tyler and Luci both

nodded and joined hands. They exchanged vows and when the pastor pronounced them man and wife, everyone got up to clap and cheer for them.

After the ceremony, they planned a small reception and danced the night away under the stars and she had to admit, she couldn't imagine her wedding any better than it turned out. Tyler and she had planned the day together and it fit both of them so well.

He held her in his arms, swaying to the music and when he smiled down at her and told her that he loved her, she knew that she had found her forever. "I love you too, Ty," she said.

"I can't believe that we're starting our lives together, here on the same land that we'll be building our lives and our family on. Who knew that when I walked into your bank that day that I'd meet the woman of my dreams?" he asked. She sighed and laid her head on his shoulder as he stroked her red hair from her face. "My wife," he breathed. "My nerdy submissive," he teased.

Luci giggled, "Always," she agreed.

HIS STUBBORN SUBMISSIVE

FORD

Ford Dixon watched as the sexy little brunette left the restaurant on the arm of some asshole and he wanted to get up and follow her the fuck out of there. Journey Ross had been his walking wet dream for as long as he could remember. Hell, he'd known her his whole life—she was his younger sister's best friend since they were all just kids, and that was exactly why she should be off-limits. The problem was his dick didn't get the memo that he needed to keep his hands off his sister's best friend.

The question was, who the fuck was the asshat she was having dinner with? Ford had spent the better part of his adult life asking Journey out. Every damn time he asked her to go to dinner or even just come over to his place for some drinks and to watch a movie, she turned him down flat. Once, he got up the nerve to ask her why and she told him that she just didn't have time for dating. She was a journalist for CNN and spent a lot of time traveling, chasing down the next story. He knew how busy she was, but he tried timing asking her out around her work schedule. He had even asked her out for tonight and she said that she had to work all weekend, to meet a deadline for an article, that was already past due. He was such a fool for believing her, but that was his own fault. He let his feelings cloud his assessment of Journey and she pulled one over on him once again.

Ford quickly paid his bar tab and followed her out into the parking lot, against his better judgment, to confront Journey. He stepped out into the cold evening air and quickly looked around the half-empty parking lot. He spotted Journey standing next to her SUV, door open, and smiling her best, "Get the fuck away from me smile," at the guy she had dinner with. Yeah —that pissed him off. He wanted to walk over to them and punch the asshole in the face, but he needed to remember that Journey made her choice to go out with the guy instead of him. She made her bed and now, she needed to figure her shit out. Keeping his nose out of her business was going to be difficult for two reasons though. One, she saw him across the parking lot and made eye contact with him. He saw the pleading in her dark eyes and knew he wouldn't be able to walk away from her. The second reason had to do with the fact that his pick-up was parked right next to her SUV and there would be no possible way for him to avoid her.

Ford casually walked up to his truck; his heartfelt about ready to beat out of his chest and nodded to Journey. That seemed to be the only recognition she needed. "Ford," she almost squealed. "Good to see you." Her fake smile was still in place, and he could tell that something was up.

"Journey," he breathed. "Good to see you too. I thought you were going to be working on an article all weekend," he said. Letting her off the hook wasn't something he was ready to do.

She nodded, and he knew she was going to ignore his snide comment. "Actually, I just had an impromptu meeting with my boss," she said, pointing to the guy who was standing a little too close to her as if marking his territory. "This is Andrew Tinsley," she said. "Andrew, this is one of my oldest friends, Ford Dixon." The guy held out his hand but made no move toward

Ford. He was being tested, and that was just fine with him. He was used to dealing with assholes who thought that he was beneath their station. In the military, he learned fast how to take orders and kiss ass when necessary. The thing was, he didn't need to kiss Andrew Tinsley's ass. Andrew dropped his arm back to his side when he realized that Ford wasn't going to make a move to accept his hand.

"Good to meet you, Ford," Andrew said.

"Likewise," Ford lied.

"Um, I'm glad that I ran into you, Ford. Your sister just called me and that's why I've had to cut our work dinner short. She needs me to run over to her place with some soup. Poor Lucinda said that she is not feeling well and I want to take her some chicken noodle soup. That always makes me feel better when I'm sick." She smiled at him and subtly winked. Yeah, she was lying. He knew that his sister wasn't ill. In fact, he stopped by her place on the way to the restaurant and he knew that Lucinda was just fine. She and Ty were planning a romantic night in, and he couldn't get out of their place fast enough. The two of them grossed him out and made him long for stuff he never thought he wanted. He had a feeling that Journey was trying to get rid of her dinner date and for just a split second, he was thinking about letting her suffer on her own. But that would be cruel. Almost as cruel as she was to him every time he asked her out and she turned him down flat.

"I'd like to check on my sister too," he said, playing along. "You want to ride with me?" he asked.

"Well, I have my car," she said nodding to her SUV. And if she left in her car, her boss would probably follow her home and insist on a nightcap.

"Right, but this way you can run in and pick up the soup, from that little place that Lucinda likes, and you won't have to fight for parking," he insisted. He was hoping she'd catch on, but he could see that she was ready to give him a fight.

"Or I could just take you over to see your friend. We could

take my car, and then finish our meeting back at your place," Andrew offered. It was almost as if Ford could see the lightbulb go off in her head when she realized what he was trying to do.

"Oh no, that won't be necessary," Journey said. "I wouldn't want to expose you to whatever Luci has. Besides, she'd kill me if I brought someone over when she's not at her best."

She turned her back to Andrew and mouthed, "Thank you," to Ford. "I'd love a ride, Ford. Thank you," she said. "I'll see you at the office, Andrew," she said, effectively dismissing her boss. Ford noticed the flash of anger in the guy's eyes just before his easy smile was back in place.

"Not a big deal," Andrew lied. "I hope your friend is feeling better soon. I'll see you at the office on Monday," he said. Andrew leaned in to kiss her cheek and she pulled away from him before he could pull her into his body for a hug. For a boss, the guy was pretty handsy and Ford wondered if there might be some history between Journey and her employer.

"See you Monday," she said. Andrew crossed the parking lot and got into his very expensive, overly pretentious car. He made no move to start his car or leave the parking lot.

Journey looked back over her shoulder and back to Ford. "What now? He's not going to leave while we're standing here. I can't just get into my car and leave because then he'll know I was lying."

"Are you sleeping with your boss, Journey?" Ford asked. Sure, it wasn't any of his business but he just couldn't help himself.

"What? No," she spat. "I've never slept with him. How unprofessional would that make me?" she asked.

"Yeah—I have a feeling that your boss is an HR nightmare," Ford said.

"So, you're not with that guy?" he asked, nodding to where Andrew still sat, watching them.

"No," she breathed as he took a few steps closer to Journey. He was so close to her that he could feel her breath on his face.

God, he had wanted to kiss her his whole life, and he never just took a leap of faith and took what he wanted from her. He was a coward and playing the nice guy was getting him nowhere with her.

"Good," Ford breathed. "Then, he won't mind if I do this." He pulled her up against his body and didn't give her a chance to protest. He knew she would give him a fight, but that was part of what turned him on. Ford crushed his mouth to hers and took what he had wanted from her for so long. He kissed her with every ounce of the pent-up desire that he had felt for her since they were just kids and she tasted like sunshine and honey. Journey tasted like home.

JOURNEY

Journey wasn't sure how her night had ended with her standing in the parking lot of her favorite restaurant, kissing the man she had wanted her whole life. He had asked her out so many times and she turned him down each time, out of fear that if she told him yes, she'd lose her best friend. Lucinda and she had made a pack when they were nine that they'd never let a boy come between them and Journey was pretty sure that dating Luci's brother would fall under that pact.

And now, she was standing in the parking lot, kissing Ford Dixon. When she allowed herself to relax and wrapped her arms around his neck, he deepened the kiss and God, could he kiss. She felt as though she had been waiting her whole life for Ford to kiss her. The only reason he broke their kiss was because her asshole boss started his sports car and revved the engine. Ford ended their kiss, leaving her needy and breathless, panting for air.

"Wow," she breathed.

"Fucking right, wow," he agreed. "I've been waiting a damn long time to do that, Journey," he whispered. He looked back over her shoulder to where her boss still sat in his car, his smile was almost mean. "We need to get going. I don't think that our audience is too happy with our little show." She looked back at Andrew and could tell that he was pissed. She was going to have to deal with him on Monday and knowing her boss, he was going to give her a load of shit and a good bit of attitude.

Journey loved her job as a journalist for CNN. Sure, she got the shitty assignments, but everyone had to cut their teeth in the industry and she knew that sooner or later, her big break would come along and she'd be able to launch her career. Working for Andrew Tinsley was something that she hated though. He had a reputation in the industry for being a cad, but when she interviewed for the job, she decided to look past his past indiscretions and take the assignment. She wanted it and working for CNN, no matter how lowly the position, gave her bragging rights with all her old college friends. She had gone on numerous job interviews and was just about flat-broke when Andrew's office called to interview her. She was waiting tables at a local diner and just about ready to give up on her dreams. Journey had college bills about to come due and was out of money and options. She thought that Andrew's offer was a sign that things were looking up. Journey knew that believing the gossip she heard around the industry was never a good idea. People talked and most of the time the stories were just that—stories. She chose to believe that the stories about Andrew were made up by women who were scorned by him not assigning a story they wanted, but she quickly came to realize that he was everything the stories made him out to be and so much more. The first time Andrew came on to her, she thought about going to HR but then he sent her out on her first dream assignment. Looking back, he did it to shut her up about him cornering her in his office and running his hands up under her skirt. Like a fool, she forgave him for what he called, "His lapse in judgment," and he sent her on her way. Things were good for months until he tried the same shit with her again. The problem was, she couldn't go to HR now that so much time had passed and so many indiscretions had occurred. The time for complaining about his bad behavior had passed and she'd just have to learn how to figure out her shit on her own.

Ford was right, she needed to get out of there and come up with a good story for Monday morning. Luckily for her, she had the entire weekend ahead of her to come up with something good. Right now, she'd let Ford come to her rescue and get her out of there. Later, she'd find a ride back to the restaurant to get her SUV. Ford helped her up into his pick-up and shut the door. She watched as he rounded his truck and got in on the driver's side. She always thought he was a good-looking guy, but his time in the military, and the twenty-five pounds of muscle he put on, made him hot as hell.

"I hate to tell you this, Honey," he breathed, "but, your boss looks pissed." She looked back at Andrew's car one last time and nodded. He did look pretty upset by their little display.

"Yeah—he's an ass," she whispered under her breath. She wasn't even sure that Ford had heard her until he chuckled. "He likes to get handsy and well, I'm pretty sure that he expected more from tonight's little working dinner. You rescued me," she admitted. "Thank you."

Ford reached across the center console and took her hand into his own. He always had a calming effect on her and even now, when she deserved his wrath, he was granting her his comfort. Even when they were kids, he was always taking care of her and his sister. They were a couple of years younger than he was and Ford could have treated them both like nuisances, but he didn't. He was always kind to her and when she was old enough to notice boys, he was one of the first she had a crush on.

"You never have to thank me for helping you out, Journey," he said.

"After all the hell I've put you through. All the times that you asked me out and I told you no, you should hate me, Ford," she whispered.

"Why did you lie to me about this weekend?" he asked. "You said you couldn't go out with me tonight because you were going to be working all weekend."

"I didn't lie," she defended. "I was working. I was supposed to be at the office late, working on my article, but then Andrew found me in my little cubicle and insisted that I go to dinner with him. He told me that he wanted to troubleshoot a few problem areas of my article and I was foolish enough to believe him again."

"Again?" he asked. "You mean that this has happened before?"

Journey almost didn't want to admit that it had. Doing so would only make her look weak and foolish—two things she never wanted to be in front of Ford. "Yes," she said. "Let's just say that my boss is very persuasive and leave it at that."

"Fuck," Ford growled. "I want to turn around and beat the shit out of him now," he admitted.

She put her hand on his forearm, noting the tension in his muscles. "That would do neither of us any good, Ford. He'll press charges against you and he'll have full access to me then. This way is for the best. I've gotten pretty good at dodging his advances. I just need a little more time to figure out how to handle him. Plus, I'm up for a promotion at work and if I get it, Andrew won't be my boss any more. I'm just hoping for that to happen, so I won't have to deal with him anymore."

"Why don't you tell anyone—you know, like HR?" he asked.

"Because it would only put a black mark on my file with HR and I'd become a problem. I'm just a lowly reporter, Ford. If I cause waves, they'll take away my assignments and I'll never get to where I want to be." Ford ran his thumb over her hand and squeezed it into his own.

"I'm sorry that you have to deal with all that, Honey," he

said. "You know if there's ever anything I can do; all you have to do is say the word."

"I know that Ford, and I appreciate it. But I need to do this on my own. Thank you though," she said.

"Again, you never have to thank me," he said.

"I guess you can take me back to my car now. I think Andrew would have moved on as soon as we took off." They had gotten about two miles down the road and Ford checked his rearview.

"Can't," he breathed. "He's following us, and I'm betting he's hoping I'll take you back for your car. Andrew seems to be a smart guy. He's probably worked out that we aren't going to Luci's with some soup."

Journey looked through the back window and saw his car trailing them a few links back. Her gasp filled the cabin, and he squeezed her hand into his own again. "What will we do then?" she asked.

"I can think of a few things I'd like to do with you, Journey. But for now, I'm going to drive for a bit and see if he stays on our tail. If he does, I'm going to take you back to my place. But there is no fucking way I'm going to take you back to your car or your house. I think we might have pissed your boss off more than we intended. I won't let him touch you again. You good with that?" Journey knew she should have told him no. She should have protested that their being together wouldn't ever work. That it wasn't fair to her best friend for them to even consider everything that Ford started in the parking lot of the restaurant. But she had no more fight left and telling Ford no; denying what she wanted for so long, wasn't something she was strong enough to do anymore.

FORD

They had been driving around in circles for almost thirty minutes and her boss didn't seem to be the kind of guy to just give up. "He's still following us, isn't he?" Journey asked.

"He is," Ford admitted, "he's a persistent fucker, I'll give him that."

"You have no idea," she mumbled. Ford wanted to ask her what she meant by that, but he had a feeling that he didn't really want to know. He'd want to beat the hell out of the guy, and as Journey already pointed out, that wouldn't end well for him.

"Why do you work for that asshole?" Ford asked.

"Because I needed a job. I know this might shock you, but my landlord doesn't let me live in my apartment for free. He kind of likes to get paid and that means that I need a job." She shook her head at him and all he could do was smile like a loon at her. "Why the hell are you smiling at me?"

"Because you've always been a smart ass. It's nice to see that some things don't change," he said. When he enlisted in the Army, Journey, and his sister were just kids. They were still in high school and even though Journey followed him around like a puppy, he couldn't give in to his basic desires and ask her out. She was four years younger than he was and he was about to go away for years. Ford didn't know when he would be back, and Journey was still underage and off-limits, not that his cock got that memo.

"You've been gone for a long time, Ford," she said. "You don't really know who I am anymore." She was right. He didn't know her anymore, but he wanted to. That was why he kept asking her out and why he was so disappointed to find her out with her boss tonight. He just wanted his chance with her and now, he was hoping to finally get it.

"You're right, Journey," he agreed, "I don't know you anymore. I'd like to get the chance to know you though. Say you'll go on a date with me."

She hesitated, looking out the passenger window at the passing scenery. He thought for sure that she was going to tell him no and he hated that she was going to turn him down again. "Just say yes, Journey," he whispered.

"What about Lucinda?" she asked. "She's my best friend and I don't want to lose her."

"Why would you lose my sister?" Ford asked. "You two have been inseparable since you were in the second grade."

"Right, but you're her brother and I'm betting she doesn't want us to date. I mean, what if things go south between us and we end up hating each other? What am I supposed to do about being friends with Lucinda? It would be awkward." Maybe she was right and it would be awkward, but he didn't give a damn about any of that. He wanted his chance with her and hearing her excuses to turn him down again was only pissing him off.

"Why do things have to go south between the two of us?" he asked. "I mean, we haven't even gotten together yet and you're breaking us up already. At least give us a chance before you end us. We don't have to tell my sister that we're going out on a date if you're worried about her. We can go on a date, see if we click, and then, you can decide when or if you want to tell her. I'll leave that up to you."

"You want me to lie to her?" Journey asked.

"Of course not," Ford insisted, "I'm just saying that we don't have to tell her right away about us. Let's take some time and get to know each other again, and then, you can tell her." He was sure that she was going to turn him down completely, but she didn't and when she nodded her agreement, he felt like the luckiest man on the planet.

"Really?" he asked. "You'll go out with me?"

"I will, as long as you're really okay with not telling Lucinda," she said. "I don't want to upset her if there's no reason to do so." He wanted to insist that there would be a reason to tell his sister about the two of them because once he got Journey into his bed, he never planned on letting her back out again.

"You got it," he agreed. "I won't say a word to my sister until you're ready to do so."

"Thank you. So, when would you like to go on this date?" she asked.

He checked his rearview mirror again and looked back at her. "How about now?" he asked. "Your boss is still a few cars back and I'm betting he won't give up following us tonight unless we give him a reason to. How about we drop by that little deli, that has my sister's favorite soup, pick up some desserts, and take them back to my place? He'll never know that we're not taking it to my sister's since he has no idea where either of us lives."

"But how will I get my SUV and go home later?" she asked. He was honestly hoping to get her to agree to stick around and spend the night with him, but he wouldn't push Journey into something that she might not be ready for.

"Once your boss gives up and goes home, I'll run you back to your SUV and follow you back to your apartment," he offered.

"Why would you follow me back to my place?" she asked. "I don't need an escort."

"I'm sure that you can handle yourself, but I'm also betting that your boss knows where you live. Do you honestly believe that he'd follow us around for the past thirty minutes to only give up once you're in my place? He'll probably check to make sure that you got home, and I'd bet he'd even want to talk to you personally to see that you're okay and make his next move. He seems like the type of guy who doesn't like to take no for an answer."

"He's not the kind of guy who takes no for an answer. I think that's why he keeps trying to trick me into spending time with him. He's probably hoping that I'll eventually give in and give him what he wants." She shivered next to him, and he pulled her hand up into his own, running his lips over her knuckles.

"I won't let that happen, honey," he promised. There was no fucking way that Ford would ever let some asshole like Andrew Tinsley lay one finger on her. He didn't care who the guy was to her—she could find another job if necessary.

❄

They ran downtown to the deli that was his sister's favorite, not that Journey's boss would know the difference. He loved that deli too, and Ford knew that they had fantastic desserts. All he could think about was eating chocolate cake off of Journey's naked body while she was in his bed, but he was pretty sure that wasn't something that she was ready for. He was still going to ask. Journey had to know how he felt about her. God, that kiss nearly set him on fire and he wanted more of that with her. He just hoped like hell that she felt the same way.

They ordered a few desserts and headed back out to his truck to find her asshole boss parked down the street watching them. He told her to pretend not to see him, but all Ford wanted to do was walk down the road, pull the guy out of his pretentious car, and beat the hell out of him. But that wouldn't do either of them any good. The guy would just press charges and he'd end up behind bars leaving Journey vulnerable for the night.

"He's not going to give up, is he?" she asked.

"I'm afraid not. I've known guys like your boss and I'm betting that he'll follow us back to your car and then show up at your place," Ford said.

"Shit, I can't have that happen. I should have reported him when he tried to stick his hand up under my skirt the first time, but I was afraid that I'd lose my job. I'm such an idiot," Journey groaned. The thought of that asshole touching her anywhere made him sick. Honestly, the thought of any man touching Journey filled him with rage that he hadn't felt in a damn long time—since his time in the Army really.

"He touched you more than once?" Ford asked.

"Careful, Ford," she spat, "you sound as if you are accusing me of wrongdoing here. I'm not the slimeball boss who's made up fake meetings to get me in the corner. I told him to keep his hands to himself after that first time and he immediately apologized. And yeah, I was a fool to believe him and didn't go to HR as I should have, but I was young and naive. I was so new to the business, I believed him."

"Until he did it again," Ford guessed.

"Yeah," she breathed.

"For the record, I wasn't blaming you for that asshole's behavior. I'd never do that, Journey. I know you, even if we haven't seen each other these past few years. You're the same sweet girl who used to follow me around before I left for basic training."

"Thank you for saying that," she whispered. "I should have gone to HR after he pulled the same crap again, but I was ashamed of not reporting him the first time. I felt like an idiot, and I just didn't want anyone to know what had happened, so I ignored his bad behavior, and look where that's gotten me. I'm effectively trapped in a car with you, driving around town, pretending to be heading to my best friend's house to deliver her soup. I've fucked everything up and now, I've gotten you involved in my mess. I'm so sorry."

"I'm not and I'd gladly spend every evening trapped in my truck with you if it means getting to spend time with you, honey," Ford said.

"You don't have to be so nice to me, Ford. I'm sure that you had other things you wanted to do tonight besides babysitting me," Journey insisted.

"Not a thing," he assured. "In fact, I was going to ask you to spend the whole evening with me."

"The whole evening?" she choked.

"Well, I can't let you go home knowing that your boss will be waiting there for you to return. And first thing tomorrow, I'm driving you to work and you're going to report that ass to HR. It's never too late to do the right thing," he said. "And reporting him is the right thing to do. What if he takes things too far with you or goes after another young woman in your office? Don't you want to stop him?"

"Yes, but there's one flaw with your plan," she said. He thought over what he had just said and couldn't see one thing wrong with his plan.

"What's that?" he asked.

"Tomorrow is Saturday, and my office is closed for the weekend. Plus, you can't babysit me for the whole weekend. I won't take up your time that way, Ford," she insisted. He wanted her to take up all of his time for the rest of his damn life, but there was no way that he'd admit that to her—not yet anyway. Ford had only just gotten her to agree to go on a date with him, and that took him months to do. He had only been home for six months now, and every damn week, he asked Journey out on a date, and she turned him down flat. Tonight was the first glimmer of hope that she had given him, and he wasn't about to fuck that all up.

"First of all, please stop calling the two of us spending time together me babysitting you, Journey. I might be older than you, but you sure in hell don't need a babysitter anymore. I want to spend time with you. Hell, you should have picked that up from me asking you out every damn week since I've been back. I want to spend the weekend with you, Journey. Say that you'll stay with me," he begged. He wasn't above begging either. He'd beg her for everything if it meant that she'd continue to give him a chance.

"You can't be serious," she insisted.

"Sure I can be," he said. "Spend the weekend with me, Journey," he asked again.

"I don't have any of my stuff," she said.

"We can run by your place now and pack a bag for you. I'll be with you the whole time, so I'm betting your boss won't make a move. Hell, maybe he'll even get the hint that we're together and leave you the fuck alone," Ford growled.

"But we're not together," she insisted.

"Give me the chance to prove you wrong," he whispered. "Let me show you how good we can be together," he asked. She looked out her window again and he was sure that she was going to turn him down—but she didn't. Instead, she turned and smiled the most beautiful smile he'd ever seen and nodded her head. She was finally giving him the chance that he had wanted with her, and he wasn't going to screw it up—not this time.

JOURNEY

Journey couldn't remember a time when she didn't want Ford Dixon. God, the man was in her dreams every night and that made her life a living hell. When he joined the Army, she was just a kid—a freshman in high school. She spent most of her teen years moping around, wondering why she wasn't good enough for Ford. She shut herself off from other boys her age, even turning down going to her senior prom—something that Lucinda was still pissed at her about. She couldn't tell her best friend why she didn't want to go to the prom with Billy Yates. Hell, she knew that half of the senior class believed the rumors about her that she was a lesbian because she turned down every boy who had ever asked her out in hopes that Ford would return home and sweep her off her feet. That never happened, and when he finally returned a year after she finished college and moved back home, she knew that she had played the fool.

When he finally asked her out, she knew that saying yes to him could never happen because then, she'd have to tell Lucinda about her massive crush on her older brother. She could never tell her best friend that she had kept that from her all of those years—it would hurt Lucinda and she wouldn't do that to her.

The only problem now was trying to find a way forward and stop wanting Ford. Seeing him around town all the time again and having him ask her out every week was wearing down her defenses. Seeing her best friend happily married was making her want things she thought that she could live without. Having Ford come to her rescue tonight was the final straw and honestly, telling him no anymore wasn't something that she wanted to do. When he asked her to spend the whole weekend with him, her head was telling her to say, no, but her heart nearly jumped out of her chest. She couldn't deny what he was asking her to do because she wanted it more than she wanted her next breath.

As promised, Ford had stopped at her apartment and waited for her to pack a bag. He looked around her living room while she painfully went through her closet analyzing everything in her wardrobe, trying to decide if she should bring it along or not. Trying to figure out if she should pack her good panties and bra or her old ones was the biggest hang-up for her. If she packed her good stuff, Ford would know that she was expecting to end up in his bed this weekend. And, if she packed her old stuff, he'd know that she wasn't hoping to end up in his bed, but she'd look raggedy when all she wanted from him was for Ford to find her sexy. Did he though? He did kiss her in the parking lot in front of her boss, and God that kiss scorched her soul. Did Ford want more from her? If he did, she wanted to be ready, so she tossed her good panties and bra into her bag, found her favorite t-shirt that she liked to sleep in, threw that in on top, and zipped up her bag. She was done second-guessing her every move when it came to Ford, and if things actually worked out with him, she'd find a way to admit to her best friend that she had been in love with her older brother for years now.

"Ready," she said.

"Your place is nice," he said. She looked around her dinky little apartment and laughed.

"You're an awful liar, but I can afford the rent and that's enough for me, for now," she said. "I would have cleaned up a bit if I knew that I'd be having company," she said.

"Well, I think that it's cozy. It feels like you, Journey," he said. She wanted to remind him that he really didn't know her —not the grown-up woman she had become, but he seemed to hate every time she pointed that fact out to him.

"Thanks," she said. She peeked out her kitchen window that looked down on the complex's parking lot and saw that her boss's car was still parked in the back.

"I take it from the look on your face that he's still out there," he said.

"Yeah, he's just not going to stop, is he?" she asked.

"No, and that's why it's best for you to spend the weekend at my place," he said. She wanted to ask him if that was the only reason he wanted her to spend the night—to protect her from her boss, but she was too much of a chicken to point blank ask him.

"Well, I appreciate you putting me up, Ford. I wouldn't feel safe here with my boss circling the block out there. You're a good friend." She picked up her purse and jacket and Ford closed the distance between the two of them, tugging the bag, her purse, and jacket from her arms. He pulled her against his body and sealed his mouth over hers again without any warning. Journey felt as though her heart was going to beat out of her chest again and she was sure that kissing Ford Dixon was something that she'd never get tired of. He broke their kiss, leaving her breathless and feeling a bit weak in the knees. Geeze, when did she become such a cliché?

"What was that for?" she asked raising a shaky hand to her swollen, wet lips.

"That was to show you that I'm not putting you up, Journey. I didn't ask you over to protect you from your boss—that's just a bonus. I asked you to spend the weekend with me because I want you. I have for a damn long time now, and I don't care if my sister finds out or not." She was about to protest him telling Lucinda when he pressed his fingers to her lips. "I won't tell her until you are ready, but I'm only keeping it a secret from her for you. I want you to spend the weekend with me—in my bed, preferably naked."

Her gasp filled the room, and he threw back his head and laughed. God, he was beautiful. "Now you're getting it, honey."

"You want me to be naked?" she stuttered. Journey had hoped but hearing him say it made her crazy with lust.

"It's all I've wanted for a long time now, Journey. If it's not what you wanted from this weekend, tell me now. I will still take you home with me, but I'll try harder to keep my hands to myself."

"I don't want you to do that," she quickly admitted. The thought of his hands all over her body made her hot. "I want your hands on me."

"Good to know," he said. Ford released her and picked up her bag, handing her back her purse and jacket. "Ready?" he asked. She suddenly felt too hot and flustered to answer him. Instead, she just nodded and tried to paste on a smile.

"I'm just glad I decided to pack my good panties and bras," she whispered.

Ford laughed, "So, you were thinking about getting naked and spending the weekend in my bed then?" he asked. All she could do was nod again. How did she admit that to him without sounding desperate? Maybe they were well past that and desperate was what Ford was into. Now, all she had to do was find a way to tell Ford that she was a virgin, but she had at least twenty minutes to figure that all out.

❋

Ford drove like a crazy person back to his place. He nearly ran a red light until she shouted that the light was about to change. "What the hell is your hurry, Ford?" she asked. He shot her a sheepish grin and shrugged.

"Sorry," he breathed. "I guess you finally giving me a chance has me a bit excited to get you back to my place. I'm worried that you might change your mind."

"I'm not going to change my mind, Ford, but you might after I tell you what I need to say." She worried that by spilling her guts and admitting that she was a twenty-three-year-old virgin, he might turn his truck back around and take her straight back to her apartment.

"You're scaring me," he said. "What is it that you need to tell me, Journey?" He pulled into his townhome's garage and cut the engine, waiting her out to tell him what she needed to. She was the one who started this. She should have at least kept her mouth shut until they got into his place. At least then, she'd have a fighting chance of him letting her stay the night until she could work out what to do about her boss. With the promise of sex looming over her, she had to tell Ford though. It was the right thing to do even if it made her completely uncomfortable. It wouldn't be fair to let him find out on his own that she had been saving herself.

Journey took a deep breath and spilled her guts. "I'm a virgin," she breathed. The words seemed to tumble out before she was really ready to give them, but at least she had that part over with. Poor Ford looked a bit confused and completely shocked by her news. "Oh, come on," she grumbled. "It's not that bad, right?"

"You're twenty-three," he insisted, "and, you went to college."

"Right, both of which have nothing to do with me having sex. I mean, there really isn't an age requirement, right? And I'm pretty sure that I didn't have to have sex to get my degree, although, if that was the case, they gave it to me anyway."

"That's not what I mean," Ford insisted. "Why haven't you had sex yet?" he asked.

"Um, I was saving myself for you," she said, "as stupid as that sounds. I guess it's pretty lame. I mean, hearing the words come out of my own mouth makes me feel lame. I don't know, I guess I just had this crazy notion that one day, you'd notice me, and I didn't want any other boy."

"You didn't go out with anyone in high school?" he asked.

"I mean, I went on a few dates with a couple of guys, but that's where it ended, really. Your sister was pretty pissed off at me when I turned down prom date offers from guys during senior year. They all started spreading rumors about me that I was a lesbian, and honestly, I let them. Your poor sister got the bum rap of that deal because everyone said that the two of us were dating, even though Lucinda dated guys in high school. They said that we were secretly in love because we were always together."

"Kids are so cruel," he said, "I'm sorry that you had to go through all of that."

"I'm sorry that Lucinda had to endure any of that on my behalf," she said. "I guess it's why I became so protective of her and still am."

"I get it—you and my sister were always close, but for the record, I don't think you're a secret lesbian," he said.

"Gee, thanks," she giggled. "Are you saying that because you don't want it to be true?" she asked.

"Maybe," he smirked. "Are you sure that you still want to do all of this?" he asked. "I mean, I don't want to push you into something that you're not ready for."

"I'm ready," she said, taking his hand into her own. "I've waited for you my whole life, Ford. The question is, are you still willing to do this? I mean, you probably don't want a virgin," she mumbled.

"Bullshit," he shouted, "I want you, Journey. I don't give a fuck if you are a virgin or not. I'm flattered that you waited all this time for me. But why did you turn me down every time I asked you out these past six months?"

"As I said, I'm protective of your sister. I didn't want to hurt her, and I thought that being with you might do that to her. It's why I asked you to keep this thing between us a secret."

"Right, and you're worried that we won't work out—but I have to warn you, Journey, if we do this, I won't want to let you go. If you agree to be with me, in my bed, I'll want you in my life too. Are you going to be able to tell Lucinda about us eventually? I mean, sooner or later, she'll figure it out." He was right. Lucinda was a smart woman and she'd look at Journey and know that she had been with her brother. But giving up her chance with Ford now that they had come so far wasn't a possibility for her.

"I'll have to come to terms with telling Lucinda at some point. Just give me this weekend to figure it out. I'm sure that we can come up with something if we put our heads together."

"I'm sure that we can," he agreed. "So, we're good?" he asked.

"We're good," she agreed. "Can I just ask you one favor?" she asked.

"Anything," he offered.

"Can we take tonight slowly? I've waited a long time for this —for you and I don't want to rush things."

"Honey, we can go as quickly or as slowly as you'd like. I'll leave that up to you, Journey," he promised. Hearing him make her any promises made her tummy feel as though it was full of butterflies. She felt like a giddy schoolgirl, and she just couldn't help it. She had waited so long for Ford, and she was finally getting her chance with him. Journey's inner schoolgirl was jumping up and down like a damn cheerleader.

FORD

Hearing Journey say that she had been saving herself all these years for him made him crazy with lust. He had spent the entire ride from her apartment hard, and that was probably why he had nearly run a red light to get her back to his place. But hearing that she was a virgin and wanted to give herself to him—well, it took all of his willpower not to jump her in his truck. Journey deserved more than that. She deserved the promise that he made her to take their time tonight, even if it might just kill him.

Ford helped her into his townhouse and dropped her bag by the steps. "I'll give you a tour," he offered, noting the smirk on her face.

"That would be great, but you don't have to come up with activities for us to do instead of heading up to your bedroom—I mean, if that's where you want to have sex."

"I know, but I promised to take things slow. I thought you'd want to know your way around here for the weekend," he said. "As for where I'd like to have sex, the bedroom is fine with me, if that's where you'll be comfortable."

"I guess that's fine. I mean, I don't have much experience

with where I like to have sex, since I never had it before," she said. Ford bit back his groan and she giggled. "I can't figure out if you're mad that I'm a virgin or okay with it." Ford took a chance and grabbed her hand into his own, tugging it down to his cock. He loved the way that Journey slyly ran her fingers over his bulge. She had some idea of what to do with him and that completely turned him on.

"I'm more than okay with it," Ford insisted. "The fact that you saved yourself for me turns me completely inside out with need. I want you so fucking bad right now, I'm going to split right out of my damn pants."

"Ford," she whispered. Journey groped his cock through his jeans and every caress made him want to push her against the wall and fuck her in his entryway. "Can I see you?" she asked.

"You'll see all of me, honey, but first, I need to take care of you," he said. "I want you ready to take me, Journey—all of me." Her breath hitched and he knew that she was just as turned on by the whole scene as he was.

"How about we skip the tour for now, and you take me up to your bedroom, Ford? Maybe we could take things a little faster if you're up for that."

"I won't rush you, Journey. I made you a promise," he said.

"Please, Ford," she whispered, "I want you." He didn't want her begging him for anything. He wanted to give Journey everything that she wanted and needed from him. Ford scooped her up into his arms and grabbed her bag on the way up his steps. He took them two at a time, causing her to giggle again. He always thought that her laugh was magical, but now, it turned him on.

He flicked on his bedroom light and carried her over to his bed, laying her across it. "You are so fucking beautiful," he whispered. Ford looked her body over as if trying to decide what his first move should be. If she was any other woman, he'd have her naked and panting out his name by now, but Journey wasn't like any other woman. If he had his way, she would be

THE woman—the one he'd spend the rest of his life with. But he was getting ahead of himself and that wasn't going to help with the nerves that he was suddenly feeling.

"Just love me, Ford," she whispered, reaching for him as if picking up on all of his indecision.

"That's all I want to do, I'm just worried that I'm going to blow it. I've waited for you too, Journey, in so many ways. I've wanted you for so long, even when it wasn't right for me to want you."

"You have?" she asked. He laid down next to her on the bed and she curled into his side. Ford knew that not giving her the whole truth after she told him hers, was something he couldn't do.

"I have. I started noticing you when you were just a kid. God, that made me feel like a complete pervert, but I just couldn't help myself. I was almost relieved when I joined the Army and went away so that I wouldn't be hanging around here every day wishing for something that could never be. You were just a kid, Journey," he said.

She framed his face with her hands and smiled, "I'm not a kid anymore, Ford. You're only four years older than me. We both just needed to grow up a bit before this could happen," she said.

"How did you get to be so wise?" he asked.

She giggled and pointed at herself, "College education at its finest," she teased. "If it helps you to feel better, I wanted you back then too. When you left for the Army, all I could think about was you coming back for me. I had these fantasies that you'd come back to town, tell me that you couldn't live without me, and take me away with you. How's that for crazy?" she asked. It didn't sound crazy to him at all. In fact, it sounded like a damn good plan right about now, especially with her boss stalking her the way that he was.

"It sounds perfect," he breathed. "I just hope that's something that you still want, honey because it's exactly what I plan to do with you. I want you to be mine, Journey," he admitted.

"Oh Ford, I've been yours for a long time now. I'm just done fighting with myself and ready to admit it," she said. Hearing her promise him made him realize that he had been worrying for nothing. Ford rolled her under his body and kissed her like a starving man and when he finally let her up for air, to work his way down her body, he was sure that a more perfect woman had never existed. She responded to him as if she was made for him.

It didn't take him long to get her naked and when he finally settled between her legs and looked up at her sexy body, he could tell that she was worried about what he was about to do to her next. Journey had closed her eyes so tightly that she looked like she was terrified.

"Open your eyes and look at me, baby," he crooned. "I won't hurt you. We can slow down if that's what you need." He hoped like hell that she didn't ask him to do that though. His cock was screaming to be released to get inside of her.

"I've just never," she breathed. He kissed his way up the inside of her thigh, and she moaned. "I don't want you to stop, Ford," she said, giving him the green light to move the rest of the way up her sexy curves. He settled between her legs and when he parted her wet folds to lick through them, Journey nearly bucked both of them off of the damn bed.

"Hold still, honey," he said, holding her down with his body. "Can you be still for me?" he asked. Journey whimpered and nodded, and he was sure that it was the most adorable thing he'd ever seen in his life.

He loved watching her as she writhed on his bed for him, trying to hold still, as promised, but failing miserably. She was sexy as hell to watch and when she found her release, he nearly came in his damn pants. God, she was perfect, and all he wanted to do was make her his completely.

He stood from the bed, loving the way that she watched him through her sex-fueled haze as he stripped. Journey sat up and eagerly reached for his zipper and he backed away from her. "If I let you do that, this will be over before I even get started," he admitted. She pouted and laid back on his bed, waiting him out. "Are you sure that you're ready?" he asked. As soon as his cock sprang free from his jeans, her eyes roamed his body and he could see the uncertainty.

"Um, that's going to fit inside of me?" she asked.

"We'll fit," he promised. They had to because giving her up now wasn't an option. She nodded and held out her arms for him. Ford laid down on the bed next to her and pulled her on top of him. "I want you to be on top," he said.

"Why?" she asked.

"So that we can take this at your pace," he said. "I don't want to rush you." She nodded and covered his shaft with her drenched folds. Ford couldn't help his moan or the way that his eager cock tried to push inside of her.

He felt as though he was holding his damn breath, waiting for her to make a move, and when she slowly inched down onto his cock, he found himself panting out her name. "Ford," she moaned. "I need you to do it, please."

"Are you sure?" he asked. She nodded and he rolled her back under his body. "I'm sorry," he whispered against her neck as he quickly finished filling her. She cried out and Ford stilled inside of her.

"I'm okay," she assured him before he could even ask. "I just need a second."

"Just say when, honey." He was trying for casual even though he felt anything but. They lay like that for what felt like an eternity, their hearts beating wildly while their ragged breaths filled the air, and Ford was sure that he had never felt so connected to another person in his life.

He peppered her face with kisses. "I'm ready," she whispered. "Move, please, Ford," she begged. He slowly pulled almost completely out of her pussy and slammed back into her, setting a pace that he was sure would have her sore in the morning. But the primal beast in him wanted to mark her, make her his so that she'd remember everything that he did to her the night before.

Ford knew that he wasn't going to last and he wanted her with him. He snaked his hand down between where his and Journey's bodies were joined and ran the pad of his thumb over her sensitive clit until she cried out his name again. The way that she felt while coming around his cock was all that he needed to finally lose himself inside of her. Journey was finally his and now, there would be no taking that back. She belonged to him and Ford's whole life finally felt right.

❈

"Your phone is going crazy again," Ford said holding it up for her to see. Journey was in his shower, and she wiped her eyes to peek out at it as if she didn't believe him or something.

"Is it your sister again?" she asked.

"Yes, it's your best friend," he countered. It had been two weeks since Journey had spent the weekend with him. She really never left once their weekend was over. He was careful to drive her to work and back to her place to pick up more of her things, but always insisted on her spending the night with him. Her boss's advancements toward her made convincing her to stay with him easy.

The asshole had really stepped up his game since Ford convinced Journey to go to HR and report her boss for sexual harassment. Of course, they took down her complaint and promised that there would be a thorough investigation, but Journey said that she wasn't holding her breath. She said that the HR representative told her that she should have come forward when it first happened, and he worried that might be a sticking point in her allegations against her boss.

The idea of Journey having to spend time with that asshole, in the same office space, made him sick. Ford found himself stopping by to check on her just about every day, making up some excuse for being in the area even if he wasn't. He had just started his new job across town, as head of security for a law firm, but he made sure to use his lunch break to check up on his girl.

He planned on enrolling in some college courses, and Journey told him that was a fantastic idea, but he couldn't live on his money from his time in the Army forever. He had to get a job and something in security felt like it might be the right thing for him after spending so much time in the military.

"You do know that you're going to have to talk to her sooner or later," he warned.

"I know that," she said, "just not now," Journey insisted. She shut off the shower as the call went to voicemail and he held his breath waiting for Lucinda to call back. That was how she usually played things. His sister wasn't a patient woman and the fact that she had let Journey avoid her for two weeks was a pretty impressive feat for her.

"I just haven't figured out how to tell her about us yet," Journey admitted. "All this stuff with my boss and me practically moving in here—it's all so fast. I just need to let the dust settle and wrap my head around all of it."

"Are you having second thoughts?" he asked, instantly regretting his question. If she was, he really didn't want to know it.

"No, of course not," she insisted. "The night that you asked me to be yours, I knew what I was getting into. I want you, Ford—all of you. I just haven't figured out a way to tell your sister that I've been pining for her older brother my entire life."

"Maybe it's best that you leave that part out," he offered. "I mean, just tell her that this thing between us kind of just happened."

"Lucinda is smart enough to figure out when I'm lying," she said. "She'll see right through me and then what will I do?"

"I guess you tell the truth," he said. "Is that really so hard?

Just tell my sister that we're together and that I'm in love with you and have been for a damn long time. Hell, let me tell her that and everything will be out in the open."

Her gasp filled the bathroom, and he pulled Journey into his arms. He loved that he was able to take her by surprise and telling her that he had fallen in love with her wasn't hard for him to do, since it was true. "You love me?"

"Yep, and don't forget the part where I said that I have for a long time. I don't want to play games with you, Journey. I've done enough of that. I left town, all those years ago, to avoid my feelings for you."

"Well, we also both needed some time to grow up. Don't forget that part," she said. How could he forget that part? It was agony waiting for Journey to come of age and then, he still wasted time, telling himself that she wasn't supposed to be his. Making Journey his was the best decision that he'd ever made, and one that he'd not regret—ever.

"So, you're good with me telling you that I'm in love with you?" he asked. Ford could tell by her beautiful smile that she was more than fine with his admission.

"I think that I can live with it," she teased, wrapping her arms around his neck. "Since I'm in love with you too and have been since I was just a girl."

"Good to know," he growled. "How about we figure out a way to tell my sister about us then, since I plan on never letting you go again, Journey."

"I'll figure out how to tell Lucinda," she promised. "Just give me a day or two to work up the nerve. She's my best friend and I can't lose her," she said.

"I don't think that you will. My sister might be hard-headed, but she's also reasonable. I'm betting that Lucinda will even surprise you," he assured.

"I hope so," Journey said.

"How about I help take your mind off of my sister for a while?" he asked.

"And just how will you do that?" she asked.

"Oh, I think that I can come up with a few ideas." Ford pulled her towel free from her curvy body, loving the giggles that filled the bathroom.

"You are very good at the art of distraction," she teased. Ford planned to help her forget all of her troubles for the rest of the night, and if she'd allow it, for the rest of her life.

JOURNEY

Journey was sitting on Ford's back patio, sipping the coffee that he had brought her, and thinking about how she could get used to his pampering her when Lucinda came walking through the kitchen door and into the backyard. A part of her panicked, and she thought about running, but the jig was up, her best friend had finally found her.

"I can't believe that you've been avoiding me for two weeks now, and this is where I find you. Has my brother been covering for you this whole time?" Lucinda asked.

"Covering for me?" Journey asked. "Why would Ford cover for me?"

"Because for some reason, you're mad at me and you're avoiding me. I know that I haven't been around a lot since getting married, but I promise that I'll do better. I'll be a better friend, I swear," she promised. Oh God, Lucinda thought that she was mad at her because she was feeling neglected. She couldn't let her feel that way, but telling her the truth meant telling Lucinda everything—even the stuff about her sleeping with Ford.

"What's going on out here?" Ford asked, coming from inside the house. Shit—this was exactly what she didn't need before she could figure out what she was going to do about Lucinda. "I can hear you shouting from inside the house, Sis. You okay?" he looked at Journey but kept his distance and she was thankful that Ford seemed to be taking her lead in all of this.

"I've been ghosted by my best friend," she said.

"Don't be so dramatic, Lucinda," Journey said. "I haven't ghosted you."

"No, you feel as though I've ghosted you, and now, you're angry with me. I can't blame you, really. But you shouldn't have to hang out with Ford just to get back at me. Why didn't you just come over to my place and talk to me instead of turning to my brother?" Ford barked out his laugh and Journey shot him a dirty look. He grinned and shrugged and God, it was hard not to find him completely irresistible, but at this moment she had bigger fish to fry.

"I haven't been hiding out over here or using Ford to get back at you. I'd never do that." Journey took a deep breath and let it out. "I've been staying here with Ford for two weeks now."

"You've been staying here? What's wrong with your apartment?" Lucinda asked.

"Nothing's wrong with it," Journey said, "unless you count my crazy boss stalking it."

"Wait, Andrew is stalking your apartment?" Lucinda asked.

"And me," Journey said.

"Tell me that you finally went to HR about that slimeball," Lucinda asked.

"You knew about her boss giving her trouble and you didn't bother to offer that advice earlier?" Ford asked. Journey didn't need him getting involved in this mess. He promised to let her handle things with Lucinda.

"Journey insisted that she could handle Andrew on her own, and she's an adult, so I believed her," Lucinda insisted.

"Thank you," Journey said, "but, I kind of blew it. I thought that he wanted to go over my latest article, so I had dinner with him. That's the night that Ford rescued me and helped me to see that Andrew was stalking me. I went to HR the next Monday, but they said that my window to report him was when the incidents first happened."

"Which is bullshit," Ford growled.

"Right, so I've been staying here, laying low, and buying time until I can figure out what to do about him," Journey said. Ford wanted her to quit her job, but that wasn't going to happen. She had worked too hard to get a leg up in CNN. She wasn't about to give all of that up now because her boss was a pig. No, there had to be another way around this mess—she just needed to find it.

"You could have come to me," Lucinda insisted. "I would have loved for you to stay with me and Ty."

"You two are disgustingly in love and I just didn't want to be around all of that. Besides, Ford and I are doing just fine here on our own," Journey said. Ford grumbled something about her being a giant chicken, and maybe she was, but she couldn't seem to find the words to tell her best friend that she was in love with her older brother.

Lucinda looked from Ford to Journey and back again. "Something is going on here that you're not telling me. Do I need to invoke the best friend rules and demand to know the truth, or do you just want to spill your guts?"

Honestly, Journey didn't like either of those options. "Is there a third option?" she squeaked.

"No," Ford barked. "It's time to tell her, Journey." He was right, but the way that Luci was staring her down intimidated the hell out of her. "Fine, I'll be the one to tell you. Journey and I are together. We're in love and she's been not only hiding out here to avoid her boss's stalking her, but also to avoid telling you about the two of us. I've been in love with her for a while now, and she made me promise not to tell you."

"Yet, here you are telling her," Journey grumbled. She really couldn't blame him. Ford had granted her more than enough time to get up the nerve to tell Lucinda. In fact, he had kept up his end of the bargain, letting her live with him until she could work up the nerve to come clean with her best friend. But he sure wasted no time spilling his guts to his sister about the two of them.

"Well, you weren't going to tell her, were you?" he countered. She wasn't. In fact, she was avoiding telling Luci at all costs.

"No, I wasn't," Journey said.

"Hold up here," Lucinda shouted, "you're with him?" she asked Journey, pointing at her brother as if accusing him of some wrongdoing.

"Yes," Journey almost whispered. "I know that I should have told you."

"How long have you liked my brother, Journey?" Lucinda asked.

She shrugged, "For as long as I can remember."

"And you never thought to tell me? All those years that the kids in high school taunted the two of us for being lesbians. They thought that we were together because you never dated and that was because you were holding out hope that my brother would come home and declare his undying love for you?" Luci asked. She sounded pissed and the way she recounted their childhood was harsh.

"That about sums it up," Journey said, "but, you have to believe that I never meant for you to get hurt in all of this. I never thought that the kids would think that we were together because you were always with some guy."

"But they did think that we were together, and you just let them instead of telling me and everyone else the way you felt about Ford."

"Go easy on her," Ford said, "she was just a kid."

"Right, and you were in love with her even back then?

What kind of man does that make you, Ford?" Lucinda spat. Ford took two steps back from his sister as if she had just slapped him. This was what Journey was trying to avoid, but now, there would be no getting around it. Lucinda knew everything and she wasn't going to let either of them off the hook for the way that they felt about each other.

"Don't say that to him," Journey defended. She stood and blocked Ford from Luci as if acting as his shield. "Ford would never do anything like that. It's why he left to join the Army. He was avoiding his feelings for me, and in the meantime, I've grown up," she said, holding her arms wide for her best friend to get a look. "He asked me to go on dates since coming home and I turned him down, believing that I couldn't date your older brother without hurting you, but that was just hurting me, Luci. I wasn't happy, but Ford makes me happy now. I just hope that someday, you'll be able to see that we're good together and be happy for the both of us. Until that time, I won't let you blame Ford for all of this. He's been nothing but a gentleman. I was the one who kept my feelings from you. I should have told you that I liked your brother, but I never thought that my feelings would matter."

"Why would you believe that I wouldn't take your feelings into consideration?" Lucinda asked.

"I guess a part of me never felt good enough to be considered a part of your family. I thought that wanting Ford would only end in heartache for me, so I resolved to squash my feelings and tell myself to stop hoping for something that would never happen. I'm done with that kind of self-doubt. I'm in love with your brother, Luci, and I hope that someday, you'll be able to accept that."

"I need some time," Lucinda muttered. "I have to go, Ty's meeting me for dinner."

"Can I call you later?" Journey asked.

"No, I think it's best if you let me call you when I'm ready," Luci insisted. She wanted to tell her friend that she was acting childish, but she also knew that giving Lucinda some time and space to think things through might be the best plan. All Journey could do was nod and watch her best friend leave Ford's house. She felt lost until his arms were around her, reminding her that she wasn't lost or alone anymore.

"She'll come around," he promised.

"I hope so," was all she could say.

FORD

Ford hadn't let Journey out of his sight for almost a month. The only time that he left her was when they both needed to go to work, and even that involved some strategically placed security cameras and an undercover guard. There was no way that he was going to let Journey be alone in a building with her boss, even if she assured him that she was completely safe. He had known slime balls like Journey's boss and the thought of him trying to touch her again made Ford want to kill the fucker.

HR had been no help to Journey. They told her that she should have reported her boss's behavior when it originally happened and that if she felt that they were being unfair, she could hire a lawyer. He thought that was a damn good idea, even if Journey didn't. She didn't want to lose her job at CNN and if that meant that she had to keep working for that asshole, she was going to. Ford had never felt so helpless in his life, and the one person whom he usually turned to for advice in situations like these, was not talking to him.

Lucinda had let all of his messages go unanswered and his calls go to voicemail, and it was really starting to piss him off.

He wished that they could put all of the negativity behind them and move on. He wanted his sister to be happy not only for him but also for Journey. He saw the sadness in her eyes every time she checked her phone and realized that Lucinda hadn't called her.

"Hey," she shouted from the front door. "I'd really love some help. I stopped at the grocery store."

"You didn't have to do that," he said. "I could have gone." She had been working nonstop at the office, trying to land some of the bigger stories with her boss constantly shooting her down. He was hoping to find a way to make her life easier, but that might require some begging and a whole lot of convincing on his part. He wanted Journey to move in with him. They had been going back and forth between her place and his, mostly spending nights at his townhome since it was bigger than her apartment. Ford could tell that all of the going back and forth was really beginning to take its toll on her.

"I know that I didn't have to, but I'm practically living here, and I'd really love to help out as much as I can." He took the two big bags from her and carried them into the kitchen. Journey scrunched up her nose and smiled, "There are two more in the trunk if you wouldn't mind grabbing them."

"Not at all," he agreed. "You know," he said, "instead of practically living here, why not actually live here?" he asked.

"Are you asking me to move in with you?" she asked.

He shrugged, trying for casual. "Sure," he said. "I mean, you said it yourself, you are already practically living here. Why not just move in with me so we don't have to keep killing ourselves going back and forth?"

"Gee, how romantic," she drawled. "You want me to move in with you to make things easier on us?"

"Not exactly," he said. "I want you to move in because I'm in love with you and I'm hoping that you'll want to live with me."

"Well, that's better," she teased. "I mean, more romantic and all that stuff." She giggled and he couldn't help his smile.

"I'm glad that you think so," he teased. "So, how about it? Will you move in here with me and make this thing between us more official?"

"I'd love to," she agreed. "But what do you think Lucinda will say about us living with each other?"

"I really don't care what my sister thinks about us living together. Honestly, I'm pissed off at her for not calling us back. It's been a month and she's acting like a child."

"I agree, but it still hurts," she admitted. "I thought that she'd come around before now." He did too, but he wasn't about to admit that to her.

"Well, when she does come around, we'll tell her our good news. Until then, I just want to concentrate on us. How does that sound?" Ford asked.

"It sounds perfect," Journey agreed. He was glad that she thought so because he thought it was a perfect plan too—even if he was the one who had come up with it. Having Journey in his life and his space felt right. His life felt right for the first time in a damn long time, and he wasn't about to let his sister or anyone else ruin that for him.

※

Ford was never one to borrow trouble, but after a few months of living with Journey, he was sure that he was going to have to stir up some shit if he wanted to get Lucinda back into their lives. His first step was to call Ty, his brother-in-law, to put their heads together and come up with a plan.

He called Ty and almost choked when he answered the phone saying, "It's about damn time."

"What the hell does that mean?" Ford asked.

"It means that our women haven't been talking for about

four months and it's about damn time we put a stop to it. They're both being bullheaded," Ty said.

"My sister is the one who's not talking to Journey or me. You would think she'd be happy for us since we're both happy."

"Are you happy, man?" Ty asked.

"I am," Ford said. "I've loved Journey for a damn long time now, and she's moved in with me. I've never been this happy in my life, and it pisses me off that Lucinda can't accept that."

"I get it, but you have to put yourself in her shoes. She's upset that you and Journey had feelings for each other this whole time and never told her how you felt."

"That's because we never admitted how we felt about each other. Hell, I joined the military before to avoid my feelings for Journey. We were both in denial and that had everything to do with not wanting to hurt Luci," Ford admitted.

"And it probably had a bit to do with the fact that when you left for the Army, Journey was still underage," Ty reminded.

"But we're both adults now, and Luci should see that and be happy for us both. This not speaking to us thing is getting ridiculous."

"I agree, and that's why I'm glad you called me," Ty said.

"You have a plan?"

"Not really, other than getting Journey and Luci in a room together to talk things out. I'm betting that if we can do that, they'll find a way to work everything out and then, we can get on with being a happy family, as we should be," Ford said.

"Speaking of family," Ty breathed, "I shouldn't be the one to tell you this, but you're going to be an uncle. Luci is pregnant."

"Wow," For said. "That's fantastic. Congratulations."

"Thanks, man," Ty said. "So, it's important that we patch things up before the little one gets here."

"Agreed," Ford said. The idea of being an uncle was one that had him thinking about his own future family. He wondered if Journey would be ready to discuss having kids and a future with him—the whole nine yards. He was really hoping that she would be ready to talk about everything that he wanted with her in the future because he had already wasted enough time with Journey. He was ready to start their future now.

"Give me a day or two to work out a place for us to meet and I'll give you a callback," Ford said. "We'll get this worked out one way or another. I don't care if we have to lock them in a room together until they both come out hugging. I want my family back, man."

"Agreed," Ty said. "Talk soon." He ended the call and Ford tossed his cell phone to the counter. All he had to do now was come up with a way to get his sister and his girlfriend in the same room to work out their differences—piece of cake.

JOURNEY

Journey wasn't sure how Andrew had convinced the news department at CNN to send her on the assignment of a lifetime, but he had. It would be a life-changing story if she could land it and all she had to do was fly into a war zone and stay alive long enough to report back what she had witnessed. Her only problem was that Andrew had convinced CNN to send him along with her. Well, that wasn't her only problem. Her biggest was the tiny secret that was hidden deep inside of her—a secret that she planned on telling Ford about tonight.

She didn't mean to get pregnant, not that she expected Ford to believe her. Honestly, she was scared to death to tell him about the baby, but there would be no hiding it. She was about two months pregnant, according to her OBGYN. She wasn't ever regular, so when she missed a couple of periods, she thought nothing of it until she started getting sick every morning. She could tell that Ford was worried about her every time she ran to the bathroom to be sick. When he asked her to go to the doctor, she never imagined that she'd have to report back to him that she was pregnant with his baby. She was going to be a mom, and she wasn't sure how she felt about that fact. The question was, how would Ford take the news that he was going to be a dad? She texted to check if he was at home, and when he told her that he was making dinner for them, and to hurry home, her tummy did a little flip-flop. Journey was going to face the music at some point, might as well be tonight.

"Hey," she breathed, walking into his kitchen. He pulled her in for a hug and quickly released her.

"What's wrong?" he asked, reading her like an open book.

"I have news," she said.

"Good or bad news?" Ford asked.

"It depends on how you look at it," she said. Journey took a deep breath and let it out. "I got offered the biggest assignment of my career. It's the break that I've always wanted."

"That's wonderful, honey," he said. "I mean, I'm not sure how you're looking at it, but I think it's great news."

She held up her hand, "Let me finish," she said. "I would have to travel with Andrew," she whispered. "And that's not the worst of it. It's in a war zone."

"No fucking way," Ford shouted. "There is no fucking way that you're going anywhere with that asshole. Not after everything he's done to you in the past four months, we've been together. Hell, we think that he broke into our home to try to get to you." A week ago, someone had broken into the townhouse but left no trace of evidence behind. They were sure that it was Andrew and told the police so when they showed up to take their statements. Since nothing was missing, just tossed about the place, the cops said that there was nothing that they could really do, especially since they had caught nothing on the security cameras.

"Right, but with no proof, there's no way to prove that he was the one in our home, Ford," she reminded. She hated that Andrew was smart enough to bypass Ford's security system and get into their home. It creeped her out knowing that he had gone through her things while they weren't home. But there was no way to prove that it was him. He'd never confess to being in their place and that was the only way to put him behind bars.

"I know that, Journey. But you and I both know that it was him." He had all but admitted it to her when she questioned him in his office. His smug smile in place as he told her that he was disappointed in her for believing that he could do something like that. Her boss was a piece of work.

"Well, I've already turned down the job, if it makes you feel any better," she spat.

"It doesn't make me feel better," he said. "I hate that you can't take the assignment of a lifetime because of some asshole stalker. I want you to do what you love, but I can't let that man anywhere near you, honey."

She nodded and took another deep breath. "Are you going to ask me why I'm not taking the job?" she asked.

He shrugged, "I thought it was because you'd have to travel with your boss," he said. "Was there another reason?"

"Yes," she said, "I told you that it's in a war zone, right?" she asked, trying to remember what she had already told him. Everything was starting to get jumbled up in her head, and she was having a hard time coming up with the words that she needed to tell him.

"You did," he said, "but, that wouldn't stop you, Journey. So, if it's not about your boss, then why are you not taking the assignment?"

"Because it's not safe for me and our baby," she whispered. She couldn't look up at him, her eyes fixated on the kitchen floor. She was afraid of what she'd see in his eyes if she looked up at him.

"Our baby," he breathed. Ford hooked his finger under her chin, forcing her to look him in the eyes.

She nodded, "Yes, I'm so sorry, Ford. I didn't mean to get pregnant. It wasn't a part of my plan. You know how important my job is to me, and a baby isn't really something that I've thought about. But he or she is in there, ready or not," she said, pointing to her still flat tummy.

"How long have you known?" he asked.

"I went to the doctor this morning. You know that I've been getting sick in the morning and I decided to go get checked out. I missed two periods but never really gave it much thought because I've never been very regular. I thought it was just a stomach bug, but I was wrong. I'm sorry."

"Why are you sorry?" Ford asked.

"Because I don't want you to think that I planned this or am trying to trap you," she admitted. That was the last thing she wanted him to think about her.

"I've already told you that I'm in love with you, honey. Hell, you even gave up your place to move in with me. Where did you think this was going?" he asked.

"I don't know," she said. "I mean, I'd like to think that you want a future with me, but this whole thing with Lucinda has us both on edge. I guess I'm worried about what will happen to the two of us if she decides never to talk to either of us again."

"My sister is being an ass," he breathed. "And what happens between Luci and us has nothing to do with what's going on between you and me," Ford insisted.

"It doesn't?" she asked.

"No," he whispered, "I love you, Journey, and I love that you're pregnant with my baby." He pulled her against his body and gently kissed her forehead. She wasn't sure if she was relieved or wanted to burst into tears. Unfortunately, her new hormones chose the latter and she found herself crying uncontrollably all over Ford's t-shirt.

"Hey, why are you crying?" he crooned.

"Because I'm happy," she sobbed. "The doctor said that this could happen."

"I wish you would have told me that you were going to the doctor, I would have gone with you, honey," he said.

"Again," she said, wiping her nose on her sleeve, "I thought that I had a stomach virus. I thought that they'd tell me to take a pill or something and I'd be fine. I had no idea I'd be hearing news that would forever change both of our lives. If it makes you feel any better, I have another appointment in three weeks. You can go with me to that," she said.

"I'd love to," he agreed. "I guess we're going to have to figure out what to do with a baby next," he said. Her tears started again, and this time, she wasn't sure that she'd be able to make them stop.

"Ugh, why are you crying again, honey?" he asked.

"Because I have no clue what to do with a baby. I'm an only child and my parents are both gone. Who do I ask about these things? I wish I could tell Lucinda, but she won't take my calls."

"Yeah, well, that's going to stop," Ford insisted.

"What do you mean?" she asked.

"I didn't want to get your hopes up, but I talked to Tyler yesterday. We've come up with a plan to get Lucinda over this stubborn stand she's taking against you and me being together. I didn't want to be the one to tell you this, but Luci's pregnant too. They just found out a few weeks ago. I'm betting that our news will have my sister turning into a slobbery mess, just like you, and she'll want to talk to us both."

"She's pregnant and she hasn't called to tell me?" Journey asked. She pulled free from his arms to sit down at the table, needing some space. "How could she do that? We've always told each other everything."

"You did keep your feelings about me from her," he reminded. "And as I've already pointed out, my sister can be quite stubborn." Ford was right. She did keep her best friend in the dark about how she felt about her brother. It wasn't fair of Journey to do that. Luci and she were best friends and were supposed to tell each other everything. She broke her best friend's trust and now, she was going to have to get over her own hurt and make amends with Luci.

"Don't tell her about the baby," Journey said. "I think that I should be the one to tell her our news, right after I apologize to her for keeping my feelings for you a secret."

"Are you sure?" Ford asked. "Tyler and I had this whole plan hatched to get you both in the same room. We want our kids growing up together and you and my sister not talking is kind of ruining that plan, now that you're pregnant." She couldn't help her smile. Luci and she had always dreamed of raising their kids together and Ford was right, now that they were both pregnant, there was no time to waste to reconcile.

"How about you and Tyler get us in the same room together, and I'll take it from there. I have a lot to tell your sister and after I'm done begging her to forgive me, we can tell her about the baby together."

"I'd like that," he said, pulling her up from her seat. "So, you're going to be a mom," he breathed, pressing his forehead to hers.

"Yep, and you're going to be a dad," she said. "Are you really happy about the baby?" she asked.

"I am," he admitted. "I know that everything feels a bit rushed, but I've known you your whole life. If you look at things that way, this kid was a long time coming."

"I like the way that you think," she said.

"You hungry?" he asked. "After dinner, I'll need to run back to the office for a few hours, if you're good."

"I'm good, and actually, I am hungry," she said. "It's a nice change of pace considering that I spent every morning this past week hovered over the toilet. I guess this kid doesn't like breakfast or something."

"Well, I can start making you dinner in the morning, if it helps," he offered.

"Already spoiling our baby," she teased. She didn't expect any different from Ford since he liked to spoil her rotten—and she wouldn't want it any other way.

FORD

The next morning Ford decided to call Tyler to put their plan into motion. It was a good plan and it had to work now that both his sister and the woman he loved were both expecting. Plus, he couldn't wait to tell Tyler about the baby. He and Luci's husband grew up together and were best friends, something that he almost blew when he found out that Luci and Ty were together. He acted like an ass back then, so a part of him understood why his sister was so upset about him and Journey. Once he accepted his best friend with his sister, he had to admit that they were good together. He was sure that if Luci gave him a chance to prove it to her, she'd see that he and Journey were good together too.

He was on his way to work when his cell phone chimed with a message from Tyler to call him when he got a chance. He quickly dialed Ty's number and noted the panic in his friend's voice when he answered.

"What's wrong?" Ford asked.

"Luci is in the ER," Tyler said.

"Wait—what?" Ford asked.

"She started having cramps and her doctor told me to bring her in to be checked. I'm scared, man," Tyler admitted. "I'm worried about her and the baby."

"I'm on my way over," Ford assured. "I have to tell Journey about this. She'll kill me if I don't tell her."

"Do what you have to do but get your ass to the hospital. Luci needs you both," Tyler ordered.

"We'll be there," Ford promised, ending the call. He took a deep breath in and let it out while calling Journey.

"Hey," she answered.

"Honey, I have something to tell you, and I need to know that you're sitting down," he said.

"What's wrong?" she asked. "Just tell me," she ordered.

"Luci is in the hospital. She was having cramps and Ty had to take her to the ER. She's there now," he said.

"Oh God, we have to go to her," Journey said. "How could I have been so stupid—I shouldn't have pushed her the way that I did."

"What are you talking about?" Ford asked.

"I called her last night when you ran to the office for a few hours. I thought about what you said—you know about our kids growing up together, and when my call went to voicemail, I decided to leave a message."

"What did you say?" he asked.

"I told her that I was sorry about keeping my feelings for you a secret from her all these years. Then, I told her that I was pregnant and that I knew that she was too, and I reminded her about our dream of having our kids grow up together. And before I ended the call, I told her that she was being stubborn and that we were wasting precious time that we'll never be able to get back."

"That's a lot, honey," he said.

"Well, it had to be said," she defended. "I just never thought that she'd end up in the ER after listening to my message."

"Let's not jump to conclusions," he said. Ford didn't need Journey ending up in the ER bed next to Lucinda's. He needed her to stay calm. "We don't even know if she listened to the message. Let's get over to the hospital and then, we'll figure it all out."

"You're right," she said. "Let me grab my purse and jacket. I'll meet you in the garage. Just get here fast." Ford was about ten minutes away and knew that he could make it in about five if he took a few shortcuts.

"I'll hurry. We'll take my truck," he said. "Are you sure you're all right?" he asked.

"I will be, as soon as I check on Luci," she said. He felt the same way, but he didn't want to let on how worried he was about his sister. For now, he'd have to stay positive for Journey —they'd get through the rest together.

※

Tyler met them in the emergency waiting room and he looked worse for wear. "How's she doing?" Ford asked. Ty pulled them both in for a quick hug.

"She's okay for now. They are monitoring both her and the baby," he said. "I was so worried that we were going to lose her, but they said that the baby's heartbeat is strong."

"Her?" Journey squeaked.

"Yeah, we found out that we're having a girl. Listen, I know that you want to see Luci, but she can't have any stress. Do you think that you can keep things lite?" he asked.

"We can," Ford promised. "If she seems to get upset, we'll leave."

"Okay, let me talk to the nurse about getting you back there. Give me a minute," Ty said. Ford watched his brother-in-law as he pointed back to them and talked to the nurse who seemed to be in charge of the waiting room. She nodded and Ty motioned for them to follow him back into the ER. Ford felt as though his heart might beat out of his damn chest as he followed Ty and Journey down the long corridor.

They walked into the second to last room and found Luci sleeping on the small bed. She was hooked up to a bunch of machines and he could hear the baby's fast heartbeat filling the room around them. Ford wondered if that was what his baby's heartbeat would sound like and a part of him couldn't wait to find out.

"Hey sis," he said, gently nudging her shoulder to wake her. "Journey and I are here; can you wake up?" He looked back to find Journey standing in the corner of the room and he reached out his hand to her. She hesitated at first, but when Luci began to stir, Journey joined in, taking his hand.

"What are you two doing here?" Luci asked, peeping her eyes open.

"I called them," Ty said. "They should be here for you, honey. This thing needs to end."

"You mean, I should get over my best friend and brother both betraying me? I should just move on?" Luci asked, sitting up a bit.

"No, that's not what he's saying," Journey said. "Ty called us to let us know that you were in the ER, but it was our choice to come to see you. I'm so sorry—this is all my fault. I shouldn't have left you that message. It upset you and now you're here."

"I told you that it's not your fault, honey," Ford said.

"What are you two talking about?" Luci asked. "What message?"

"I left you a message last night and it upset you, I'm so sorry, Luci. I should have told you how I felt about Ford. I shouldn't have kept it from you all these years," Journey said.

"No, you shouldn't have," Luci agreed, "but, I'm not here because of a message you left. I never got your message."

Ty shot his wife a sheepish grin and Ford had a feeling that he was the reason why she never got her message from Journey.

"You didn't get it because I deleted it," he said. "You were in the shower when it came in and I didn't want you to be upset. Plus, if you had listened to that message, you would have ruined my and Ford's plan to put you two back together."

"You and my brother came up with a plan to get me and Journey back together?" she asked.

"We did, but then this happened, and I thought, why not just have you two talk things out here," Ty admitted.

"What did your message say?" Luci asked. At least she was talking to them both. Ford had a feeling that telling her about the message would only serve to upset her, but she asked.

"I apologized for not telling you about Ford and me. You're my best friend and I should have told you. I just didn't want to hurt you," Journey said.

"It feels like you lied to me our whole lives," Luci said.

"I know, I feel awful about it. I just never thought that I'd have a chance with your brother and bringing up my feelings wouldn't matter. If he never wanted me, then why spill my guts about crushing on him?"

"You should have told me anyway because that's what best friends do. We tell each other everything," Luci said.

"I know that asking you to forgive me now seems trite, but I'm here to do just that. I want our kids to grow up together," Journey said, cupping her tummy.

"Kids," Lucinda repeated. "Wait—you're pregnant?"

"I am. I just found out that Ford and I are going to have a baby. I'm about two months along," Journey said.

"We're going to have kids about a month apart," Luci whispered.

"We are," Ford said. "I don't want our baby not to know his or her aunt and uncle because of a stupid feud, sis," he said. "Can't we just start over? I'm in love with your best friend and I won't apologize for that. I'll never apologize for loving Journey. I want a life with her—I plan on marrying her."

"You do?" both Journey and Luci asked in unison.

"I do," he admitted. "We have so much to look forward to, can't we stop looking backward?"

Tyler cleared his throat, "For the record, I agree with Ford," he said.

"Of course you do," Luci grumbled. He worried that his sister was too stubborn to accept any of their apologies, but when she smiled and reached for Journey's hand, he knew that she was willing to try. "I think I agree with Ford too, even though it pains me to say so. As you know, I never like to agree with anything that my brother says."

They all laughed and the nurse from the front desk walked into the room. "You all are being too loud," she chided.

"Sorry," Luci said, "we just found out that my brother and my best friend are going to have a baby too. We were just celebrating."

"Congratulations but celebrate quieter." The nurse turned to leave the room and another walked in behind her.

"Well, I have some good news," she said.

"Do I get to go home?" Luci asked.

"Not yet," the nurse said. "But you seem to be out of the woods. We're going to admit you for the night and keep an eye on you and your little one. You should be good to go home tomorrow if you do well throughout the night."

"Will I be able to stay with her?" Ty asked.

"Yes," the nurse said. "There is a sofa in each of the maternity rooms that you'll be able to sleep on."

"We can run over to your place to grab what you'll need for the night," Ford offered.

"How about if you two boys run back to our place and get what we'll need, and Journey and I can spend some time catching up?" Luci asked.

"You good with that, honey?" Ford asked. Journey smiled over at him and nodded, and God, she was crying again. "Again with the crying?" he asked. She and Luci both giggled and

Journey sat down next to his sister. It was good to see the two of them together again. He worried that might not happen, but they needed each other. Journey was the sister that Luci never had—and if he had his way, she'd become her sister-in-law very soon.

JOURNEY

Journey spent most of the weekend hanging out at Lucinda's place once she was out of the hospital. It was like old times being with her best friend, and she could tell that Ford was relieved to have his sister and his best friend back. Of course, he and Ty spent most of their weekend watching football while Journey and Luci discussed nursery decorating ideas. It felt good to have her best friend back.

She went to work on Monday morning and turned down the "Story of a lifetime" as Andrew liked to call it. Really, it wasn't a hard decision to make. She knew that if she took the job, she'd be putting her unborn child in danger, not that she was about to tell her boss that. She was only telling a select few people about the pregnancy. Journey knew that she still had a couple of months until she'd have to make the big announcement and give up her dreams of landing the "Hard news" stories. She would be put on fluff pieces, but it was a price she was willing to pay until after her baby was born. Honestly, it wouldn't be that different from what she was reporting now. She was sent out on human interest stories, and she really didn't mind. But a part of her wished to be a part of the big leagues, reporting on the hard-hitting world news, not just local fluff pieces.

For the most part, Andrew had been leaving her alone. Journey was hoping that he had finally taken the hint that she wasn't interested and never would be. She had made it very clear that she was with Ford. Of course, he helped with that, showing up at her office and bringing her flowers or coffee. Ford always made a point to put on quite the display, kissing her goodbye at her desk, making sure that Andrew saw them. At first, it only seemed to piss him off, but after a while, he began to take less of an interest in her and her love life. Andrew hadn't asked her to dinner in weeks, and that had to be some kind of record.

Andrew poked his head out of his office, "Can I see you for a minute, Journey?" he asked. She avoided going into his office alone with him at all costs. She quickly looked around the office and realized that everyone else was missing from their desks. Most of them hadn't even made it to work yet. She was an early bird, always was, and usually was the first reporter into the office.

"Um, sure," she squeaked. She grabbed her phone and walked into his office, sitting as far away from him on the other side of the room. "What's up?" she asked, trying for casual.

"How about you tell me," he said. He seemed pissed and she wondered what that was about.

"I'm not sure that I know what you mean," she said with a shrug.

"I've been trying to figure out if the rumors that I've heard around the office are true about you," he said. Andrew was trying to trap her and she wasn't about to play into his hands.

"What rumors are you hearing about me?" she asked.

"That you've moved in with your boyfriend," he spat.

"Well, that's hardly a rumor or a secret. I have moved in with Ford," she said.

"When you introduced him to me in the parking lot after

our dinner date, you said he was just a friend," Andrew reminded. Ford was just her friend back then, but so much had changed so quickly.

"First, it wasn't a date, Andrew. We met over dinner to discuss my story. Second, Ford and I have been friends since we were just kids. It blossomed into more, not that it's any of your business." She was pushing him, she knew it, but she just couldn't help herself.

"Listen, I think that we got off on the wrong foot. I'd love to sit down with you and talk about your future with CNN," Andrew said.

"What's that supposed to mean?" She spat. "Are you threatening my job here, because I won't give it up without a fight? You want to fire me, you'll have a lawsuit on your hands." He stood from behind his desk and took a step toward her. She backed into the wall and worried that he was going to keep pushing her, with nowhere else to go.

"I didn't mean it that way," he insisted. "I wish you'd just give me a chance here and listen to me."

"I don't need to listen to you anymore," Journey said. "My life and whom I'm living with isn't any of your business. It's personal and our relationship is purely business. I'm sure that HR will agree with me."

"So, now you're threatening me?" he asked.

"I'm not threatening you, Andrew. I'm telling you that if you keep asking me personal questions, I'm going to report you to HR," she said.

"Again," he said, "you're going to report me to HR again. I know all about you running to HR about me. What did you tell them again? Oh, yes, that I made unwanted sexual advanced to you. If I remember correctly, you agreed to have dinner with me, and you seemed just fine with my behavior before your boyfriend stopped by and ruined our evening."

"I was never all right with what you did to me. The only reason why I accepted your dinner invitation was that I thought that we were going to be working on my last article. As for Ford, he's none of your business. Our living situation is none of your business either. Am I clear?" she asked. He took another step toward her, his smile mean, and she realized that she had nowhere to run. She was trapped in his office with him, and no one was going to come to her rescue.

"You know, it's cute when you act all bossy," he whispered. "But you and I both know that HR won't believe a word you run to tell them, right?" He was right, even if it made her sick to admit it.

Her world started spinning and she closed her eyes, trying to remain upright. She really didn't want to pass out in front of her boss, especially when he was practically on top of her. "I need some air," she whispered.

"You can go get your air, but we're not done here," he promised. Andrew stepped to the side, letting her pass as she ran out of his office. Journey ran out of the office, practically plowing down the guy who was walking in the front door.

"Sorry," she said over her shoulder as he grunted his response.

She pulled her cell phone from her pocket to call Ford. "You okay, honey?" he answered.

"No," she breathed, "I'm not okay. Can you come to get me?" she asked.

"What happened?" he asked.

"Andrew," she whispered into her phone. "He found out that I moved in with you and he's angrier than usual."

"I'm on my way," he promised. "I'll be there in less than ten minutes. You wait outside of the building. Don't go back in there," he ordered.

"I won't," she said, "but, my bag is in there."

"I'll grab your bag when I get there. You just stay safe and wait for me," he ordered.

"I will," she assured. "See you soon," she breathed, ending the call.

Ford pulled up to the front of her office building minutes later and looked mad enough to kill someone. Journey worried that he'd do just that if he went into her building to get her bag.

He got out of his truck and rounded the front, pulling her into his arms as soon as he reached her. "Get into the truck and wait for me," he ordered.

"Ford," she whispered. "Don't go in there and do something stupid. It will give Andrew what he wants. You'll play right into his hands."

"I'm not going to touch the asshole," he assured, though Journey didn't believe a word he was saying. He looked about ready to beat Andrew into a bloody stump.

"You promise?" she asked. Two police cars pulled up to the curb and parked behind Ford's pickup. "What have you done?" she asked.

"What had to be done," he growled. "I won't lay a hand on him, but you're going to press charges against him. It's only right," he said. "You need to make this stop, Journey. You're the only one who can do that. If HR won't do anything about it, you need to. File charges against that fucker so that this can end now." Ford looked so desperate, she couldn't tell him no. How could she do that to him? She needed to start thinking about him and their baby—the family that they were building together. It was the only way to have the future that she wanted with Ford. She was holding onto a dead-end job, and she knew that sooner or later, she'd have to give up on it. Her whole life, all she wanted was a future with Ford. Now, she was finally going to have that and she was foolishly throwing it away to do puff pieces for a news organization that didn't take her word that her boss was making unwanted passes at her.

She nodded, "I'll file a complaint against him, but it might not do any good. His side of the story is that I wanted him to touch me and ask me out. He just said as much when he trapped me in his office. How can I fight a man like that?" she asked.

"With me by your side," Ford offered. "I won't let him touch you again. Hell, I'll quit my job and camp out here if I have to," he promised.

"That won't be necessary," she assured. "I'm going to quit my job."

"You can't quit your job, honey," he insisted. "You love your job."

"No, I love the idea of my job. I hate that the company that I work for doesn't believe a word that I say because my boss has called me a liar. I hate that I've worked my ass off trying to get ahead, and never make any leeway. I'm ready to move on," she said.

"What will you do?" he asked.

"Well, I think that I'm going to concentrate on the baby for now. Then, I've been looking into freelancing. I think that I'd like to write articles for magazines, but I've really not given it much thought. If you don't mind me taking some time to consider my options, I'd like to think things over for now."

"I don't mind at all. In fact, I think that it's a great idea. It will give you time to plan our wedding and everything before the baby gets here," he said.

"Our wedding?" she squeaked. "Are you asking me to marry you, Ford?"

"I am," he simply answered. "I've loved you forever, Journey. Say that you'll marry me and let me spend the rest of my life making you happy."

"I've loved you forever too, Ford. I'll marry you," she breathed. He pulled her against his body, sealing his mouth over hers. He kissed her until a police officer cleared his throat behind them.

"I hate to break this up, but I need to take your statement, ma'am." She looked into the lobby of her building, all of her coworkers standing there watching her, and she took a deep breath when she got to Andrew who was staring her down, shooting daggers at her and Ford.

"I will gladly give you my statement, just give me one minute," she said. She pulled free from Ford's arms and started for the building.

"What are you doing?" Ford asked.

"What I need to do, and I need to do this alone," she said. "I won't be long. We have our whole future to plan, and I don't want to waste another second." She gently kissed his cheek and turned back to the building she had basically called home for so many years now. She stared down Andrew the whole time, not wanting to let his intimidating stare get to her. He wouldn't intimidate her ever again.

As soon as she walked into the lobby, the sea of onlookers parted and she walked right up to her boss. "I quit, Andrew," she said.

"You what?" he asked.

"You heard me. I quit and I'll also be filing charges against you for sexual misconduct. You won't ever touch me or pressure me into spending one on one time with you to keep my job, ever again." She turned to walk away from him, and he grabbed her arm, tugging her back. She looked through the window to see Ford's murderous expression and she shook her head at him. The last thing she needed was for him to storm into the lobby and start a fight with her boss-well, ex-boss.

"Let go of me, or I will add assault to my statement," she spat. "You need to learn to take no for an answer, Andrew. I don't want you; I never did. Maybe you should learn to ask a lady before you just assume."

Journey pulled her arm free and started for the front door, hoping like hell that she didn't fall on her face and ruin her grand exit. Applause broke out around her and Journey looked around at all of the smiling women who were cheering her on. She walked out onto the street and straight into Ford's arms. "I'm so fucking proud of you, honey," he said. "I love you."

"Love you too," she whispered, "don't let go of me until this is over," she said.

"You don't have to worry about that, honey," he said. "I don't plan on ever letting go of you again." He walked her over to the police officer who was waiting to take her statement. She was looking forward to forever with Ford. It was something that she never dreamed possible—a lifetime with her best friend's older brother. Ford Dixon was her dream come true and she would never deny her feelings for him again.

"I'm going to hold you to that promise," she whispered to him.

The End

ABOUT K.L. RAMSEY & BE KELLY

***Romance Rebel fighting for
Happily Ever After!***

K. L. Ramsey currently resides in West Virginia (Go Mountaineers!). In her spare time, she likes to read romance novels, go to WVU football games and attend book club (aka-drink wine) with girlfriends. K. L. enjoys writing Contemporary Romance, Erotic Romance, and Sexy Ménage! She loves to write strong, capable women and bossy, hot as hell alphas, who fall ass over tea kettle for them. And of course, her stories always have a happy ending. But wait—there's more!

Somewhere along the writing path, K.L. developed a love of ALL things paranormal (but has a special affinity for shifters <YUM!!>)!! She decided to take a chance and create another persona- BE Kelly- to bring you all of her yummy shifters, seers, and everything paranormal (plus a hefty dash of MC!).

K. L. RAMSEY'S SOCIAL MEDIA

Ramsey's Rebels - K.L. Ramsey's Readers Group
https://www.facebook.com/groups/ramseysrebels

KL Ramsey & BE Kelly's ARC Team
https://www.facebook.com/groups/klramseyandbekellyarcteam

KL Ramsey and BE Kelly's Newsletter
https://mailchi.mp/4e73ed1b04b9/authorklramsey/

KL Ramsey and BE Kelly's Website
https://www.klramsey.com

- facebook.com/kl.ramsey.58
- instagram.com/itsprivate2
- bookbub.com/profile/k-l-ramsey
- twitter.com/KLRamsey5
- amazon.com/K.L.-Ramsey/e/B0799P6JGJ

BE KELLY'S SOCIAL MEDIA

[BE Kelly's Reader's group](https://www.facebook.com/groups/kellsangelsreadersgroup/)
https://www.facebook.com/groups/kellsangelsreadersgroup/

- facebook.com/be.kelly.564
- instagram.com/bekellyparanormalromanceauthor
- twitter.com/BEKelly9
- bookbub.com/profile/be-kelly
- amazon.com/BE-Kelly/e/B081LLD38M

WORKS BY K. L. RAMSEY

The Relinquished Series Box Set

Love Times Infinity

Love's Patient Journey

Love's Design

Love's Promise

Harvest Ridge Series Box Set

Worth the Wait

The Christmas Wedding

Line of Fire

Torn Devotion

Fighting for Justice

Last First Kiss Series Box Set

Theirs to Keep

Theirs to Love

Theirs to Have

Theirs to Take

Second Chance Summer Series

True North

The Wrong Mister Right

Ties That Bind Series

Saving Valentine

Blurred Lines

Dirty Little Secrets

Ties That Bind Box Set

Taken Series

Double Bossed

Double Crossed

Double The Mistletoe

Double Down

Owned

His Secret Submissive

His Reluctant Submissive

His Cougar Submissive

His Nerdy Submissive

His Stubborn Submissive

Alphas in Uniform

Hellfire

Royal Bastards MC

Savage Heat

Whiskey Tango

Can't Fix Cupid

Ratchet's Revenge

Patched for Christmas

Love at First Fight

Dizzy's Desire

Possessing Demon

Mistletoe and Mayhem

Legend

Savage Hell MC Series

Roadkill

REPOssession

Dirty Ryder

Hart's Desire

Axel's Grind

Razor's Edge

Trista's Truth

Thorne's Rose

Lone Star Rangers

Don't Mess With Texas

Sweet Adeline

Dash of Regret

Austin's Starlet

Ranger's Revenge

Heart of Stone

Smokey Bandits MC Series

Aces Wild

Queen of Hearts

Full House

King of Clubs

Joker's Wild

Betting on Blaze

Tirana Brothers (Social Rejects Syndicate

Llir

Altin

Veton

Dirty Desire Series

Torrid

Clean Sweep

No Limits

Mountain Men Mercenary Series

Eagle Eye

Hacker

Widowmaker

Deadly Sins Syndicate (Mafia Series)

Pride

Envy

Greed

Lust

Wrath

Sloth

Gluttony

Forgiven Series

Confession of a Sinner

Confessions of a Saint

Confessions of a Rebel

Chasing Serendipity Series

Kismet

Sealed With a Kiss Series

Kissable

Never Been Kissed

Garo Syndicate Trilogy

Edon

Bekim

Rovena

Billionaire Boys Club

His Naughty Assistant

His Virgin Assistant

His Nerdy Assistant

His Curvy Assistant

His Bossy Assistant

His Rebellious Assistant

Grumpy Mountain Men Series

Grizz

Jed

Axel

A Grumpy Mountain Man for Xmas

The Bridezilla Series

Happily Ever After- Almost

Picture Perfect

Haunted Honeymoon for One

Rope 'Em and Ride 'Em Series

Saddle Up

A Cowboy for Christmas

WORKS BY BE KELLY (K.L.'S ALTER EGO...)

Reckoning MC Seer Series
Reaper

Tank

Raven

Reckoning MC Series Box Set

Perdition MC Shifter Series
Ringer

Rios

Trace

Perdition 3 Book Box Set

Silver Wolf Shifter Series
Daddy Wolf's Little Seer

Daddy Wolf's Little Captive

Daddy Wolf's Little Star

Rogue Enforcers
Juno

Blaze

Elite Enforcers
A Very Rogue Christmas Novella

One Rogue Turn

Graystone Academy Series

Eden's Playground

Violet's Surrender

Holly's Hope (A Christmas Novella)

Renegades Shifter Series

Pandora's Promise

Kinsley's Pact

Leader of the Pack Series

Wren's Pack

Printed in Great Britain
by Amazon